enemies

Svetlana Chmakova

enemies

SVETLANA CHMAKOVA

Coloring assistants: Effie Lealand, Melissa McCommon
Inking assistants: Effie Lealand, Young Kim
Lettering: JY Editorial

Copyright © 2022 Svetlana Chmakova

Yen Press, LLC supports the right to free expression and the value of copyright. The purpose of copyright is to encourage writers and artists to produce the creative works that enrich our culture.

The scanning, uploading, and distribution of this book without permission is a theft of the author's intellectual property. If you would like permission to use material from the book (other than for review purposes), please contact the publisher. Thank you for your support of the author's rights.

JY
150 West 30th Street, 19th Floor
New York, NY 10001

Visit us at jyforkids.com
facebook.com/jyforkids
twitter.com/jyforkids
jyforkids.tumblr.com
instagram.com/jyforkids

First JY Edition: September 2022

JY is an imprint of Yen Press, LLC.
The JY name and logo are trademarks of Yen Press, LLC.

The publisher is not responsible for websites (or their content) that are not owned by the publisher.

Library of Congress Control Number: 2022940170

ISBNs: 978-1-9753-1279-4 (hardcover)
978-1-9753-1272-5 (paperback)
978-1-9753-1278-7 (ebook)

1 3 5 7 9 10 8 6 4 2

LSC-C

Printed in the United States of America

Table of Contents

CHAPTER 1

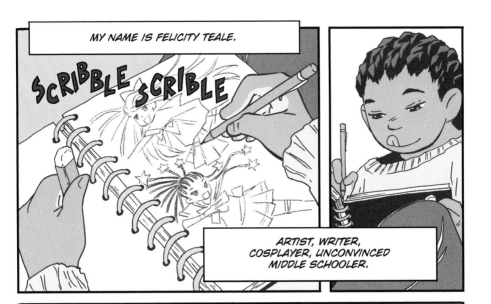

MY NAME IS FELICITY TEALE.

SCRIBBLE SCRIBBLE

ARTIST, WRITER, COSPLAYER, UNCONVINCED MIDDLE SCHOOLER.

SITTING HERE, PLOTTING AWESOME THINGS I'M GONNA DO.

AFTER I'M DONE WATCHING TV WITH THE FAM. (FOR **RESEARCH!**)

...YOU KNOW THAT SHOW PIRANHA PIT, WHERE PEOPLE PITCH THEIR BUSINESSES TO BIG-SHOT INVESTORS...

...TRYING TO GET A DEAL?

TAP TAP

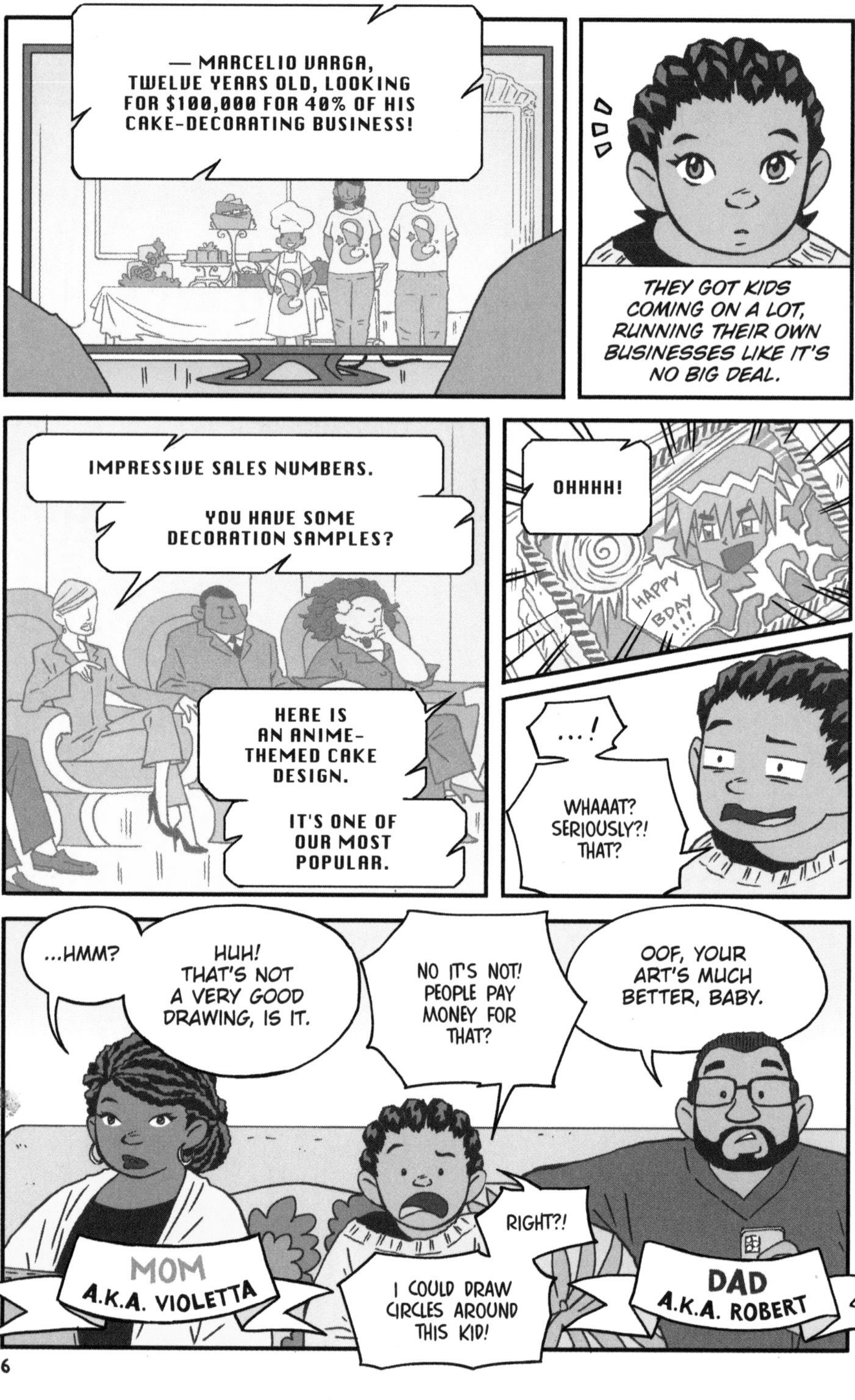
— MARCELIO VARGA, TWELVE YEARS OLD, LOOKING FOR $100,000 FOR 40% OF HIS CAKE-DECORATING BUSINESS!
THEY GOT KIDS COMING ON A LOT, RUNNING THEIR OWN BUSINESSES LIKE IT'S NO BIG DEAL.
IMPRESSIVE SALES NUMBERS.
YOU HAVE SOME DECORATION SAMPLES?
HERE IS AN ANIME-THEMED CAKE DESIGN.
IT'S ONE OF OUR MOST POPULAR.
OHHHH!
HAPPY BDAY!!!
...!
WHAAAT? SERIOUSLY?! THAT?
...HMM?
HUH! THAT'S NOT A VERY GOOD DRAWING, IS IT.
NO IT'S NOT! PEOPLE PAY MONEY FOR THAT?
OOF, YOUR ART'S MUCH BETTER, BABY.
RIGHT?!
I COULD DRAW CIRCLES AROUND THIS KID!
MOM A.K.A. VIOLETTA
DAD A.K.A. ROBERT

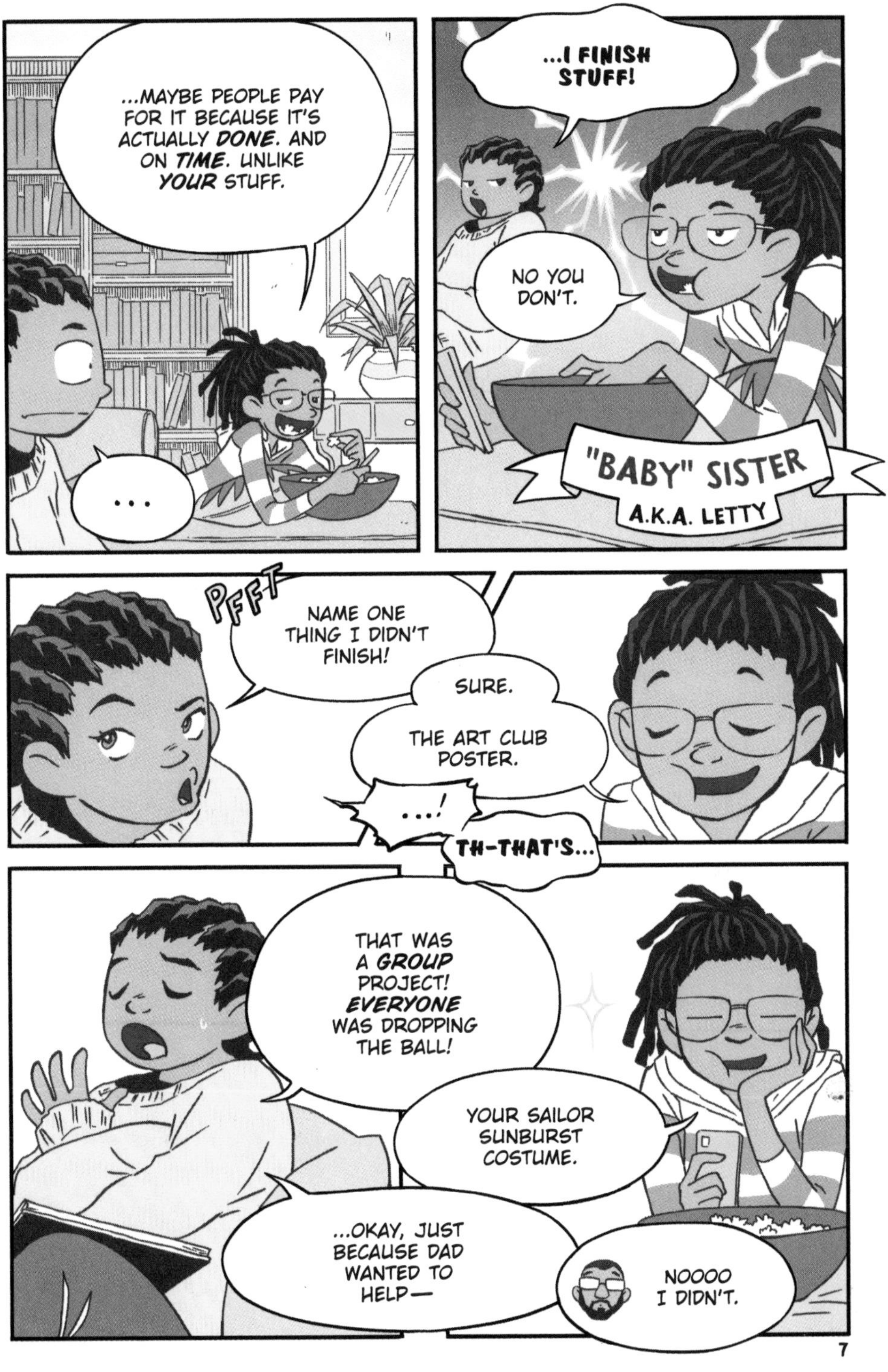
...MAYBE PEOPLE PAY FOR IT BECAUSE IT'S ACTUALLY DONE. AND ON TIME. UNLIKE YOUR STUFF.
...
...I FINISH STUFF!
NO YOU DON'T.
"BABY" SISTER
A.K.A. LETTY
PFFT
NAME ONE THING I DIDN'T FINISH!
SURE.
THE ART CLUB POSTER.
...!
TH-THAT'S...
THAT WAS A GROUP PROJECT! EVERYONE WAS DROPPING THE BALL!
YOUR SAILOR SUNBURST COSTUME.
...OKAY, JUST BECAUSE DAD WANTED TO HELP—
NOOOO I DIDN'T.

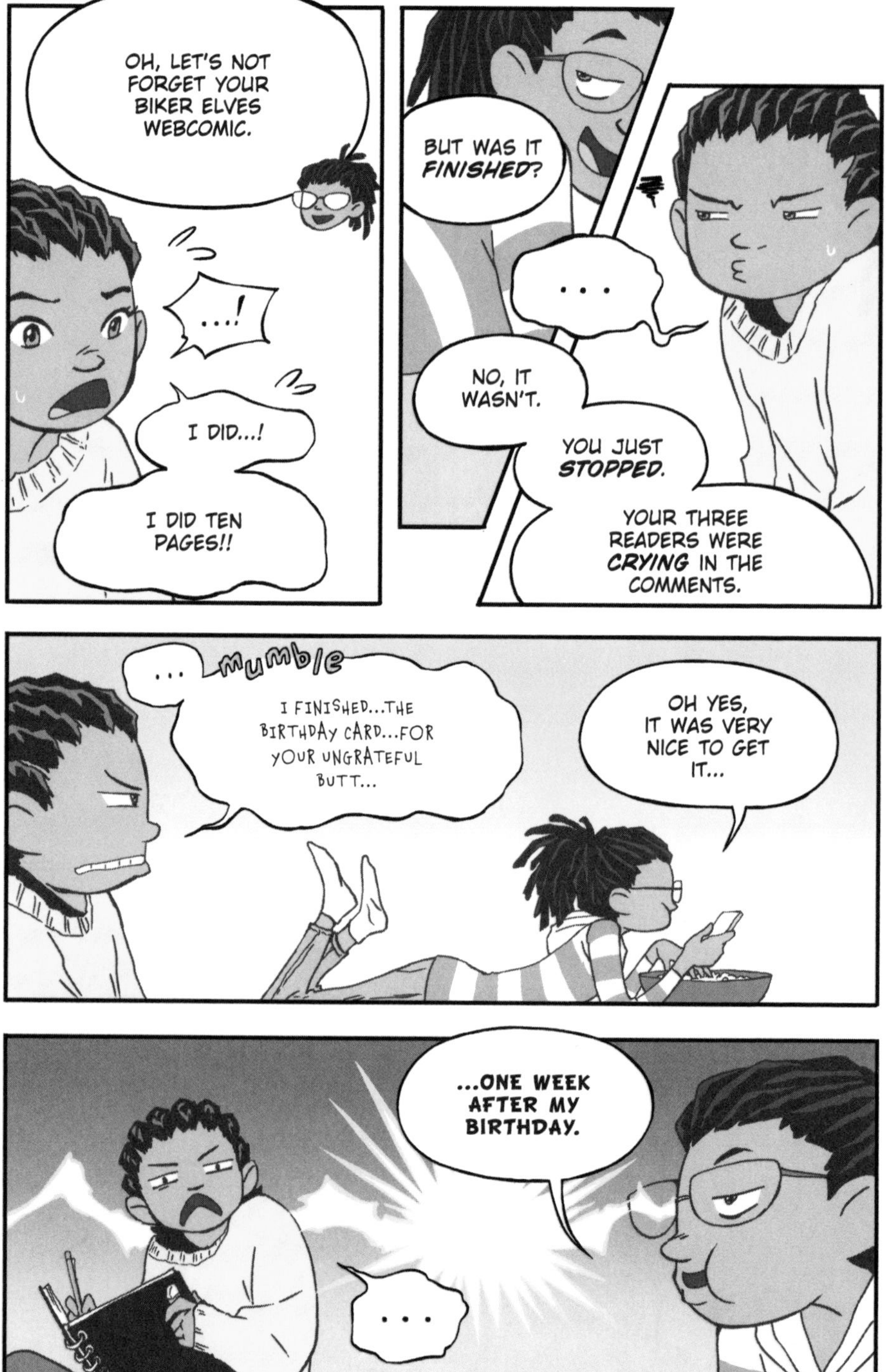
OH, LET'S NOT FORGET YOUR BIKER ELVES WEBCOMIC.
...!
I DID...!
I DID TEN PAGES!!
BUT WAS IT FINISHED?
...
NO, IT WASN'T.
YOU JUST STOPPED.
YOUR THREE READERS WERE CRYING IN THE COMMENTS.
...
mumble
I FINISHED...THE BIRTHDAY CARD...FOR YOUR UNGRATEFUL BUTT...
OH YES, IT WAS VERY NICE TO GET IT...
...ONE WEEK AFTER MY BIRTHDAY.
...

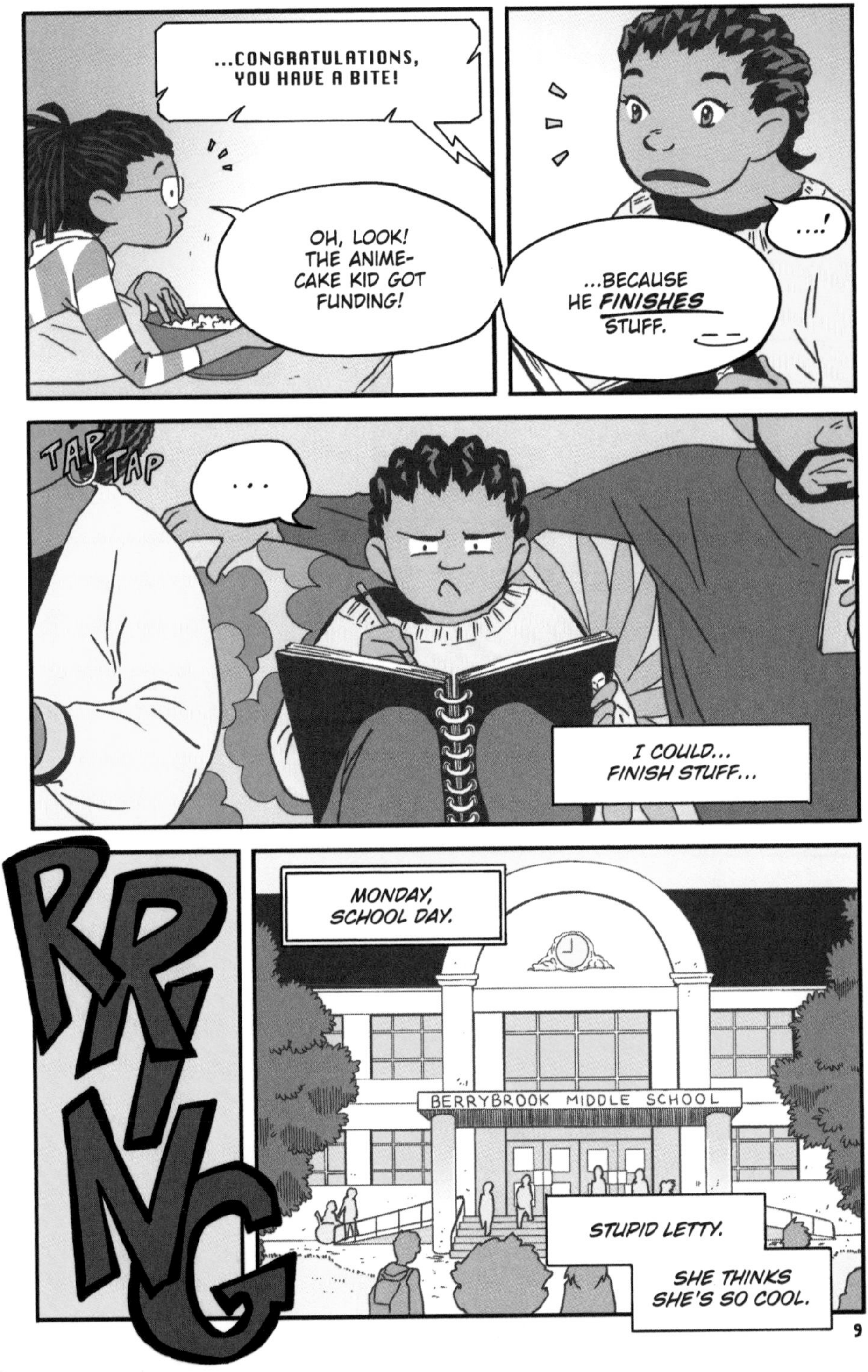
...CONGRATULATIONS, YOU HAVE A BITE!
OH, LOOK! THE ANIME-CAKE KID GOT FUNDING!
...!
...BECAUSE HE FINISHES STUFF.
TAP TAP
...
I COULD... FINISH STUFF...
RRING
MONDAY, SCHOOL DAY.
BERRYBROOK MIDDLE SCHOOL
STUPID LETTY.
SHE THINKS SHE'S SO COOL.

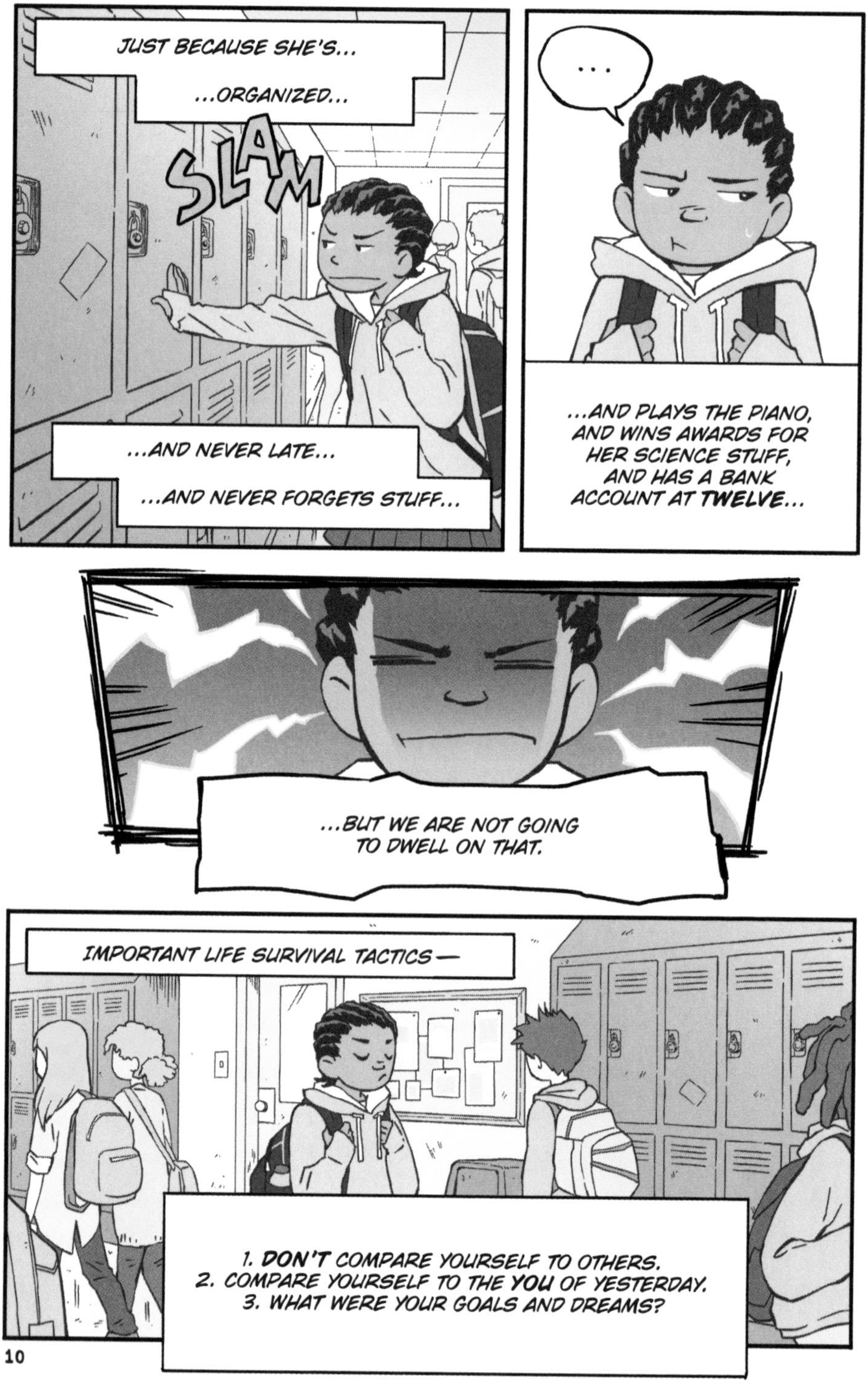
JUST BECAUSE SHE'S...
...ORGANIZED...
SLAM
...AND NEVER LATE...
...AND NEVER FORGETS STUFF...
...
...AND PLAYS THE PIANO, AND WINS AWARDS FOR HER SCIENCE STUFF, AND HAS A BANK ACCOUNT AT TWELVE...
...BUT WE ARE NOT GOING TO DWELL ON THAT.
IMPORTANT LIFE SURVIVAL TACTICS—
1. DON'T COMPARE YOURSELF TO OTHERS.
2. COMPARE YOURSELF TO THE YOU OF YESTERDAY.
3. WHAT WERE YOUR GOALS AND DREAMS?

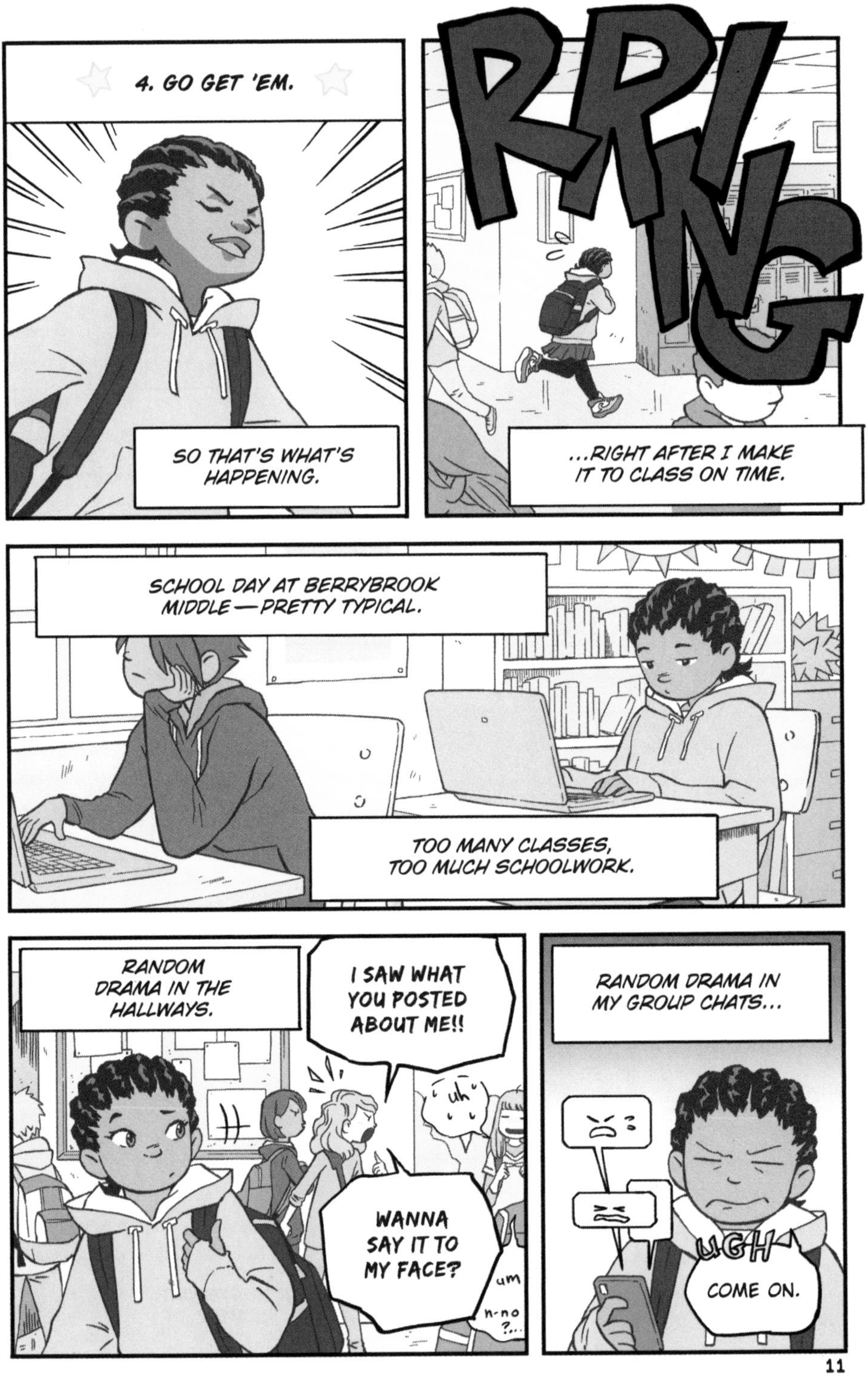

4. GO GET 'EM.
SO THAT'S WHAT'S HAPPENING.
RRRING
...RIGHT AFTER I MAKE IT TO CLASS ON TIME.
SCHOOL DAY AT BERRYBROOK MIDDLE—PRETTY TYPICAL.
TOO MANY CLASSES, TOO MUCH SCHOOLWORK.
RANDOM DRAMA IN THE HALLWAYS.
I SAW WHAT YOU POSTED ABOUT ME!!
uh
WANNA SAY IT TO MY FACE?
um
n-no ?...
RANDOM DRAMA IN MY GROUP CHATS...
UGH
COME ON.

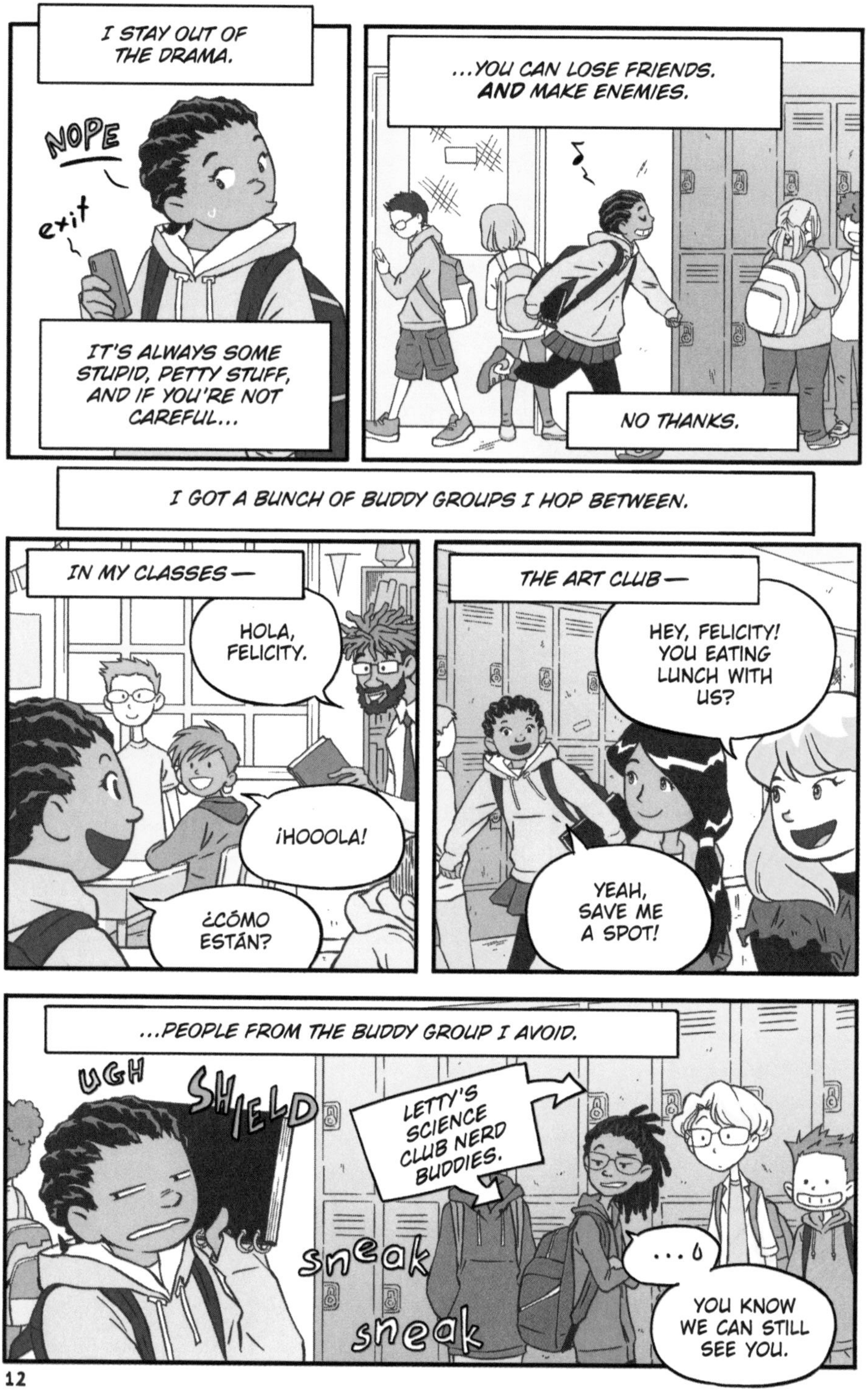

I STAY OUT OF THE DRAMA.
NOPE
exit
IT'S ALWAYS SOME STUPID, PETTY STUFF, AND IF YOU'RE NOT CAREFUL...
...YOU CAN LOSE FRIENDS. AND MAKE ENEMIES.
NO THANKS.
I GOT A BUNCH OF BUDDY GROUPS I HOP BETWEEN.
IN MY CLASSES—
HOLA, FELICITY.
¡HOOOLA!
¿CÓMO ESTÁN?
THE ART CLUB—
HEY, FELICITY! YOU EATING LUNCH WITH US?
YEAH, SAVE ME A SPOT!
...PEOPLE FROM THE BUDDY GROUP I AVOID.
UGH
SHIELD
LETTY'S SCIENCE CLUB NERD BUDDIES.
sneak
sneak
...
YOU KNOW WE CAN STILL SEE YOU.

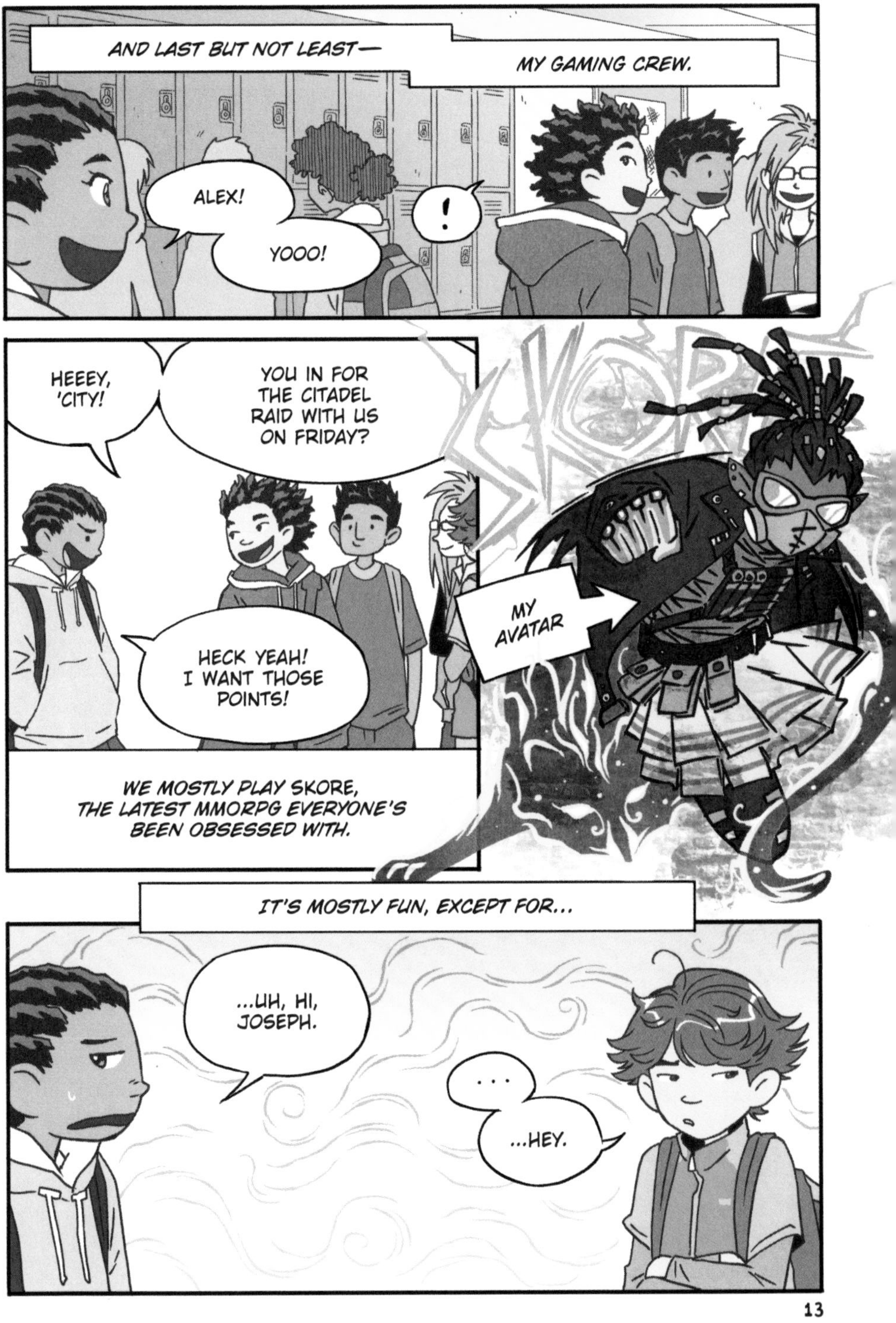
AND LAST BUT NOT LEAST—
MY GAMING CREW.
ALEX!
YOOO!
!
HEEEY, 'CITY!
YOU IN FOR THE CITADEL RAID WITH US ON FRIDAY?
HECK YEAH! I WANT THOSE POINTS!
WE MOSTLY PLAY SKORE, THE LATEST MMORPG EVERYONE'S BEEN OBSESSED WITH.
MY AVATAR
IT'S MOSTLY FUN, EXCEPT FOR...
...UH, HI, JOSEPH.
. . .
...HEY.

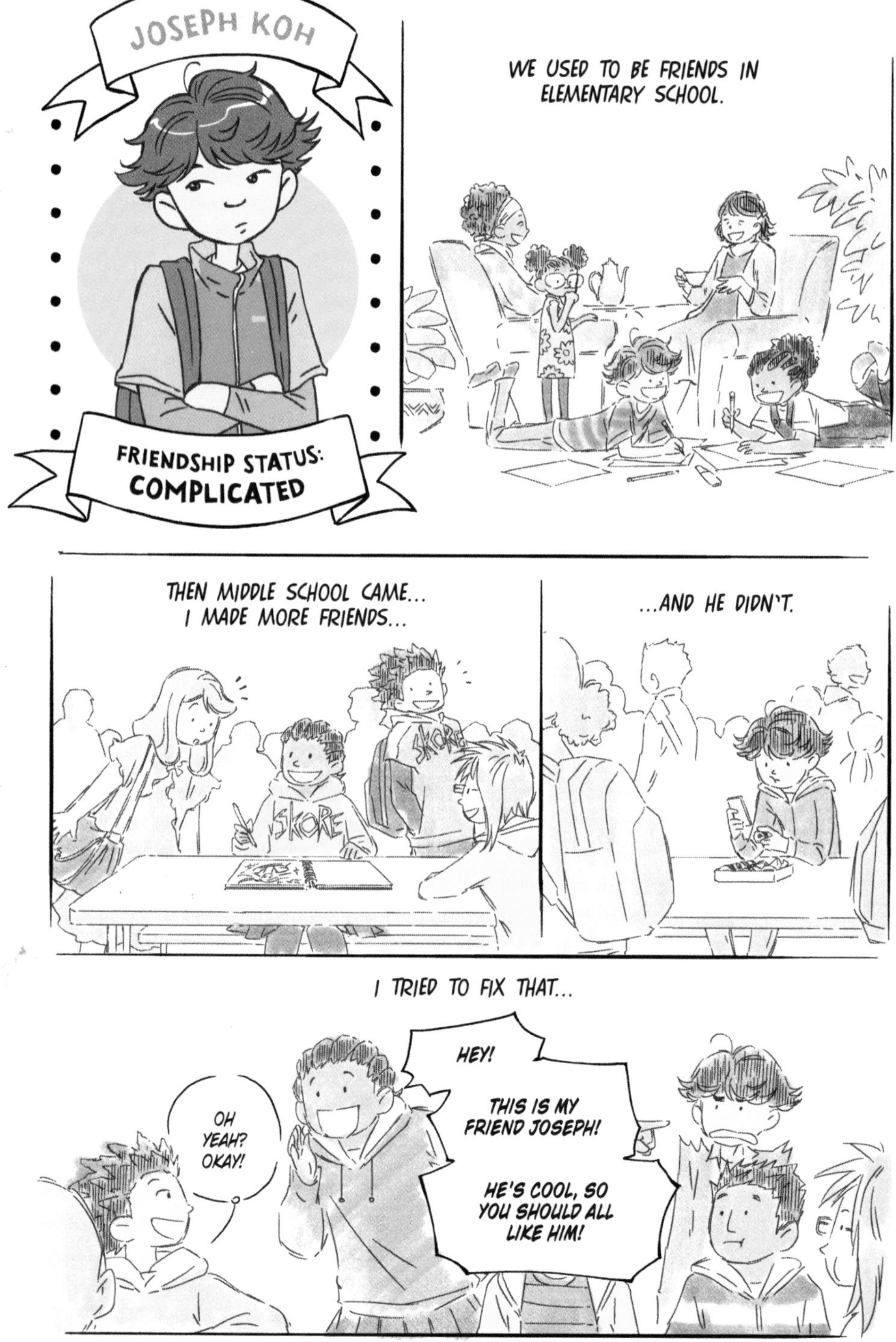
JOSEPH KOH
FRIENDSHIP STATUS:
COMPLICATED
WE USED TO BE FRIENDS IN ELEMENTARY SCHOOL.
THEN MIDDLE SCHOOL CAME... I MADE MORE FRIENDS...
SKORE
...AND HE DIDN'T.
I TRIED TO FIX THAT...
HEY!
THIS IS MY FRIEND JOSEPH!
HE'S COOL, SO YOU SHOULD ALL LIKE HIM!
OH YEAH? OKAY!

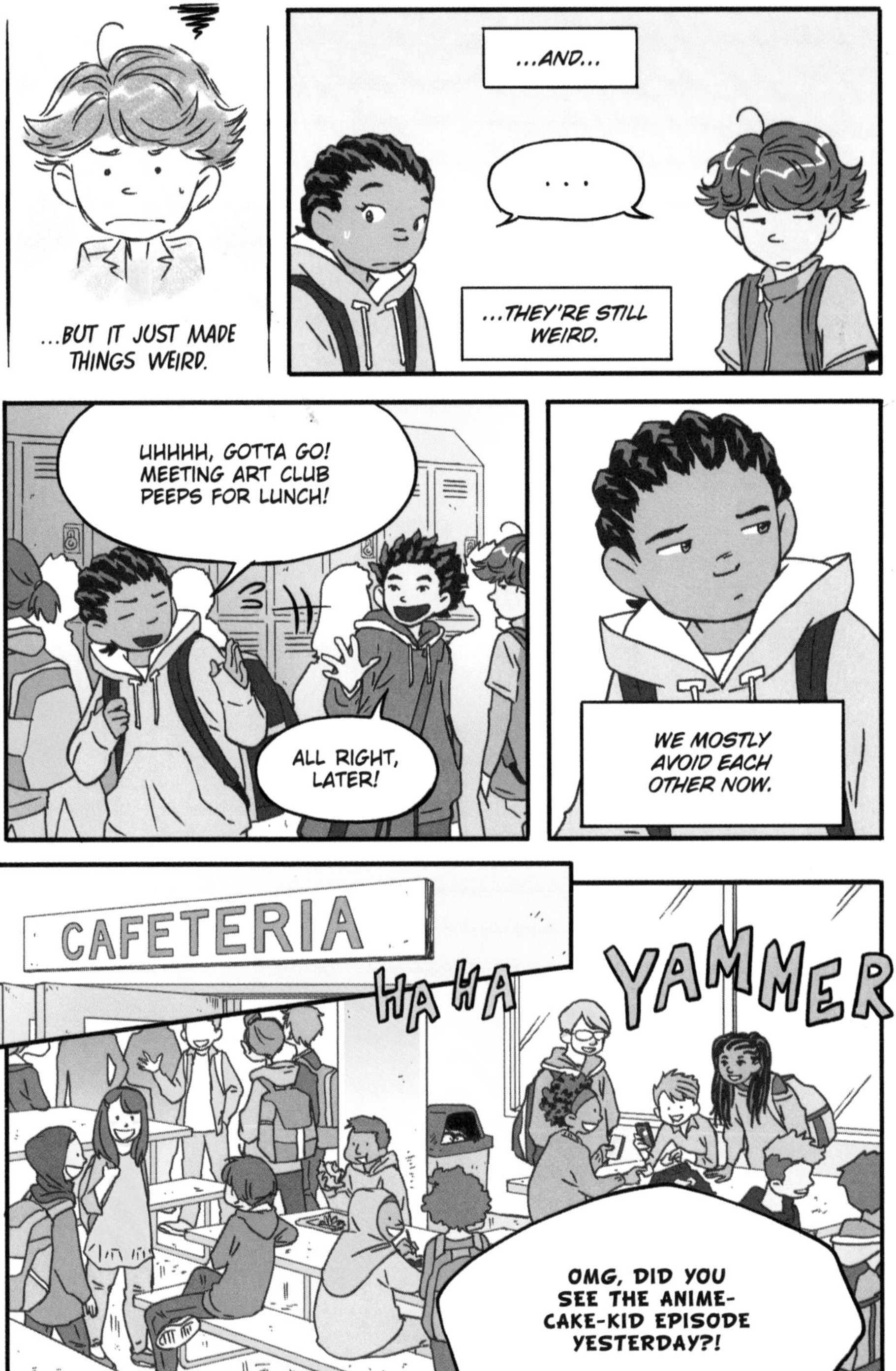

...BUT IT JUST MADE THINGS WEIRD.
...AND...
. . .
...THEY'RE STILL WEIRD.
UHHHH, GOTTA GO! MEETING ART CLUB PEEPS FOR LUNCH!
ALL RIGHT, LATER!
WE MOSTLY AVOID EACH OTHER NOW.
CAFETERIA
HA HA
YAMMER
OMG, DID YOU SEE THE ANIME-CAKE-KID EPISODE YESTERDAY?!

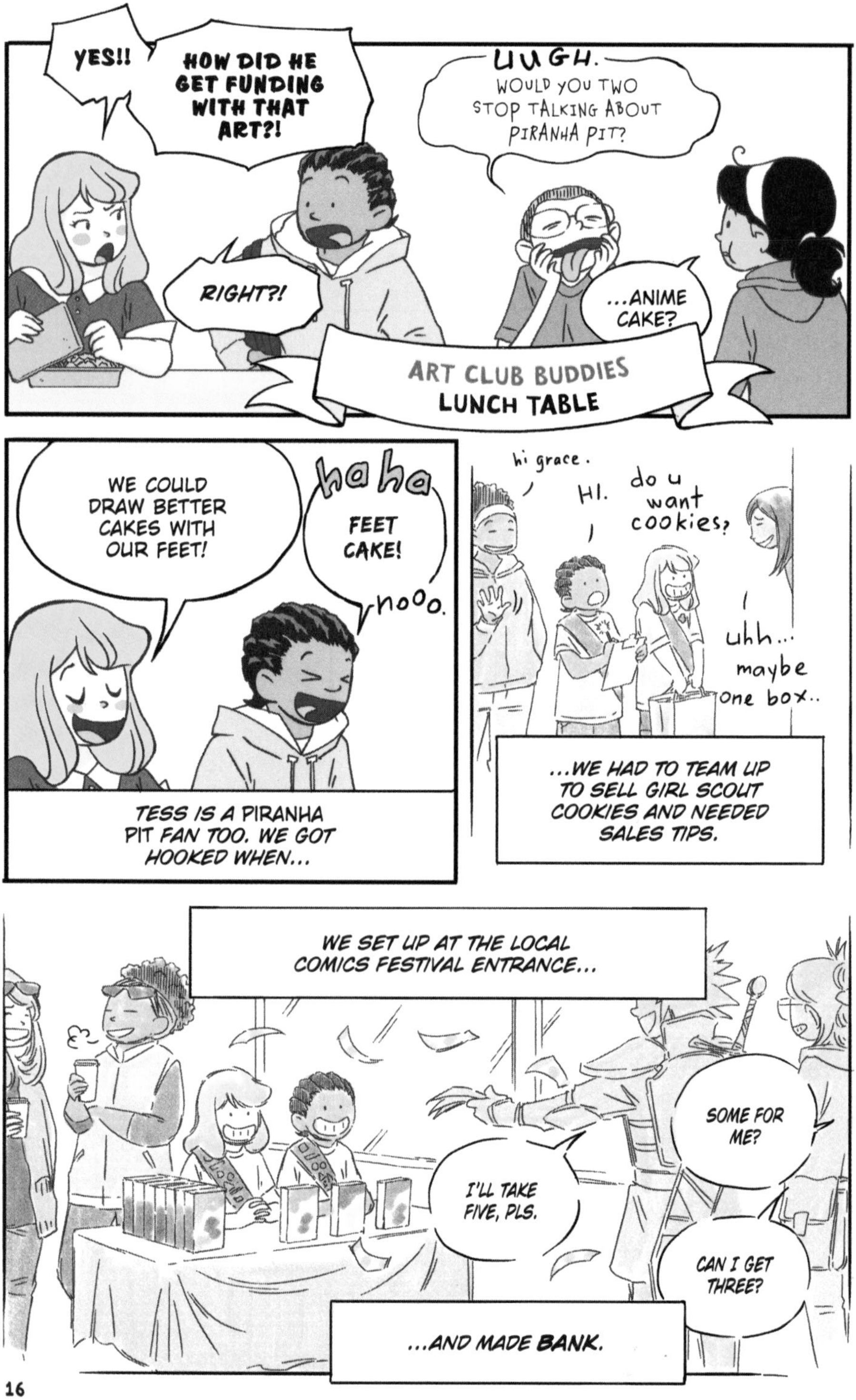
YES!!
HOW DID HE GET FUNDING WITH THAT ART?!
UUGH.
WOULD YOU TWO STOP TALKING ABOUT PIRANHA PIT?
RIGHT?!
...ANIME CAKE?
ART CLUB BUDDIES
LUNCH TABLE
WE COULD DRAW BETTER CAKES WITH OUR FEET!
haha
FEET CAKE!
nooo.
TESS IS A PIRANHA PIT FAN TOO. WE GOT HOOKED WHEN...
hi grace.
HI.
do u want cookies?
uhh... maybe one box..
...WE HAD TO TEAM UP TO SELL GIRL SCOUT COOKIES AND NEEDED SALES TIPS.
WE SET UP AT THE LOCAL COMICS FESTIVAL ENTRANCE...
SOME FOR ME?
I'LL TAKE FIVE, PLS.
CAN I GET THREE?
...AND MADE BANK.

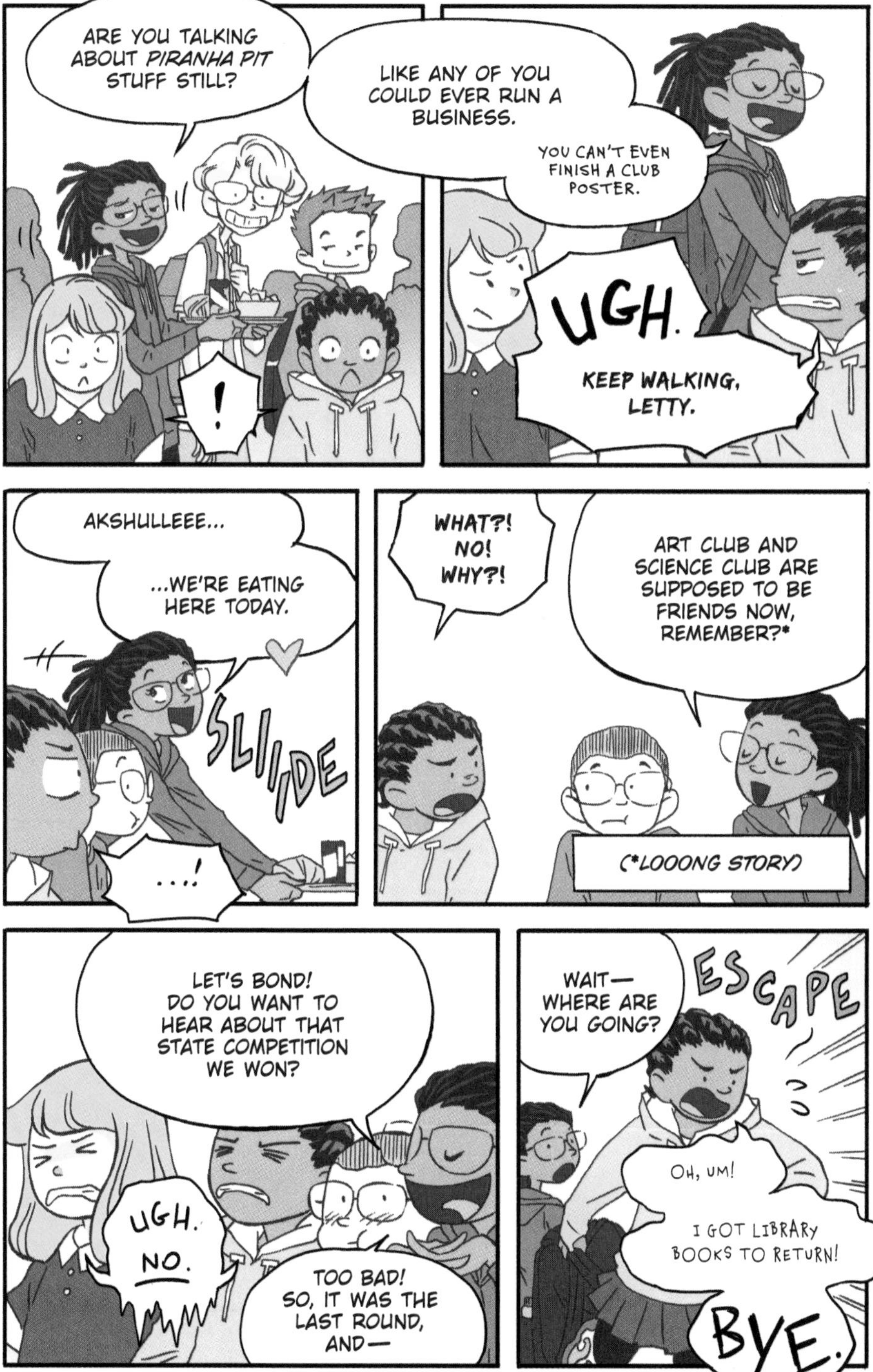

ARE YOU TALKING ABOUT *PIRANHA PIT* STUFF STILL?
LIKE ANY OF YOU COULD EVER RUN A BUSINESS.
YOU CAN'T EVEN FINISH A CLUB POSTER.
!
UGH.
KEEP WALKING, LETTY.
AKSHULLEEE...
...WE'RE EATING HERE TODAY.
SLIIIDE
...!
WHAT?! NO! WHY?!
ART CLUB AND SCIENCE CLUB ARE SUPPOSED TO BE FRIENDS NOW, REMEMBER?*
(*LOOONG STORY)
LET'S BOND! DO YOU WANT TO HEAR ABOUT THAT STATE COMPETITION WE WON?
UGH. NO.
TOO BAD! SO, IT WAS THE LAST ROUND, AND—
WAIT— WHERE ARE YOU GOING?
ESCAPE
OH, UM!
I GOT LIBRARY BOOKS TO RETURN!
BYE.

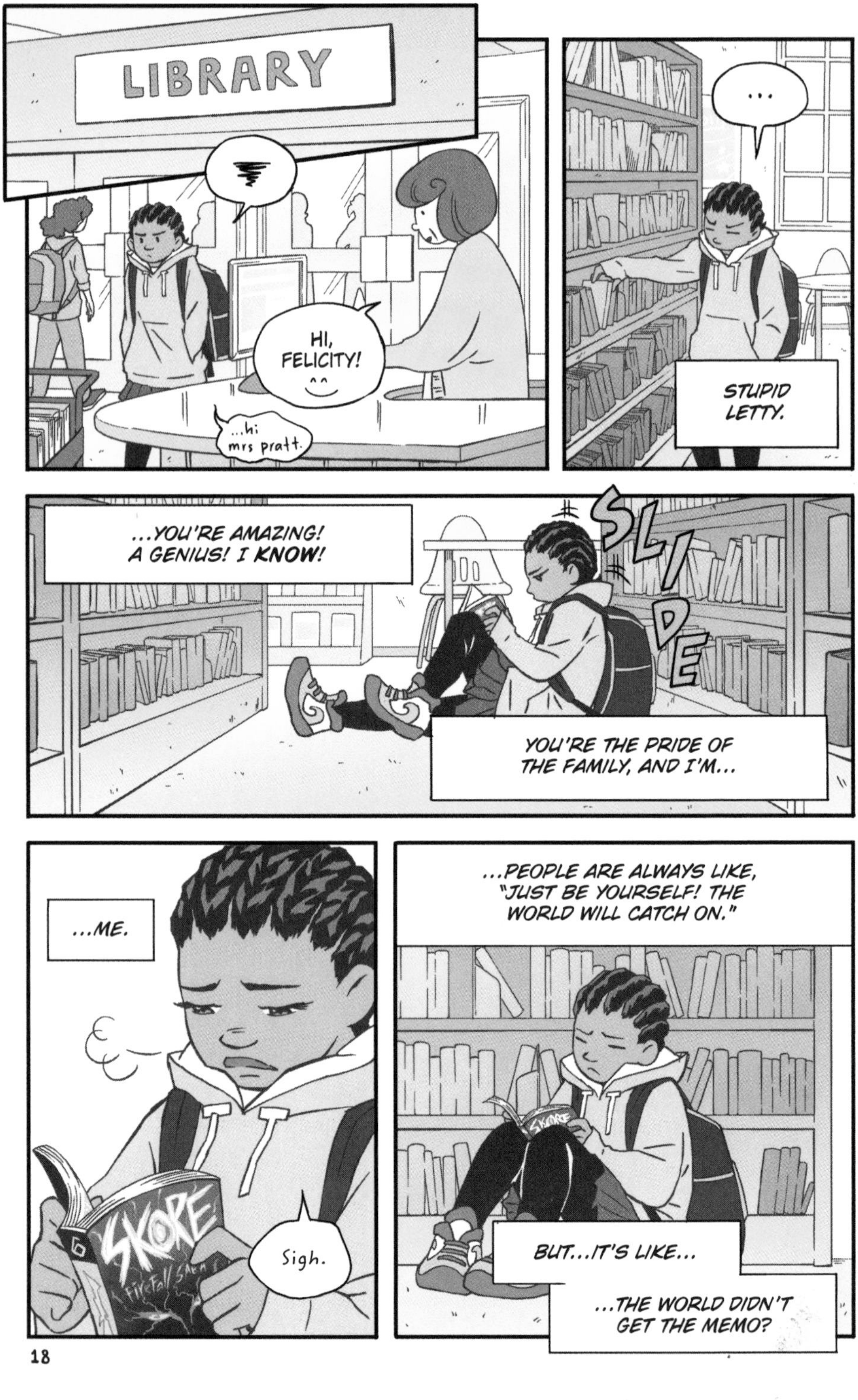
LIBRARY
HI, FELICITY! ^^
...hi mrs pratt.
...
STUPID LETTY.
...YOU'RE AMAZING! A GENIUS! I KNOW!
SLIDE
YOU'RE THE PRIDE OF THE FAMILY, AND I'M...
...ME.
SKORE
Sigh.
...PEOPLE ARE ALWAYS LIKE, "JUST BE YOURSELF! THE WORLD WILL CATCH ON."
SKORE
BUT...IT'S LIKE...
...THE WORLD DIDN'T GET THE MEMO?

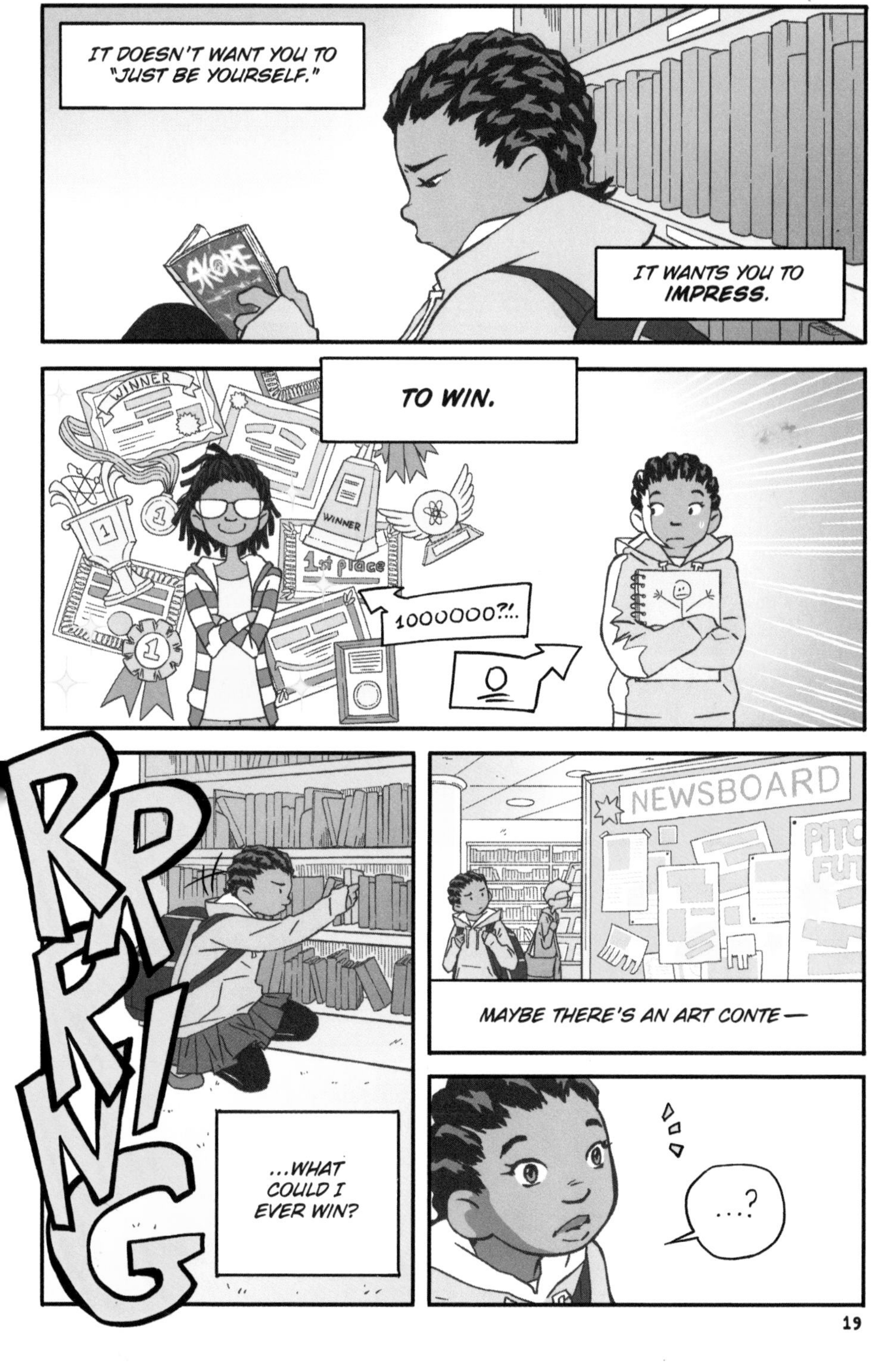
IT DOESN'T WANT YOU TO "JUST BE YOURSELF."
SKORE
IT WANTS YOU TO IMPRESS.
TO WIN.
WINNER
WINNER
1st place
1000000?!..
0
RRRIIING
...WHAT COULD I EVER WIN?
NEWSBOARD
MAYBE THERE'S AN ART CONTE—
...?

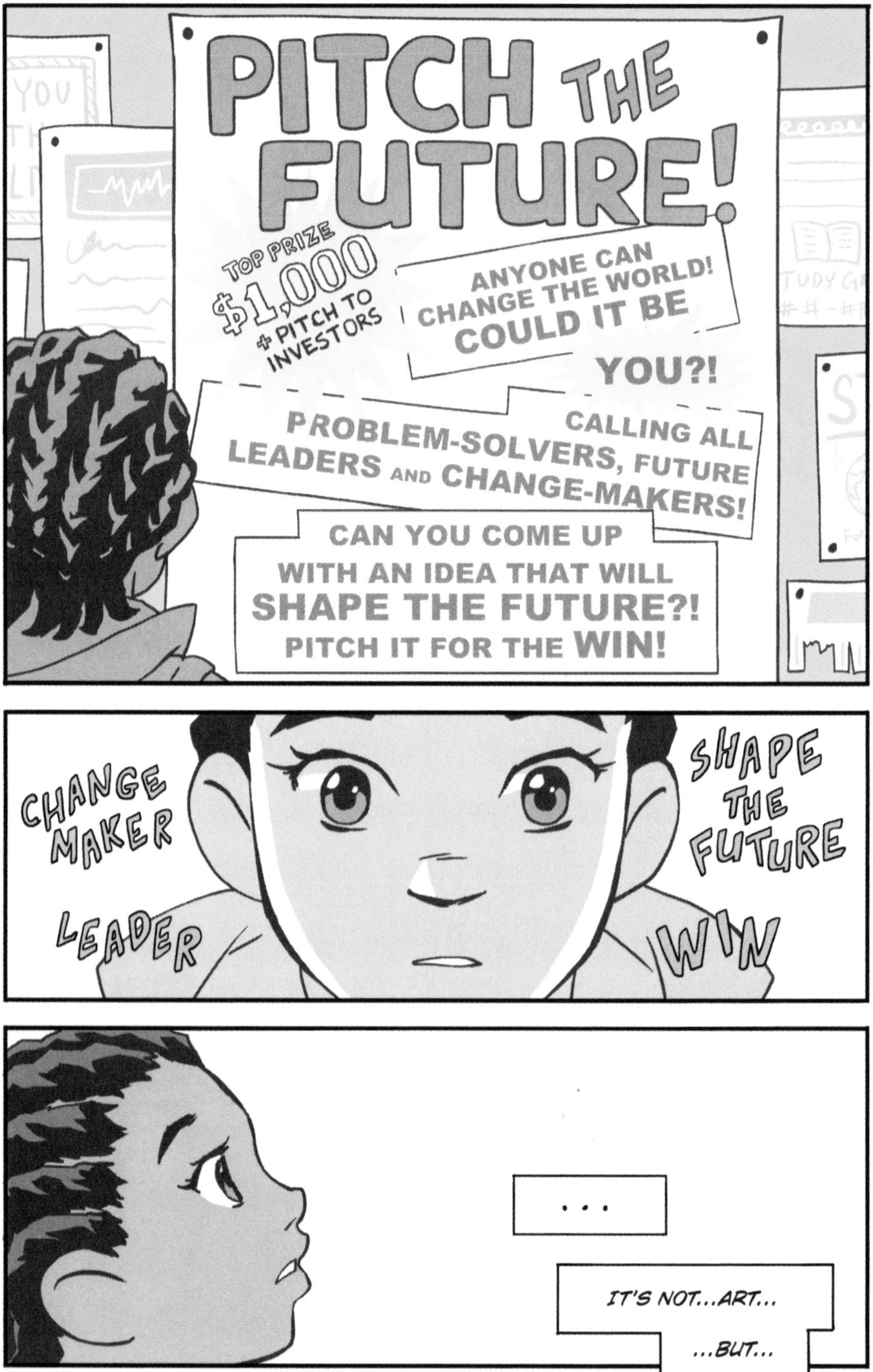
PITCH THE FUTURE!
TOP PRIZE $1,000 + PITCH TO INVESTORS
ANYONE CAN CHANGE THE WORLD! COULD IT BE YOU?!
CALLING ALL PROBLEM-SOLVERS, FUTURE LEADERS AND CHANGE-MAKERS!
CAN YOU COME UP WITH AN IDEA THAT WILL SHAPE THE FUTURE?! PITCH IT FOR THE WIN!
CHANGE MAKER
SHAPE THE FUTURE
LEADER
WIN
. . .
IT'S NOT...ART...
...BUT...

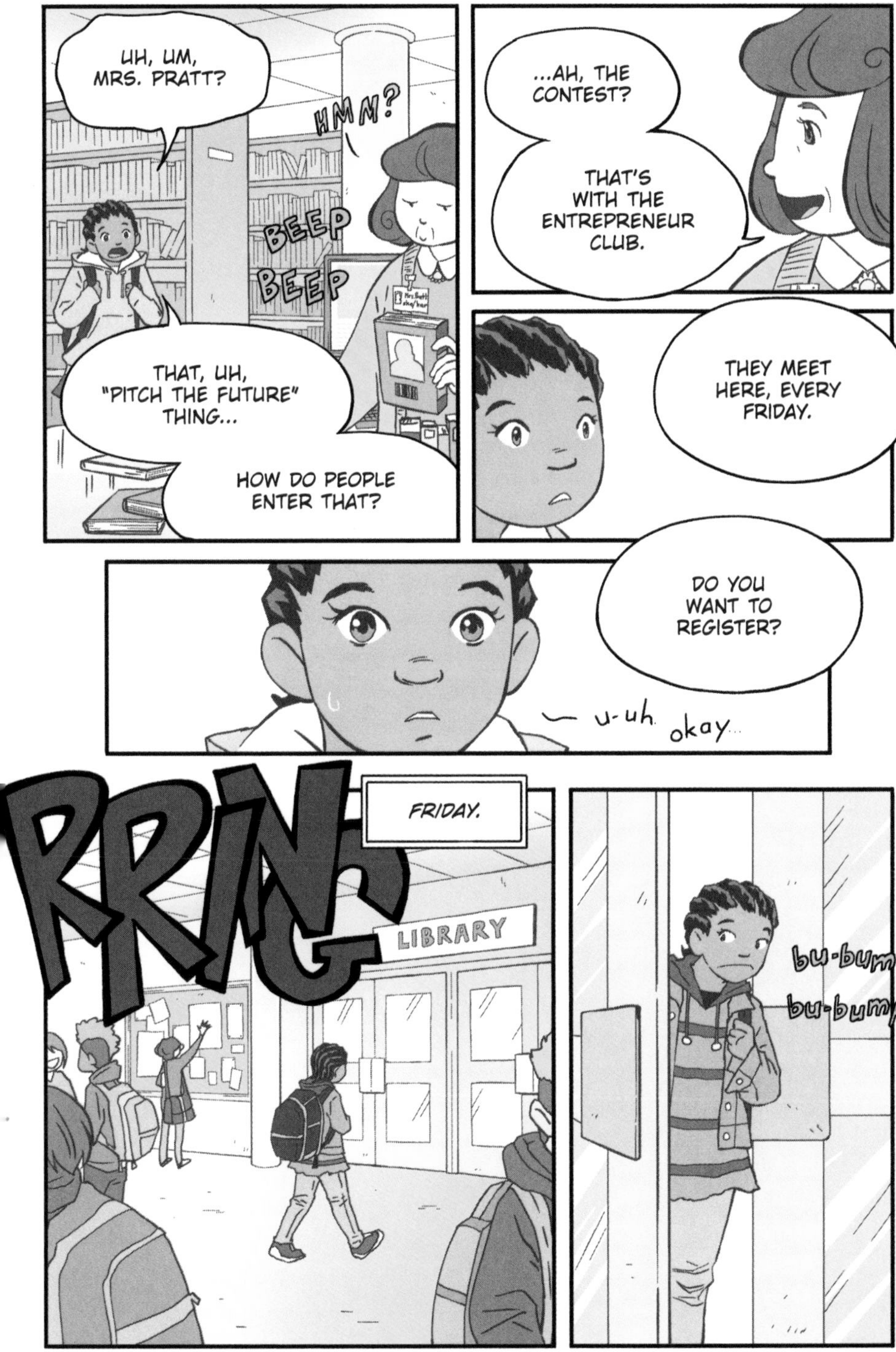
UH, UM, MRS. PRATT?
HMM?
BEEP
BEEP
THAT, UH, "PITCH THE FUTURE" THING...
HOW DO PEOPLE ENTER THAT?
...AH, THE CONTEST?
THAT'S WITH THE ENTREPRENEUR CLUB.
THEY MEET HERE, EVERY FRIDAY.
DO YOU WANT TO REGISTER?
u-uh. okay...
RRING
FRIDAY.
LIBRARY
bu-bump
bu-bump

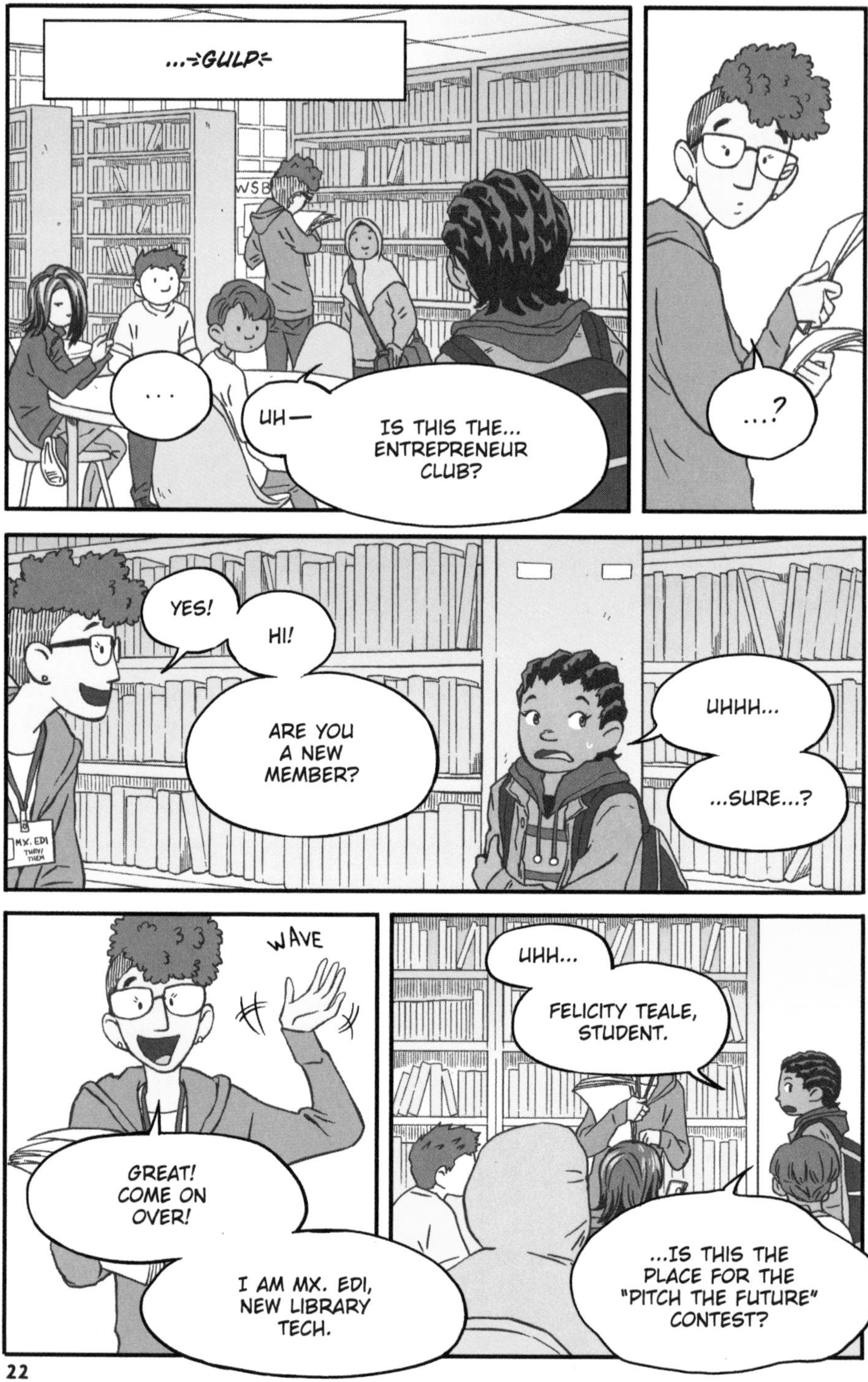
...GULP
...
UH—
IS THIS THE... ENTREPRENEUR CLUB?
...?
YES!
HI!
ARE YOU A NEW MEMBER?
UHHH...
...SURE...?
MX. EDI THEY/THEM
WAVE
GREAT! COME ON OVER!
I AM MX. EDI, NEW LIBRARY TECH.
UHH...
FELICITY TEALE, STUDENT.
...IS THIS THE PLACE FOR THE "PITCH THE FUTURE" CONTEST?

IT SURE IS!!

WELCOME!

EEEEE

WE WERE JUST ABOUT TO START!

HERE'S THE CONTEST-INFO BOOKLET...

...AND THE WORKBOOK WE'RE USING.

GRAB A SEAT!

NOW, LET'S PICK UP WHERE WE LEFT OFF LAST WEEK!

SCRAPE

WE WENT OVER THE RULES, WE BRAINSTORMED IDEAS...

NOW LET'S TALK FORMAT!

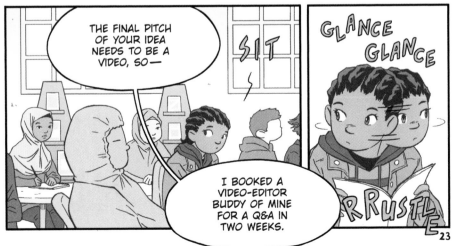

THE FINAL PITCH OF YOUR IDEA NEEDS TO BE A VIDEO, SO—

SIT

GLANCE GLANCE

I BOOKED A VIDEO-EDITOR BUDDY OF MINE FOR A Q&A IN TWO WEEKS.

RRUSTLE

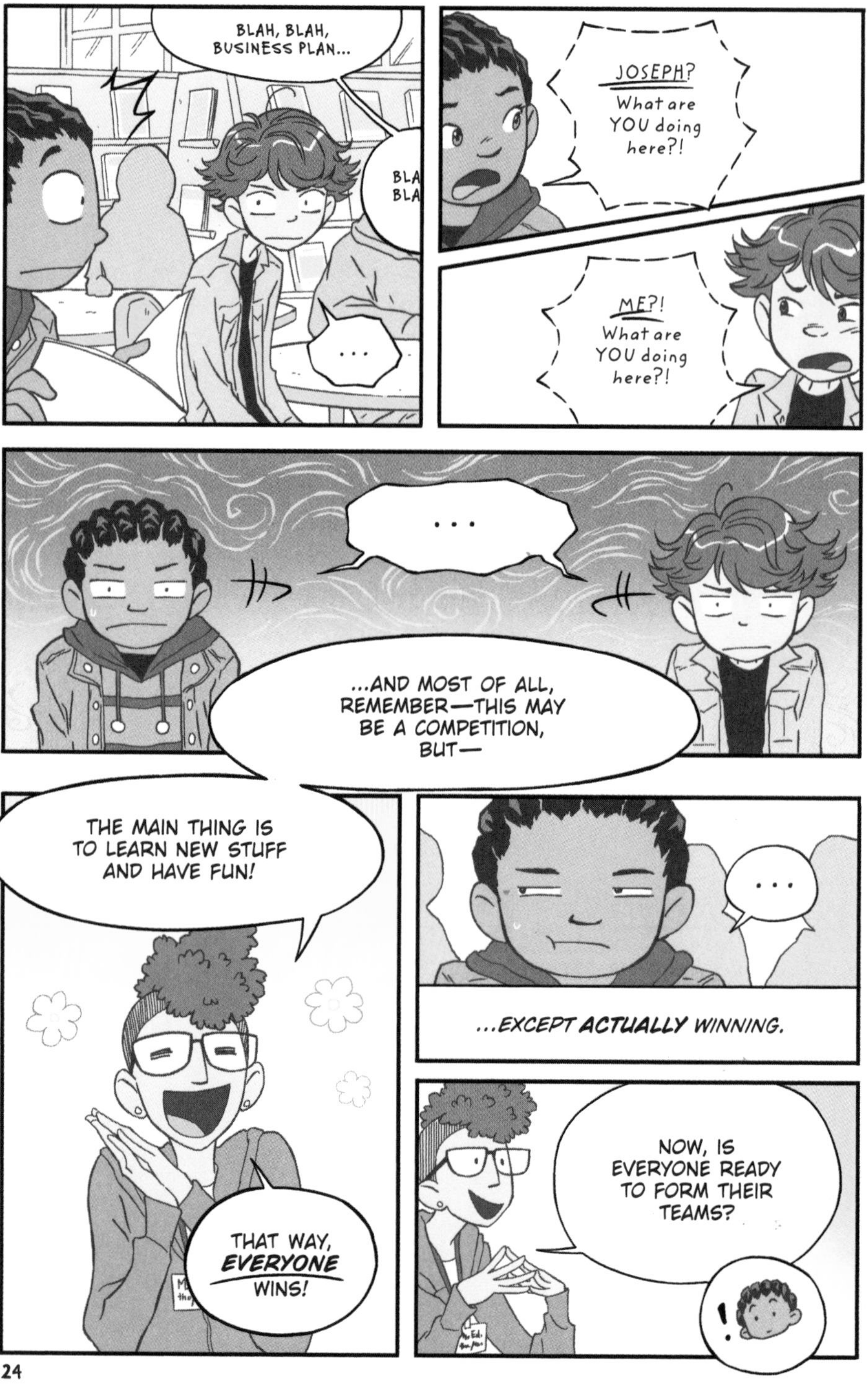
BLAH, BLAH, BUSINESS PLAN...
...
JOSEPH? What are YOU doing here?!
ME?! What are YOU doing here?!
...
...AND MOST OF ALL, REMEMBER—THIS MAY BE A COMPETITION, BUT—
THE MAIN THING IS TO LEARN NEW STUFF AND HAVE FUN!
THAT WAY, EVERYONE WINS!
...
...EXCEPT ACTUALLY WINNING.
NOW, IS EVERYONE READY TO FORM THEIR TEAMS?
!

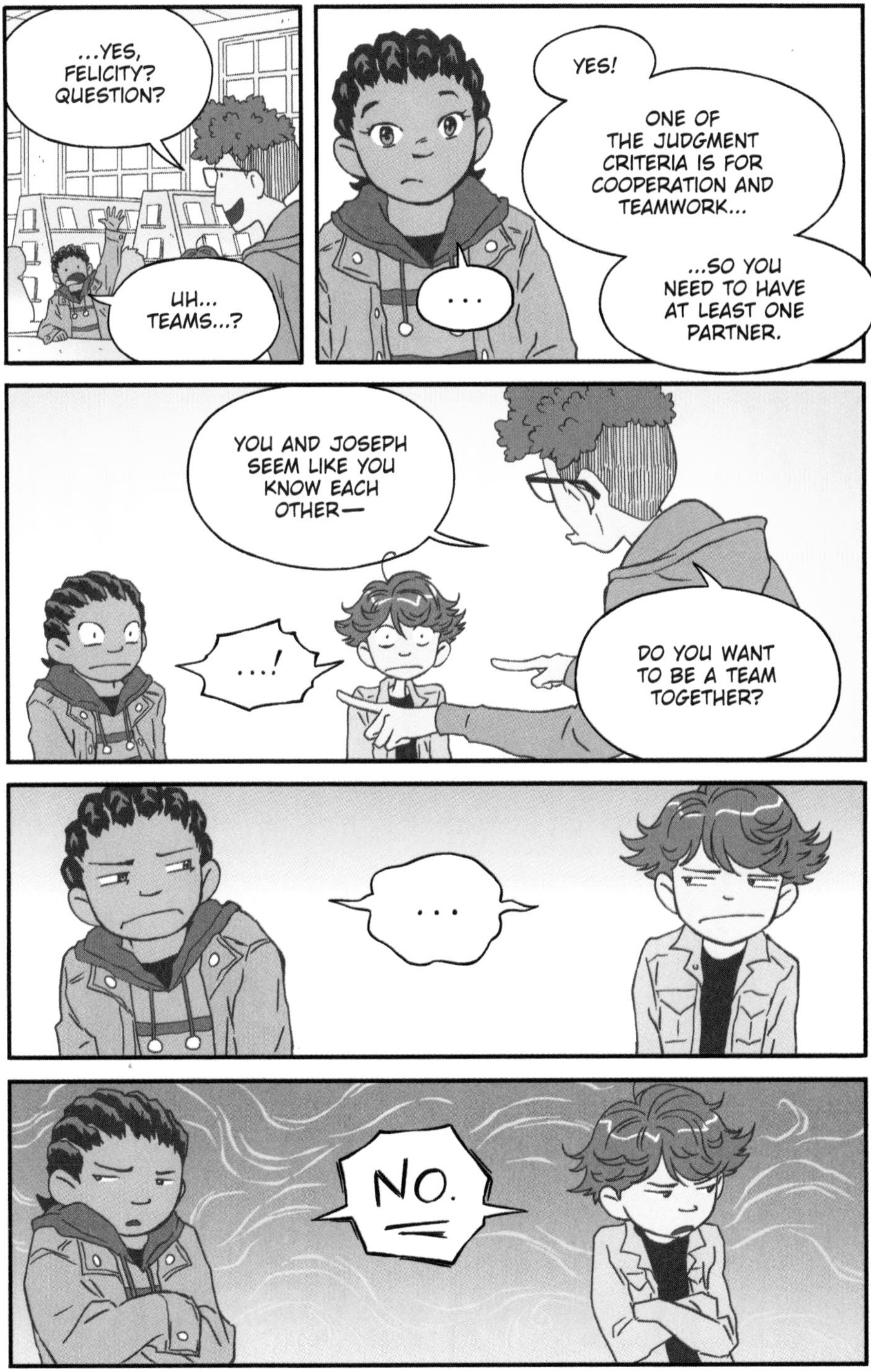
...YES, FELICITY? QUESTION?
UH... TEAMS...?
YES!
ONE OF THE JUDGMENT CRITERIA IS FOR COOPERATION AND TEAMWORK...
...
...SO YOU NEED TO HAVE AT LEAST ONE PARTNER.
YOU AND JOSEPH SEEM LIKE YOU KNOW EACH OTHER—
DO YOU WANT TO BE A TEAM TOGETHER?
...!
...
NO.

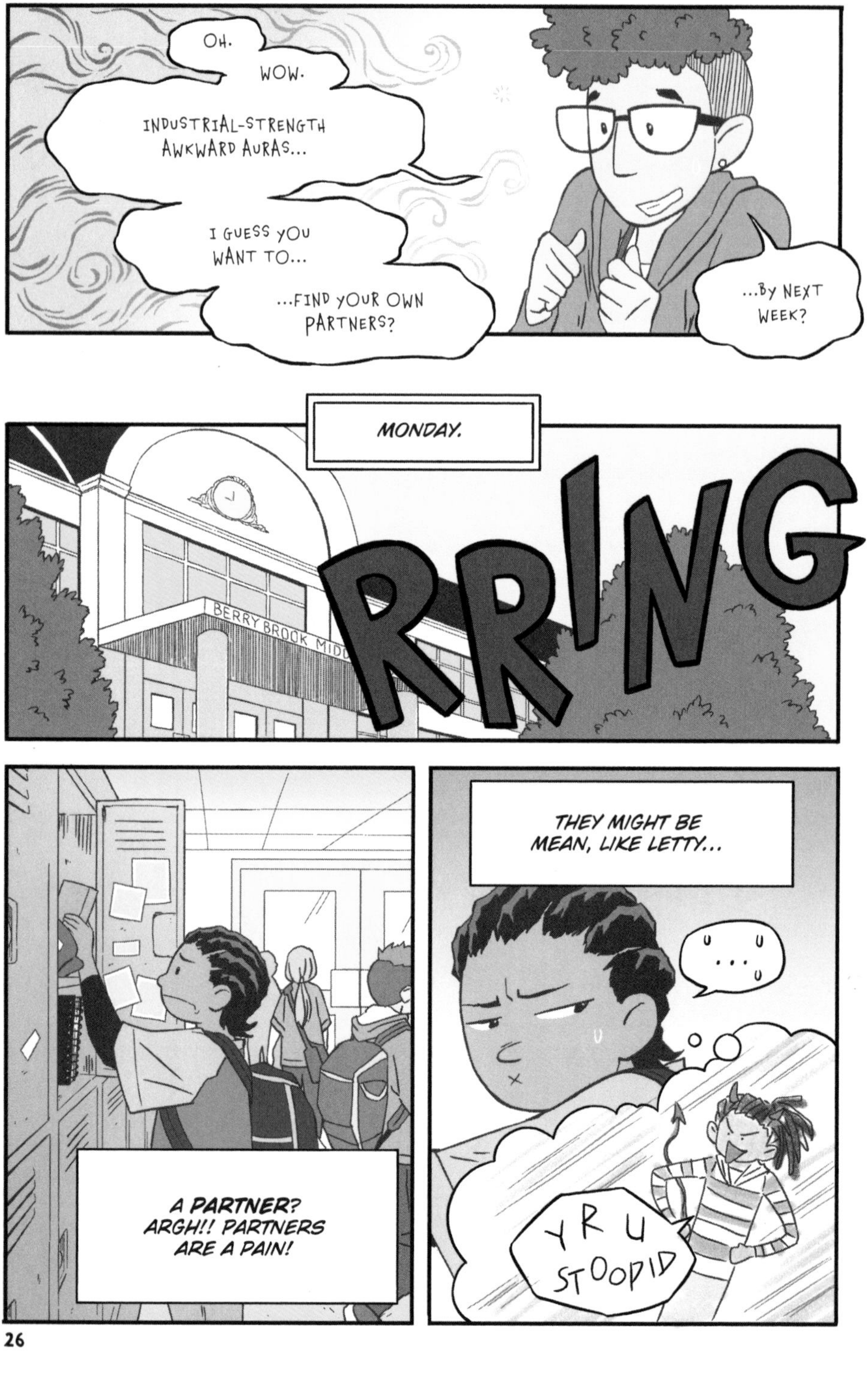

OH.
WOW.
INDUSTRIAL-STRENGTH AWKWARD AURAS...
I GUESS YOU WANT TO...
...FIND YOUR OWN PARTNERS?
...BY NEXT WEEK?
MONDAY.
RRING
BERRY BROOK MIDD
A PARTNER? ARGH!! PARTNERS ARE A PAIN!
THEY MIGHT BE MEAN, LIKE LETTY...
...
Y R U STOOPID

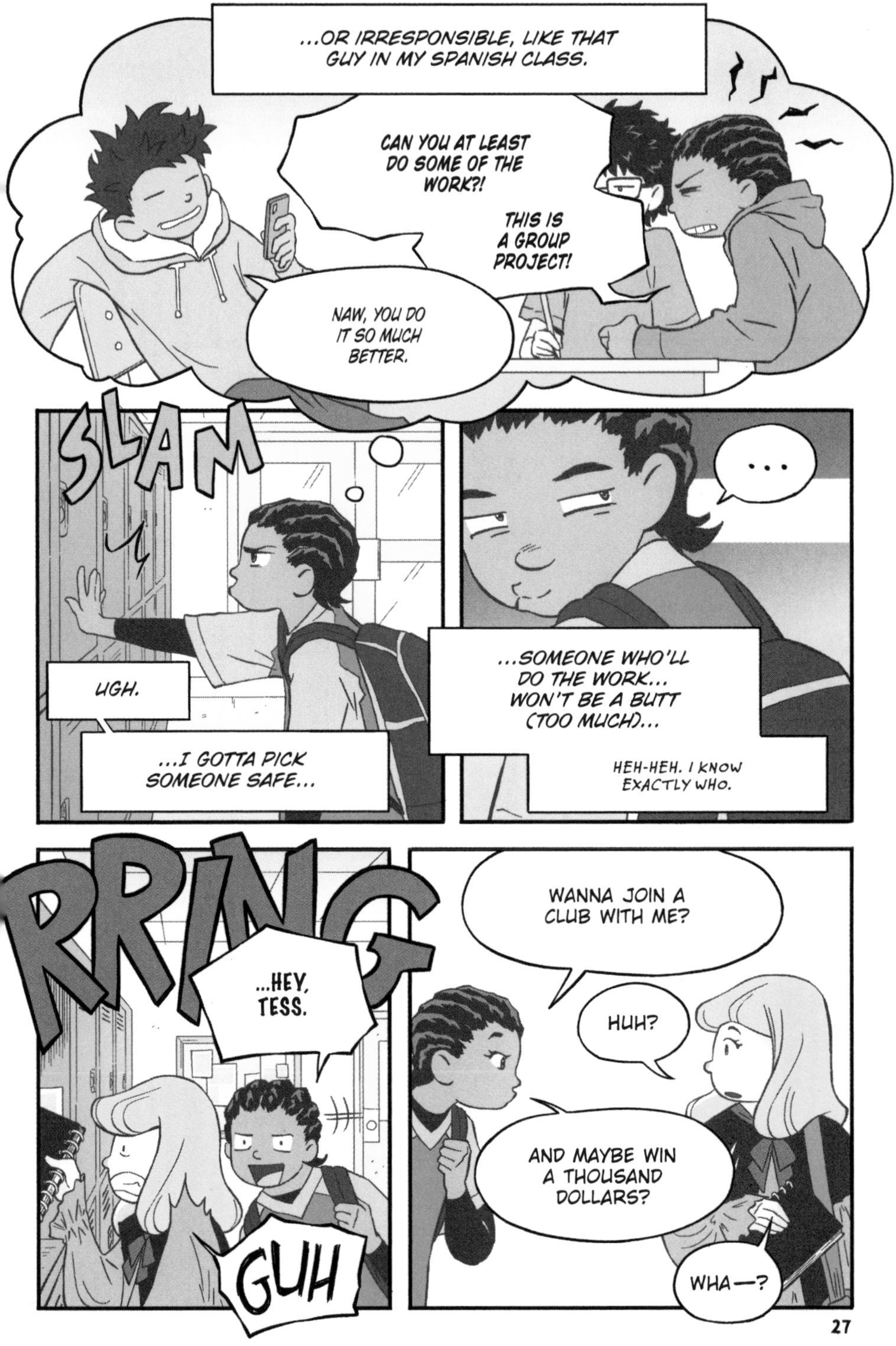
...OR IRRESPONSIBLE, LIKE THAT GUY IN MY SPANISH CLASS.
CAN YOU AT LEAST DO SOME OF THE WORK?!
THIS IS A GROUP PROJECT!
NAW, YOU DO IT SO MUCH BETTER.
SLAM
UGH.
...I GOTTA PICK SOMEONE SAFE...
...
...SOMEONE WHO'LL DO THE WORK... WON'T BE A BUTT (TOO MUCH)...
HEH-HEH. I KNOW EXACTLY WHO.
RRING
...HEY, TESS.
GUH
WANNA JOIN A CLUB WITH ME?
HUH?
AND MAYBE WIN A THOUSAND DOLLARS?
WHA—?

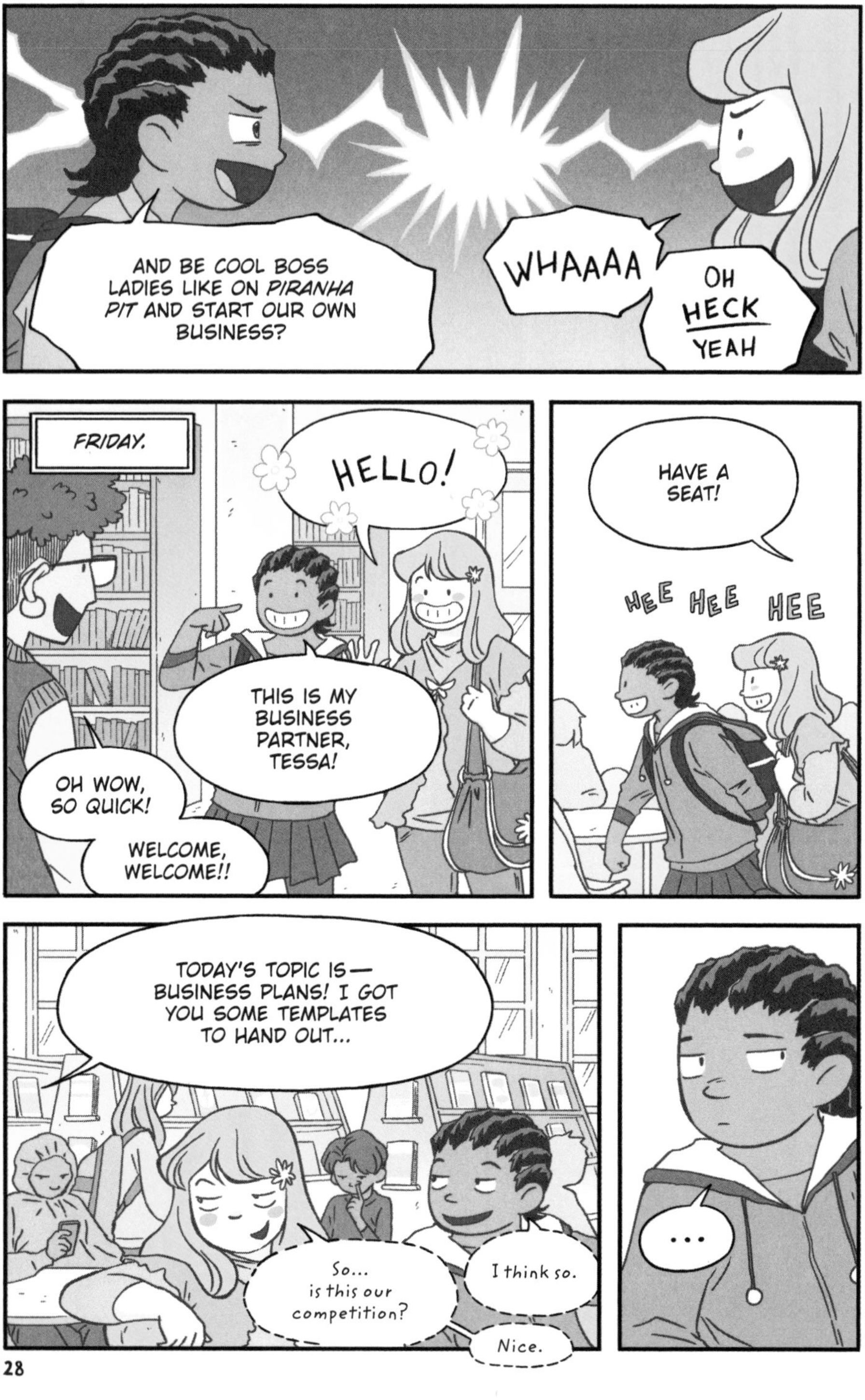
AND BE COOL BOSS LADIES LIKE ON *PIRANHA PIT* AND START OUR OWN BUSINESS?
WHAAAA
OH HECK YEAH
FRIDAY.
HELLO!
THIS IS MY BUSINESS PARTNER, TESSA!
OH WOW, SO QUICK!
WELCOME, WELCOME!!
HAVE A SEAT!
HEE HEE HEE
TODAY'S TOPIC IS— BUSINESS PLANS! I GOT YOU SOME TEMPLATES TO HAND OUT...
So... is this our competition?
I think so.
Nice.
...

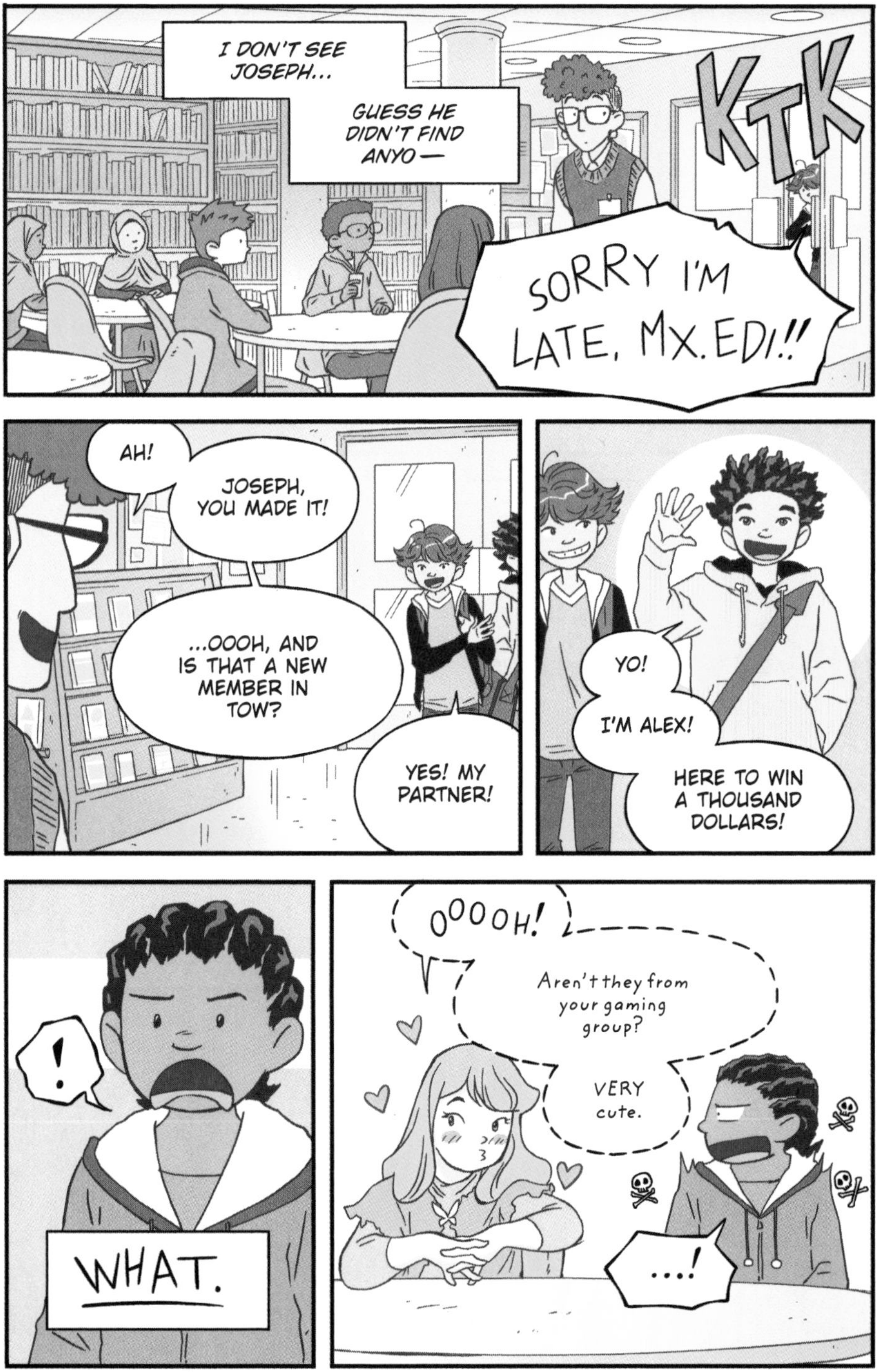
I DON'T SEE JOSEPH...
GUESS HE DIDN'T FIND ANYO—
KTK
SORRY I'M LATE, MX. EDI!!
AH!
JOSEPH, YOU MADE IT!
...OOOH, AND IS THAT A NEW MEMBER IN TOW?
YES! MY PARTNER!
YO!
I'M ALEX!
HERE TO WIN A THOUSAND DOLLARS!
!
WHAT.
OOOOH!
Aren't they from your gaming group?
VERY cute.
...!

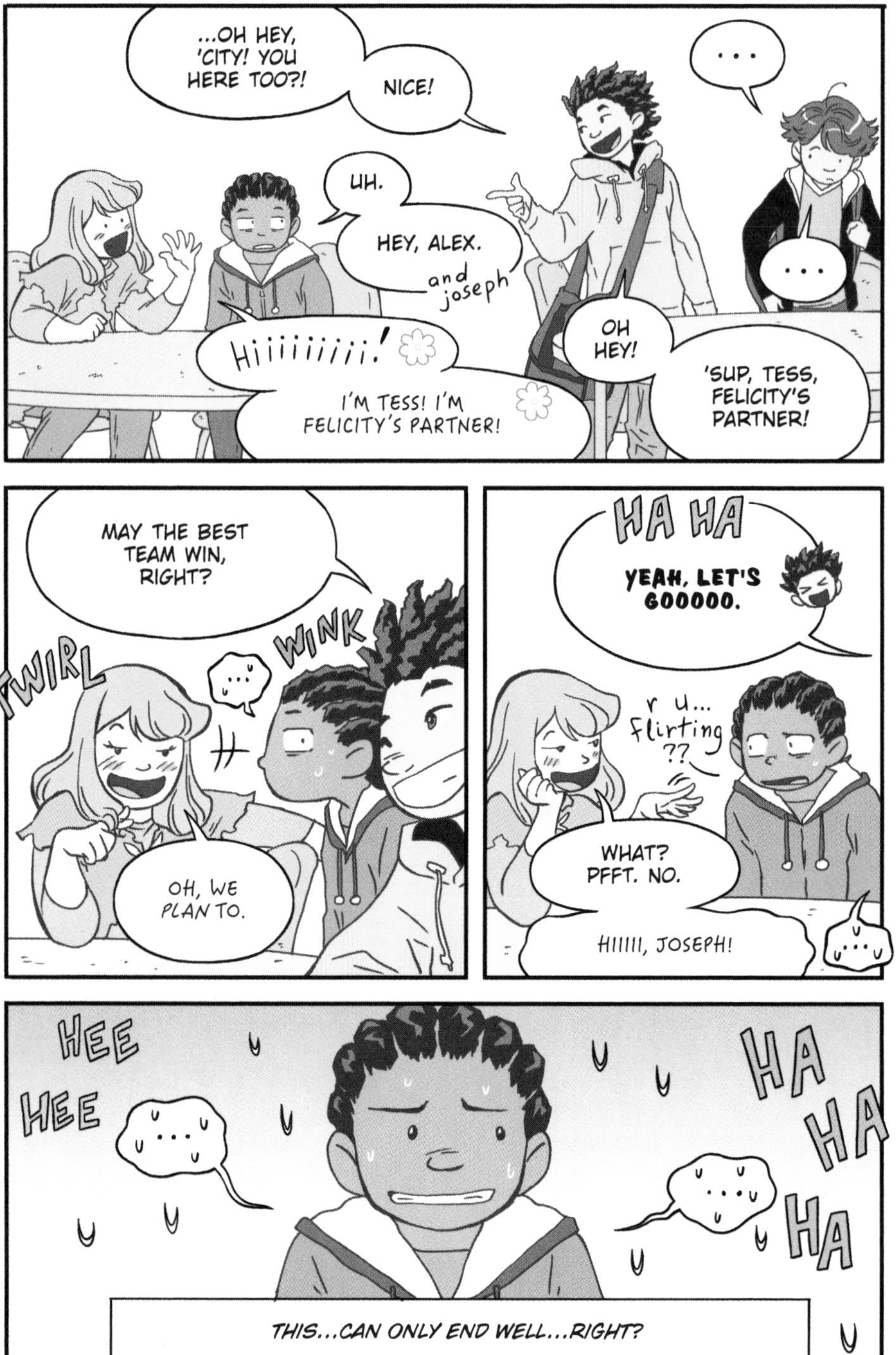
...OH HEY, 'CITY! YOU HERE TOO?!
NICE!
...
UH.
HEY, ALEX.
and joseph
...
Hiiiiiiiii!
I'M TESS! I'M FELICITY'S PARTNER!
OH HEY!
'SUP, TESS, FELICITY'S PARTNER!
MAY THE BEST TEAM WIN, RIGHT?
TWIRL
WINK
...
OH, WE PLAN TO.
HA HA
YEAH, LET'S GOOOOO.
r u... flirting ??
WHAT? PFFT. NO.
HIIIII, JOSEPH!
...
HEE HEE
...
HA HA HA
...
THIS...CAN ONLY END WELL...RIGHT?

CHAPTER 2

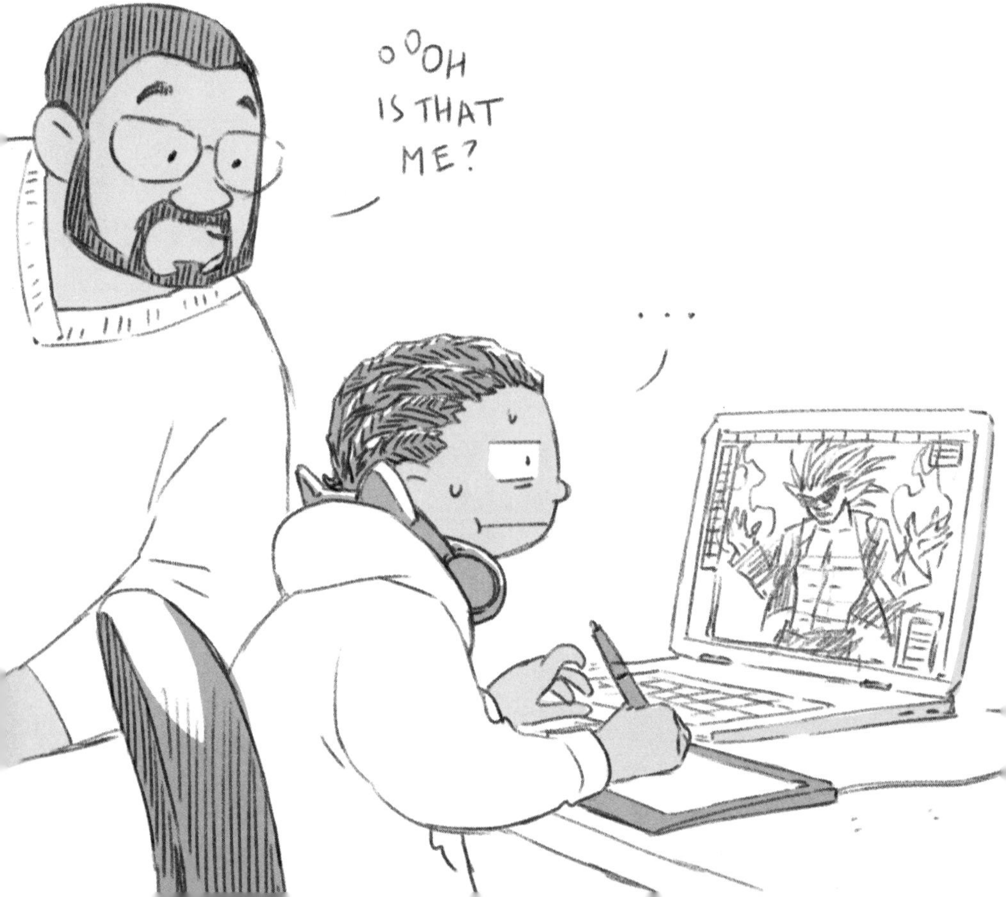
OOOH IS THAT ME?
...

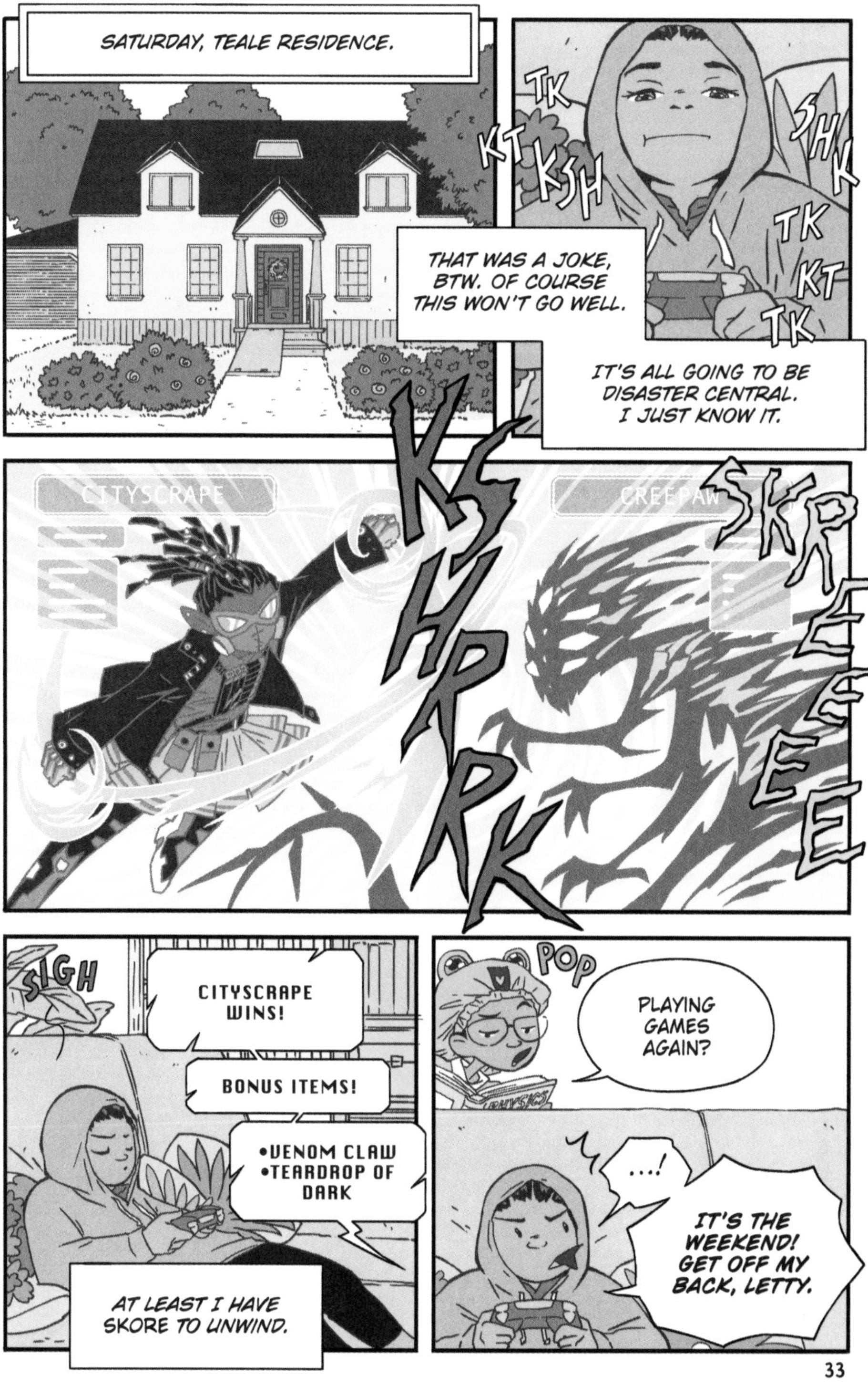
SATURDAY, TEALE RESIDENCE.
TK
KT
KSH
SHK
TK
KT
TK
THAT WAS A JOKE, BTW. OF COURSE THIS WON'T GO WELL.
IT'S ALL GOING TO BE DISASTER CENTRAL. I JUST KNOW IT.
CITYSCRAPE
CREEPAW
KSHRK
SKREEEE
SIGH
CITYSCRAPE WINS!
BONUS ITEMS!
•VENOM CLAW
•TEARDROP OF DARK
AT LEAST I HAVE SKORE TO UNWIND.
POP
PLAYING GAMES AGAIN?
...!
IT'S THE WEEKEND! GET OFF MY BACK, LETTY.

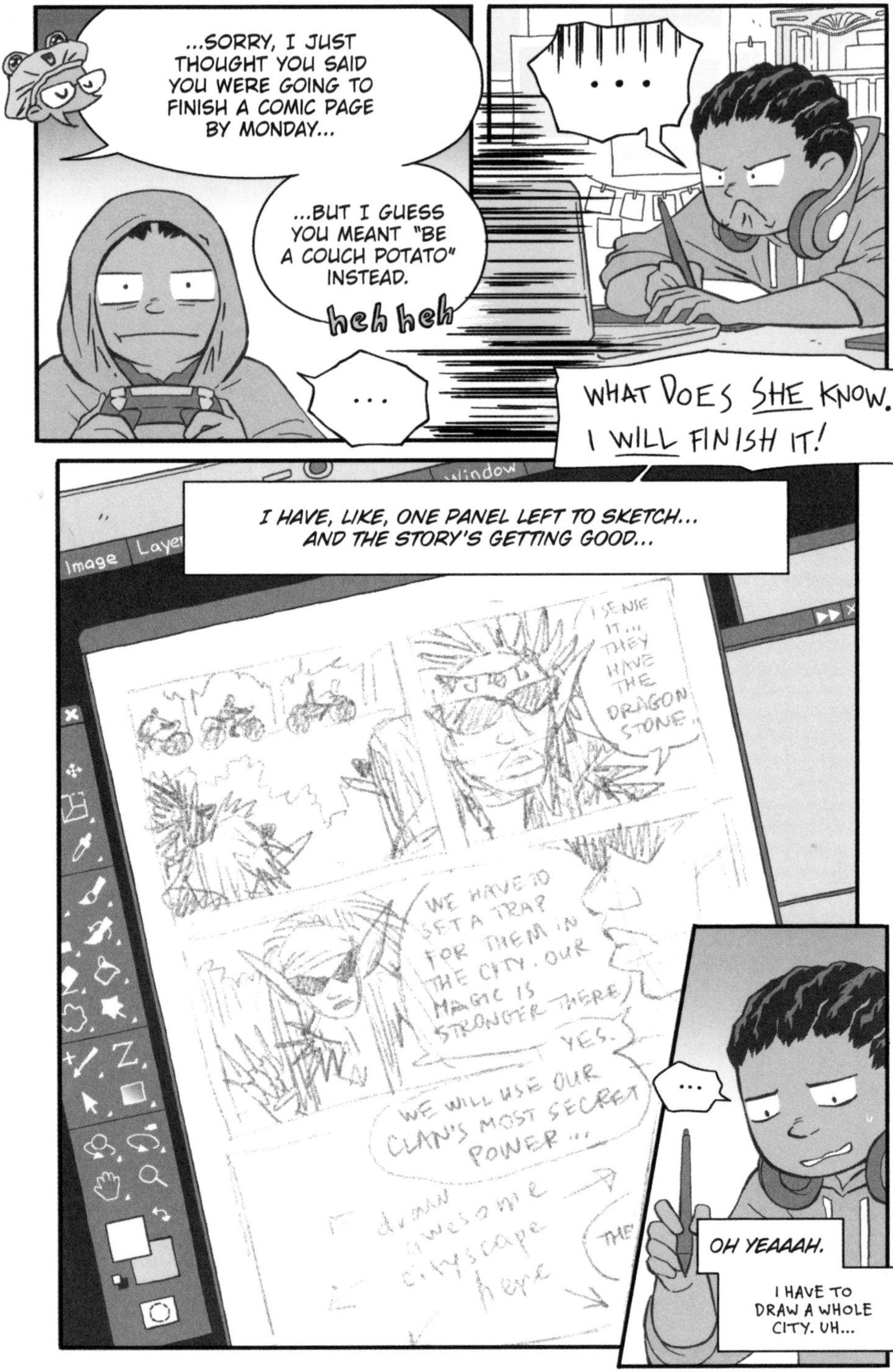
...SORRY, I JUST THOUGHT YOU SAID YOU WERE GOING TO FINISH A COMIC PAGE BY MONDAY...
...BUT I GUESS YOU MEANT "BE A COUCH POTATO" INSTEAD.
heh heh
...
...
WHAT DOES SHE KNOW. I WILL FINISH IT!
I HAVE, LIKE, ONE PANEL LEFT TO SKETCH... AND THE STORY'S GETTING GOOD...
Image
Window
I SENSE IT... THEY HAVE THE DRAGON STONE.
WE HAVE TO SET A TRAP FOR THEM IN THE CITY. OUR MAGIC IS STRONGER THERE.
YES.
WE WILL USE OUR CLAN'S MOST SECRET POWER...
draw awesome cityscape here
...
OH YEAAAH.
I HAVE TO DRAW A WHOLE CITY. UH...

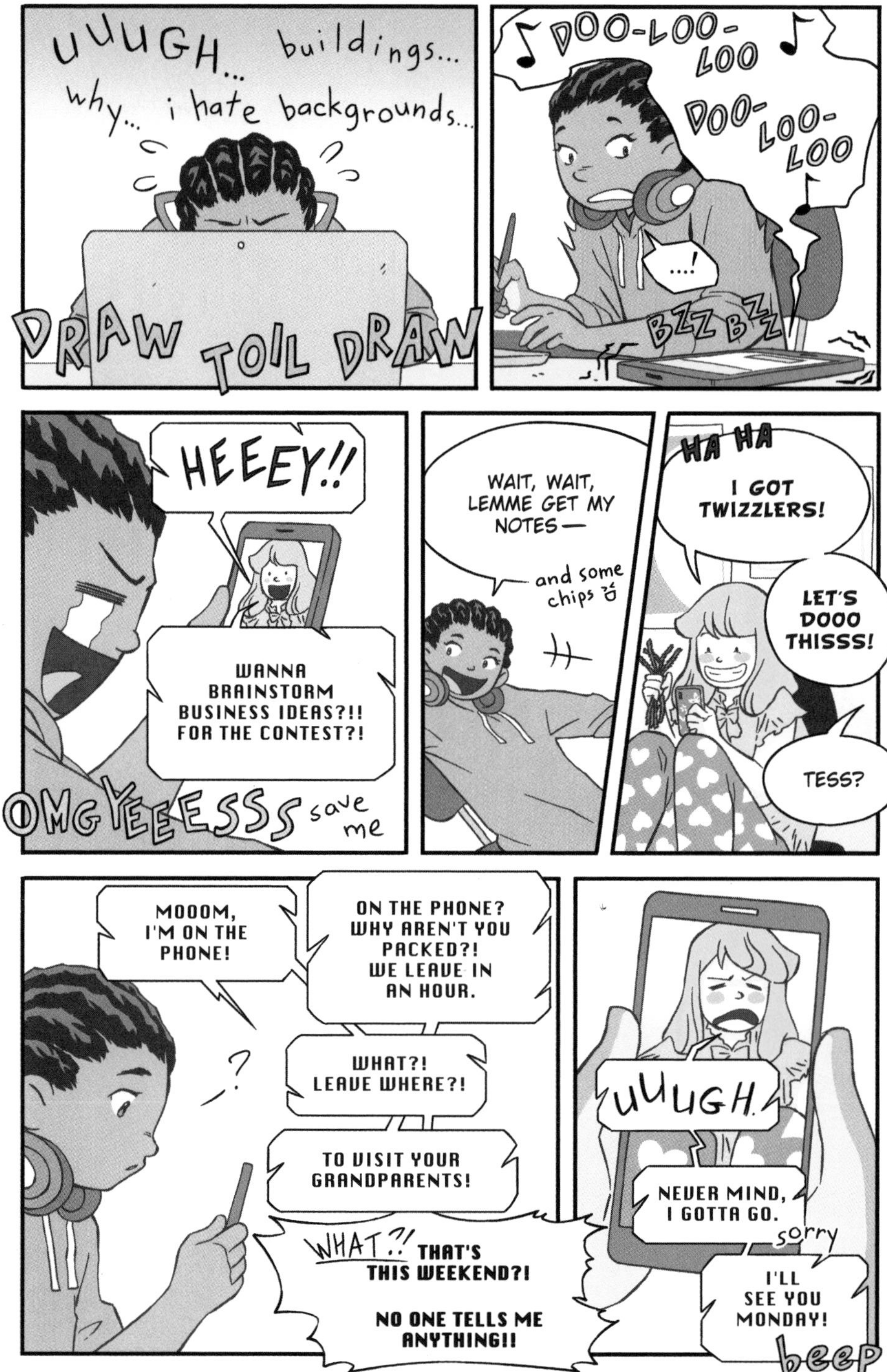

UUUGH... buildings...
why... i hate backgrounds...
DRAW TOIL DRAW
DOO-LOO-LOO
DOO-LOO-LOO
...!
BZZ BZZ
HEEEY!!
WANNA BRAINSTORM BUSINESS IDEAS?!! FOR THE CONTEST?!
OMGYEEESSS save me
WAIT, WAIT, LEMME GET MY NOTES—
and some chips
HA HA
I GOT TWIZZLERS!
LET'S DOOO THISSS!
TESS?
MOOOM, I'M ON THE PHONE!
ON THE PHONE? WHY AREN'T YOU PACKED?! WE LEAVE IN AN HOUR.
WHAT?! LEAVE WHERE?!
TO VISIT YOUR GRANDPARENTS!
WHAT?! THAT'S THIS WEEKEND?!
NO ONE TELLS ME ANYTHING!!
UUUGH.
NEVER MIND, I GOTTA GO.
sorry
I'LL SEE YOU MONDAY!
beep

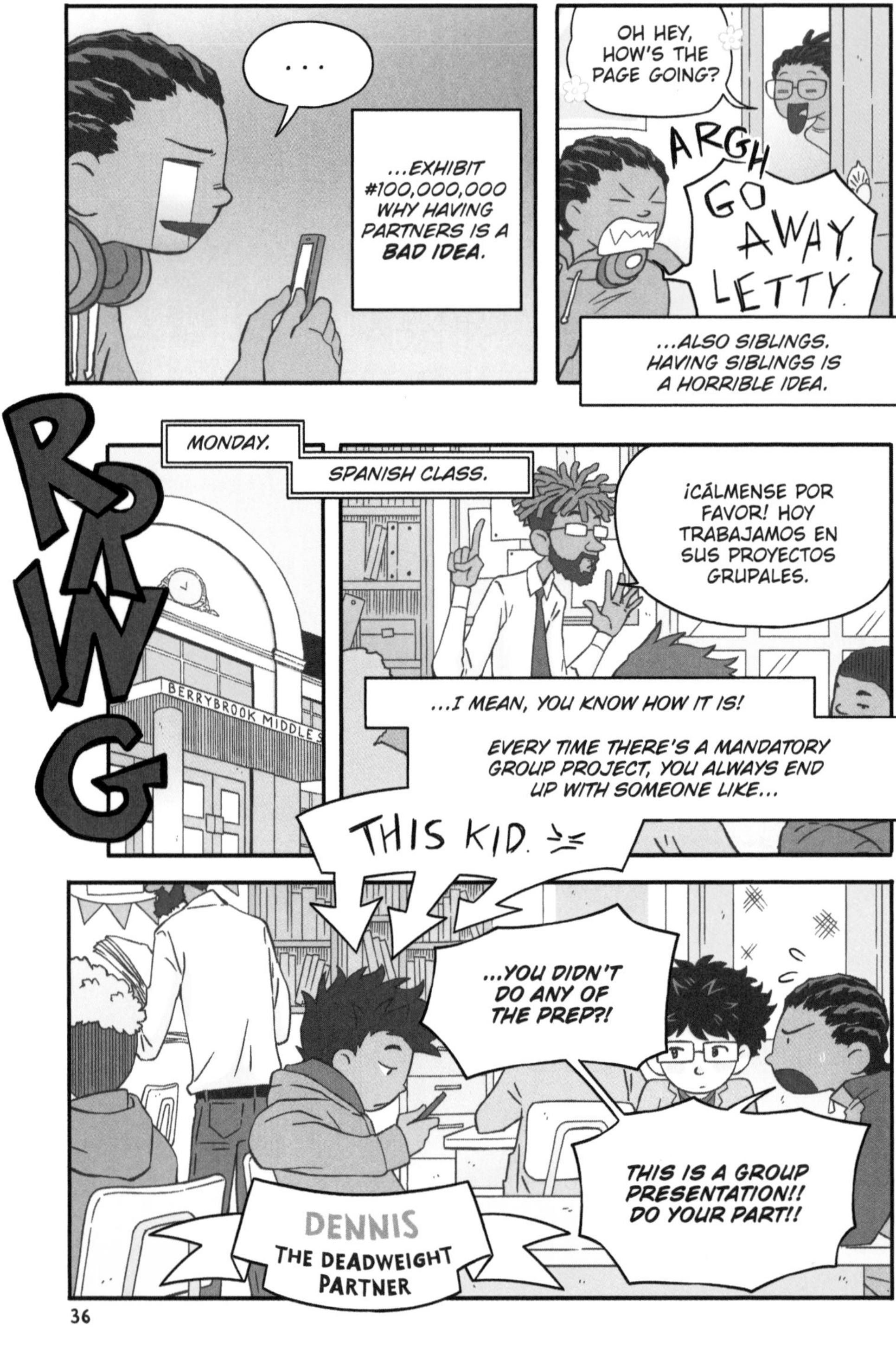

...
...EXHIBIT #100,000,000 WHY HAVING PARTNERS IS A BAD IDEA.
OH HEY, HOW'S THE PAGE GOING?
ARGH GO AWAY. LETTY.
...ALSO SIBLINGS. HAVING SIBLINGS IS A HORRIBLE IDEA.
RRRWG
MONDAY.
SPANISH CLASS.
BERRYBROOK MIDDLE S
¡CÁLMENSE POR FAVOR! HOY TRABAJAMOS EN SUS PROYECTOS GRUPALES.
...I MEAN, YOU KNOW HOW IT IS!
EVERY TIME THERE'S A MANDATORY GROUP PROJECT, YOU ALWAYS END UP WITH SOMEONE LIKE...
THIS KID.
...YOU DIDN'T DO ANY OF THE PREP?!
THIS IS A GROUP PRESENTATION!! DO YOUR PART!!
DENNIS
THE DEADWEIGHT PARTNER

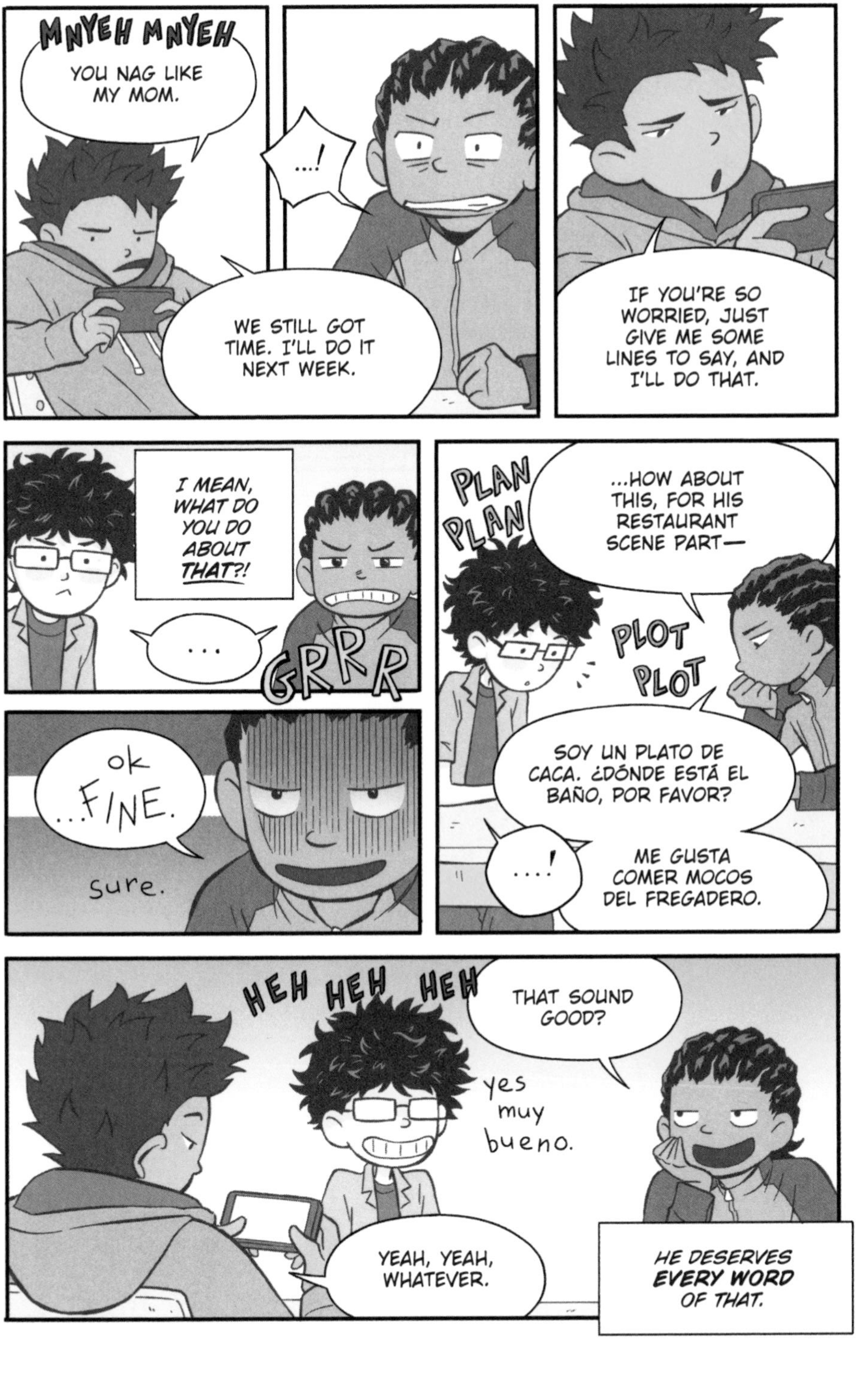
MNYEH MNYEH
YOU NAG LIKE MY MOM.
...!
WE STILL GOT TIME. I'LL DO IT NEXT WEEK.
IF YOU'RE SO WORRIED, JUST GIVE ME SOME LINES TO SAY, AND I'LL DO THAT.
I MEAN, WHAT DO YOU DO ABOUT THAT?!
...
GRRR
ok ...FINE. sure.
PLAN PLAN
...HOW ABOUT THIS, FOR HIS RESTAURANT SCENE PART—
PLOT PLOT
SOY UN PLATO DE CACA. ¿DÓNDE ESTÁ EL BAÑO, POR FAVOR?
...!
ME GUSTA COMER MOCOS DEL FREGADERO.
HEH HEH HEH
THAT SOUND GOOD?
yes muy bueno.
YEAH, YEAH, WHATEVER.
HE DESERVES EVERY WORD OF THAT.

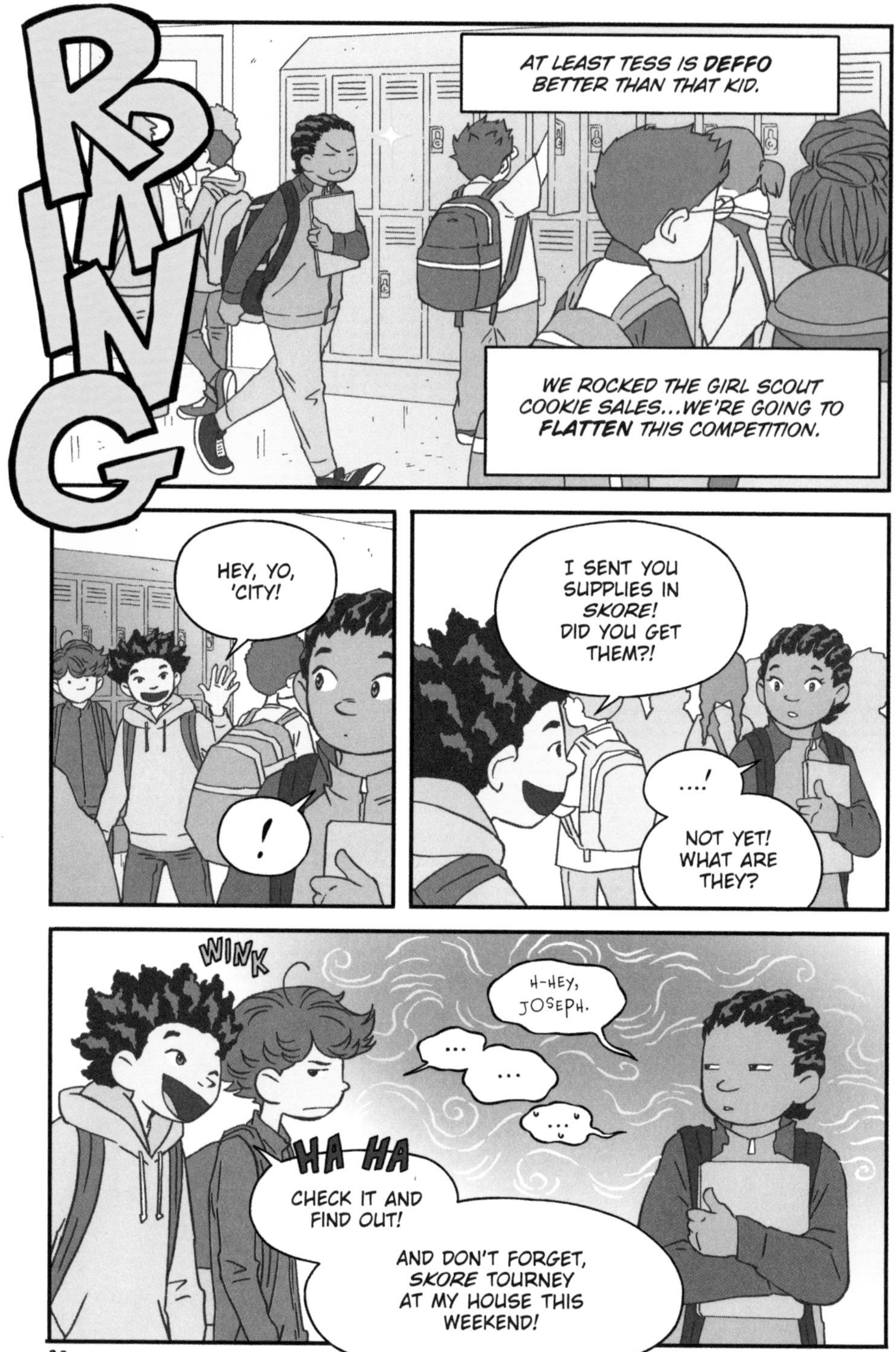
RRING
AT LEAST TESS IS DEFFO BETTER THAN THAT KID.
WE ROCKED THE GIRL SCOUT COOKIE SALES...WE'RE GOING TO FLATTEN THIS COMPETITION.
HEY, YO, 'CITY!
!
I SENT YOU SUPPLIES IN SKORE! DID YOU GET THEM?!
...!
NOT YET! WHAT ARE THEY?
WINK
H-HEY, JOSEPH.
...
...
...
HA HA
CHECK IT AND FIND OUT!
AND DON'T FORGET, SKORE TOURNEY AT MY HOUSE THIS WEEKEND!

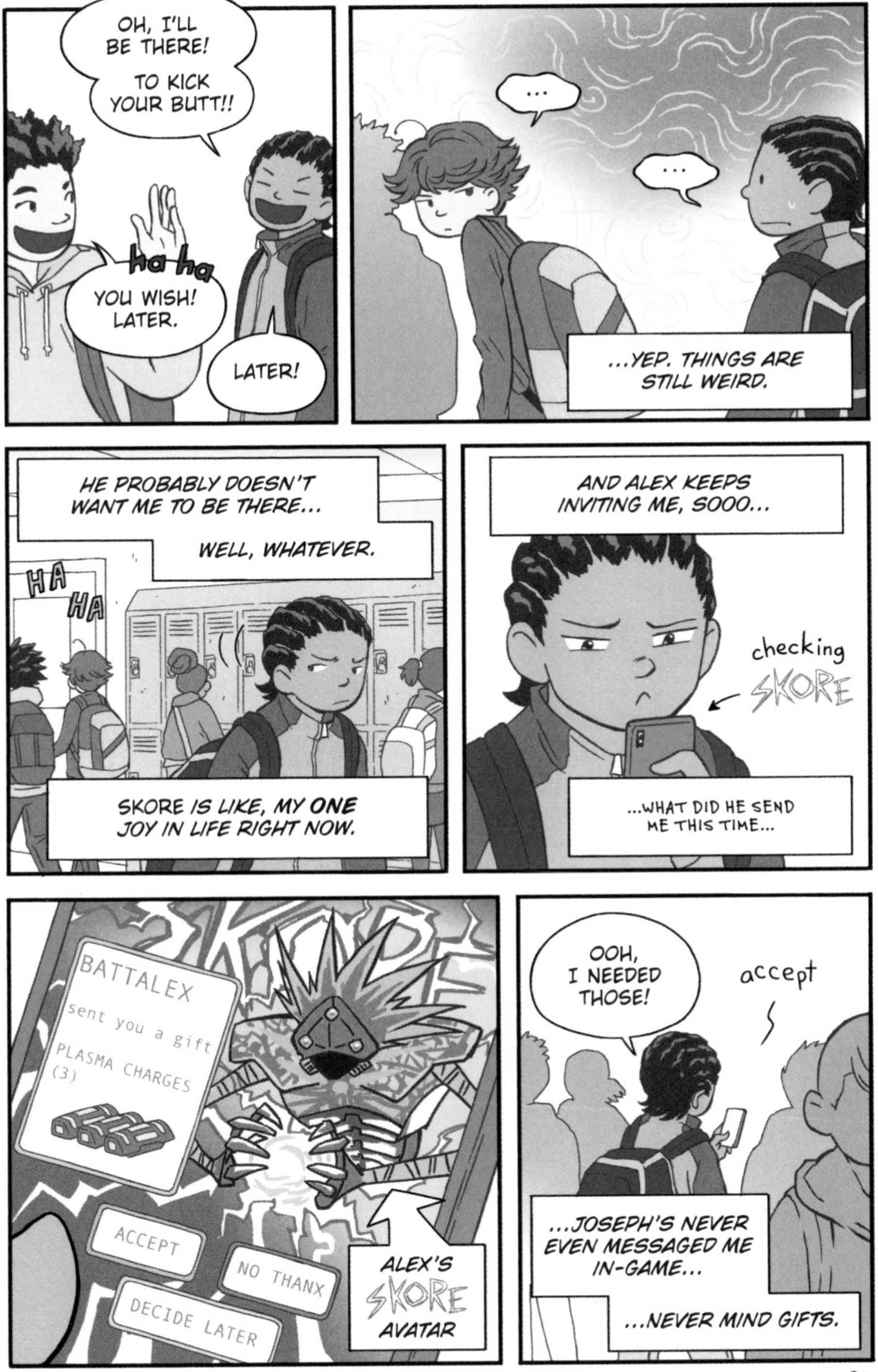
OH, I'LL BE THERE!
TO KICK YOUR BUTT!!
ha ha
YOU WISH! LATER.
LATER!
...
...
...YEP. THINGS ARE STILL WEIRD.
HE PROBABLY DOESN'T WANT ME TO BE THERE...
WELL, WHATEVER.
HA
HA
SKORE IS LIKE, MY ONE JOY IN LIFE RIGHT NOW.
AND ALEX KEEPS INVITING ME, SOOO...
checking SKORE
...WHAT DID HE SEND ME THIS TIME...
BATTALEX
sent you a gift
PLASMA CHARGES
(3)
ACCEPT
NO THANX
DECIDE LATER
ALEX'S SKORE AVATAR
OOH, I NEEDED THOSE!
accept
...JOSEPH'S NEVER EVEN MESSAGED ME IN-GAME...
...NEVER MIND GIFTS.

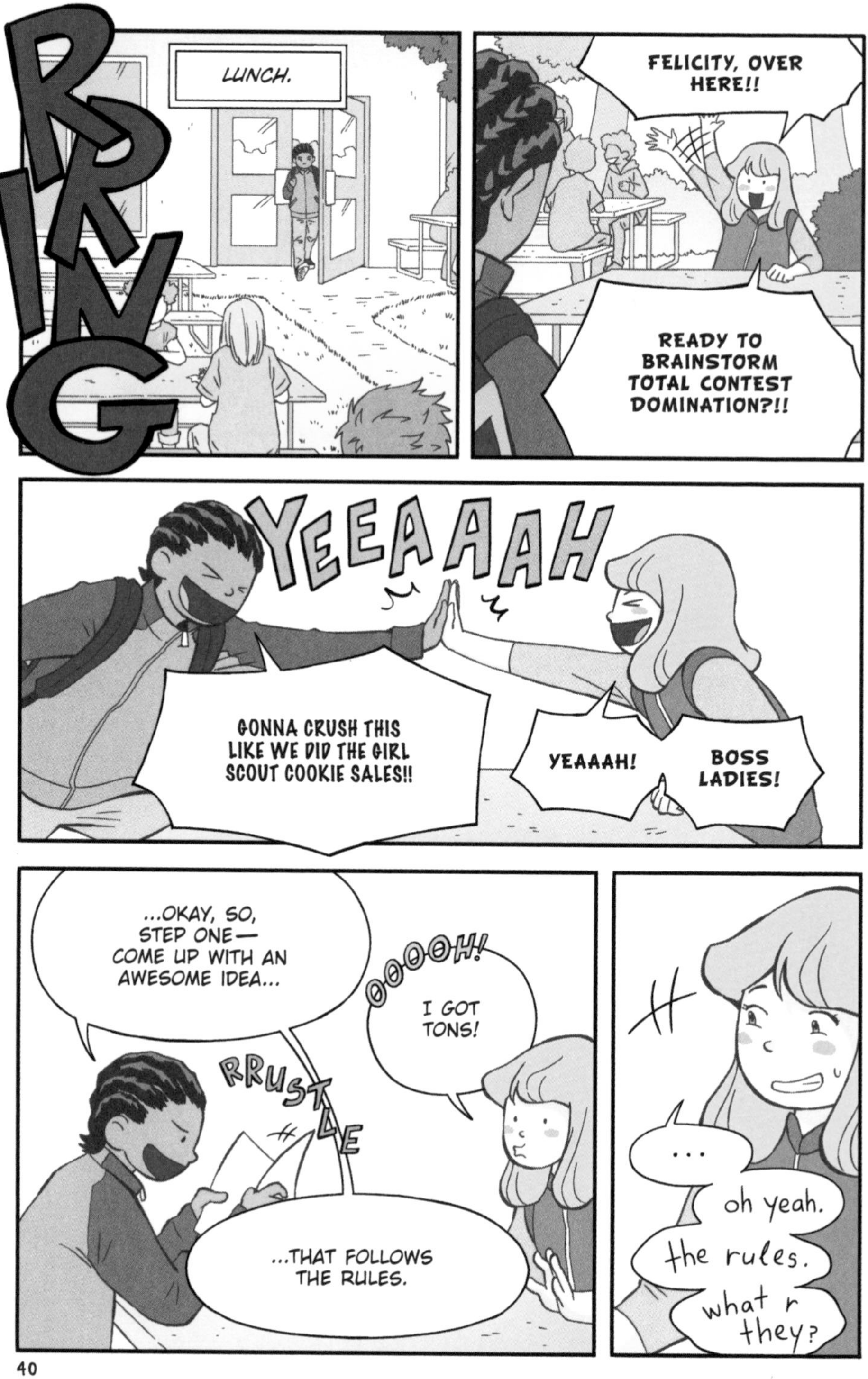
RRRING
LUNCH.
FELICITY, OVER HERE!!
READY TO BRAINSTORM TOTAL CONTEST DOMINATION?!!
YEEAAAH
GONNA CRUSH THIS LIKE WE DID THE GIRL SCOUT COOKIE SALES!!
YEAAAH!
BOSS LADIES!
...OKAY, SO, STEP ONE— COME UP WITH AN AWESOME IDEA...
OOOOH!
I GOT TONS!
RRUSTLE
...THAT FOLLOWS THE RULES.
...
oh yeah.
the rules.
what r they?

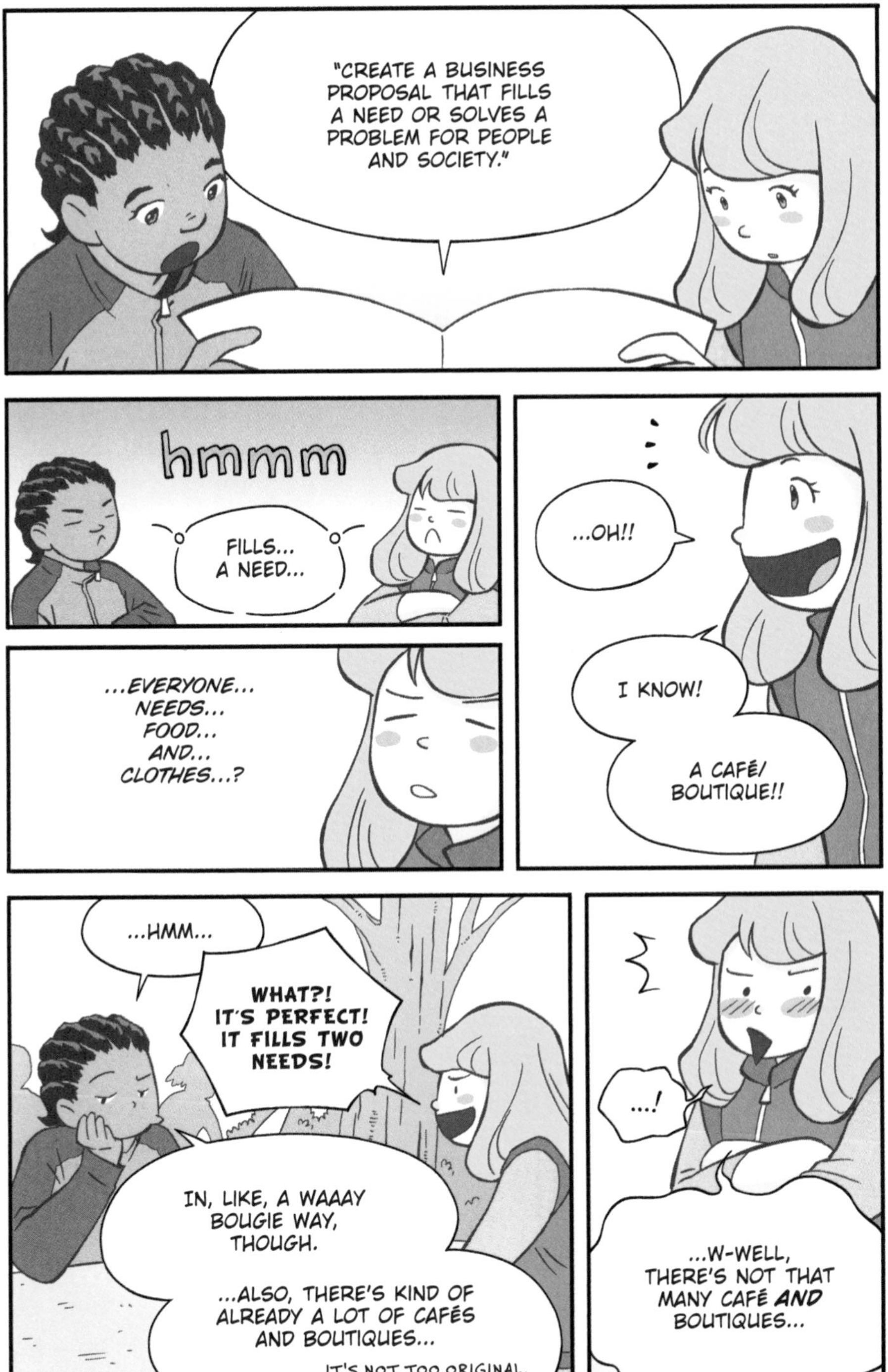
"CREATE A BUSINESS PROPOSAL THAT FILLS A NEED OR SOLVES A PROBLEM FOR PEOPLE AND SOCIETY."
hmmm
FILLS... A NEED...
...EVERYONE... NEEDS... FOOD... AND... CLOTHES...?
...OH!!
I KNOW!
A CAFÉ/ BOUTIQUE!!
...HMM...
WHAT?! IT'S PERFECT! IT FILLS TWO NEEDS!
IN, LIKE, A WAAAY BOUGIE WAY, THOUGH.
...ALSO, THERE'S KIND OF ALREADY A LOT OF CAFÉS AND BOUTIQUES...
IT'S NOT TOO ORIGINAL.
....!
...W-WELL, THERE'S NOT THAT MANY CAFÉ ***AND*** BOUTIQUES...

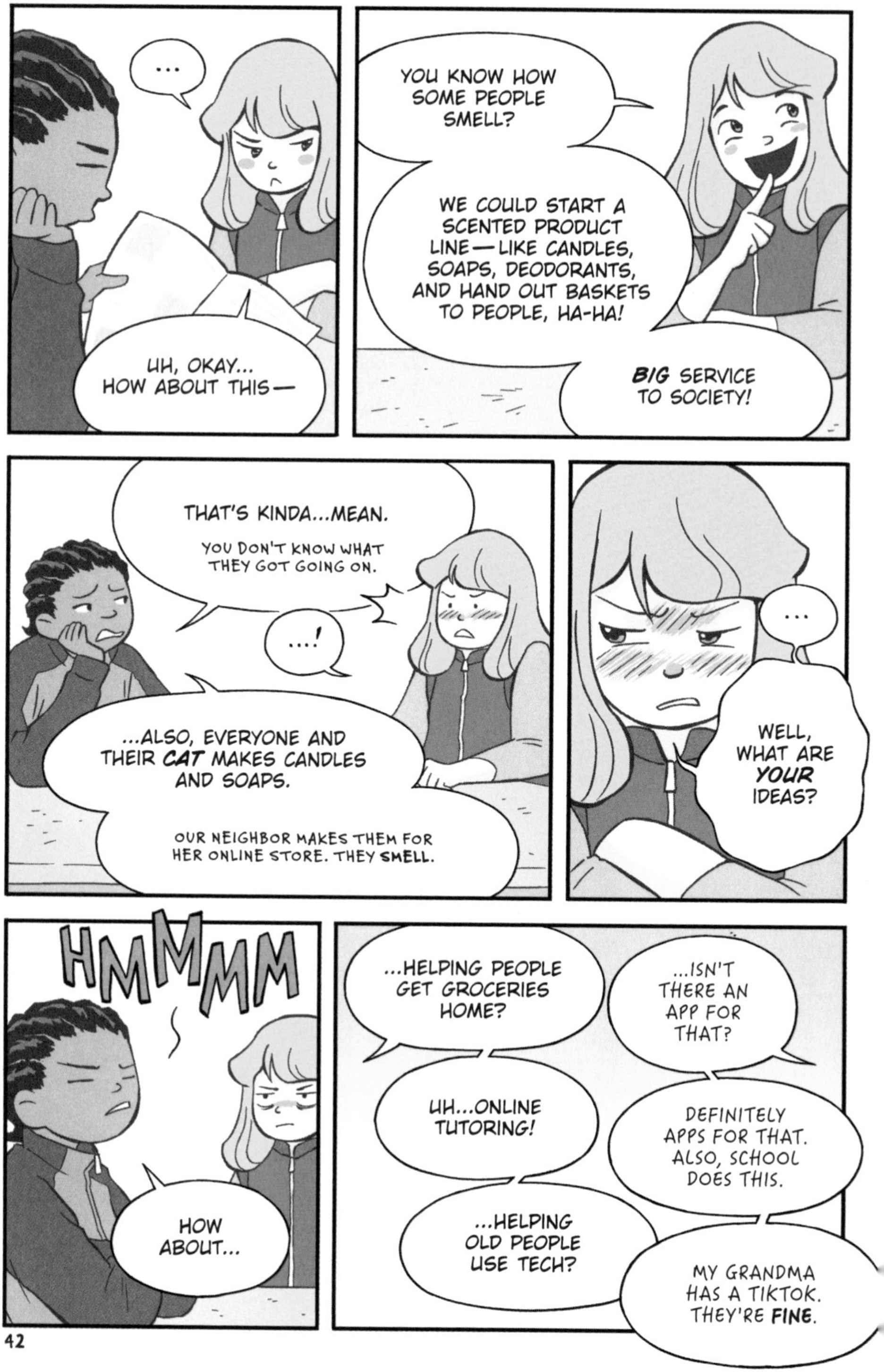
...
UH, OKAY... HOW ABOUT THIS—
YOU KNOW HOW SOME PEOPLE SMELL?
WE COULD START A SCENTED PRODUCT LINE—LIKE CANDLES, SOAPS, DEODORANTS, AND HAND OUT BASKETS TO PEOPLE, HA-HA!
BIG SERVICE TO SOCIETY!
THAT'S KINDA...MEAN.
YOU DON'T KNOW WHAT THEY GOT GOING ON.
...!
...ALSO, EVERYONE AND THEIR CAT MAKES CANDLES AND SOAPS.
OUR NEIGHBOR MAKES THEM FOR HER ONLINE STORE. THEY SMELL.
...
WELL, WHAT ARE YOUR IDEAS?
HMMMM
HOW ABOUT...
...HELPING PEOPLE GET GROCERIES HOME?
...ISN'T THERE AN APP FOR THAT?
UH...ONLINE TUTORING!
DEFINITELY APPS FOR THAT. ALSO, SCHOOL DOES THIS.
...HELPING OLD PEOPLE USE TECH?
MY GRANDMA HAS A TIKTOK. THEY'RE FINE.

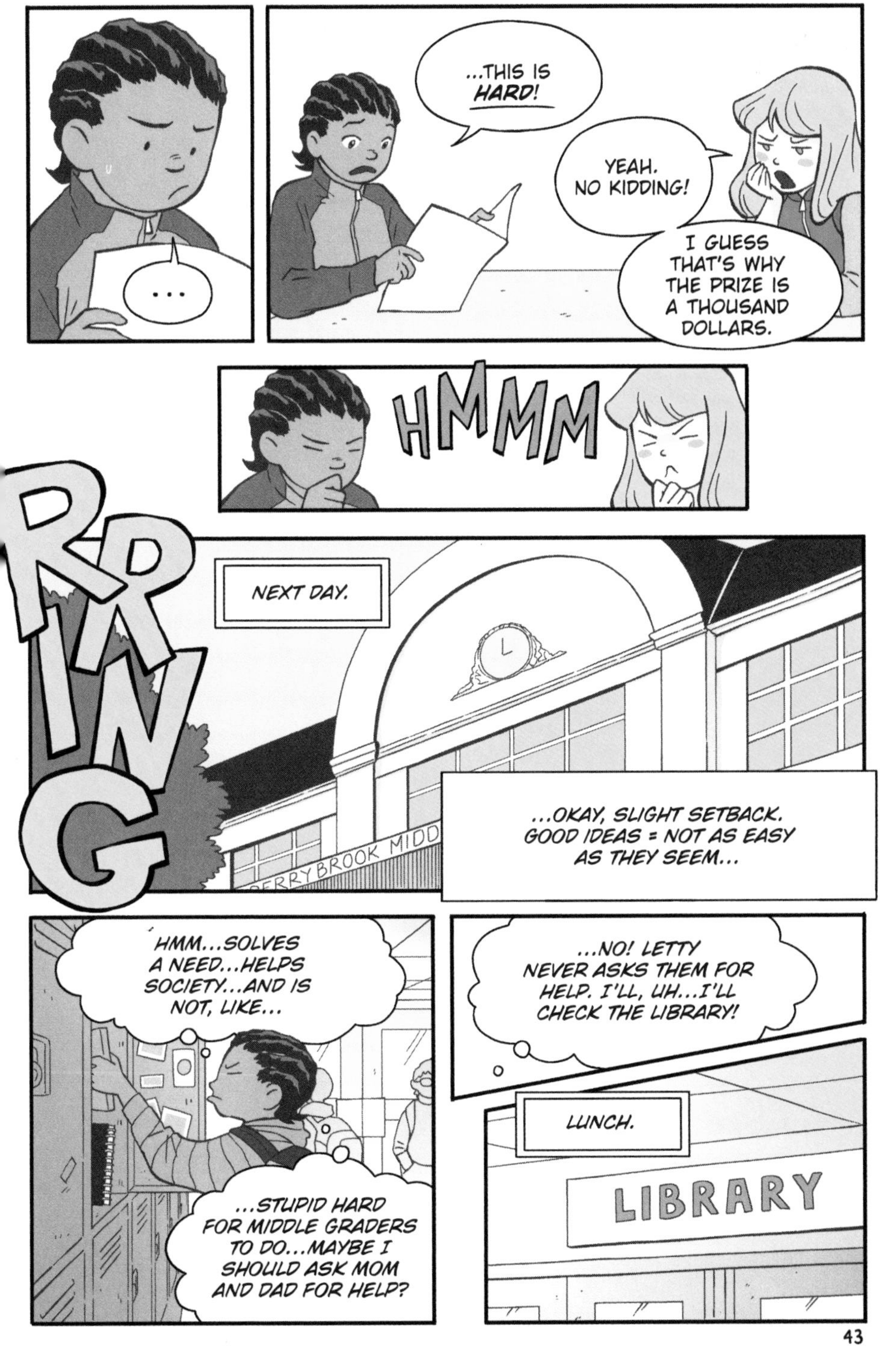

...
...THIS IS HARD!
YEAH. NO KIDDING!
I GUESS THAT'S WHY THE PRIZE IS A THOUSAND DOLLARS.
HMMM
RRING
NEXT DAY.
...OKAY, SLIGHT SETBACK. GOOD IDEAS = NOT AS EASY AS THEY SEEM...
HMM...SOLVES A NEED...HELPS SOCIETY...AND IS NOT, LIKE...
...STUPID HARD FOR MIDDLE GRADERS TO DO...MAYBE I SHOULD ASK MOM AND DAD FOR HELP?
...NO! LETTY NEVER ASKS THEM FOR HELP. I'LL, UH...I'LL CHECK THE LIBRARY!
LUNCH.
LIBRARY

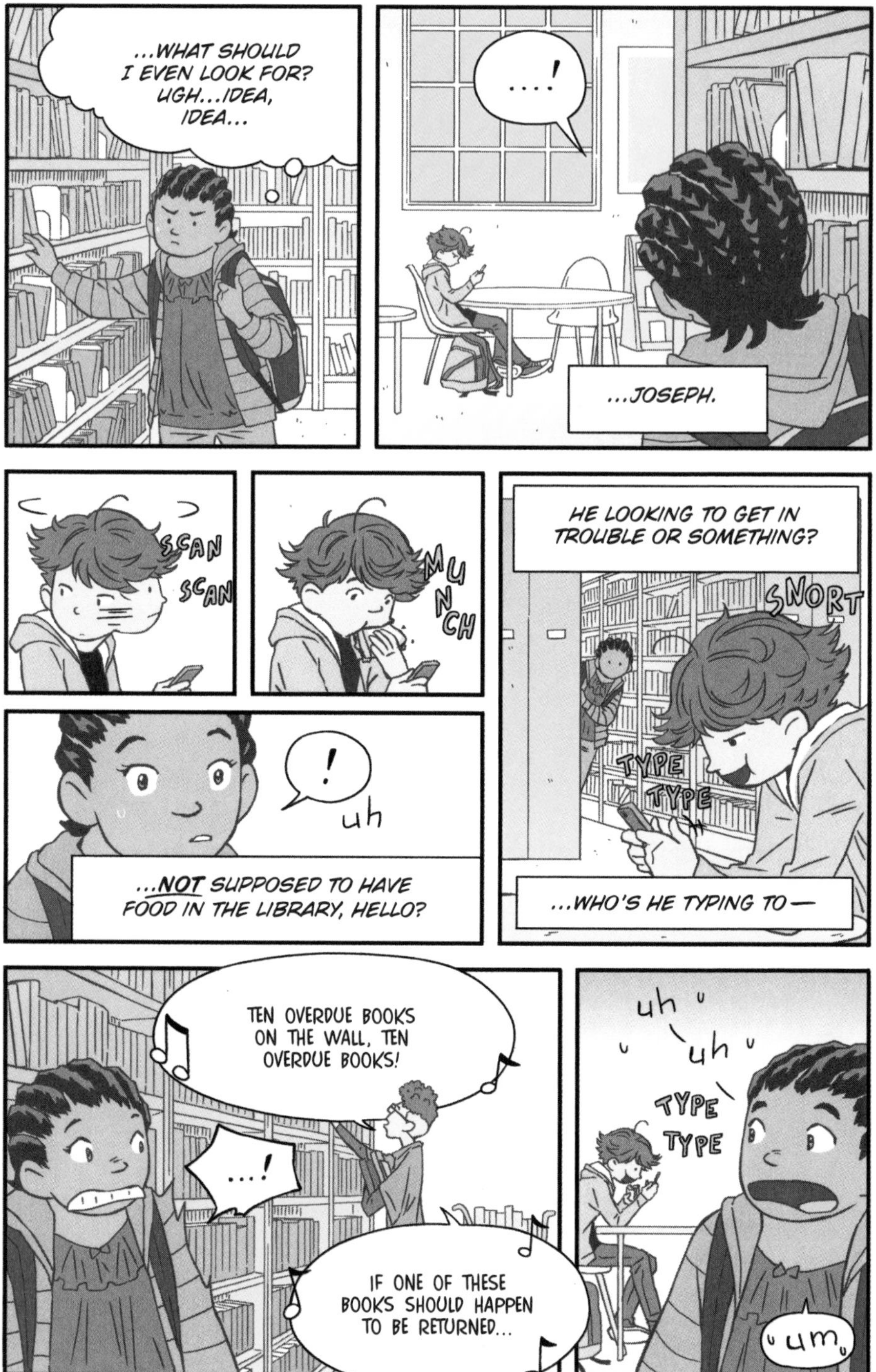
...WHAT SHOULD I EVEN LOOK FOR? UGH...IDEA, IDEA...
....!
...JOSEPH.
SCAN
SCAN
MUNCH
HE LOOKING TO GET IN TROUBLE OR SOMETHING?
SNORT
TYPE
TYPE
...WHO'S HE TYPING TO—
!
uh
...**NOT** SUPPOSED TO HAVE FOOD IN THE LIBRARY, HELLO?
TEN OVERDUE BOOKS ON THE WALL, TEN OVERDUE BOOKS!
...!
IF ONE OF THESE BOOKS SHOULD HAPPEN TO BE RETURNED...
uh
uh
TYPE
TYPE
um

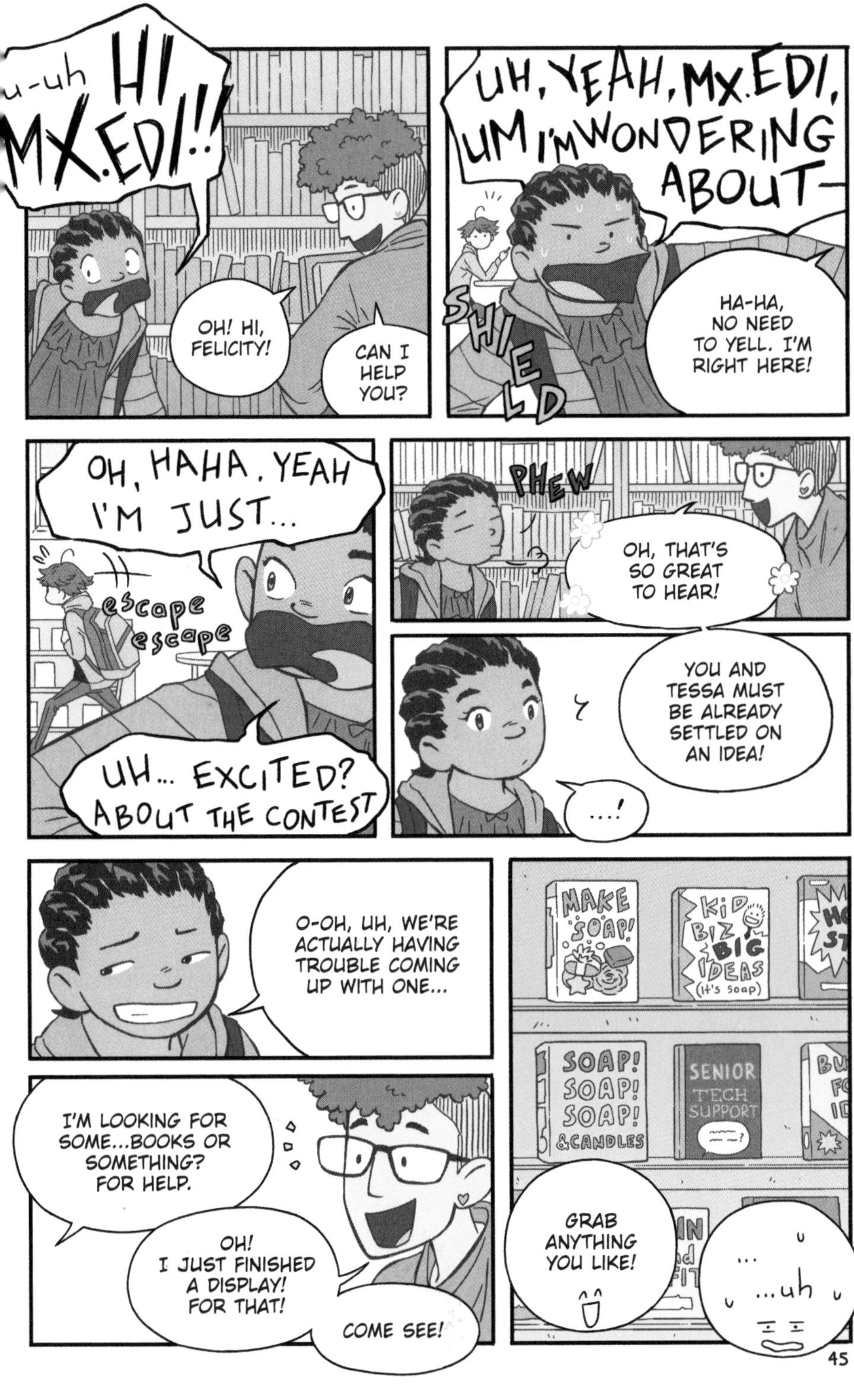
u-uh HI MX.EDI!!
OH! HI, FELICITY!
CAN I HELP YOU?
UH, YEAH, MX.EDI, UM I'M WONDERING ABOUT—
SHIELD
HA-HA, NO NEED TO YELL. I'M RIGHT HERE!
OH, HAHA. YEAH I'M JUST...
escape escape
UH... EXCITED? ABOUT THE CONTEST
PHEW
OH, THAT'S SO GREAT TO HEAR!
YOU AND TESSA MUST BE ALREADY SETTLED ON AN IDEA!
...!
O-OH, UH, WE'RE ACTUALLY HAVING TROUBLE COMING UP WITH ONE...
I'M LOOKING FOR SOME...BOOKS OR SOMETHING? FOR HELP.
OH! I JUST FINISHED A DISPLAY! FOR THAT!
COME SEE!
MAKE SOAP!
KID BIZ BIG IDEAS (it's soap)
SOAP! SOAP! SOAP! &CANDLES
SENIOR TECH SUPPORT
GRAB ANYTHING YOU LIKE!
... ...uh

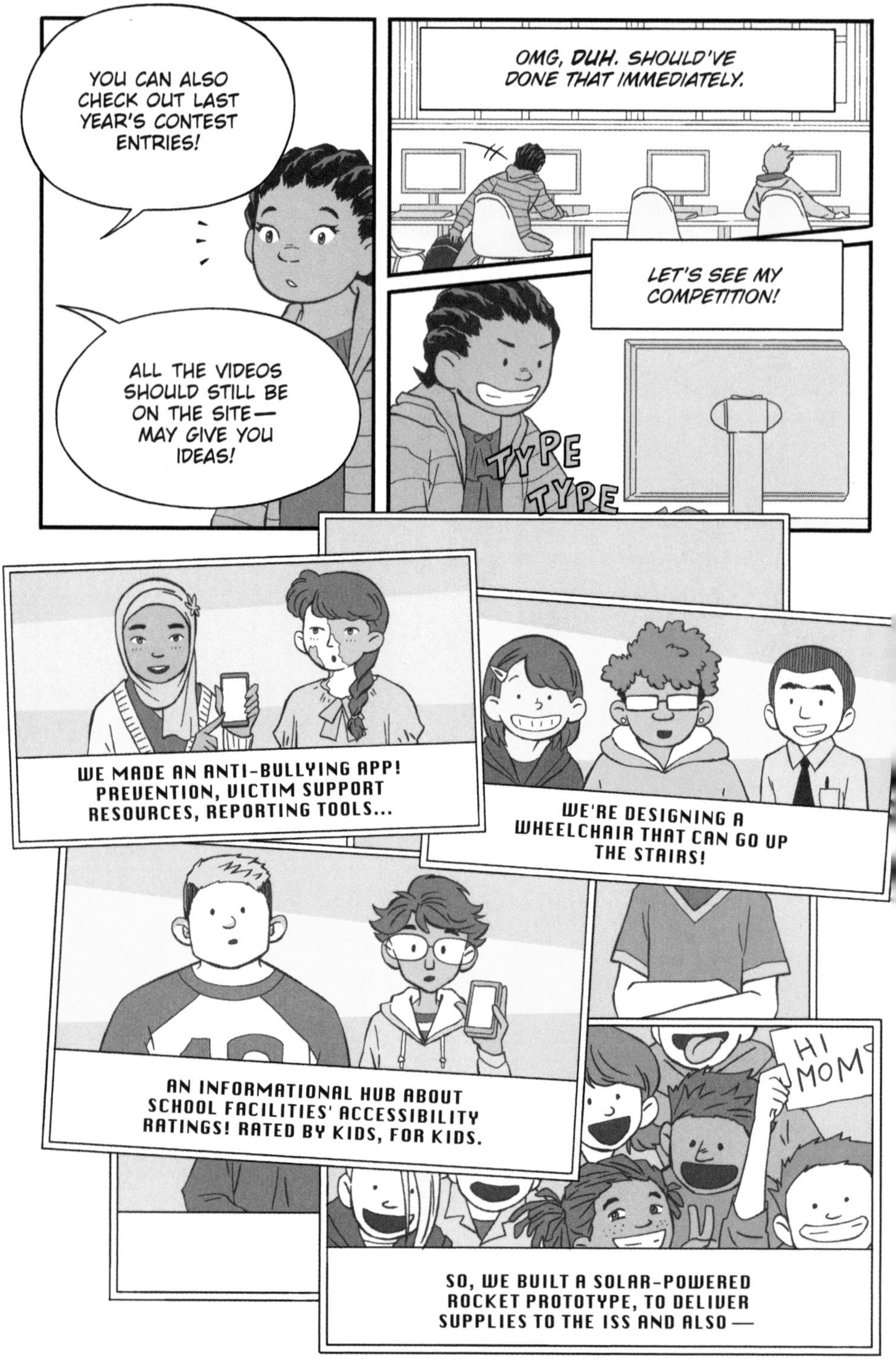

YOU CAN ALSO CHECK OUT LAST YEAR'S CONTEST ENTRIES!
ALL THE VIDEOS SHOULD STILL BE ON THE SITE— MAY GIVE YOU IDEAS!
OMG, DUH. SHOULD'VE DONE THAT IMMEDIATELY.
LET'S SEE MY COMPETITION!
TYPE TYPE
WE MADE AN ANTI-BULLYING APP! PREVENTION, VICTIM SUPPORT RESOURCES, REPORTING TOOLS...
WE'RE DESIGNING A WHEELCHAIR THAT CAN GO UP THE STAIRS!
AN INFORMATIONAL HUB ABOUT SCHOOL FACILITIES' ACCESSIBILITY RATINGS! RATED BY KIDS, FOR KIDS.
HI MOM
SO, WE BUILT A SOLAR-POWERED ROCKET PROTOTYPE, TO DELIVER SUPPLIES TO THE ISS AND ALSO—

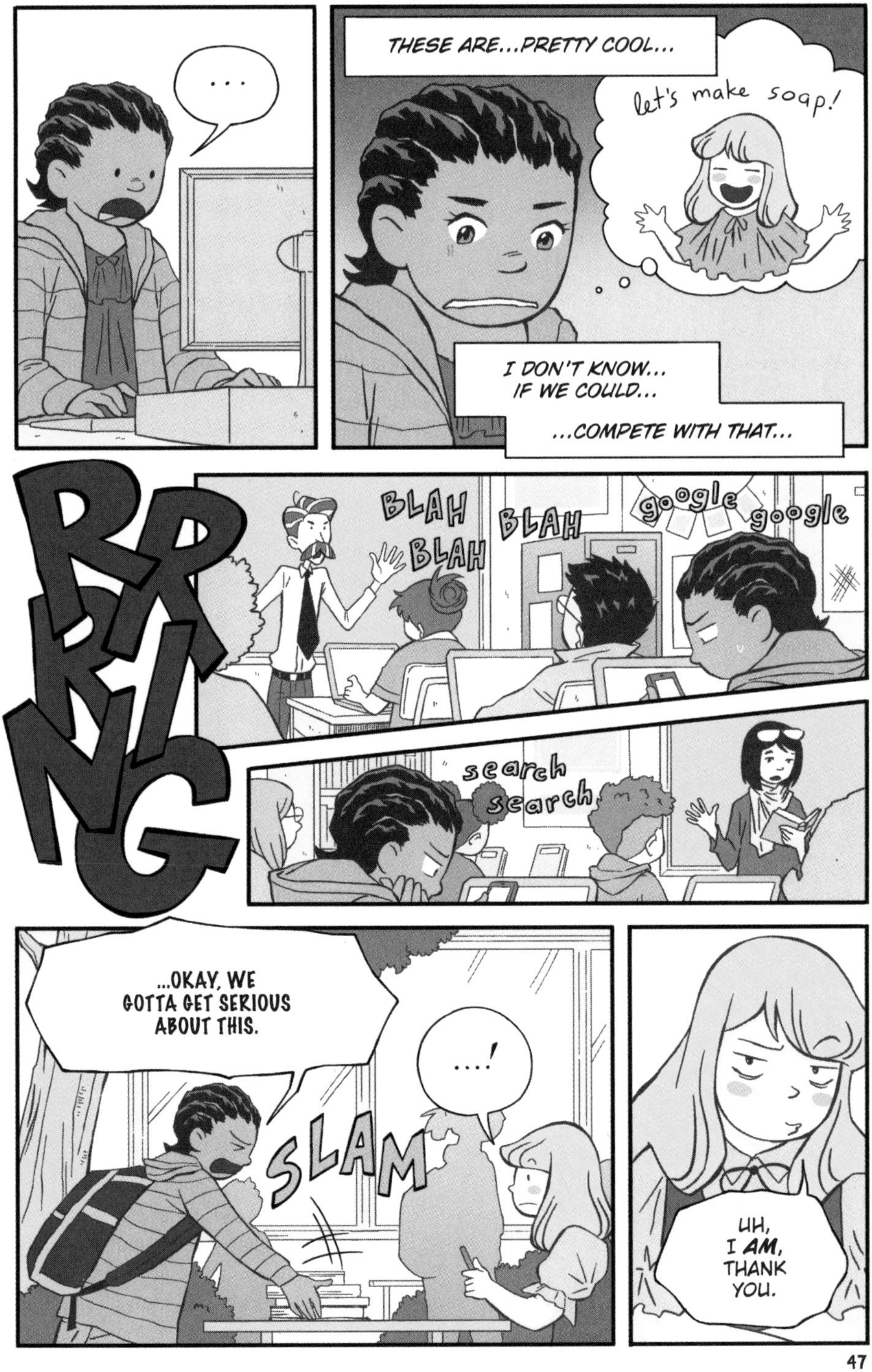
...
THESE ARE...PRETTY COOL...
let's make soap!
I DON'T KNOW... IF WE COULD...
...COMPETE WITH THAT...
RRRING
BLAH BLAH
BLAH
google google
search search
...OKAY, WE GOTTA GET SERIOUS ABOUT THIS.
SLAM
...!
UH, I AM, THANK YOU.

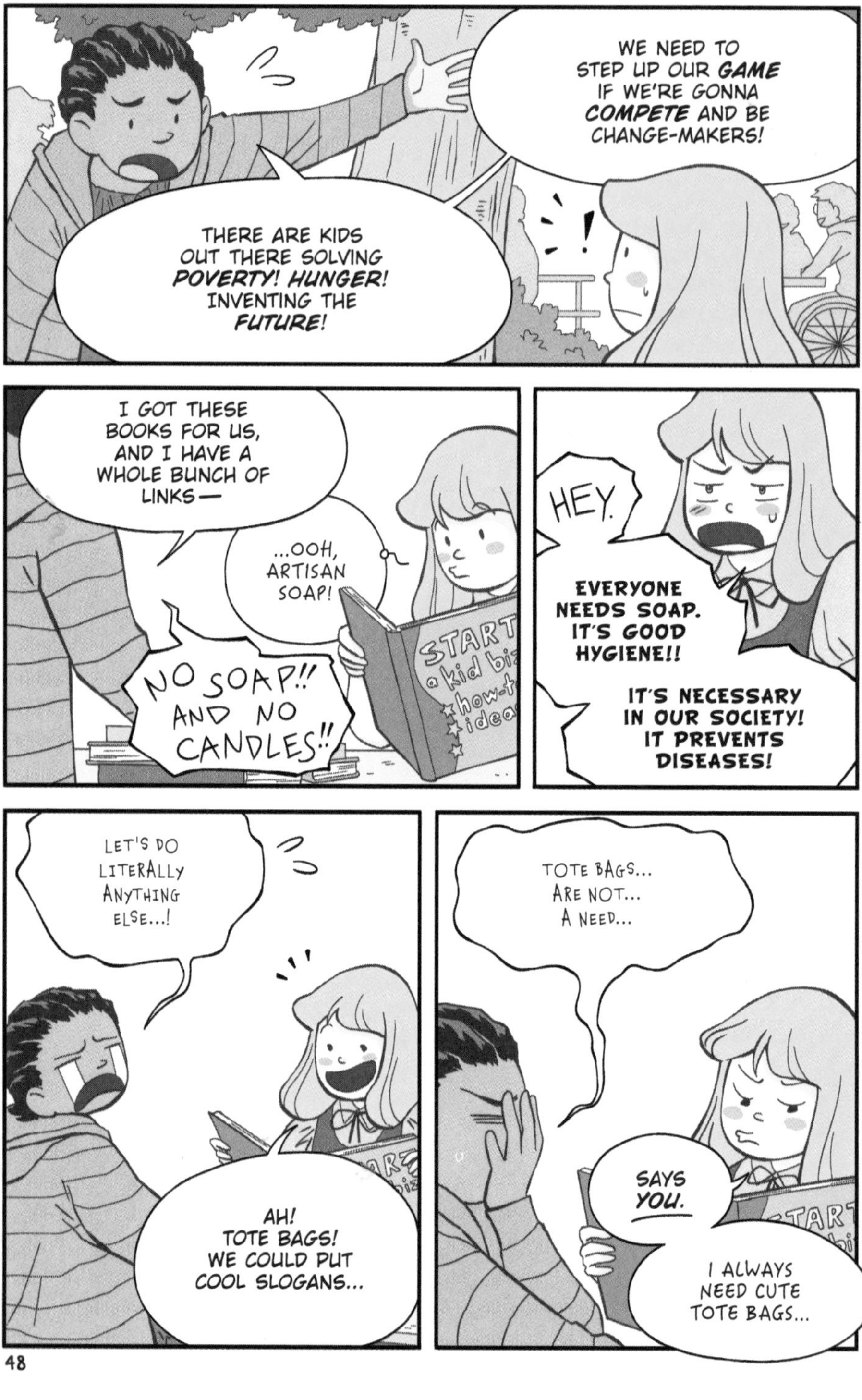
WE NEED TO STEP UP OUR **GAME** IF WE'RE GONNA **COMPETE** AND BE CHANGE-MAKERS!
THERE ARE KIDS OUT THERE SOLVING **POVERTY! HUNGER!** INVENTING THE **FUTURE!**
I GOT THESE BOOKS FOR US, AND I HAVE A WHOLE BUNCH OF LINKS—
...OOH, ARTISAN SOAP!
NO SOAP!! AND NO CANDLES!!
START a kid biz how-to ideas
HEY.
EVERYONE NEEDS SOAP. IT'S GOOD HYGIENE!!
IT'S NECESSARY IN OUR SOCIETY! IT PREVENTS DISEASES!
LET'S DO LITERALLY ANYTHING ELSE...!
AH! TOTE BAGS! WE COULD PUT COOL SLOGANS...
TOTE BAGS... ARE NOT... A NEED...
SAYS **YOU.**
I ALWAYS NEED CUTE TOTE BAGS...

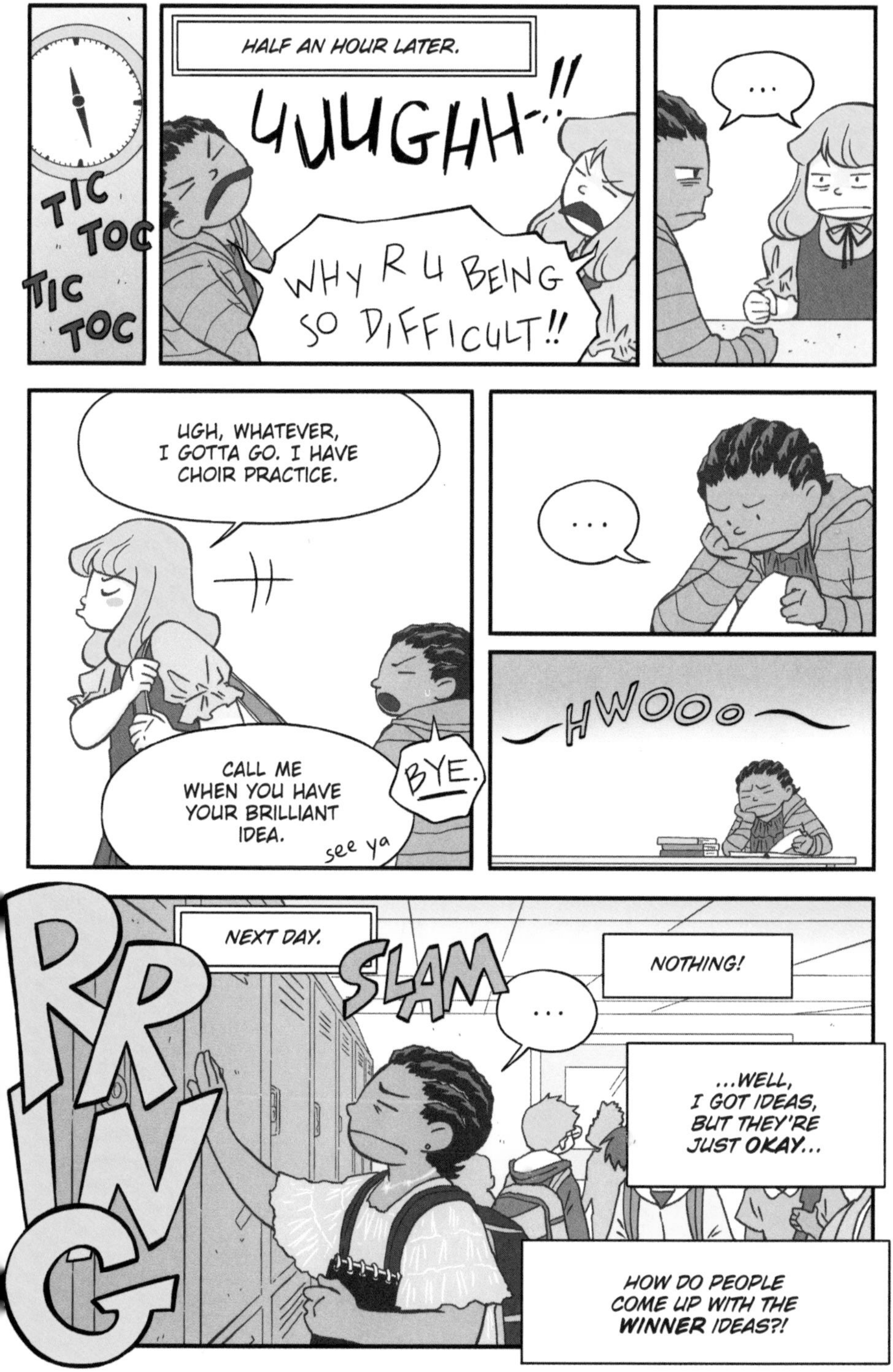
TIC TOC TIC TOC
HALF AN HOUR LATER.
UUUGHH-!!
WHY R U BEING SO DIFFICULT!!
...
UGH, WHATEVER, I GOTTA GO. I HAVE CHOIR PRACTICE.
CALL ME WHEN YOU HAVE YOUR BRILLIANT IDEA.
see ya
BYE.
...
HWOOo
NEXT DAY.
RRING
SLAM
...
NOTHING!
...WELL, I GOT IDEAS, BUT THEY'RE JUST OKAY...
HOW DO PEOPLE COME UP WITH THE WINNER IDEAS?!

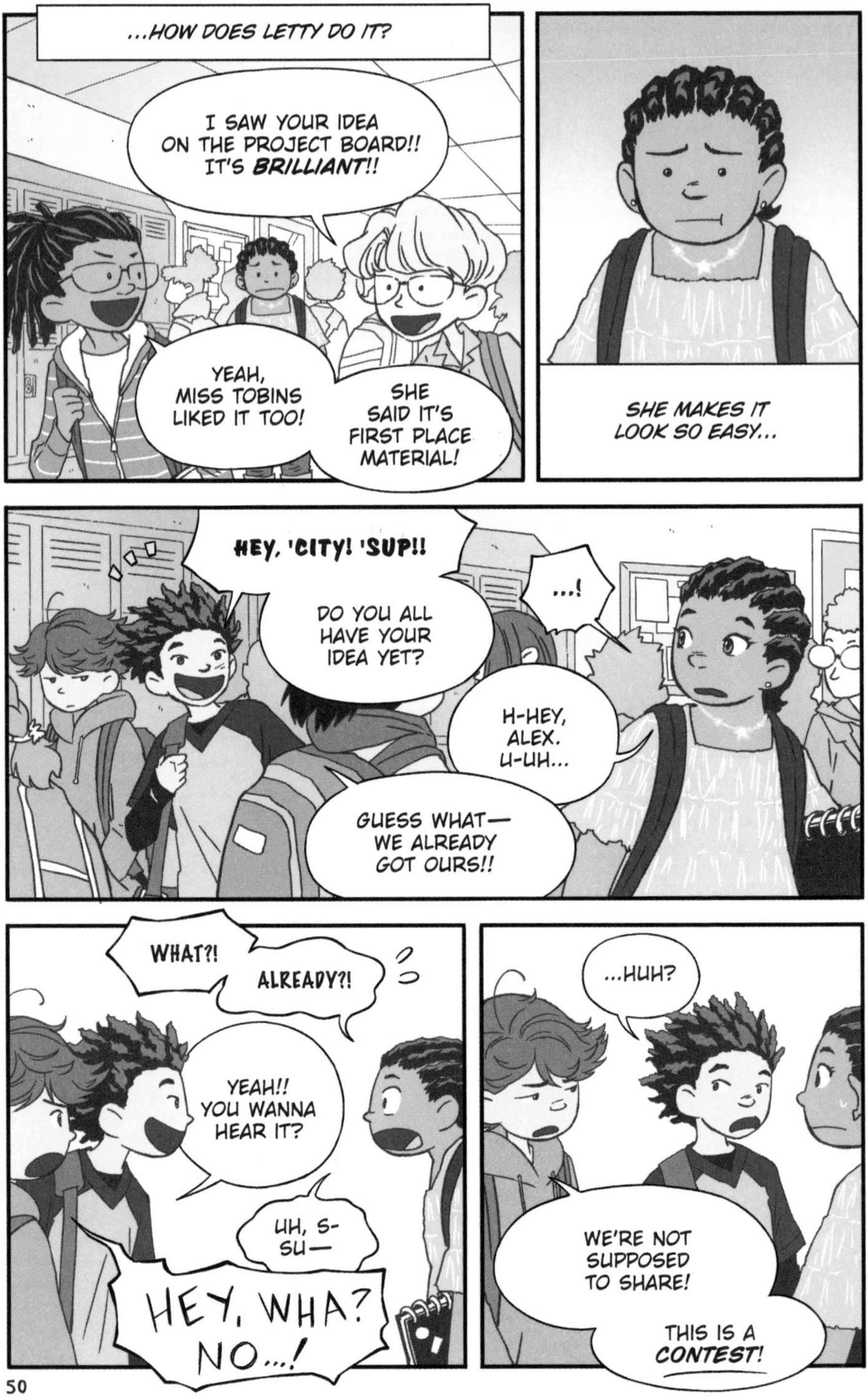
...HOW DOES LETTY DO IT?
I SAW YOUR IDEA ON THE PROJECT BOARD!! IT'S BRILLIANT!!
YEAH, MISS TOBINS LIKED IT TOO!
SHE SAID IT'S FIRST PLACE MATERIAL!
SHE MAKES IT LOOK SO EASY...
HEY, 'CITY! 'SUP!!
DO YOU ALL HAVE YOUR IDEA YET?
...!
H-HEY, ALEX. U-UH...
GUESS WHAT— WE ALREADY GOT OURS!!
WHAT?!
ALREADY?!
YEAH!! YOU WANNA HEAR IT?
UH, S-SU—
HEY, WHA? NO...!
...HUH?
WE'RE NOT SUPPOSED TO SHARE!
THIS IS A CONTEST!

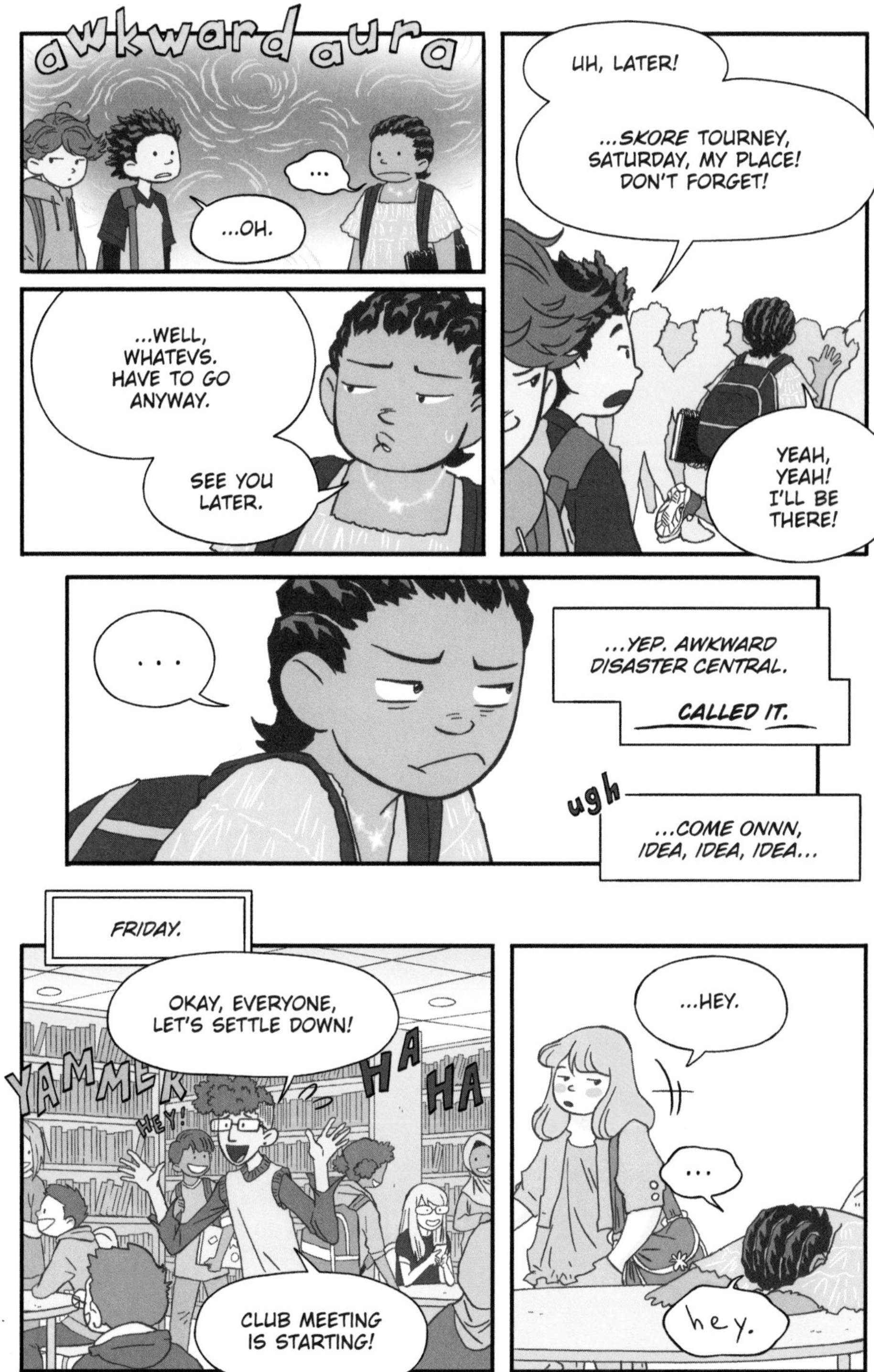
awkward aura
...
...OH.
UH, LATER!
...SKORE TOURNEY, SATURDAY, MY PLACE! DON'T FORGET!
...WELL, WHATEVS. HAVE TO GO ANYWAY.
SEE YOU LATER.
YEAH, YEAH! I'LL BE THERE!
. . .
...YEP. AWKWARD DISASTER CENTRAL.
CALLED IT.
ugh
...COME ONNN, IDEA, IDEA, IDEA...
FRIDAY.
OKAY, EVERYONE, LET'S SETTLE DOWN!
YAMMER
HEY!
HA HA
CLUB MEETING IS STARTING!
...HEY.
...
hey.

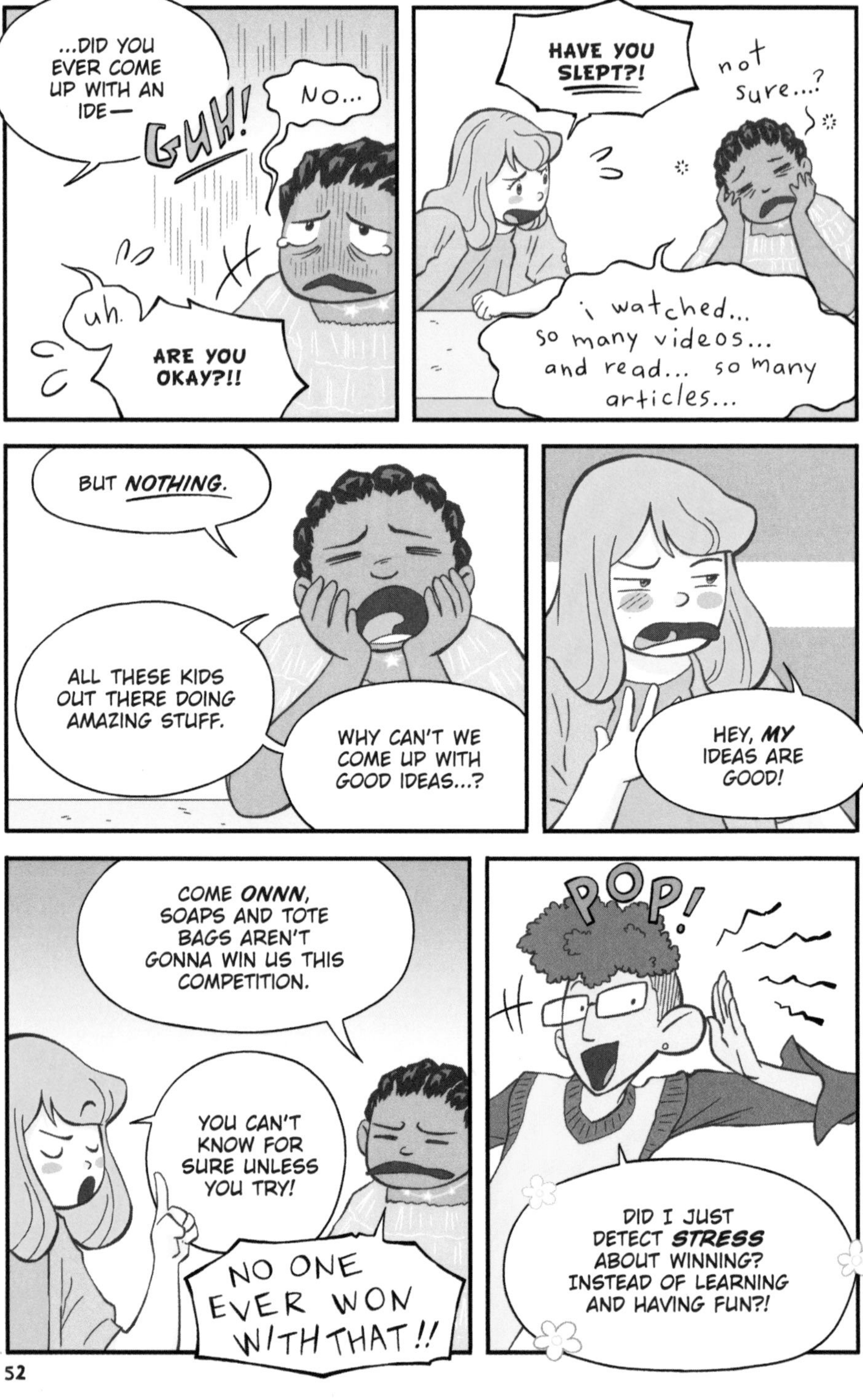
...DID YOU EVER COME UP WITH AN IDE—
GUH!
NO...
uh.
ARE YOU OKAY?!!
HAVE YOU SLEPT?!
not sure...?
i watched... so many videos... and read... so many articles...
BUT NOTHING.
ALL THESE KIDS OUT THERE DOING AMAZING STUFF.
WHY CAN'T WE COME UP WITH GOOD IDEAS...?
HEY, MY IDEAS ARE GOOD!
COME ONNN, SOAPS AND TOTE BAGS AREN'T GONNA WIN US THIS COMPETITION.
YOU CAN'T KNOW FOR SURE UNLESS YOU TRY!
NO ONE EVER WON WITH THAT!!
POP!
DID I JUST DETECT STRESS ABOUT WINNING? INSTEAD OF LEARNING AND HAVING FUN?!

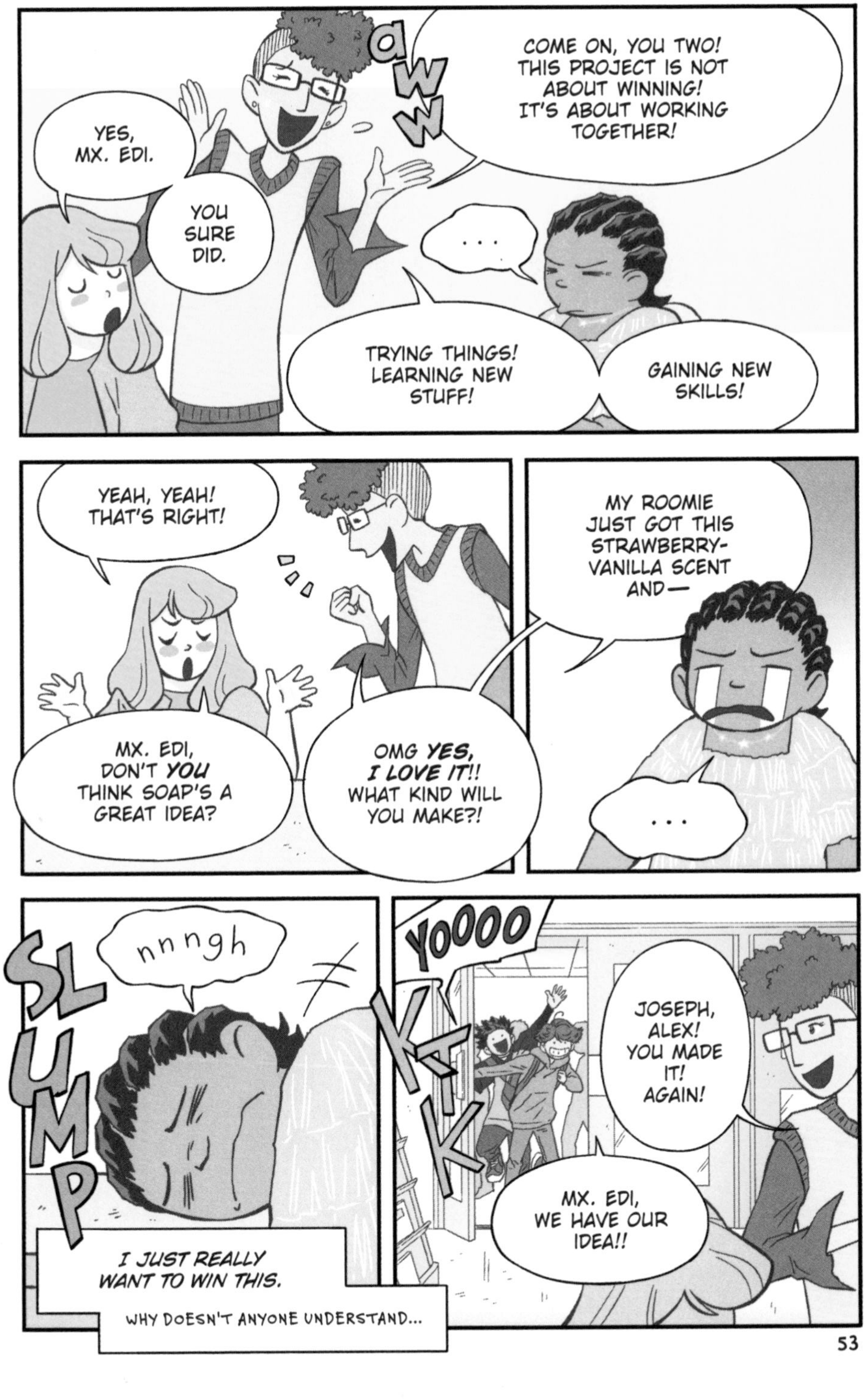
aww
COME ON, YOU TWO! THIS PROJECT IS NOT ABOUT WINNING! IT'S ABOUT WORKING TOGETHER!
YES, MX. EDI.
YOU SURE DID.
. . .
TRYING THINGS! LEARNING NEW STUFF!
GAINING NEW SKILLS!
YEAH, YEAH! THAT'S RIGHT!
MX. EDI, DON'T *YOU* THINK SOAP'S A GREAT IDEA?
OMG ***YES, I LOVE IT***!! WHAT KIND WILL YOU MAKE?!
MY ROOMIE JUST GOT THIS STRAWBERRY-VANILLA SCENT AND—
. . .
SLUMP
nnngh
I JUST REALLY WANT TO WIN THIS.
WHY DOESN'T ANYONE UNDERSTAND...
YOOOO
KTAK
JOSEPH, ALEX! YOU MADE IT! AGAIN!
MX. EDI, WE HAVE OUR IDEA!!

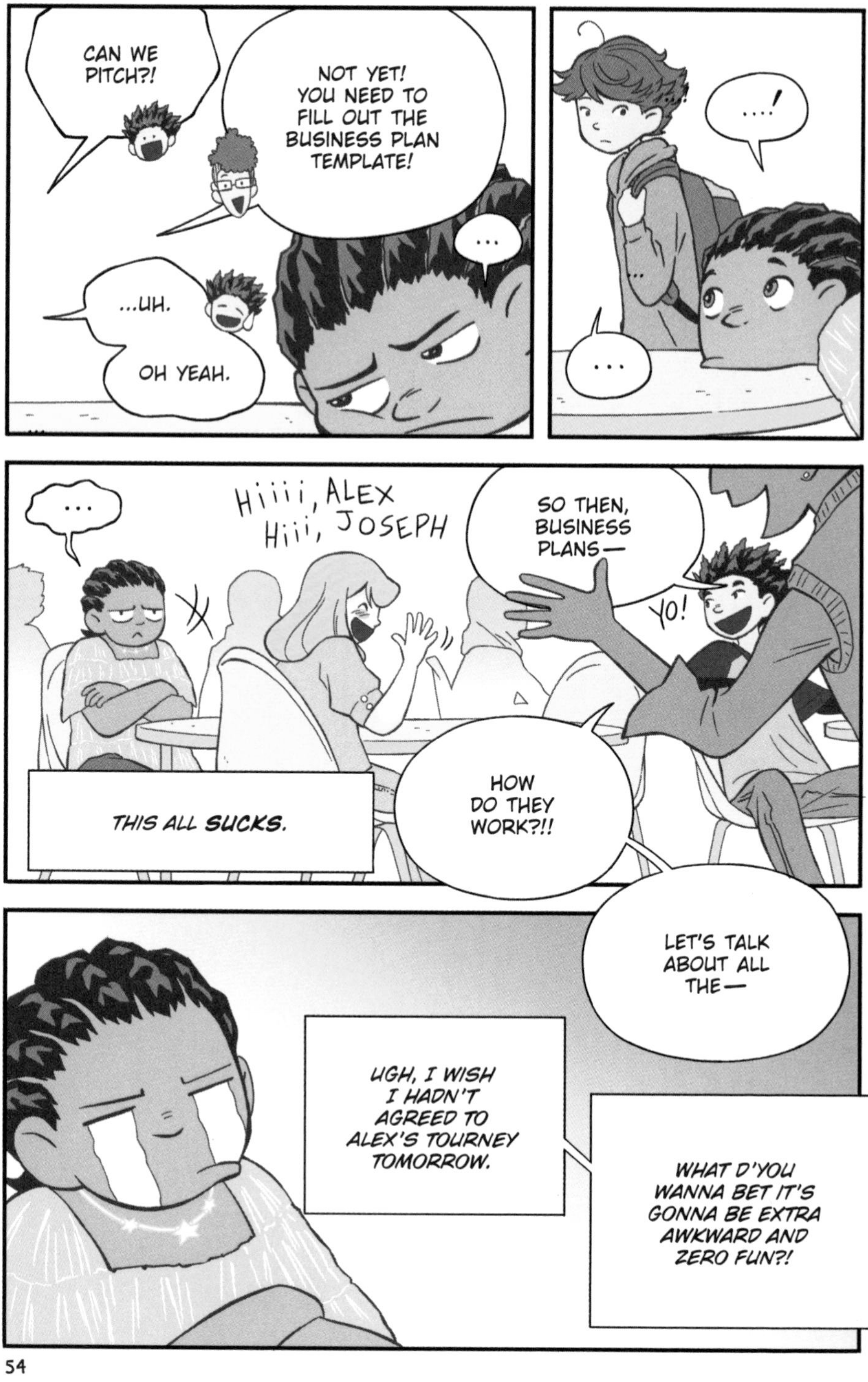
CAN WE PITCH?!
NOT YET! YOU NEED TO FILL OUT THE BUSINESS PLAN TEMPLATE!
...UH.
OH YEAH.
...
....!
...
...
Hiiii, ALEX
Hiii, JOSEPH
SO THEN, BUSINESS PLANS—
YO!
THIS ALL SUCKS.
HOW DO THEY WORK?!!
LET'S TALK ABOUT ALL THE—
UGH, I WISH I HADN'T AGREED TO ALEX'S TOURNEY TOMORROW.
WHAT D'YOU WANNA BET IT'S GONNA BE EXTRA AWKWARD AND ZERO FUN?!

CHAPTER 3

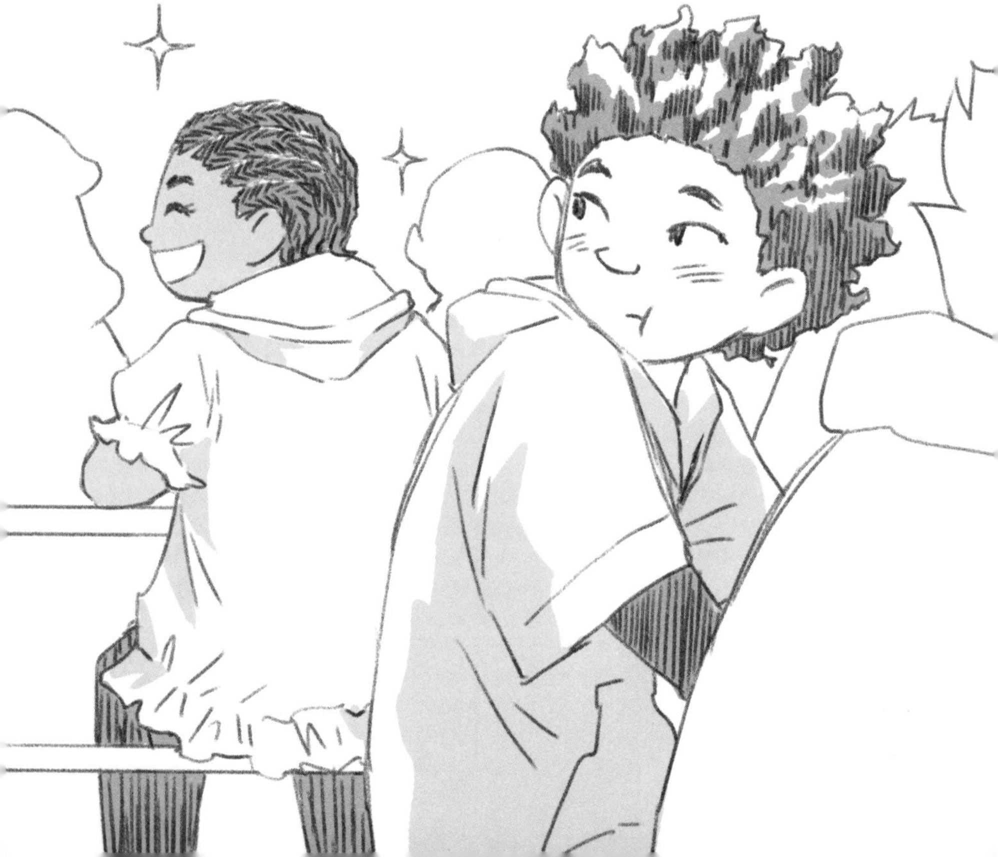

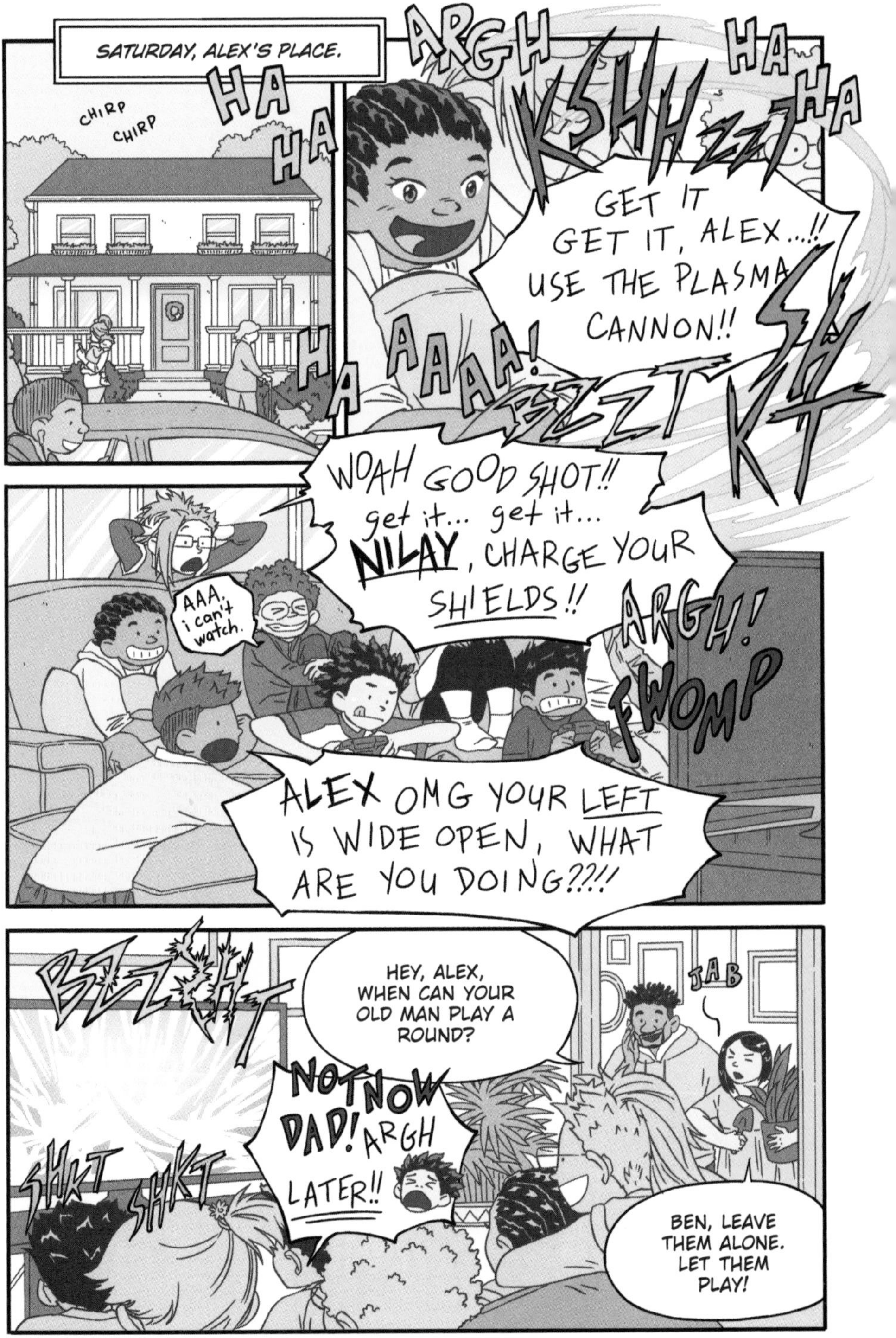
SATURDAY, ALEX'S PLACE.
CHIRP
CHIRP
HA
HA
ARGH
KSHHZZZ
HA
HA
HA
GET IT
GET IT, ALEX...!!
USE THE PLASMA
CANNON!!
HA
HA
AAAA!
BZZZT
SH
KT
WOAH GOOD SHOT!!
get it... get it...
NILAY, CHARGE YOUR
SHIELDS!!
AAA,
i can't
watch.
ARGH!
FWOMP
ALEX OMG YOUR LEFT
IS WIDE OPEN, WHAT
ARE YOU DOING??!!
BZZSHT
HEY, ALEX,
WHEN CAN YOUR
OLD MAN PLAY A
ROUND?
JAB
NOT NOW
DAD! ARGH
LATER!!
SHKT
SHKT
BEN, LEAVE
THEM ALONE.
LET THEM
PLAY!

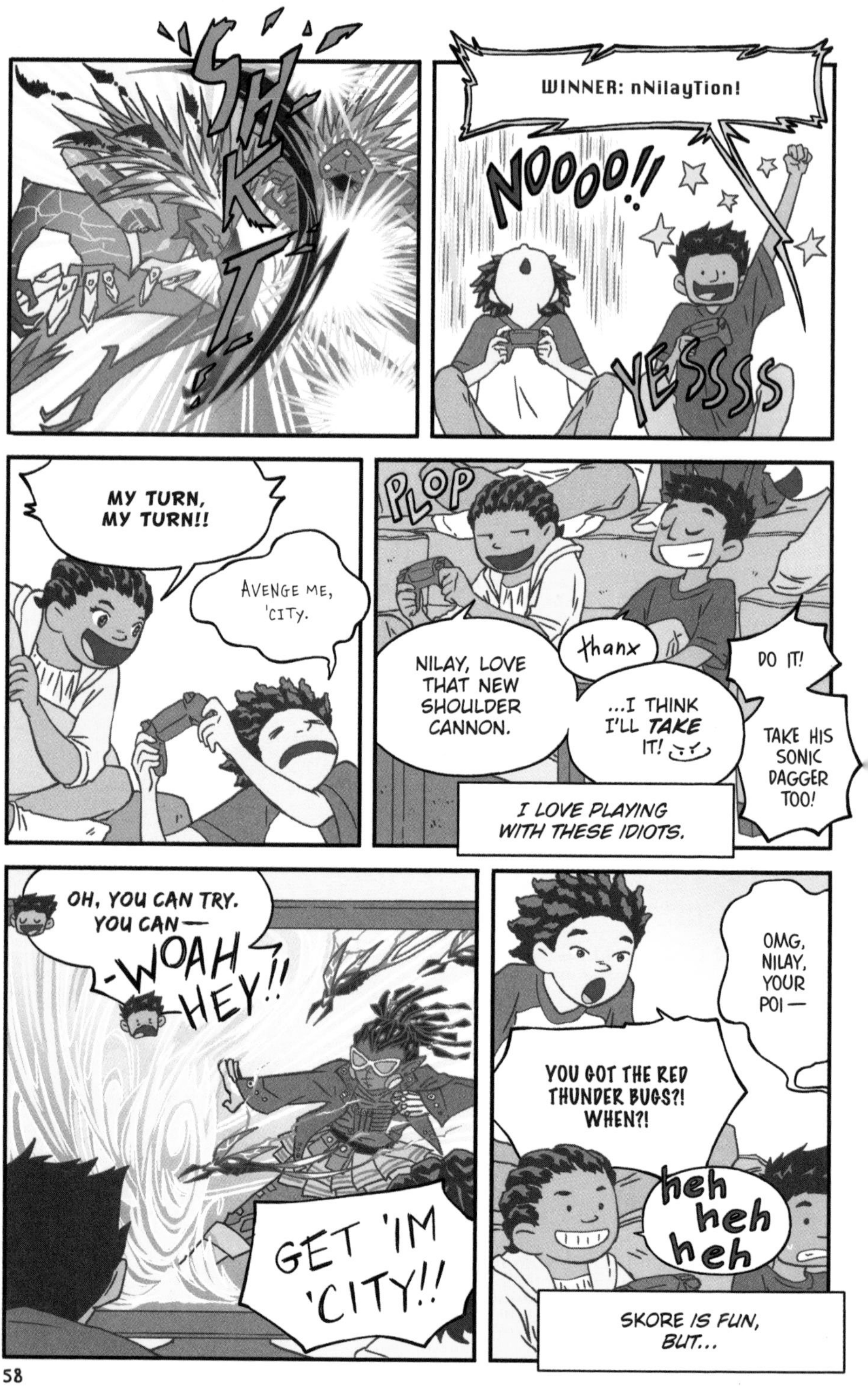
SHKT!
WINNER: nNilayTion!
NOOOO!!
YESSSS
MY TURN, MY TURN!!
AVENGE ME, 'CITY.
PLOP
NILAY, LOVE THAT NEW SHOULDER CANNON.
thanx
...I THINK I'LL TAKE IT!
DO IT!
TAKE HIS SONIC DAGGER TOO!
I LOVE PLAYING WITH THESE IDIOTS.
OH, YOU CAN TRY. YOU CAN—
-WOAH HEY!!
GET 'IM 'CITY!!
OMG, NILAY, YOUR POI—
YOU GOT THE RED THUNDER BUGS?! WHEN?!
heh heh heh
SKORE IS FUN, BUT...

...EVEN TIC-TAC-TOE WOULD BE, WITH THIS CREW.

(EXTRA FUN, SINCE JOSEPH DIDN'T SHOW UP, I GUESS.)

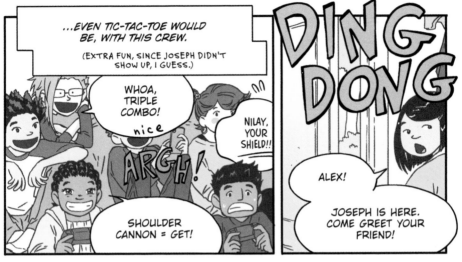

WHOA, TRIPLE COMBO!

nice

NILAY, YOUR SHIELD!!

ARGH!

SHOULDER CANNON = GET!

DING DONG

ALEX!

JOSEPH IS HERE. COME GREET YOUR FRIEND!

JO, FINALLY!!

C'MON, GET IN HERE!

...

YOU ALMOST MISSED IT!!

WE'RE DOING LIGHTNING ROUNDS— 'CITY'S ABOUT TO WIPE THE FLOOR WITH NILAY!

'CITY, WATCH OUT!!

SHKT

-2,000

+5,000

SHKT

...GUH!!

DUDE, WHAT ARE YOU DOING?! PUT UP YOUR SHIELDS!!

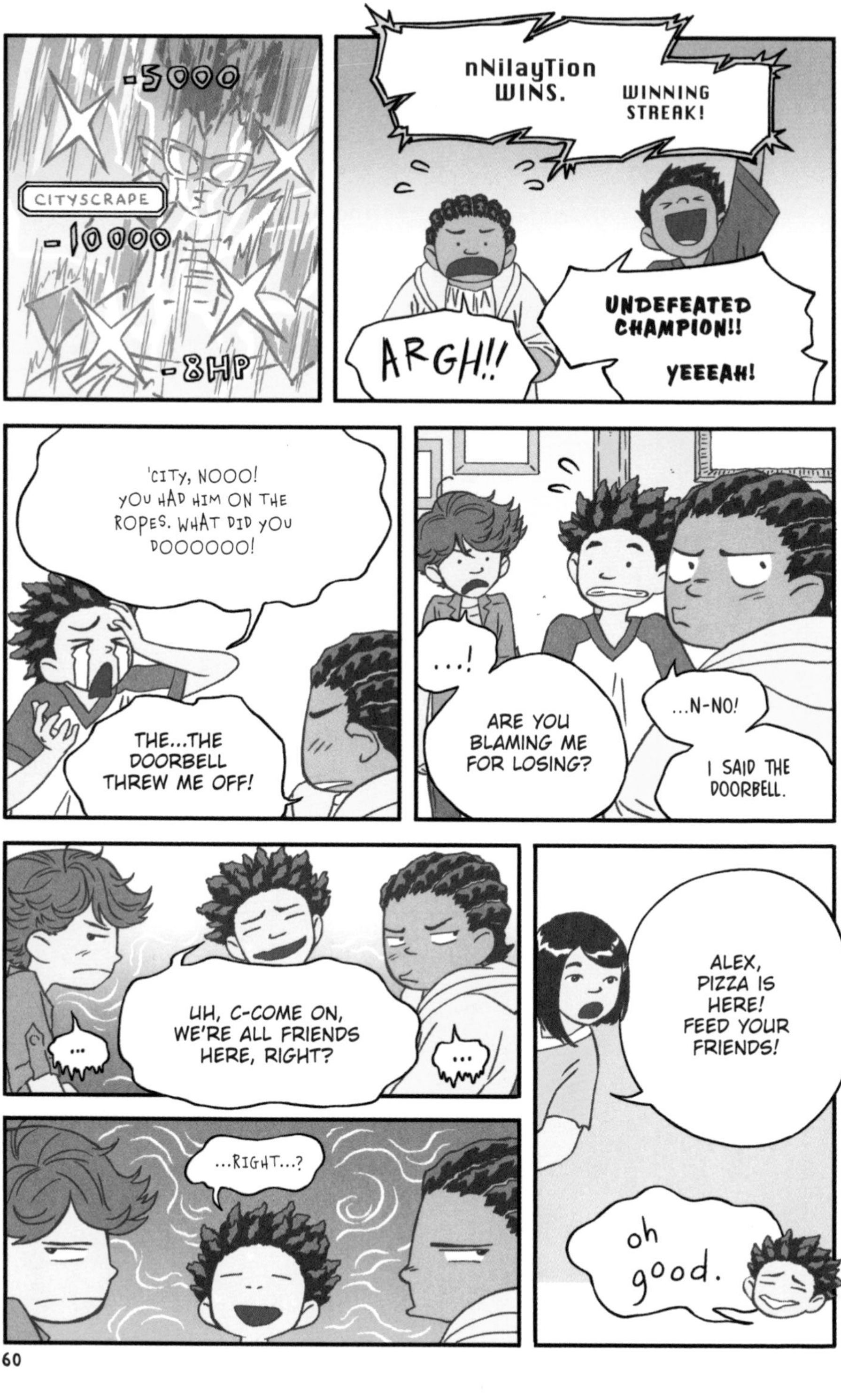
-5000
CITYSCRAPE
-10000
-8HP
nNilayTion WINS.
WINNING STREAK!
UNDEFEATED CHAMPION!!
YEEEAH!
ARGH!!
'CITY, NOOO! YOU HAD HIM ON THE ROPES. WHAT DID YOU DOOOOOO!
THE...THE DOORBELL THREW ME OFF!
...!
ARE YOU BLAMING ME FOR LOSING?
...N-NO!
I SAID THE DOORBELL.
...
UH, C-COME ON, WE'RE ALL FRIENDS HERE, RIGHT?
...
...RIGHT...?
ALEX, PIZZA IS HERE! FEED YOUR FRIENDS!
oh good.

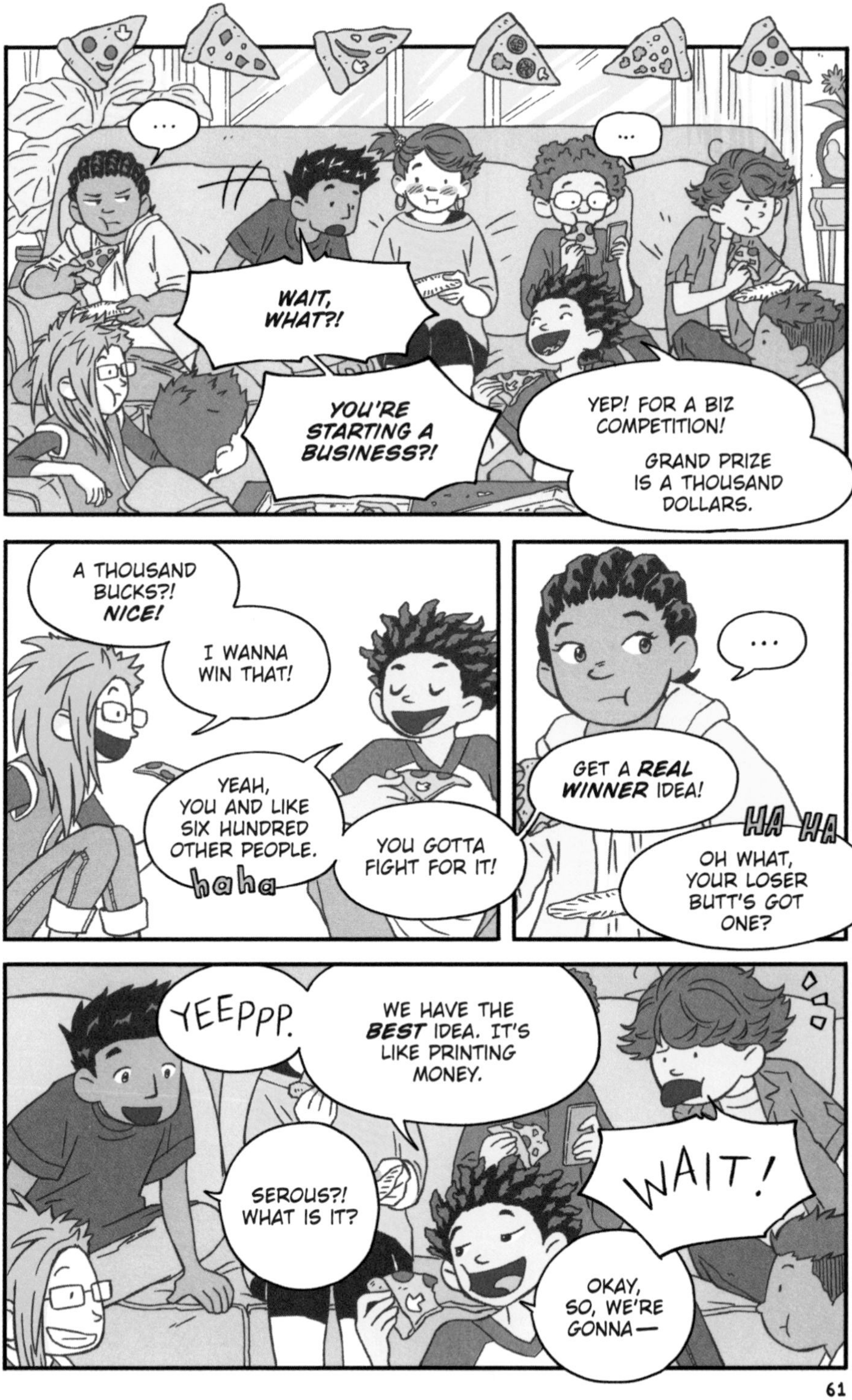
...
WAIT, WHAT?!
...
YOU'RE STARTING A BUSINESS?!
YEP! FOR A BIZ COMPETITION!
GRAND PRIZE IS A THOUSAND DOLLARS.
A THOUSAND BUCKS?! NICE!
I WANNA WIN THAT!
YEAH, YOU AND LIKE SIX HUNDRED OTHER PEOPLE.
haha
YOU GOTTA FIGHT FOR IT!
...
GET A REAL WINNER IDEA!
HA HA
OH WHAT, YOUR LOSER BUTT'S GOT ONE?
YEEPPP.
WE HAVE THE BEST IDEA. IT'S LIKE PRINTING MONEY.
SEROUS?! WHAT IS IT?
WAIT!
OKAY, SO, WE'RE GONNA—

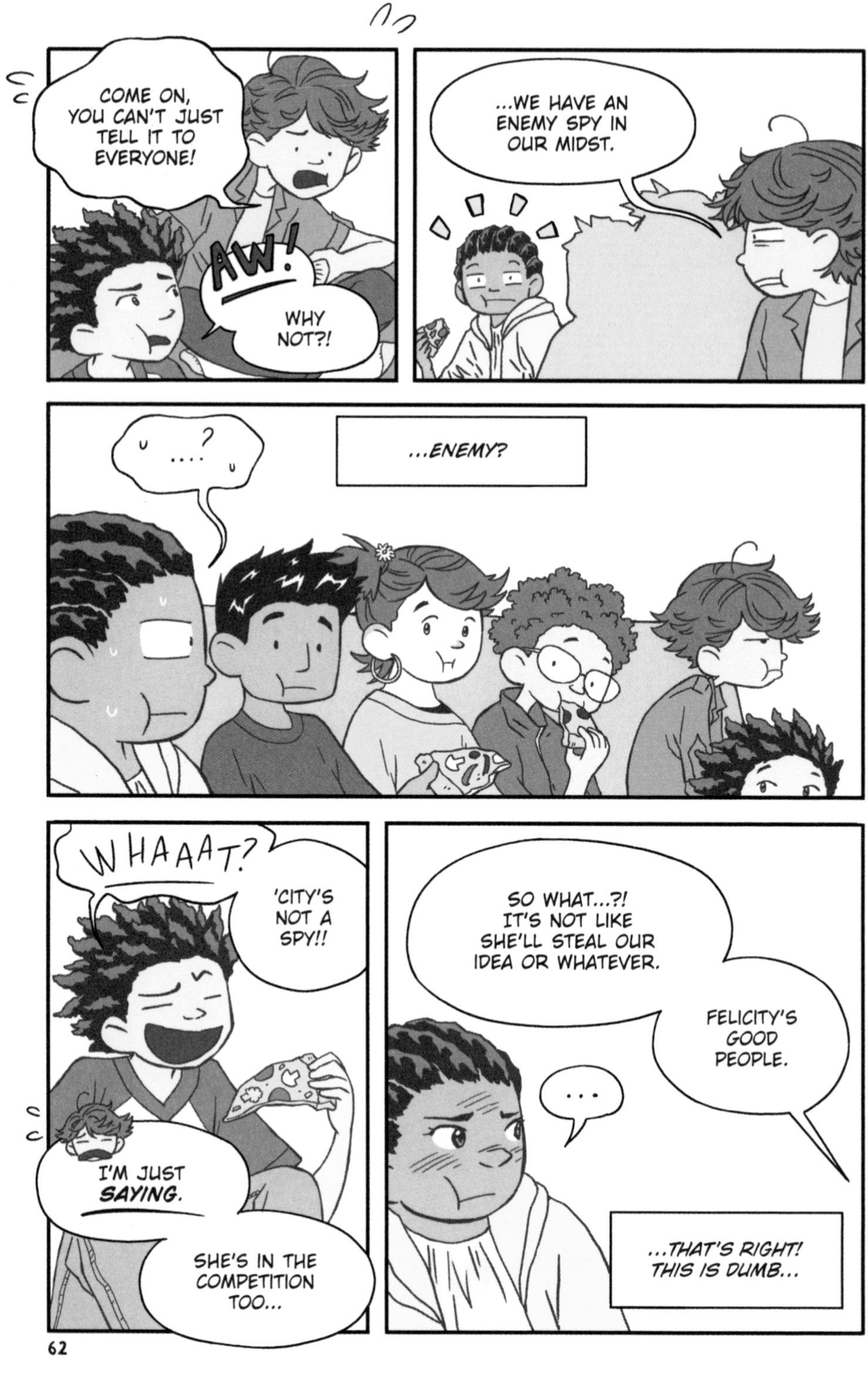
COME ON, YOU CAN'T JUST TELL IT TO EVERYONE!
AW!
WHY NOT?!
...WE HAVE AN ENEMY SPY IN OUR MIDST.
...?
...ENEMY?
WHAAAT?
'CITY'S NOT A SPY!!
I'M JUST SAYING.
SHE'S IN THE COMPETITION TOO...
SO WHAT...?! IT'S NOT LIKE SHE'LL STEAL OUR IDEA OR WHATEVER.
FELICITY'S GOOD PEOPLE.
...
...THAT'S RIGHT! THIS IS DUMB...

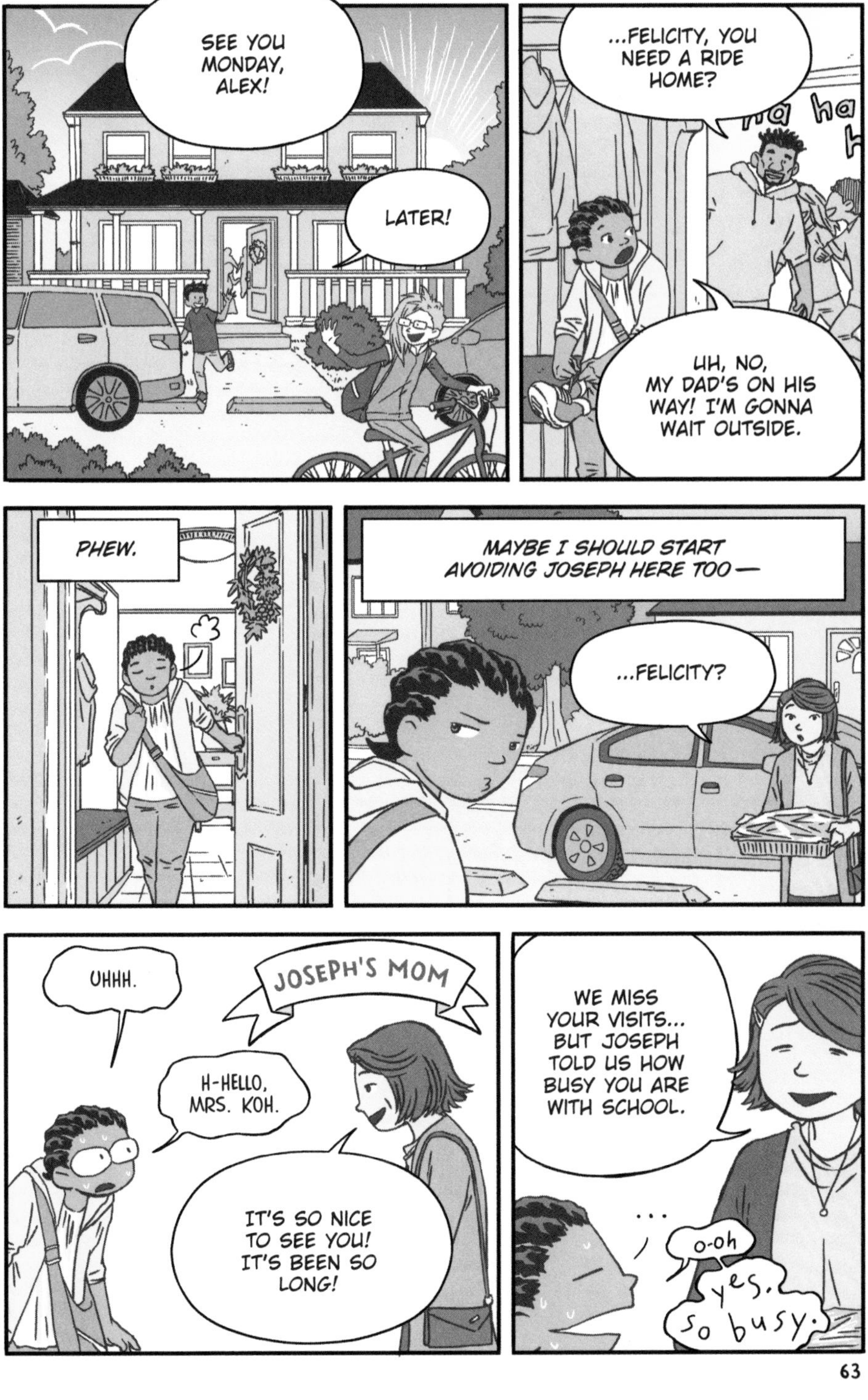
SEE YOU MONDAY, ALEX!
LATER!
...FELICITY, YOU NEED A RIDE HOME?
ha ha
UH, NO, MY DAD'S ON HIS WAY! I'M GONNA WAIT OUTSIDE.
PHEW.
MAYBE I SHOULD START AVOIDING JOSEPH HERE TOO—
...FELICITY?
UHHH.
JOSEPH'S MOM
H-HELLO, MRS. KOH.
IT'S SO NICE TO SEE YOU! IT'S BEEN SO LONG!
WE MISS YOUR VISITS... BUT JOSEPH TOLD US HOW BUSY YOU ARE WITH SCHOOL.
...
o-oh
yes. so busy.

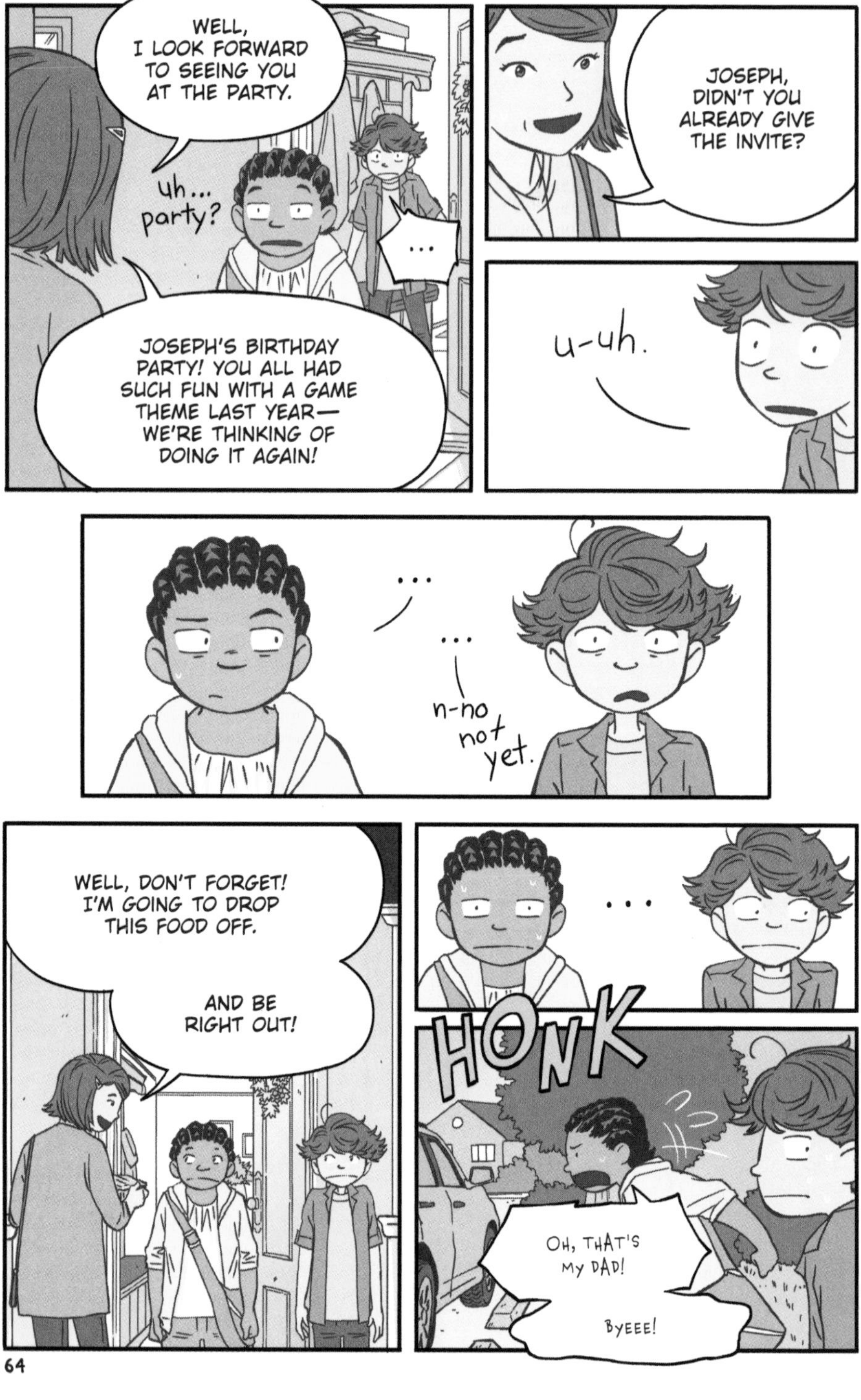
WELL, I LOOK FORWARD TO SEEING YOU AT THE PARTY.
uh... party?
...
JOSEPH'S BIRTHDAY PARTY! YOU ALL HAD SUCH FUN WITH A GAME THEME LAST YEAR— WE'RE THINKING OF DOING IT AGAIN!
JOSEPH, DIDN'T YOU ALREADY GIVE THE INVITE?
u-uh.
...
...
n-no not yet.
WELL, DON'T FORGET! I'M GOING TO DROP THIS FOOD OFF.
AND BE RIGHT OUT!
...
HONK
OH, THAT'S MY DAD!
BYEEE!

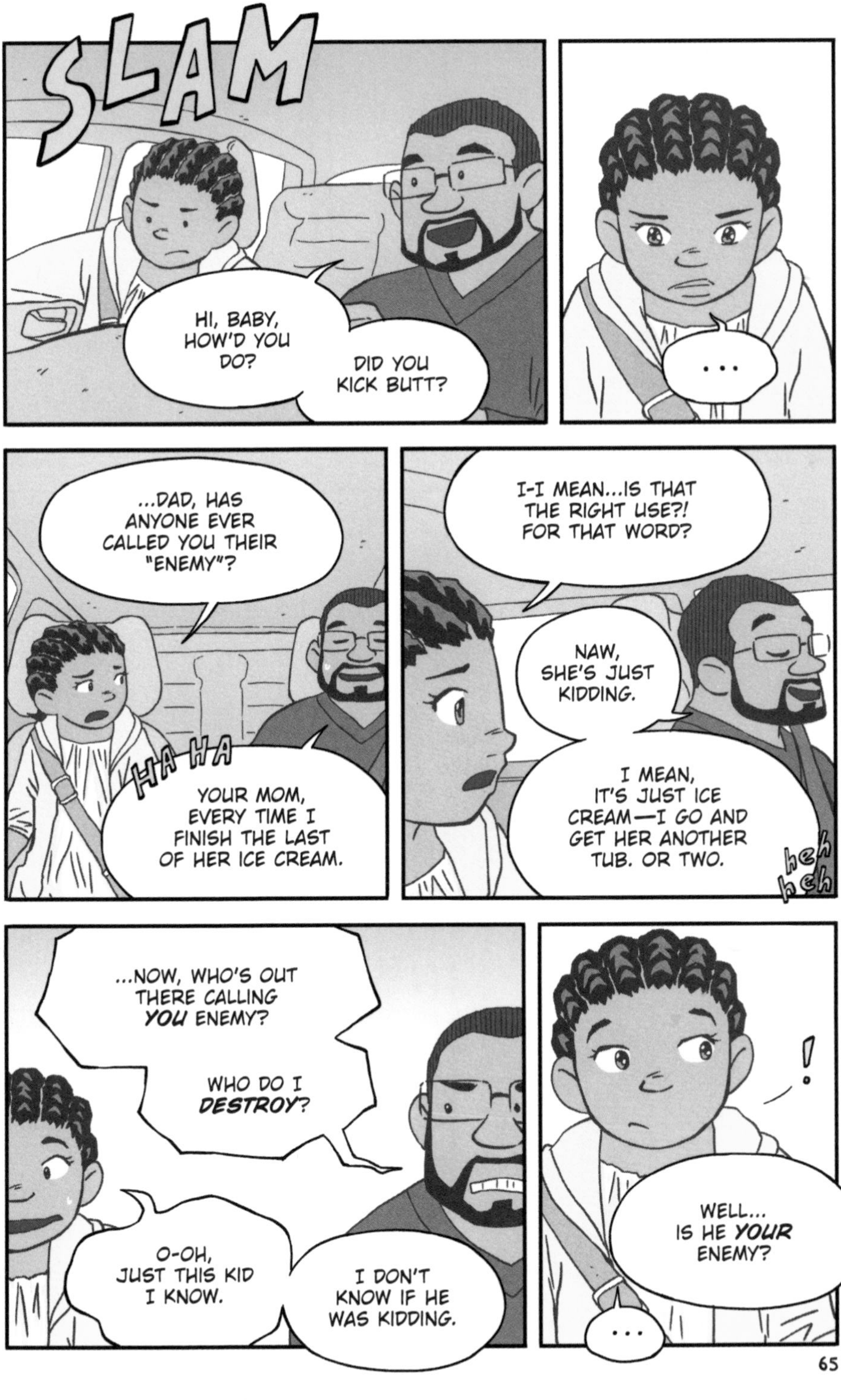
SLAM
HI, BABY, HOW'D YOU DO?
DID YOU KICK BUTT?
...
...DAD, HAS ANYONE EVER CALLED YOU THEIR "ENEMY"?
HA HA
YOUR MOM, EVERY TIME I FINISH THE LAST OF HER ICE CREAM.
I-I MEAN...IS THAT THE RIGHT USE?! FOR THAT WORD?
NAW, SHE'S JUST KIDDING.
I MEAN, IT'S JUST ICE CREAM—I GO AND GET HER ANOTHER TUB. OR TWO.
heh heh
...NOW, WHO'S OUT THERE CALLING *YOU* ENEMY?
WHO DO I *DESTROY*?
O-OH, JUST THIS KID I KNOW.
I DON'T KNOW IF HE WAS KIDDING.
!
WELL... IS HE *YOUR* ENEMY?
...

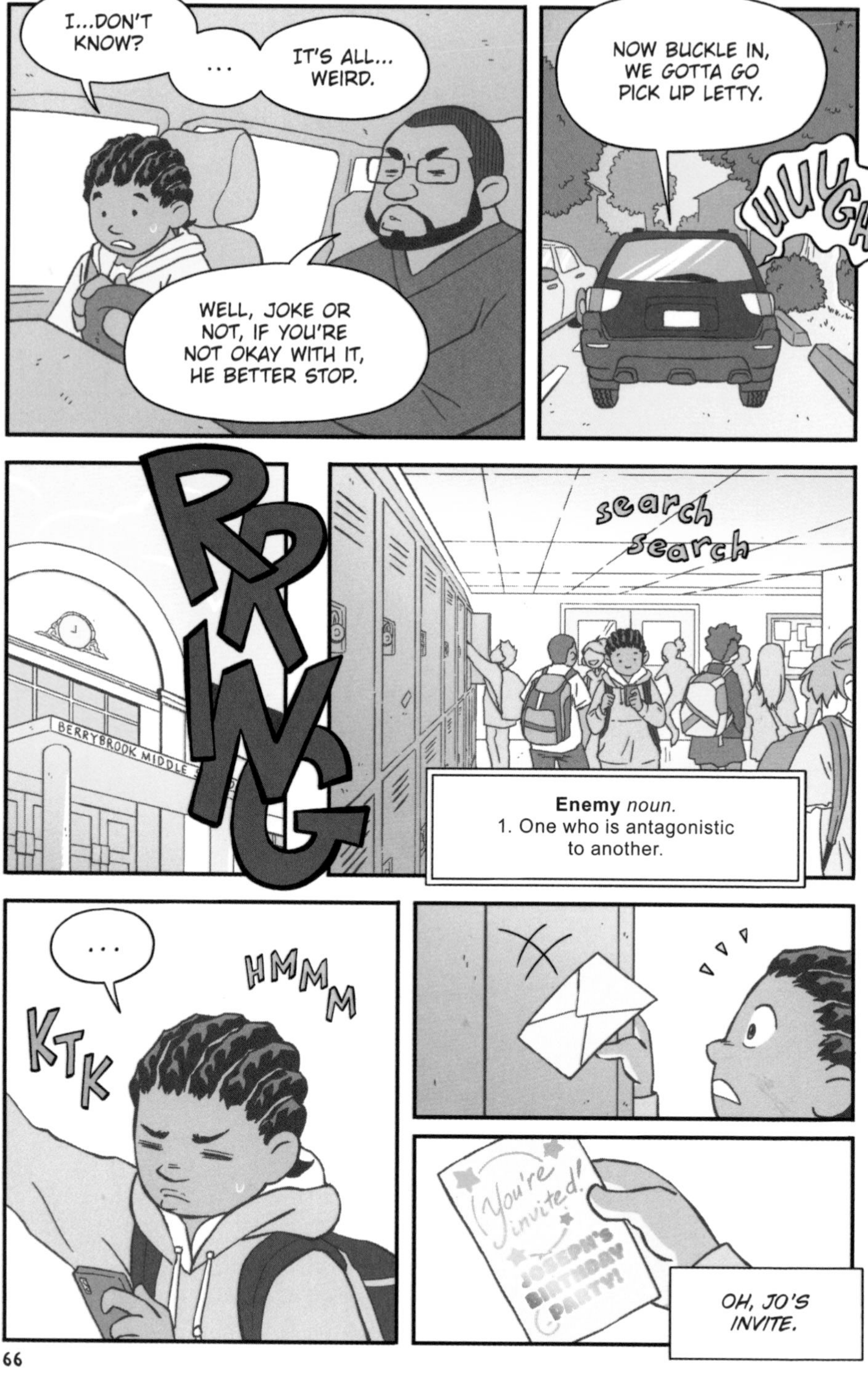
I...DON'T KNOW?
...
IT'S ALL... WEIRD.
WELL, JOKE OR NOT, IF YOU'RE NOT OKAY WITH IT, HE BETTER STOP.
NOW BUCKLE IN, WE GOTTA GO PICK UP LETTY.
UUUGH
RRIING
BERRYBROOK MIDDLE
search search
Enemy *noun.*
1. One who is antagonistic to another.
...
KTK
HMMM
You're invited!
JOSEPH'S BIRTHDAY PARTY!
OH, JO'S INVITE.

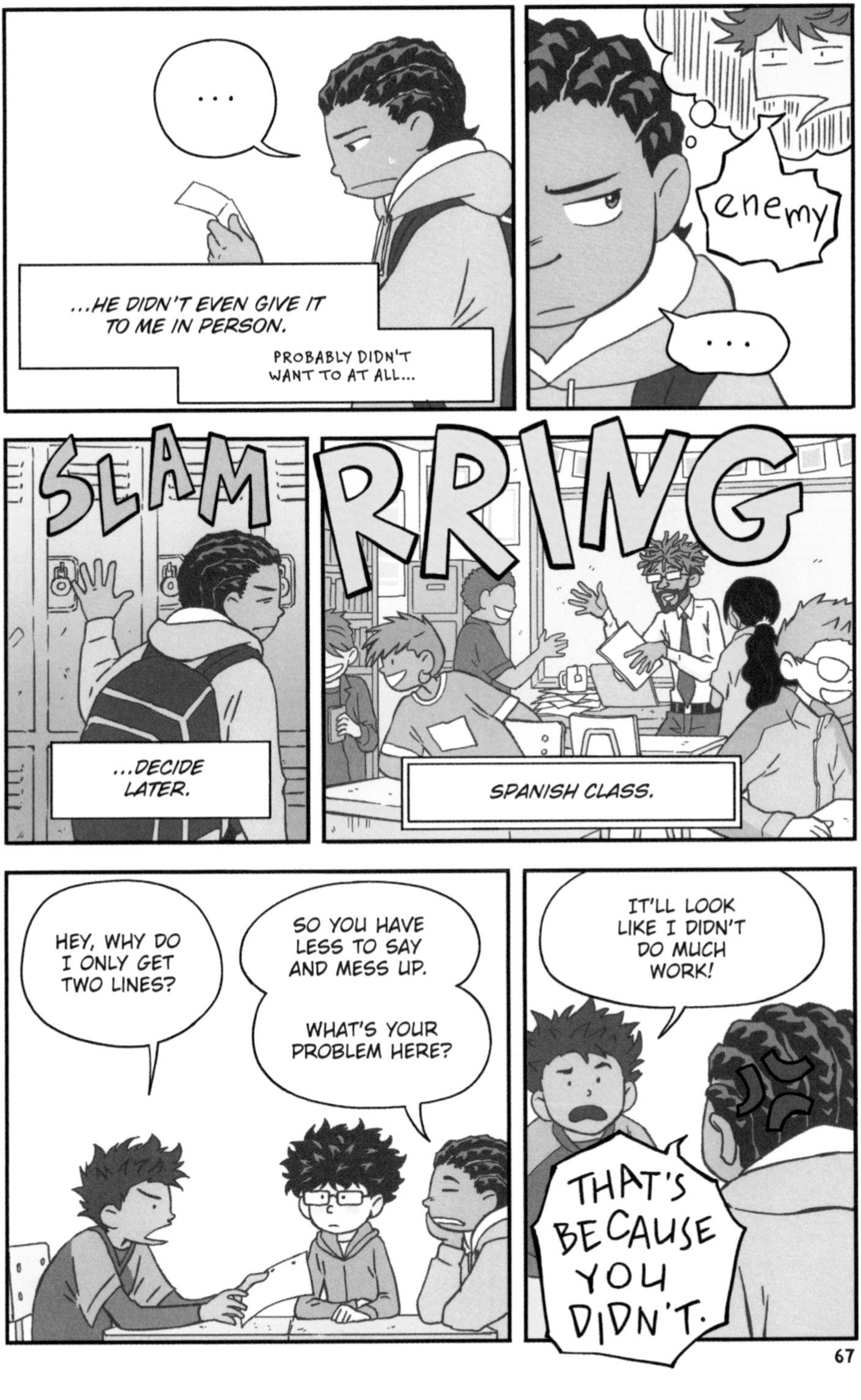
...
...HE DIDN'T EVEN GIVE IT TO ME IN PERSON.
PROBABLY DIDN'T WANT TO AT ALL...
enemy
...
SLAM
...DECIDE LATER.
RRING
SPANISH CLASS.
HEY, WHY DO I ONLY GET TWO LINES?
SO YOU HAVE LESS TO SAY AND MESS UP.
WHAT'S YOUR PROBLEM HERE?
IT'LL LOOK LIKE I DIDN'T DO MUCH WORK!
THAT'S BECAUSE YOU DIDN'T.

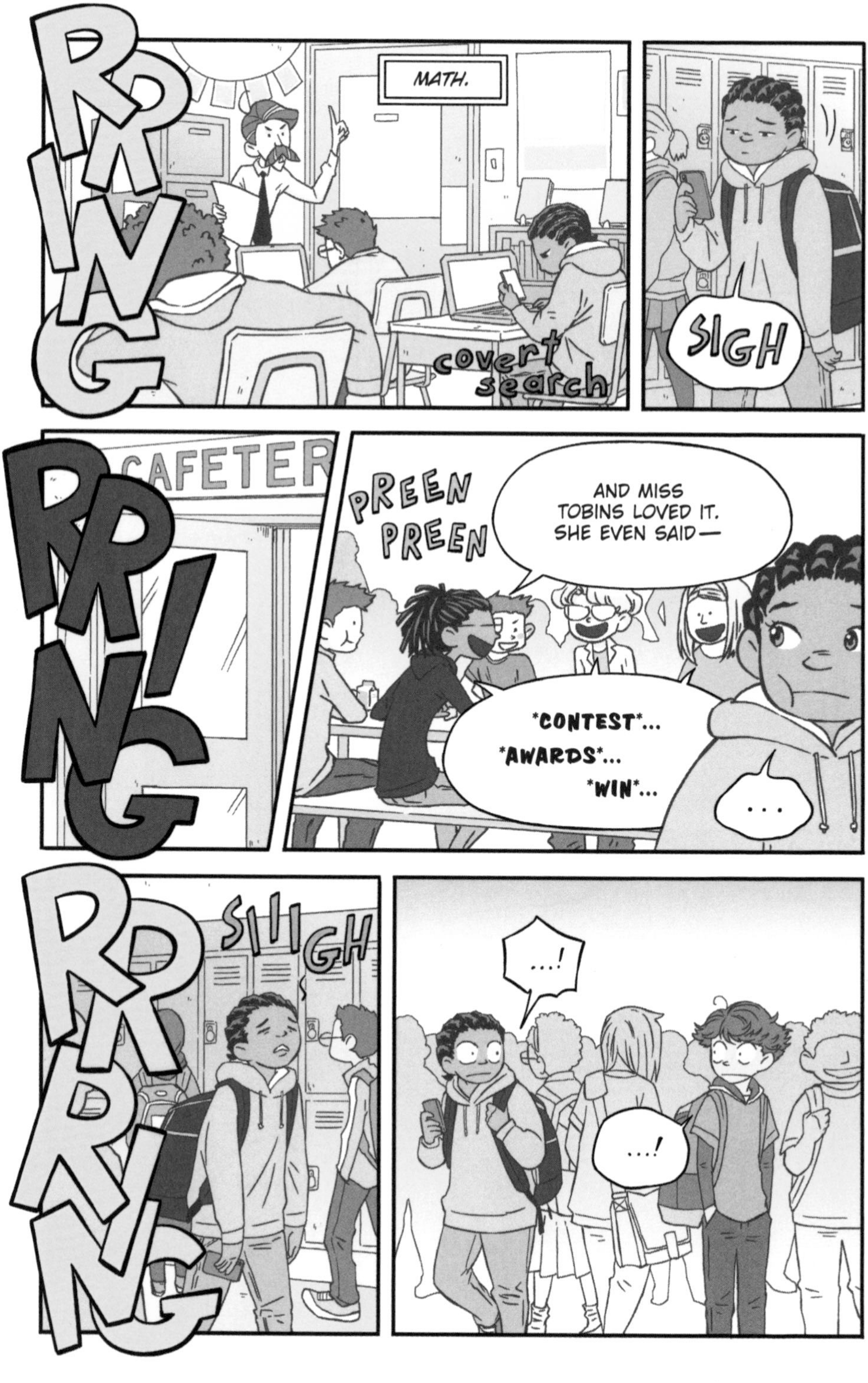
RRING
MATH.
covert search
SIGH
RRRING!
CAFETER
PREEN PREEN
AND MISS TOBINS LOVED IT. SHE EVEN SAID—
CONTEST... *AWARDS*... *WIN*...
. . .
RRRRING
SIIIGH
...!
...!

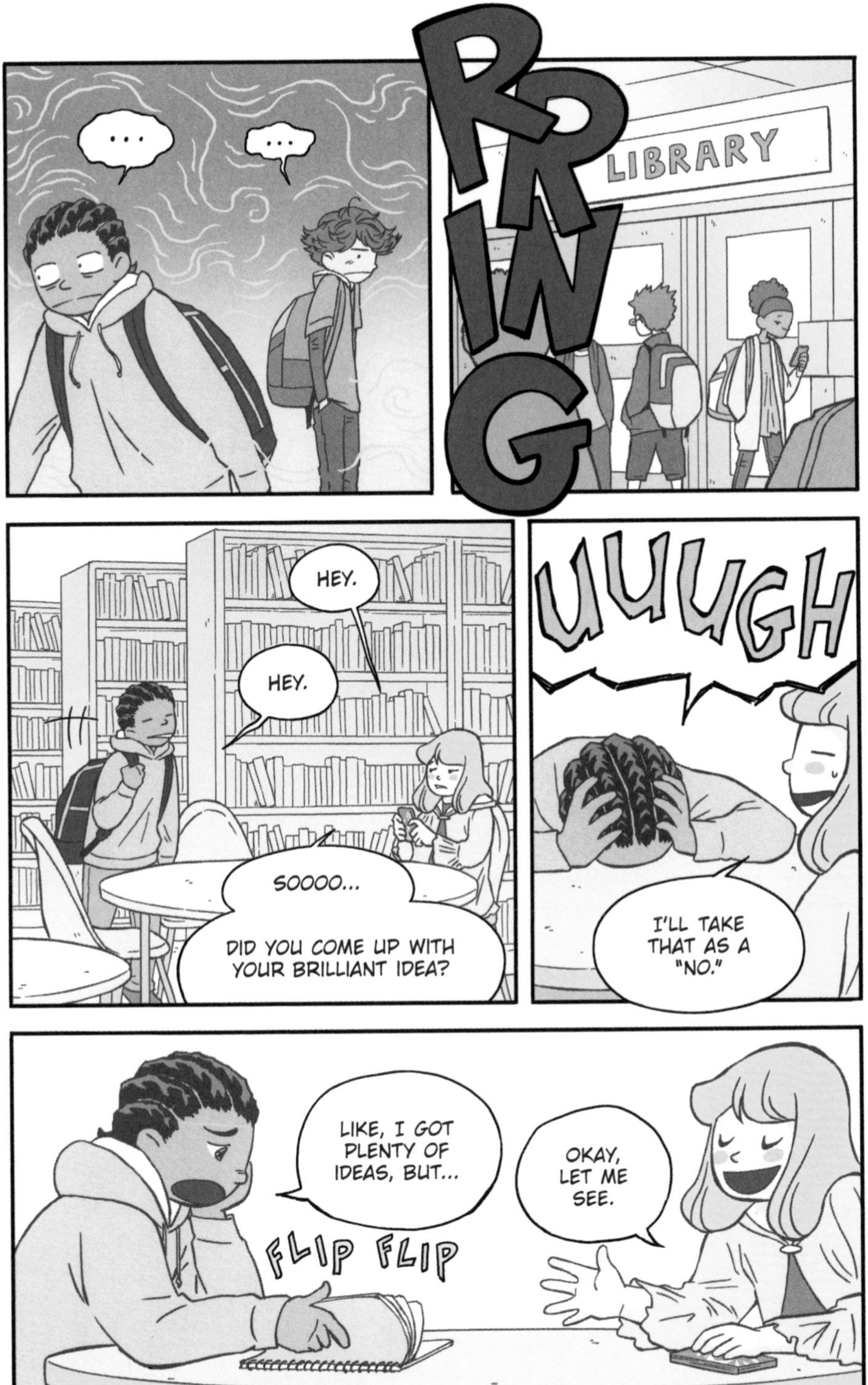
...
...
RRING
LIBRARY
HEY.
HEY.
SOOOO...
DID YOU COME UP WITH YOUR BRILLIANT IDEA?
UUUGH
I'LL TAKE THAT AS A "NO."
LIKE, I GOT PLENTY OF IDEAS, BUT...
FLIP FLIP
OKAY, LET ME SEE.

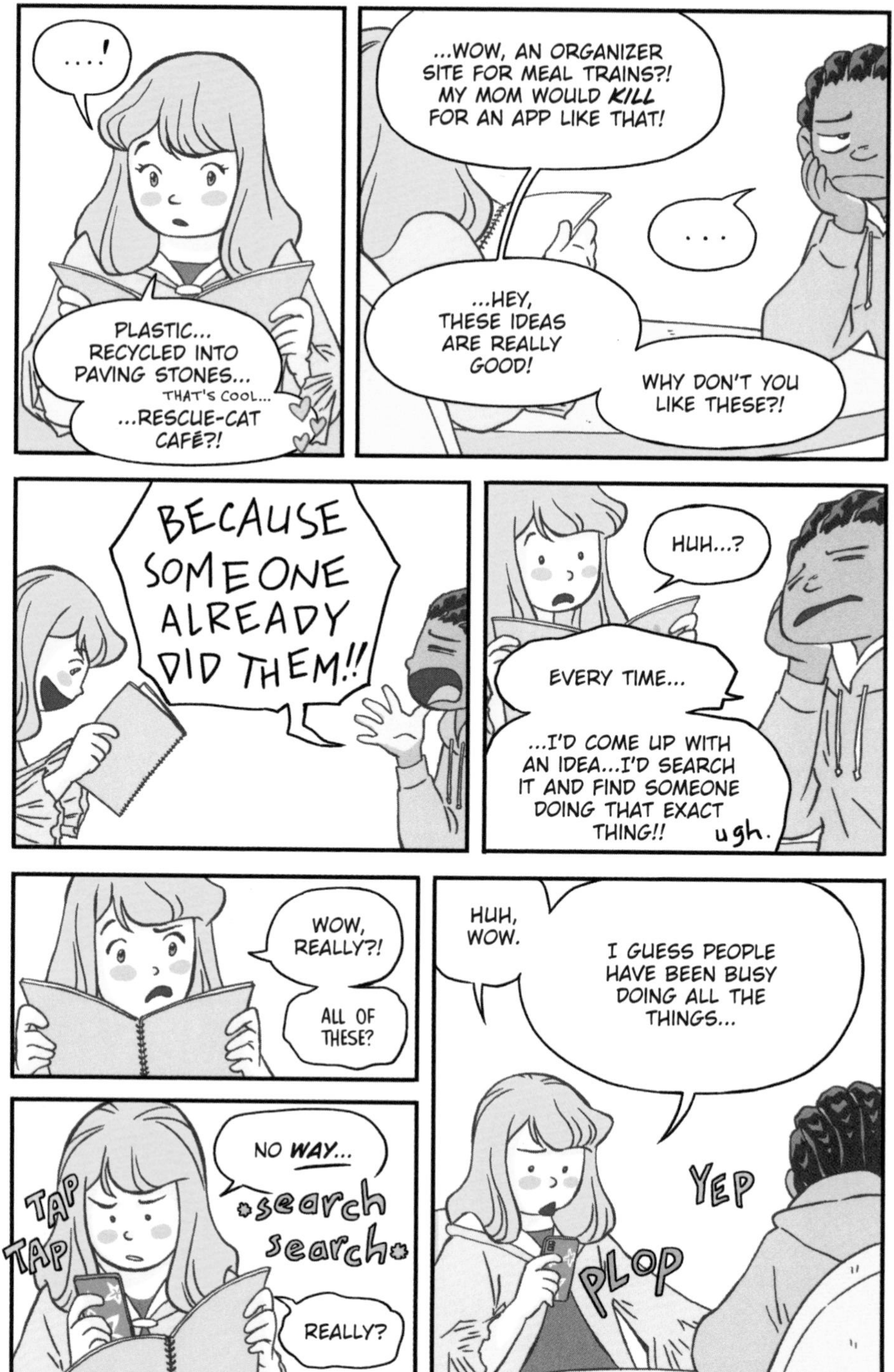

....!
...WOW, AN ORGANIZER SITE FOR MEAL TRAINS?! MY MOM WOULD KILL FOR AN APP LIKE THAT!
...
PLASTIC... RECYCLED INTO PAVING STONES...
THAT'S COOL...
...RESCUE-CAT CAFÉ?!
...HEY, THESE IDEAS ARE REALLY GOOD!
WHY DON'T YOU LIKE THESE?!
BECAUSE SOMEONE ALREADY DID THEM!!
HUH...?
EVERY TIME...
...I'D COME UP WITH AN IDEA...I'D SEARCH IT AND FIND SOMEONE DOING THAT EXACT THING!!
ugh.
WOW, REALLY?!
ALL OF THESE?
HUH, WOW.
I GUESS PEOPLE HAVE BEEN BUSY DOING ALL THE THINGS...
NO WAY...
TAP TAP
search search
REALLY?
YEP
PLOP

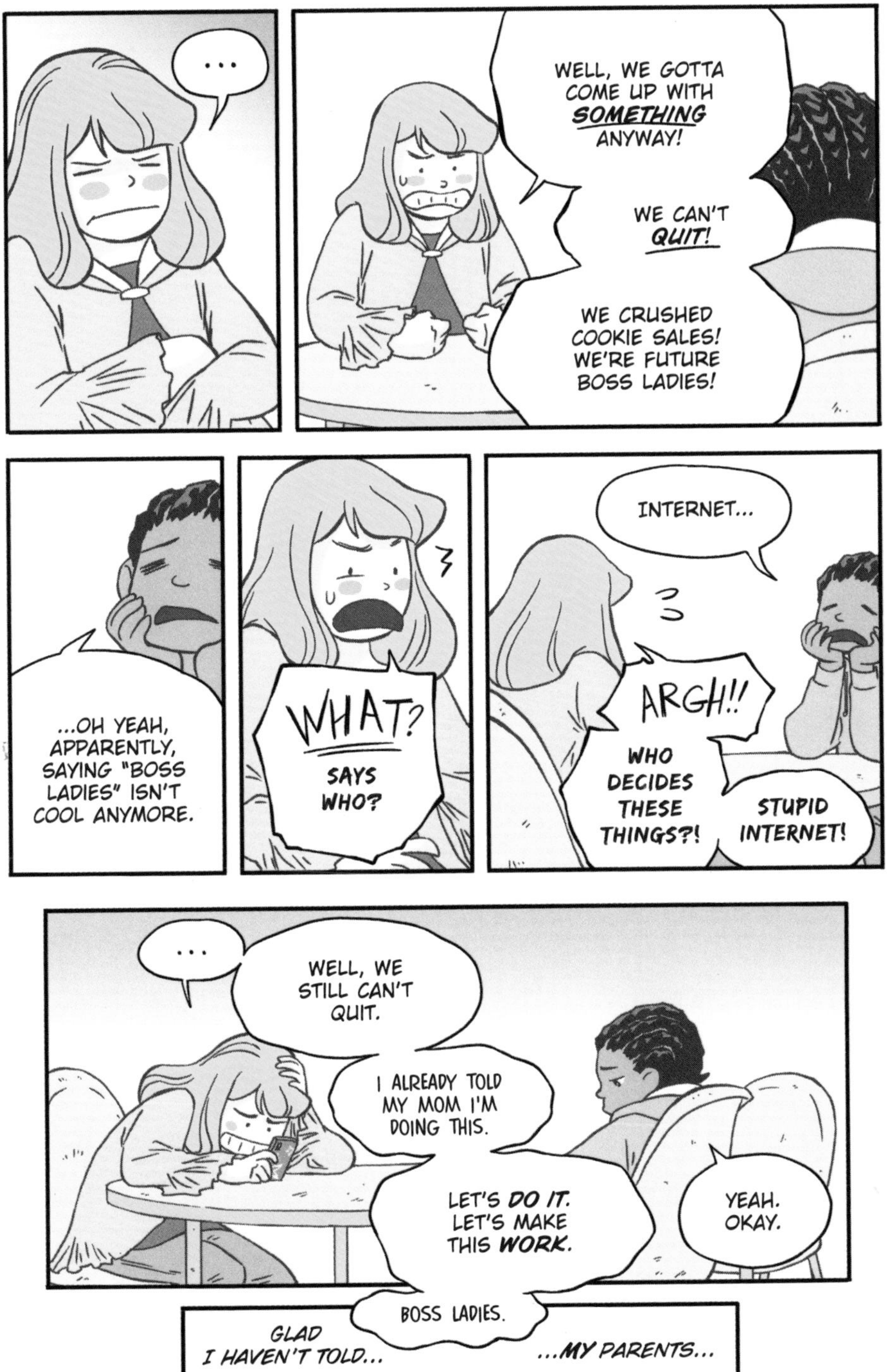
...
WELL, WE GOTTA COME UP WITH SOMETHING ANYWAY!
WE CAN'T QUIT!
WE CRUSHED COOKIE SALES! WE'RE FUTURE BOSS LADIES!
...OH YEAH, APPARENTLY, SAYING "BOSS LADIES" ISN'T COOL ANYMORE.
WHAT?
SAYS WHO?
INTERNET...
ARGH!!
WHO DECIDES THESE THINGS?!
STUPID INTERNET!
...
WELL, WE STILL CAN'T QUIT.
I ALREADY TOLD MY MOM I'M DOING THIS.
LET'S DO IT. LET'S MAKE THIS WORK.
YEAH. OKAY.
BOSS LADIES.
GLAD I HAVEN'T TOLD...
...MY PARENTS...

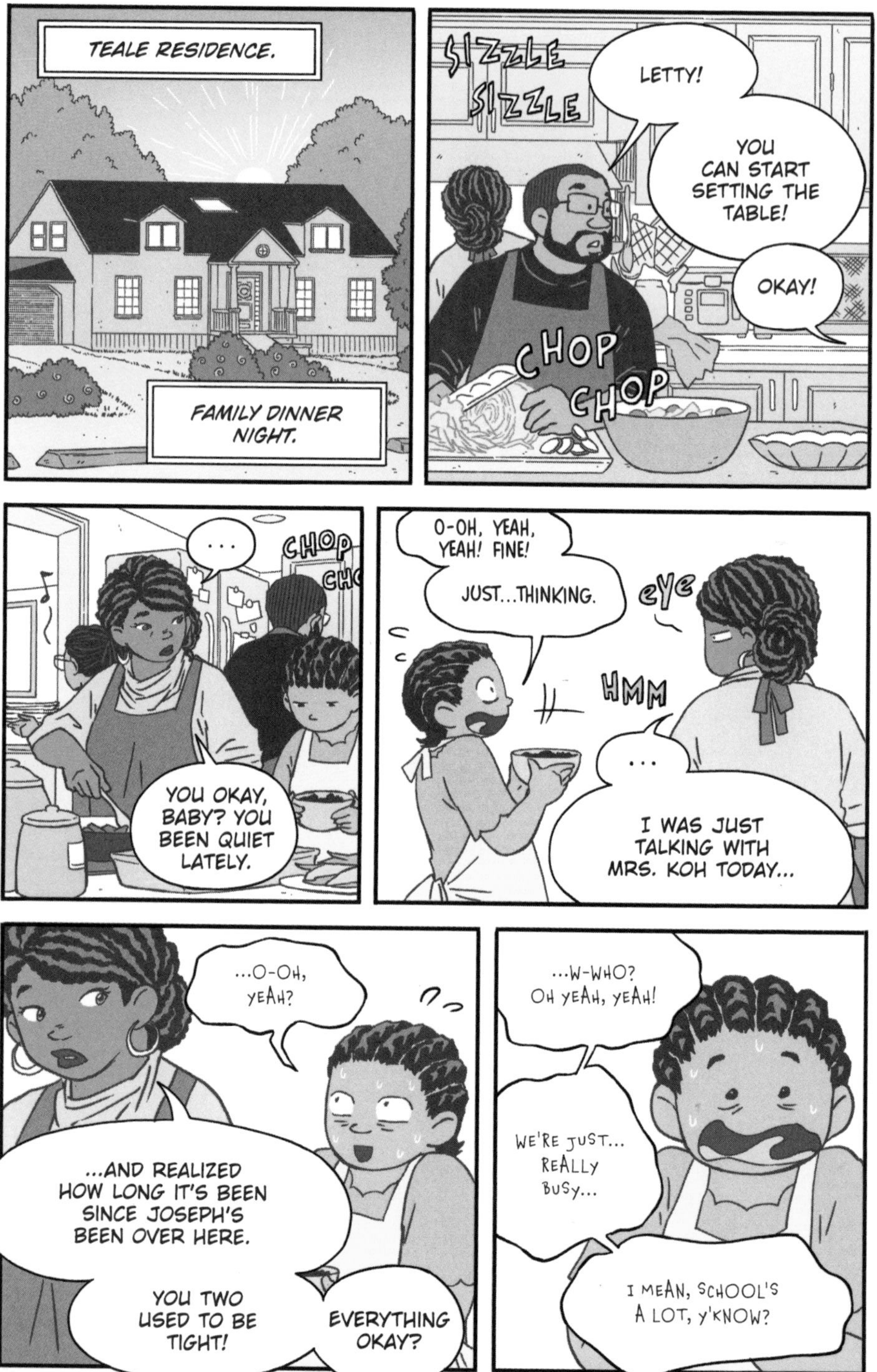
TEALE RESIDENCE.
FAMILY DINNER NIGHT.
SIZZLE SIZZLE
LETTY!
YOU CAN START SETTING THE TABLE!
OKAY!
CHOP CHOP
...
CHOP CHO
YOU OKAY, BABY? YOU BEEN QUIET LATELY.
O-OH, YEAH, YEAH! FINE!
JUST...THINKING.
eye
HMM
...
I WAS JUST TALKING WITH MRS. KOH TODAY...
...AND REALIZED HOW LONG IT'S BEEN SINCE JOSEPH'S BEEN OVER HERE.
...O-OH, YEAH?
YOU TWO USED TO BE TIGHT!
EVERYTHING OKAY?
...W-WHO? OH YEAH, YEAH!
WE'RE JUST... REALLY BUSY...
I MEAN, SCHOOL'S A LOT, Y'KNOW?

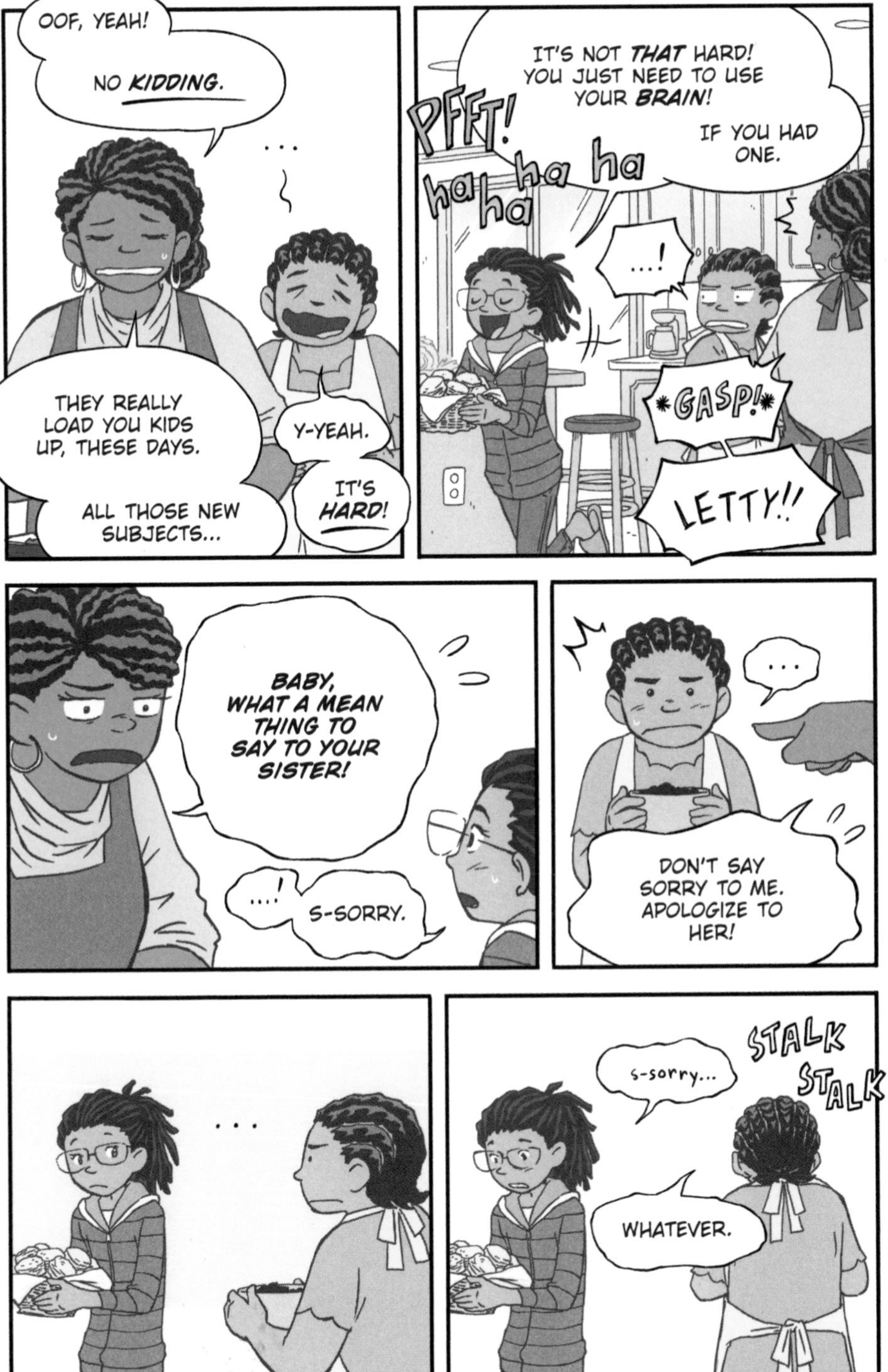
OOF, YEAH!
NO KIDDING.
...
THEY REALLY LOAD YOU KIDS UP, THESE DAYS.
ALL THOSE NEW SUBJECTS...
Y-YEAH.
IT'S HARD!
IT'S NOT THAT HARD! YOU JUST NEED TO USE YOUR BRAIN!
IF YOU HAD ONE.
PFFT!
ha ha ha ha
...!
GASP!
LETTY!!
BABY, WHAT A MEAN THING TO SAY TO YOUR SISTER!
...!
S-SORRY.
...
DON'T SAY SORRY TO ME. APOLOGIZE TO HER!
...
s-sorry...
STALK
STALK
WHATEVER.

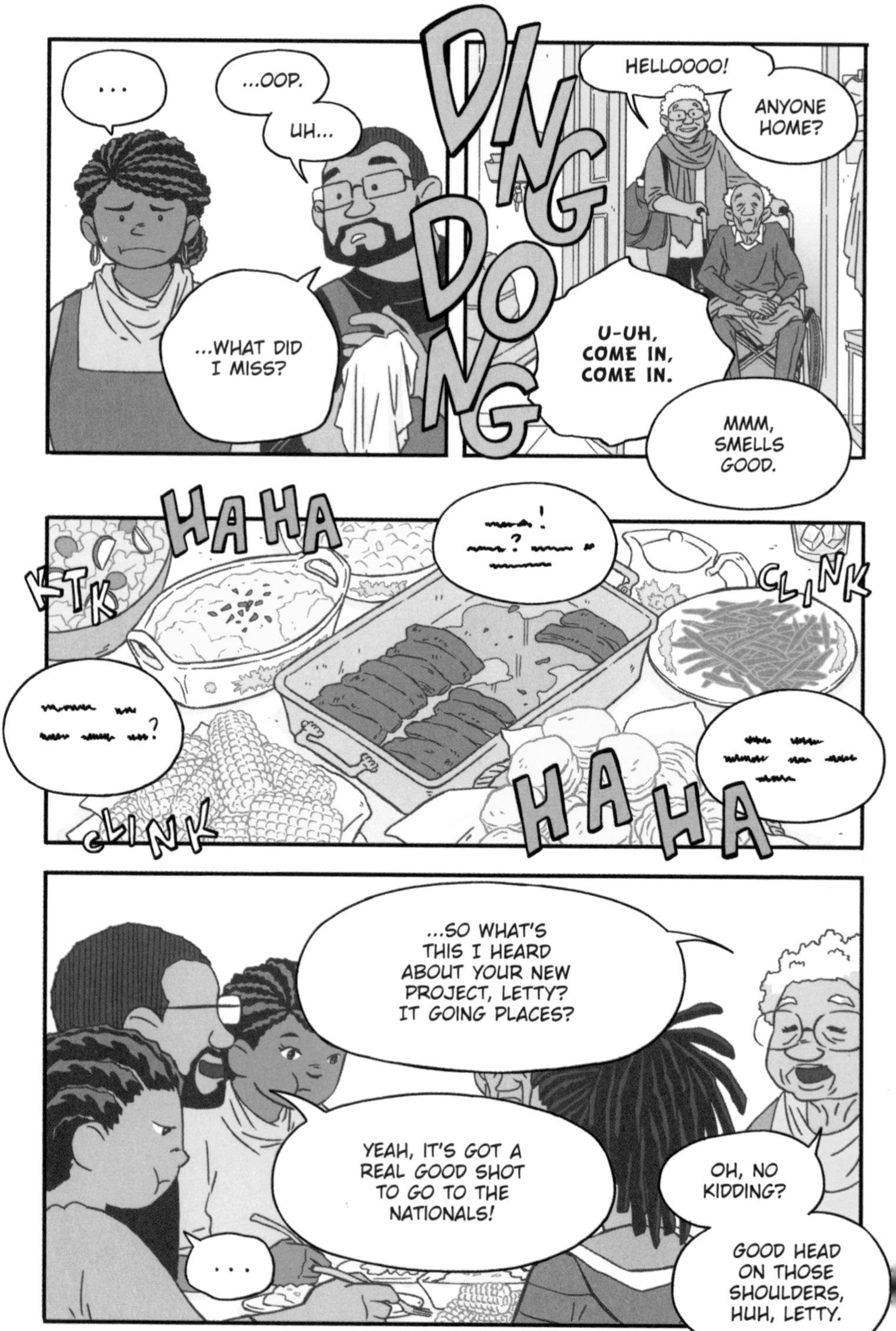
...
...OOP.
UH...
...WHAT DID I MISS?
DING DONG
HELLOOOO!
ANYONE HOME?
U-UH, COME IN, COME IN.
MMM, SMELLS GOOD.
HAHA
KTK
CLINK
HAHA
CLINK
...SO WHAT'S THIS I HEARD ABOUT YOUR NEW PROJECT, LETTY? IT GOING PLACES?
YEAH, IT'S GOT A REAL GOOD SHOT TO GO TO THE NATIONALS!
OH, NO KIDDING?
GOOD HEAD ON THOSE SHOULDERS, HUH, LETTY.
...

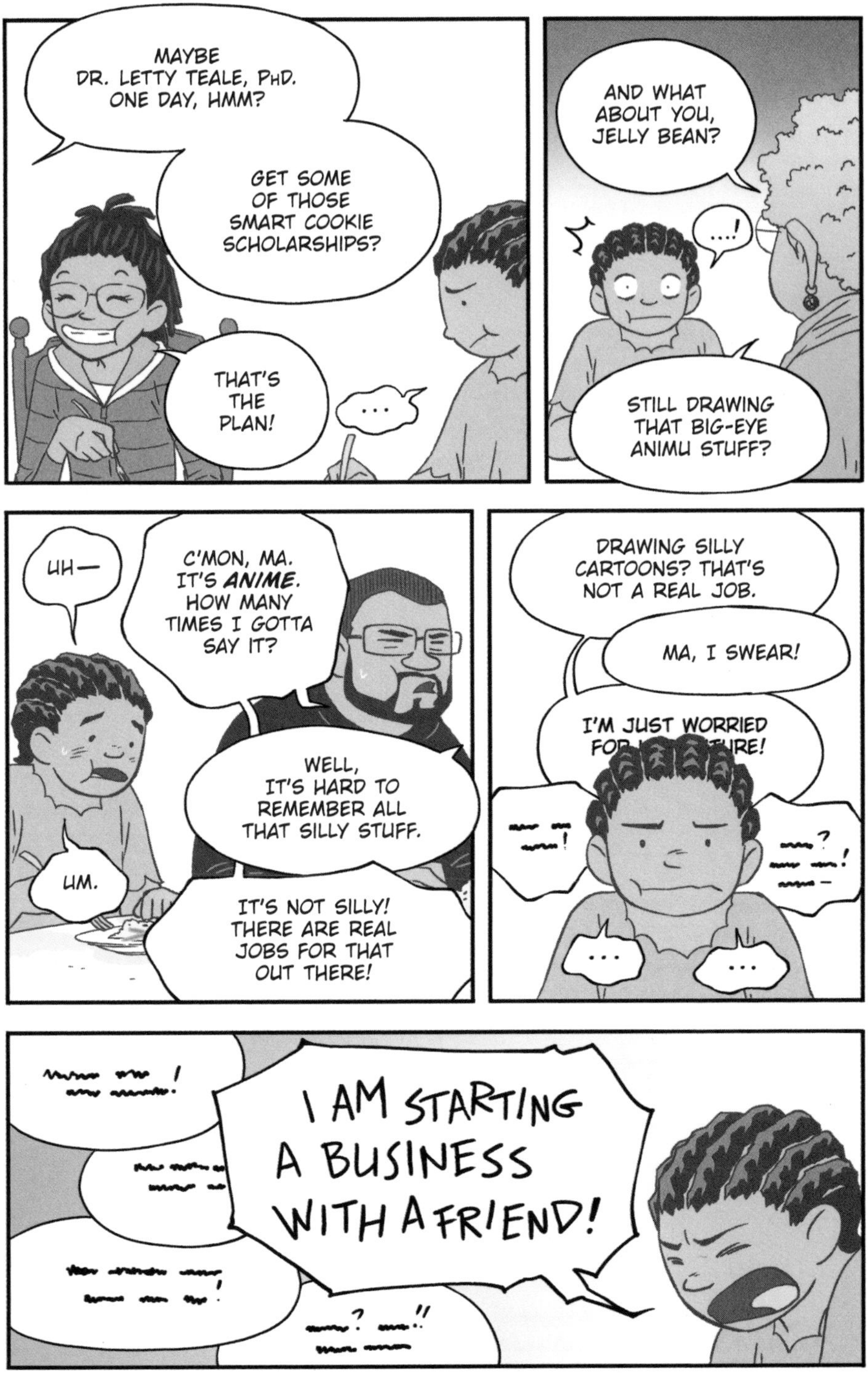
MAYBE DR. LETTY TEALE, PHD. ONE DAY, HMM?
GET SOME OF THOSE SMART COOKIE SCHOLARSHIPS?
THAT'S THE PLAN!
...
AND WHAT ABOUT YOU, JELLY BEAN?
....!
STILL DRAWING THAT BIG-EYE ANIMU STUFF?
UH—
C'MON, MA. IT'S ANIME. HOW MANY TIMES I GOTTA SAY IT?
WELL, IT'S HARD TO REMEMBER ALL THAT SILLY STUFF.
UM.
IT'S NOT SILLY! THERE ARE REAL JOBS FOR THAT OUT THERE!
DRAWING SILLY CARTOONS? THAT'S NOT A REAL JOB.
MA, I SWEAR!
I'M JUST WORRIED
...
...
I AM STARTING A BUSINESS WITH A FRIEND!

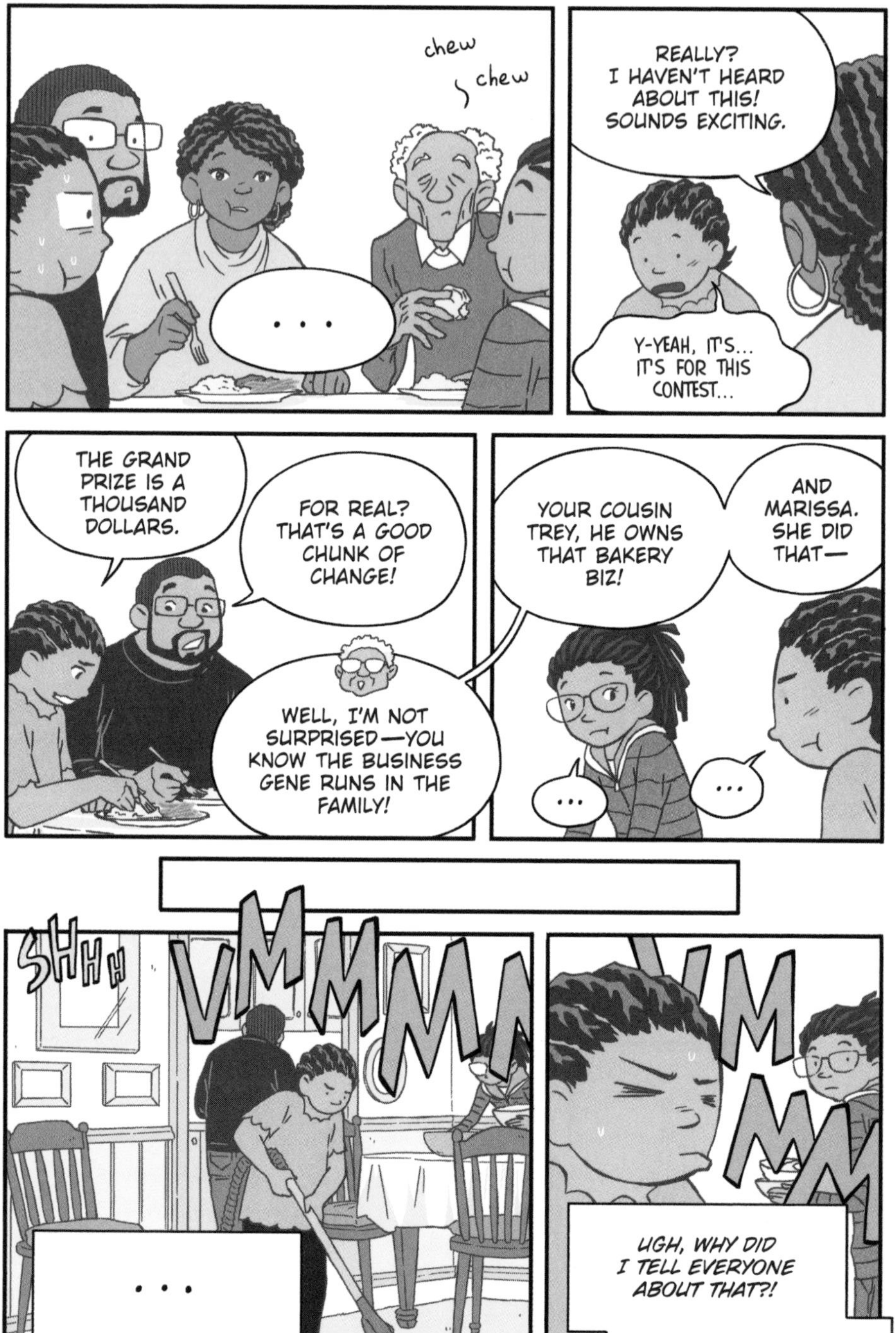
chew
chew
...
REALLY? I HAVEN'T HEARD ABOUT THIS! SOUNDS EXCITING.
Y-YEAH, IT'S... IT'S FOR THIS CONTEST...
THE GRAND PRIZE IS A THOUSAND DOLLARS.
FOR REAL? THAT'S A GOOD CHUNK OF CHANGE!
WELL, I'M NOT SURPRISED—YOU KNOW THE BUSINESS GENE RUNS IN THE FAMILY!
YOUR COUSIN TREY, HE OWNS THAT BAKERY BIZ!
AND MARISSA. SHE DID THAT—
...
...
SHHH
VMMMM
...
VMMMM
UGH, WHY DID I TELL EVERYONE ABOUT THAT?!
NOW I CAN'T SECRETLY QUIT...

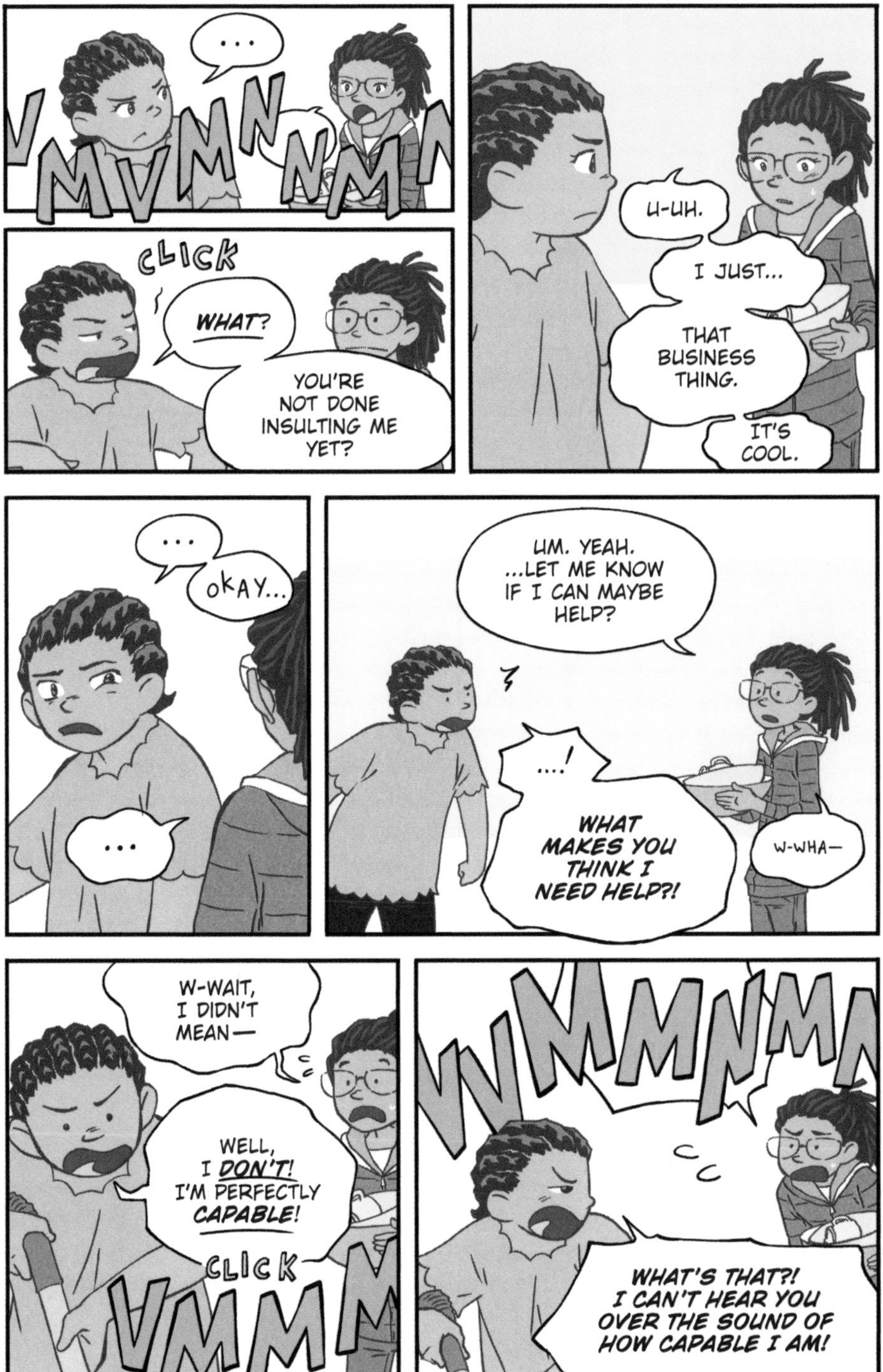
...
VMMVMNNMMN
CLICK
WHAT?
YOU'RE NOT DONE INSULTING ME YET?
U-UH.
I JUST...
THAT BUSINESS THING.
IT'S COOL.
...
OKAY...
...
UM. YEAH. ...LET ME KNOW IF I CAN MAYBE HELP?
....!
WHAT MAKES YOU THINK I NEED HELP?!
W-WHA—
W-WAIT, I DIDN'T MEAN—
WELL, I DON'T! I'M PERFECTLY CAPABLE!
CLICK
VMMM
VVMMMNNM
WHAT'S THAT?! I CAN'T HEAR YOU OVER THE SOUND OF HOW CAPABLE I AM!

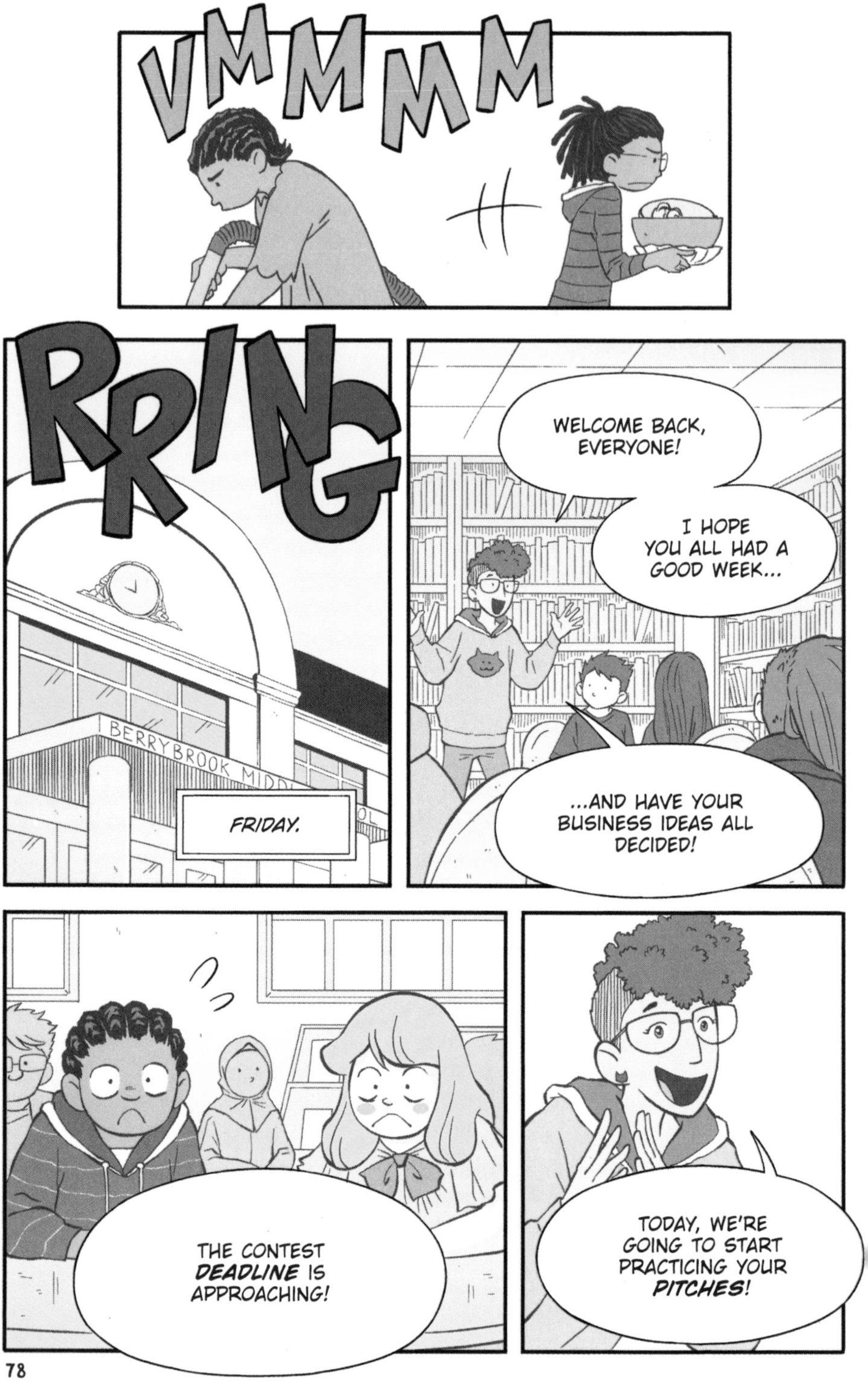
VMMMMM
RRING
BERRYBROOK MIDD
FRIDAY.
WELCOME BACK, EVERYONE!
I HOPE YOU ALL HAD A GOOD WEEK...
...AND HAVE YOUR BUSINESS IDEAS ALL DECIDED!
THE CONTEST DEADLINE IS APPROACHING!
TODAY, WE'RE GOING TO START PRACTICING YOUR PITCHES!

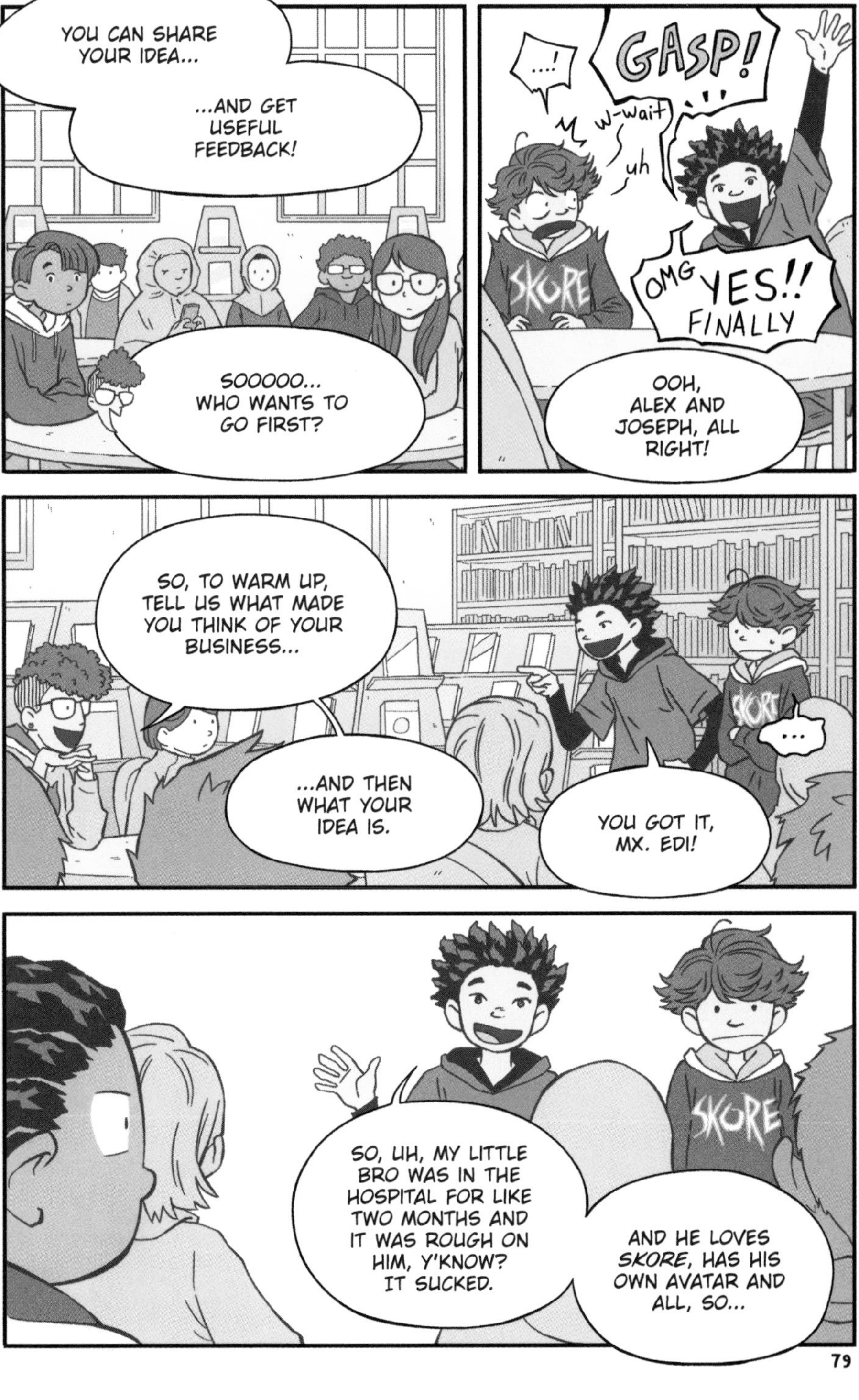
YOU CAN SHARE YOUR IDEA...
...AND GET USEFUL FEEDBACK!
SOOOOO... WHO WANTS TO GO FIRST?
...!
GASP!
W-wait
uh
OMG YES!! FINALLY
OOH, ALEX AND JOSEPH, ALL RIGHT!
SO, TO WARM UP, TELL US WHAT MADE YOU THINK OF YOUR BUSINESS...
...AND THEN WHAT YOUR IDEA IS.
YOU GOT IT, MX. EDI!
...
SO, UH, MY LITTLE BRO WAS IN THE HOSPITAL FOR LIKE TWO MONTHS AND IT WAS ROUGH ON HIM, Y'KNOW? IT SUCKED.
AND HE LOVES *SKORE*, HAS HIS OWN AVATAR AND ALL, SO...

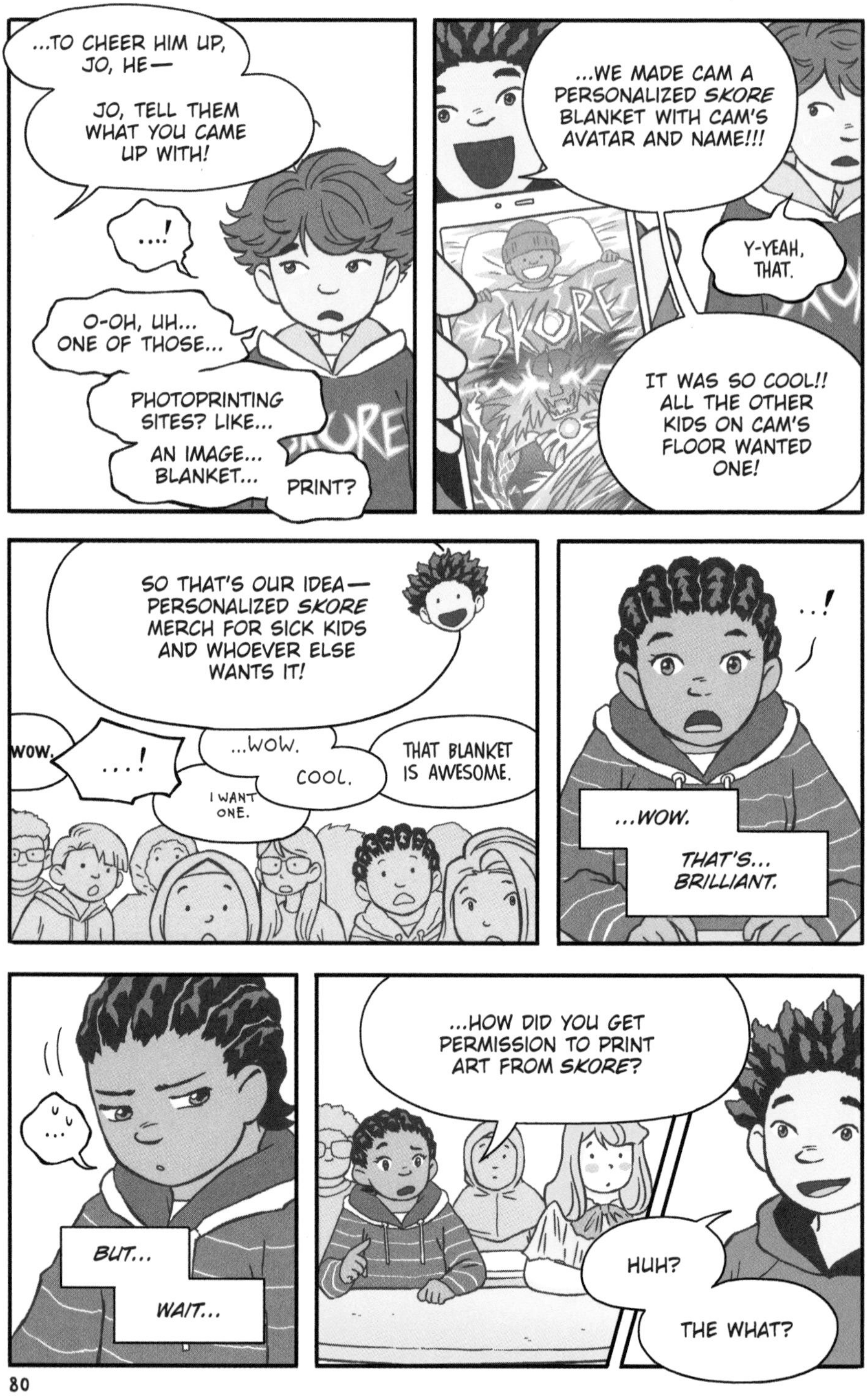

...TO CHEER HIM UP, JO, HE—
JO, TELL THEM WHAT YOU CAME UP WITH!
...!
O-OH, UH... ONE OF THOSE...
PHOTOPRINTING SITES? LIKE...
AN IMAGE... BLANKET...
PRINT?
...WE MADE CAM A PERSONALIZED SKORE BLANKET WITH CAM'S AVATAR AND NAME!!!
Y-YEAH, THAT.
SKORE
IT WAS SO COOL!! ALL THE OTHER KIDS ON CAM'S FLOOR WANTED ONE!
SO THAT'S OUR IDEA— PERSONALIZED SKORE MERCH FOR SICK KIDS AND WHOEVER ELSE WANTS IT!
WOW.
...!
...WOW.
COOL.
THAT BLANKET IS AWESOME.
I WANT ONE.
..!
...WOW.
THAT'S... BRILLIANT.
...
BUT...
WAIT...
...HOW DID YOU GET PERMISSION TO PRINT ART FROM SKORE?
HUH?
THE WHAT?

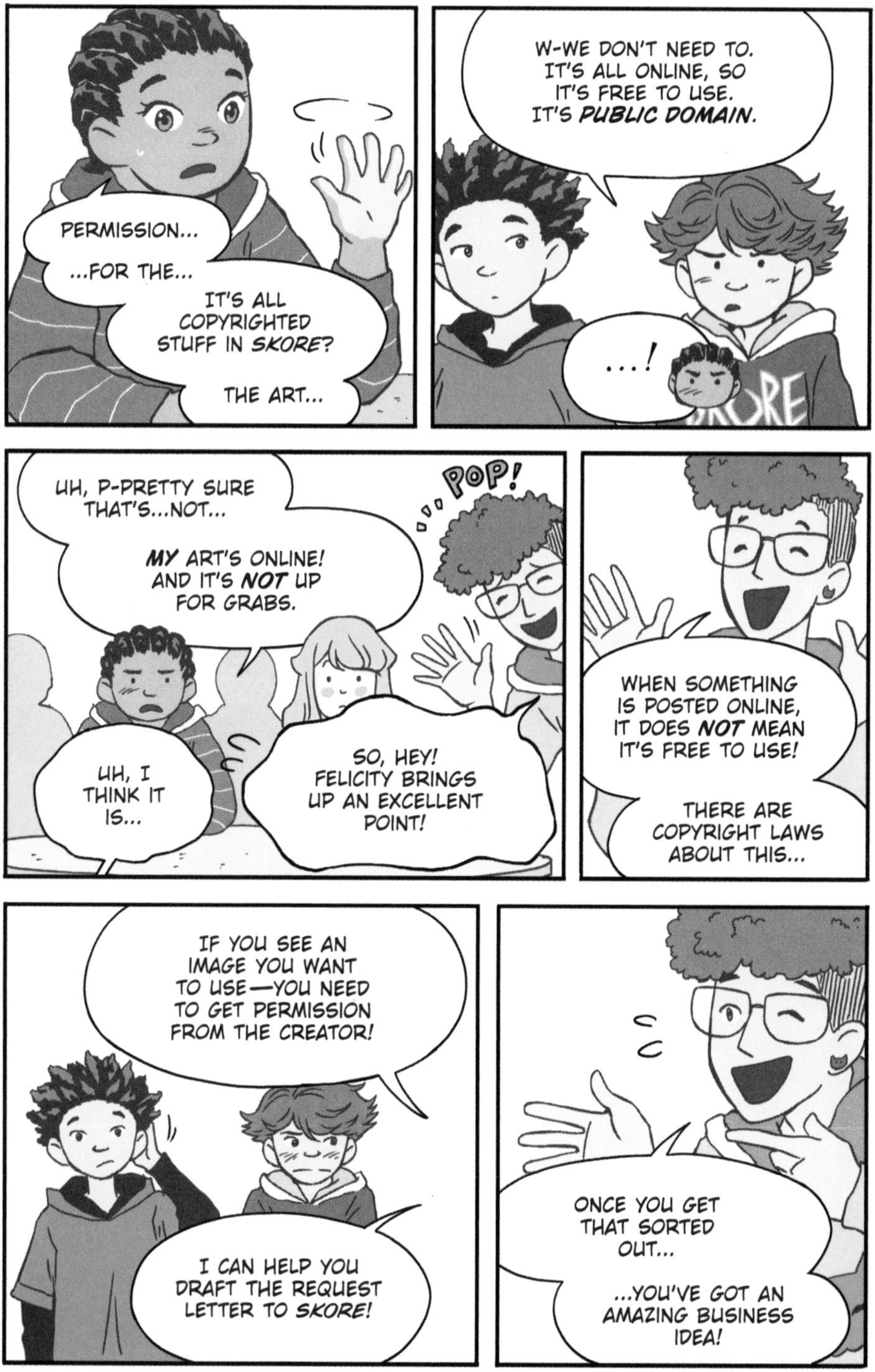
PERMISSION...
...FOR THE...
IT'S ALL COPYRIGHTED STUFF IN SKORE?
THE ART...
W-WE DON'T NEED TO. IT'S ALL ONLINE, SO IT'S FREE TO USE. IT'S PUBLIC DOMAIN.
...!
SKORE
UH, P-PRETTY SURE THAT'S...NOT...
MY ART'S ONLINE! AND IT'S NOT UP FOR GRABS.
POP!
UH, I THINK IT IS...
SO, HEY! FELICITY BRINGS UP AN EXCELLENT POINT!
WHEN SOMETHING IS POSTED ONLINE, IT DOES NOT MEAN IT'S FREE TO USE!
THERE ARE COPYRIGHT LAWS ABOUT THIS...
IF YOU SEE AN IMAGE YOU WANT TO USE—YOU NEED TO GET PERMISSION FROM THE CREATOR!
I CAN HELP YOU DRAFT THE REQUEST LETTER TO SKORE!
ONCE YOU GET THAT SORTED OUT...
...YOU'VE GOT AN AMAZING BUSINESS IDEA!

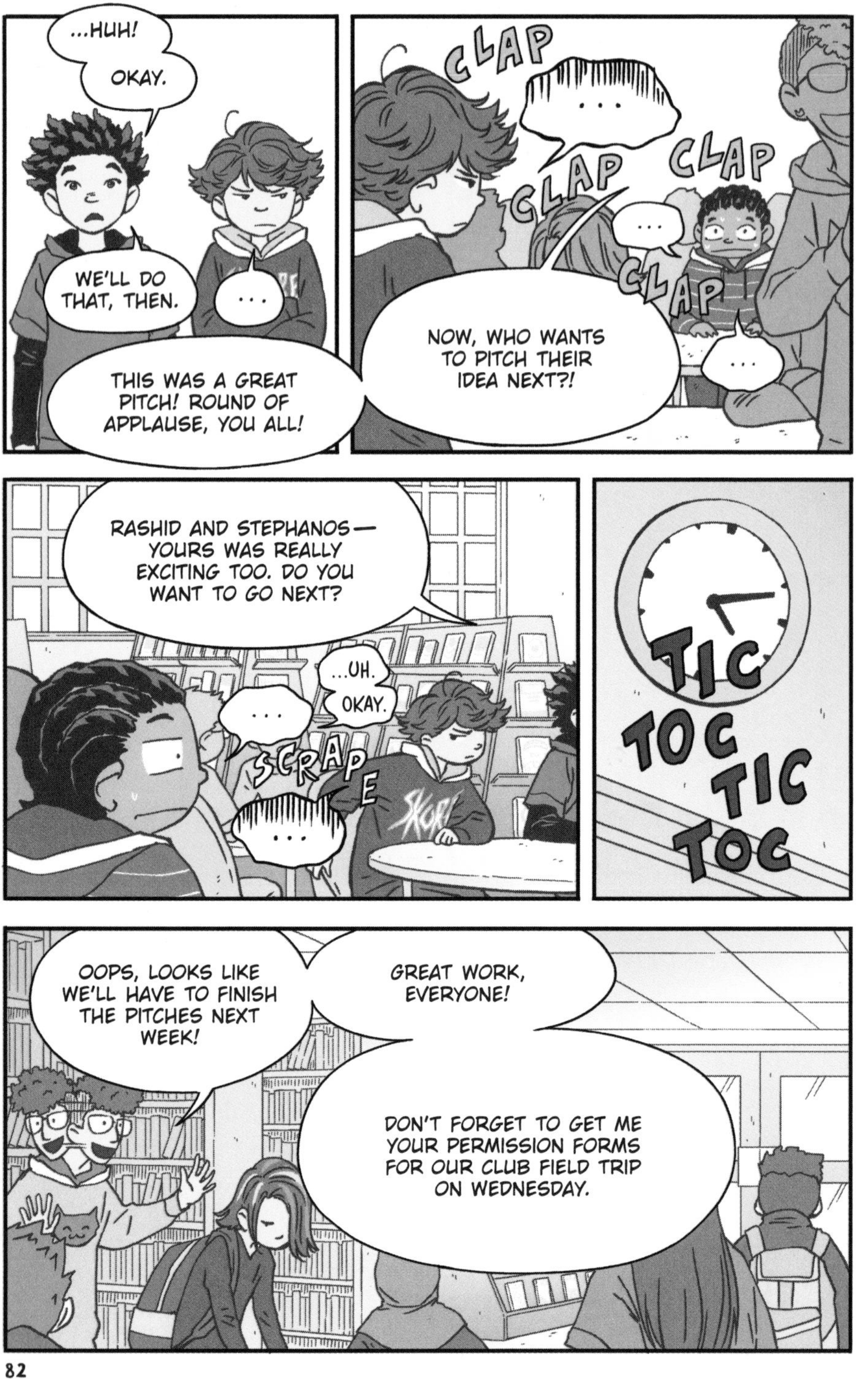
...HUH!
OKAY.
WE'LL DO THAT, THEN.
...
THIS WAS A GREAT PITCH! ROUND OF APPLAUSE, YOU ALL!
CLAP
...
CLAP
CLAP
...
CLAP
NOW, WHO WANTS TO PITCH THEIR IDEA NEXT?!
...
RASHID AND STEPHANOS— YOURS WAS REALLY EXCITING TOO. DO YOU WANT TO GO NEXT?
...
...UH.
OKAY.
SCRAPE
...
TIC
TOC
TIC
TOC
OOPS, LOOKS LIKE WE'LL HAVE TO FINISH THE PITCHES NEXT WEEK!
GREAT WORK, EVERYONE!
DON'T FORGET TO GET ME YOUR PERMISSION FORMS FOR OUR CLUB FIELD TRIP ON WEDNESDAY.

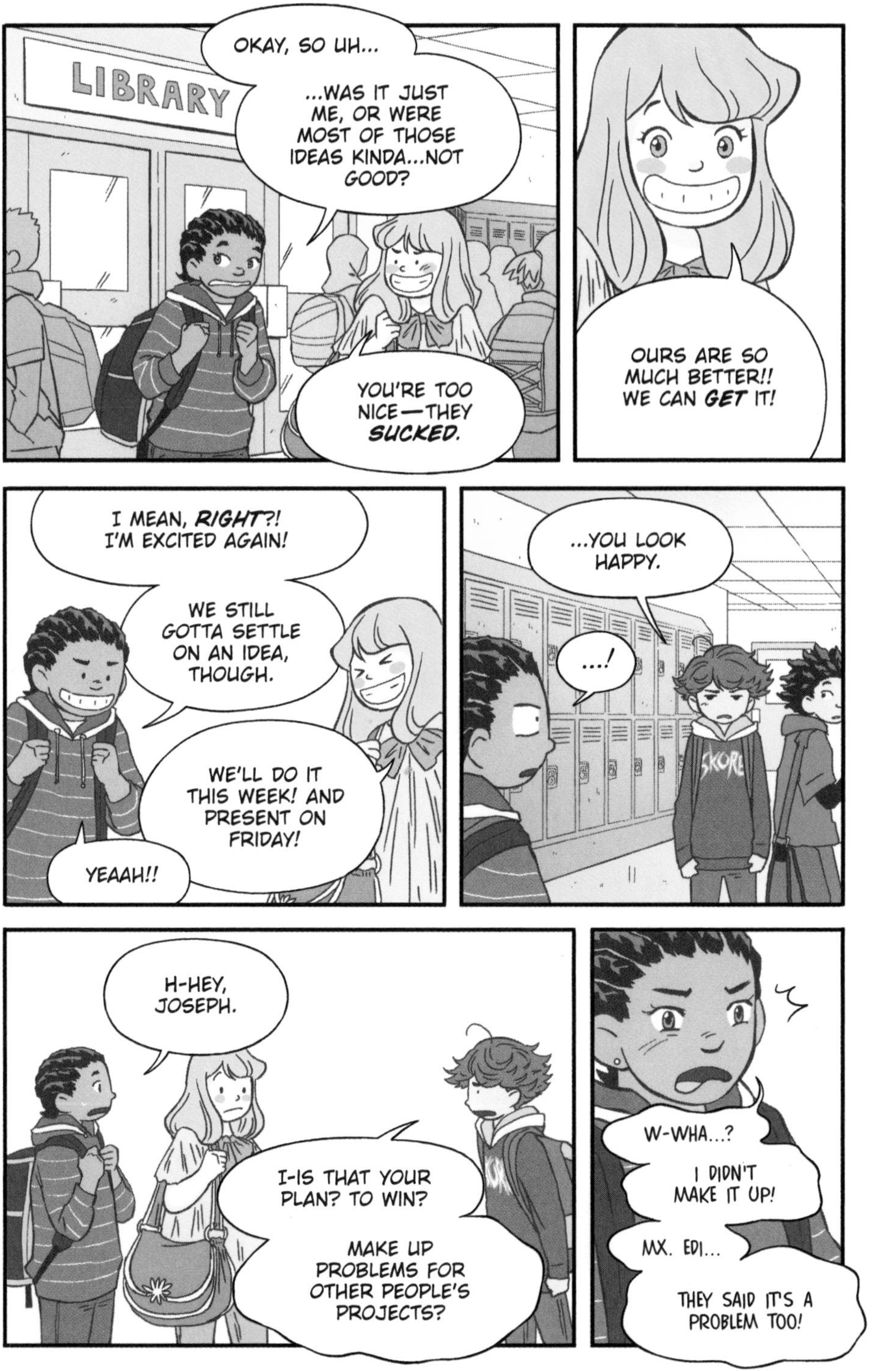
LIBRARY
OKAY, SO UH...
...WAS IT JUST ME, OR WERE MOST OF THOSE IDEAS KINDA...NOT GOOD?
YOU'RE TOO NICE—THEY ***SUCKED***.
OURS ARE SO MUCH BETTER!! WE CAN ***GET*** IT!
I MEAN, ***RIGHT***?! I'M EXCITED AGAIN!
WE STILL GOTTA SETTLE ON AN IDEA, THOUGH.
WE'LL DO IT THIS WEEK! AND PRESENT ON FRIDAY!
YEAAH!!
...YOU LOOK HAPPY.
...!
SKORE
H-HEY, JOSEPH.
I-IS THAT YOUR PLAN? TO WIN?
MAKE UP PROBLEMS FOR OTHER PEOPLE'S PROJECTS?
W-WHA...?
I DIDN'T MAKE IT UP!
MX. EDI...
THEY SAID IT'S A PROBLEM TOO!

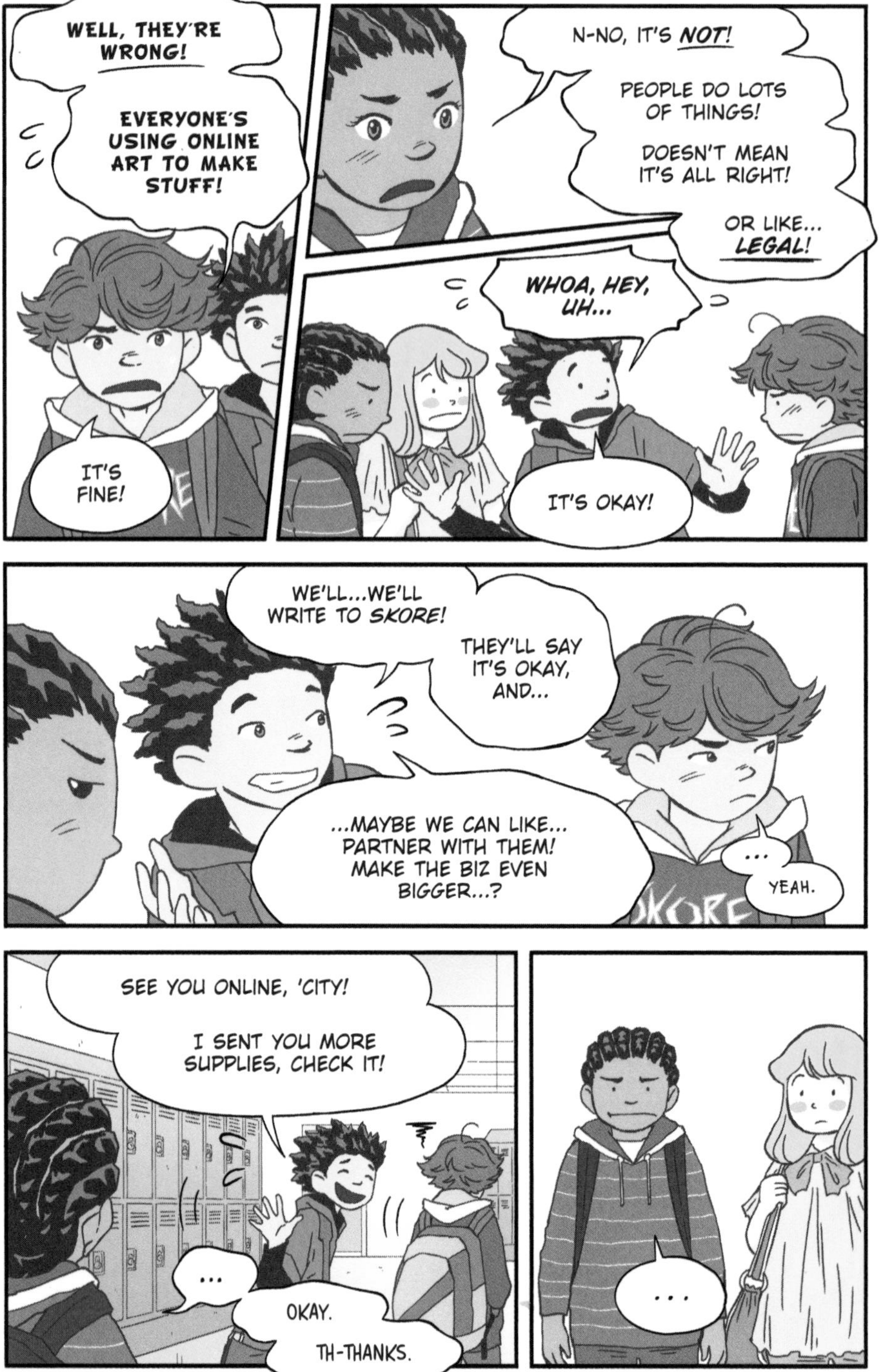
WELL, THEY'RE WRONG!
EVERYONE'S USING ONLINE ART TO MAKE STUFF!
IT'S FINE!
N-NO, IT'S NOT!
PEOPLE DO LOTS OF THINGS!
DOESN'T MEAN IT'S ALL RIGHT!
OR LIKE... LEGAL!
WHOA, HEY, UH...
IT'S OKAY!
WE'LL...WE'LL WRITE TO SKORE!
THEY'LL SAY IT'S OKAY, AND...
...MAYBE WE CAN LIKE... PARTNER WITH THEM! MAKE THE BIZ EVEN BIGGER...?
...
YEAH.
SEE YOU ONLINE, 'CITY!
I SENT YOU MORE SUPPLIES, CHECK IT!
...
OKAY.
TH-THANKS.
...

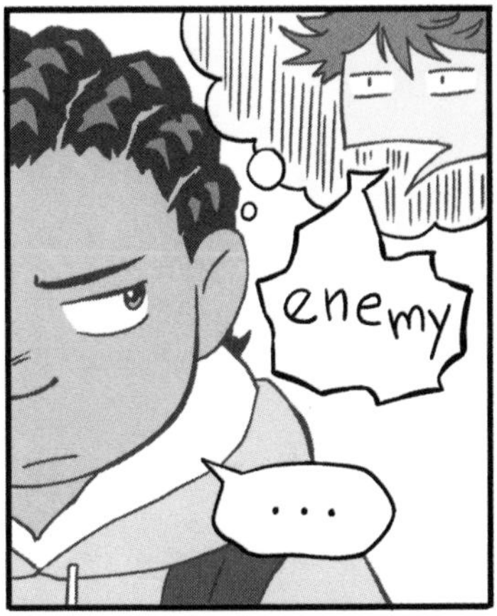
enemy
...

CHAPTER 4

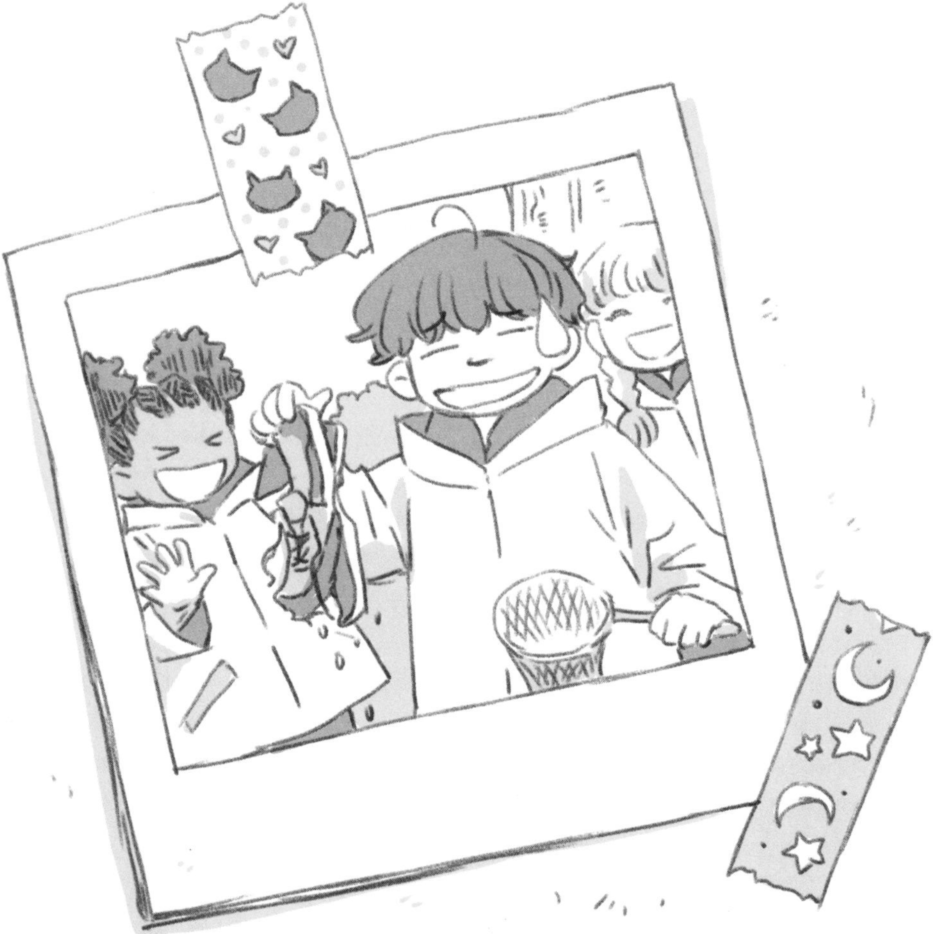

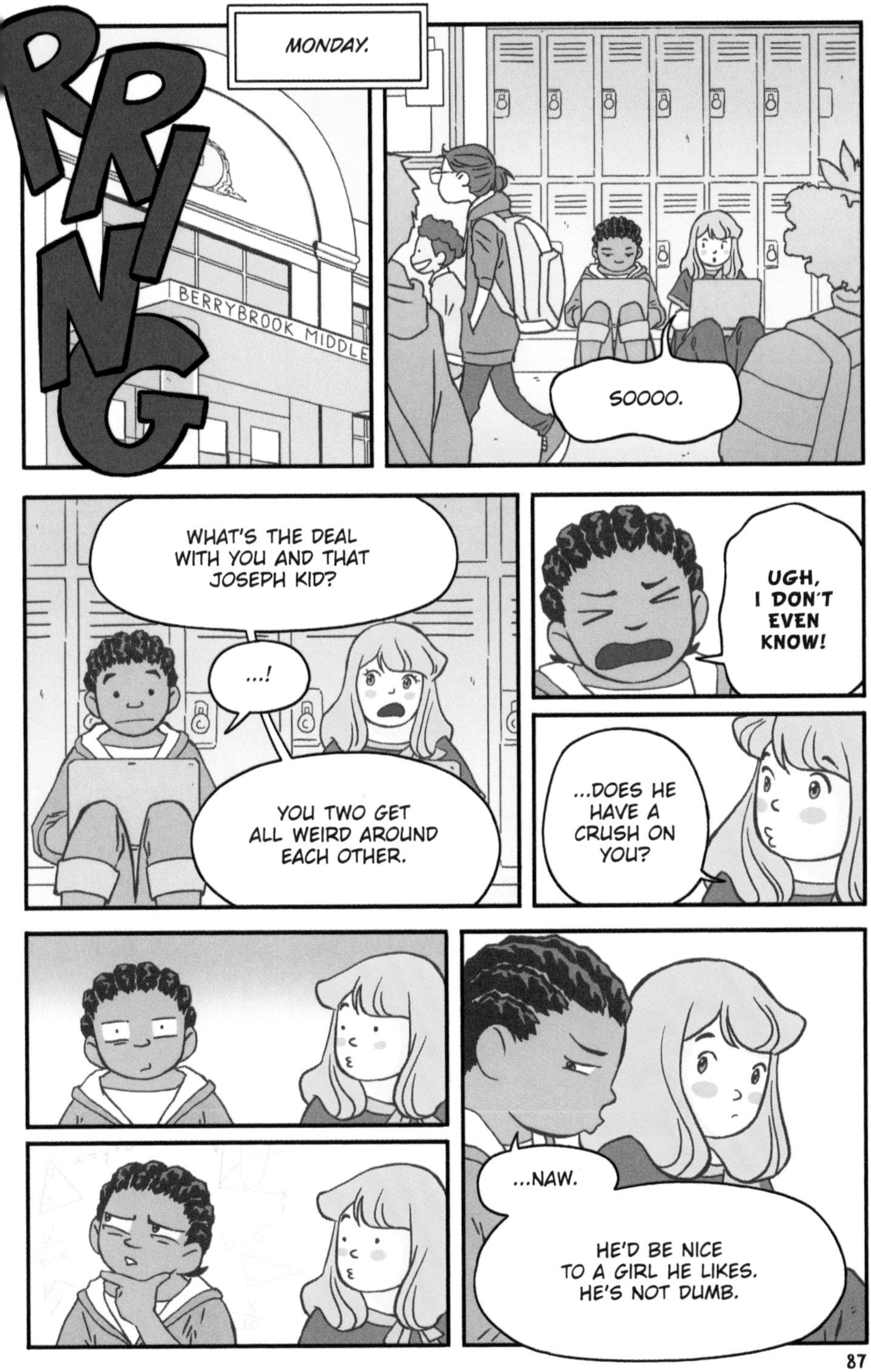
RRING
MONDAY.
BERRYBROOK MIDDLE
SOOOO.
WHAT'S THE DEAL WITH YOU AND THAT JOSEPH KID?
...!
YOU TWO GET ALL WEIRD AROUND EACH OTHER.
UGH, I DON'T EVEN KNOW!
...DOES HE HAVE A CRUSH ON YOU?
...NAW.
HE'D BE NICE TO A GIRL HE LIKES. HE'S NOT DUMB.

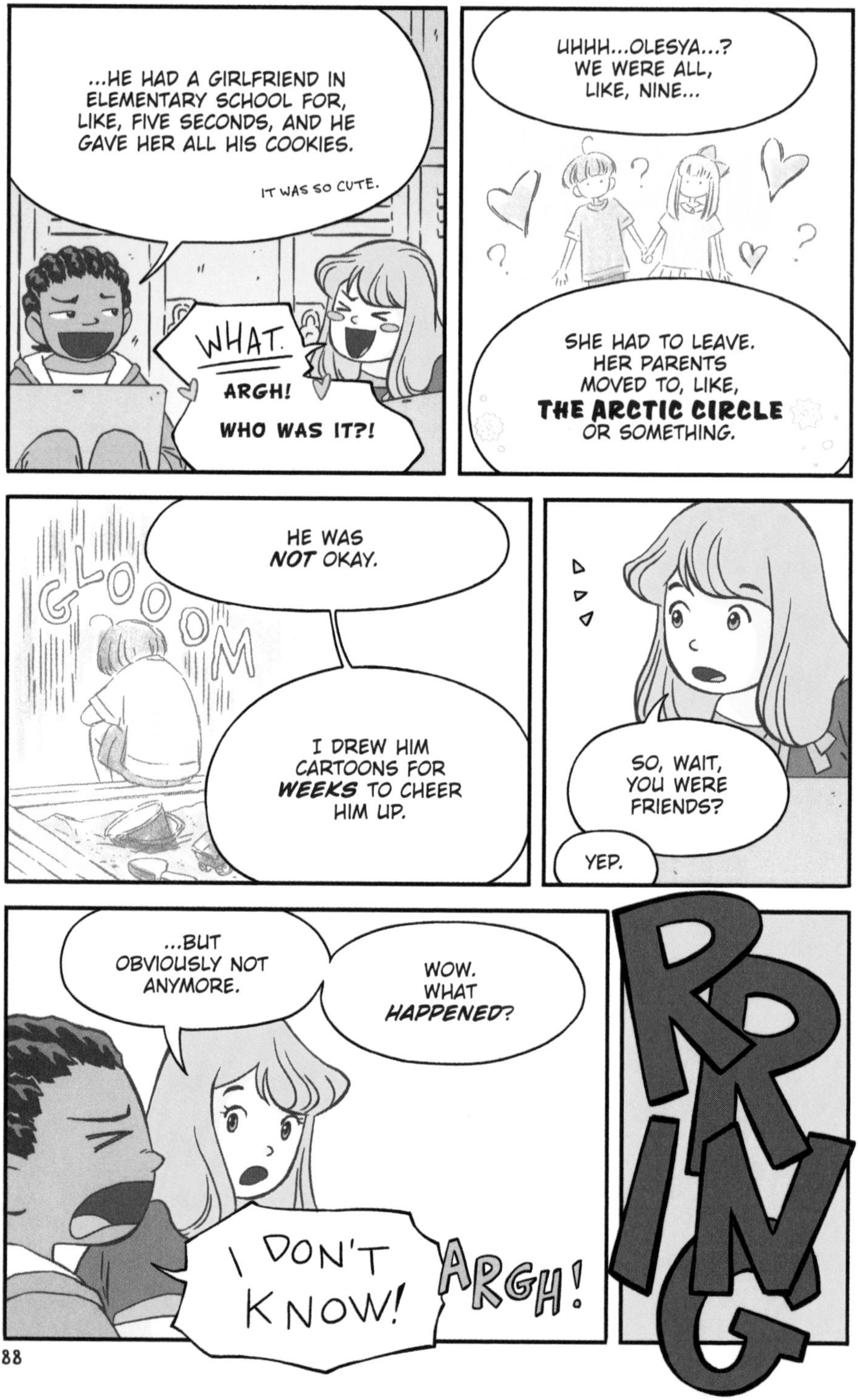
...HE HAD A GIRLFRIEND IN ELEMENTARY SCHOOL FOR, LIKE, FIVE SECONDS, AND HE GAVE HER ALL HIS COOKIES.
IT WAS SO CUTE.
WHAT.
ARGH!
WHO WAS IT?!
UHHH...OLESYA...? WE WERE ALL, LIKE, NINE...
SHE HAD TO LEAVE. HER PARENTS MOVED TO, LIKE, THE ARCTIC CIRCLE OR SOMETHING.
GLOOOM
HE WAS NOT OKAY.
I DREW HIM CARTOONS FOR WEEKS TO CHEER HIM UP.
SO, WAIT, YOU WERE FRIENDS?
YEP.
...BUT OBVIOUSLY NOT ANYMORE.
WOW. WHAT HAPPENED?
I DON'T KNOW!
ARGH!
RRRING

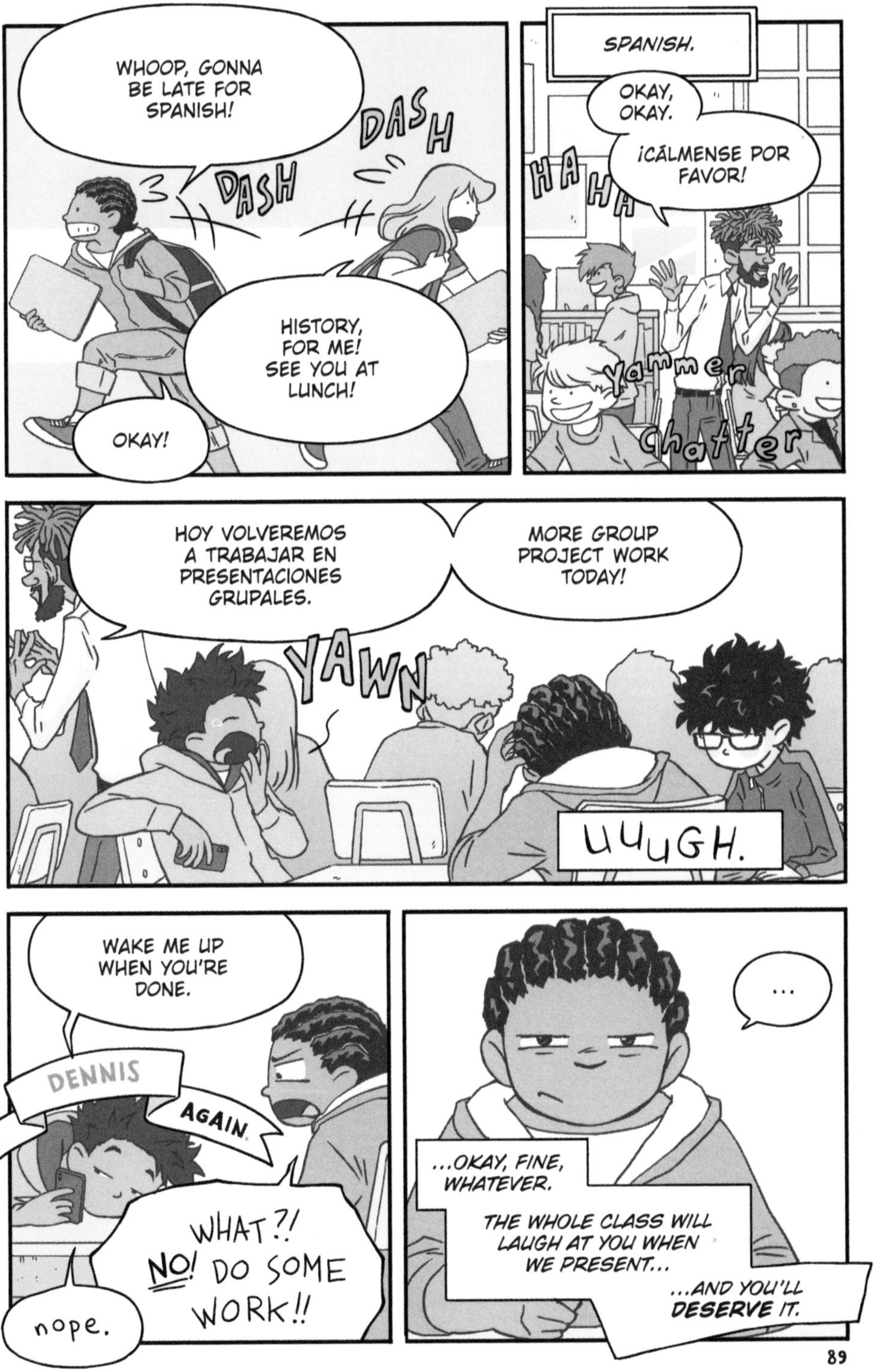
WHOOP, GONNA BE LATE FOR SPANISH!
DASH
DASH
HISTORY, FOR ME! SEE YOU AT LUNCH!
OKAY!
SPANISH.
OKAY, OKAY.
¡CÁLMENSE POR FAVOR!
HA HA HA
yammer
chatter
HOY VOLVEREMOS A TRABAJAR EN PRESENTACIONES GRUPALES.
MORE GROUP PROJECT WORK TODAY!
YAWN
UUUGH.
WAKE ME UP WHEN YOU'RE DONE.
DENNIS
AGAIN.
WHAT?! NO! DO SOME WORK!!
nope.
...
...OKAY, FINE, WHATEVER.
THE WHOLE CLASS WILL LAUGH AT YOU WHEN WE PRESENT...
...AND YOU'LL DESERVE IT.

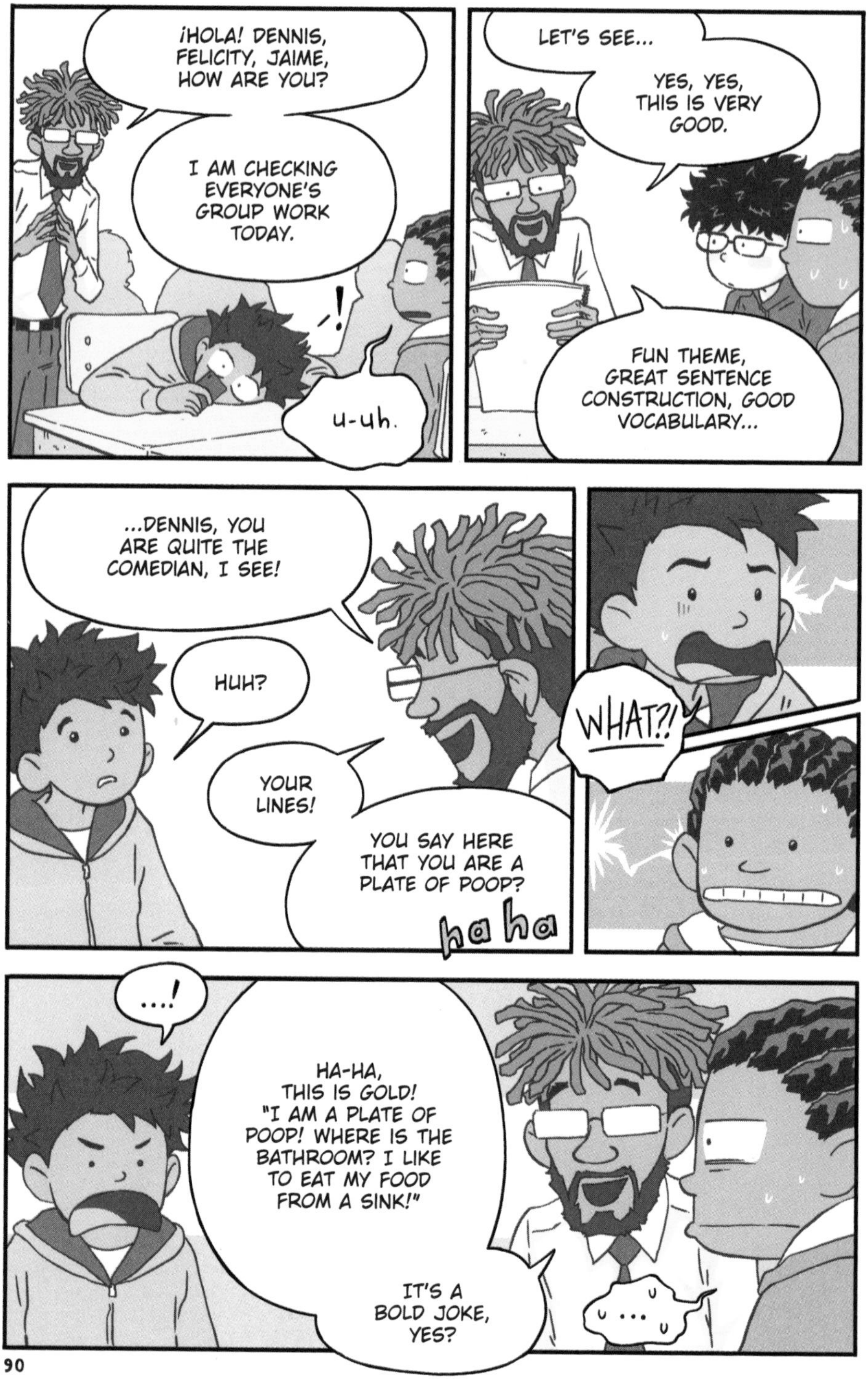
¡HOLA! DENNIS, FELICITY, JAIME, HOW ARE YOU?
I AM CHECKING EVERYONE'S GROUP WORK TODAY.
!
U-UH.
LET'S SEE...
YES, YES, THIS IS VERY GOOD.
FUN THEME, GREAT SENTENCE CONSTRUCTION, GOOD VOCABULARY...
...DENNIS, YOU ARE QUITE THE COMEDIAN, I SEE!
HUH?
YOUR LINES!
YOU SAY HERE THAT YOU ARE A PLATE OF POOP?
HA HA
WHAT?!
...!
HA-HA, THIS IS GOLD! "I AM A PLATE OF POOP! WHERE IS THE BATHROOM? I LIKE TO EAT MY FOOD FROM A SINK!"
IT'S A BOLD JOKE, YES?
...

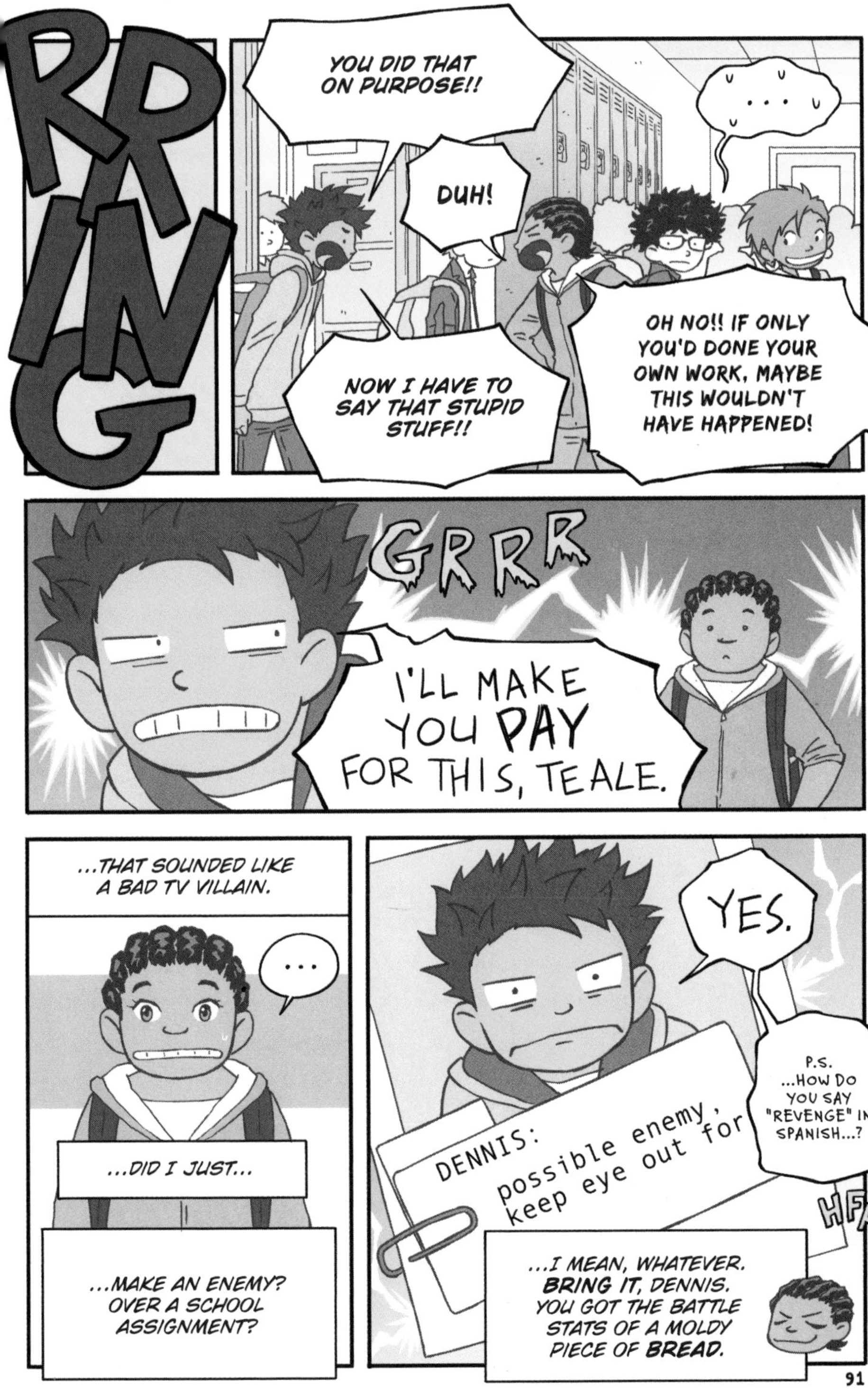
RRRING
YOU DID THAT ON PURPOSE!!
DUH!
NOW I HAVE TO SAY THAT STUPID STUFF!!
OH NO!! IF ONLY YOU'D DONE YOUR OWN WORK, MAYBE THIS WOULDN'T HAVE HAPPENED!
GRRR
I'LL MAKE YOU PAY FOR THIS, TEALE.
...THAT SOUNDED LIKE A BAD TV VILLAIN.
...
...DID I JUST...
...MAKE AN ENEMY? OVER A SCHOOL ASSIGNMENT?
YES.
DENNIS: possible enemy, keep eye out for
P.S. ...HOW DO YOU SAY "REVENGE" IN SPANISH...?
HFF
...I MEAN, WHATEVER. BRING IT, DENNIS. YOU GOT THE BATTLE STATS OF A MOLDY PIECE OF BREAD.

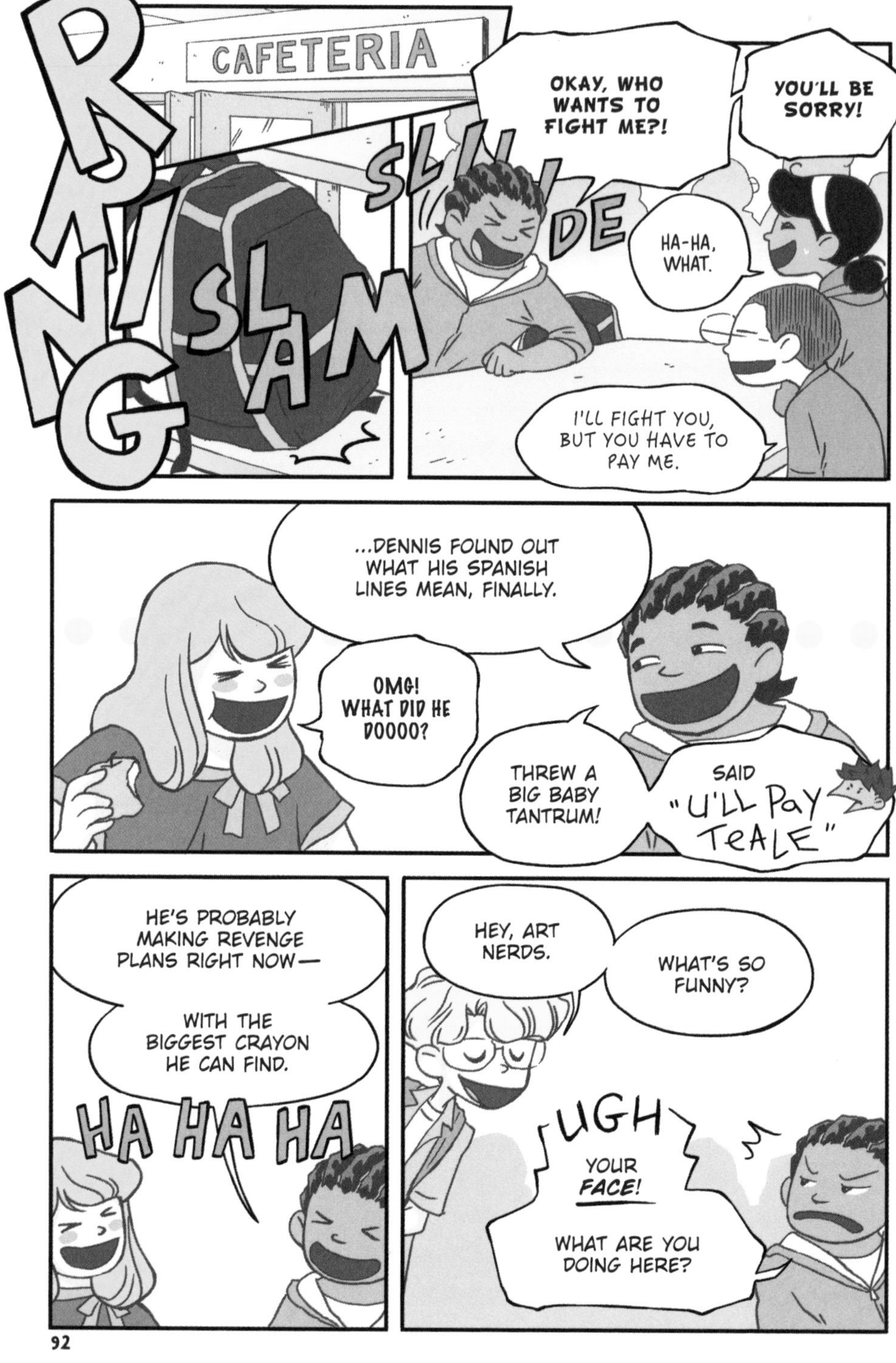
CAFETERIA
RING
SLAM
SLIIIIDE
OKAY, WHO WANTS TO FIGHT ME?!
YOU'LL BE SORRY!
HA-HA, WHAT.
I'LL FIGHT YOU, BUT YOU HAVE TO PAY ME.
...DENNIS FOUND OUT WHAT HIS SPANISH LINES MEAN, FINALLY.
OMG! WHAT DID HE DOOOO?
THREW A BIG BABY TANTRUM!
SAID "U'LL Pay TeALE"
HE'S PROBABLY MAKING REVENGE PLANS RIGHT NOW—
WITH THE BIGGEST CRAYON HE CAN FIND.
HA HA HA
HEY, ART NERDS.
WHAT'S SO FUNNY?
UGH
YOUR ***FACE!***
WHAT ARE YOU DOING HERE?

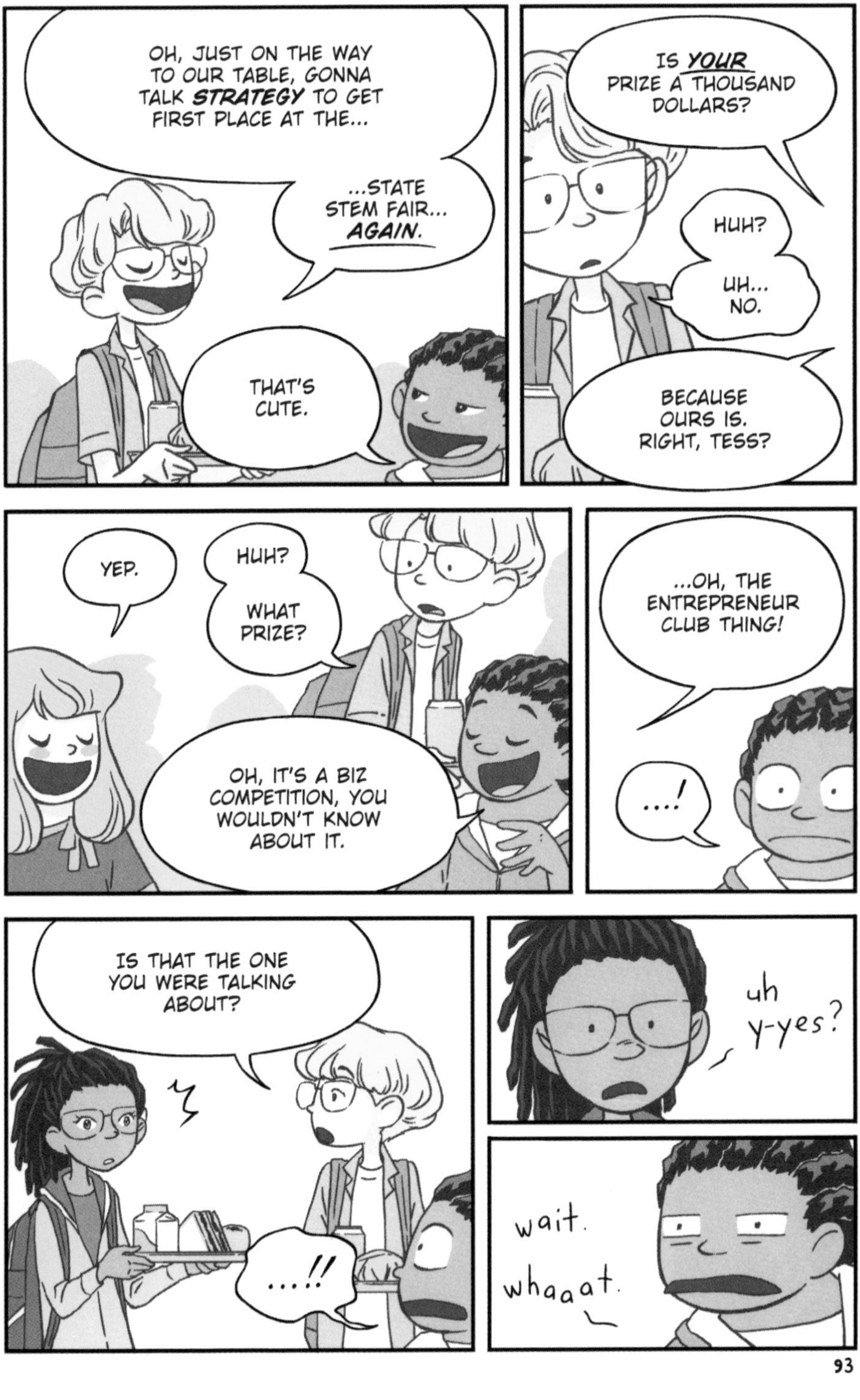
OH, JUST ON THE WAY TO OUR TABLE, GONNA TALK STRATEGY TO GET FIRST PLACE AT THE...
...STATE STEM FAIR... AGAIN.
THAT'S CUTE.
IS YOUR PRIZE A THOUSAND DOLLARS?
HUH?
UH... NO.
BECAUSE OURS IS. RIGHT, TESS?
YEP.
HUH?
WHAT PRIZE?
OH, IT'S A BIZ COMPETITION, YOU WOULDN'T KNOW ABOUT IT.
...OH, THE ENTREPRENEUR CLUB THING!
...!
IS THAT THE ONE YOU WERE TALKING ABOUT?
...!!
uh
y-yes?
wait.
whaaat.

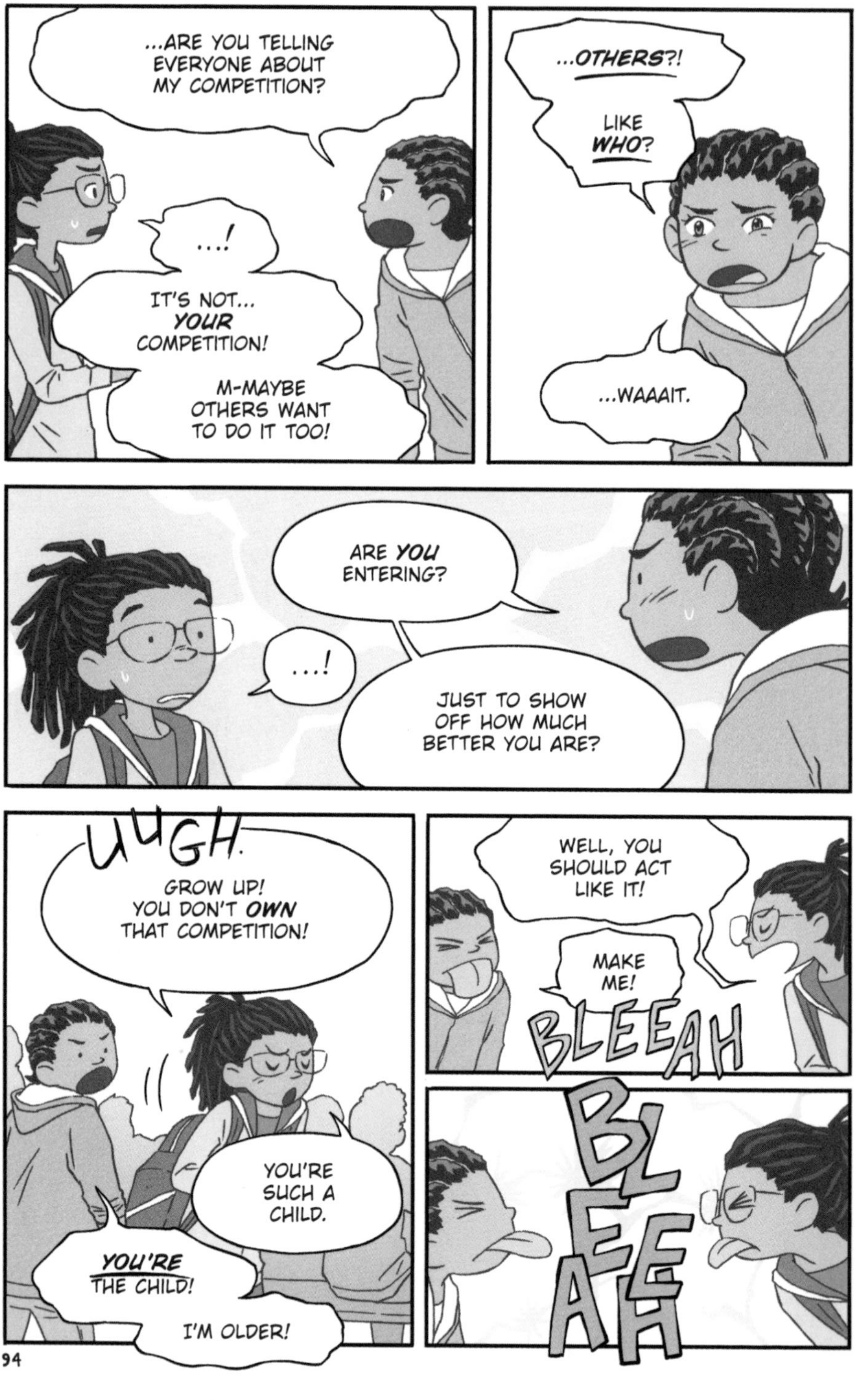
...ARE YOU TELLING EVERYONE ABOUT MY COMPETITION?
...!
IT'S NOT... YOUR COMPETITION!
M-MAYBE OTHERS WANT TO DO IT TOO!
...OTHERS?!
LIKE WHO?
...WAAAIT.
ARE YOU ENTERING?
...!
JUST TO SHOW OFF HOW MUCH BETTER YOU ARE?
UUGH.
GROW UP! YOU DON'T OWN THAT COMPETITION!
YOU'RE SUCH A CHILD.
YOU'RE THE CHILD!
I'M OLDER!
WELL, YOU SHOULD ACT LIKE IT!
MAKE ME!
BLEEAH
BLEEAH
BLEEAH

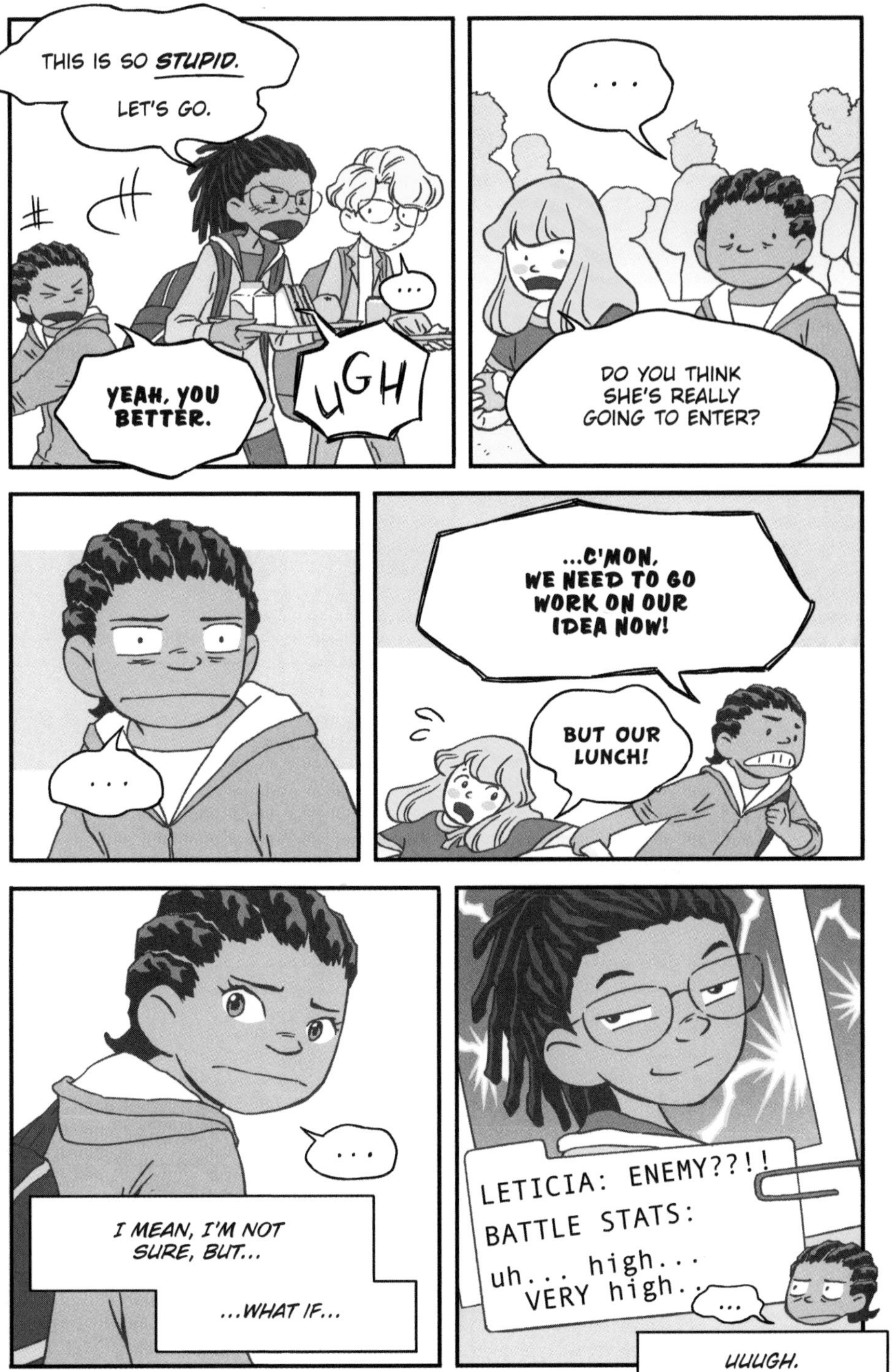

THIS IS SO STUPID.
LET'S GO.
YEAH, YOU BETTER.
UGH
...
...
DO YOU THINK SHE'S REALLY GOING TO ENTER?
...
...C'MON, WE NEED TO GO WORK ON OUR IDEA NOW!
BUT OUR LUNCH!
...
I MEAN, I'M NOT SURE, BUT...
...WHAT IF...
LETICIA: ENEMY??!!
BATTLE STATS:
uh... high...
VERY high..
...
UUUGH.

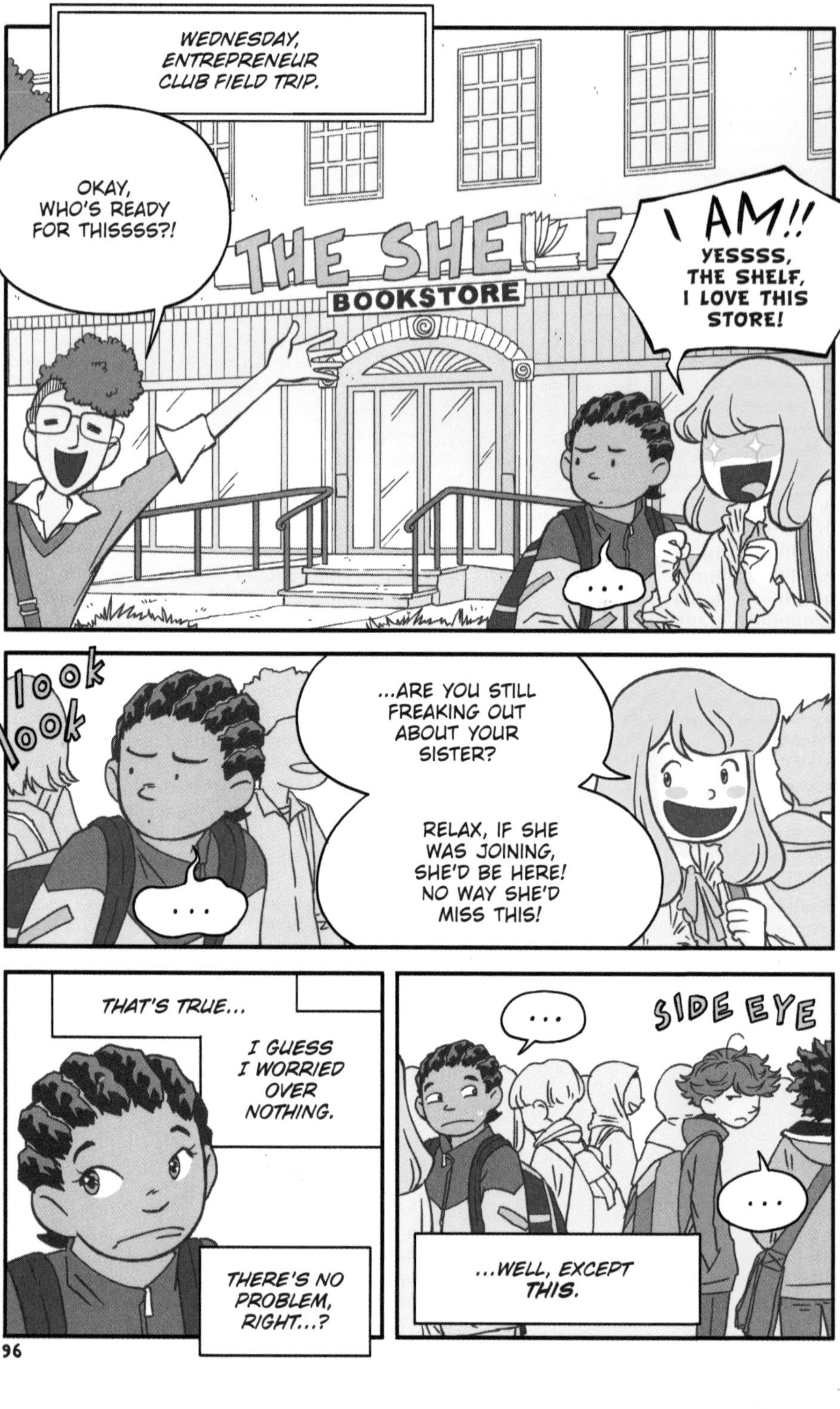
WEDNESDAY, ENTREPRENEUR CLUB FIELD TRIP.
OKAY, WHO'S READY FOR THISSSS?!
THE SHELF
BOOKSTORE
I AM!! YESSSS, THE SHELF, I LOVE THIS STORE!
...
look look
...ARE YOU STILL FREAKING OUT ABOUT YOUR SISTER?
RELAX, IF SHE WAS JOINING, SHE'D BE HERE! NO WAY SHE'D MISS THIS!
...
THAT'S TRUE...
I GUESS I WORRIED OVER NOTHING.
THERE'S NO PROBLEM, RIGHT...?
...
SIDE EYE
...
...WELL, EXCEPT THIS.

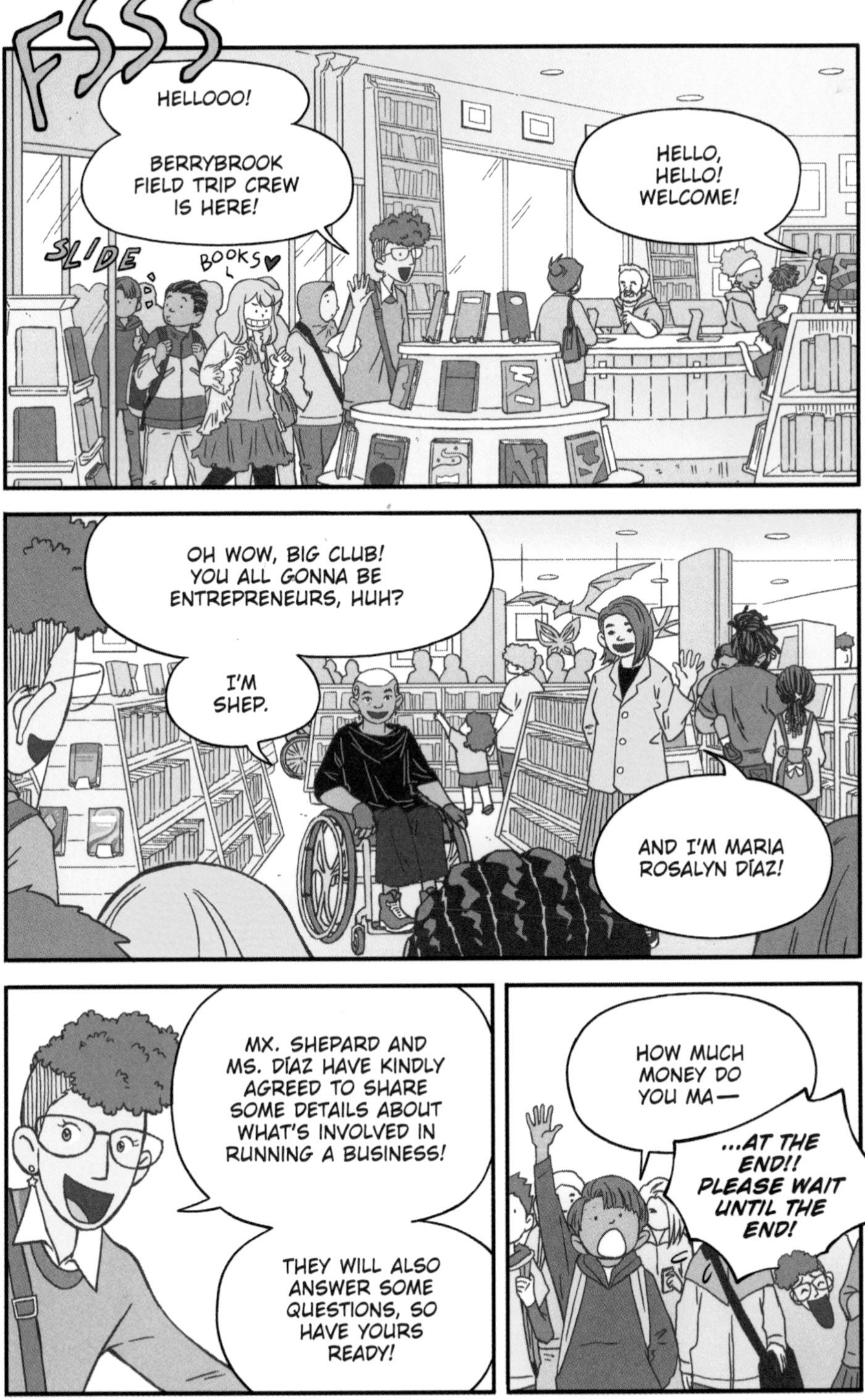
FSSS
HELLOOO!
BERRYBROOK FIELD TRIP CREW IS HERE!
SLIDE
BOOKS ♥
HELLO, HELLO! WELCOME!
OH WOW, BIG CLUB! YOU ALL GONNA BE ENTREPRENEURS, HUH?
I'M SHEP.
AND I'M MARIA ROSALYN DÍAZ!
MX. SHEPARD AND MS. DÍAZ HAVE KINDLY AGREED TO SHARE SOME DETAILS ABOUT WHAT'S INVOLVED IN RUNNING A BUSINESS!
THEY WILL ALSO ANSWER SOME QUESTIONS, SO HAVE YOURS READY!
HOW MUCH MONEY DO YOU MA—
...AT THE END!! PLEASE WAIT UNTIL THE END!

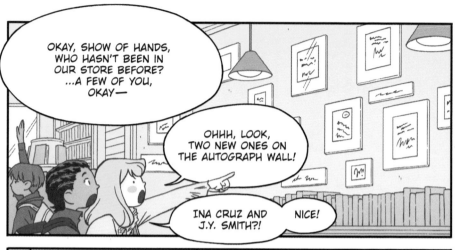

OKAY, SHOW OF HANDS, WHO HASN'T BEEN IN OUR STORE BEFORE? ...A FEW OF YOU, OKAY—

OHHH, LOOK, TWO NEW ONES ON THE AUTOGRAPH WALL!

INA CRUZ AND J.Y. SMITH?!

NICE!

TESSA, FELICITY! PLEASE STAY WITH THE GROUP FOR THE TOUR.

BLAH BLAH

BLAH

BLAH

I DON'T NEED A TOUR.

DAD'S BEEN TAKING ME AND LETTY HERE SINCE WE WERE IN DIAPERS.

OOPS, SORRY MX. EDI!

THERE'S THEIR HUGE MANGA SECTION...

...AND THERE'S THE COFFEE/SNACK BAR. (THE FUDGE BROWNIES ARE THE *BEST*.)

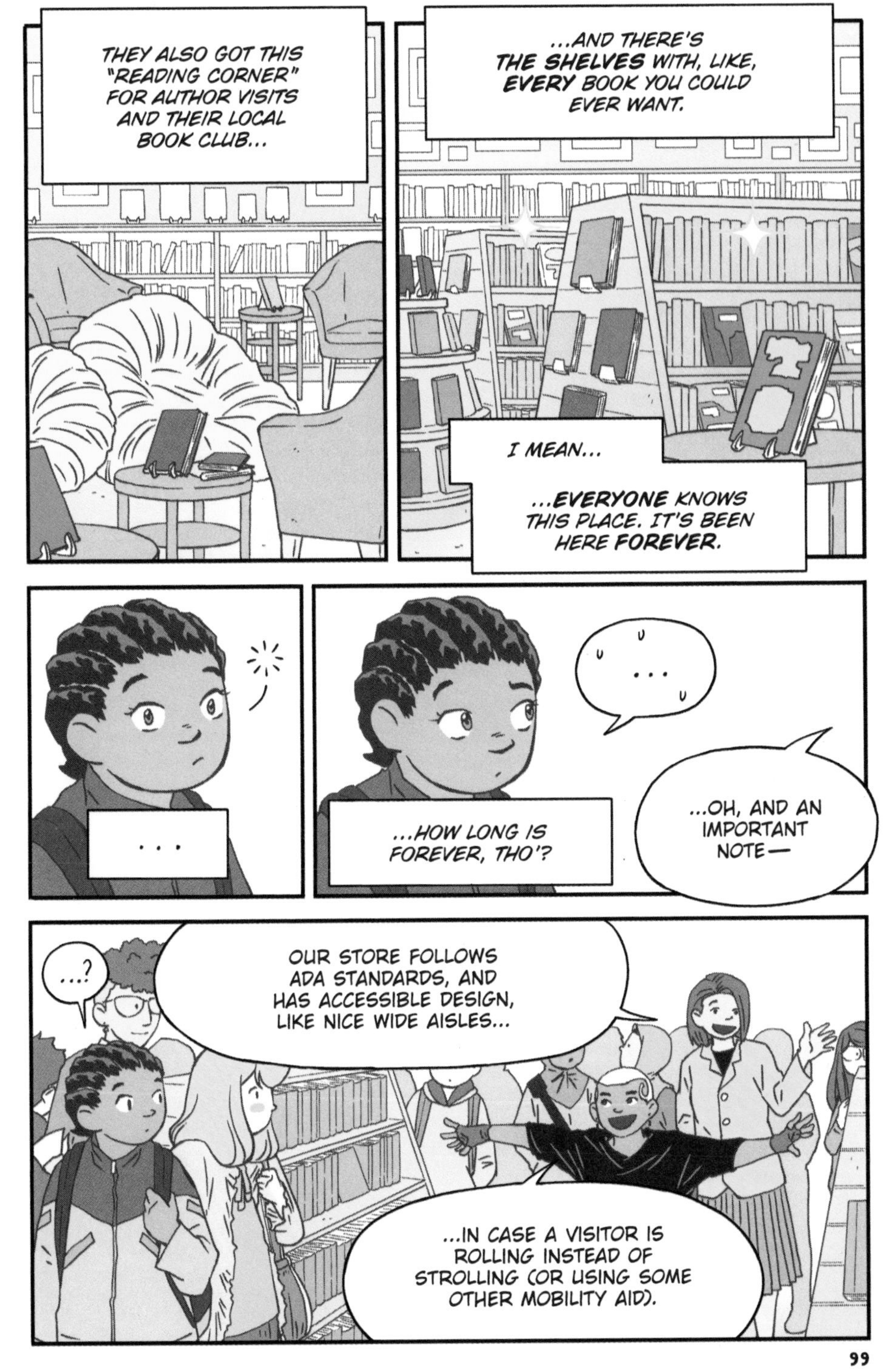

THEY ALSO GOT THIS "READING CORNER" FOR AUTHOR VISITS AND THEIR LOCAL BOOK CLUB...
...AND THERE'S THE SHELVES WITH, LIKE, EVERY BOOK YOU COULD EVER WANT.
I MEAN...
...EVERYONE KNOWS THIS PLACE. IT'S BEEN HERE FOREVER.
. . .
...HOW LONG IS FOREVER, THO'?
. . .
...OH, AND AN IMPORTANT NOTE—
...?
OUR STORE FOLLOWS ADA STANDARDS, AND HAS ACCESSIBLE DESIGN, LIKE NICE WIDE AISLES...
...IN CASE A VISITOR IS ROLLING INSTEAD OF STROLLING (OR USING SOME OTHER MOBILITY AID).

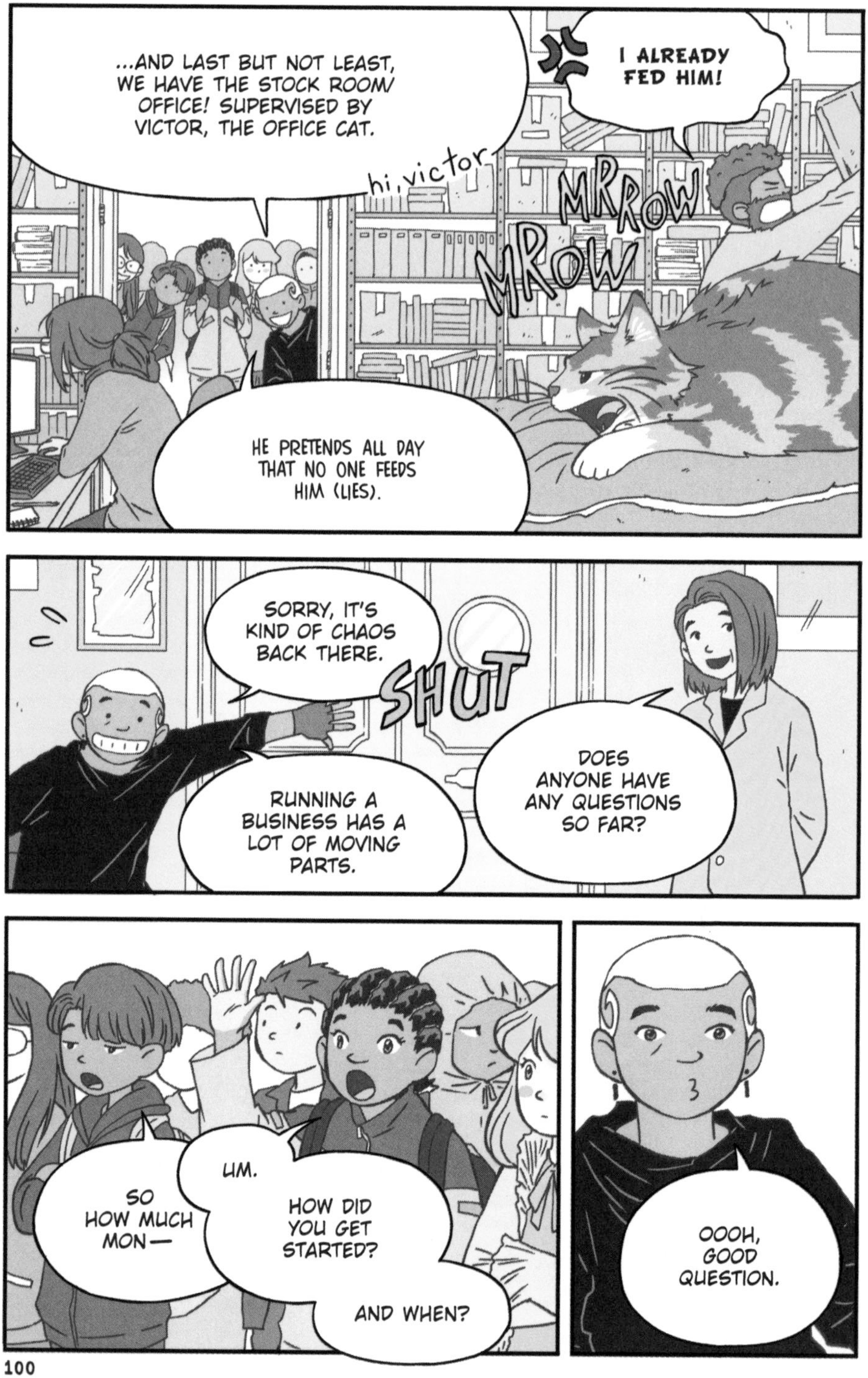
...AND LAST BUT NOT LEAST, WE HAVE THE STOCK ROOM/ OFFICE! SUPERVISED BY VICTOR, THE OFFICE CAT.
hi, victor
I ALREADY FED HIM!
MRROW
MROW
HE PRETENDS ALL DAY THAT NO ONE FEEDS HIM (LIES).
SORRY, IT'S KIND OF CHAOS BACK THERE.
SHUT
RUNNING A BUSINESS HAS A LOT OF MOVING PARTS.
DOES ANYONE HAVE ANY QUESTIONS SO FAR?
SO HOW MUCH MON—
UM.
HOW DID YOU GET STARTED?
AND WHEN?
OOOH, GOOD QUESTION.

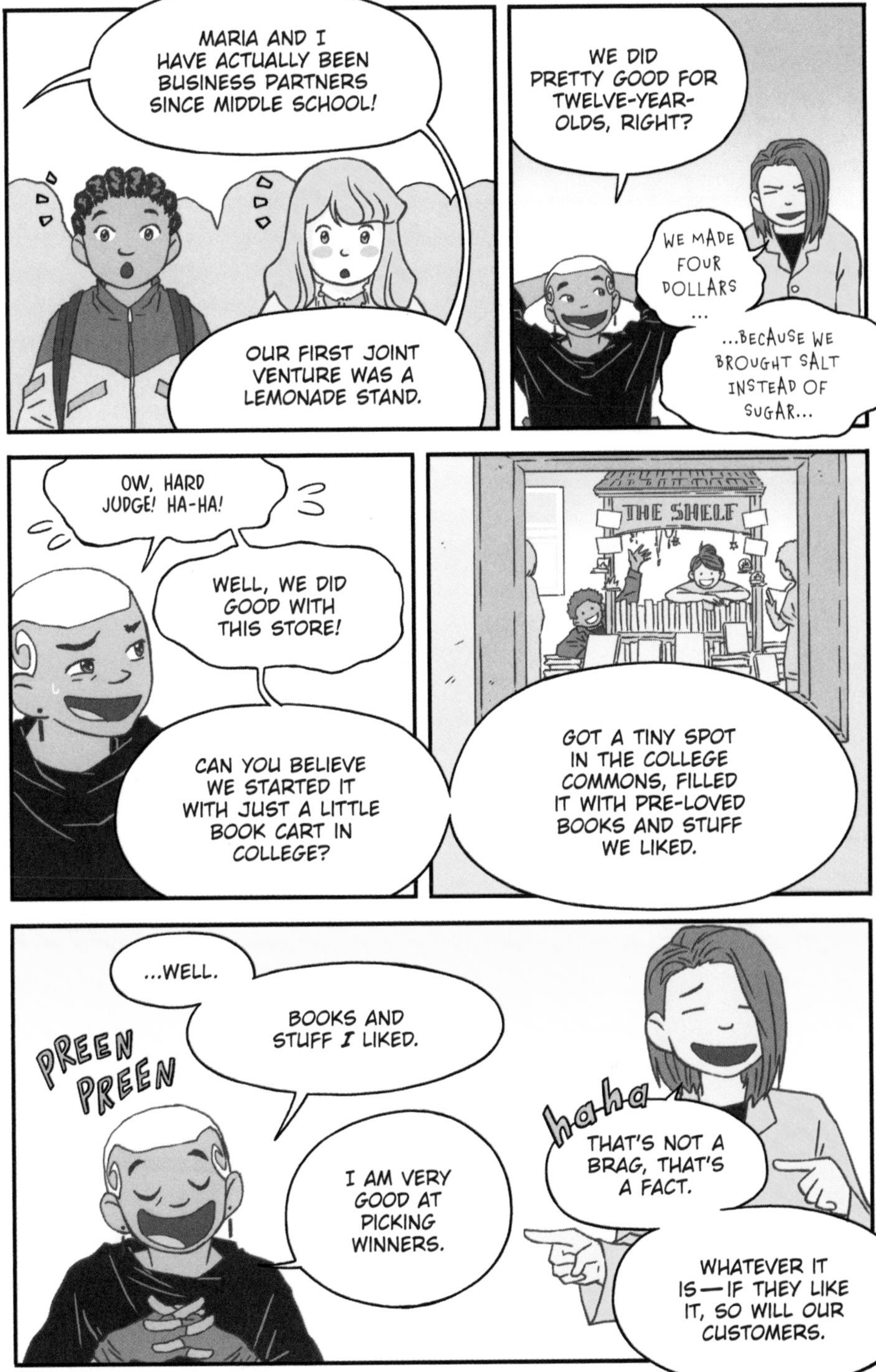
MARIA AND I HAVE ACTUALLY BEEN BUSINESS PARTNERS SINCE MIDDLE SCHOOL!
OUR FIRST JOINT VENTURE WAS A LEMONADE STAND.
WE DID PRETTY GOOD FOR TWELVE-YEAR-OLDS, RIGHT?
WE MADE FOUR DOLLARS...
...BECAUSE WE BROUGHT SALT INSTEAD OF SUGAR...
OW, HARD JUDGE! HA-HA!
WELL, WE DID GOOD WITH THIS STORE!
CAN YOU BELIEVE WE STARTED IT WITH JUST A LITTLE BOOK CART IN COLLEGE?
THE SHELF
GOT A TINY SPOT IN THE COLLEGE COMMONS, FILLED IT WITH PRE-LOVED BOOKS AND STUFF WE LIKED.
...WELL.
BOOKS AND STUFF *I* LIKED.
PREEN PREEN
I AM VERY GOOD AT PICKING WINNERS.
haha
THAT'S NOT A BRAG, THAT'S A FACT.
WHATEVER IT IS—IF THEY LIKE IT, SO WILL OUR CUSTOMERS.

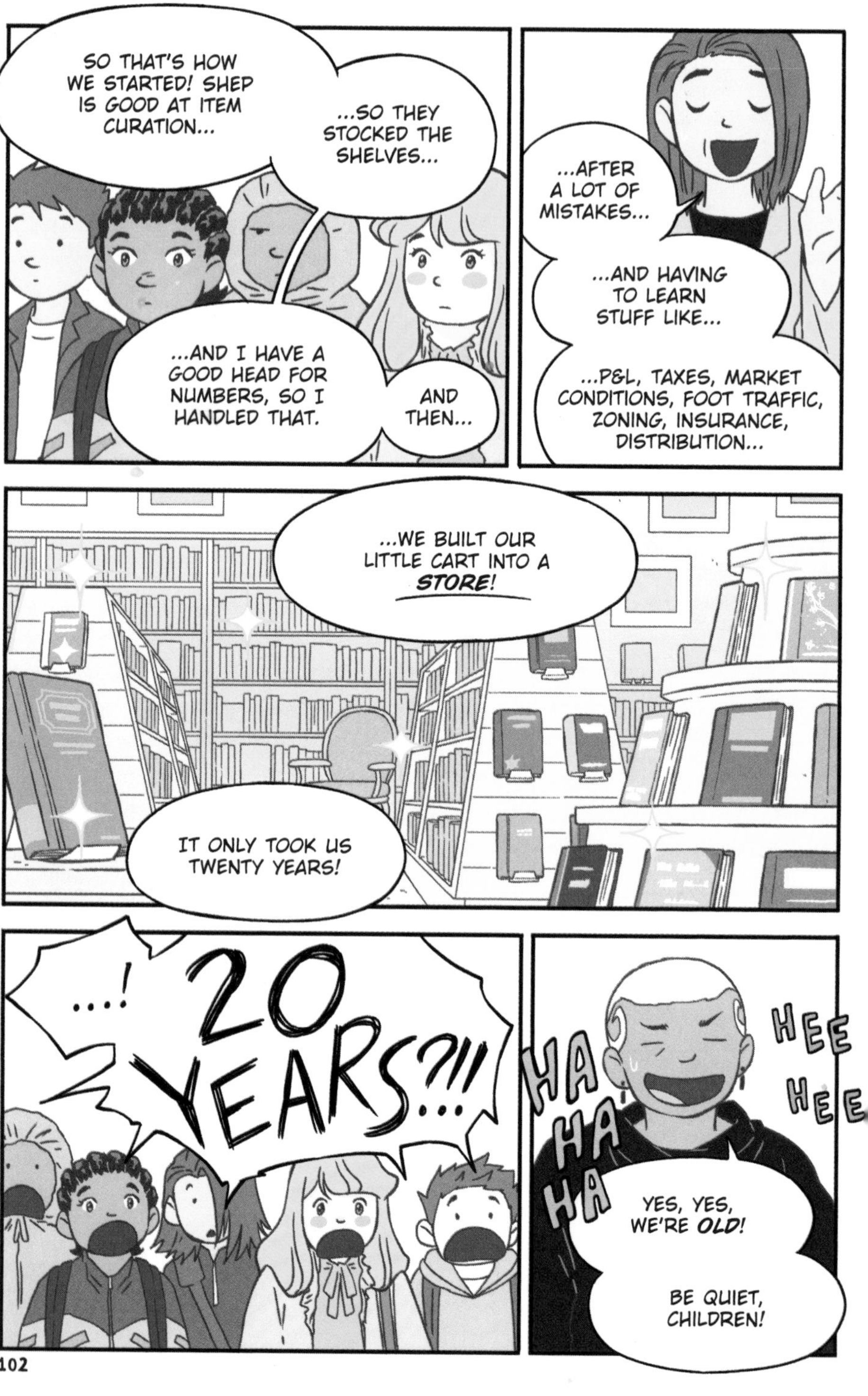
SO THAT'S HOW WE STARTED! SHEP IS GOOD AT ITEM CURATION...
...SO THEY STOCKED THE SHELVES...
...AND I HAVE A GOOD HEAD FOR NUMBERS, SO I HANDLED THAT.
AND THEN...
...AFTER A LOT OF MISTAKES...
...AND HAVING TO LEARN STUFF LIKE...
...P&L, TAXES, MARKET CONDITIONS, FOOT TRAFFIC, ZONING, INSURANCE, DISTRIBUTION...
...WE BUILT OUR LITTLE CART INTO A ***STORE***!
IT ONLY TOOK US TWENTY YEARS!
...!
20 YEARS?!!
...
HA HA HA
HEE HEE
YES, YES, WE'RE ***OLD***!
BE QUIET, CHILDREN!

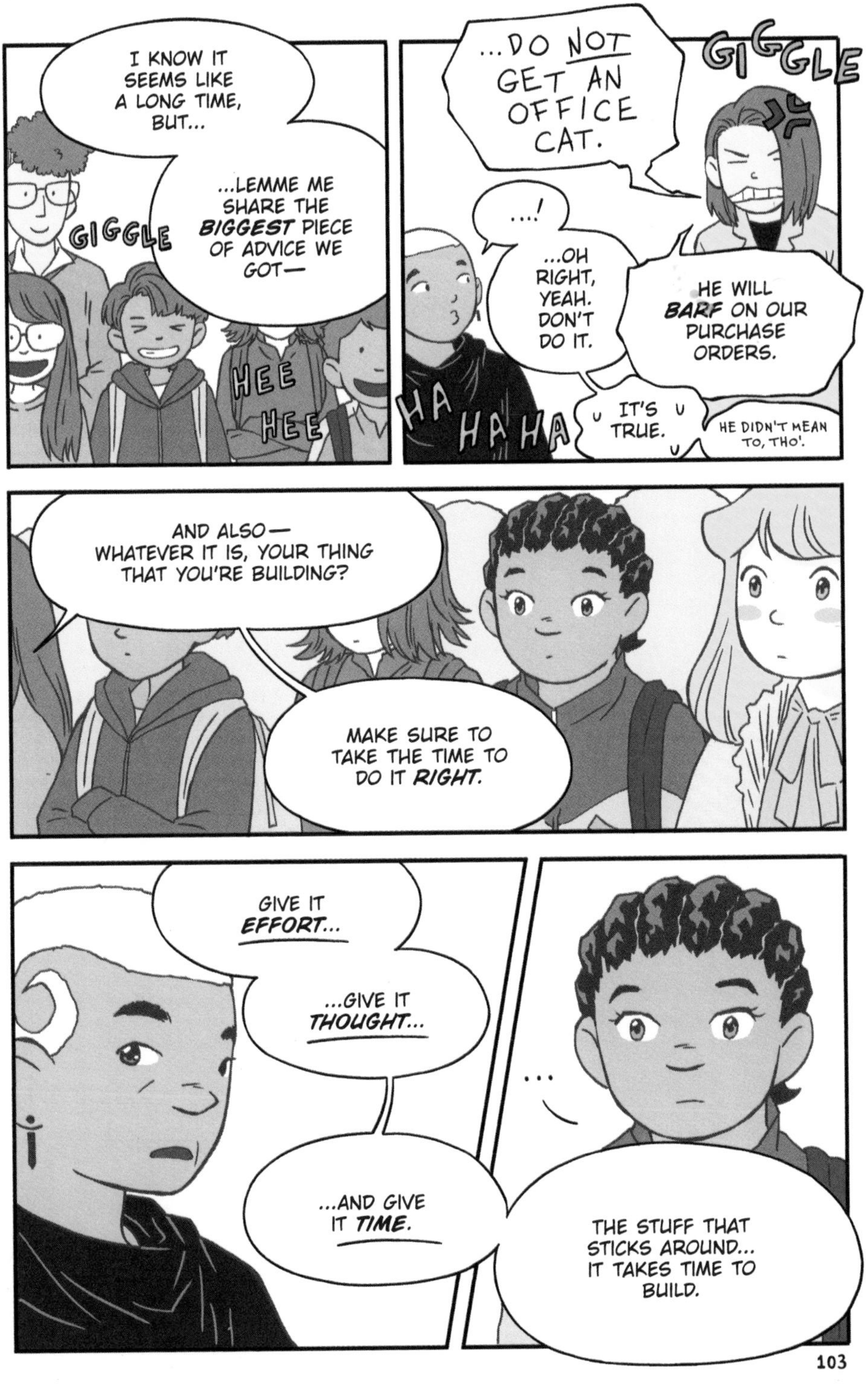
I KNOW IT SEEMS LIKE A LONG TIME, BUT...
...LEMME ME SHARE THE BIGGEST PIECE OF ADVICE WE GOT—
GIGGLE
HEE HEE
...DO NOT GET AN OFFICE CAT.
GIGGLE
....!
...OH RIGHT, YEAH. DON'T DO IT.
HE WILL BARF ON OUR PURCHASE ORDERS.
HA HAHA
IT'S TRUE.
HE DIDN'T MEAN TO, THO'.
AND ALSO— WHATEVER IT IS, YOUR THING THAT YOU'RE BUILDING?
MAKE SURE TO TAKE THE TIME TO DO IT RIGHT.
GIVE IT EFFORT...
...GIVE IT THOUGHT...
...AND GIVE IT TIME.
...
THE STUFF THAT STICKS AROUND... IT TAKES TIME TO BUILD.

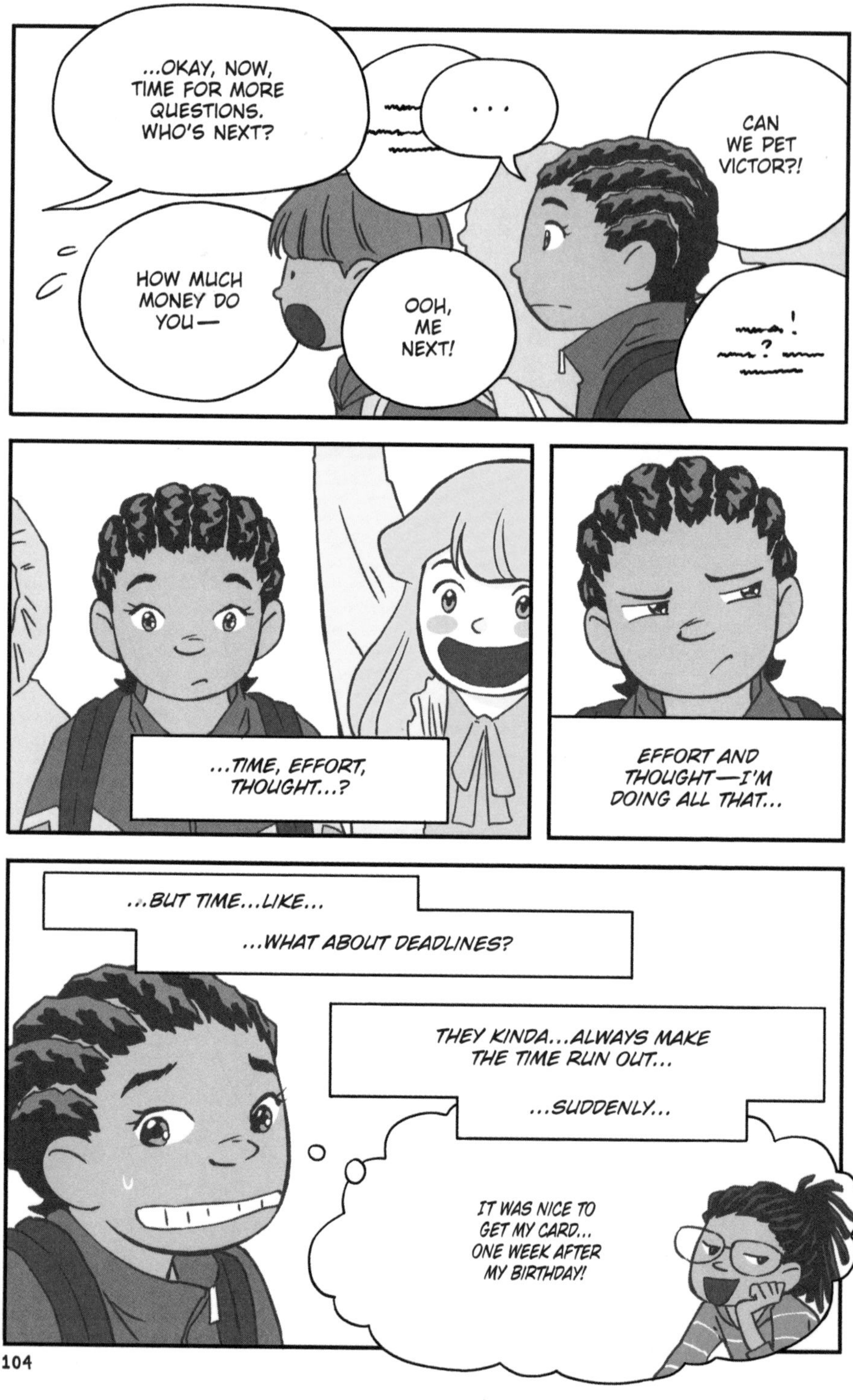
...OKAY, NOW, TIME FOR MORE QUESTIONS. WHO'S NEXT?
. . .
CAN WE PET VICTOR?!
HOW MUCH MONEY DO YOU—
OOH, ME NEXT!
...TIME, EFFORT, THOUGHT...?
EFFORT AND THOUGHT—I'M DOING ALL THAT...
...BUT TIME...LIKE...
...WHAT ABOUT DEADLINES?
THEY KINDA...ALWAYS MAKE THE TIME RUN OUT...
...SUDDENLY...
IT WAS NICE TO GET MY CARD... ONE WEEK AFTER MY BIRTHDAY!

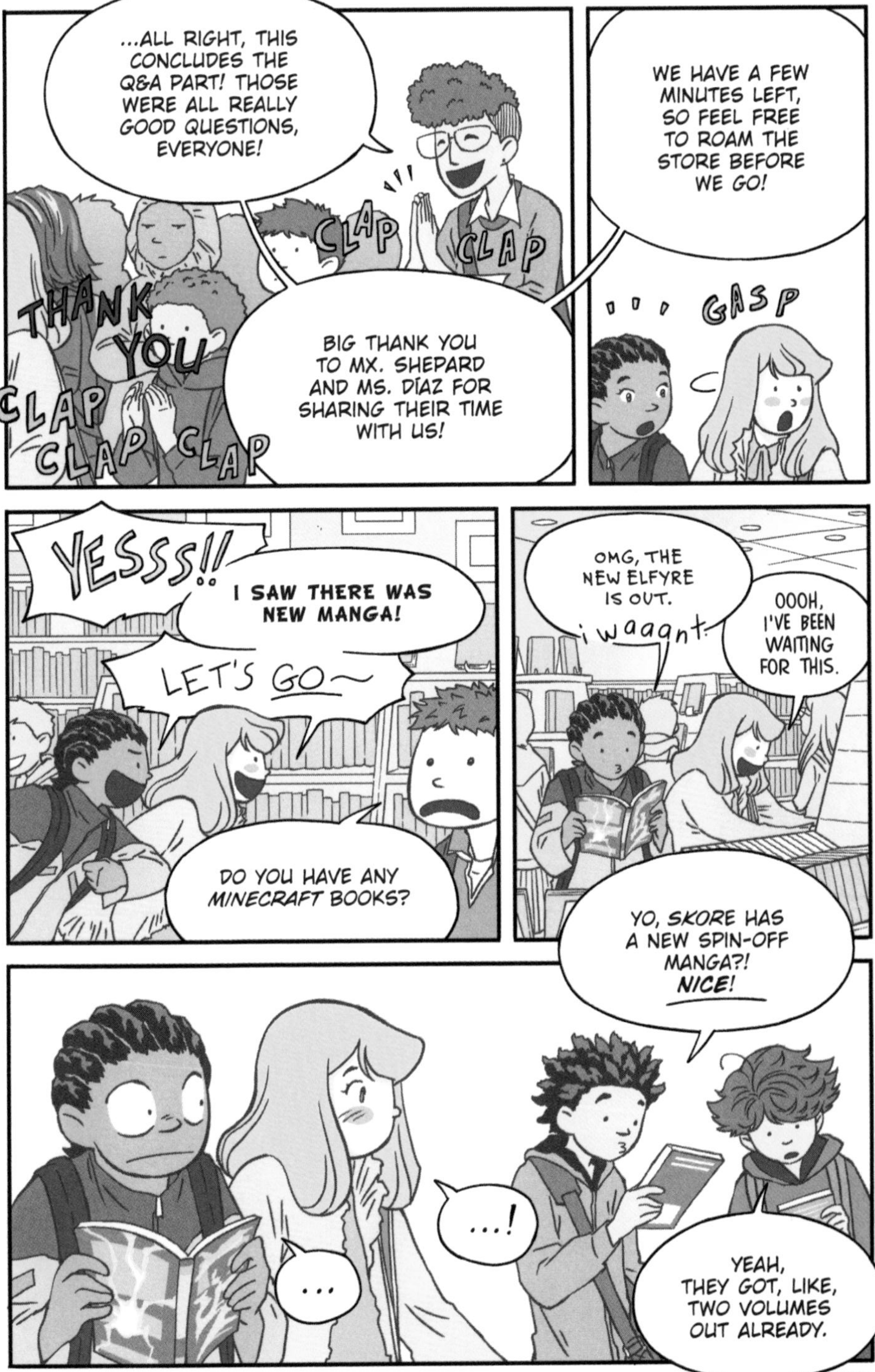
...ALL RIGHT, THIS CONCLUDES THE Q&A PART! THOSE WERE ALL REALLY GOOD QUESTIONS, EVERYONE!
CLAP
CLAP
THANK YOU
CLAP
CLAP
CLAP
BIG THANK YOU TO MX. SHEPARD AND MS. DÍAZ FOR SHARING THEIR TIME WITH US!
WE HAVE A FEW MINUTES LEFT, SO FEEL FREE TO ROAM THE STORE BEFORE WE GO!
GASP
YESSS!!
I SAW THERE WAS NEW MANGA!
LET'S GO~
DO YOU HAVE ANY *MINECRAFT* BOOKS?
OMG, THE NEW ELFYRE IS OUT.
iwaaant
OOOH, I'VE BEEN WAITING FOR THIS.
YO, *SKORE* HAS A NEW SPIN-OFF MANGA?! ***NICE!***
...!
...
YEAH, THEY GOT, LIKE, TWO VOLUMES OUT ALREADY.

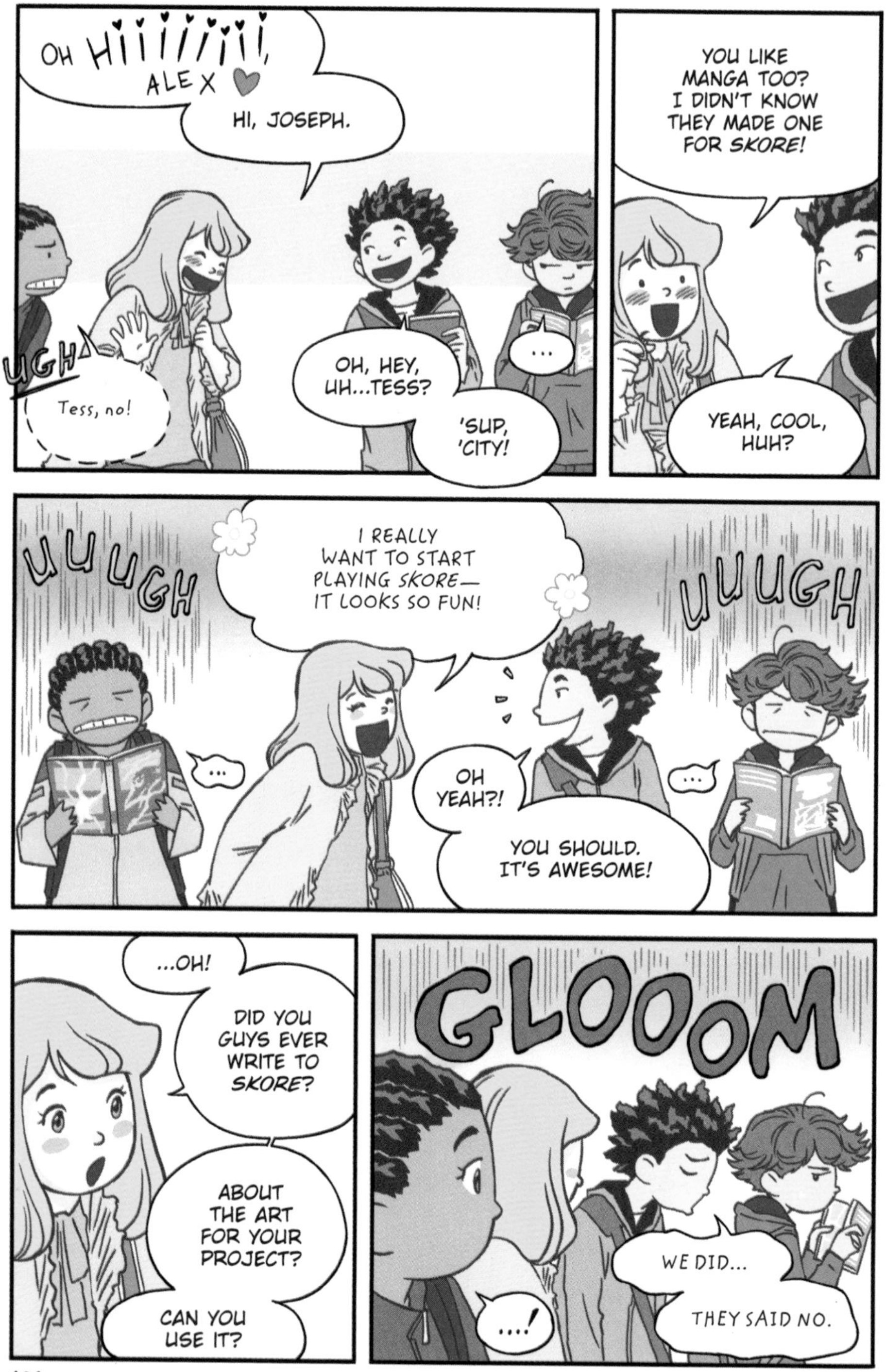

OH HIIIIIIII, ALEX
HI, JOSEPH.
UGH
Tess, no!
OH, HEY, UH...TESS?
...
'SUP, 'CITY!
YOU LIKE MANGA TOO? I DIDN'T KNOW THEY MADE ONE FOR SKORE!
YEAH, COOL, HUH?
UUUGH
I REALLY WANT TO START PLAYING SKORE— IT LOOKS SO FUN!
UUUGH
...
OH YEAH?!
YOU SHOULD. IT'S AWESOME!
...
...OH!
DID YOU GUYS EVER WRITE TO SKORE?
ABOUT THE ART FOR YOUR PROJECT?
CAN YOU USE IT?
GLOOOM
WE DID...
THEY SAID NO.
....!

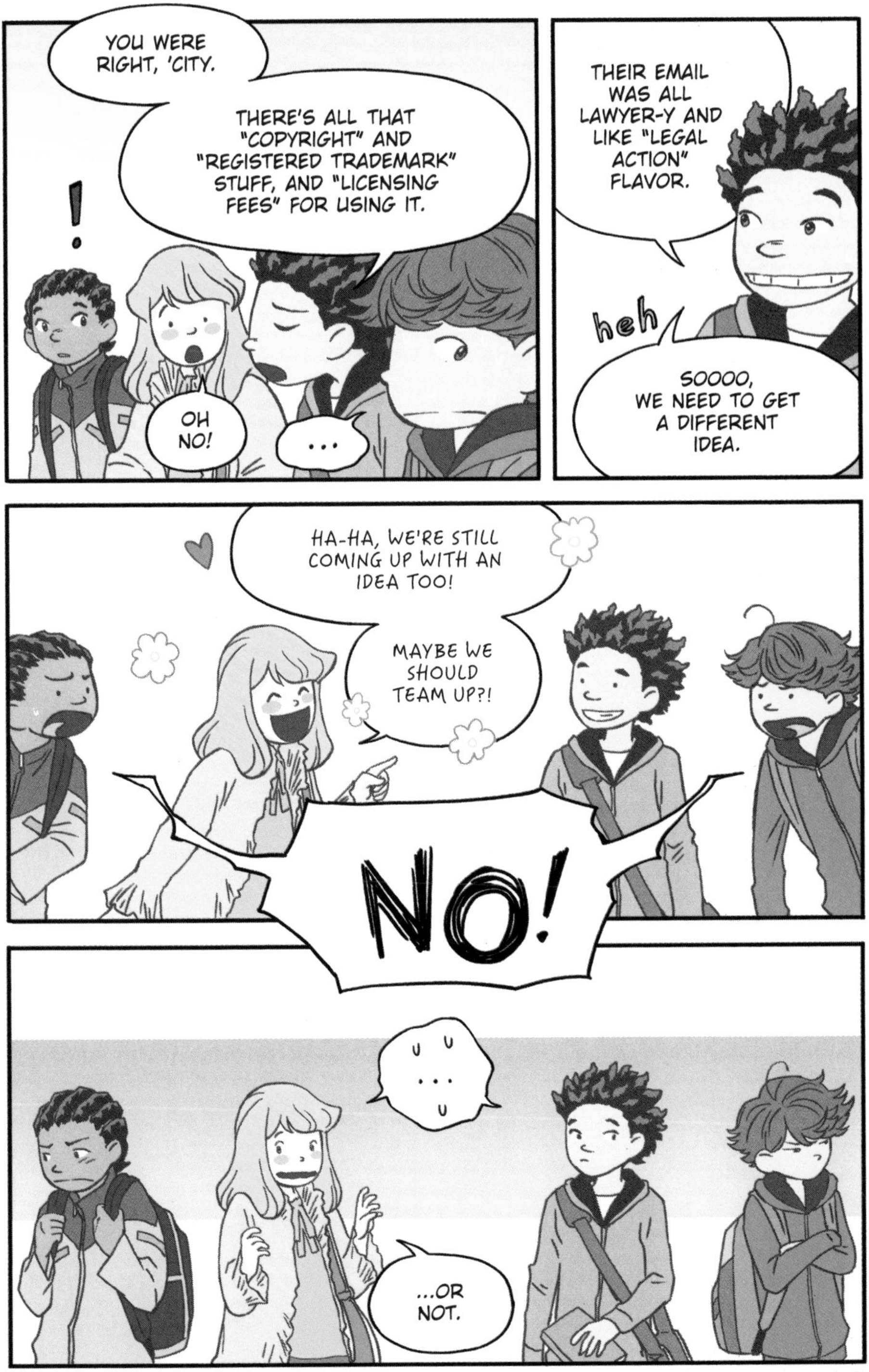
YOU WERE RIGHT, 'CITY.
THERE'S ALL THAT "COPYRIGHT" AND "REGISTERED TRADEMARK" STUFF, AND "LICENSING FEES" FOR USING IT.
!
OH NO!
...
THEIR EMAIL WAS ALL LAWYER-Y AND LIKE "LEGAL ACTION" FLAVOR.
heh
SOOOO, WE NEED TO GET A DIFFERENT IDEA.
HA-HA, WE'RE STILL COMING UP WITH AN IDEA TOO!
MAYBE WE SHOULD TEAM UP?!
NO!
...
...OR NOT.

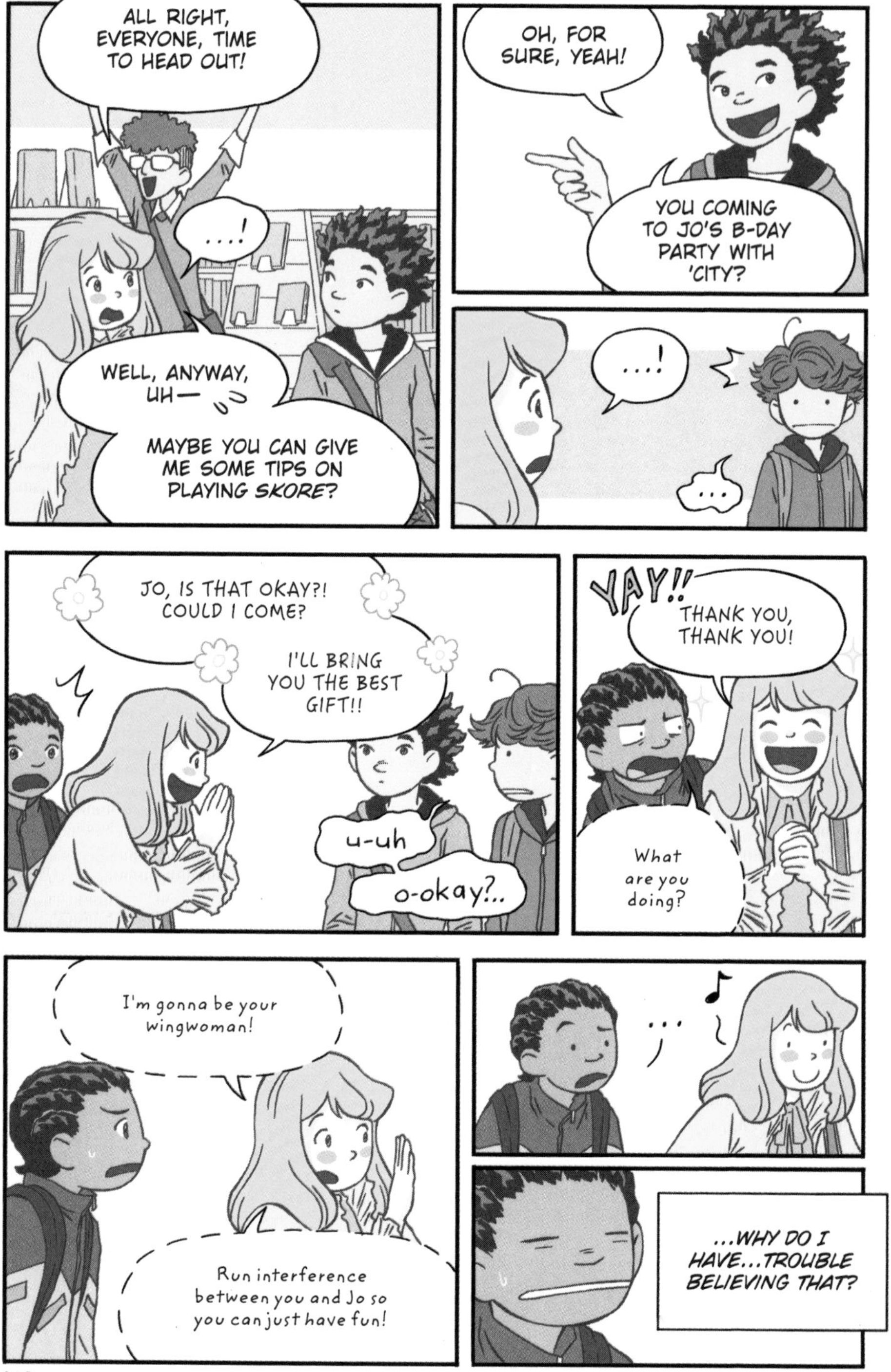
ALL RIGHT, EVERYONE, TIME TO HEAD OUT!
...!
WELL, ANYWAY, UH—
MAYBE YOU CAN GIVE ME SOME TIPS ON PLAYING *SKORE*?
OH, FOR SURE, YEAH!
YOU COMING TO JO'S B-DAY PARTY WITH 'CITY?
...!
...
JO, IS THAT OKAY?! COULD I COME?
I'LL BRING YOU THE BEST GIFT!!
u-uh
o-okay?..
YAY!!
THANK YOU, THANK YOU!
What are you doing?
I'm gonna be your wingwoman!
Run interference between you and Jo so you can just have fun!
...
...WHY DO I HAVE...TROUBLE BELIEVING THAT?

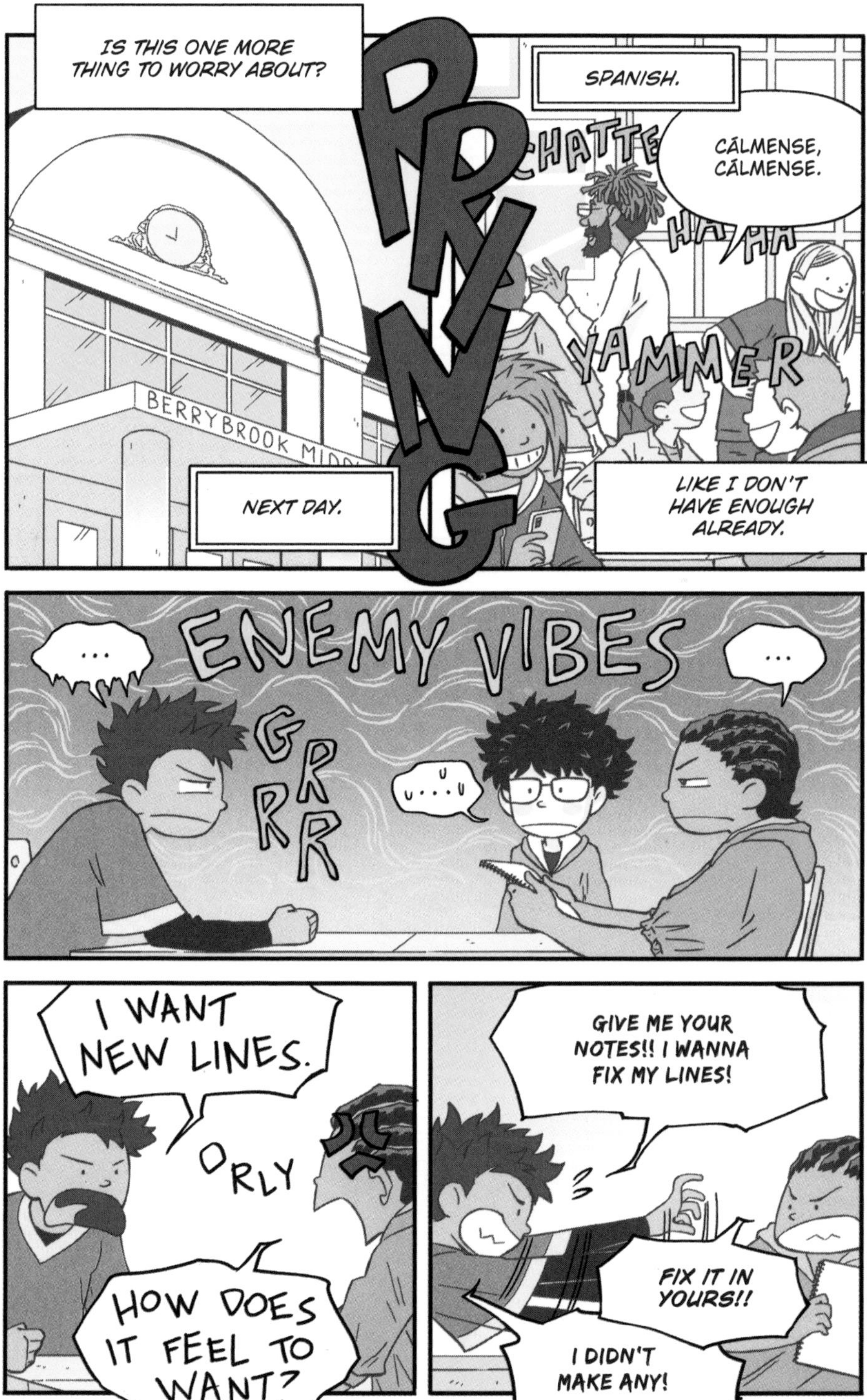
IS THIS ONE MORE THING TO WORRY ABOUT?
PRRING
BERRYBROOK MIDD
NEXT DAY.
SPANISH.
CHATTE
CÁLMENSE, CÁLMENSE.
HA HA
YAMMER
LIKE I DON'T HAVE ENOUGH ALREADY.
ENEMY VIBES
...
...
GRRR
u u... u
I WANT NEW LINES.
ORLY
HOW DOES IT FEEL TO WANT?
GIVE ME YOUR NOTES!! I WANNA FIX MY LINES!
FIX IT IN YOURS!!
I DIDN'T MAKE ANY!

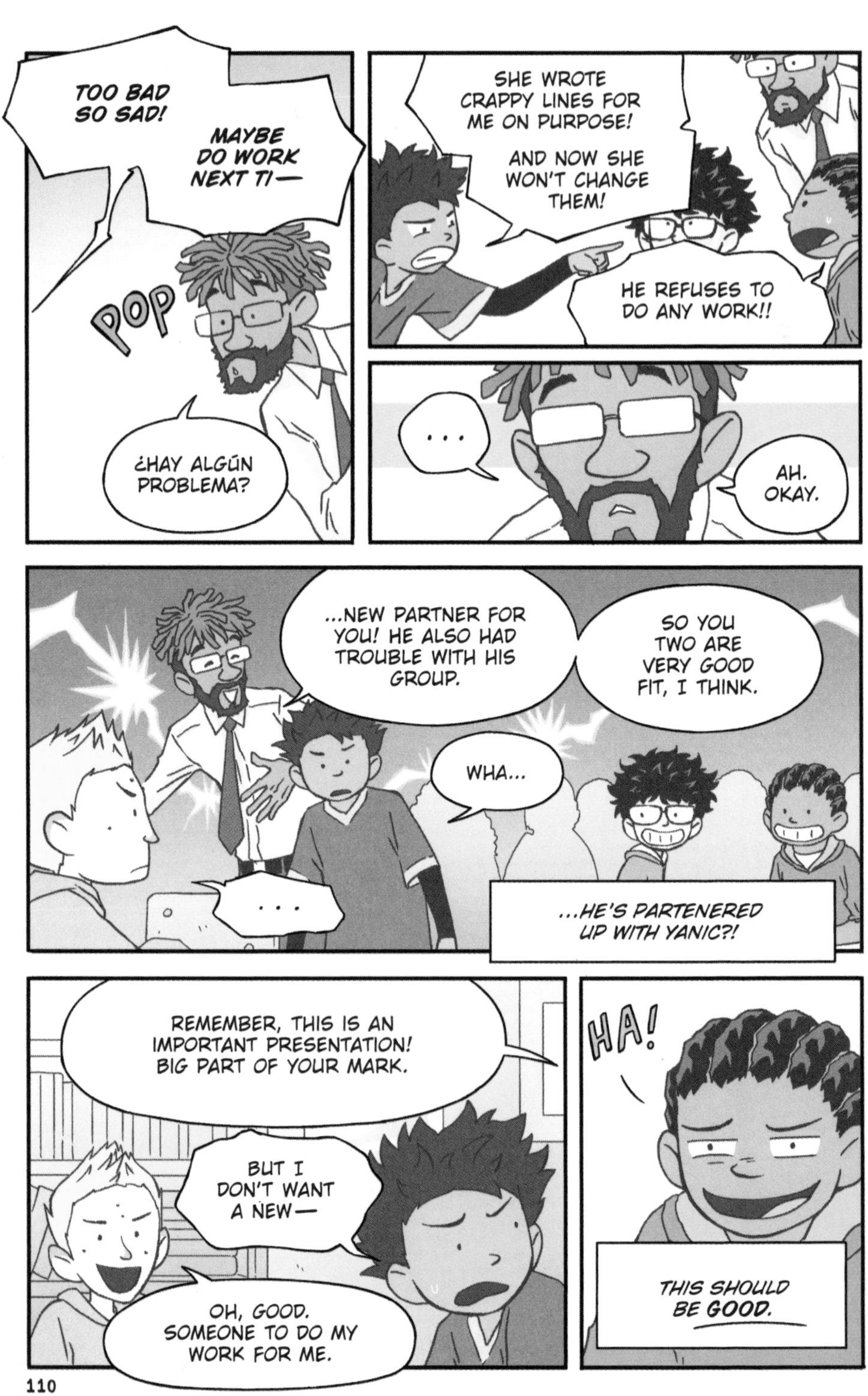
TOO BAD SO SAD!
MAYBE DO WORK NEXT TI—
POP
¿HAY ALGÚN PROBLEMA?
SHE WROTE CRAPPY LINES FOR ME ON PURPOSE!
AND NOW SHE WON'T CHANGE THEM!
HE REFUSES TO DO ANY WORK!!
. . .
AH. OKAY.
...NEW PARTNER FOR YOU! HE ALSO HAD TROUBLE WITH HIS GROUP.
SO YOU TWO ARE VERY GOOD FIT, I THINK.
WHA...
. . .
...HE'S PARTENERED UP WITH YANIC?!
REMEMBER, THIS IS AN IMPORTANT PRESENTATION! BIG PART OF YOUR MARK.
BUT I DON'T WANT A NEW—
OH, GOOD. SOMEONE TO DO MY WORK FOR ME.
HA!
THIS SHOULD BE GOOD.

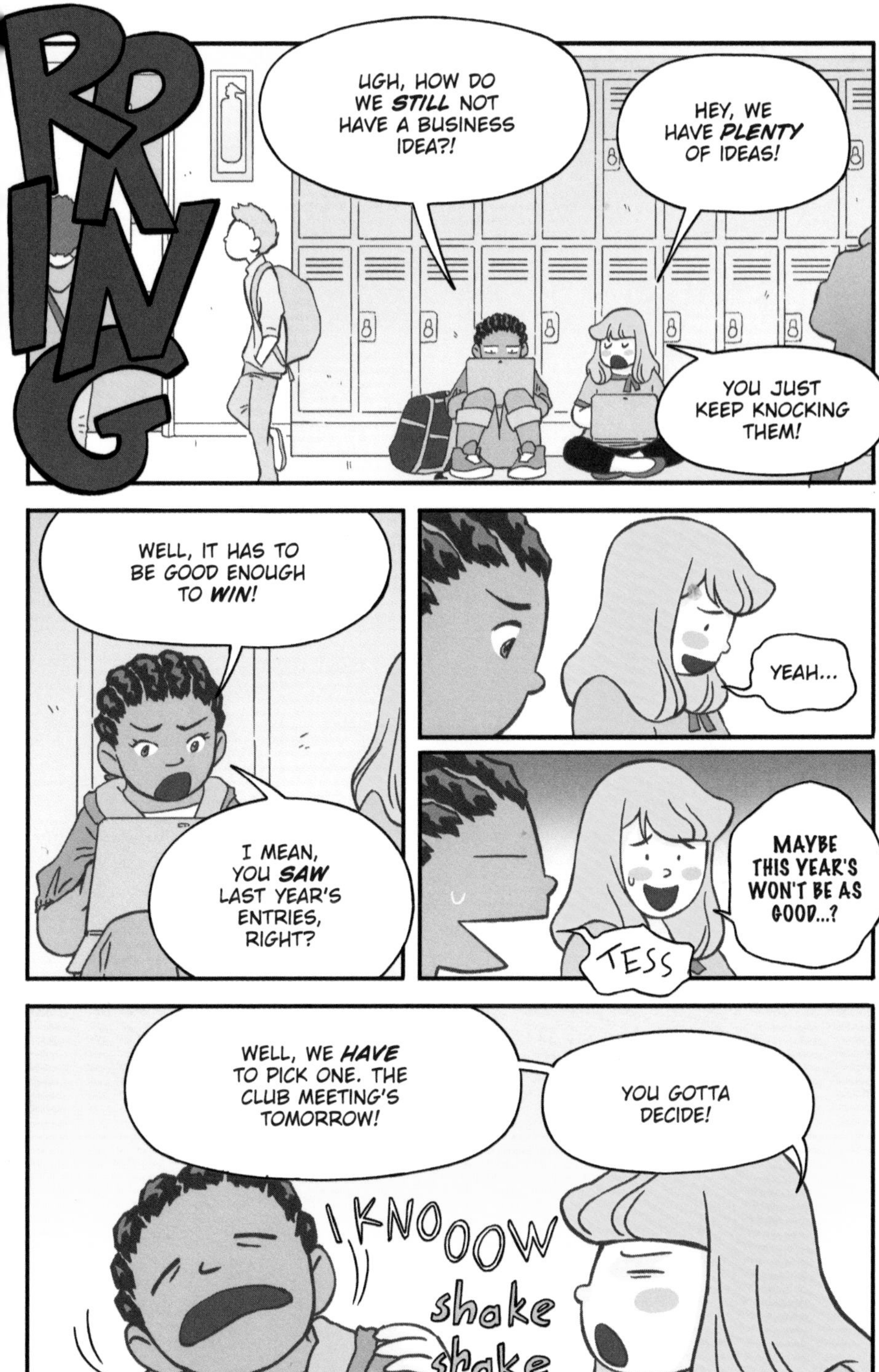
RRING
UGH, HOW DO WE STILL NOT HAVE A BUSINESS IDEA?!
HEY, WE HAVE PLENTY OF IDEAS!
YOU JUST KEEP KNOCKING THEM!
WELL, IT HAS TO BE GOOD ENOUGH TO WIN!
I MEAN, YOU SAW LAST YEAR'S ENTRIES, RIGHT?
YEAH...
MAYBE THIS YEAR'S WON'T BE AS GOOD...?
TESS
WELL, WE HAVE TO PICK ONE. THE CLUB MEETING'S TOMORROW!
YOU GOTTA DECIDE!
I KNOOOOW
shake shake

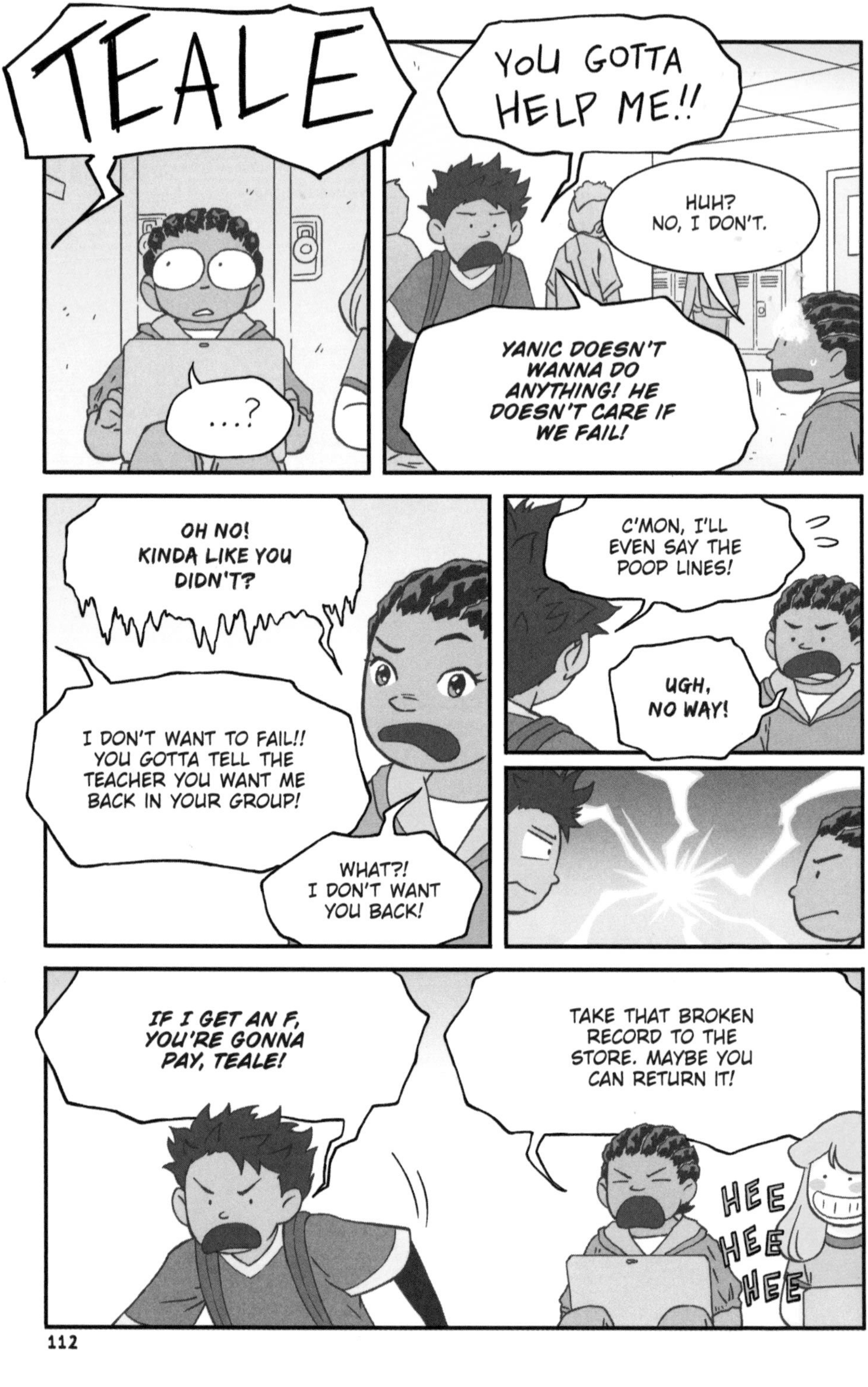
TEALE
...?
YOU GOTTA HELP ME!!
HUH? NO, I DON'T.
YANIC DOESN'T WANNA DO ANYTHING! HE DOESN'T CARE IF WE FAIL!
OH NO! KINDA LIKE YOU DIDN'T?
I DON'T WANT TO FAIL!! YOU GOTTA TELL THE TEACHER YOU WANT ME BACK IN YOUR GROUP!
WHAT?! I DON'T WANT YOU BACK!
C'MON, I'LL EVEN SAY THE POOP LINES!
UGH, NO WAY!
IF I GET AN F, YOU'RE GONNA PAY, TEALE!
TAKE THAT BROKEN RECORD TO THE STORE. MAYBE YOU CAN RETURN IT!
HEE HEE HEE

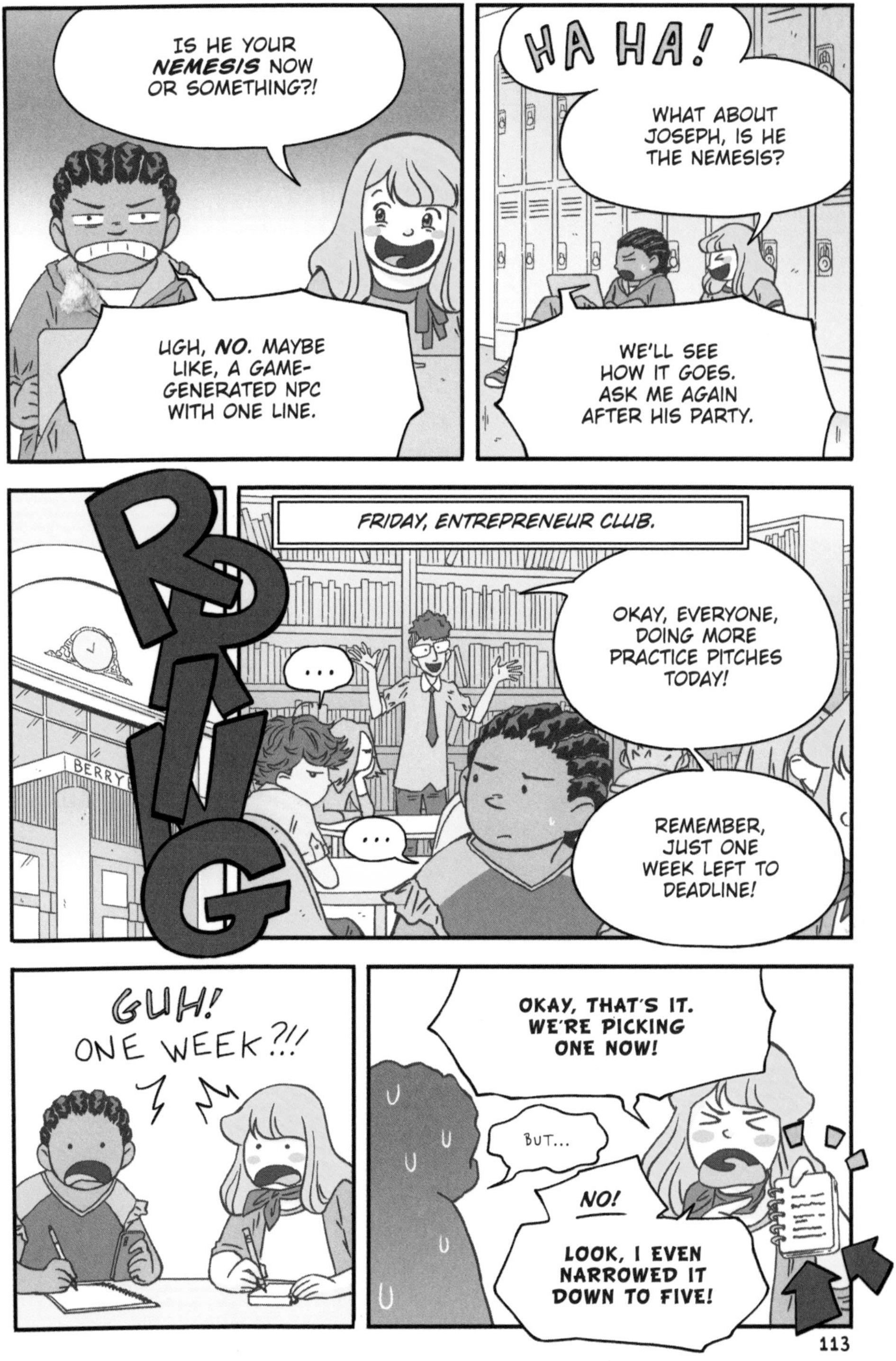
IS HE YOUR NEMESIS NOW OR SOMETHING?!
UGH, NO. MAYBE LIKE, A GAME-GENERATED NPC WITH ONE LINE.
HA HA!
WHAT ABOUT JOSEPH, IS HE THE NEMESIS?
WE'LL SEE HOW IT GOES. ASK ME AGAIN AFTER HIS PARTY.
RRING
FRIDAY, ENTREPRENEUR CLUB.
BERRY
OKAY, EVERYONE, DOING MORE PRACTICE PITCHES TODAY!
...
...
REMEMBER, JUST ONE WEEK LEFT TO DEADLINE!
GUH! ONE WEEK?!!
OKAY, THAT'S IT. WE'RE PICKING ONE NOW!
BUT...
NO!
LOOK, I EVEN NARROWED IT DOWN TO FIVE!

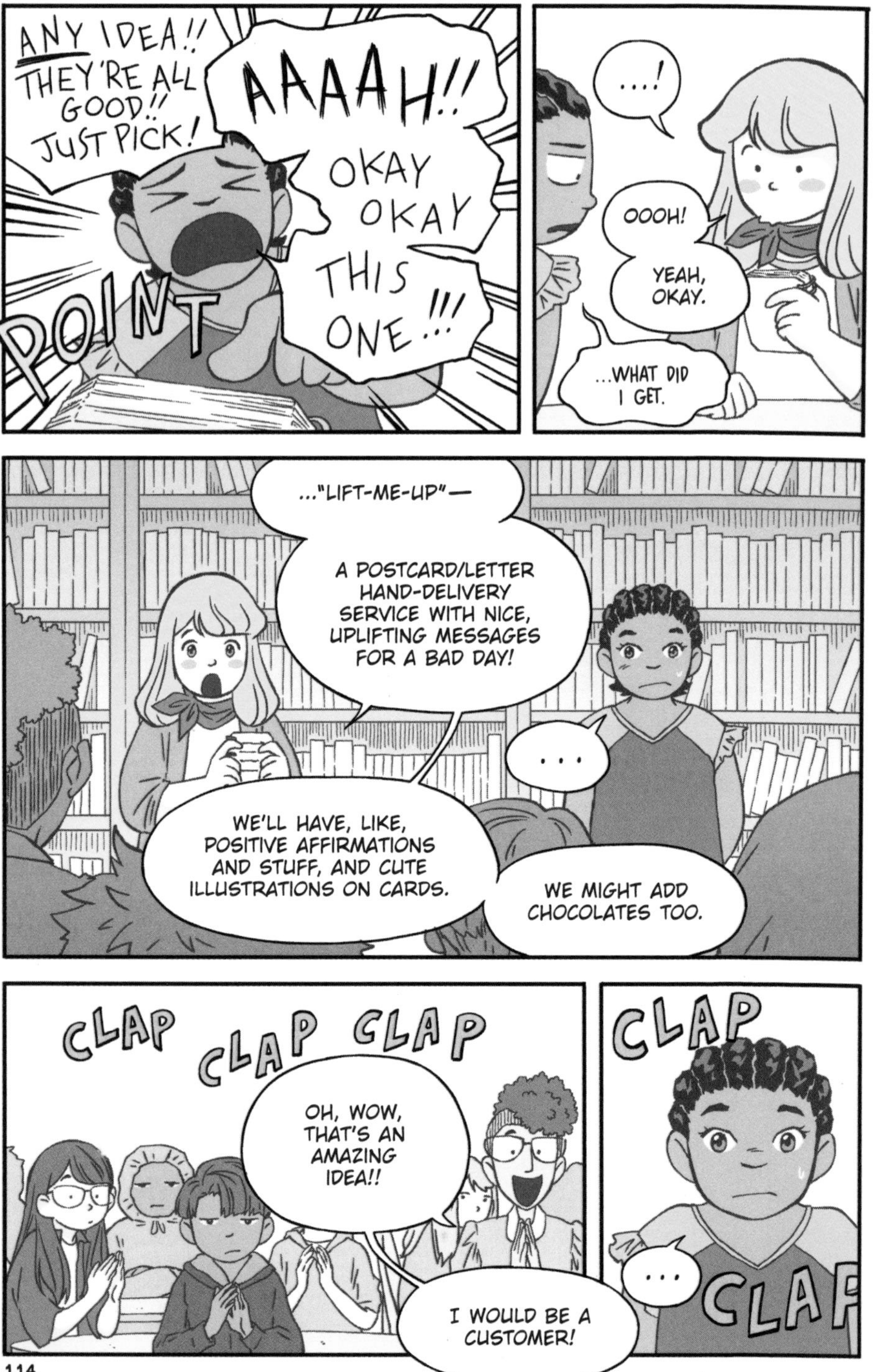
ANY IDEA!! THEY'RE ALL GOOD!! JUST PICK!
AAAAH!!
OKAY OKAY THIS ONE!!!
POINT
....!
OOOH!
YEAH, OKAY.
...WHAT DID I GET.
..."LIFT-ME-UP"—
A POSTCARD/LETTER HAND-DELIVERY SERVICE WITH NICE, UPLIFTING MESSAGES FOR A BAD DAY!
. . .
WE'LL HAVE, LIKE, POSITIVE AFFIRMATIONS AND STUFF, AND CUTE ILLUSTRATIONS ON CARDS.
WE MIGHT ADD CHOCOLATES TOO.
CLAP CLAP CLAP
OH, WOW, THAT'S AN AMAZING IDEA!!
I WOULD BE A CUSTOMER!
CLAP
. . .
CLAP

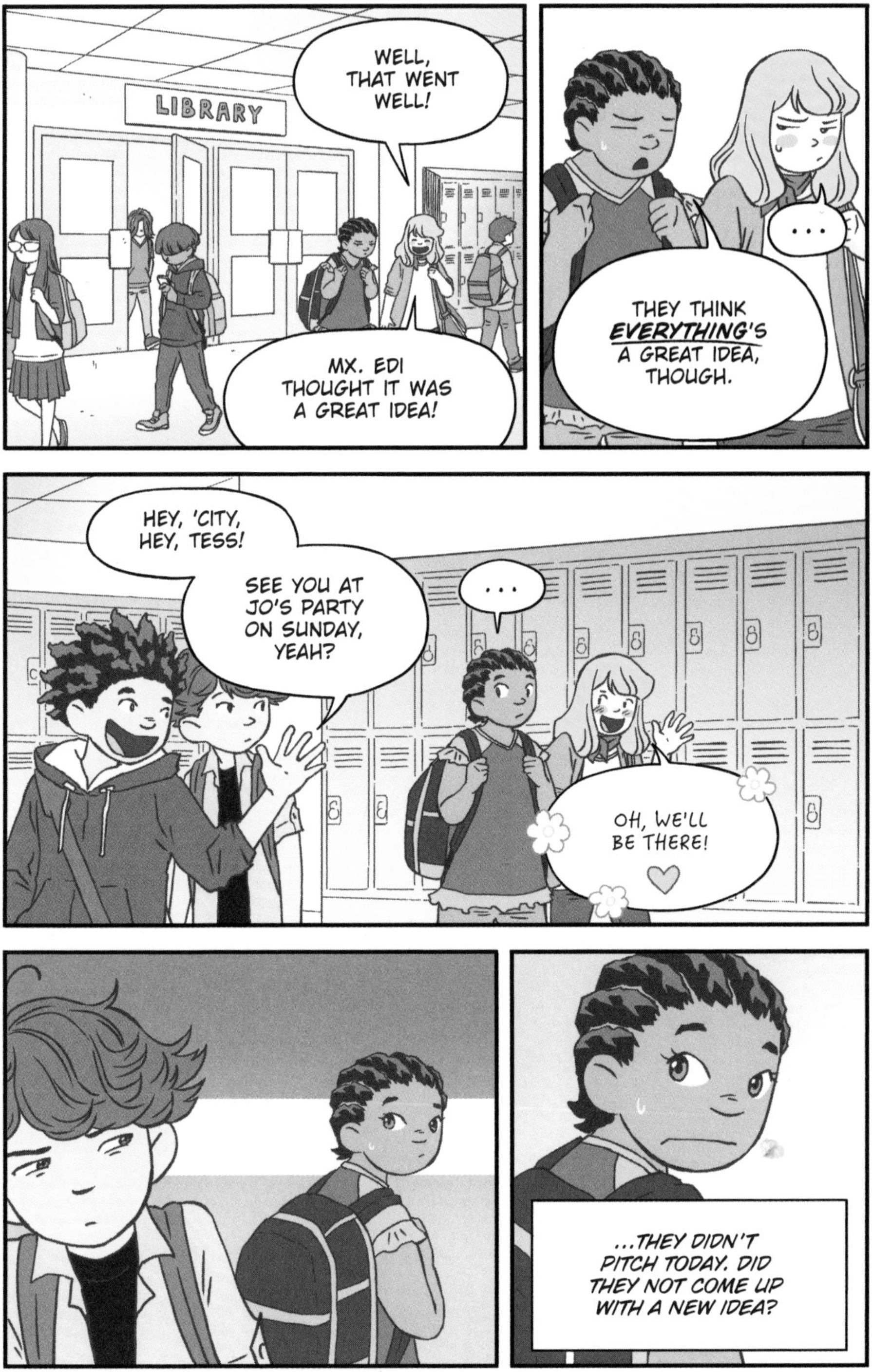
LIBRARY
WELL, THAT WENT WELL!
MX. EDI THOUGHT IT WAS A GREAT IDEA!
...
THEY THINK EVERYTHING'S A GREAT IDEA, THOUGH.
HEY, 'CITY, HEY, TESS!
SEE YOU AT JO'S PARTY ON SUNDAY, YEAH?
...
OH, WE'LL BE THERE!
...THEY DIDN'T PITCH TODAY. DID THEY NOT COME UP WITH A NEW IDEA?

CHAPTER 5

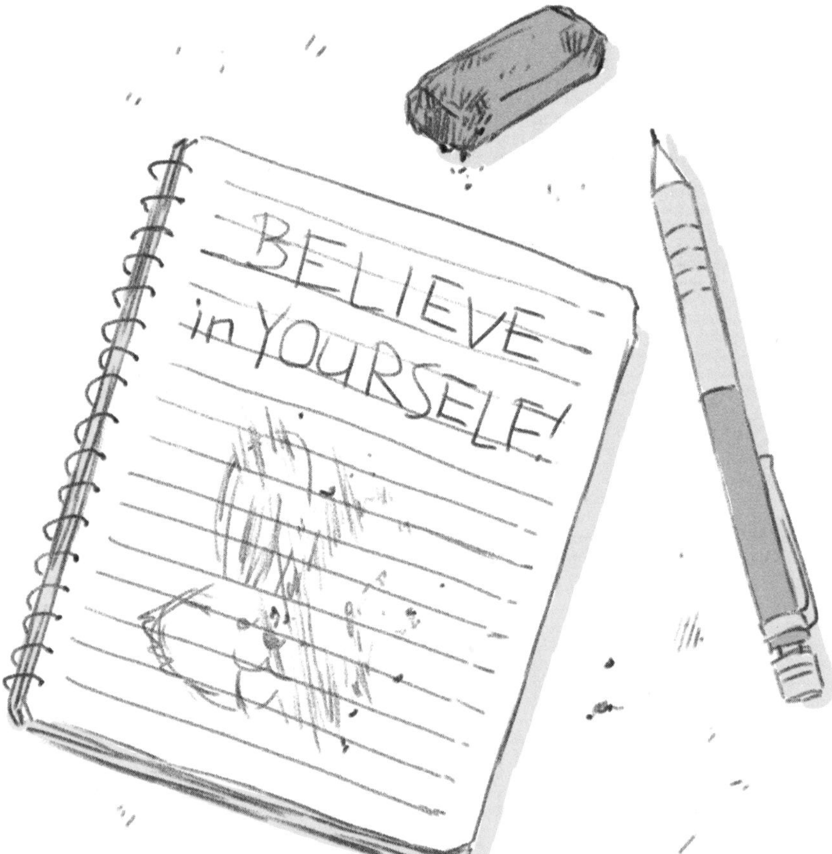
BELIEVE in YOURSELF!

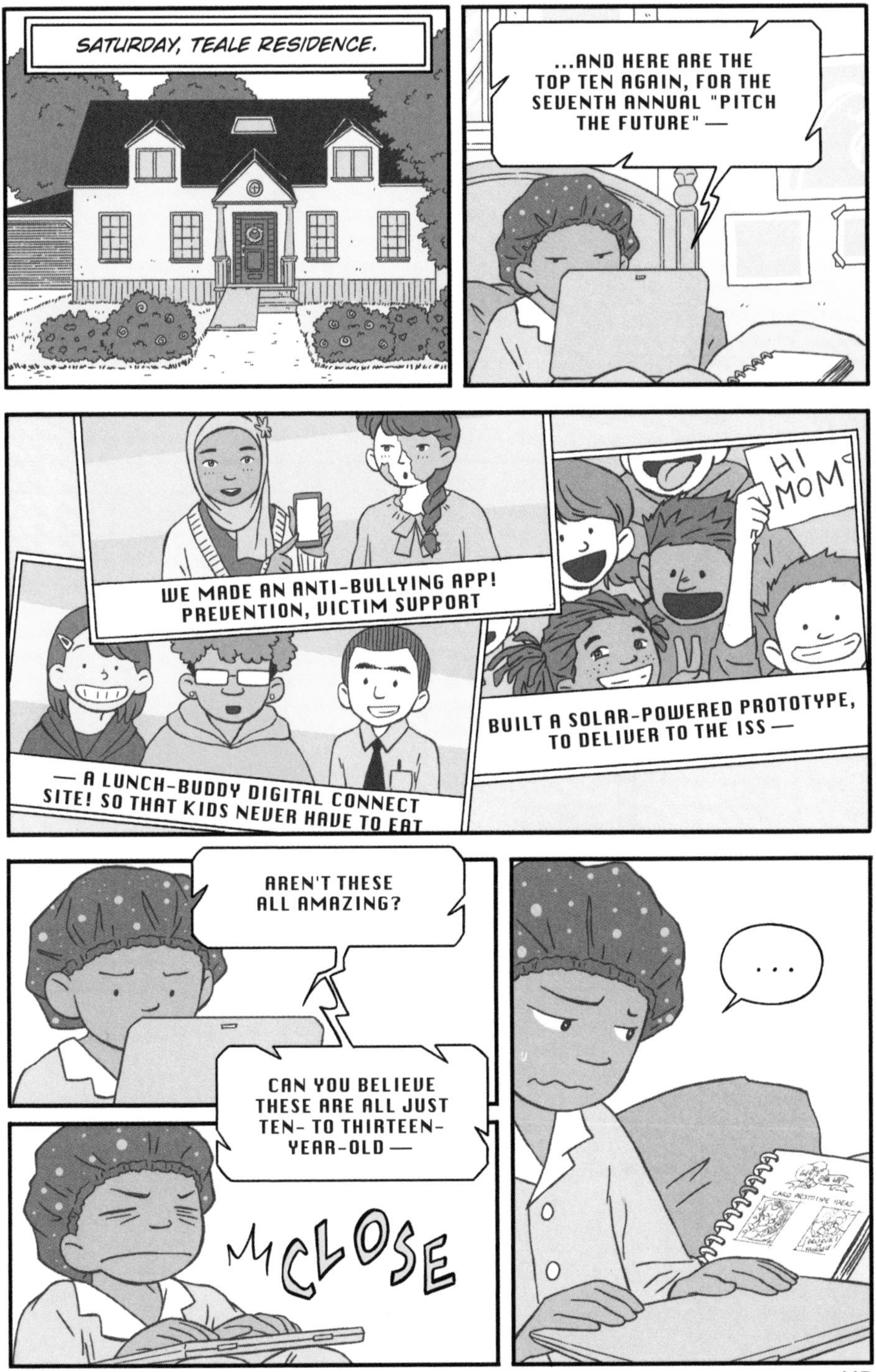
SATURDAY, TEALE RESIDENCE.
...AND HERE ARE THE TOP TEN AGAIN, FOR THE SEVENTH ANNUAL "PITCH THE FUTURE" —
WE MADE AN ANTI-BULLYING APP! PREVENTION, VICTIM SUPPORT
— A LUNCH-BUDDY DIGITAL CONNECT SITE! SO THAT KIDS NEVER HAVE TO EAT
HI MOM
BUILT A SOLAR-POWERED PROTOTYPE, TO DELIVER TO THE ISS —
AREN'T THESE ALL AMAZING?
CAN YOU BELIEVE THESE ARE ALL JUST TEN- TO THIRTEEN-YEAR-OLD —
CLOSE
. . .
CARD PROTOTYPE IDEAS

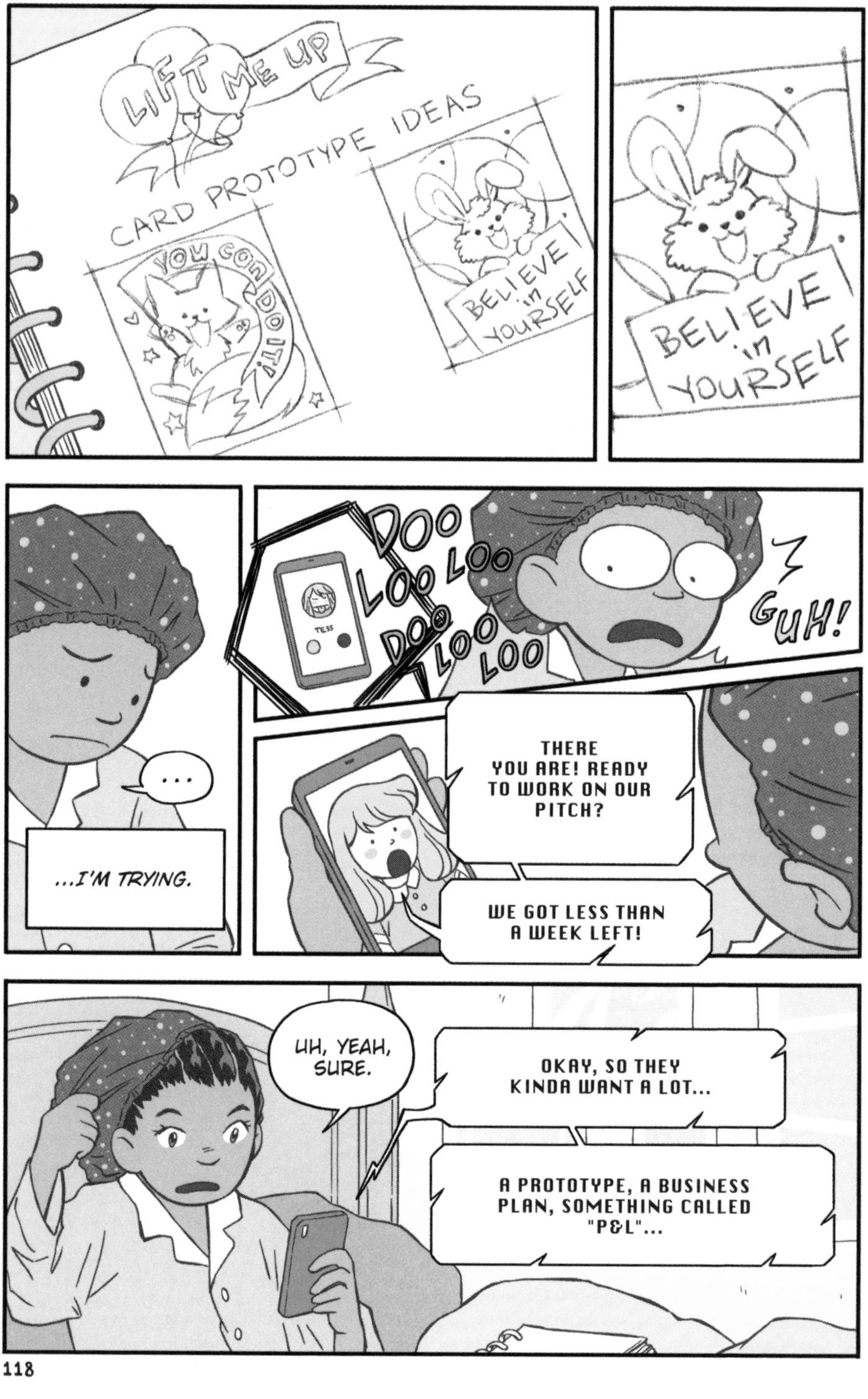
LIFT ME UP
CARD PROTOTYPE IDEAS
YOU CAN DO IT!
BELIEVE in YOURSELF
BELIEVE in YOURSELF
...
...I'M TRYING.
DOO LOO LOO DOO LOO LOO
TESS
GUH!
THERE YOU ARE! READY TO WORK ON OUR PITCH?
WE GOT LESS THAN A WEEK LEFT!
UH, YEAH, SURE.
OKAY, SO THEY KINDA WANT A LOT...
A PROTOTYPE, A BUSINESS PLAN, SOMETHING CALLED "P&L"...

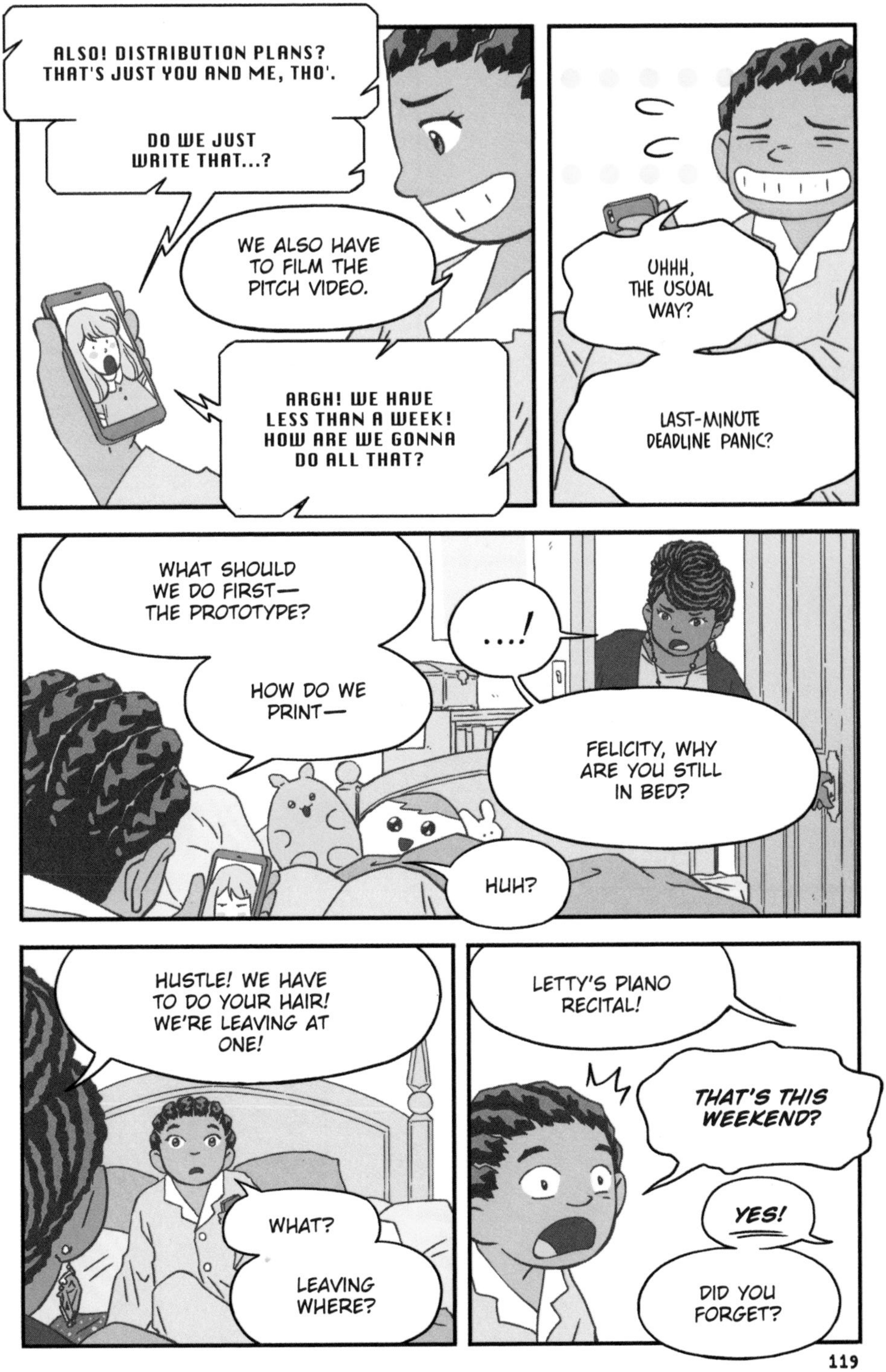
ALSO! DISTRIBUTION PLANS? THAT'S JUST YOU AND ME, THO'.
DO WE JUST WRITE THAT...?
WE ALSO HAVE TO FILM THE PITCH VIDEO.
ARGH! WE HAVE LESS THAN A WEEK! HOW ARE WE GONNA DO ALL THAT?
UHHH, THE USUAL WAY?
LAST-MINUTE DEADLINE PANIC?
WHAT SHOULD WE DO FIRST— THE PROTOTYPE?
HOW DO WE PRINT—
...!
FELICITY, WHY ARE YOU STILL IN BED?
HUH?
HUSTLE! WE HAVE TO DO YOUR HAIR! WE'RE LEAVING AT ONE!
WHAT?
LEAVING WHERE?
LETTY'S PIANO RECITAL!
THAT'S THIS WEEKEND?
YES!
DID YOU FORGET?

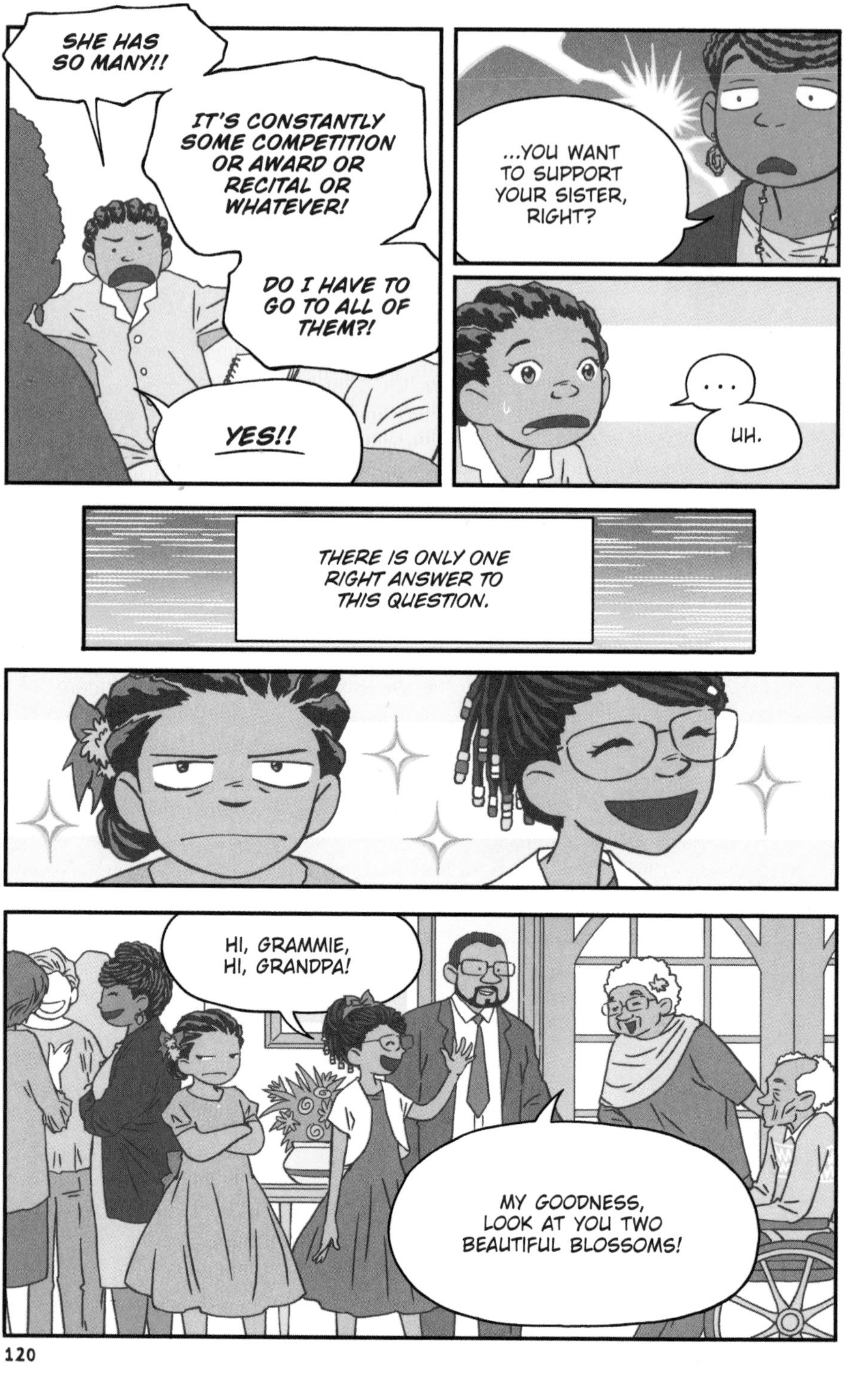
SHE HAS SO MANY!!
IT'S CONSTANTLY SOME COMPETITION OR AWARD OR RECITAL OR WHATEVER!
DO I HAVE TO GO TO ALL OF THEM?!
YES!!
...YOU WANT TO SUPPORT YOUR SISTER, RIGHT?
...
UH.
THERE IS ONLY ONE RIGHT ANSWER TO THIS QUESTION.
HI, GRAMMIE, HI, GRANDPA!
MY GOODNESS, LOOK AT YOU TWO BEAUTIFUL BLOSSOMS!

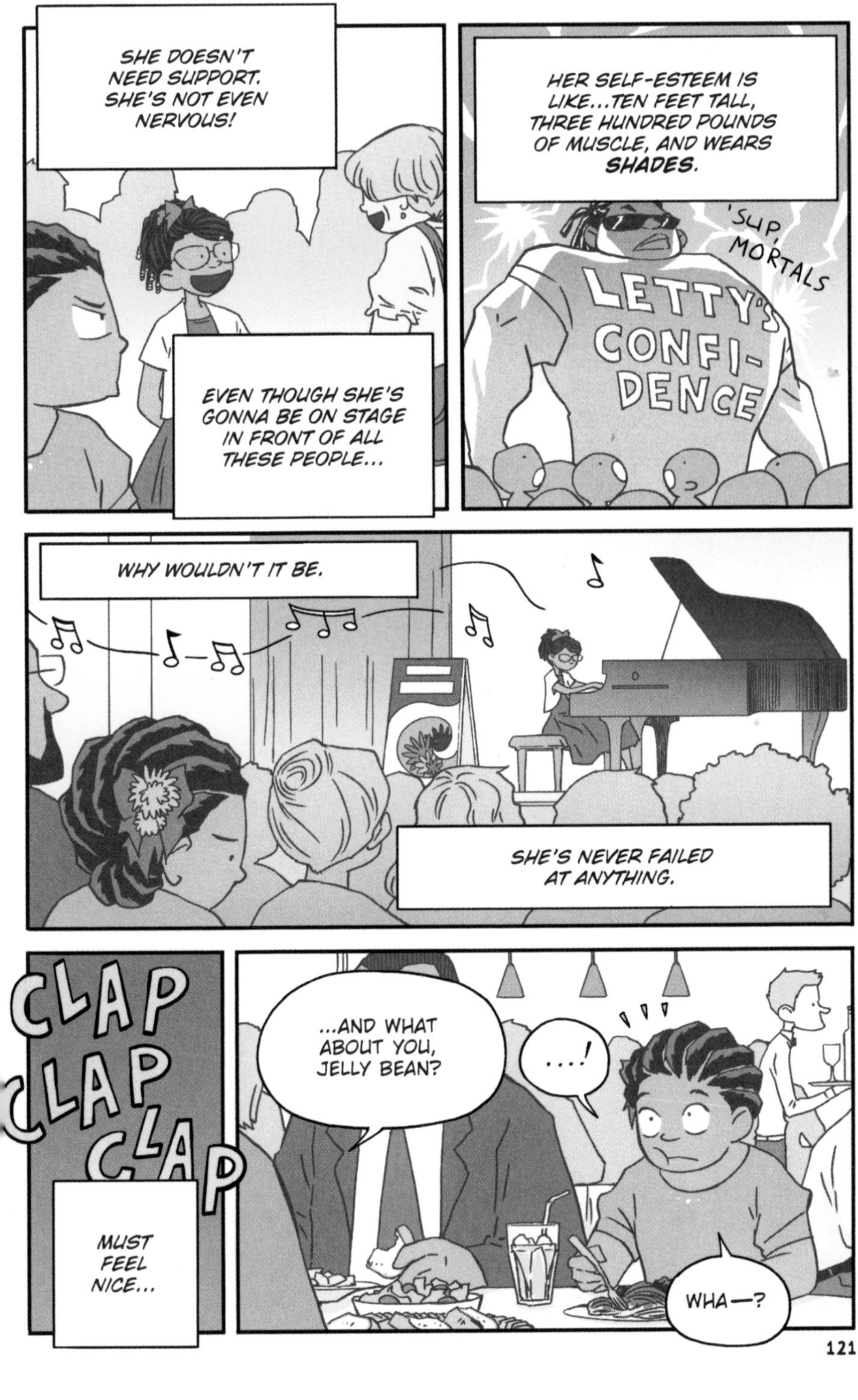
SHE DOESN'T NEED SUPPORT. SHE'S NOT EVEN NERVOUS!
EVEN THOUGH SHE'S GONNA BE ON STAGE IN FRONT OF ALL THESE PEOPLE...
HER SELF-ESTEEM IS LIKE...TEN FEET TALL, THREE HUNDRED POUNDS OF MUSCLE, AND WEARS SHADES.
'SUP, MORTALS
LETTY'S CONFI-DENCE
WHY WOULDN'T IT BE.
SHE'S NEVER FAILED AT ANYTHING.
CLAP CLAP CLAP
MUST FEEL NICE...
...AND WHAT ABOUT YOU, JELLY BEAN?
...!
WHA—?

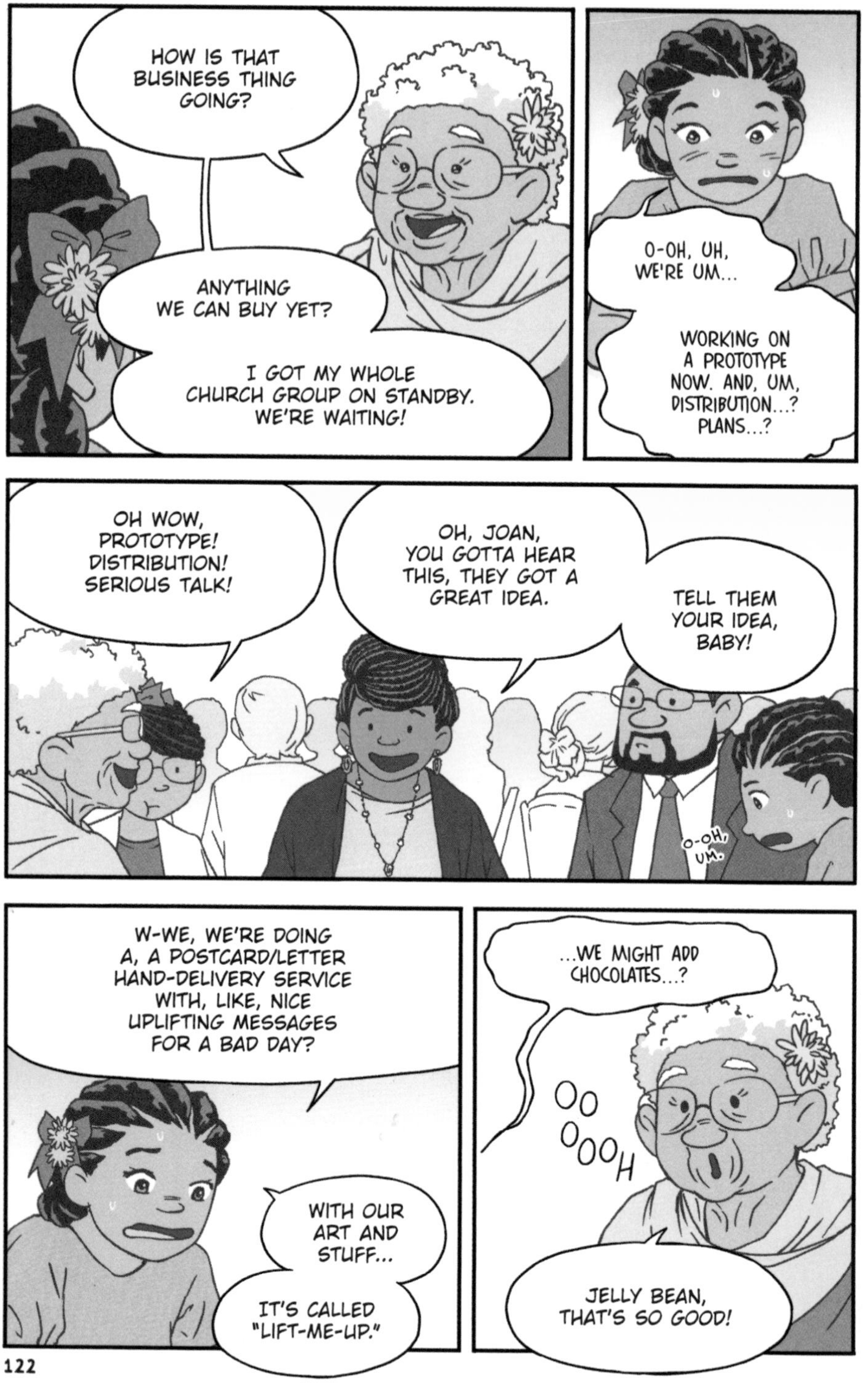
HOW IS THAT BUSINESS THING GOING?
ANYTHING WE CAN BUY YET?
I GOT MY WHOLE CHURCH GROUP ON STANDBY. WE'RE WAITING!
O-OH, UH, WE'RE UM...
WORKING ON A PROTOTYPE NOW. AND, UM, DISTRIBUTION...? PLANS...?
OH WOW, PROTOTYPE! DISTRIBUTION! SERIOUS TALK!
OH, JOAN, YOU GOTTA HEAR THIS, THEY GOT A GREAT IDEA.
TELL THEM YOUR IDEA, BABY!
O-OH, UM.
W-WE, WE'RE DOING A, A POSTCARD/LETTER HAND-DELIVERY SERVICE WITH, LIKE, NICE UPLIFTING MESSAGES FOR A BAD DAY?
WITH OUR ART AND STUFF...
IT'S CALLED "LIFT-ME-UP."
...WE MIGHT ADD CHOCOLATES...?
OOOOOH
JELLY BEAN, THAT'S SO GOOD!

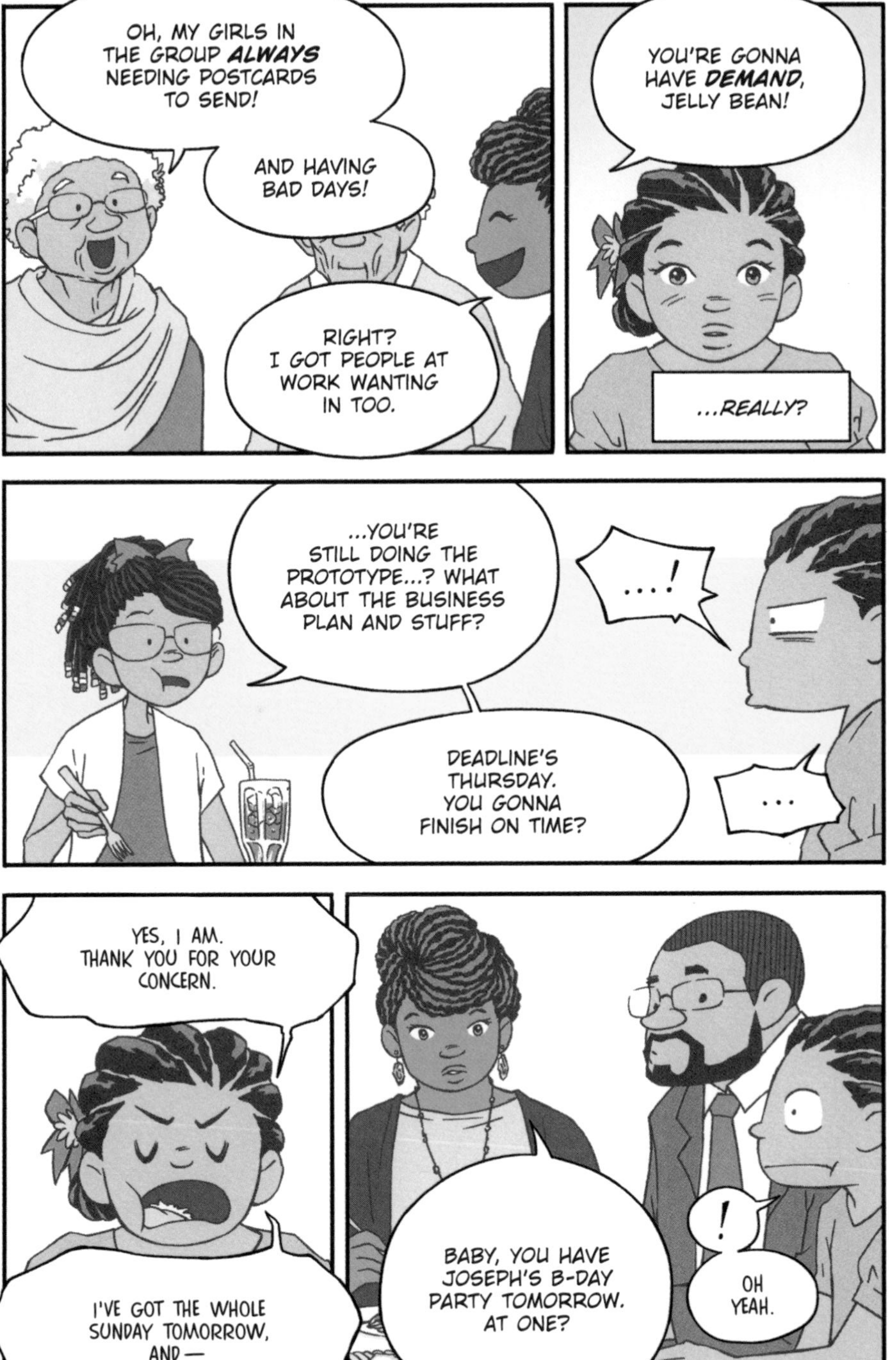
OH, MY GIRLS IN THE GROUP **ALWAYS** NEEDING POSTCARDS TO SEND!
AND HAVING BAD DAYS!
RIGHT? I GOT PEOPLE AT WORK WANTING IN TOO.
YOU'RE GONNA HAVE **DEMAND**, JELLY BEAN!
...REALLY?
...YOU'RE STILL DOING THE PROTOTYPE...? WHAT ABOUT THE BUSINESS PLAN AND STUFF?
...!
DEADLINE'S THURSDAY. YOU GONNA FINISH ON TIME?
...
YES, I AM. THANK YOU FOR YOUR CONCERN.
I'VE GOT THE WHOLE SUNDAY TOMORROW, AND—
BABY, YOU HAVE JOSEPH'S B-DAY PARTY TOMORROW. AT ONE?
!
OH YEAH.

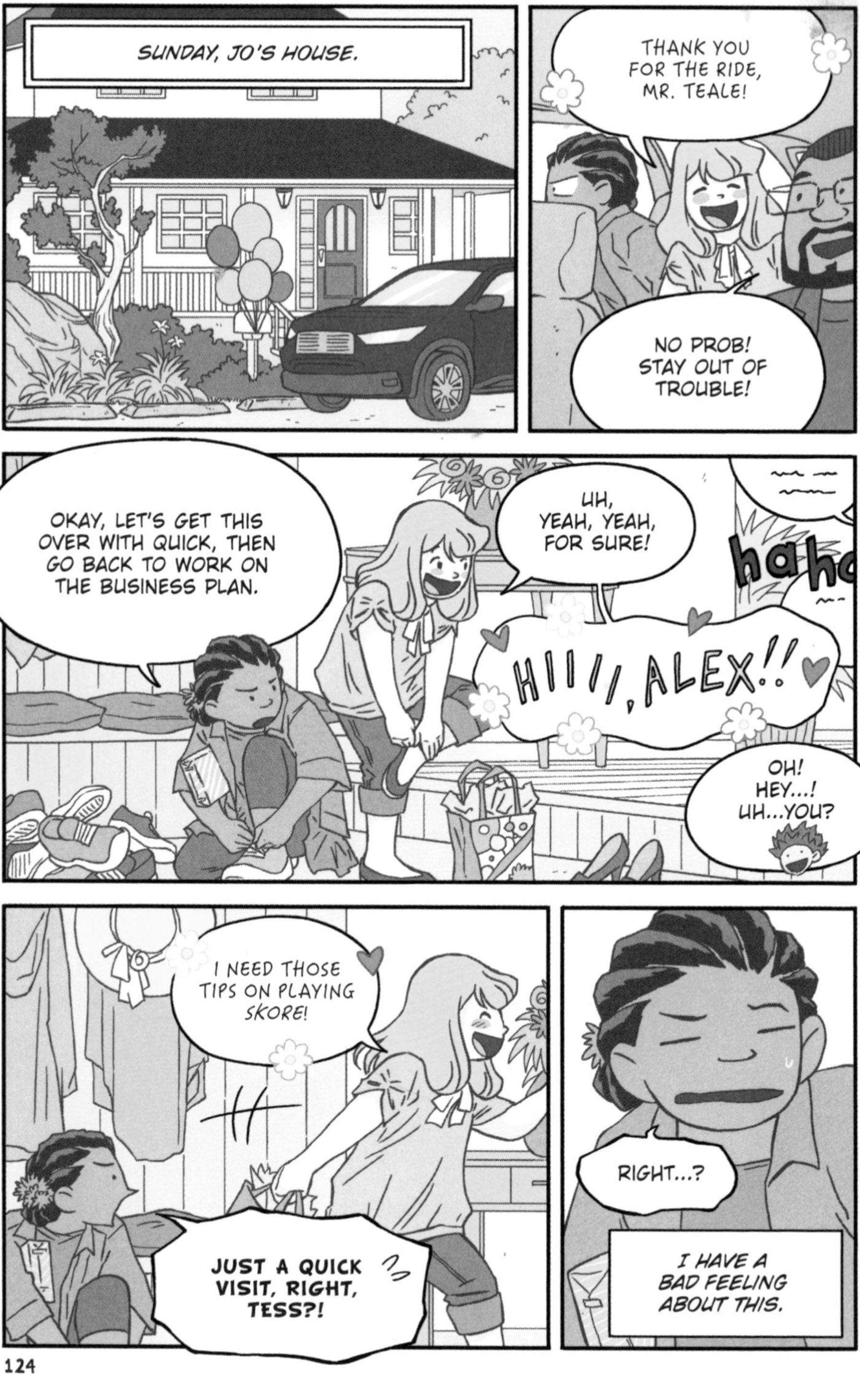
SUNDAY, JO'S HOUSE.
THANK YOU FOR THE RIDE, MR. TEALE!
NO PROB! STAY OUT OF TROUBLE!
OKAY, LET'S GET THIS OVER WITH QUICK, THEN GO BACK TO WORK ON THE BUSINESS PLAN.
UH, YEAH, YEAH, FOR SURE!
haha
HIIII, ALEX!!
OH! HEY...! UH...YOU?
I NEED THOSE TIPS ON PLAYING SKORE!
JUST A QUICK VISIT, RIGHT, TESS?!
RIGHT...?
I HAVE A BAD FEELING ABOUT THIS.

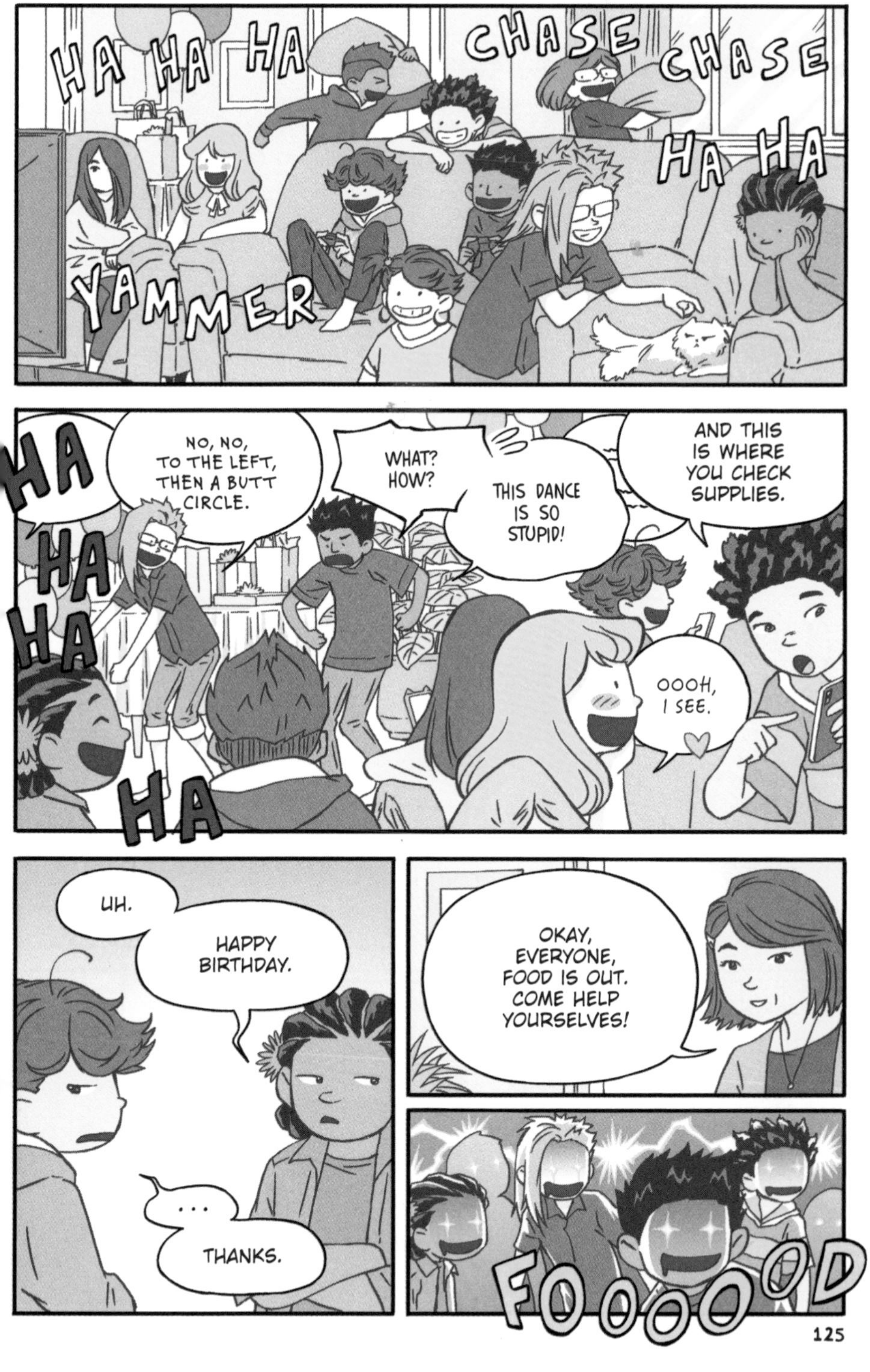
HA HA HA
CHASE
CHASE
HA HA
YAMMER
HA
HA
HA
NO, NO, TO THE LEFT, THEN A BUTT CIRCLE.
WHAT? HOW?
THIS DANCE IS SO STUPID!
AND THIS IS WHERE YOU CHECK SUPPLIES.
OOOH, I SEE.
HA
UH.
HAPPY BIRTHDAY.
...
THANKS.
OKAY, EVERYONE, FOOD IS OUT. COME HELP YOURSELVES!
FOOOOOOD

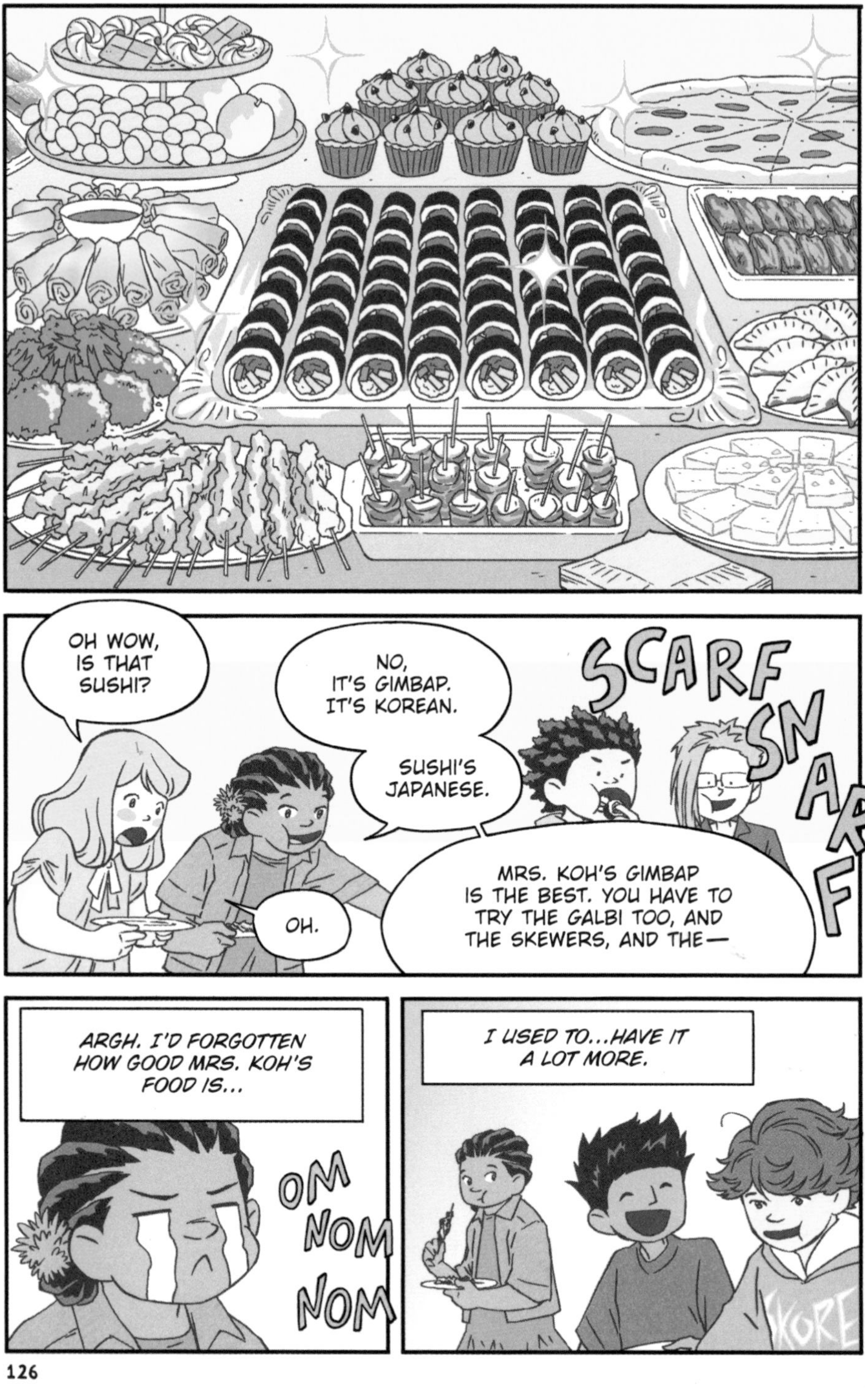
OH WOW, IS THAT SUSHI?
NO, IT'S GIMBAP. IT'S KOREAN.
SUSHI'S JAPANESE.
SCARF
SNARF
OH.
MRS. KOH'S GIMBAP IS THE BEST. YOU HAVE TO TRY THE GALBI TOO, AND THE SKEWERS, AND THE—
ARGH. I'D FORGOTTEN HOW GOOD MRS. KOH'S FOOD IS...
OM NOM NOM
I USED TO...HAVE IT A LOT MORE.
KORE

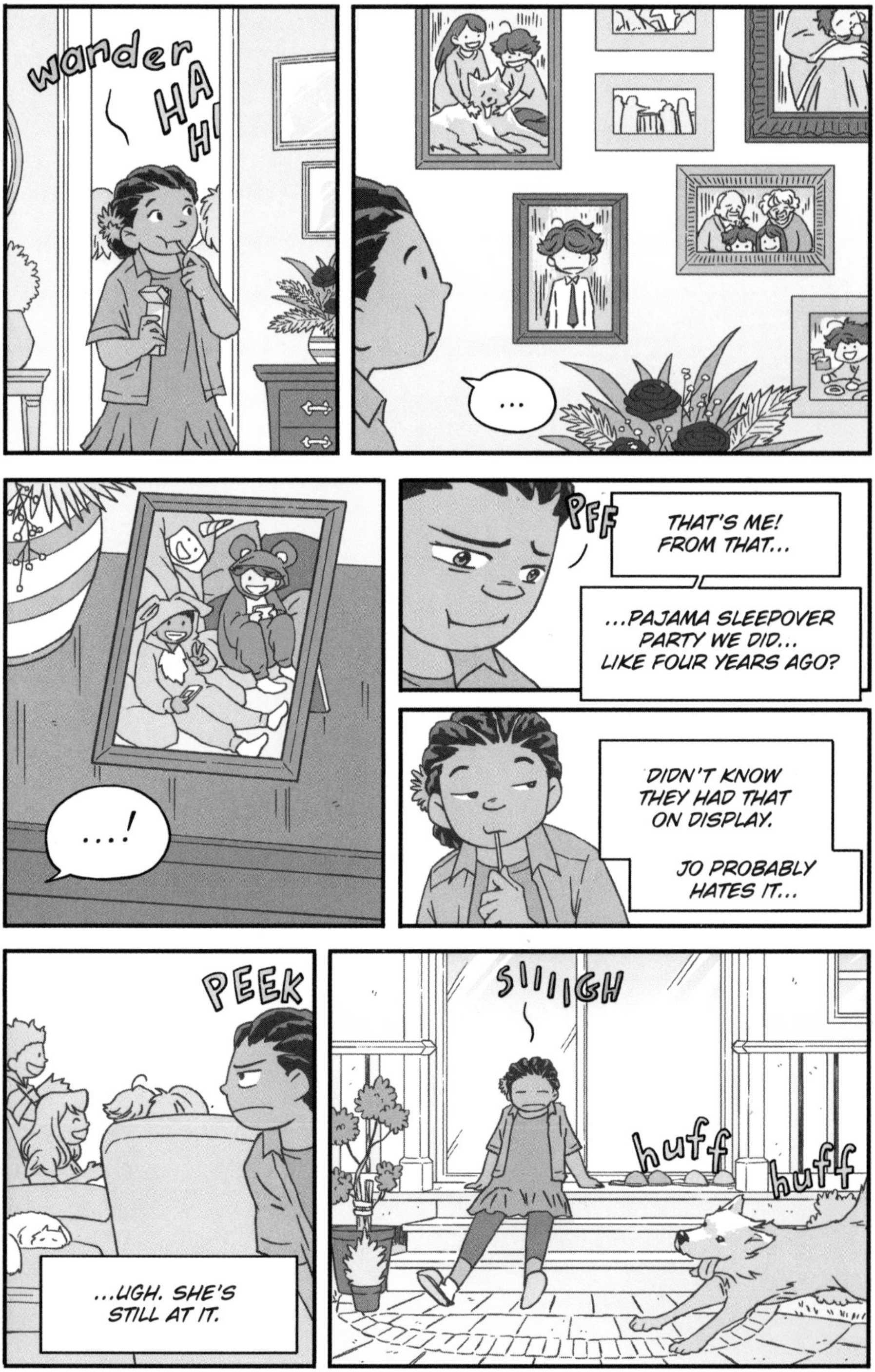
wander
HA
HI
...
...!
PFF
THAT'S ME! FROM THAT...
...PAJAMA SLEEPOVER PARTY WE DID... LIKE FOUR YEARS AGO?
DIDN'T KNOW THEY HAD THAT ON DISPLAY.
JO PROBABLY HATES IT...
PEEK
...UGH. SHE'S STILL AT IT.
SIIIIGH
huff
huff

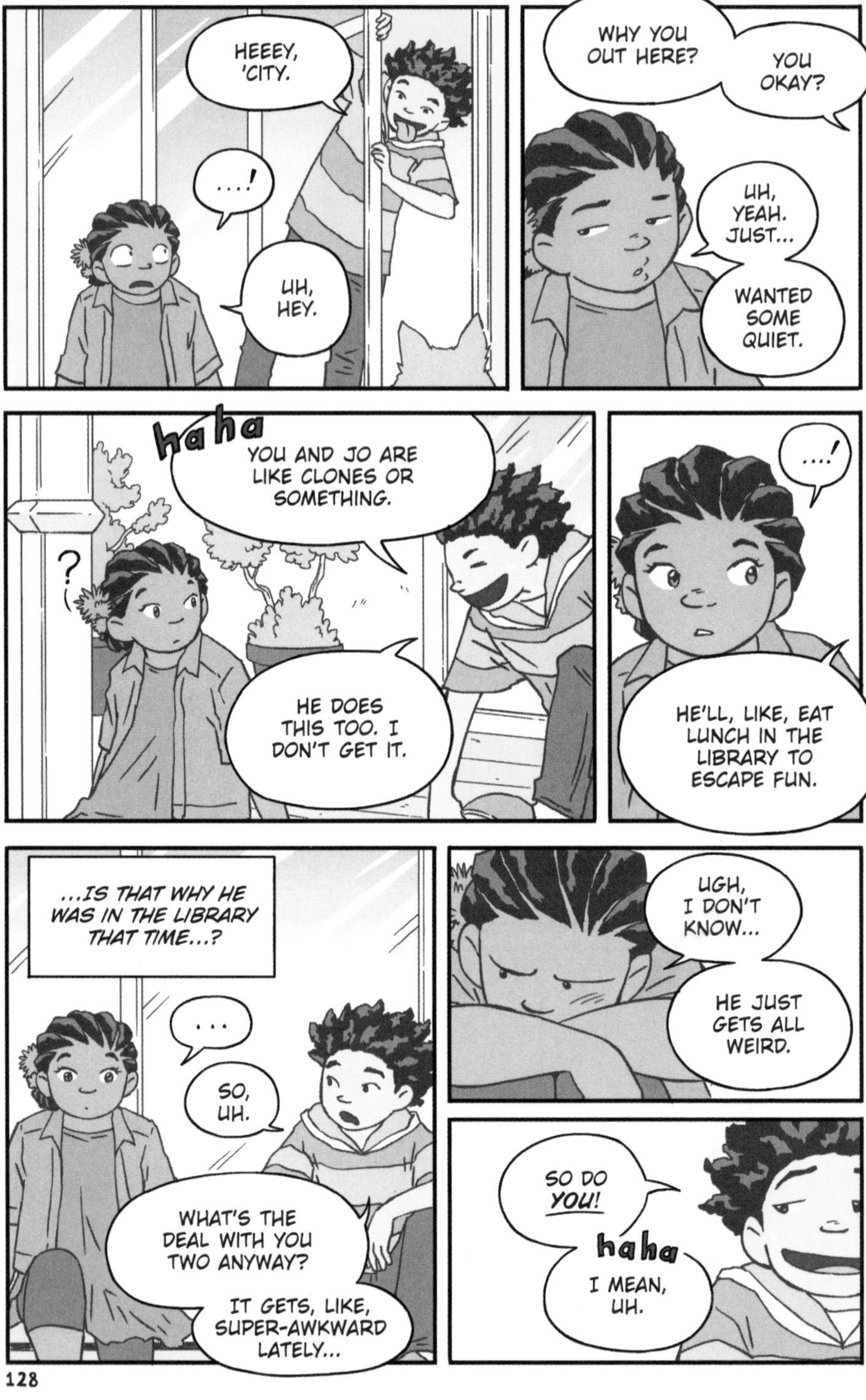
HEEEY, 'CITY.
....!
UH, HEY.
WHY YOU OUT HERE?
YOU OKAY?
UH, YEAH. JUST...
WANTED SOME QUIET.
haha
YOU AND JO ARE LIKE CLONES OR SOMETHING.
?
HE DOES THIS TOO. I DON'T GET IT.
....!
HE'LL, LIKE, EAT LUNCH IN THE LIBRARY TO ESCAPE FUN.
...IS THAT WHY HE WAS IN THE LIBRARY THAT TIME...?
...
SO, UH.
WHAT'S THE DEAL WITH YOU TWO ANYWAY?
IT GETS, LIKE, SUPER-AWKWARD LATELY...
UGH, I DON'T KNOW...
HE JUST GETS ALL WEIRD.
SO DO ***YOU!***
haha
I MEAN, UH.

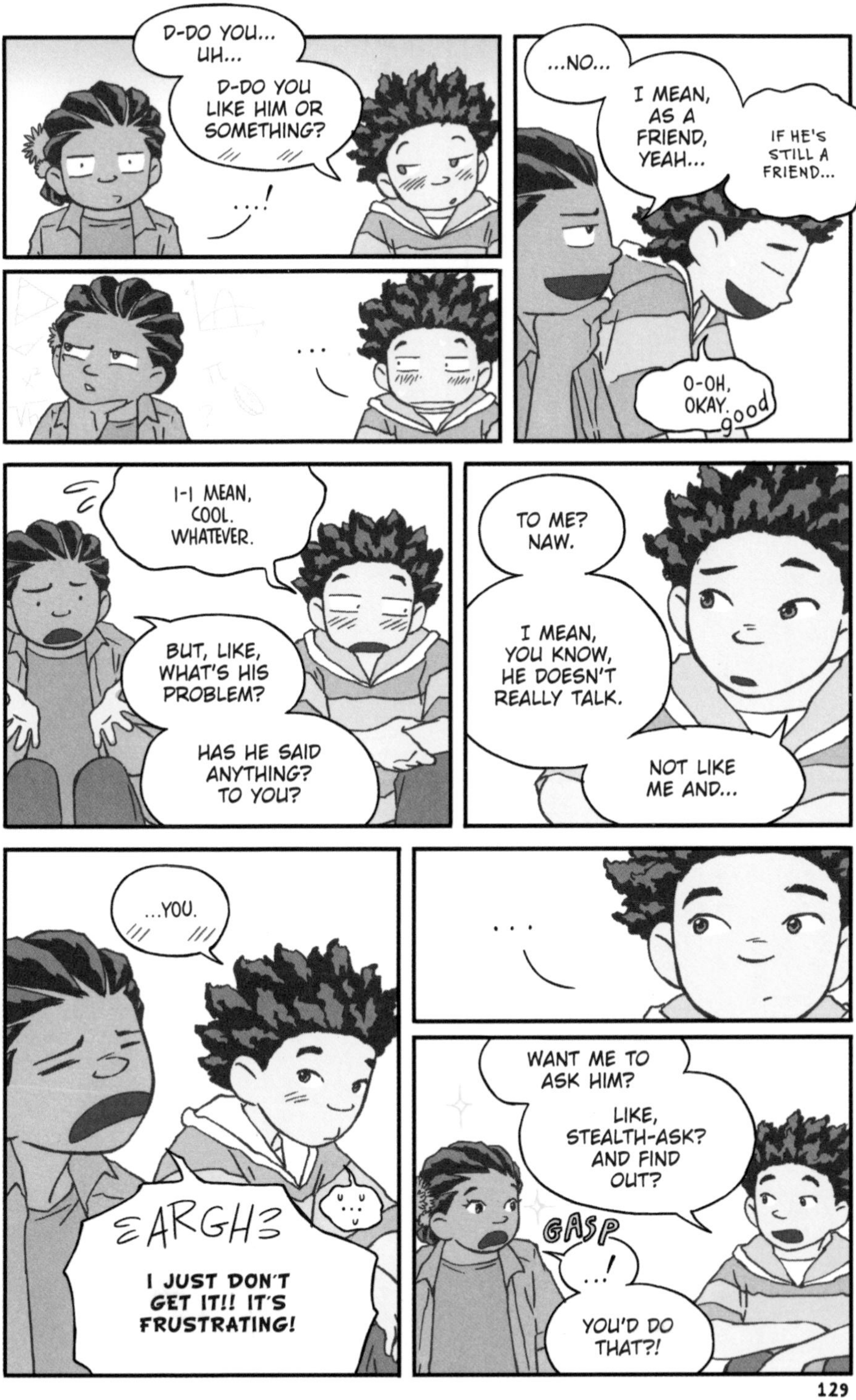
D-DO YOU... UH...
D-DO YOU LIKE HIM OR SOMETHING?
...!
...NO...
I MEAN, AS A FRIEND, YEAH...
IF HE'S STILL A FRIEND...
...
O-OH, OKAY.
good
I-I MEAN, COOL. WHATEVER.
BUT, LIKE, WHAT'S HIS PROBLEM?
HAS HE SAID ANYTHING? TO YOU?
TO ME? NAW.
I MEAN, YOU KNOW, HE DOESN'T REALLY TALK.
NOT LIKE ME AND...
...YOU.
...
ARGH
I JUST DON'T GET IT!! IT'S FRUSTRATING!
WANT ME TO ASK HIM?
LIKE, STEALTH-ASK? AND FIND OUT?
GASP
...!
YOU'D DO THAT?!

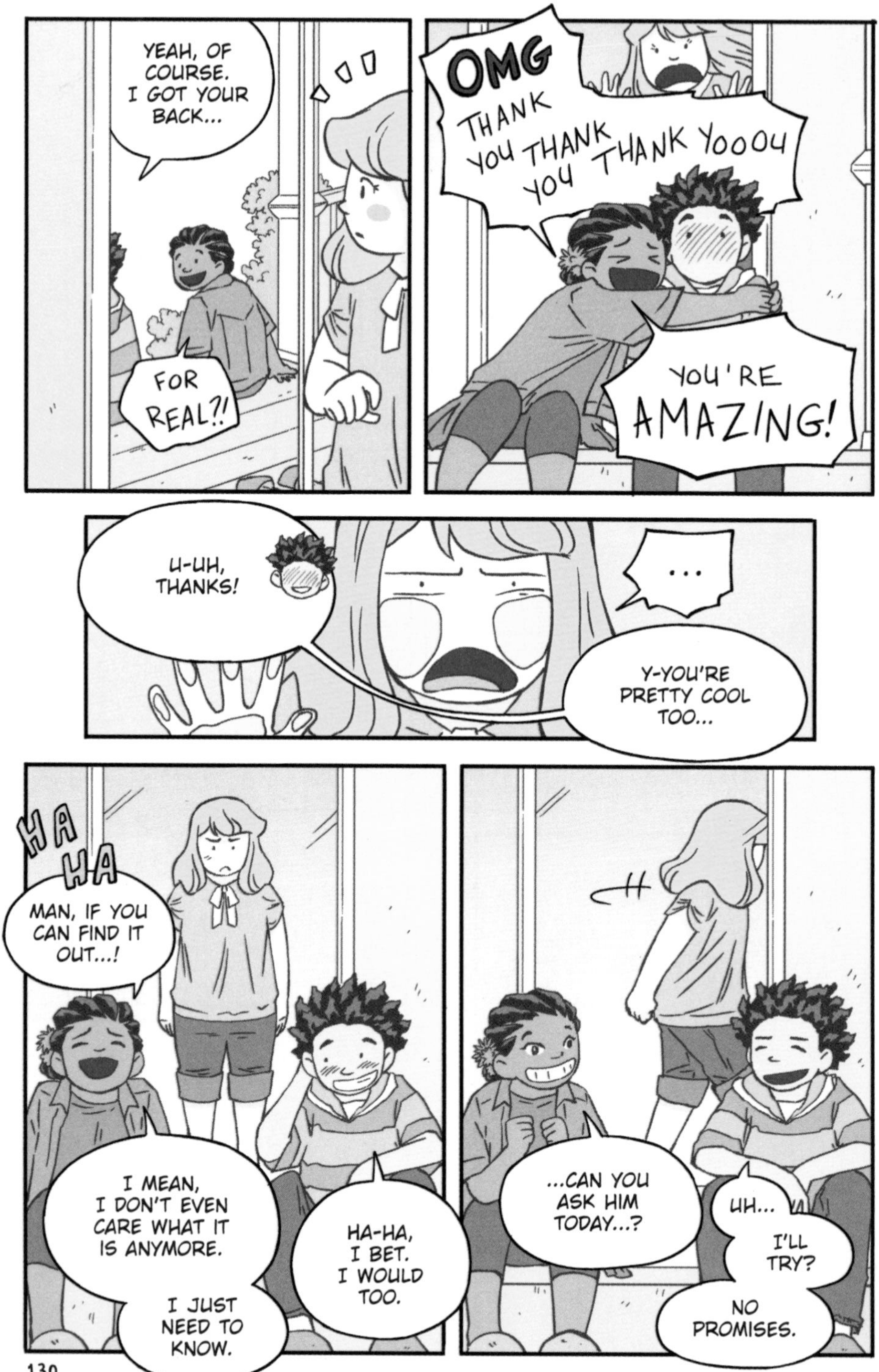
YEAH, OF COURSE. I GOT YOUR BACK...
FOR REAL?!
OMG
THANK YOU THANK YOU THANK YOU THANK YOOOU
YOU'RE AMAZING!
U-UH, THANKS!
...
Y-YOU'RE PRETTY COOL TOO...
HA HA
MAN, IF YOU CAN FIND IT OUT...!
I MEAN, I DON'T EVEN CARE WHAT IT IS ANYMORE.
I JUST NEED TO KNOW.
HA-HA, I BET. I WOULD TOO.
...CAN YOU ASK HIM TODAY...?
UH...
I'LL TRY?
NO PROMISES.

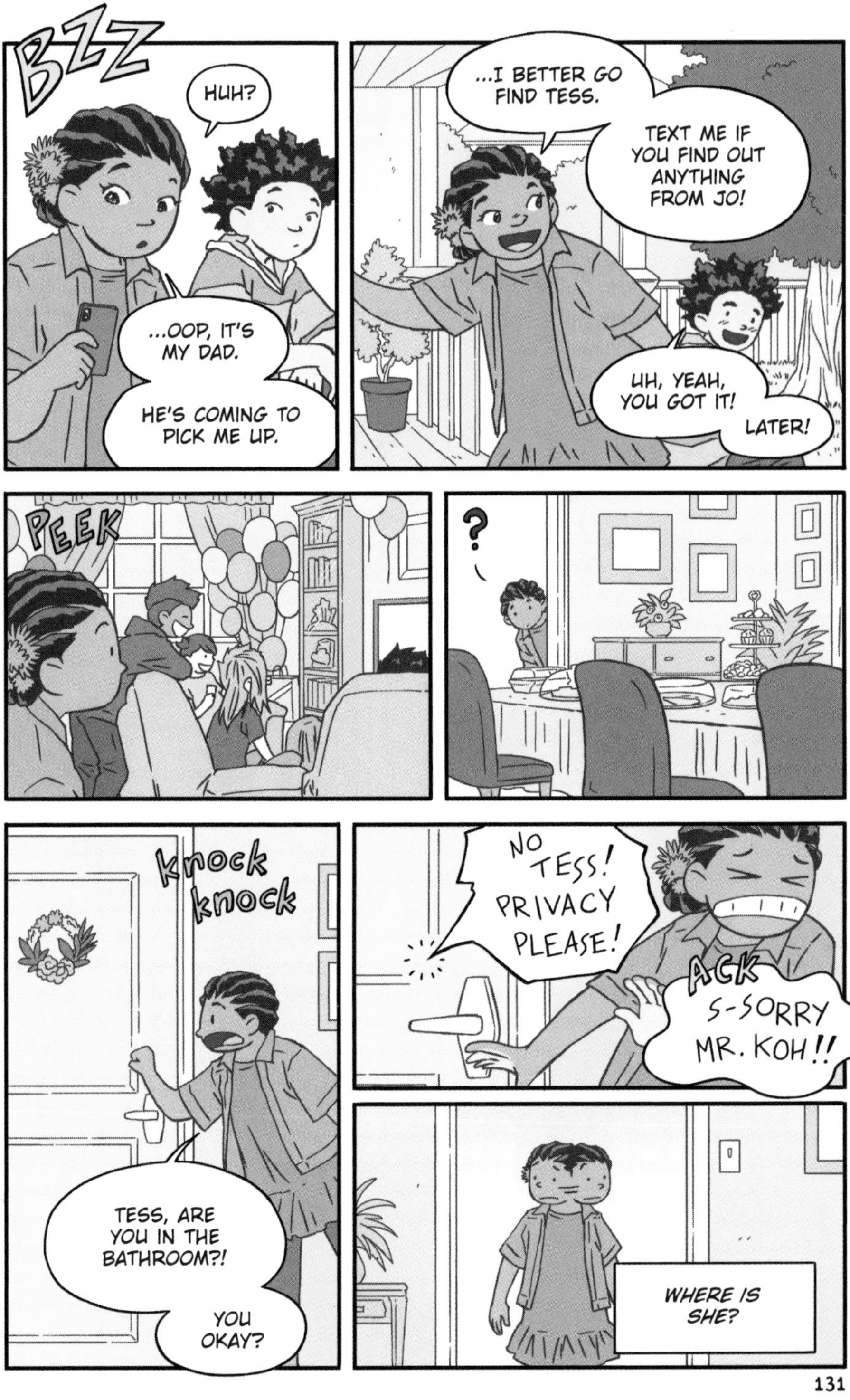
BZZ
HUH?
...OOP, IT'S MY DAD.
HE'S COMING TO PICK ME UP.
...I BETTER GO FIND TESS.
TEXT ME IF YOU FIND OUT ANYTHING FROM JO!
UH, YEAH, YOU GOT IT!
LATER!
PEEK
?
knock knock
TESS, ARE YOU IN THE BATHROOM?!
YOU OKAY?
NO TESS! PRIVACY PLEASE!
ACK
S-SORRY MR. KOH!!
WHERE IS SHE?

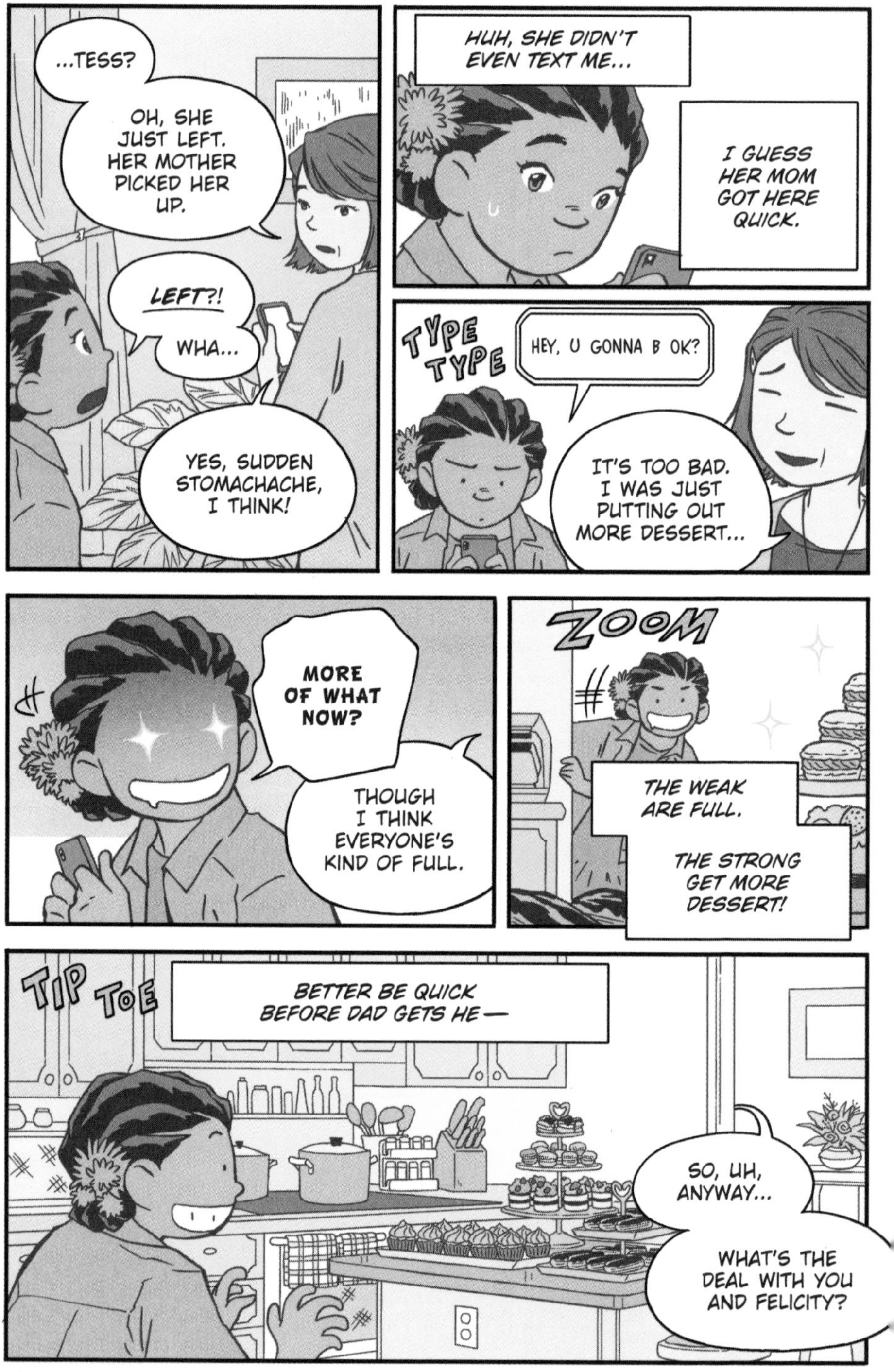
...TESS?
OH, SHE JUST LEFT. HER MOTHER PICKED HER UP.
LEFT?!
WHA...
YES, SUDDEN STOMACHACHE, I THINK!
HUH, SHE DIDN'T EVEN TEXT ME...
I GUESS HER MOM GOT HERE QUICK.
TYPE TYPE
HEY, U GONNA B OK?
IT'S TOO BAD. I WAS JUST PUTTING OUT MORE DESSERT...
MORE OF WHAT NOW?
THOUGH I THINK EVERYONE'S KIND OF FULL.
ZOOM
THE WEAK ARE FULL.
THE STRONG GET MORE DESSERT!
TIP TOE
BETTER BE QUICK BEFORE DAD GETS HE—
SO, UH, ANYWAY...
WHAT'S THE DEAL WITH YOU AND FELICITY?

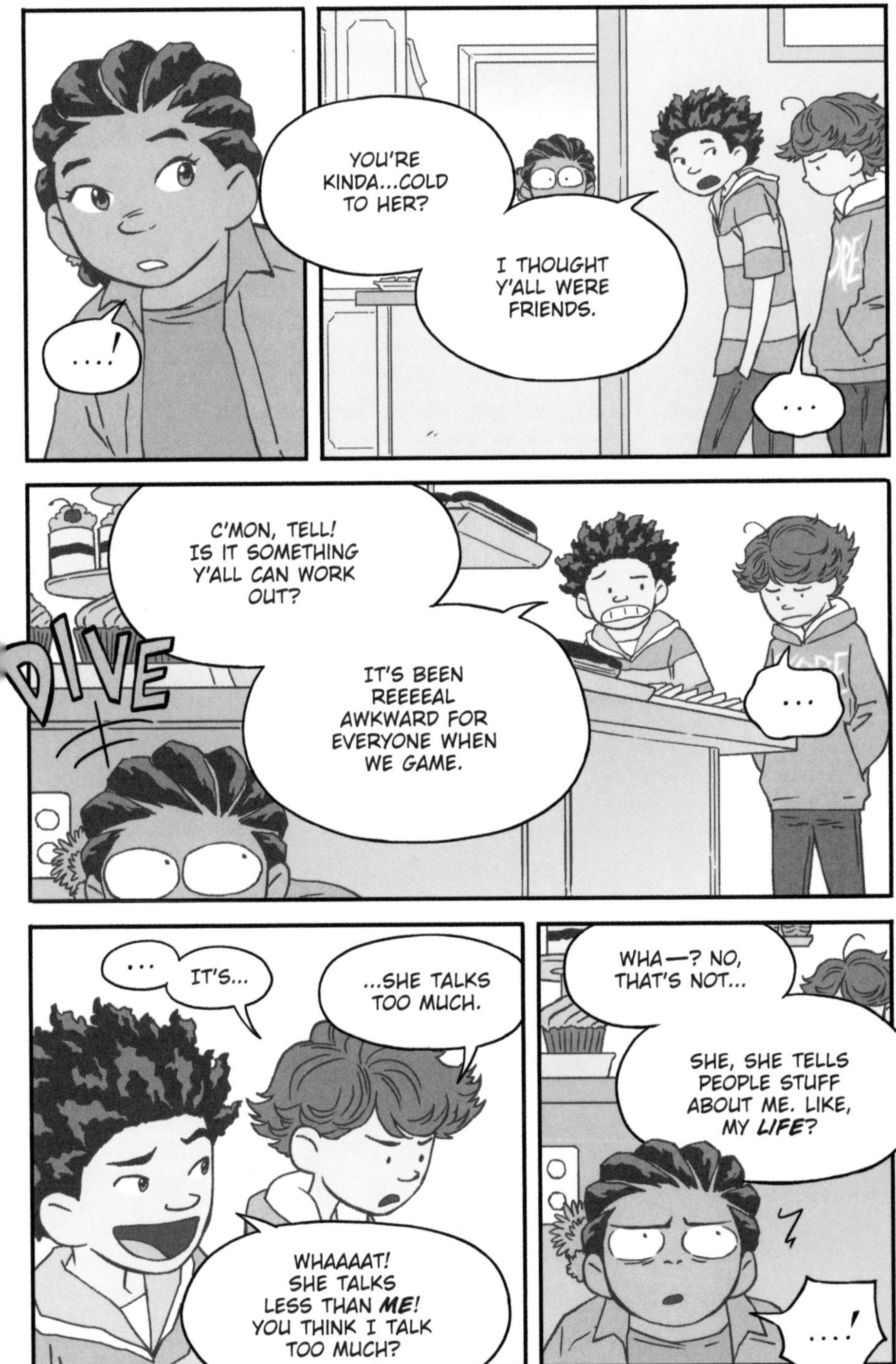

YOU'RE KINDA...COLD TO HER?
I THOUGHT Y'ALL WERE FRIENDS.
....!
...
C'MON, TELL! IS IT SOMETHING Y'ALL CAN WORK OUT?
IT'S BEEN REEEEAL AWKWARD FOR EVERYONE WHEN WE GAME.
DIVE
...
... IT'S...
...SHE TALKS TOO MUCH.
WHAAAAT! SHE TALKS LESS THAN **ME**! YOU THINK I TALK TOO MUCH?
WHA—? NO, THAT'S NOT...
SHE, SHE TELLS PEOPLE STUFF ABOUT ME. LIKE, MY ***LIFE***?
....!

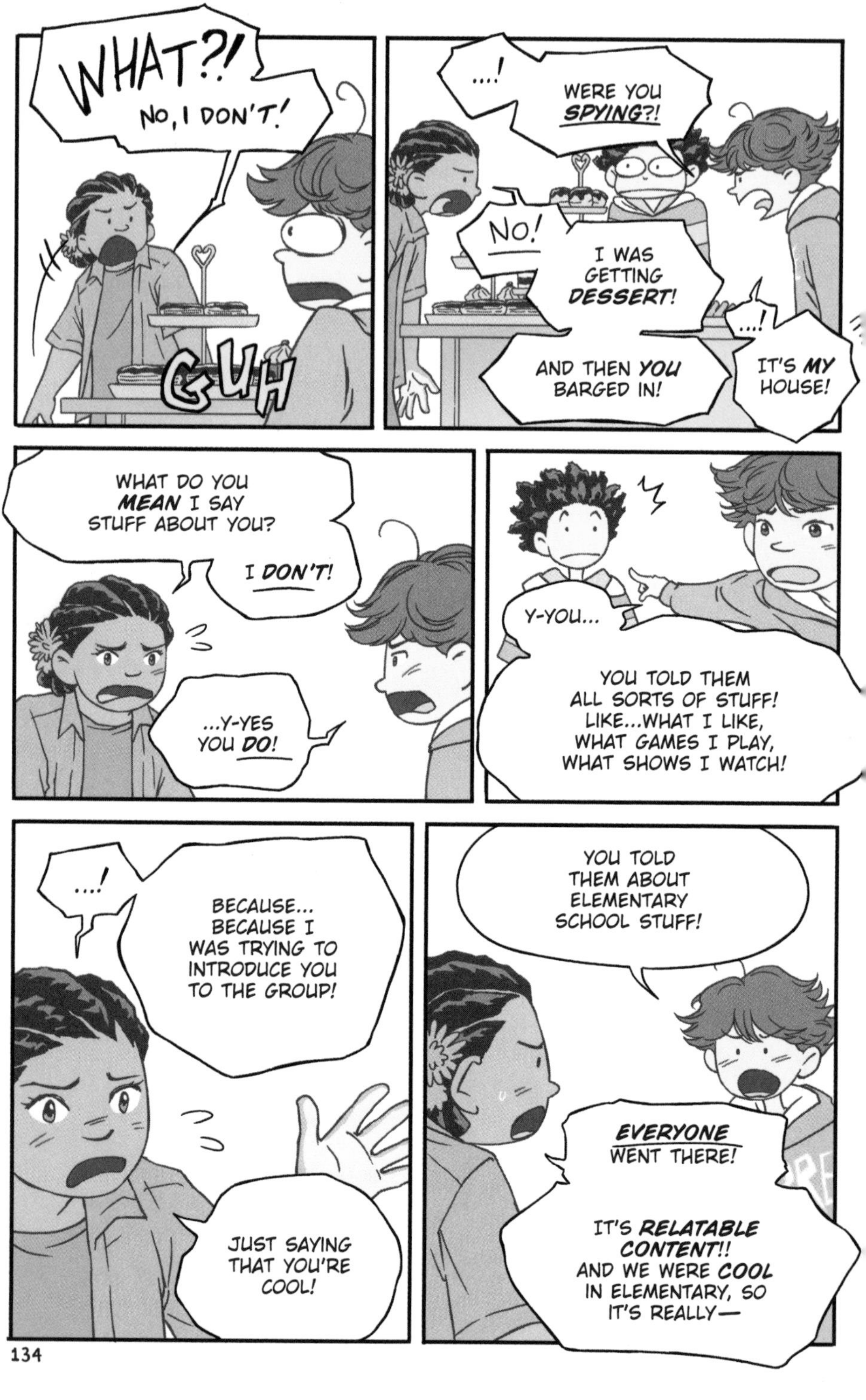
WHAT?!
NO, I DON'T!
GUH
...!
WERE YOU SPYING?!
NO!
I WAS GETTING DESSERT!
AND THEN YOU BARGED IN!
...!
IT'S MY HOUSE!
WHAT DO YOU MEAN I SAY STUFF ABOUT YOU?
I DON'T!
...Y-YES YOU DO!
Y-YOU...
YOU TOLD THEM ALL SORTS OF STUFF! LIKE...WHAT I LIKE, WHAT GAMES I PLAY, WHAT SHOWS I WATCH!
...!
BECAUSE... BECAUSE I WAS TRYING TO INTRODUCE YOU TO THE GROUP!
JUST SAYING THAT YOU'RE COOL!
YOU TOLD THEM ABOUT ELEMENTARY SCHOOL STUFF!
EVERYONE WENT THERE!
IT'S RELATABLE CONTENT!! AND WE WERE COOL IN ELEMENTARY, SO IT'S REALLY—

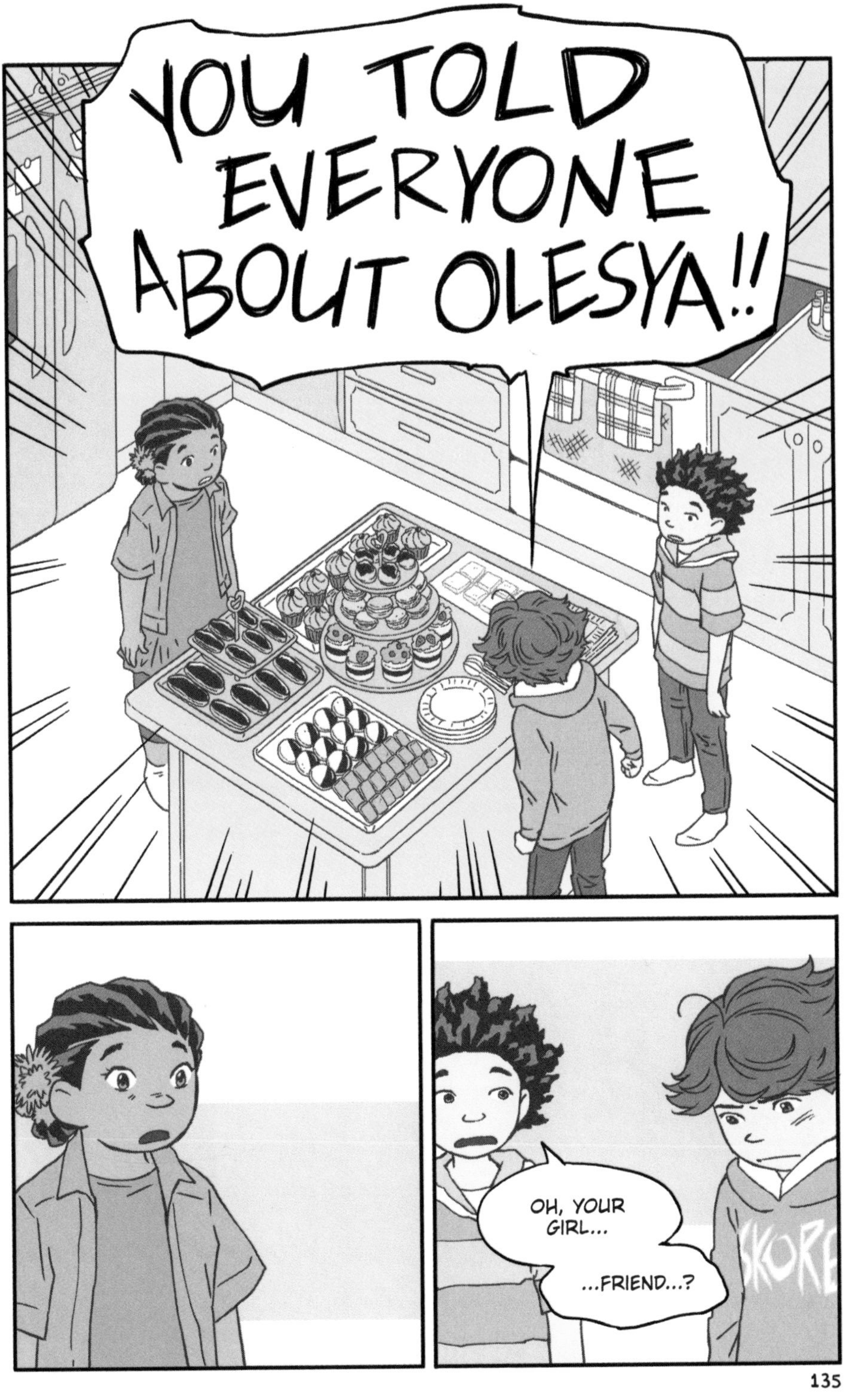
YOU TOLD EVERYONE ABOUT OLESYA!!
OH, YOUR GIRL...
...FRIEND...?
SKORE

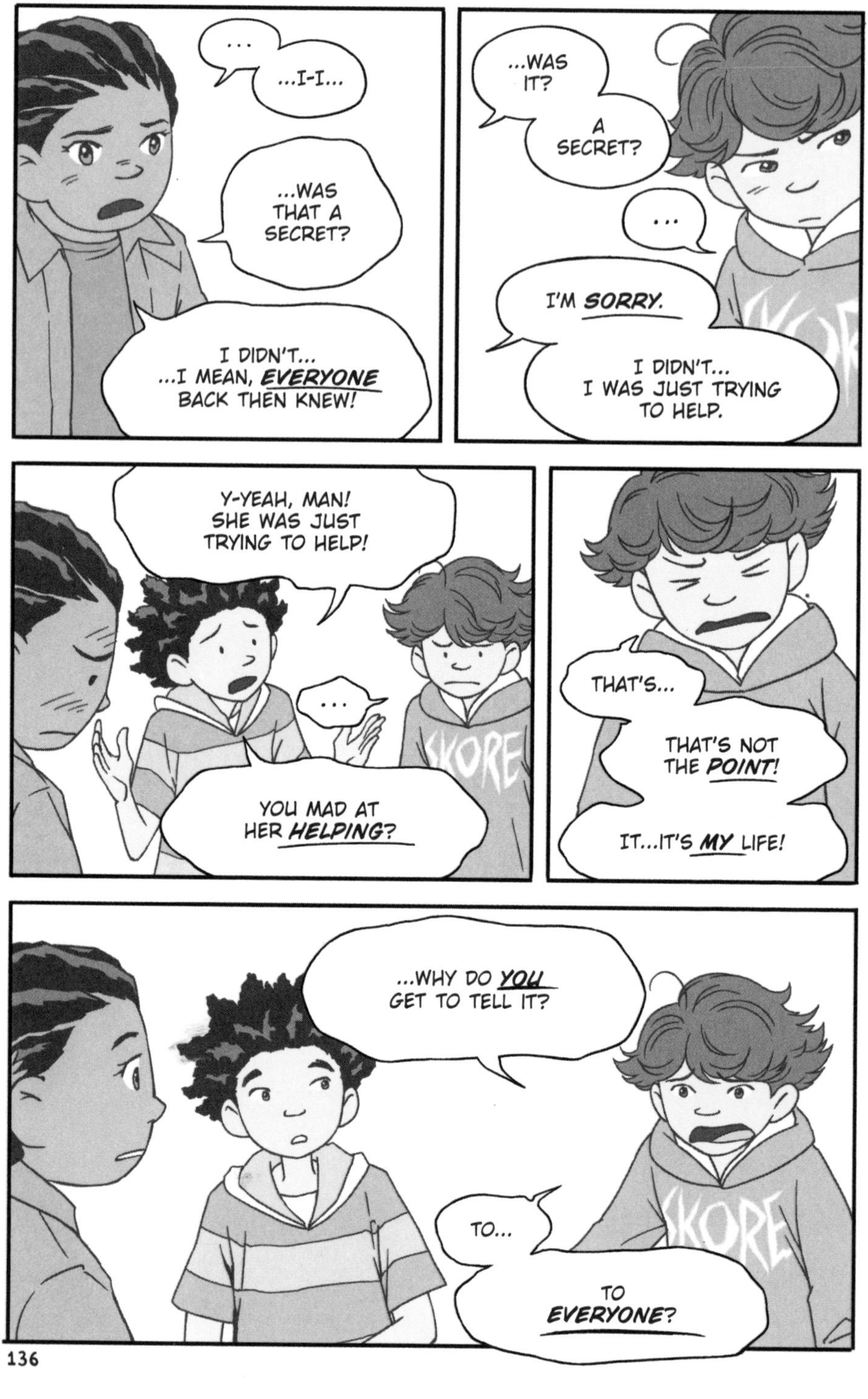
...
...I-I...
...WAS THAT A SECRET?
I DIDN'T... ...I MEAN, EVERYONE BACK THEN KNEW!
...WAS IT?
A SECRET?
...
I'M SORRY.
I DIDN'T... I WAS JUST TRYING TO HELP.
Y-YEAH, MAN! SHE WAS JUST TRYING TO HELP!
...
YOU MAD AT HER HELPING?
SKORE
THAT'S...
THAT'S NOT THE POINT!
IT...IT'S MY LIFE!
...WHY DO YOU GET TO TELL IT?
TO...
TO EVERYONE?
SKORE

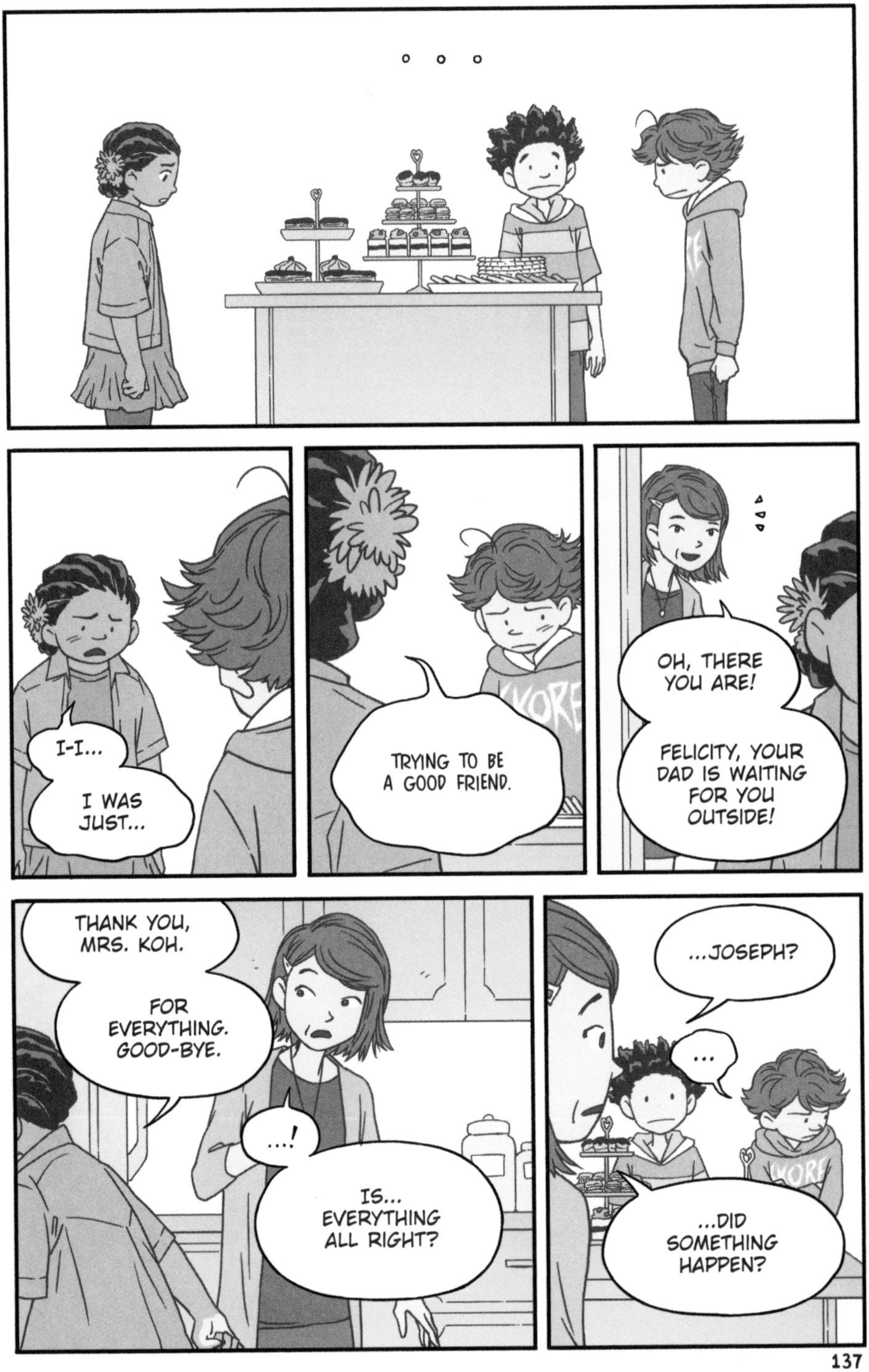

I-I...
I WAS JUST...
TRYING TO BE A GOOD FRIEND.
OH, THERE YOU ARE!
FELICITY, YOUR DAD IS WAITING FOR YOU OUTSIDE!
THANK YOU, MRS. KOH.
FOR EVERYTHING. GOOD-BYE.
...!
IS... EVERYTHING ALL RIGHT?
...JOSEPH?
...
...DID SOMETHING HAPPEN?

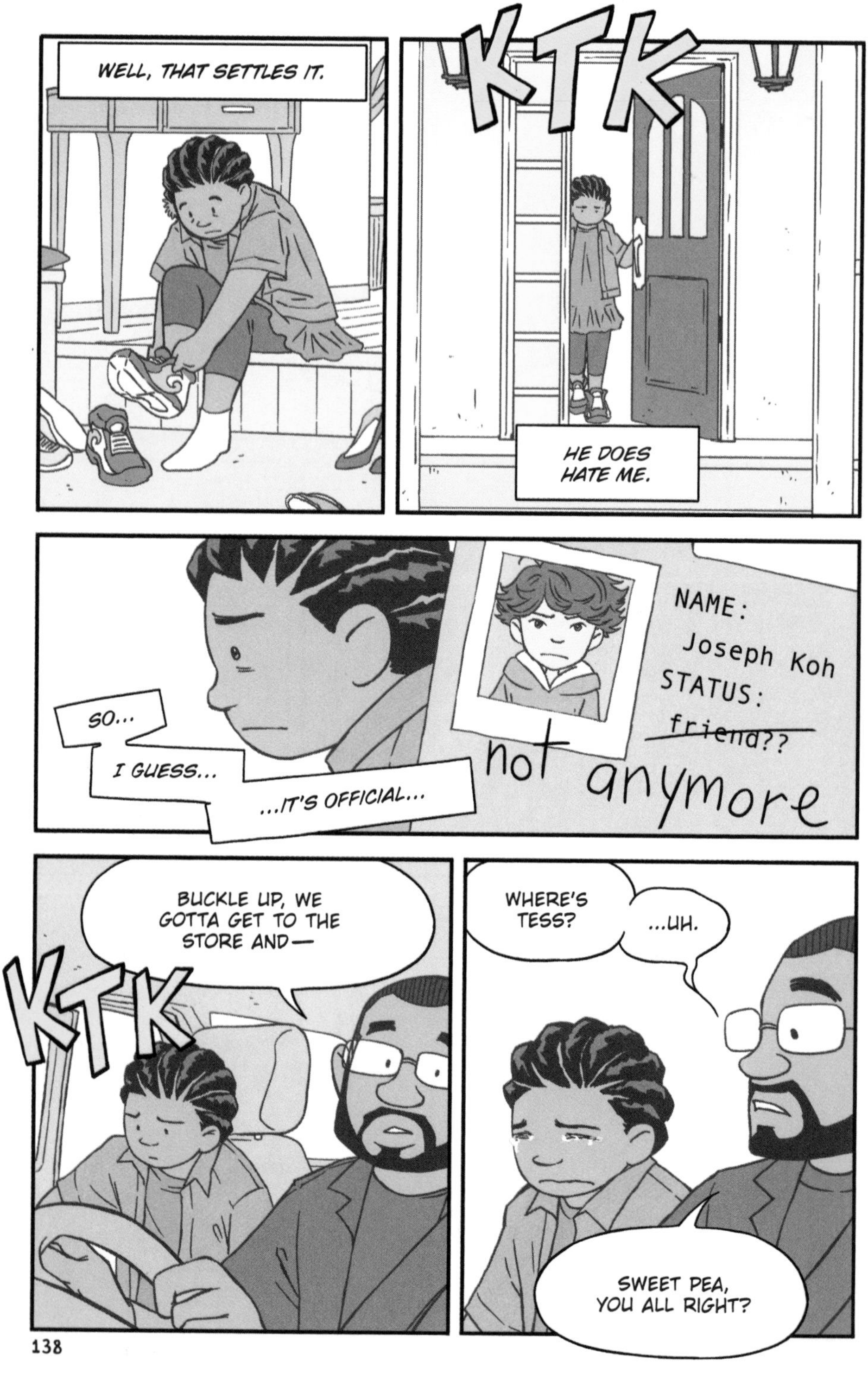
WELL, THAT SETTLES IT.
KTK
HE DOES HATE ME.
NAME:
Joseph Koh
STATUS:
friend??
not anymore
SO...
I GUESS...
...IT'S OFFICIAL...
BUCKLE UP, WE GOTTA GET TO THE STORE AND—
KTK
WHERE'S TESS?
...UH.
SWEET PEA, YOU ALL RIGHT?

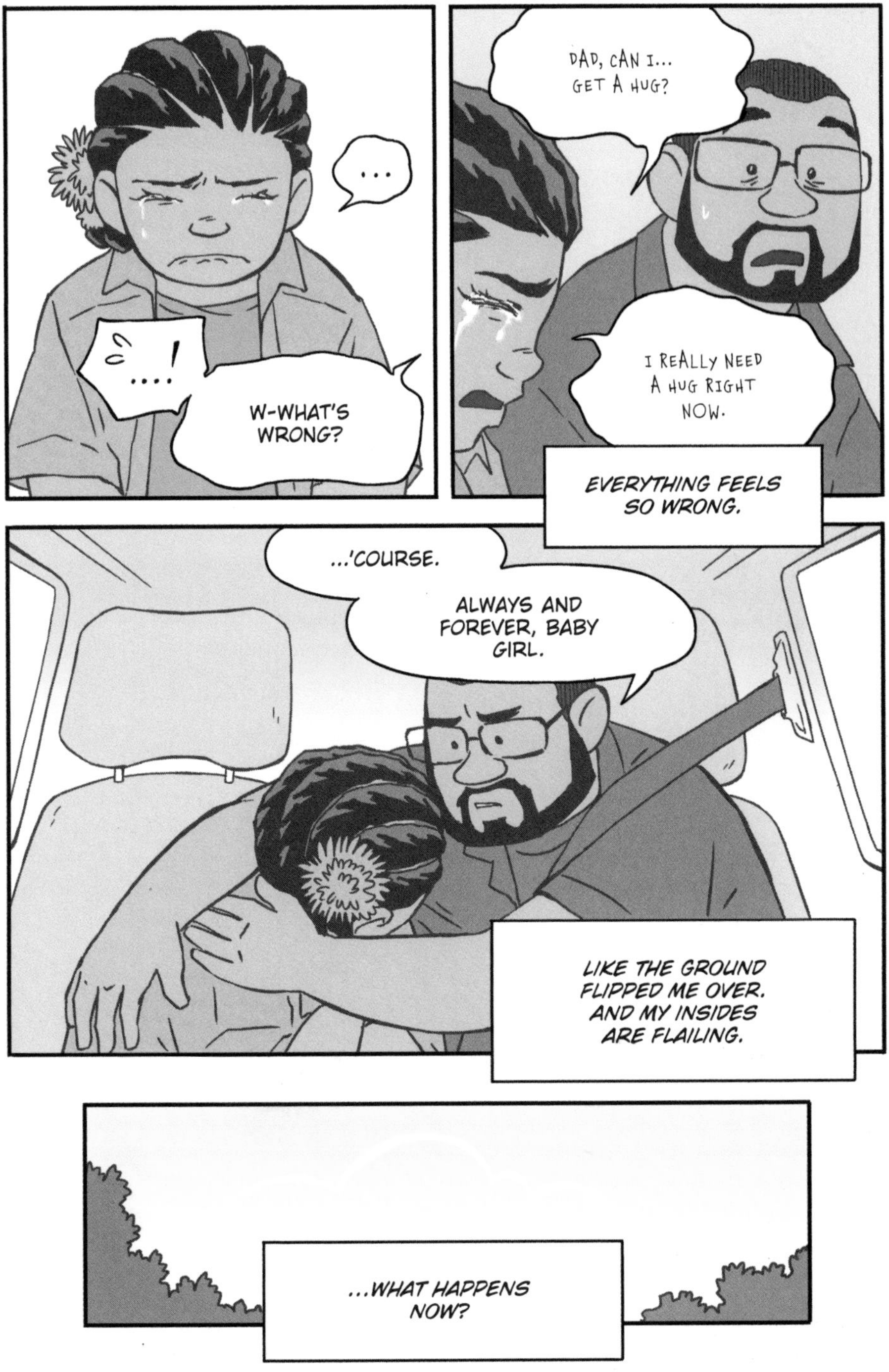
...
...!
W-WHAT'S WRONG?
DAD, CAN I... GET A HUG?
I REALLY NEED A HUG RIGHT NOW.
EVERYTHING FEELS SO WRONG.
...'COURSE.
ALWAYS AND FOREVER, BABY GIRL.
LIKE THE GROUND FLIPPED ME OVER. AND MY INSIDES ARE FLAILING.
...WHAT HAPPENS NOW?

CHAPTER 6

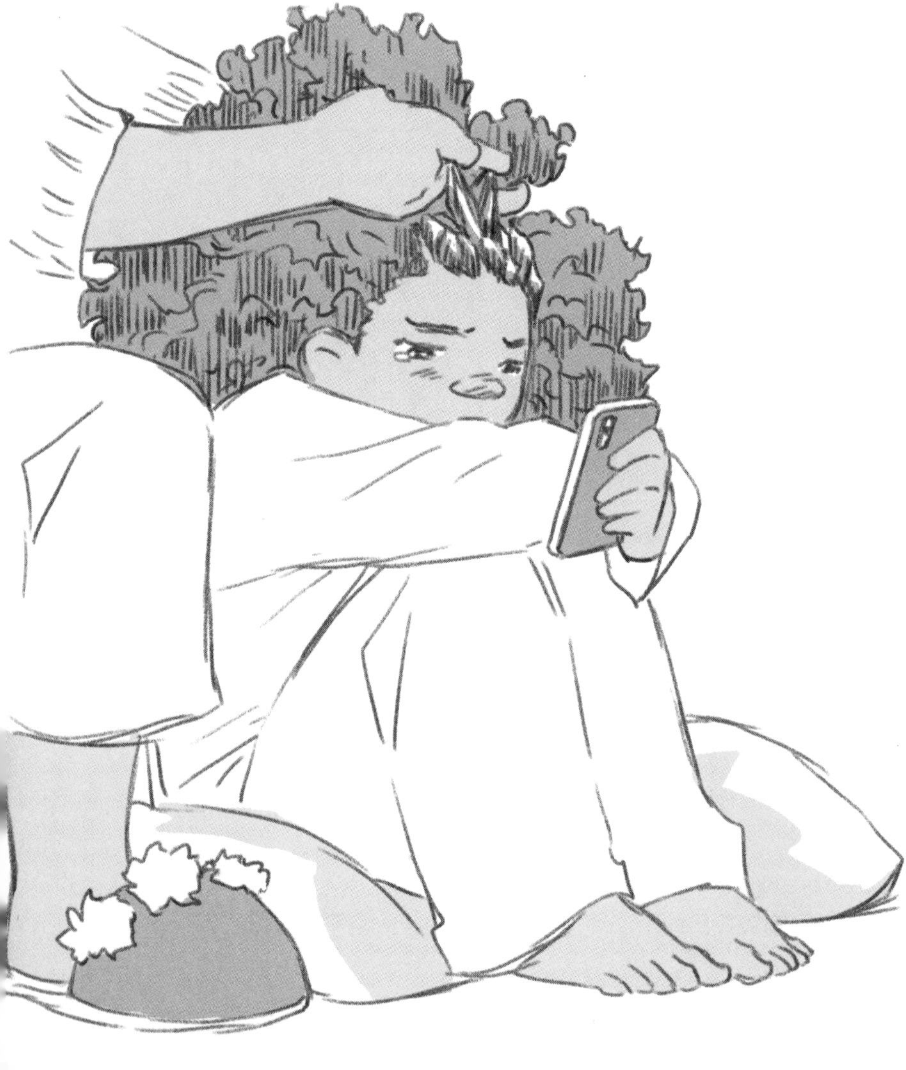

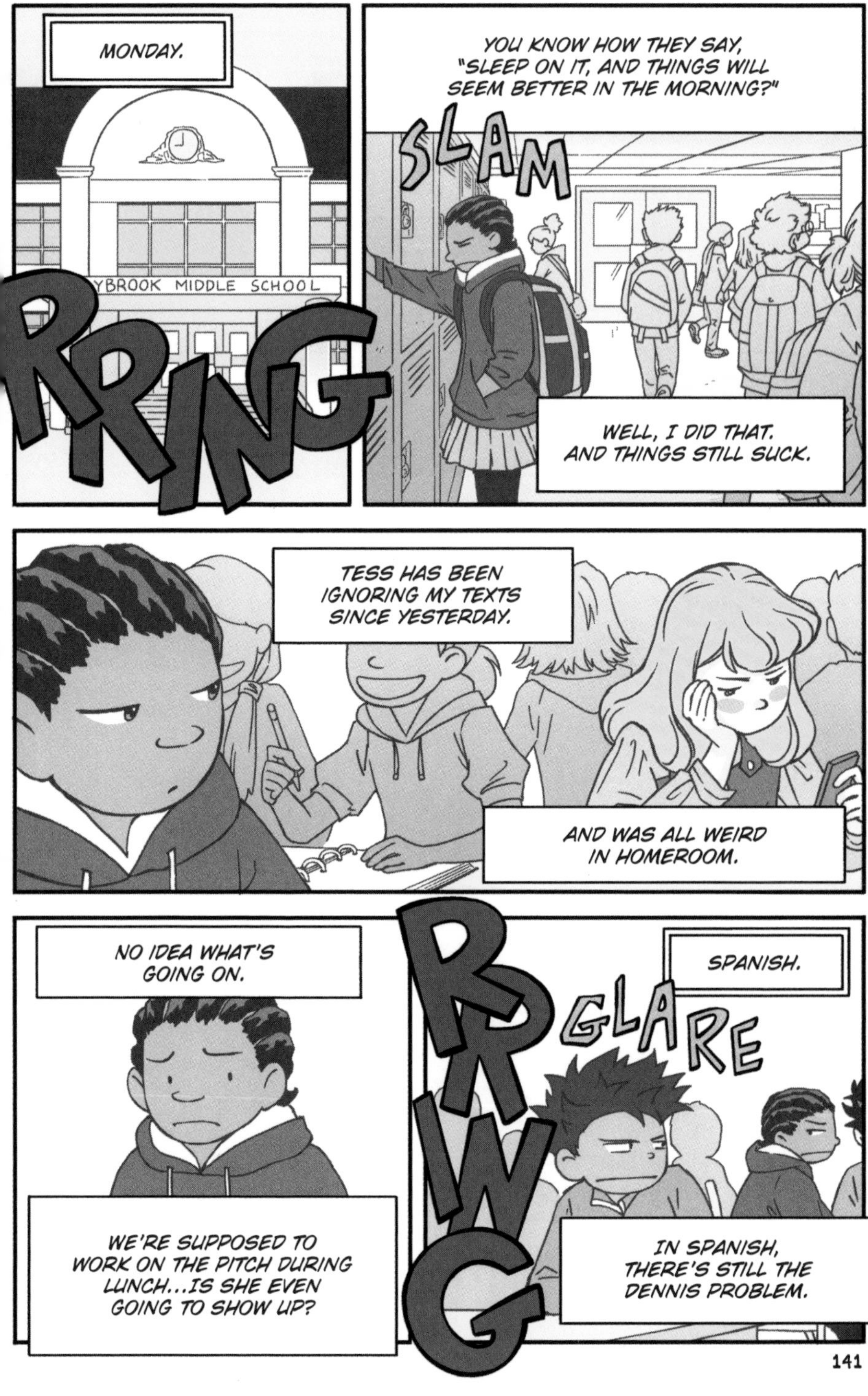
MONDAY.
YBROOK MIDDLE SCHOOL
RRING
YOU KNOW HOW THEY SAY, "SLEEP ON IT, AND THINGS WILL SEEM BETTER IN THE MORNING?"
SLAM
WELL, I DID THAT. AND THINGS STILL SUCK.
TESS HAS BEEN IGNORING MY TEXTS SINCE YESTERDAY.
AND WAS ALL WEIRD IN HOMEROOM.
NO IDEA WHAT'S GOING ON.
WE'RE SUPPOSED TO WORK ON THE PITCH DURING LUNCH...IS SHE EVEN GOING TO SHOW UP?
RRIWG
SPANISH.
GLARE
IN SPANISH, THERE'S STILL THE DENNIS PROBLEM.

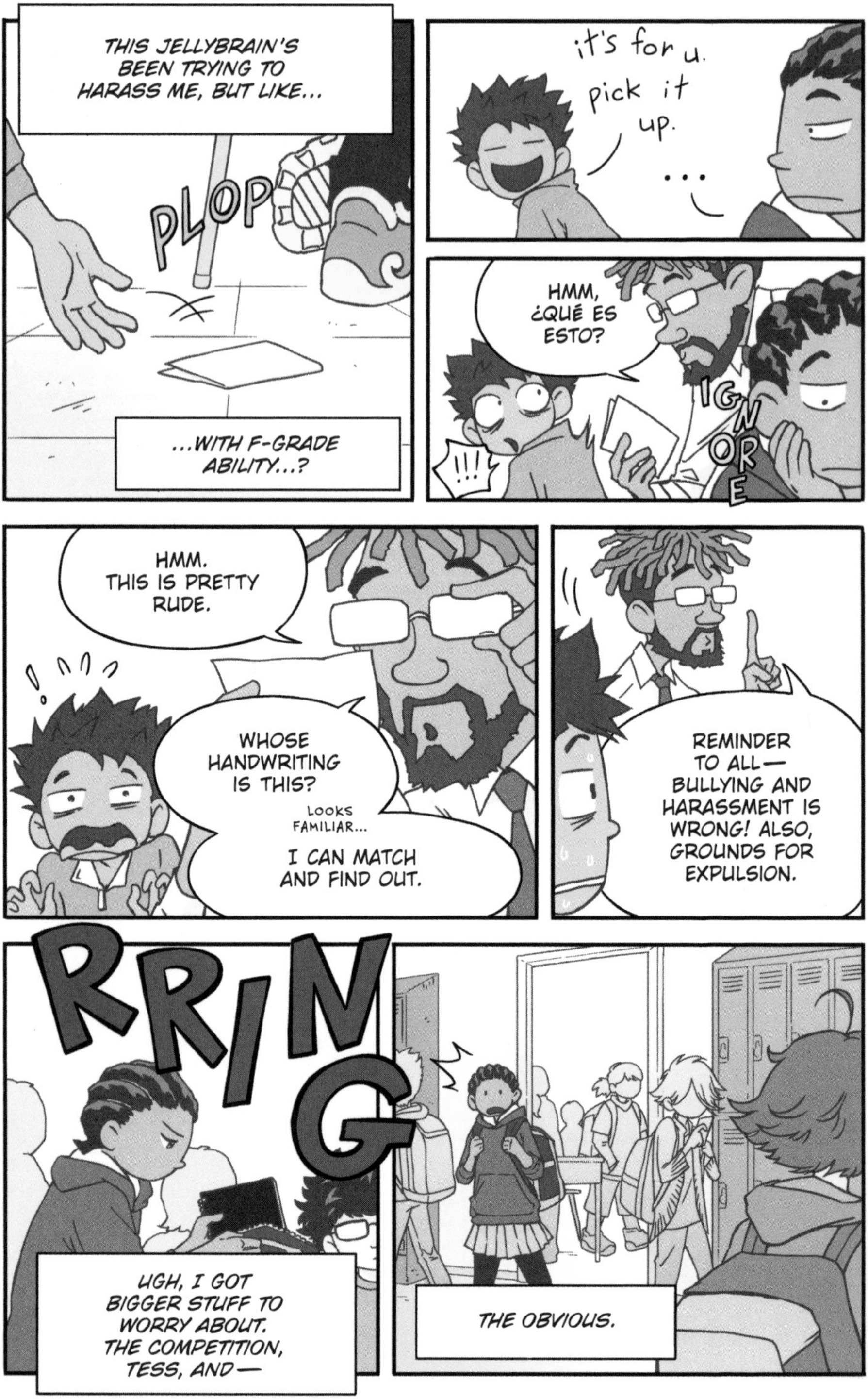
THIS JELLYBRAIN'S BEEN TRYING TO HARASS ME, BUT LIKE...
PLOP
...WITH F-GRADE ABILITY...?
it's for u. pick it up.
...
HMM, ¿QUÉ ES ESTO?
!!!
IGNORE
HMM. THIS IS PRETTY RUDE.
WHOSE HANDWRITING IS THIS?
LOOKS FAMILIAR...
I CAN MATCH AND FIND OUT.
REMINDER TO ALL— BULLYING AND HARASSMENT IS WRONG! ALSO, GROUNDS FOR EXPULSION.
RRING
UGH, I GOT BIGGER STUFF TO WORRY ABOUT. THE COMPETITION, TESS, AND—
THE OBVIOUS.

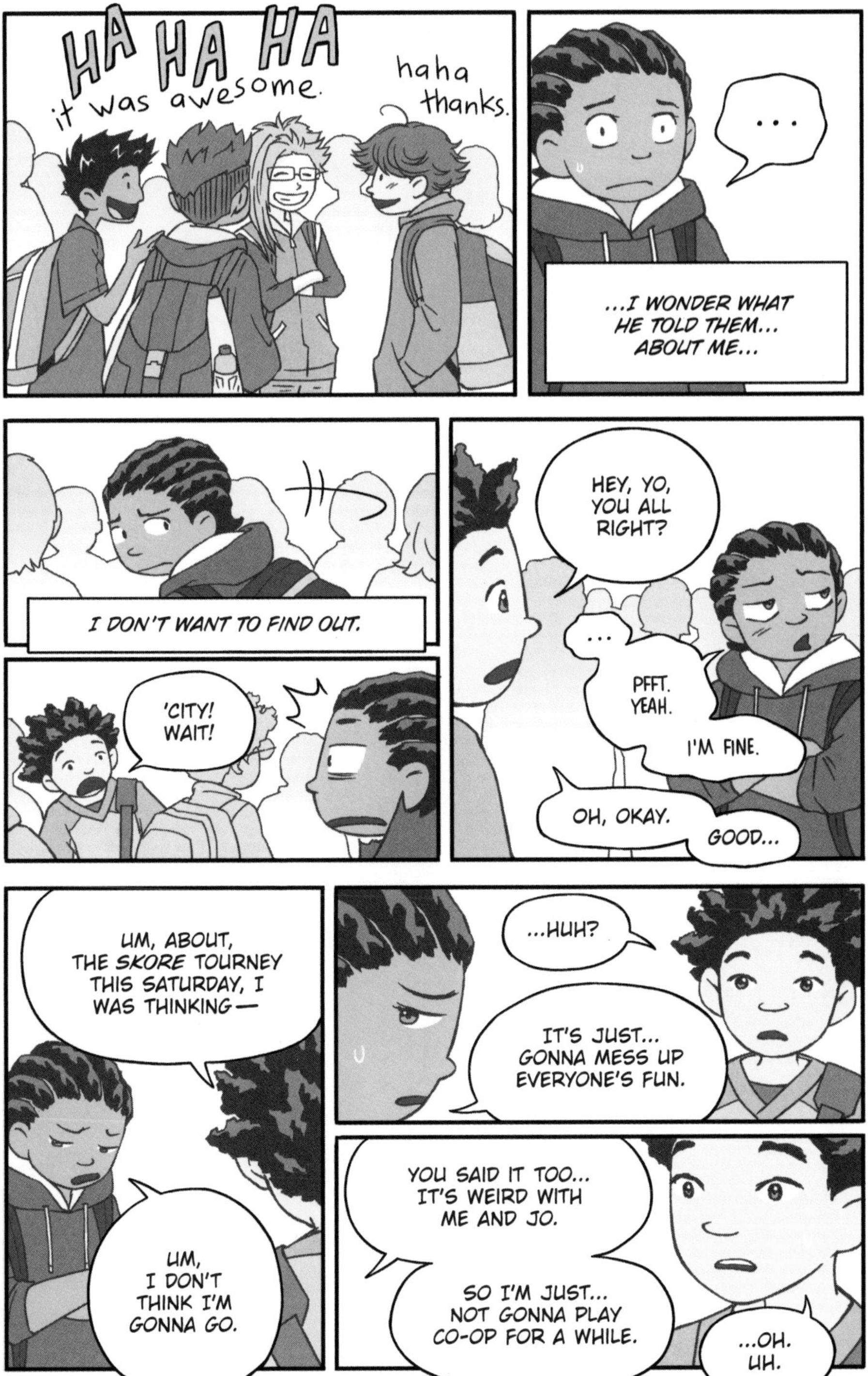
HA HA HA
it was awesome.
haha thanks.
...
...I WONDER WHAT HE TOLD THEM... ABOUT ME...
I DON'T WANT TO FIND OUT.
'CITY! WAIT!
HEY, YO, YOU ALL RIGHT?
...
PFFT. YEAH.
I'M FINE.
OH, OKAY.
GOOD...
UM, ABOUT, THE SKORE TOURNEY THIS SATURDAY, I WAS THINKING—
UM, I DON'T THINK I'M GONNA GO.
...HUH?
IT'S JUST... GONNA MESS UP EVERYONE'S FUN.
YOU SAID IT TOO... IT'S WEIRD WITH ME AND JO.
SO I'M JUST... NOT GONNA PLAY CO-OP FOR A WHILE.
...OH. UH.

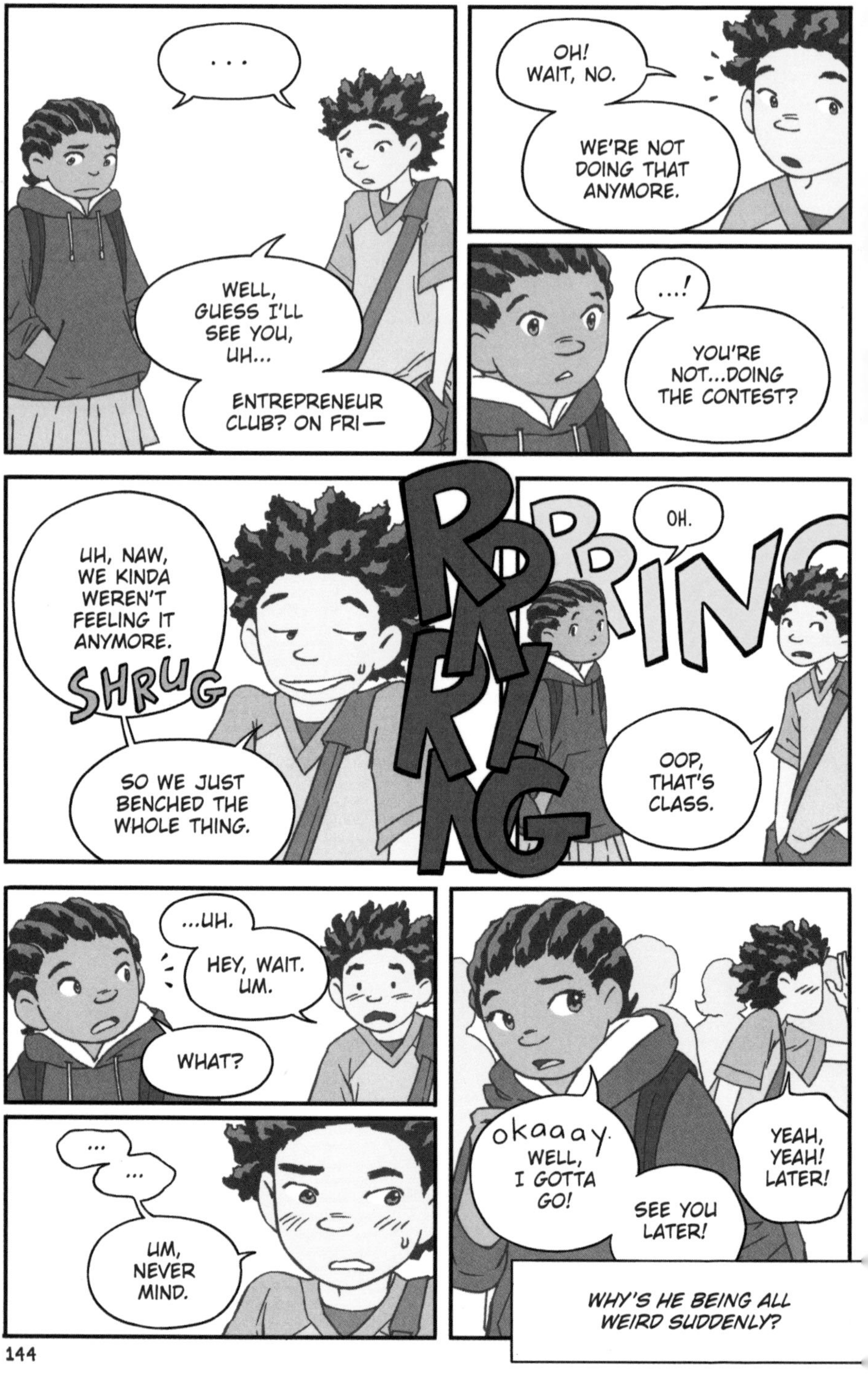
. . .
WELL, GUESS I'LL SEE YOU, UH...
ENTREPRENEUR CLUB? ON FRI—
OH! WAIT, NO.
WE'RE NOT DOING THAT ANYMORE.
....!
YOU'RE NOT...DOING THE CONTEST?
UH, NAW, WE KINDA WEREN'T FEELING IT ANYMORE.
SHRUG
SO WE JUST BENCHED THE WHOLE THING.
RRRRRING
OH.
OOP, THAT'S CLASS.
...UH.
HEY, WAIT. UM.
WHAT?
...
...
UM, NEVER MIND.
okaaay.
WELL, I GOTTA GO!
SEE YOU LATER!
YEAH, YEAH! LATER!
WHY'S HE BEING ALL WEIRD SUDDENLY?

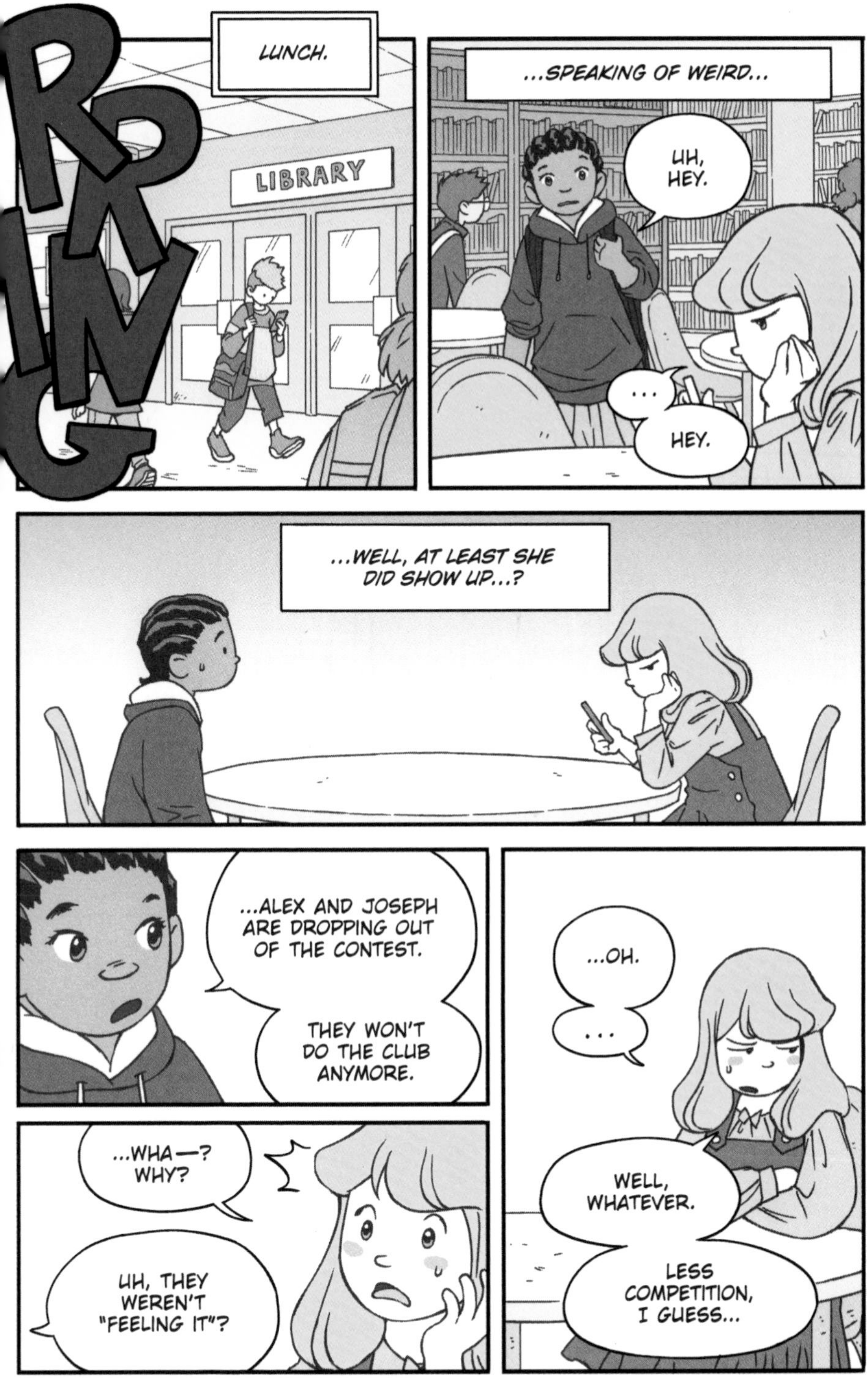
RRRING
LUNCH.
...SPEAKING OF WEIRD...
LIBRARY
UH, HEY.
...
HEY.
...WELL, AT LEAST SHE DID SHOW UP...?
...ALEX AND JOSEPH ARE DROPPING OUT OF THE CONTEST.
THEY WON'T DO THE CLUB ANYMORE.
...WHA—? WHY?
UH, THEY WEREN'T "FEELING IT"?
...OH.
...
WELL, WHATEVER.
LESS COMPETITION, I GUESS...

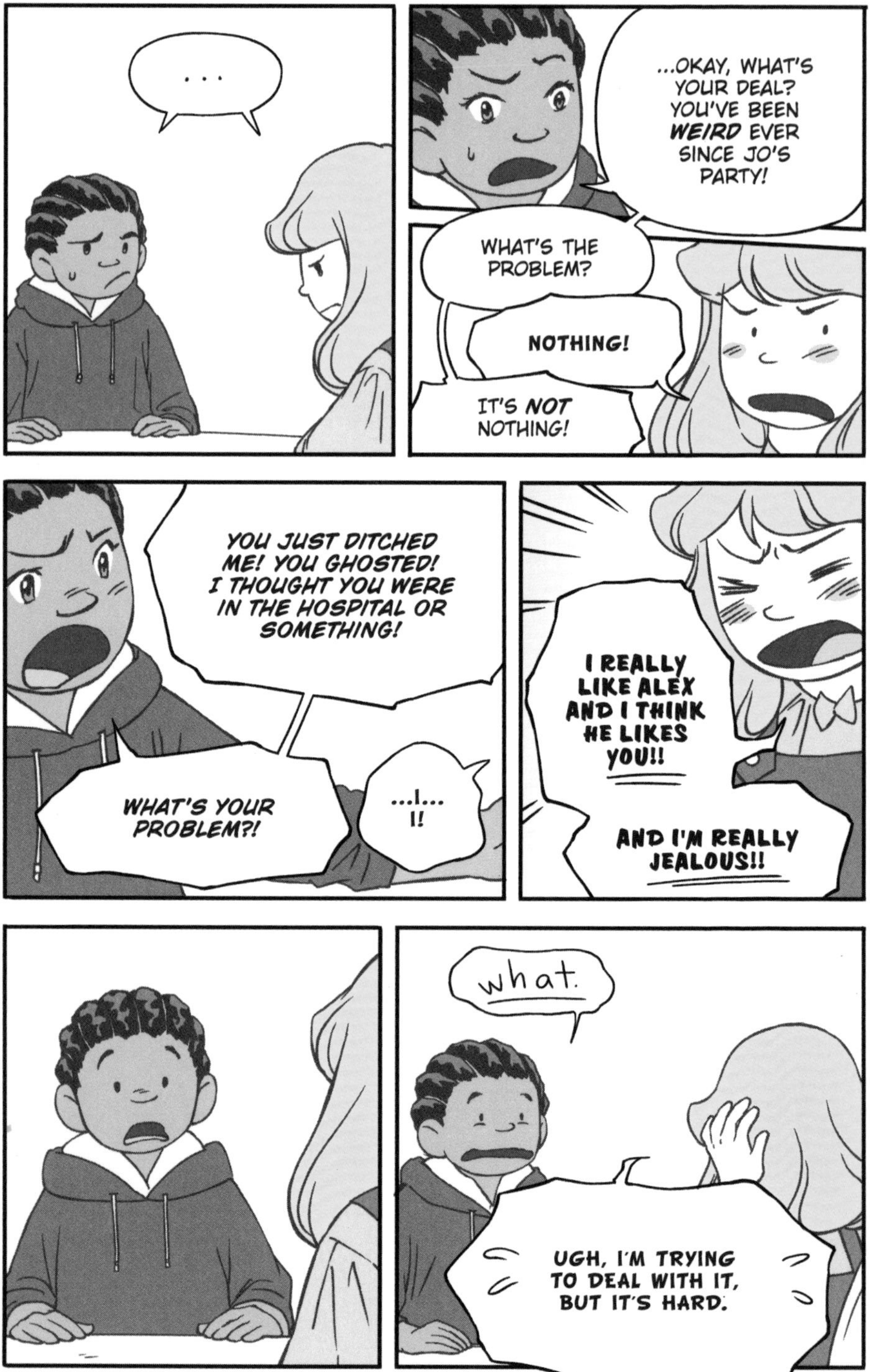
...
...OKAY, WHAT'S YOUR DEAL? YOU'VE BEEN WEIRD EVER SINCE JO'S PARTY!
WHAT'S THE PROBLEM?
NOTHING!
IT'S NOT NOTHING!
YOU JUST DITCHED ME! YOU GHOSTED! I THOUGHT YOU WERE IN THE HOSPITAL OR SOMETHING!
WHAT'S YOUR PROBLEM?!
...I... I!
I REALLY LIKE ALEX AND I THINK HE LIKES YOU!!
AND I'M REALLY JEALOUS!!
what.
UGH, I'M TRYING TO DEAL WITH IT, BUT IT'S HARD.

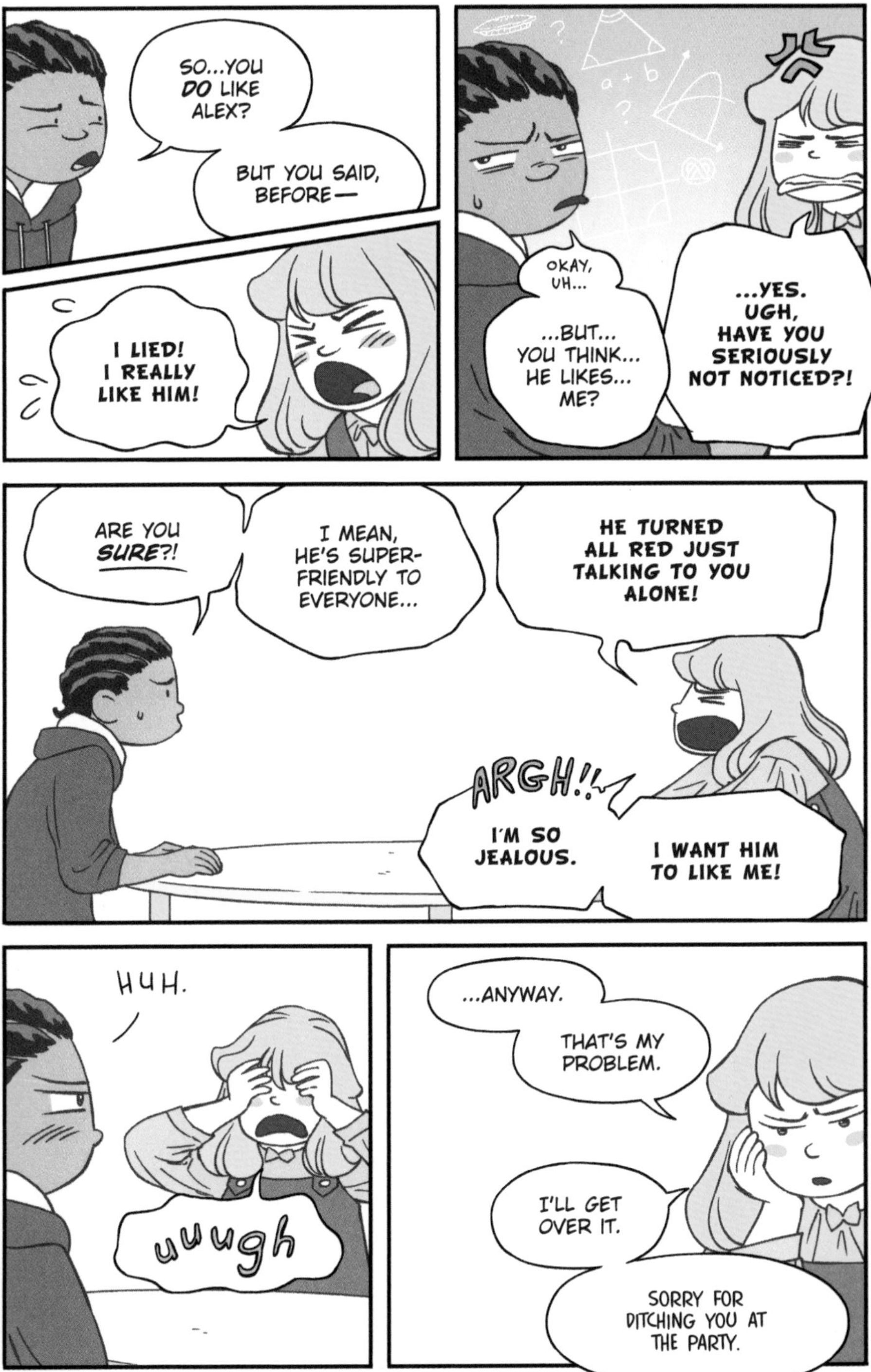
SO...YOU DO LIKE ALEX?
BUT YOU SAID, BEFORE—
I LIED! I REALLY LIKE HIM!
OKAY, UH...
...BUT... YOU THINK... HE LIKES... ME?
...YES. UGH, HAVE YOU SERIOUSLY NOT NOTICED?!
ARE YOU SURE?!
I MEAN, HE'S SUPER-FRIENDLY TO EVERYONE...
HE TURNED ALL RED JUST TALKING TO YOU ALONE!
ARGH!!
I'M SO JEALOUS.
I WANT HIM TO LIKE ME!
HUH.
uuugh
...ANYWAY.
THAT'S MY PROBLEM.
I'LL GET OVER IT.
SORRY FOR DITCHING YOU AT THE PARTY.

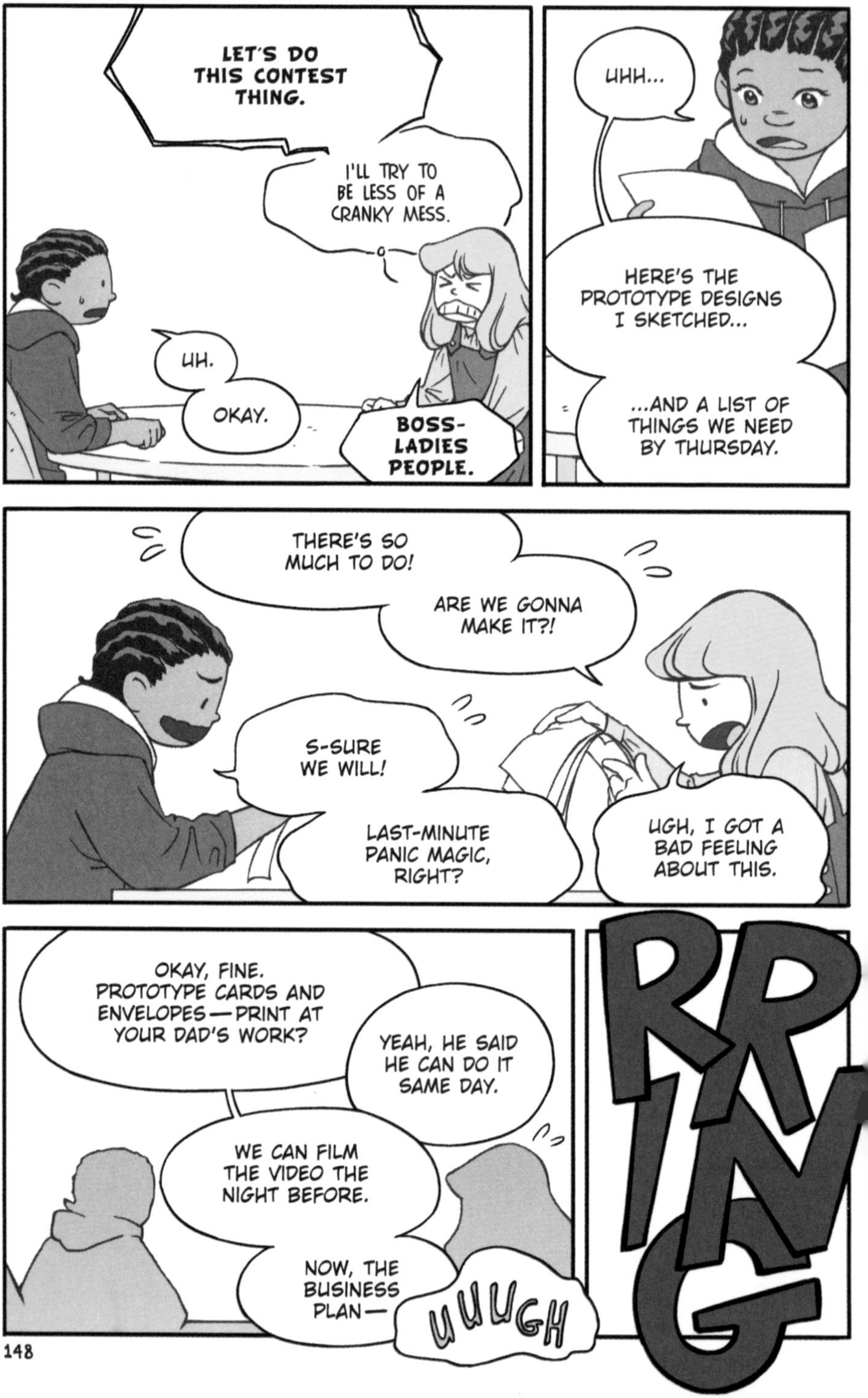
LET'S DO THIS CONTEST THING.
I'LL TRY TO BE LESS OF A CRANKY MESS.
UH.
OKAY.
BOSS-LADIES PEOPLE.
UHH...
HERE'S THE PROTOTYPE DESIGNS I SKETCHED...
...AND A LIST OF THINGS WE NEED BY THURSDAY.
THERE'S SO MUCH TO DO!
ARE WE GONNA MAKE IT?!
S-SURE WE WILL!
LAST-MINUTE PANIC MAGIC, RIGHT?
UGH, I GOT A BAD FEELING ABOUT THIS.
OKAY, FINE. PROTOTYPE CARDS AND ENVELOPES—PRINT AT YOUR DAD'S WORK?
YEAH, HE SAID HE CAN DO IT SAME DAY.
WE CAN FILM THE VIDEO THE NIGHT BEFORE.
NOW, THE BUSINESS PLAN—
UUUGH
RRING

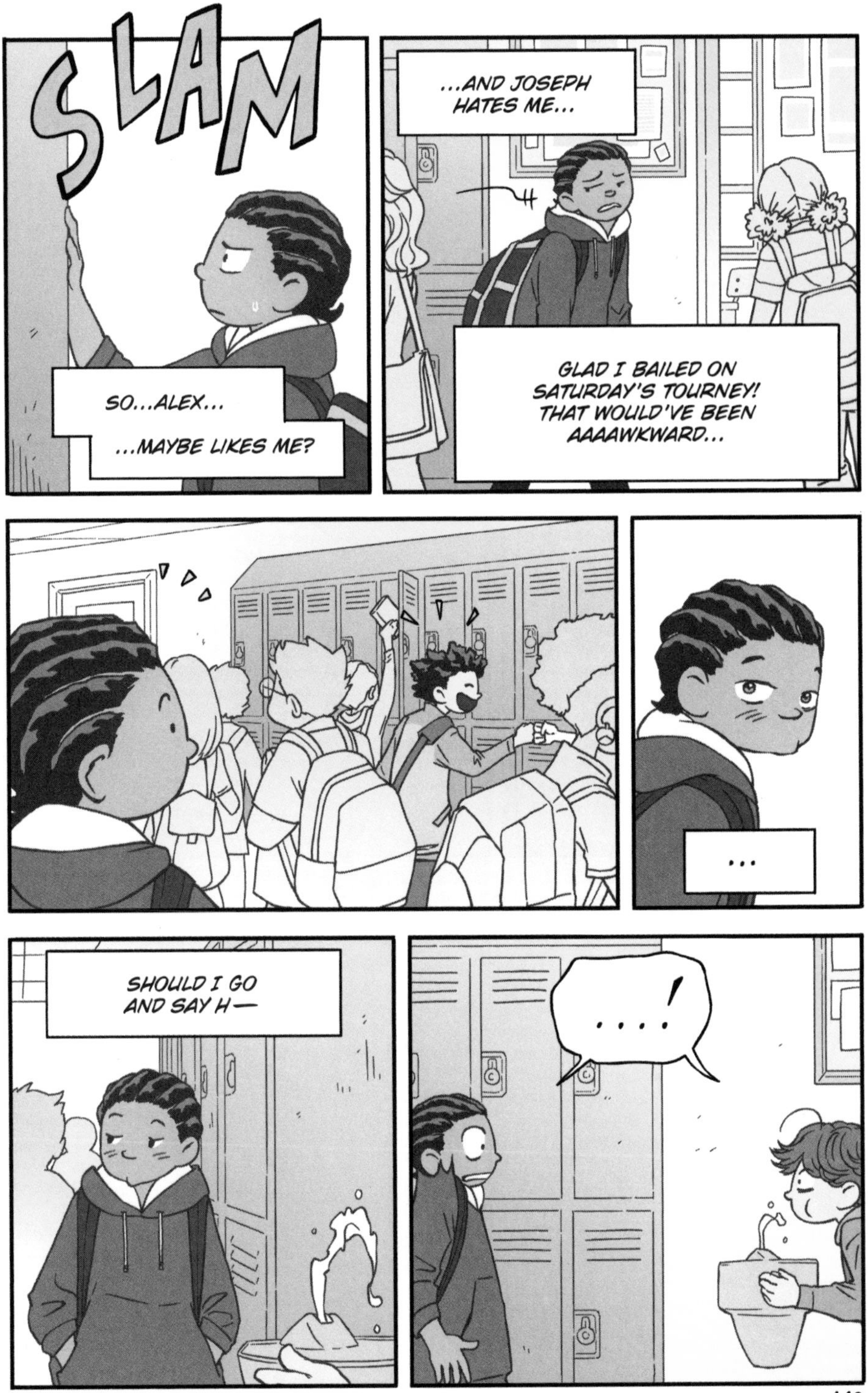
SLAM
SO...ALEX...
...MAYBE LIKES ME?
...AND JOSEPH HATES ME...
GLAD I BAILED ON SATURDAY'S TOURNEY! THAT WOULD'VE BEEN AAAAWKWARD...
...
SHOULD I GO AND SAY H—
....!

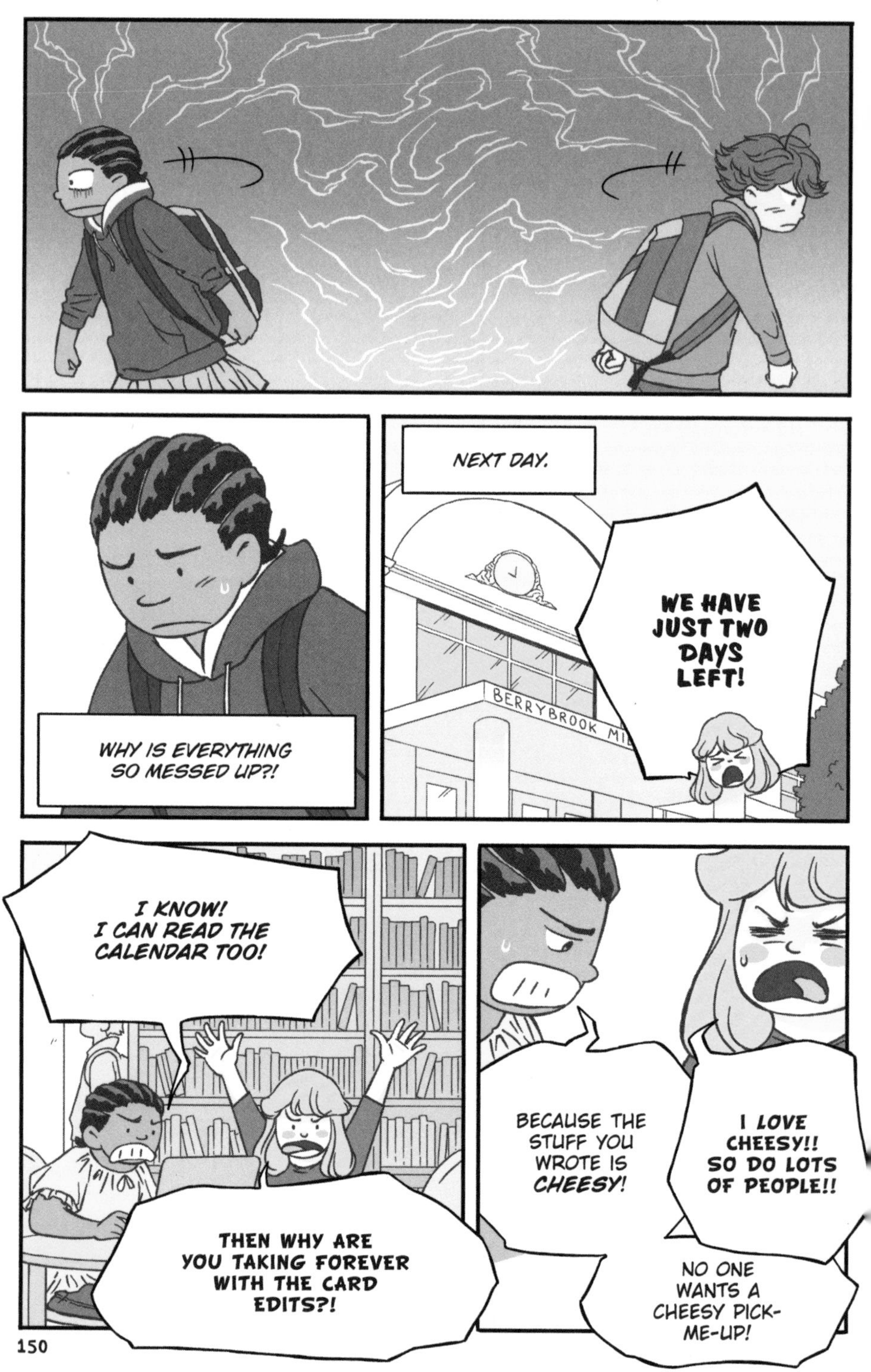
NEXT DAY.
WHY IS EVERYTHING SO MESSED UP?!
WE HAVE JUST TWO DAYS LEFT!
BERRYBROOK MI
I KNOW! I CAN READ THE CALENDAR TOO!
THEN WHY ARE YOU TAKING FOREVER WITH THE CARD EDITS?!
BECAUSE THE STUFF YOU WROTE IS CHEESY!
I LOVE CHEESY!! SO DO LOTS OF PEOPLE!!
NO ONE WANTS A CHEESY PICK-ME-UP!

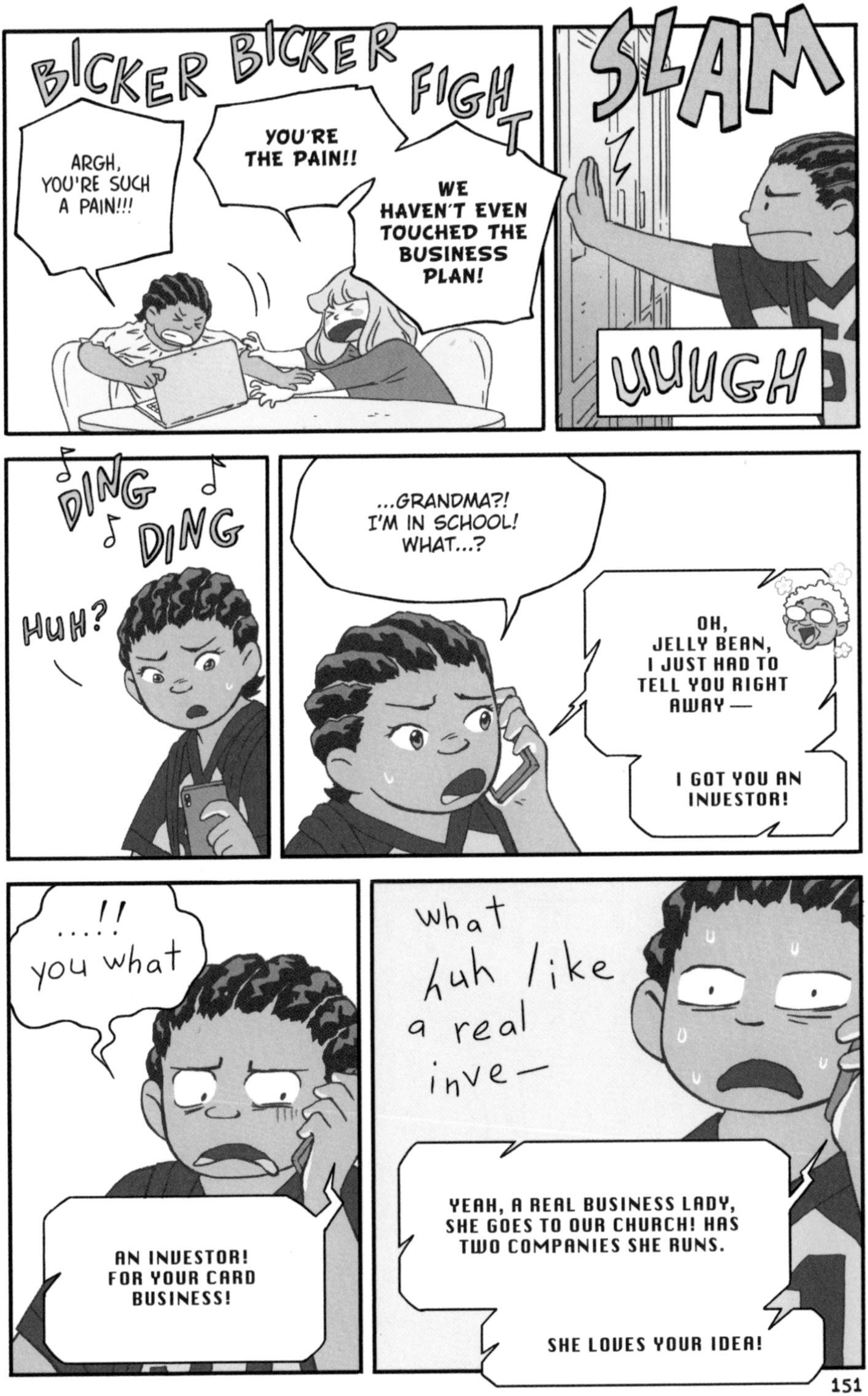
BICKER BICKER
ARGH, YOU'RE SUCH A PAIN!!!
YOU'RE THE PAIN!!
FIGHT
WE HAVEN'T EVEN TOUCHED THE BUSINESS PLAN!
SLAM
UUUGH
DING DING
HUH?
...GRANDMA?! I'M IN SCHOOL! WHAT...?
OH, JELLY BEAN, I JUST HAD TO TELL YOU RIGHT AWAY—
I GOT YOU AN INVESTOR!
...!! you what
AN INVESTOR! FOR YOUR CARD BUSINESS!
what huh like a real inve—
YEAH, A REAL BUSINESS LADY, SHE GOES TO OUR CHURCH! HAS TWO COMPANIES SHE RUNS.
SHE LOVES YOUR IDEA!

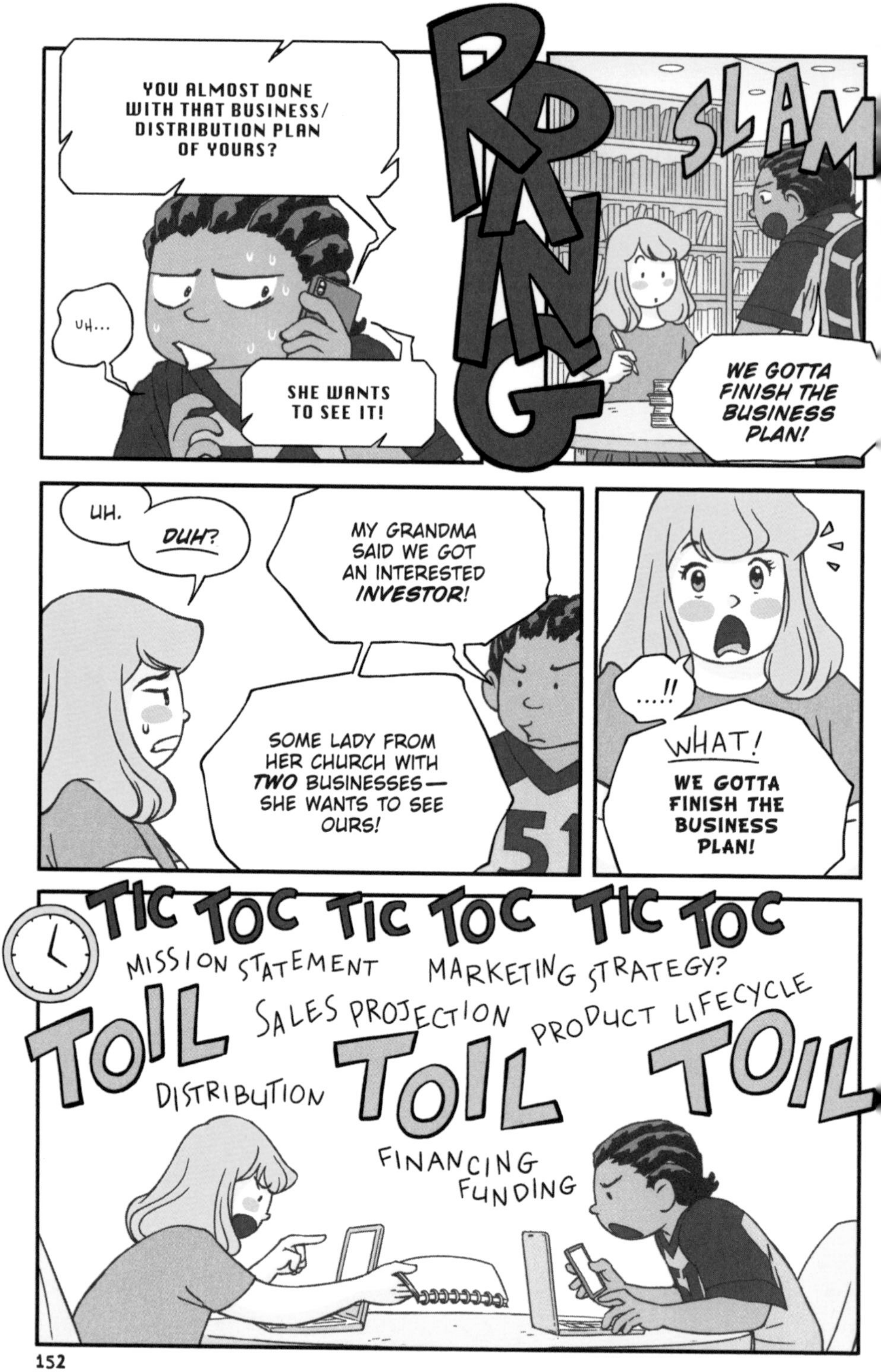
YOU ALMOST DONE WITH THAT BUSINESS/ DISTRIBUTION PLAN OF YOURS?
UH...
SHE WANTS TO SEE IT!
RRRING
SLAM
WE GOTTA FINISH THE BUSINESS PLAN!
UH. DUH?
MY GRANDMA SAID WE GOT AN INTERESTED INVESTOR!
SOME LADY FROM HER CHURCH WITH TWO BUSINESSES— SHE WANTS TO SEE OURS!
....!!
WHAT!
WE GOTTA FINISH THE BUSINESS PLAN!
TIC TOC TIC TOC TIC TOC
MISSION STATEMENT
MARKETING STRATEGY?
TOIL
SALES PROJECTION
PRODUCT LIFECYCLE
DISTRIBUTION
TOIL
TOIL
FINANCING
FUNDING

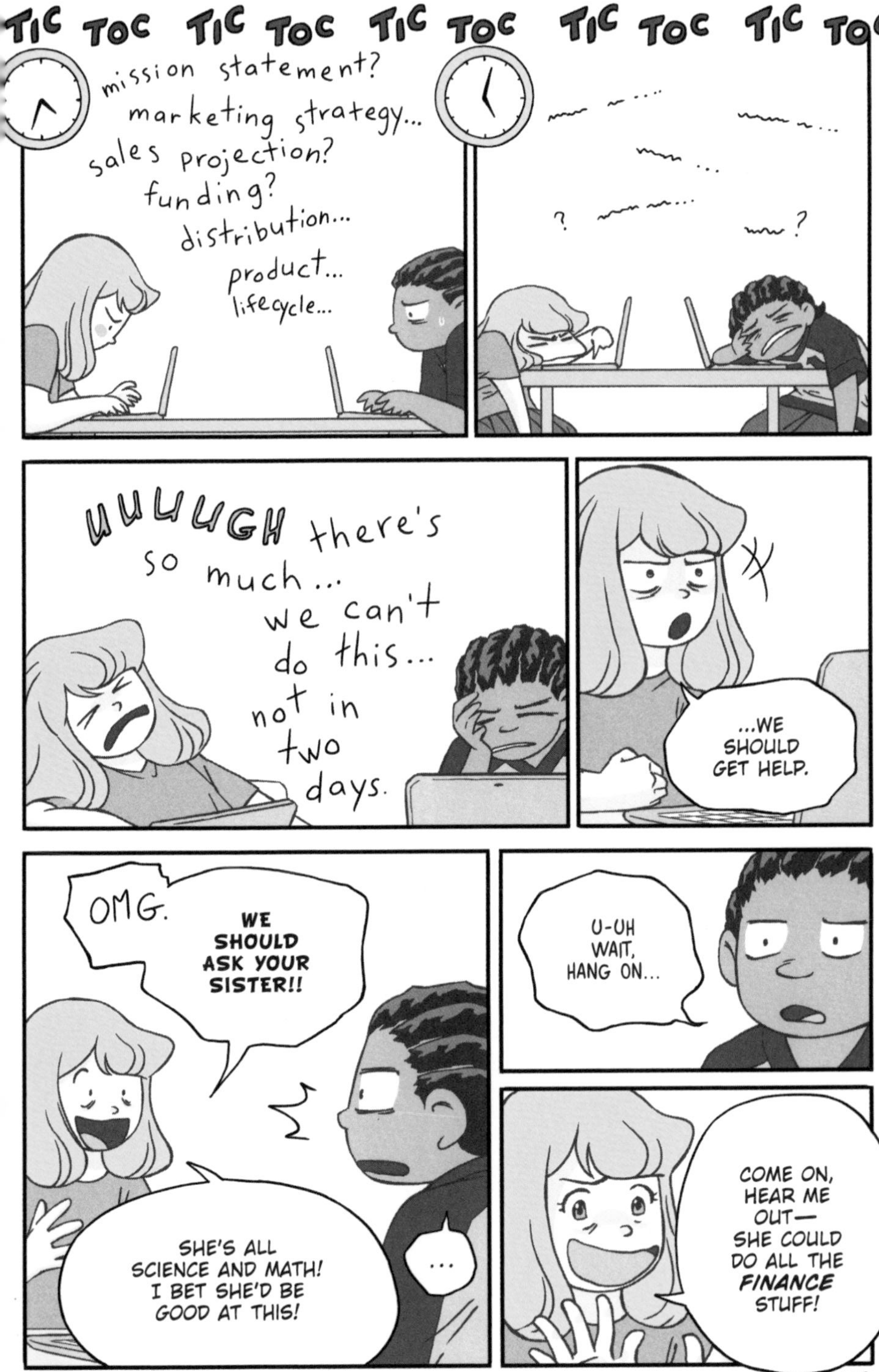
TIC TOC TIC TOC TIC TOC TIC TOC TIC TOC
mission statement?
marketing strategy...
sales projection?
funding?
distribution...
product...
lifecycle...
? ...
UUUUGH there's so much... we can't do this... not in two days.
...WE SHOULD GET HELP.
OMG.
WE SHOULD ASK YOUR SISTER!!
SHE'S ALL SCIENCE AND MATH! I BET SHE'D BE GOOD AT THIS!
...
U-UH WAIT, HANG ON...
COME ON, HEAR ME OUT— SHE COULD DO ALL THE *FINANCE* STUFF!

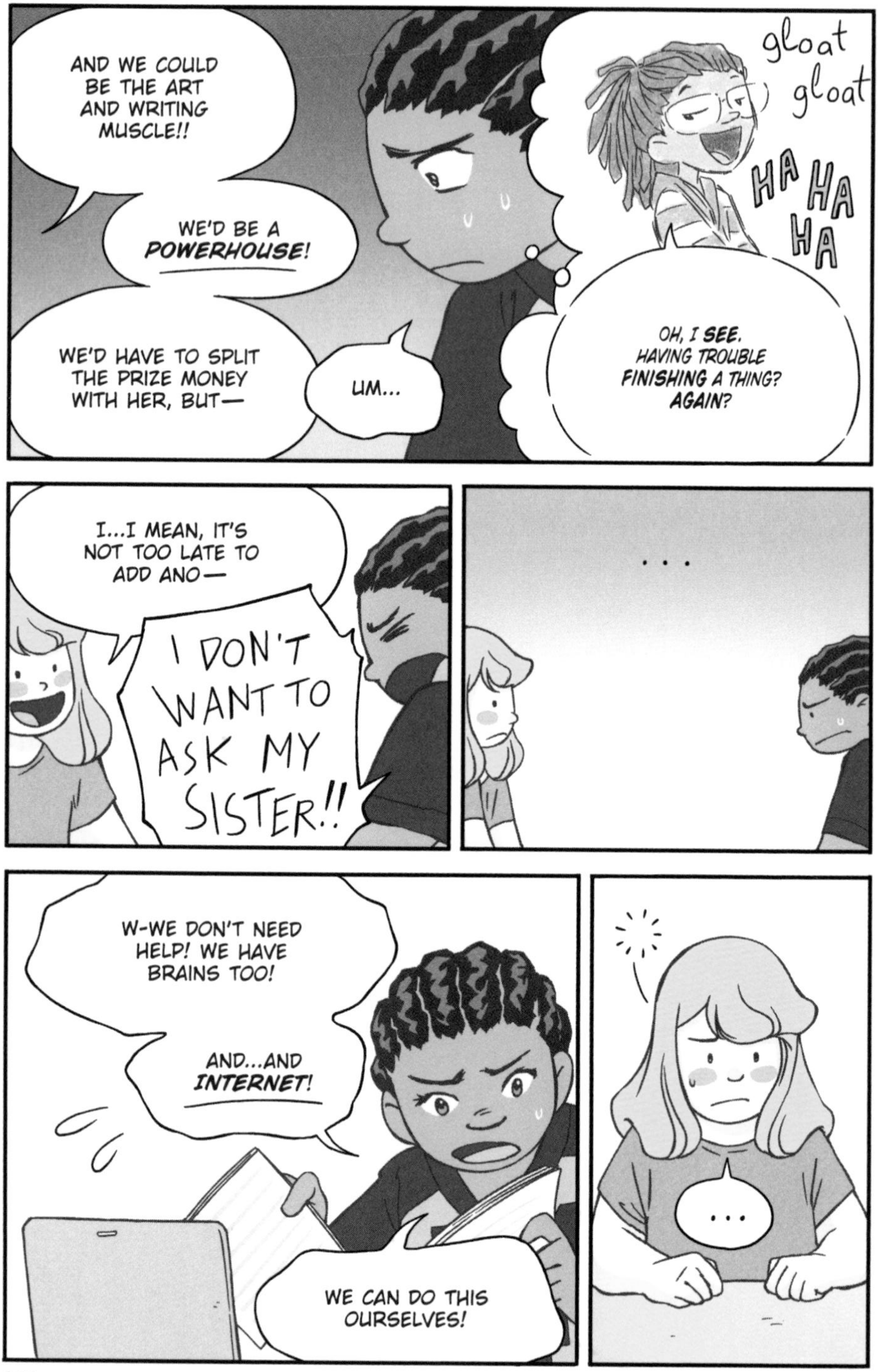
AND WE COULD BE THE ART AND WRITING MUSCLE!!
WE'D BE A **POWERHOUSE**!
WE'D HAVE TO SPLIT THE PRIZE MONEY WITH HER, BUT—
UM...
gloat gloat
HA HA HA
OH, I **SEE**. HAVING TROUBLE **FINISHING** A THING? **AGAIN**?
I...I MEAN, IT'S NOT TOO LATE TO ADD ANO—
I DON'T WANT TO ASK MY SISTER!!
...
W-WE DON'T NEED HELP! WE HAVE BRAINS TOO!
AND...AND **INTERNET**!
WE CAN DO THIS OURSELVES!
...

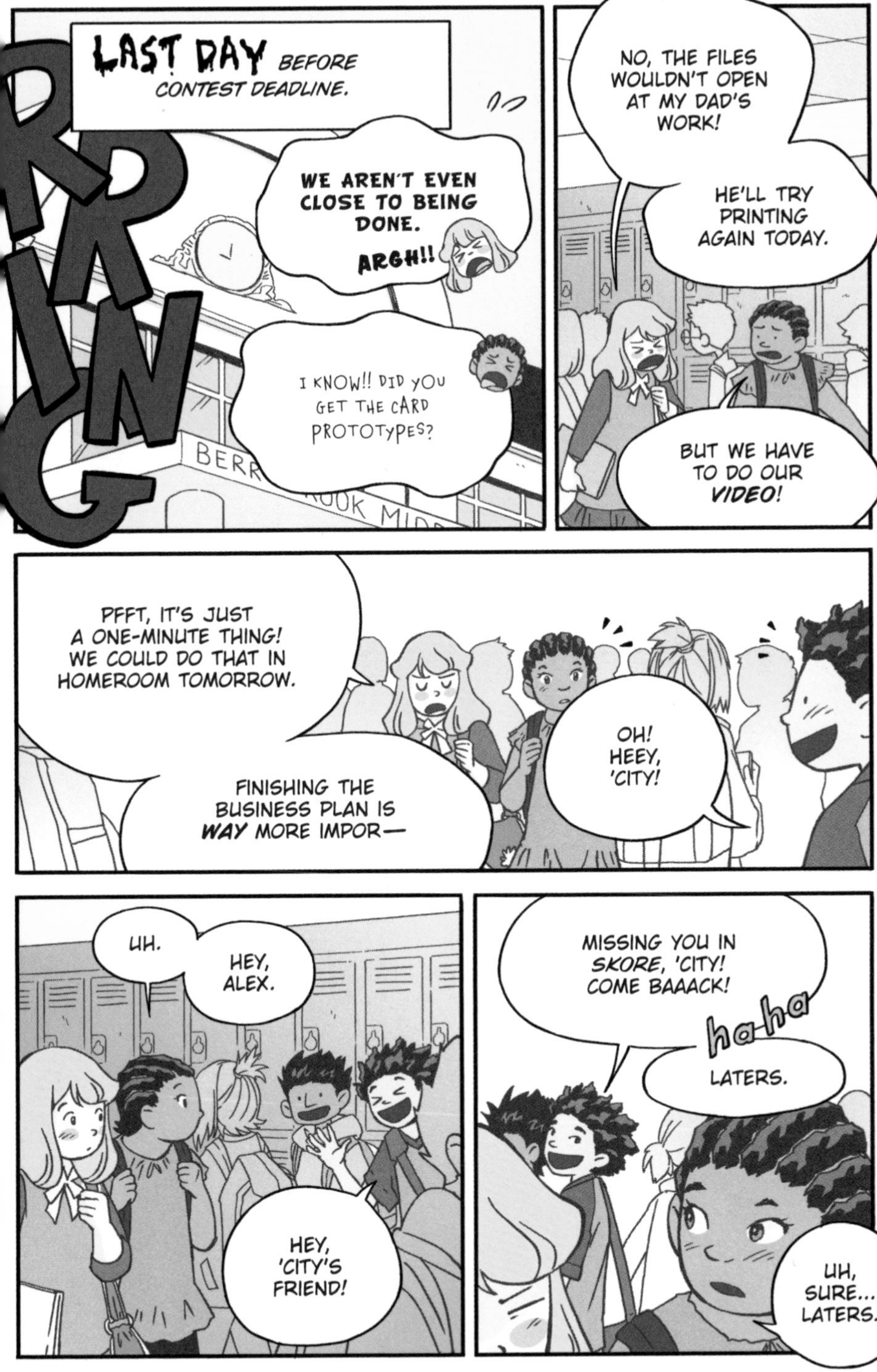
RRRING
LAST DAY BEFORE CONTEST DEADLINE.
WE AREN'T EVEN CLOSE TO BEING DONE. ARGH!!
I KNOW!! DID YOU GET THE CARD PROTOTYPES?
BERR
OOK MID
NO, THE FILES WOULDN'T OPEN AT MY DAD'S WORK!
HE'LL TRY PRINTING AGAIN TODAY.
BUT WE HAVE TO DO OUR VIDEO!
PFFT, IT'S JUST A ONE-MINUTE THING! WE COULD DO THAT IN HOMEROOM TOMORROW.
FINISHING THE BUSINESS PLAN IS WAY MORE IMPOR—
OH! HEEY, 'CITY!
UH.
HEY, ALEX.
HEY, 'CITY'S FRIEND!
MISSING YOU IN SKORE, 'CITY! COME BAAACK!
haha
LATERS.
UH, SURE... LATERS.

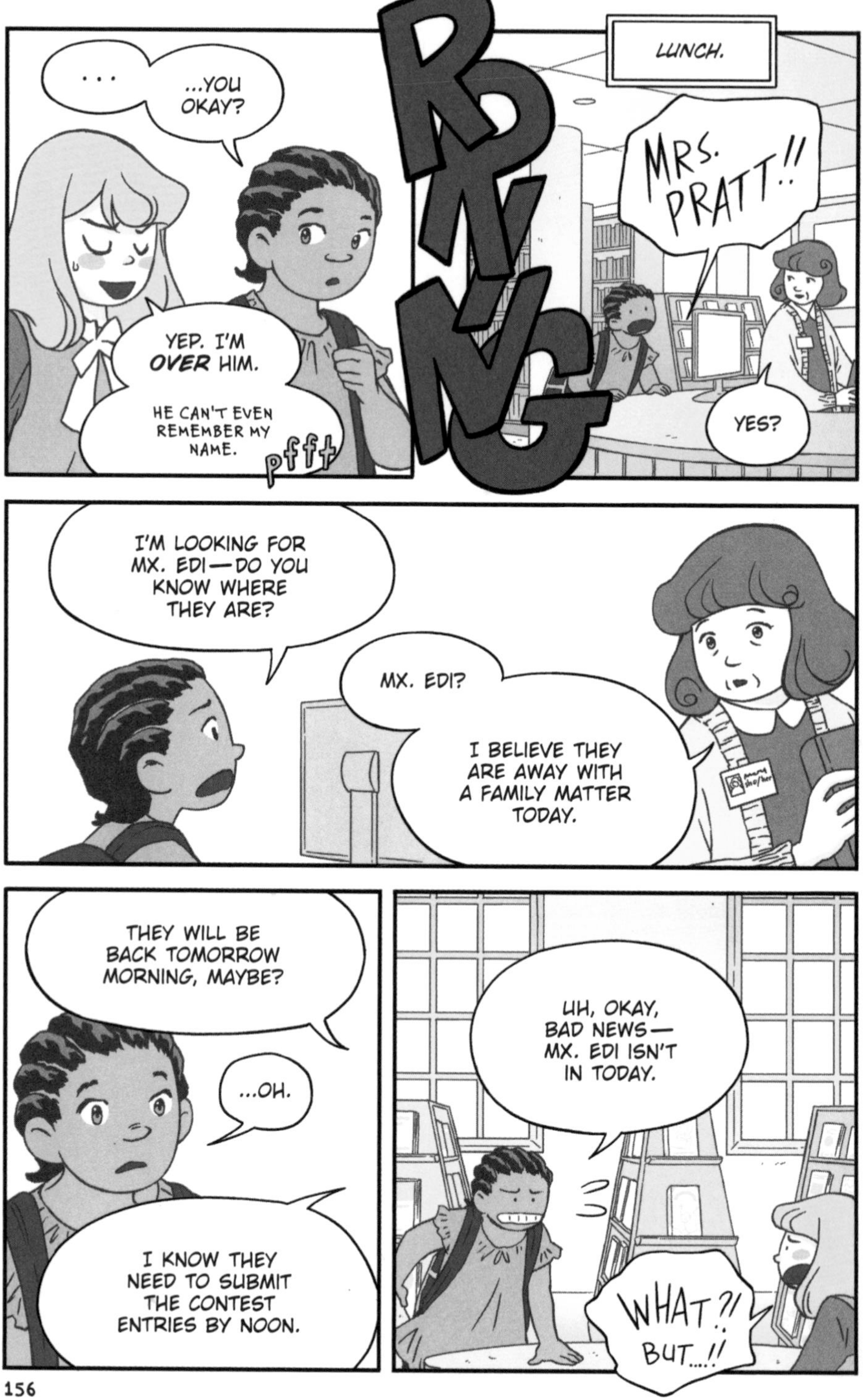
...
...YOU OKAY?
YEP. I'M **OVER** HIM.
HE CAN'T EVEN REMEMBER MY NAME.
pfft
RRRING
LUNCH.
MRS. PRATT!!
YES?
I'M LOOKING FOR MX. EDI—DO YOU KNOW WHERE THEY ARE?
MX. EDI?
I BELIEVE THEY ARE AWAY WITH A FAMILY MATTER TODAY.
THEY WILL BE BACK TOMORROW MORNING, MAYBE?
...OH.
I KNOW THEY NEED TO SUBMIT THE CONTEST ENTRIES BY NOON.
UH, OKAY, BAD NEWS—MX. EDI ISN'T IN TODAY.
WHAT?!
BUT...!!

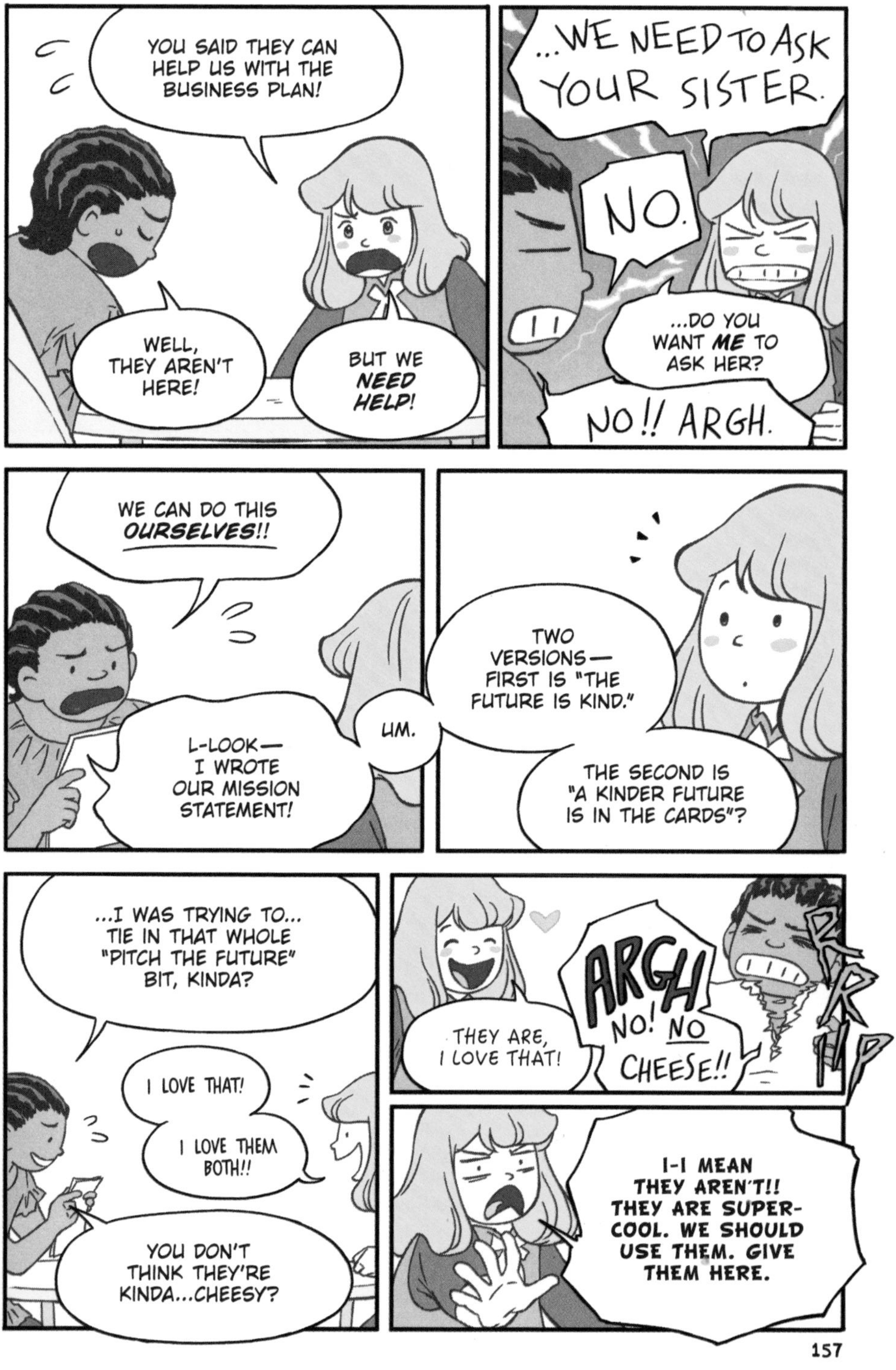
YOU SAID THEY CAN HELP US WITH THE BUSINESS PLAN!
WELL, THEY AREN'T HERE!
BUT WE NEED HELP!
...WE NEED TO ASK YOUR SISTER.
NO.
...DO YOU WANT ME TO ASK HER?
NO!! ARGH.
WE CAN DO THIS OURSELVES!!
L-LOOK— I WROTE OUR MISSION STATEMENT!
UM.
TWO VERSIONS— FIRST IS "THE FUTURE IS KIND."
THE SECOND IS "A KINDER FUTURE IS IN THE CARDS"?
...I WAS TRYING TO... TIE IN THAT WHOLE "PITCH THE FUTURE" BIT, KINDA?
I LOVE THAT!
I LOVE THEM BOTH!!
YOU DON'T THINK THEY'RE KINDA...CHEESY?
THEY ARE, I LOVE THAT!
ARGH
NO! NO CHEESE!!
RRRIP
I-I MEAN THEY AREN'T!! THEY ARE SUPER-COOL. WE SHOULD USE THEM. GIVE THEM HERE.

UUUGH

...DID YOU DO THE MARKETING/ DISTRIBUTION IDEAS LIST?

YES, I DID! TEXTING NOW. PRETTY PROUD OF THESE.

scroll scroll

...ARE YOU FOR REAL WITH THESE?

...?

...CARRIER PIGEONS...TRAINED DELIVERY CATS...?!

...SKYWRITING?!

WHAAAT! IT'LL MAKE OUR PITCH STAND OUT!

BUT THESE ARE *RIDICULOUS*!!

NO, THEY'RE OUT-OF-THE-BOX THINKING!

CONTESTS *LOVE* OUT-OF-THE-BOX STUFF!

BUT... THIS IS...

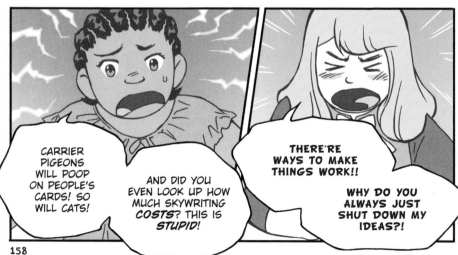

CARRIER PIGEONS WILL POOP ON PEOPLE'S CARDS! SO WILL CATS!

AND DID YOU EVEN LOOK UP HOW MUCH SKYWRITING *COSTS*? THIS IS *STUPID*!

THERE'RE WAYS TO MAKE THINGS WORK!!

WHY DO YOU ALWAYS JUST SHUT DOWN MY IDEAS?!

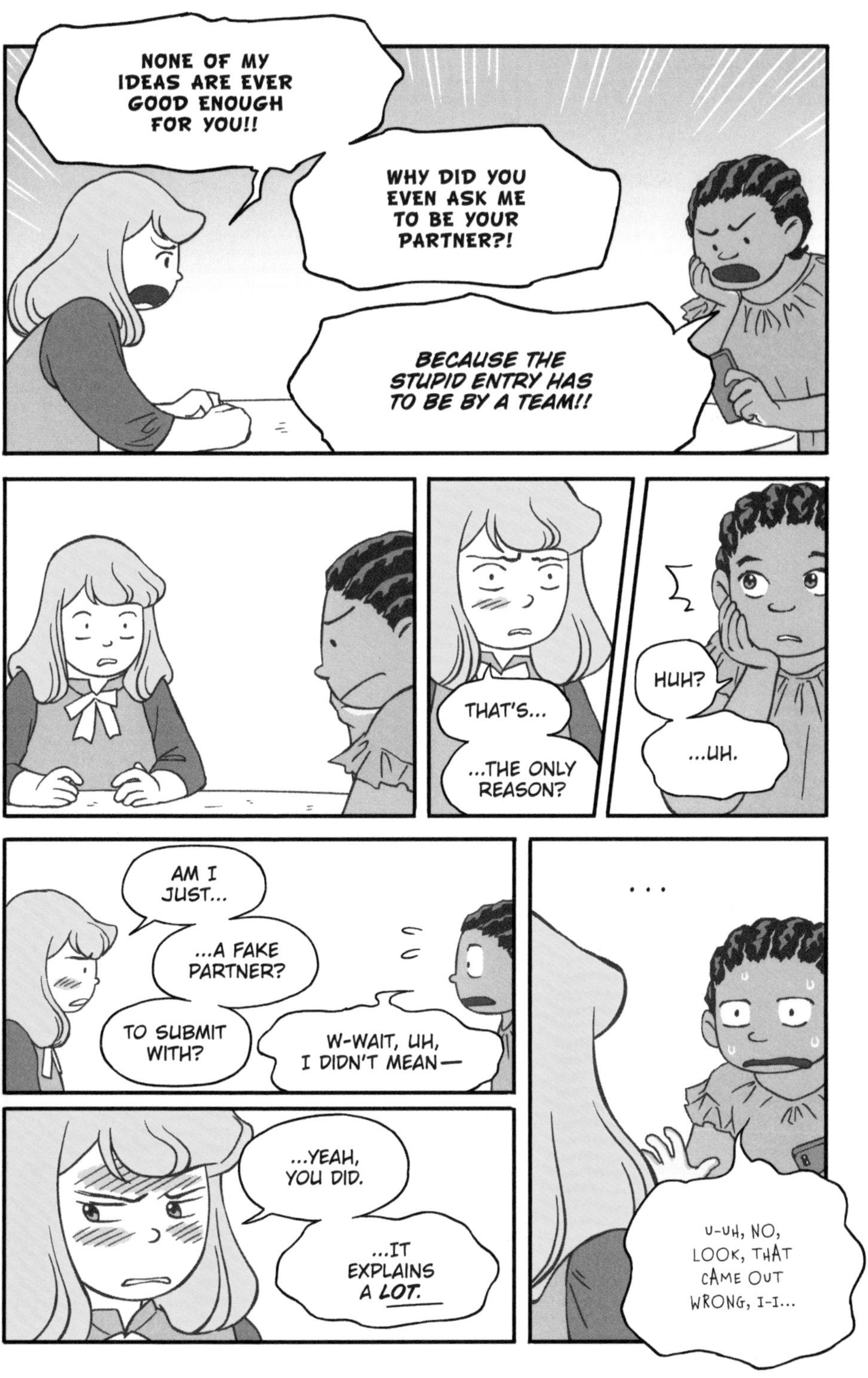
NONE OF MY IDEAS ARE EVER GOOD ENOUGH FOR YOU!!
WHY DID YOU EVEN ASK ME TO BE YOUR PARTNER?!
BECAUSE THE STUPID ENTRY HAS TO BE BY A TEAM!!
THAT'S...
...THE ONLY REASON?
HUH?
...UH.
AM I JUST...
...A FAKE PARTNER?
TO SUBMIT WITH?
W-WAIT, UH, I DIDN'T MEAN—
...YEAH, YOU DID.
...IT EXPLAINS A LOT.
. . .
U-UH, NO, LOOK, THAT CAME OUT WRONG, I-I...

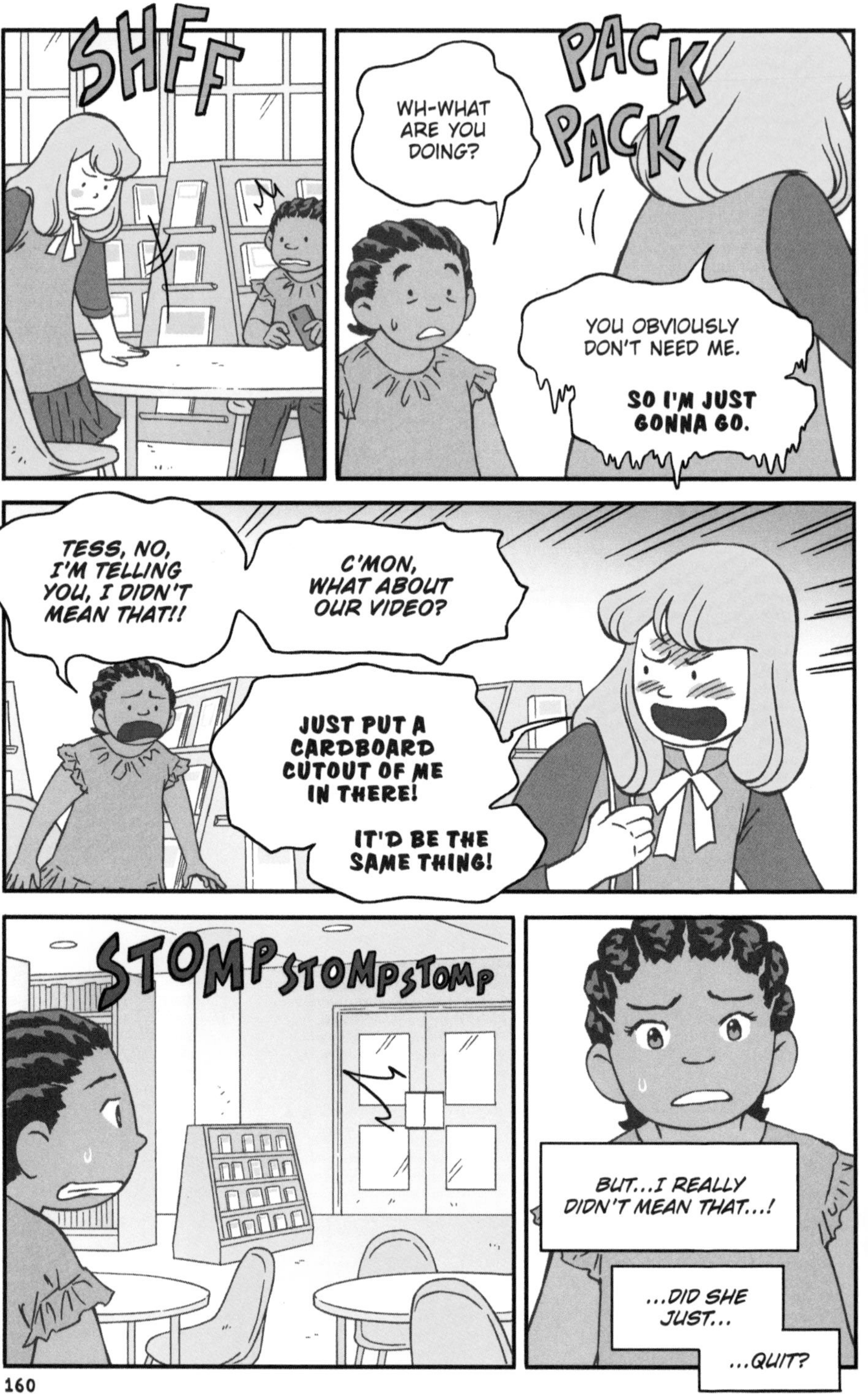
SHFF
WH-WHAT ARE YOU DOING?
PACK PACK
YOU OBVIOUSLY DON'T NEED ME.
SO I'M JUST GONNA GO.
TESS, NO, I'M TELLING YOU, I DIDN'T MEAN THAT!!
C'MON, WHAT ABOUT OUR VIDEO?
JUST PUT A CARDBOARD CUTOUT OF ME IN THERE!
IT'D BE THE SAME THING!
STOMP STOMP STOMP
BUT...I REALLY DIDN'T MEAN THAT...!
...DID SHE JUST...
...QUIT?

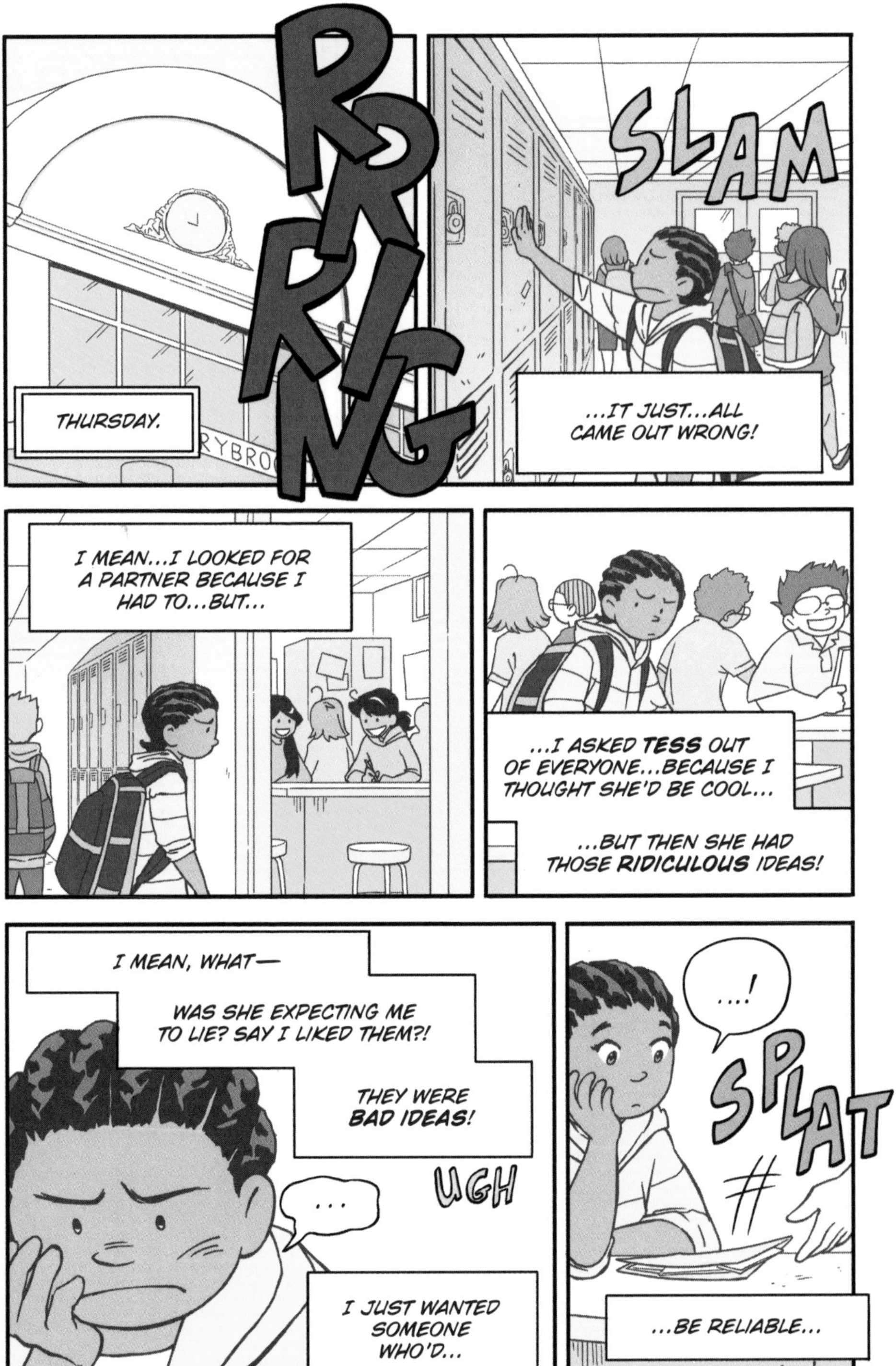
RRRIIING
THURSDAY.
RYBRO
SLAM
...IT JUST...ALL CAME OUT WRONG!
I MEAN...I LOOKED FOR A PARTNER BECAUSE I HAD TO...BUT...
...I ASKED TESS OUT OF EVERYONE...BECAUSE I THOUGHT SHE'D BE COOL...
...BUT THEN SHE HAD THOSE RIDICULOUS IDEAS!
I MEAN, WHAT—
WAS SHE EXPECTING ME TO LIE? SAY I LIKED THEM?!
THEY WERE BAD IDEAS!
UGH
...
I JUST WANTED SOMEONE WHO'D...
...!
SPLAT
...BE RELIABLE...

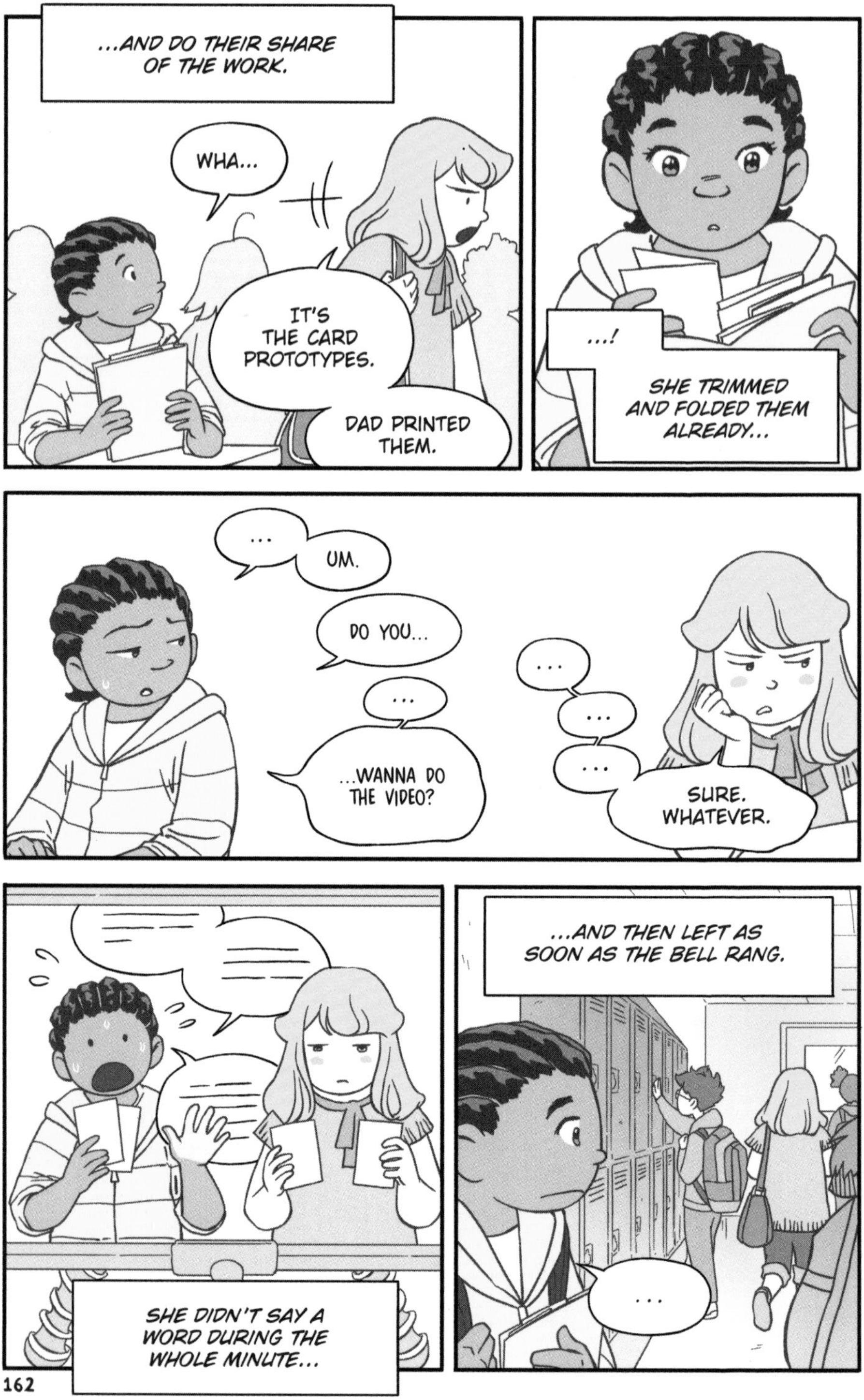
...AND DO THEIR SHARE OF THE WORK.
WHA...
IT'S THE CARD PROTOTYPES.
DAD PRINTED THEM.
...!
SHE TRIMMED AND FOLDED THEM ALREADY...
...
UM.
DO YOU...
...
...WANNA DO THE VIDEO?
...
...
...
SURE. WHATEVER.
SHE DIDN'T SAY A WORD DURING THE WHOLE MINUTE...
...AND THEN LEFT AS SOON AS THE BELL RANG.
...

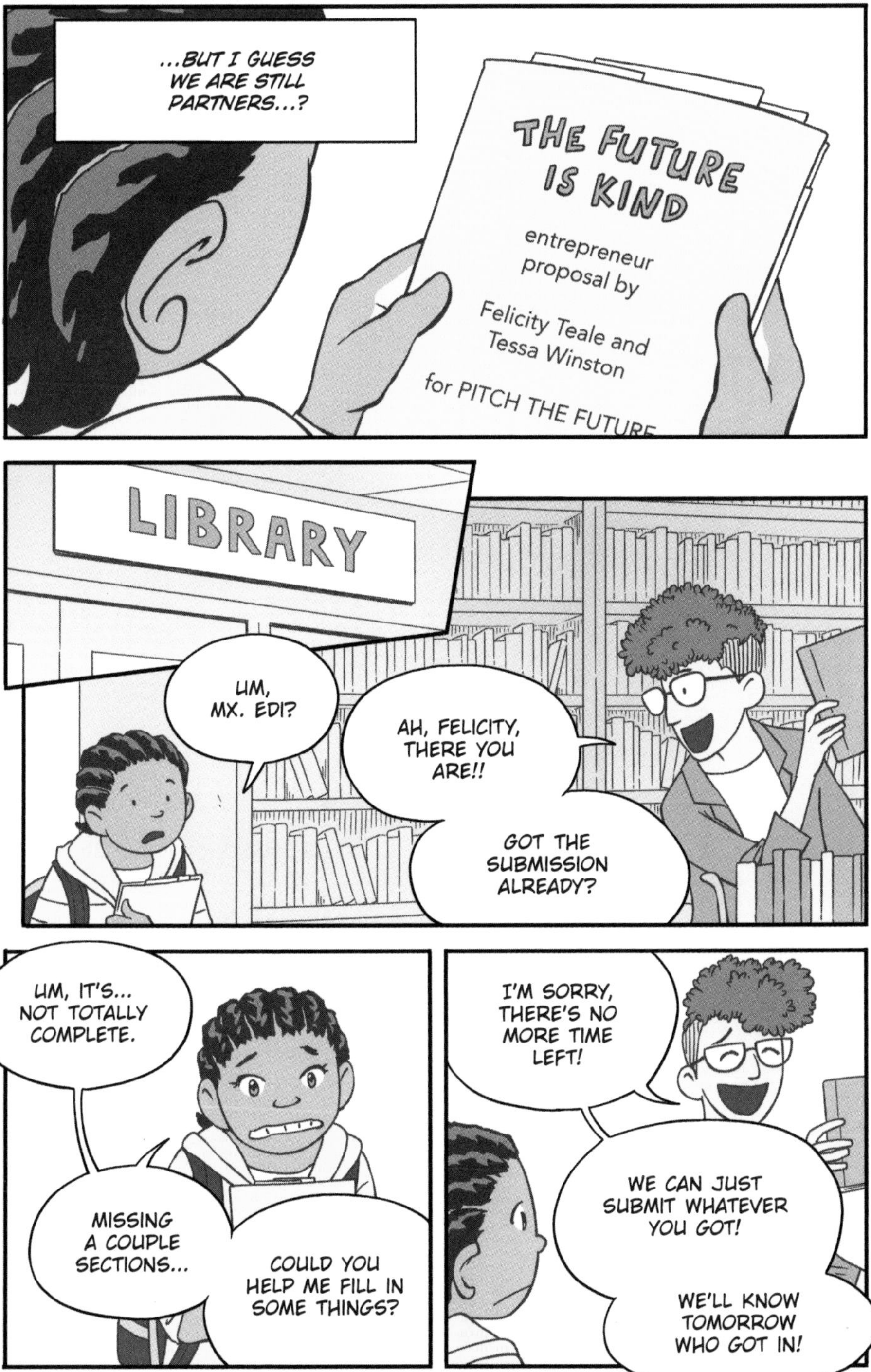
...BUT I GUESS WE ARE STILL PARTNERS...?
THE FUTURE IS KIND
entrepreneur proposal by
Felicity Teale and Tessa Winston
for PITCH THE FUTURE
LIBRARY
UM, MX. EDI?
AH, FELICITY, THERE YOU ARE!!
GOT THE SUBMISSION ALREADY?
UM, IT'S... NOT TOTALLY COMPLETE.
MISSING A COUPLE SECTIONS...
COULD YOU HELP ME FILL IN SOME THINGS?
I'M SORRY, THERE'S NO MORE TIME LEFT!
WE CAN JUST SUBMIT WHATEVER YOU GOT!
WE'LL KNOW TOMORROW WHO GOT IN!

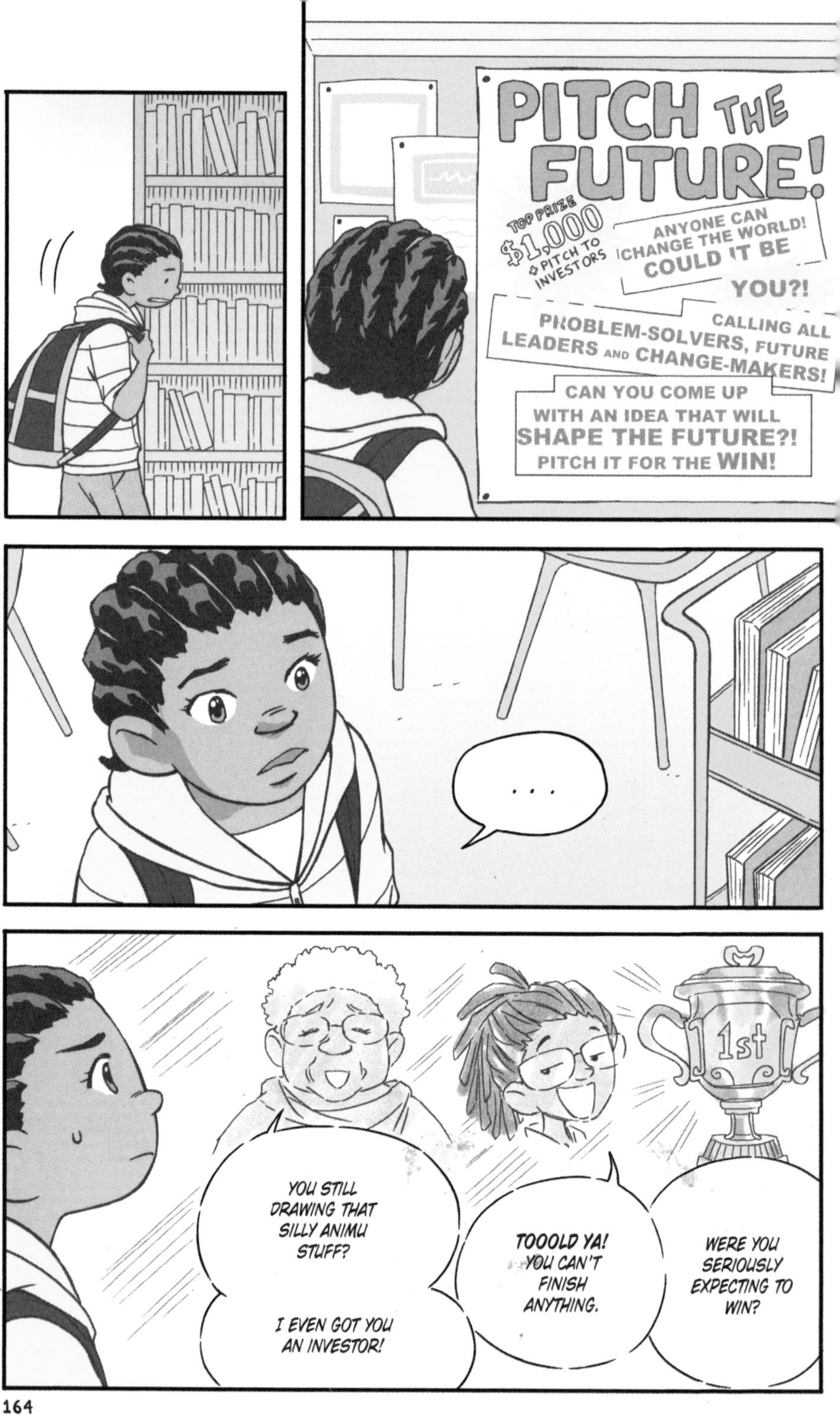
PITCH THE FUTURE!
TOP PRIZE $1,000 + PITCH TO INVESTORS
ANYONE CAN CHANGE THE WORLD! COULD IT BE YOU?!
CALLING ALL PROBLEM-SOLVERS, FUTURE LEADERS AND CHANGE-MAKERS!
CAN YOU COME UP WITH AN IDEA THAT WILL SHAPE THE FUTURE?! PITCH IT FOR THE WIN!
...
1st
YOU STILL DRAWING THAT SILLY ANIMU STUFF?
I EVEN GOT YOU AN INVESTOR!
TOOOLD YA! YOU CAN'T FINISH ANYTHING.
WERE YOU SERIOUSLY EXPECTING TO WIN?

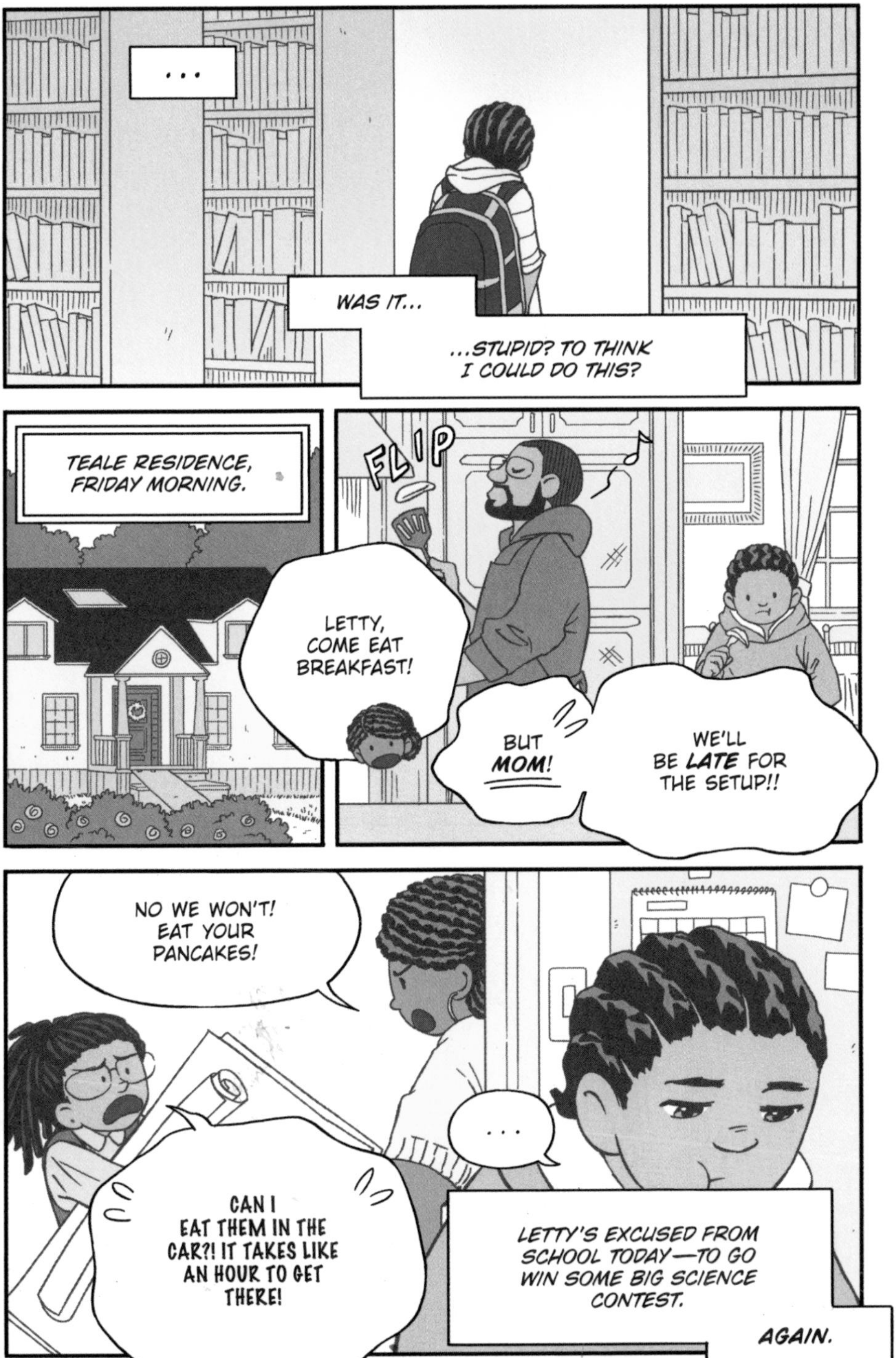
. . .
WAS IT...
...STUPID? TO THINK I COULD DO THIS?
TEALE RESIDENCE, FRIDAY MORNING.
FLIP
LETTY, COME EAT BREAKFAST!
BUT MOM!
WE'LL BE LATE FOR THE SETUP!!
NO WE WON'T! EAT YOUR PANCAKES!
CAN I EAT THEM IN THE CAR?! IT TAKES LIKE AN HOUR TO GET THERE!
. . .
LETTY'S EXCUSED FROM SCHOOL TODAY—TO GO WIN SOME BIG SCIENCE CONTEST.
AGAIN.

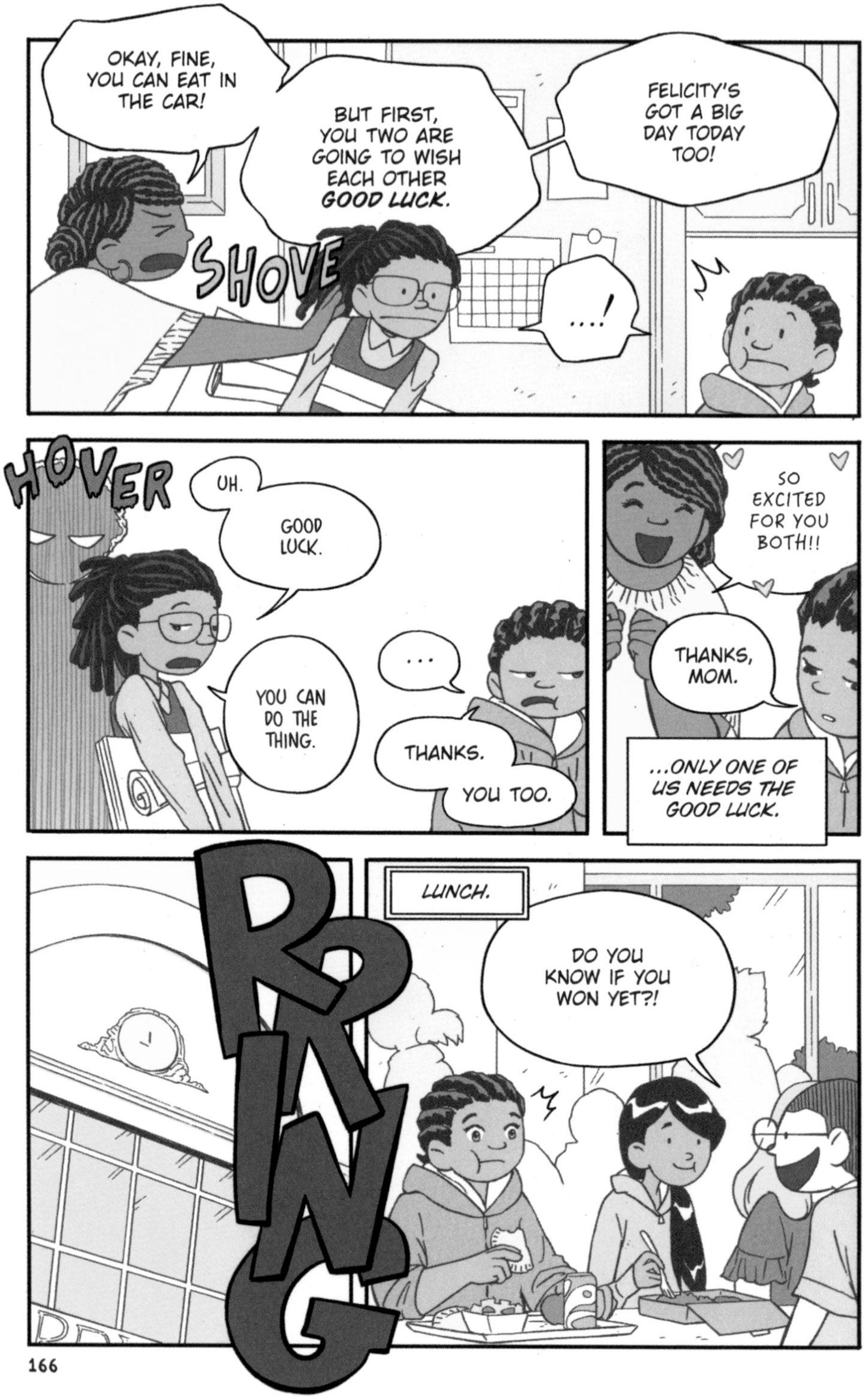
OKAY, FINE, YOU CAN EAT IN THE CAR!
BUT FIRST, YOU TWO ARE GOING TO WISH EACH OTHER GOOD LUCK.
FELICITY'S GOT A BIG DAY TODAY TOO!
SHOVE
...!
HOVER
UH.
GOOD LUCK.
YOU CAN DO THE THING.
...
THANKS.
YOU TOO.
SO EXCITED FOR YOU BOTH!!
THANKS, MOM.
...ONLY ONE OF US NEEDS THE GOOD LUCK.
RRING
LUNCH.
DO YOU KNOW IF YOU WON YET?!

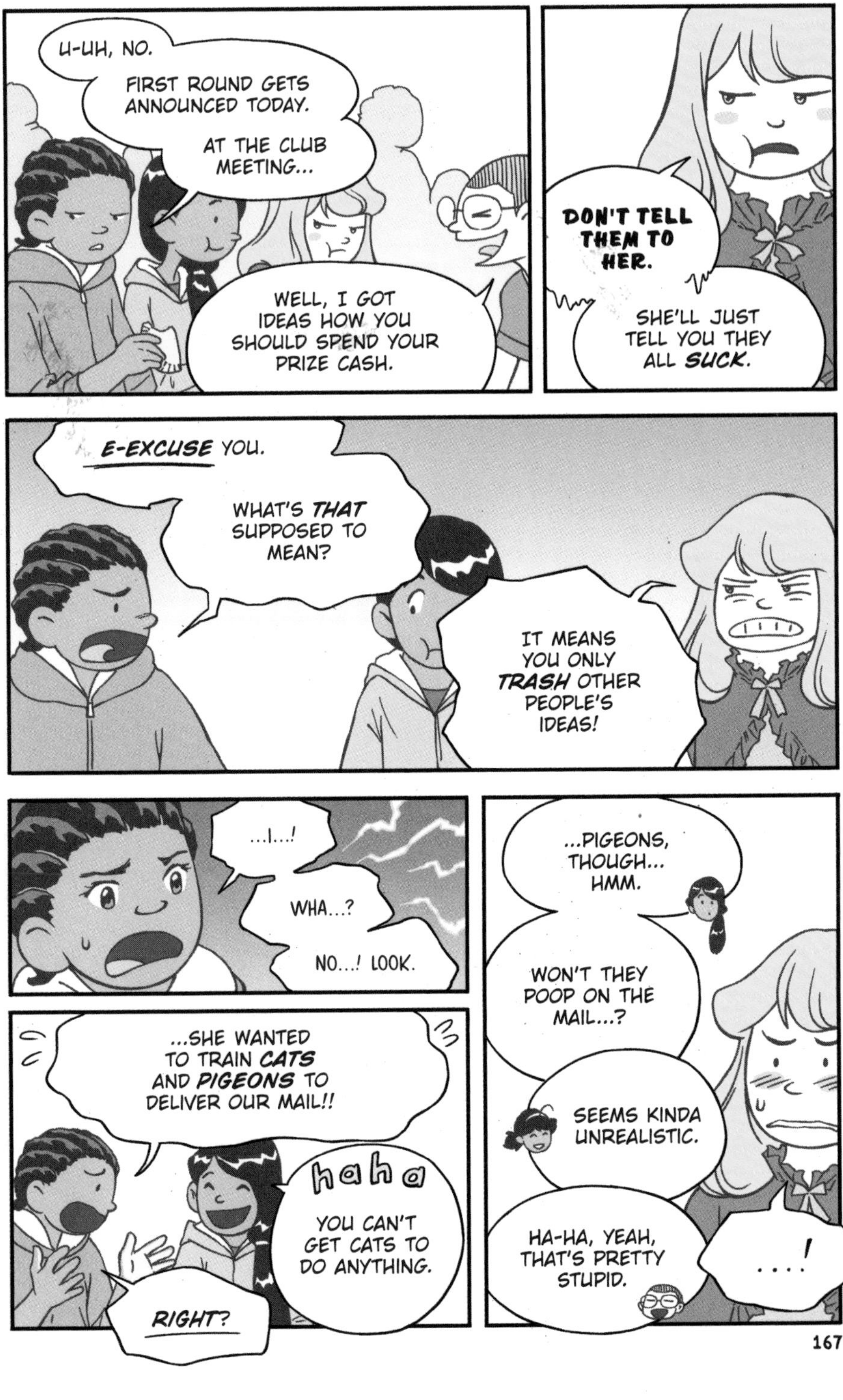
U-UH, NO.
FIRST ROUND GETS ANNOUNCED TODAY.
AT THE CLUB MEETING...
WELL, I GOT IDEAS HOW YOU SHOULD SPEND YOUR PRIZE CASH.
DON'T TELL THEM TO HER.
SHE'LL JUST TELL YOU THEY ALL SUCK.
E-EXCUSE YOU.
WHAT'S THAT SUPPOSED TO MEAN?
IT MEANS YOU ONLY TRASH OTHER PEOPLE'S IDEAS!
...I...!
WHA...?
NO...! LOOK.
...SHE WANTED TO TRAIN CATS AND PIGEONS TO DELIVER OUR MAIL!!
RIGHT?
haha
YOU CAN'T GET CATS TO DO ANYTHING.
...PIGEONS, THOUGH... HMM.
WON'T THEY POOP ON THE MAIL...?
SEEMS KINDA UNREALISTIC.
HA-HA, YEAH, THAT'S PRETTY STUPID.
...!

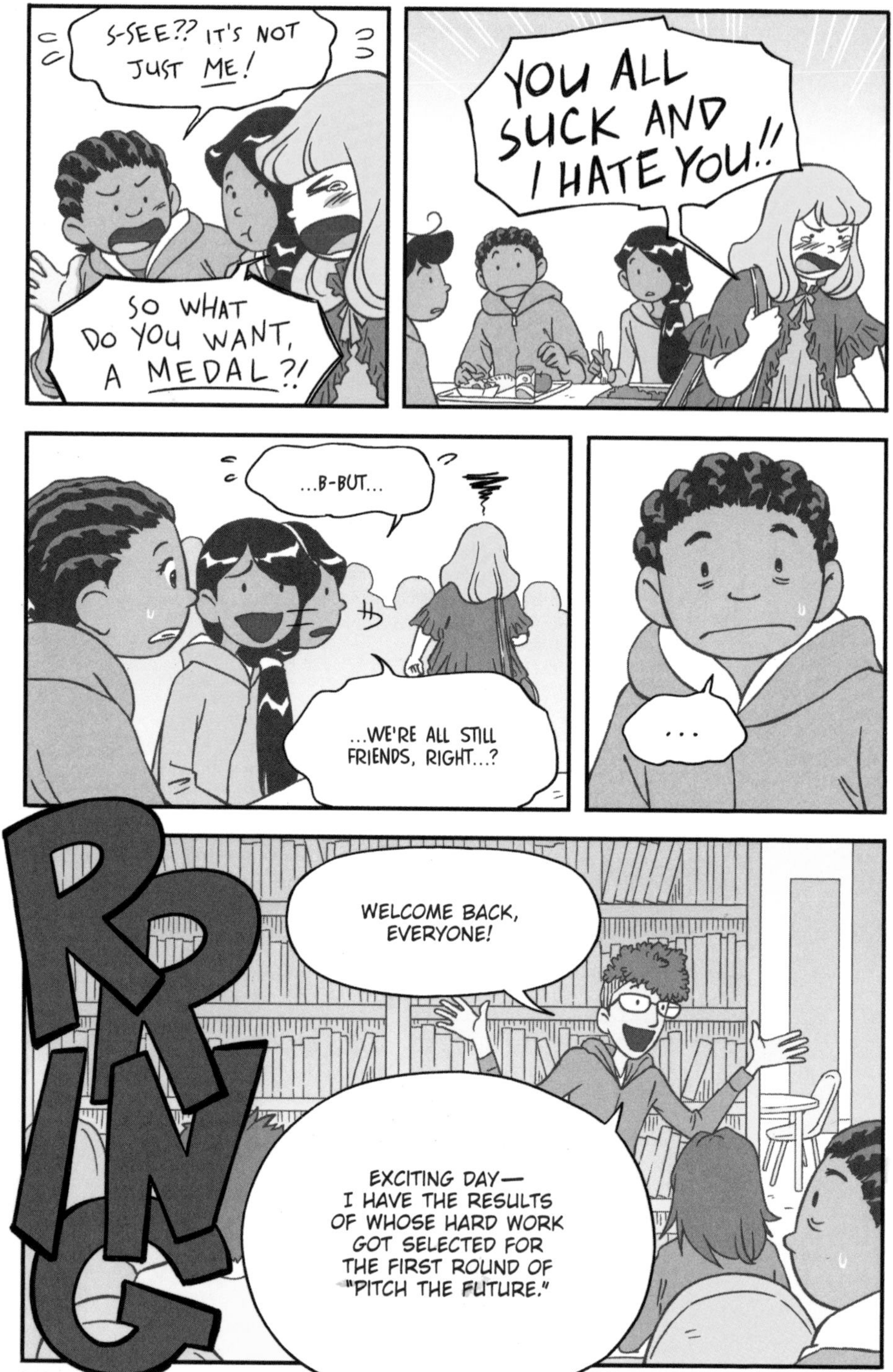
S-SEE?? IT'S NOT JUST ME!
SO WHAT DO YOU WANT, A MEDAL?!
YOU ALL SUCK AND I HATE YOU!!
...B-BUT...
...WE'RE ALL STILL FRIENDS, RIGHT...?
...
RRRING
WELCOME BACK, EVERYONE!
EXCITING DAY— I HAVE THE RESULTS OF WHOSE HARD WORK GOT SELECTED FOR THE FIRST ROUND OF "PITCH THE FUTURE."

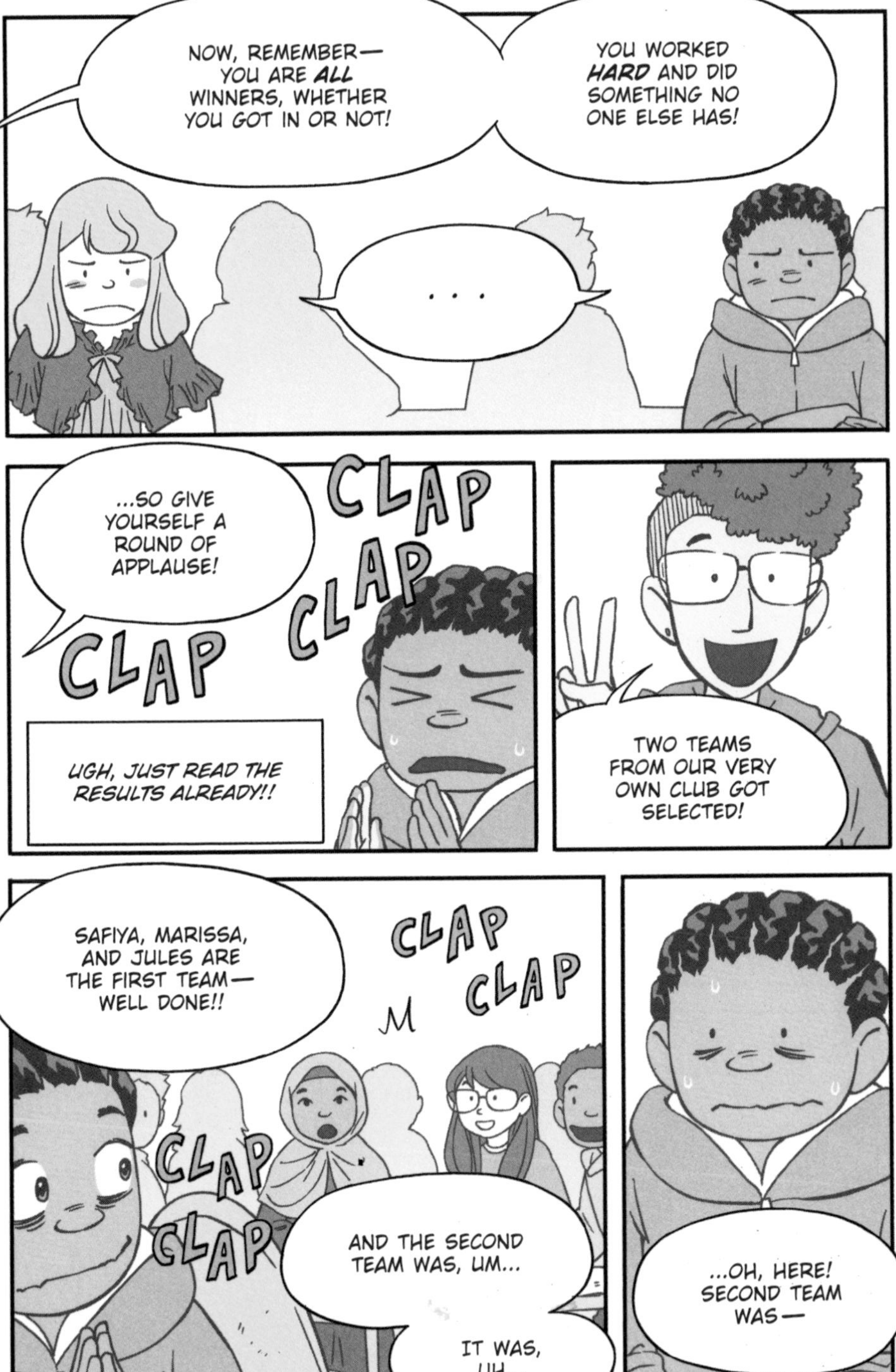
NOW, REMEMBER— YOU ARE ALL WINNERS, WHETHER YOU GOT IN OR NOT!
YOU WORKED HARD AND DID SOMETHING NO ONE ELSE HAS!
...
...SO GIVE YOURSELF A ROUND OF APPLAUSE!
CLAP
CLAP
CLAP
UGH, JUST READ THE RESULTS ALREADY!!
TWO TEAMS FROM OUR VERY OWN CLUB GOT SELECTED!
SAFIYA, MARISSA, AND JULES ARE THE FIRST TEAM— WELL DONE!!
CLAP
CLAP
M
CLAP
CLAP
AND THE SECOND TEAM WAS, UM...
IT WAS, UH...
...OH, HERE! SECOND TEAM WAS—

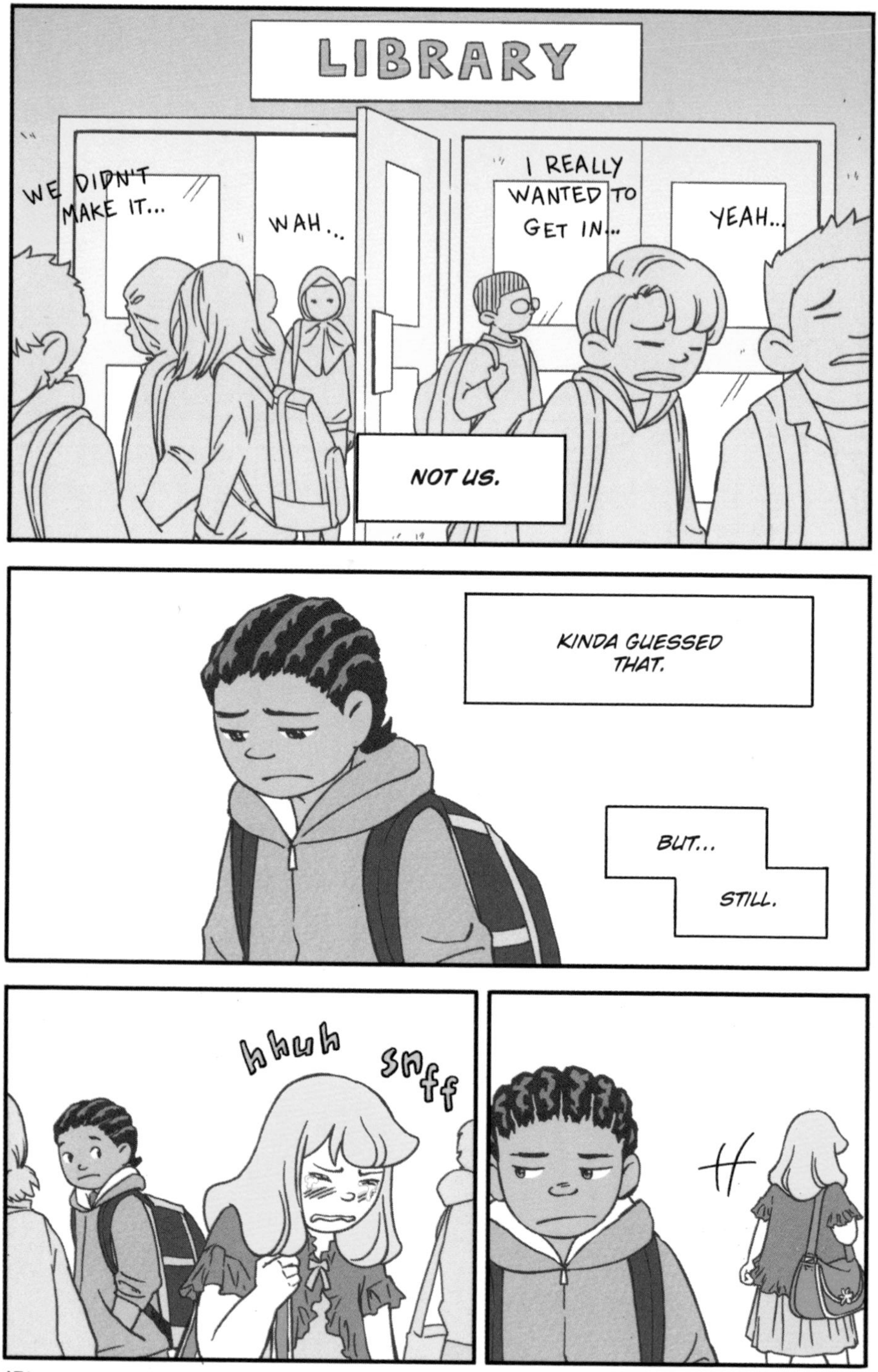
LIBRARY
WE DIDN'T MAKE IT...
WAH...
I REALLY WANTED TO GET IN...
YEAH...
NOT US.
KINDA GUESSED THAT.
BUT...
STILL.
hhuh
snff

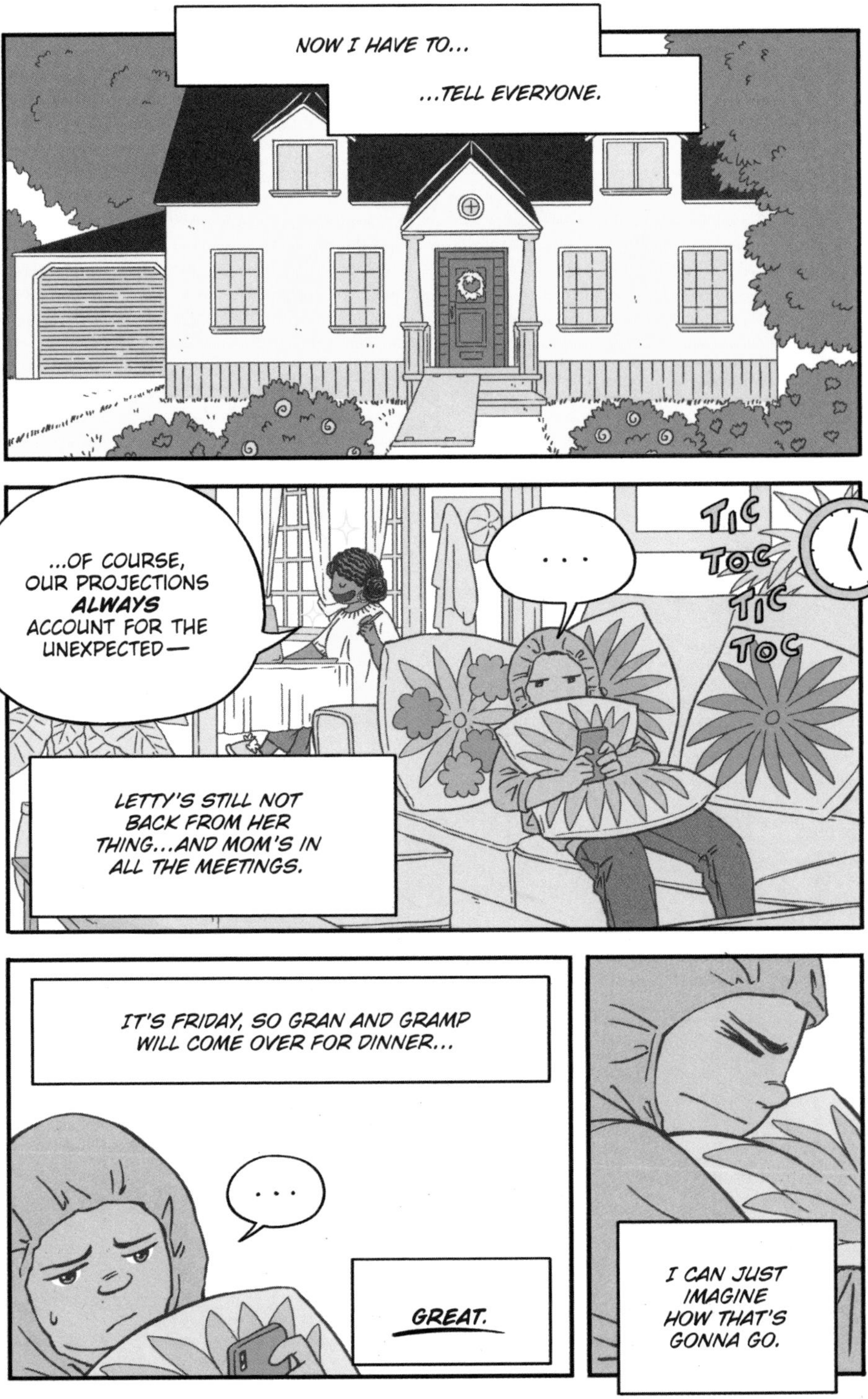
NOW I HAVE TO...
...TELL EVERYONE.
...OF COURSE, OUR PROJECTIONS ALWAYS ACCOUNT FOR THE UNEXPECTED—
. . .
TIC TOC TIC TOC
LETTY'S STILL NOT BACK FROM HER THING...AND MOM'S IN ALL THE MEETINGS.
IT'S FRIDAY, SO GRAN AND GRAMP WILL COME OVER FOR DINNER...
. . .
GREAT.
I CAN JUST IMAGINE HOW THAT'S GONNA GO.

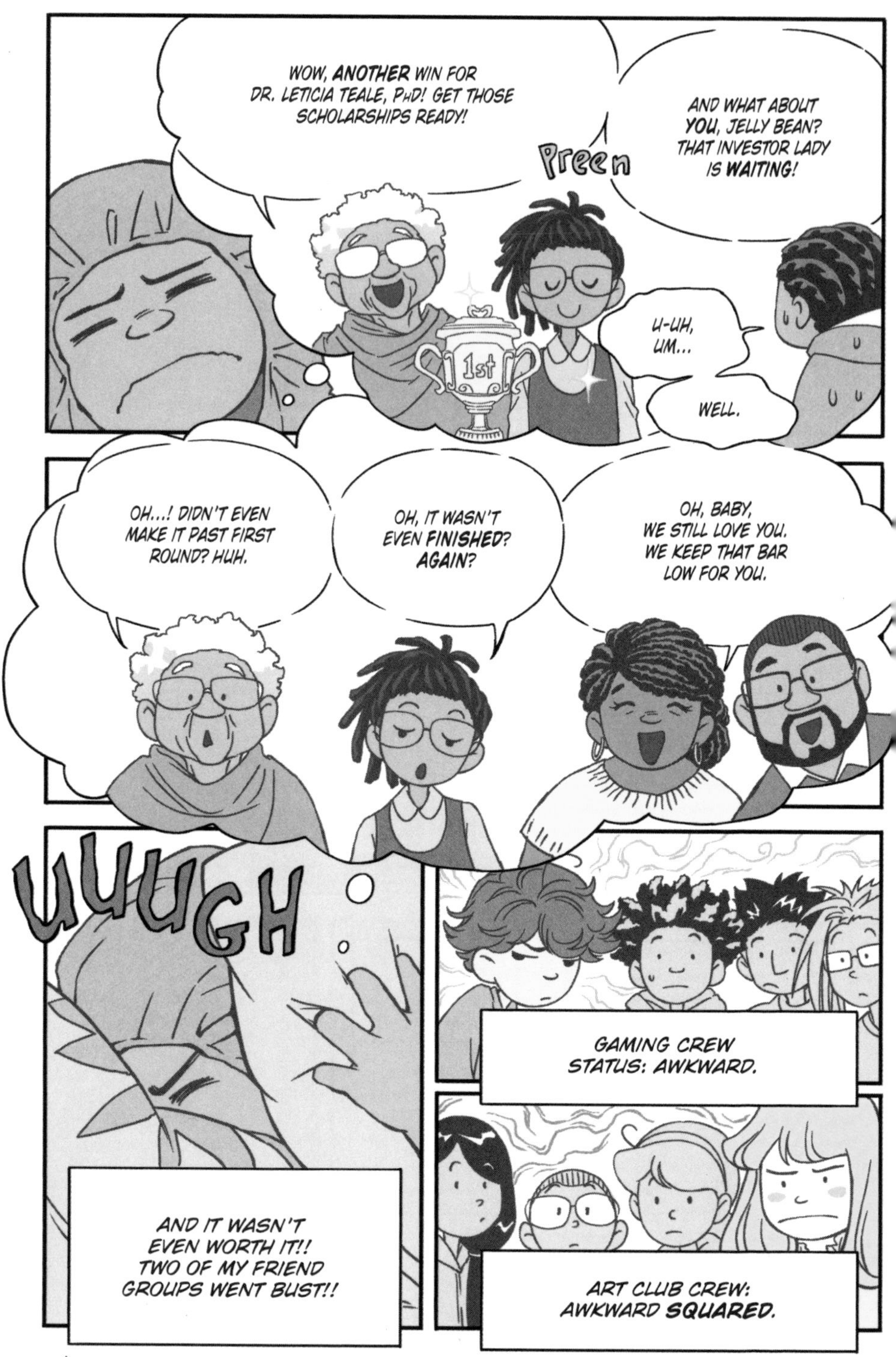
WOW, ANOTHER WIN FOR DR. LETICIA TEALE, PhD! GET THOSE SCHOLARSHIPS READY!
Preen
AND WHAT ABOUT YOU, JELLY BEAN? THAT INVESTOR LADY IS WAITING!
1st
U-UH, UM...
WELL.
OH...! DIDN'T EVEN MAKE IT PAST FIRST ROUND? HUH.
OH, IT WASN'T EVEN FINISHED? AGAIN?
OH, BABY, WE STILL LOVE YOU. WE KEEP THAT BAR LOW FOR YOU.
UUUGH
AND IT WASN'T EVEN WORTH IT!! TWO OF MY FRIEND GROUPS WENT BUST!!
GAMING CREW STATUS: AWKWARD.
ART CLUB CREW: AWKWARD SQUARED.

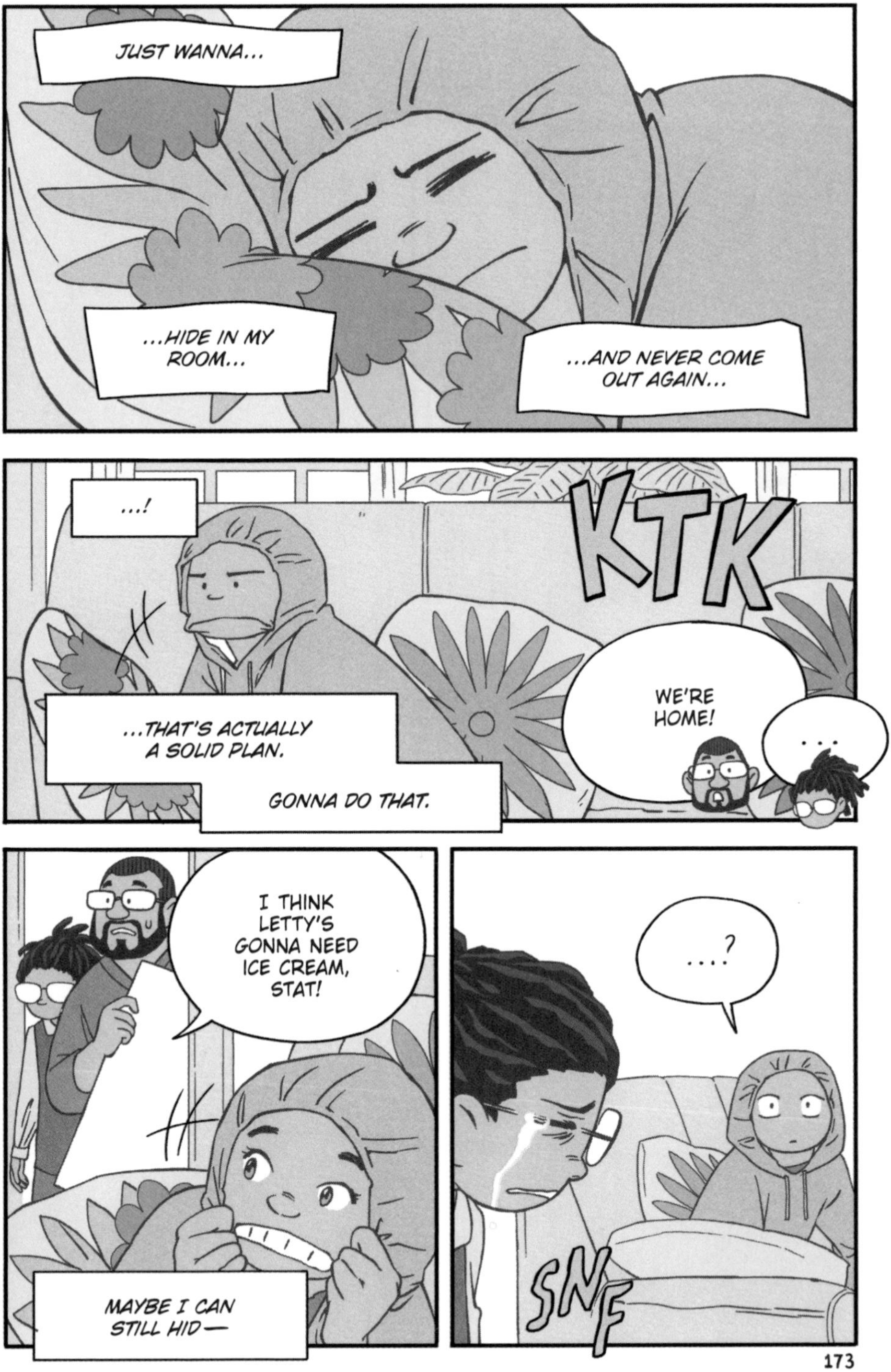

JUST WANNA...
...HIDE IN MY ROOM...
...AND NEVER COME OUT AGAIN...
...!
KTK
...THAT'S ACTUALLY A SOLID PLAN.
GONNA DO THAT.
WE'RE HOME!
...
I THINK LETTY'S GONNA NEED ICE CREAM, STAT!
MAYBE I CAN STILL HID—
...?
SNF

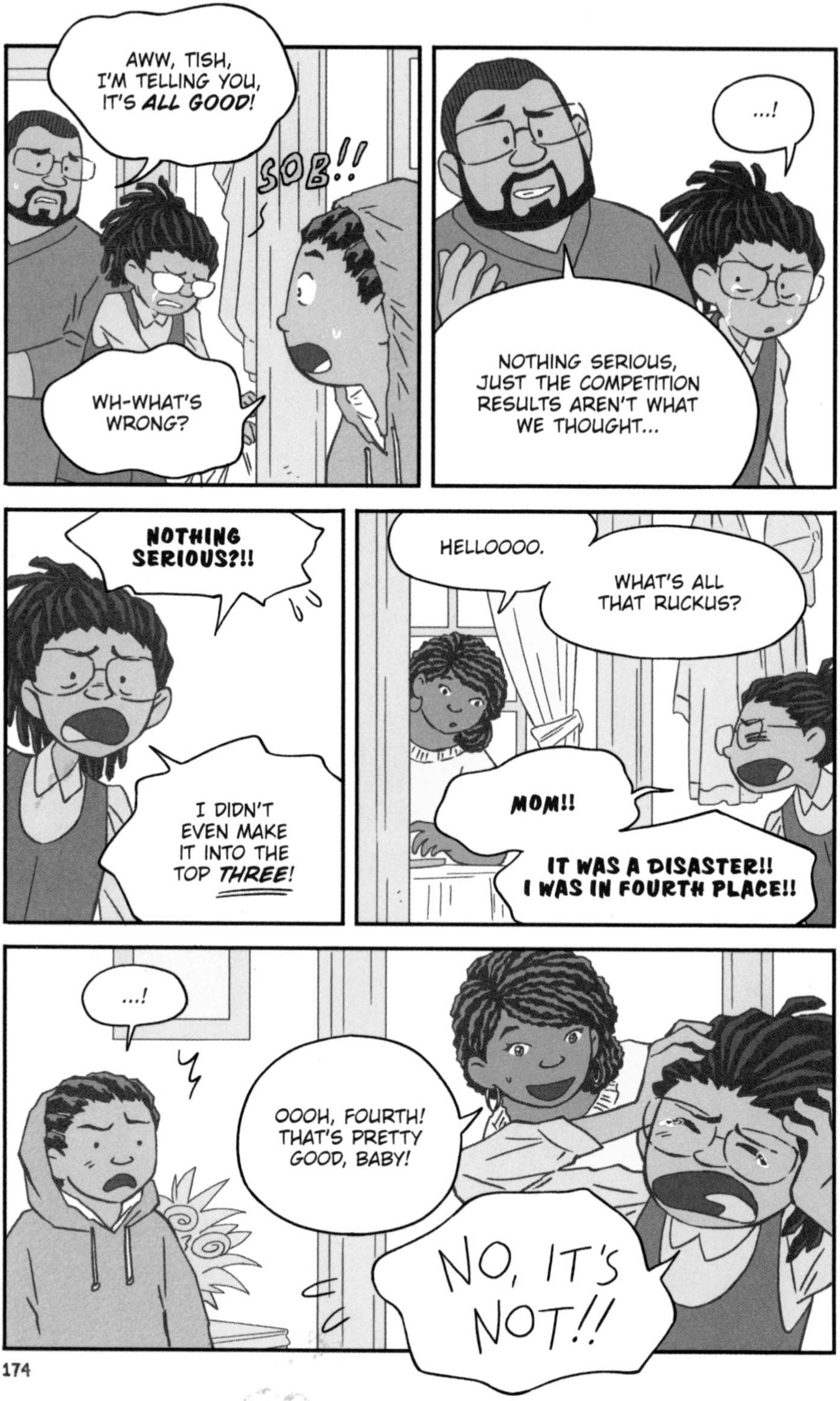
AWW, TISH, I'M TELLING YOU, IT'S **ALL GOOD**!
SOB!!
WH-WHAT'S WRONG?
...!
NOTHING SERIOUS, JUST THE COMPETITION RESULTS AREN'T WHAT WE THOUGHT...
NOTHING SERIOUS?!!
I DIDN'T EVEN MAKE IT INTO THE TOP ***THREE***!
HELLOOOO.
WHAT'S ALL THAT RUCKUS?
MOM!!
IT WAS A DISASTER!! I WAS IN FOURTH PLACE!!
...!
OOOH, FOURTH! THAT'S PRETTY GOOD, BABY!
NO, IT'S NOT!!

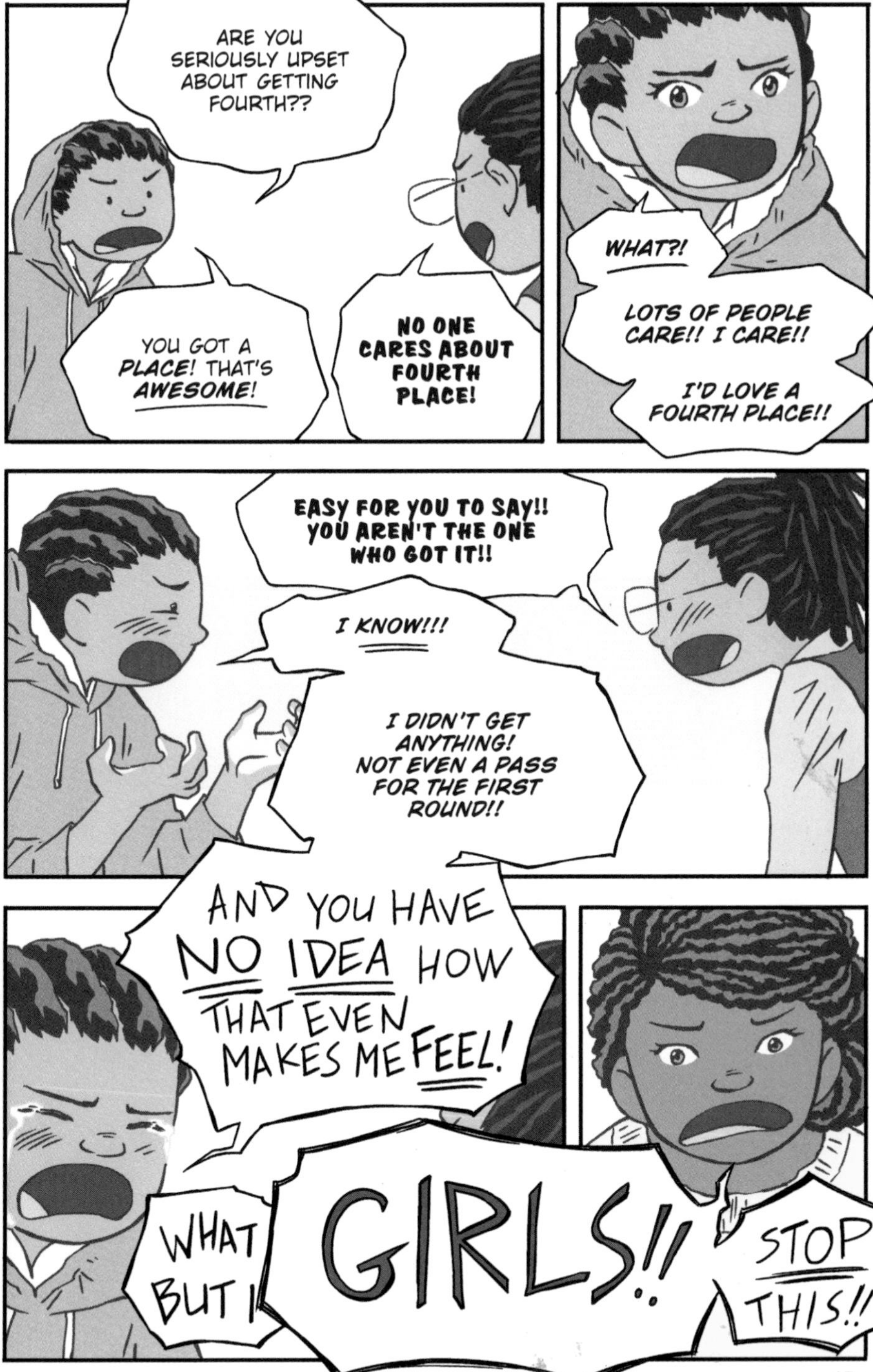
ARE YOU SERIOUSLY UPSET ABOUT GETTING FOURTH??
YOU GOT A PLACE! THAT'S AWESOME!
NO ONE CARES ABOUT FOURTH PLACE!
WHAT?!
LOTS OF PEOPLE CARE!! I CARE!!
I'D LOVE A FOURTH PLACE!!
EASY FOR YOU TO SAY!! YOU AREN'T THE ONE WHO GOT IT!!
I KNOW!!!
I DIDN'T GET ANYTHING! NOT EVEN A PASS FOR THE FIRST ROUND!!
AND YOU HAVE NO IDEA HOW THAT EVEN MAKES ME FEEL!
WHAT BUT I
GIRLS!!
STOP THIS!!

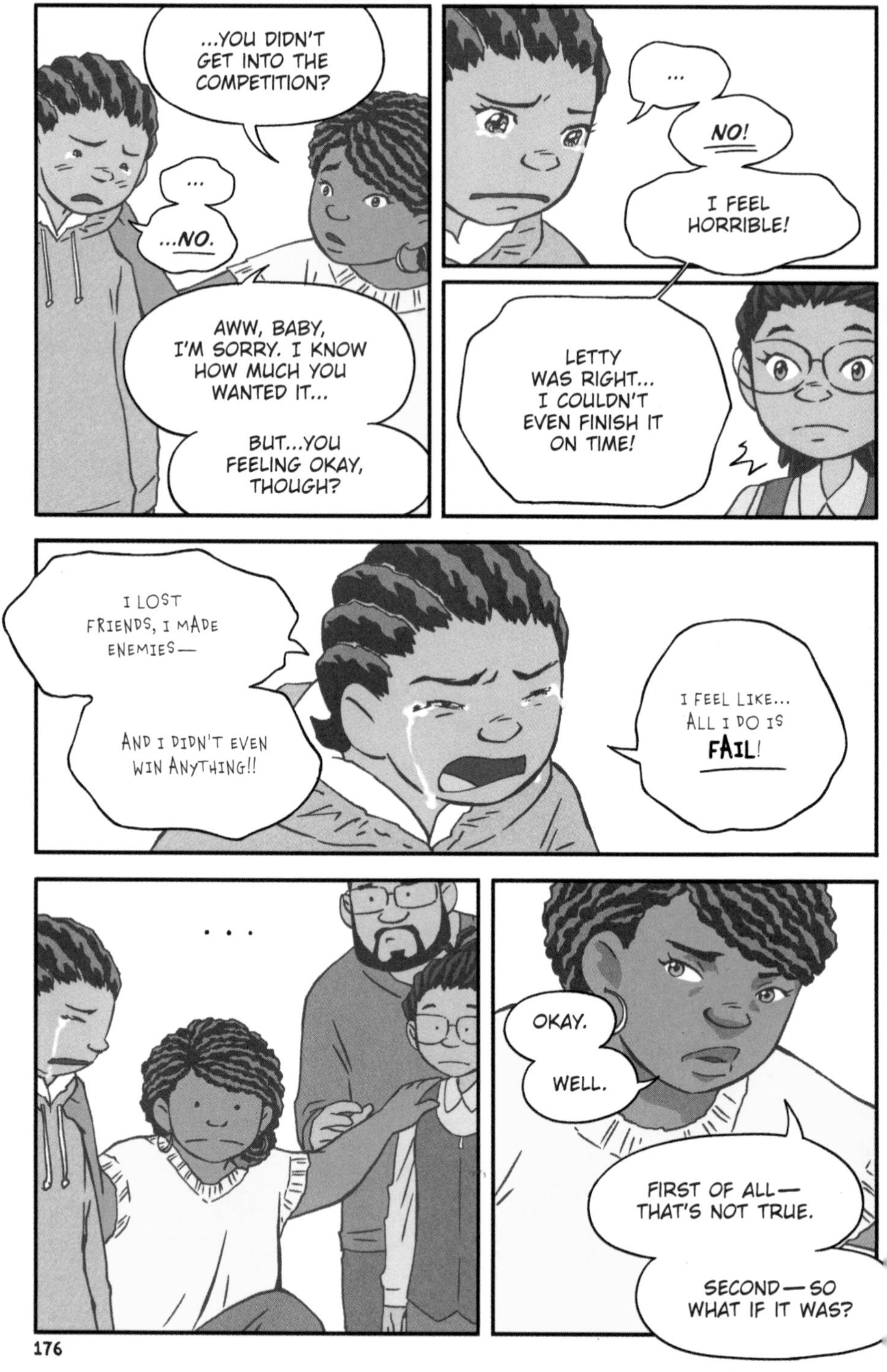
...YOU DIDN'T GET INTO THE COMPETITION?
...
...NO.
AWW, BABY, I'M SORRY. I KNOW HOW MUCH YOU WANTED IT...
BUT...YOU FEELING OKAY, THOUGH?
...
NO!
I FEEL HORRIBLE!
LETTY WAS RIGHT... I COULDN'T EVEN FINISH IT ON TIME!
I LOST FRIENDS, I MADE ENEMIES—
AND I DIDN'T EVEN WIN ANYTHING!!
I FEEL LIKE... ALL I DO IS FAIL!
. . .
OKAY.
WELL.
FIRST OF ALL— THAT'S NOT TRUE.
SECOND—SO WHAT IF IT WAS?

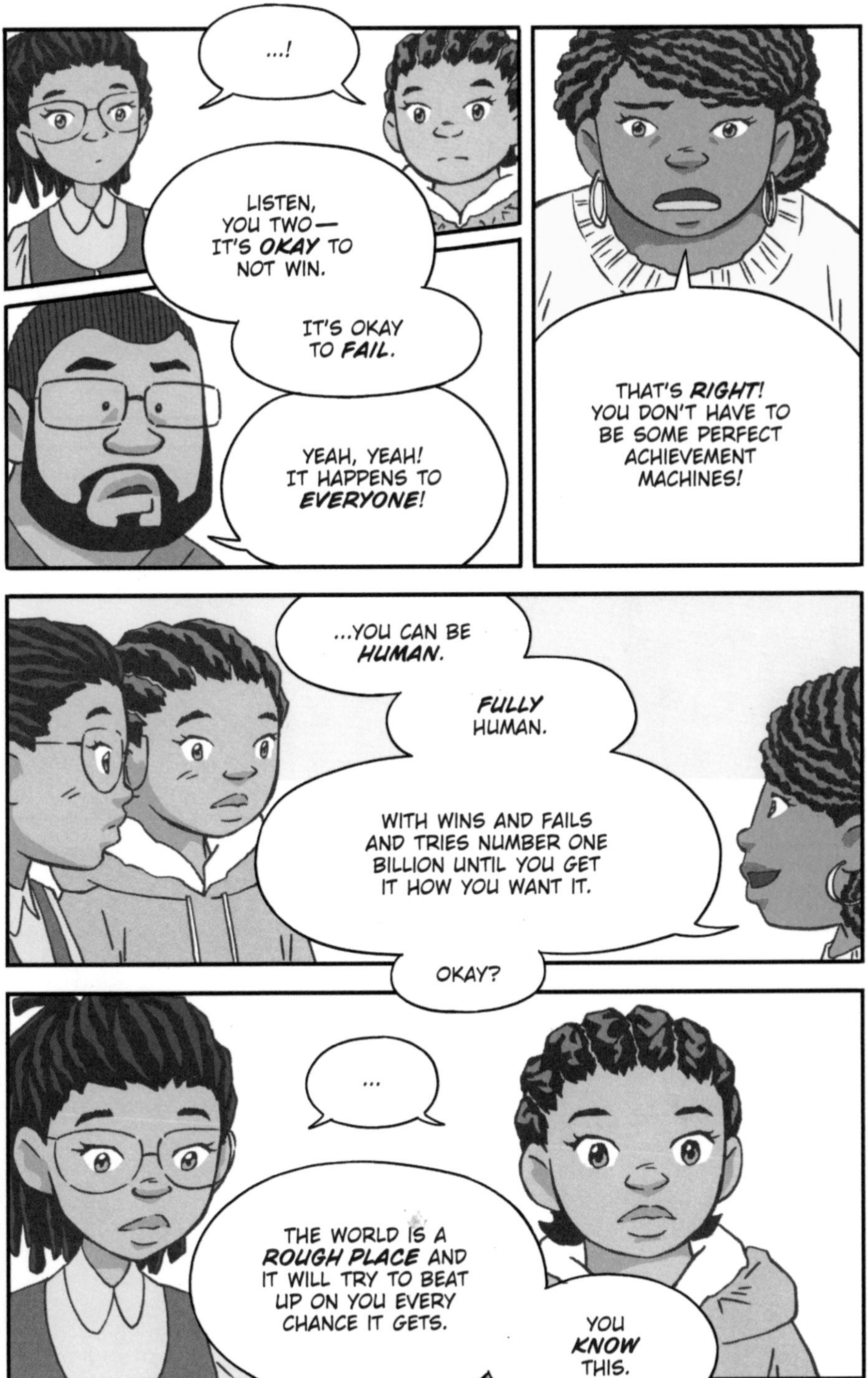
...!
LISTEN, YOU TWO— IT'S OKAY TO NOT WIN.
IT'S OKAY TO FAIL.
YEAH, YEAH! IT HAPPENS TO EVERYONE!
THAT'S RIGHT! YOU DON'T HAVE TO BE SOME PERFECT ACHIEVEMENT MACHINES!
...YOU CAN BE HUMAN.
FULLY HUMAN.
WITH WINS AND FAILS AND TRIES NUMBER ONE BILLION UNTIL YOU GET IT HOW YOU WANT IT.
OKAY?
...
THE WORLD IS A ROUGH PLACE AND IT WILL TRY TO BEAT UP ON YOU EVERY CHANCE IT GETS.
YOU KNOW THIS.

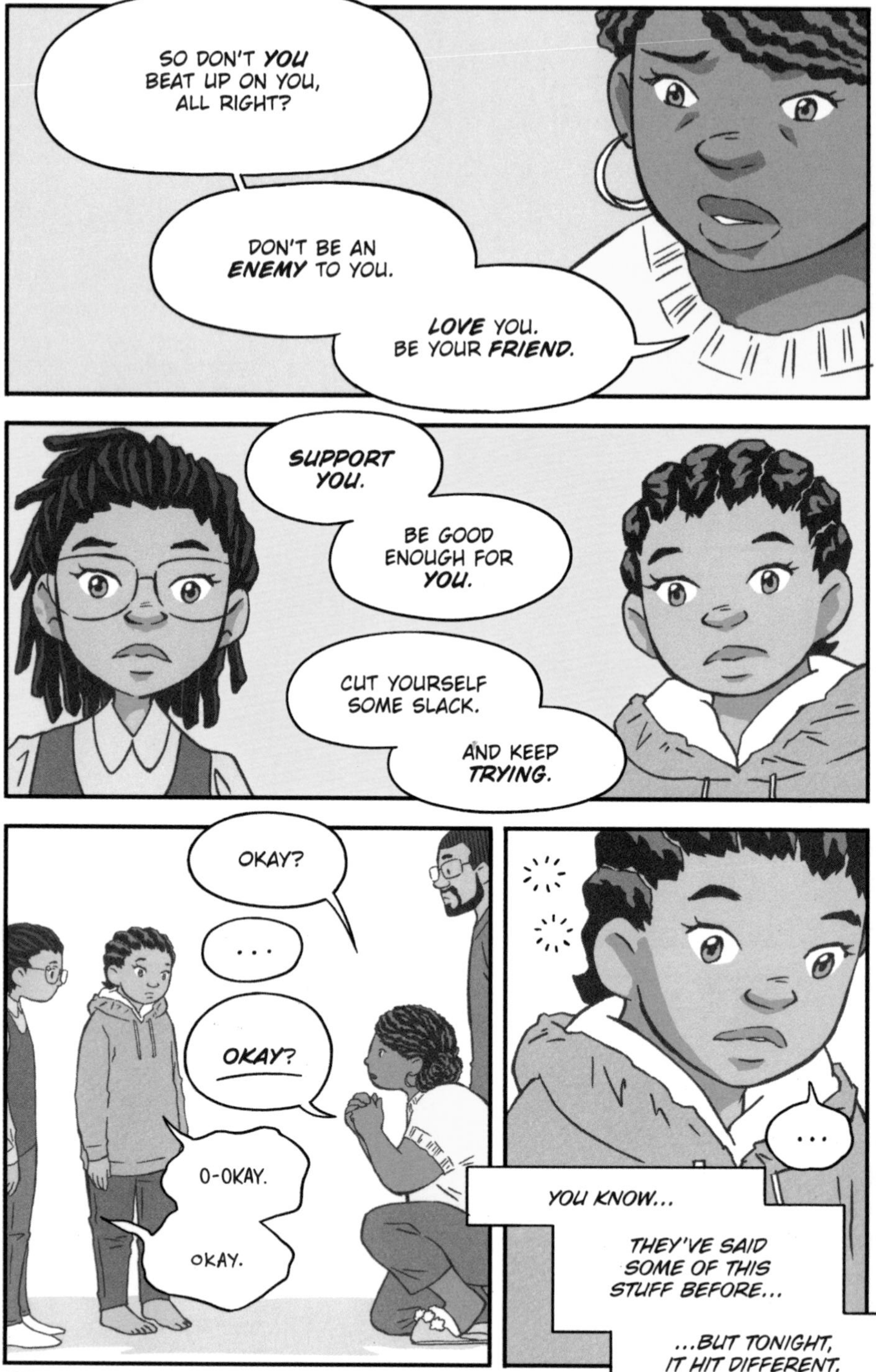
SO DON'T YOU BEAT UP ON YOU, ALL RIGHT?
DON'T BE AN ENEMY TO YOU.
LOVE YOU. BE YOUR FRIEND.
SUPPORT YOU.
BE GOOD ENOUGH FOR YOU.
CUT YOURSELF SOME SLACK.
AND KEEP TRYING.
OKAY?
. . .
OKAY?
O-OKAY.
OKAY.
. . .
YOU KNOW...
THEY'VE SAID SOME OF THIS STUFF BEFORE...
...BUT TONIGHT, IT HIT DIFFERENT.

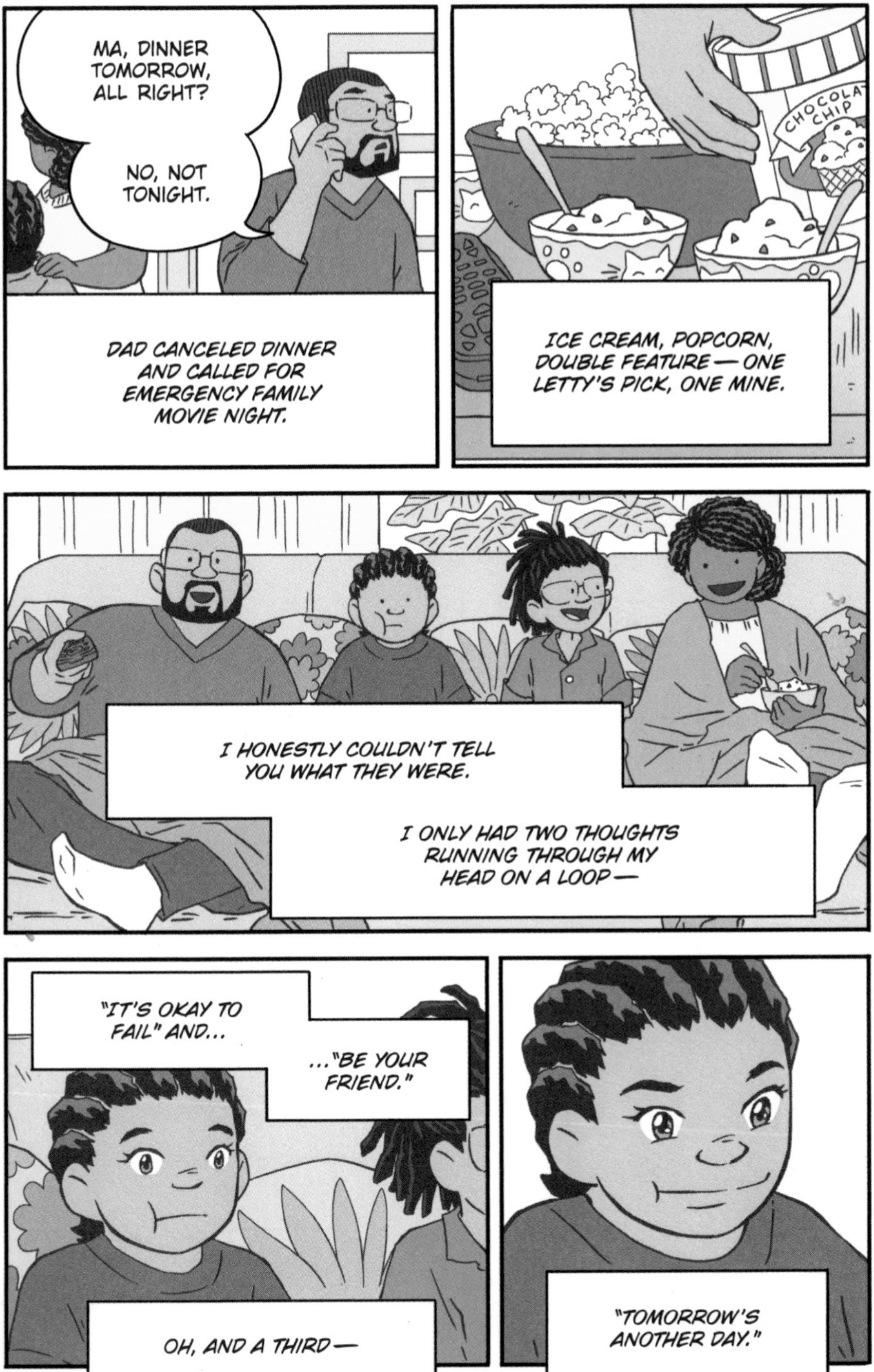
MA, DINNER TOMORROW, ALL RIGHT?
NO, NOT TONIGHT.
DAD CANCELED DINNER AND CALLED FOR EMERGENCY FAMILY MOVIE NIGHT.
CHOCOLATE CHIP
ICE CREAM, POPCORN, DOUBLE FEATURE — ONE LETTY'S PICK, ONE MINE.
I HONESTLY COULDN'T TELL YOU WHAT THEY WERE.
I ONLY HAD TWO THOUGHTS RUNNING THROUGH MY HEAD ON A LOOP—
"IT'S OKAY TO FAIL" AND...
..."BE YOUR FRIEND."
OH, AND A THIRD—
"TOMORROW'S ANOTHER DAY."

CHAPTER 7

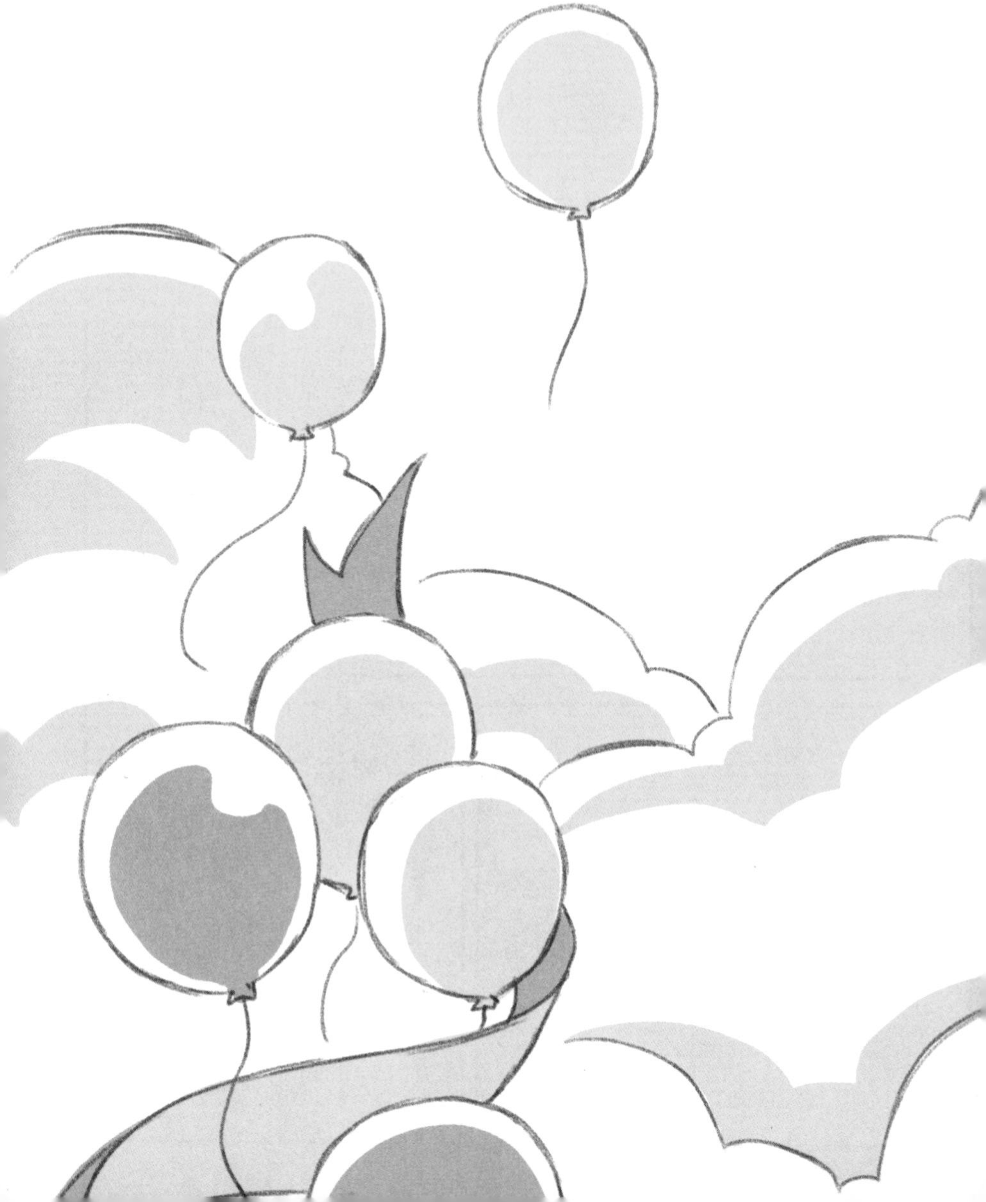

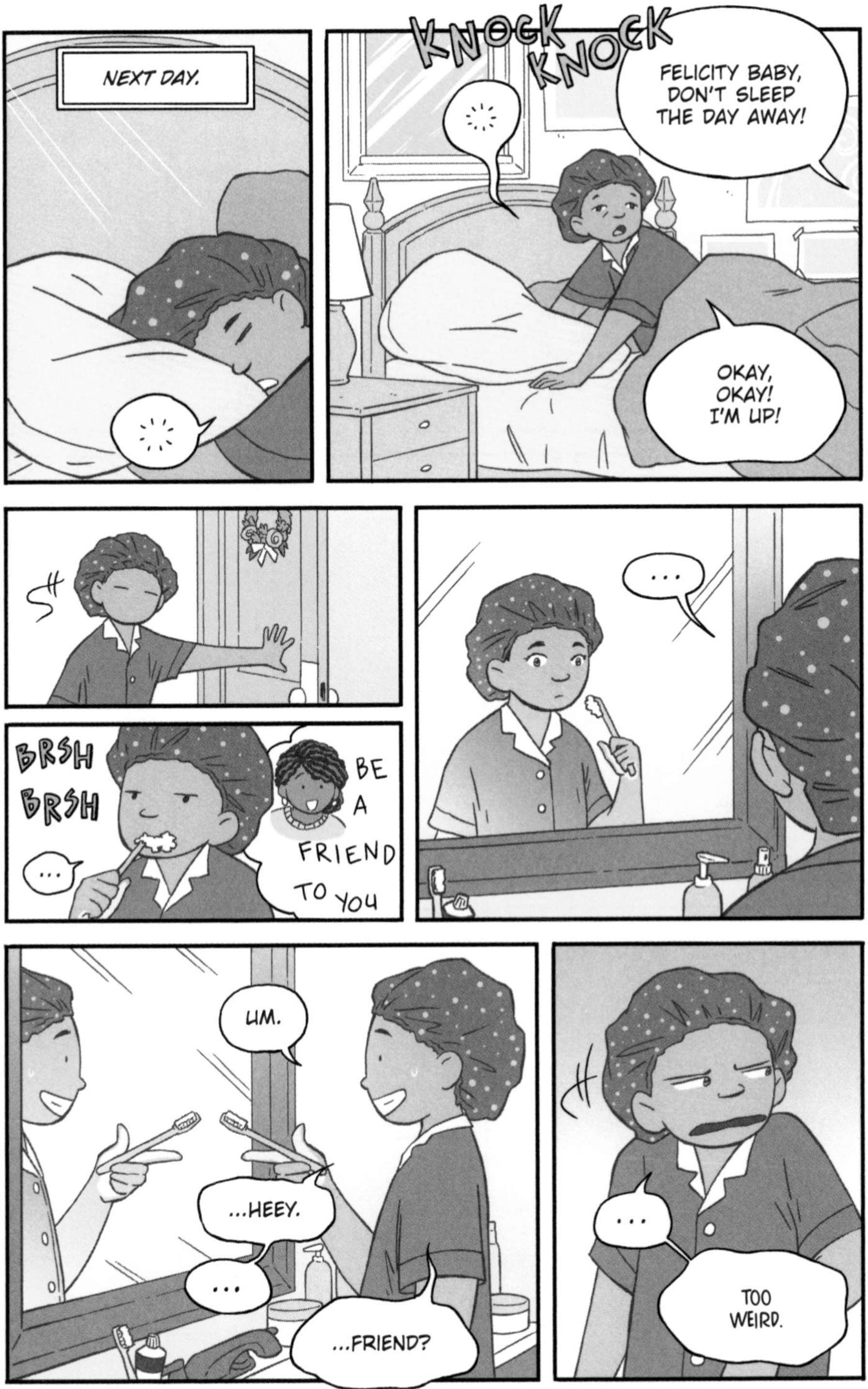
NEXT DAY.
KNOCK KNOCK
FELICITY BABY, DON'T SLEEP THE DAY AWAY!
OKAY, OKAY! I'M UP!
BRSH BRSH
...
BE A FRIEND TO YOU
...
UM.
...HEEY.
...
...FRIEND?
...
TOO WEIRD.

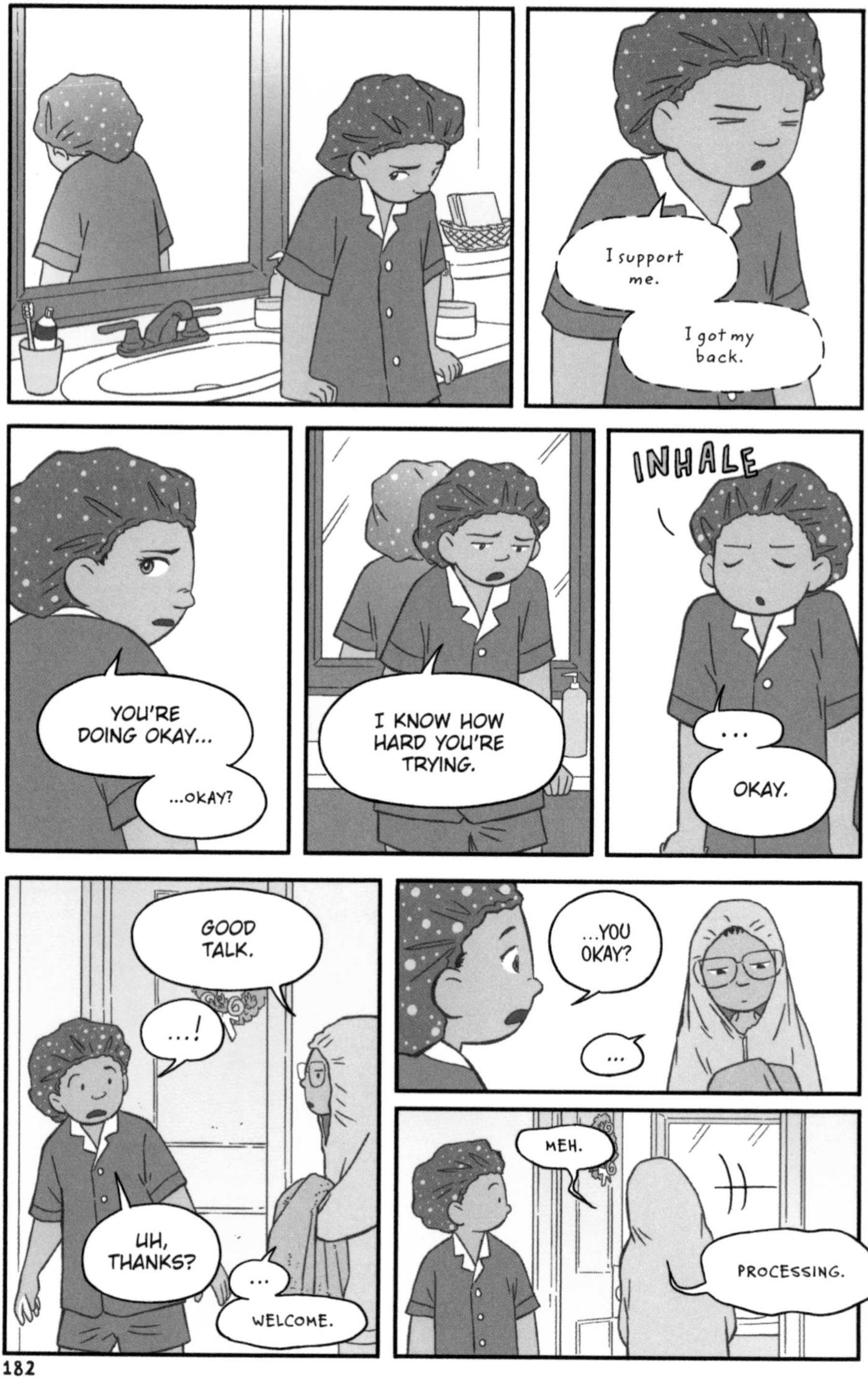
I support me.
I got my back.
YOU'RE DOING OKAY...
...OKAY?
I KNOW HOW HARD YOU'RE TRYING.
INHALE
...
OKAY.
GOOD TALK.
...!
UH, THANKS?
...
WELCOME.
...YOU OKAY?
...
MEH.
PROCESSING.

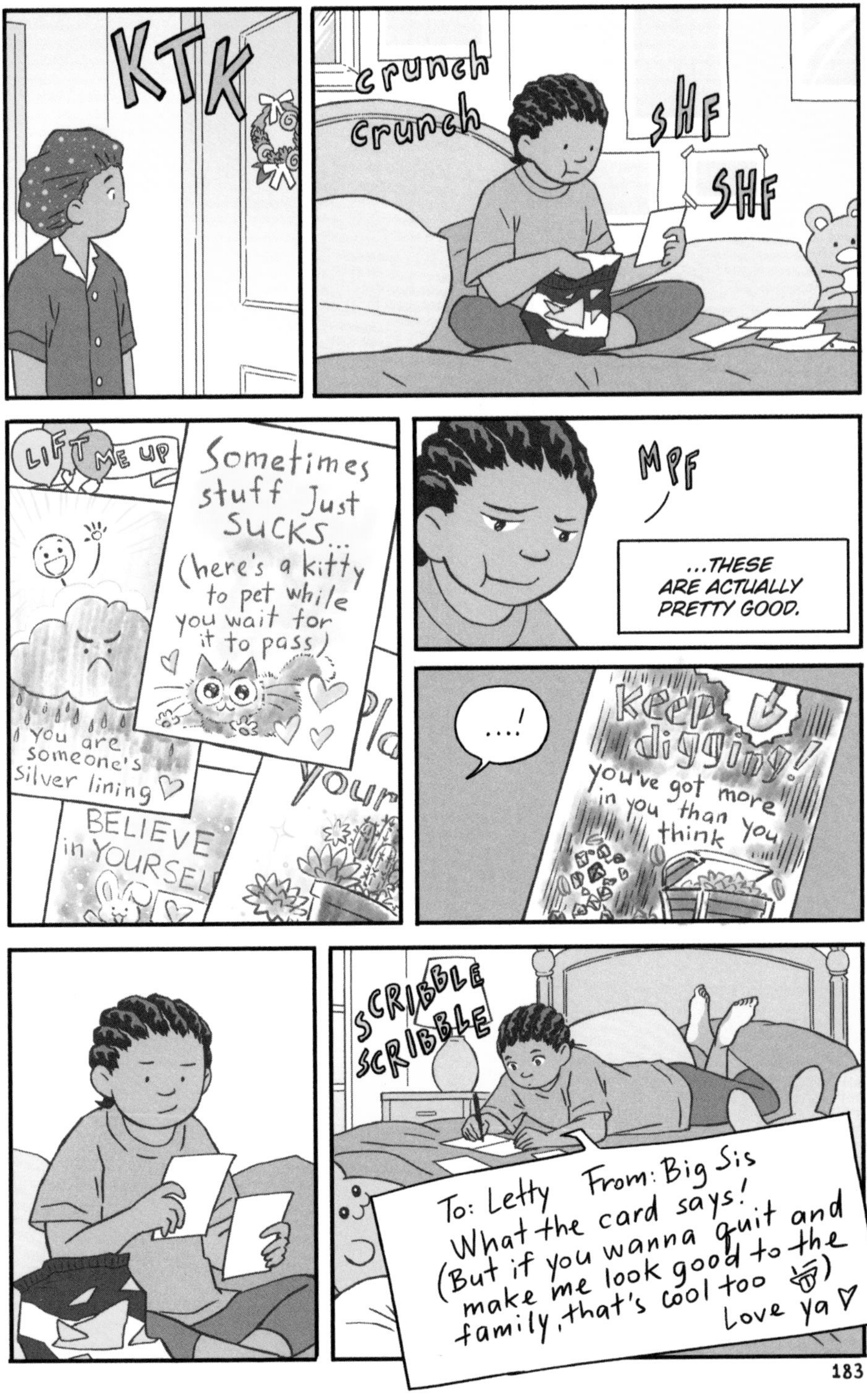
KTK
crunch
crunch
SHF
SHF
LIFT ME UP
Sometimes stuff Just SUCKS... (here's a kitty to pet while you wait for it to pass)
you are someone's silver lining
BELIEVE in YOURSELF
MPF
...THESE ARE ACTUALLY PRETTY GOOD.
....!
Keep digging! you've got more in you than you think
SCRIBBLE
SCRIBBLE
To: Letty From: Big Sis
What the card says!
(But if you wanna quit and make me look good to the family, that's cool too)
Love ya

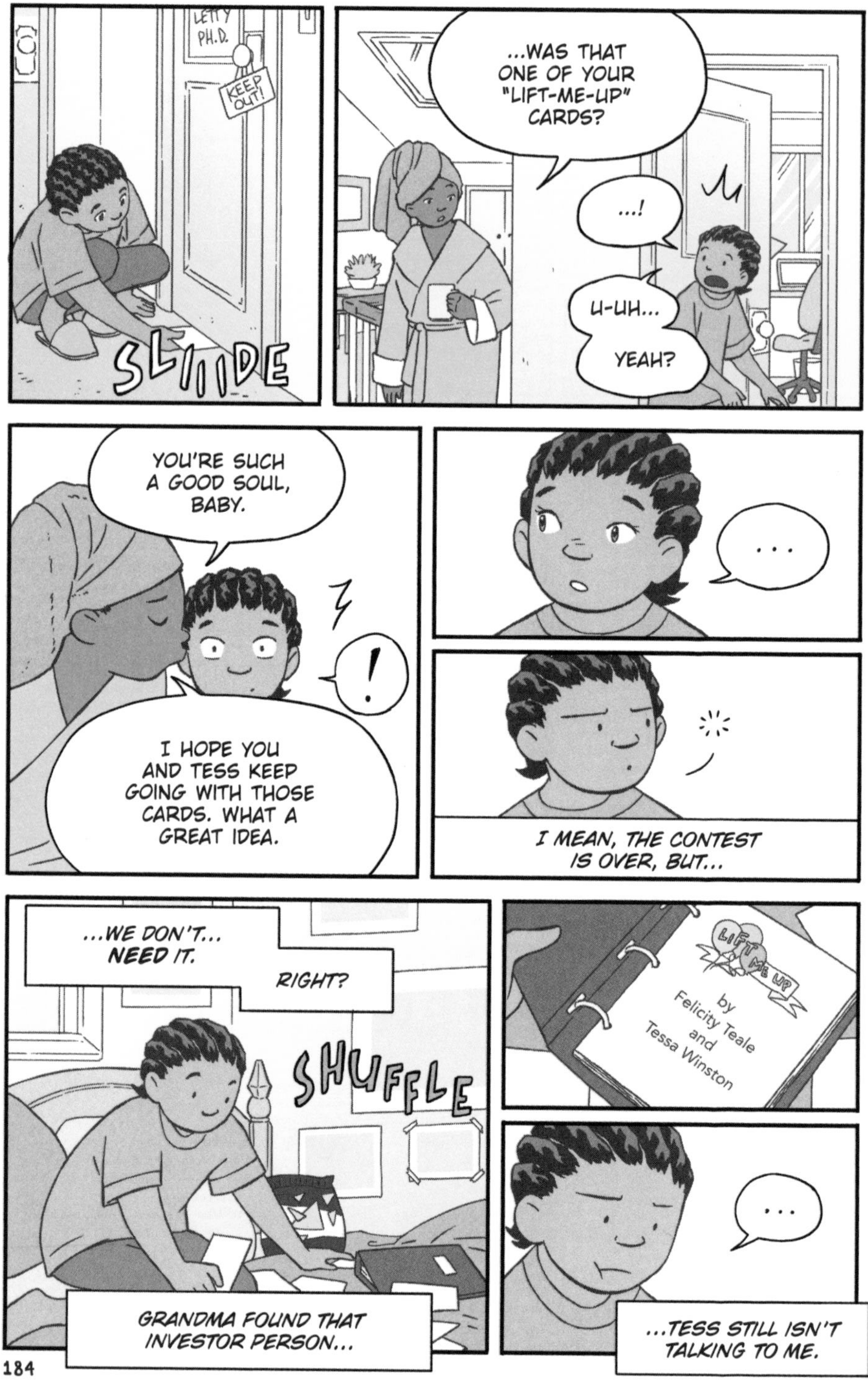
LETTY PH.D.
KEEP OUT!
SLIIIDE
...WAS THAT ONE OF YOUR "LIFT-ME-UP" CARDS?
...!
U-UH...
YEAH?
YOU'RE SUCH A GOOD SOUL, BABY.
!
I HOPE YOU AND TESS KEEP GOING WITH THOSE CARDS. WHAT A GREAT IDEA.
...
I MEAN, THE CONTEST IS OVER, BUT...
...WE DON'T... NEED IT.
RIGHT?
SHUFFLE
GRANDMA FOUND THAT INVESTOR PERSON...
LIFT ME UP
by Felicity Teale and Tessa Winston
...
...TESS STILL ISN'T TALKING TO ME.

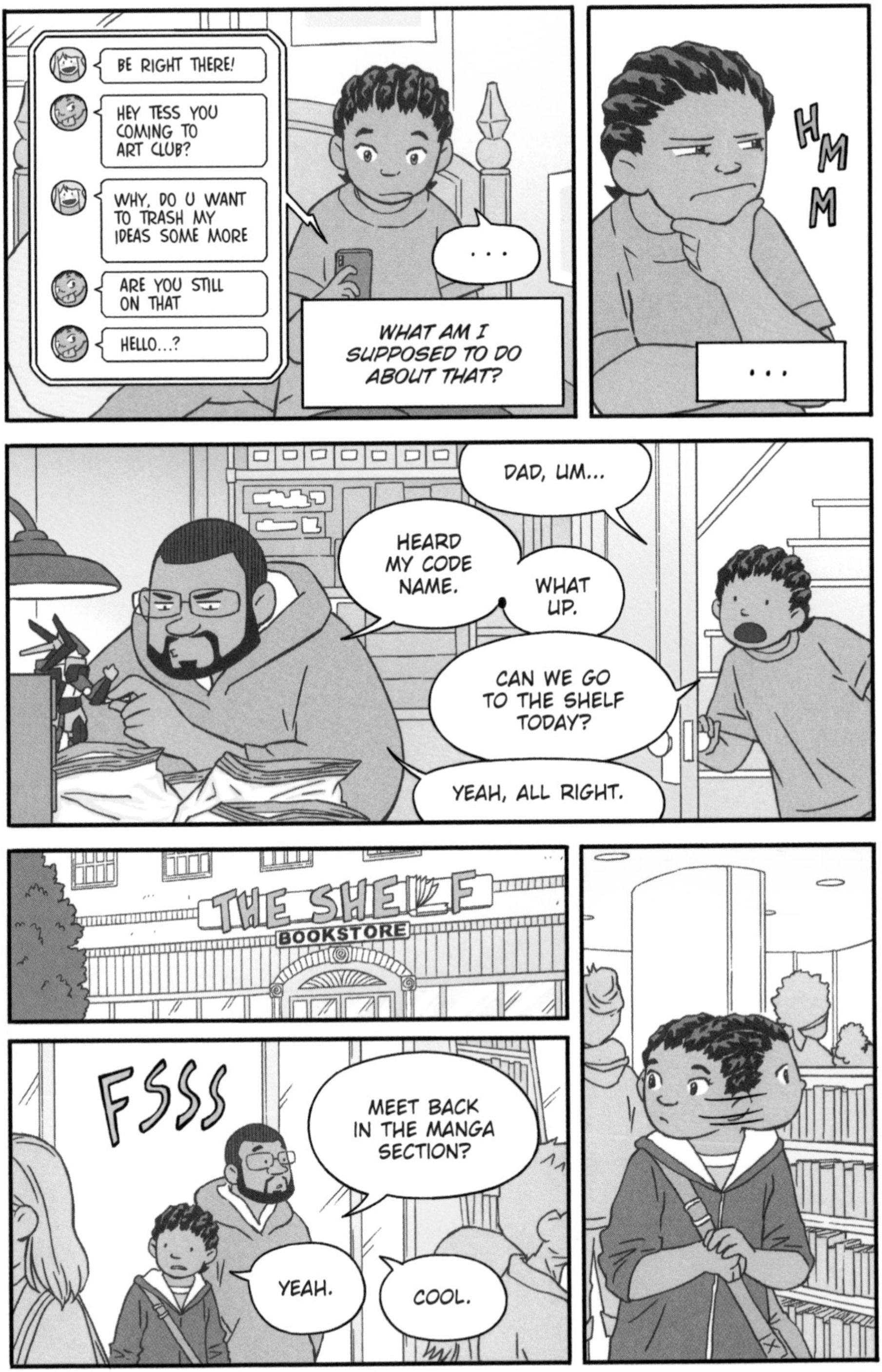
HEY TESS YOU COMING TO ART CLUB?
WHY, DO U WANT TO TRASH MY IDEAS SOME MORE
ARE YOU STILL ON THAT
HELLO...?
BE RIGHT THERE!
. . .
WHAT AM I SUPPOSED TO DO ABOUT THAT?
HMM
. . .
DAD, UM...
HEARD MY CODE NAME.
WHAT UP.
CAN WE GO TO THE SHELF TODAY?
YEAH, ALL RIGHT.
THE SHELF
BOOKSTORE
FSSS
MEET BACK IN THE MANGA SECTION?
YEAH.
COOL.

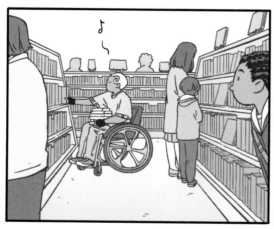

...UM, EXCUSE ME... MX. SHEPARD?

?

DO YOU... DO YOU HAVE TIME FOR A QUESTION?

HEEEY, I KNOW YOU! ONE OF EDI'S KIDPRENEURS?

U-UH, YEAH.

HI.

WELCOME BACK, FUTURE CHANGE-MAKER!

HOW'D THAT CONTEST TURN OUT?

O-OH, UM...

...MY TEAM DIDN'T GET IN.

...AH.

BUMMER.

IT KINDA WASN'T A SURPRISE. WE DIDN'T EVEN REALLY FINISH IT...

...AND I HAD THIS *HUGE* FIGHT WITH MY PARTNER...

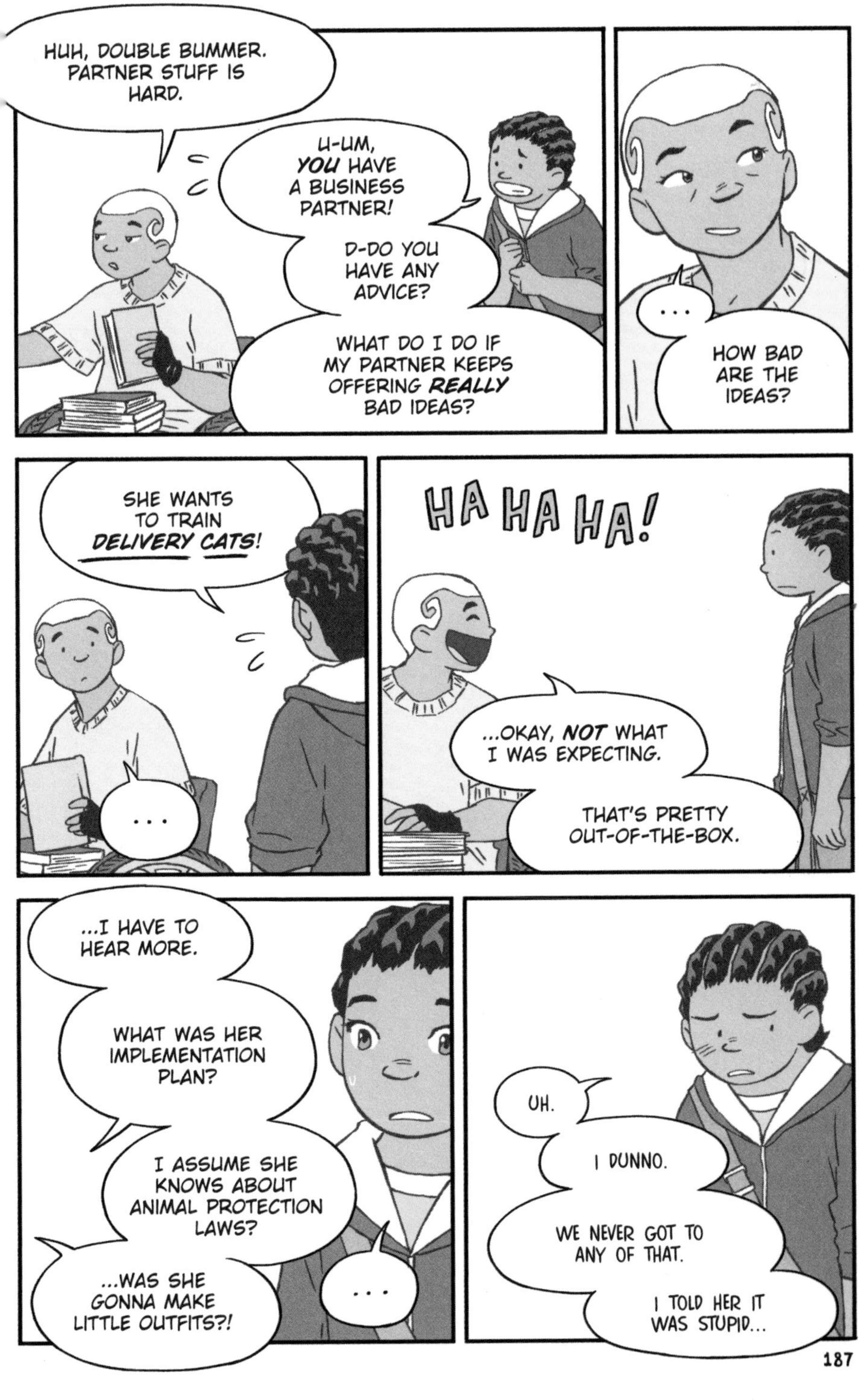
HUH, DOUBLE BUMMER. PARTNER STUFF IS HARD.
U-UM, **YOU** HAVE A BUSINESS PARTNER!
D-DO YOU HAVE ANY ADVICE?
WHAT DO I DO IF MY PARTNER KEEPS OFFERING **REALLY** BAD IDEAS?
...
HOW BAD ARE THE IDEAS?
SHE WANTS TO TRAIN **DELIVERY CATS**!
...
HA HA HA HA!
...OKAY, **NOT** WHAT I WAS EXPECTING.
THAT'S PRETTY OUT-OF-THE-BOX.
...I HAVE TO HEAR MORE.
WHAT WAS HER IMPLEMENTATION PLAN?
I ASSUME SHE KNOWS ABOUT ANIMAL PROTECTION LAWS?
...WAS SHE GONNA MAKE LITTLE OUTFITS?!
...
UH.
I DUNNO.
WE NEVER GOT TO ANY OF THAT.
I TOLD HER IT WAS STUPID...

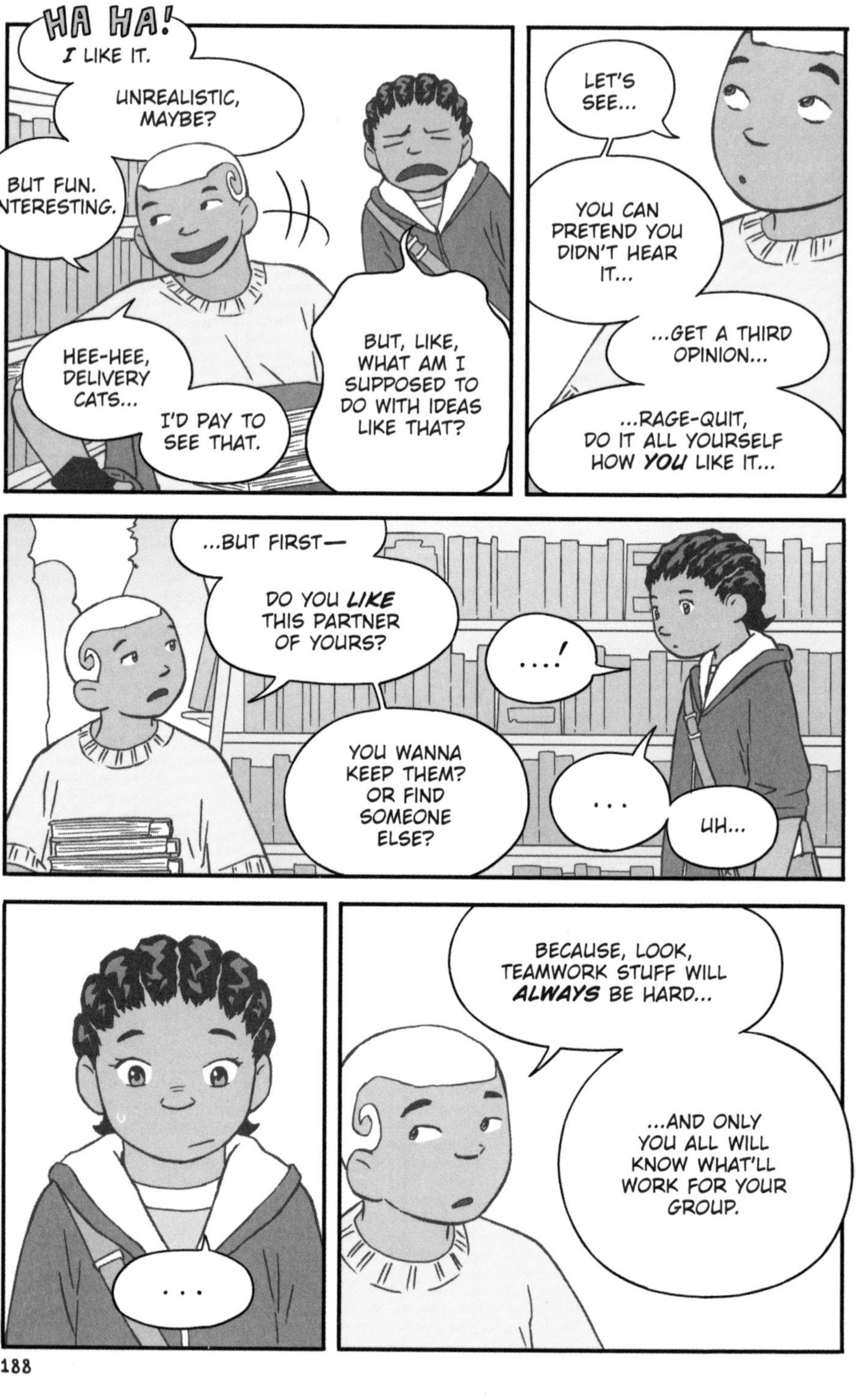
HA HA!
I LIKE IT.
UNREALISTIC, MAYBE?
BUT FUN. INTERESTING.
HEE-HEE, DELIVERY CATS...
I'D PAY TO SEE THAT.
BUT, LIKE, WHAT AM I SUPPOSED TO DO WITH IDEAS LIKE THAT?
LET'S SEE...
YOU CAN PRETEND YOU DIDN'T HEAR IT...
...GET A THIRD OPINION...
...RAGE-QUIT, DO IT ALL YOURSELF HOW YOU LIKE IT...
...BUT FIRST—
DO YOU LIKE THIS PARTNER OF YOURS?
YOU WANNA KEEP THEM? OR FIND SOMEONE ELSE?
....!
...
UH...
...
BECAUSE, LOOK, TEAMWORK STUFF WILL ALWAYS BE HARD...
...AND ONLY YOU ALL WILL KNOW WHAT'LL WORK FOR YOUR GROUP.

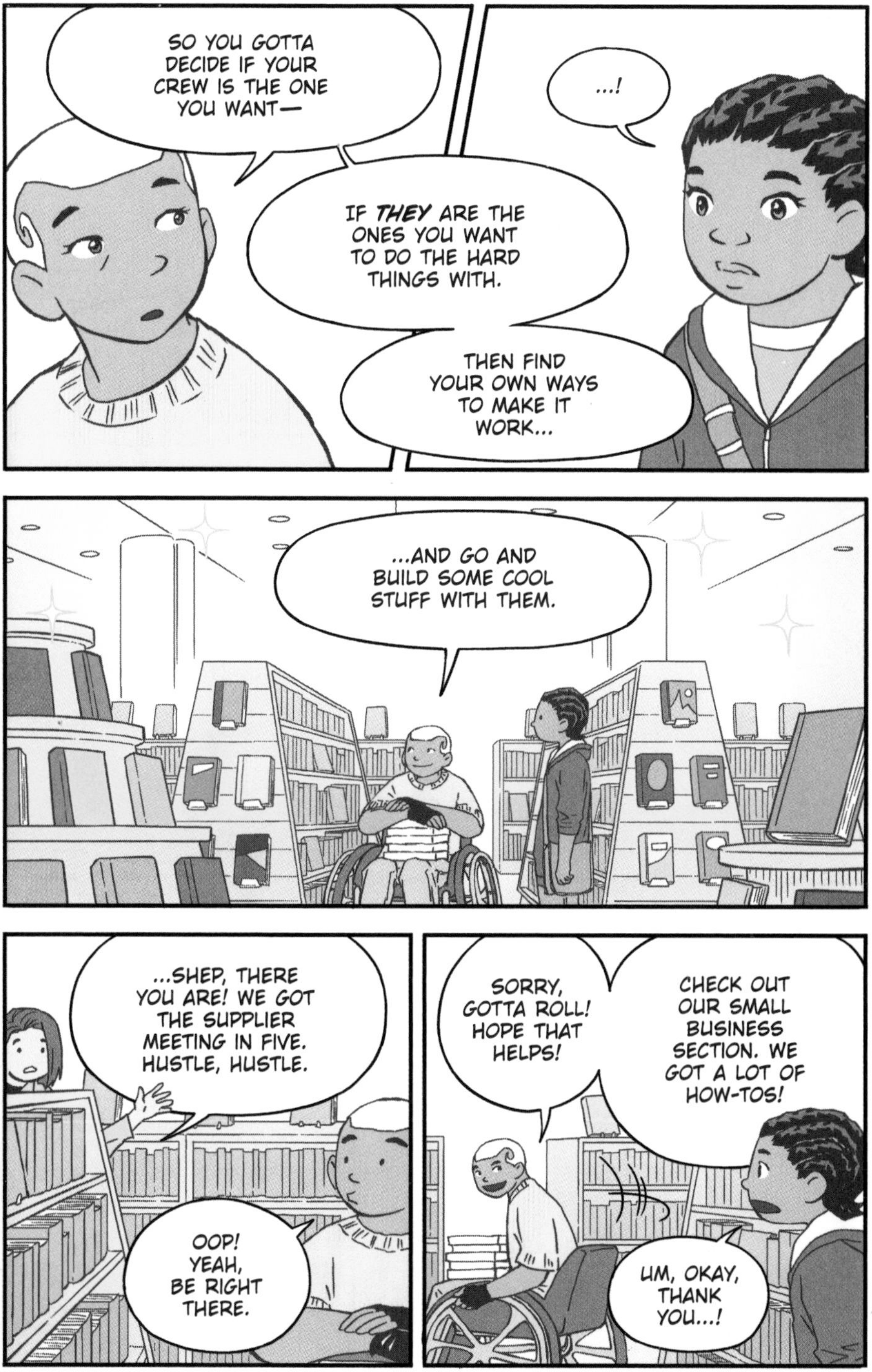
SO YOU GOTTA DECIDE IF YOUR CREW IS THE ONE YOU WANT—
...!
IF *THEY* ARE THE ONES YOU WANT TO DO THE HARD THINGS WITH.
THEN FIND YOUR OWN WAYS TO MAKE IT WORK...
...AND GO AND BUILD SOME COOL STUFF WITH THEM.
...SHEP, THERE YOU ARE! WE GOT THE SUPPLIER MEETING IN FIVE. HUSTLE, HUSTLE.
OOP! YEAH, BE RIGHT THERE.
SORRY, GOTTA ROLL! HOPE THAT HELPS!
CHECK OUT OUR SMALL BUSINESS SECTION. WE GOT A LOT OF HOW-TOS!
UM, OKAY, THANK YOU...!

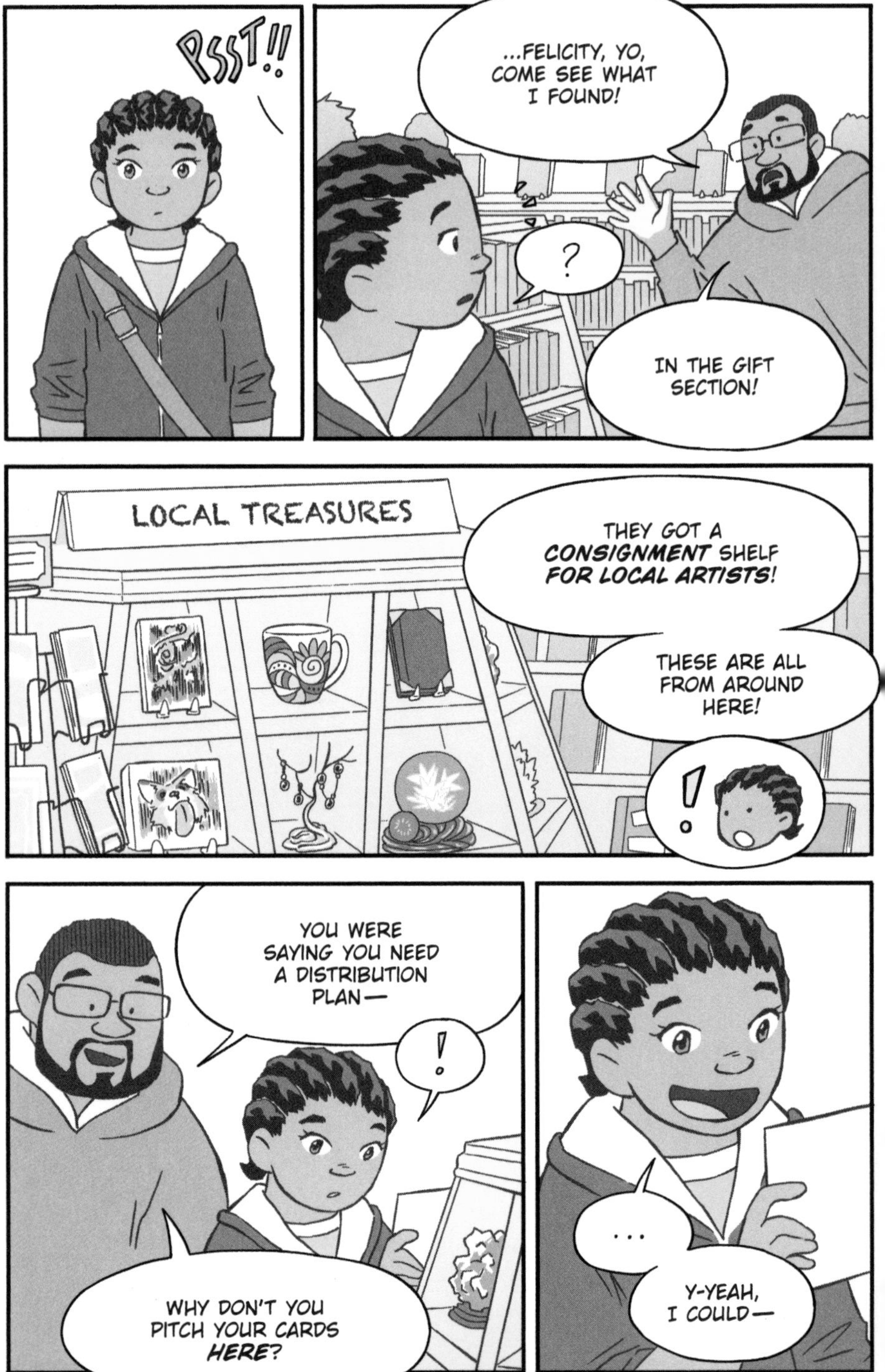
PSST!!
...FELICITY, YO, COME SEE WHAT I FOUND!
?
IN THE GIFT SECTION!
LOCAL TREASURES
THEY GOT A **CONSIGNMENT** SHELF **FOR LOCAL ARTISTS**!
THESE ARE ALL FROM AROUND HERE!
!
YOU WERE SAYING YOU NEED A DISTRIBUTION PLAN—
!
WHY DON'T YOU PITCH YOUR CARDS **HERE**?
...
Y-YEAH, I COULD—

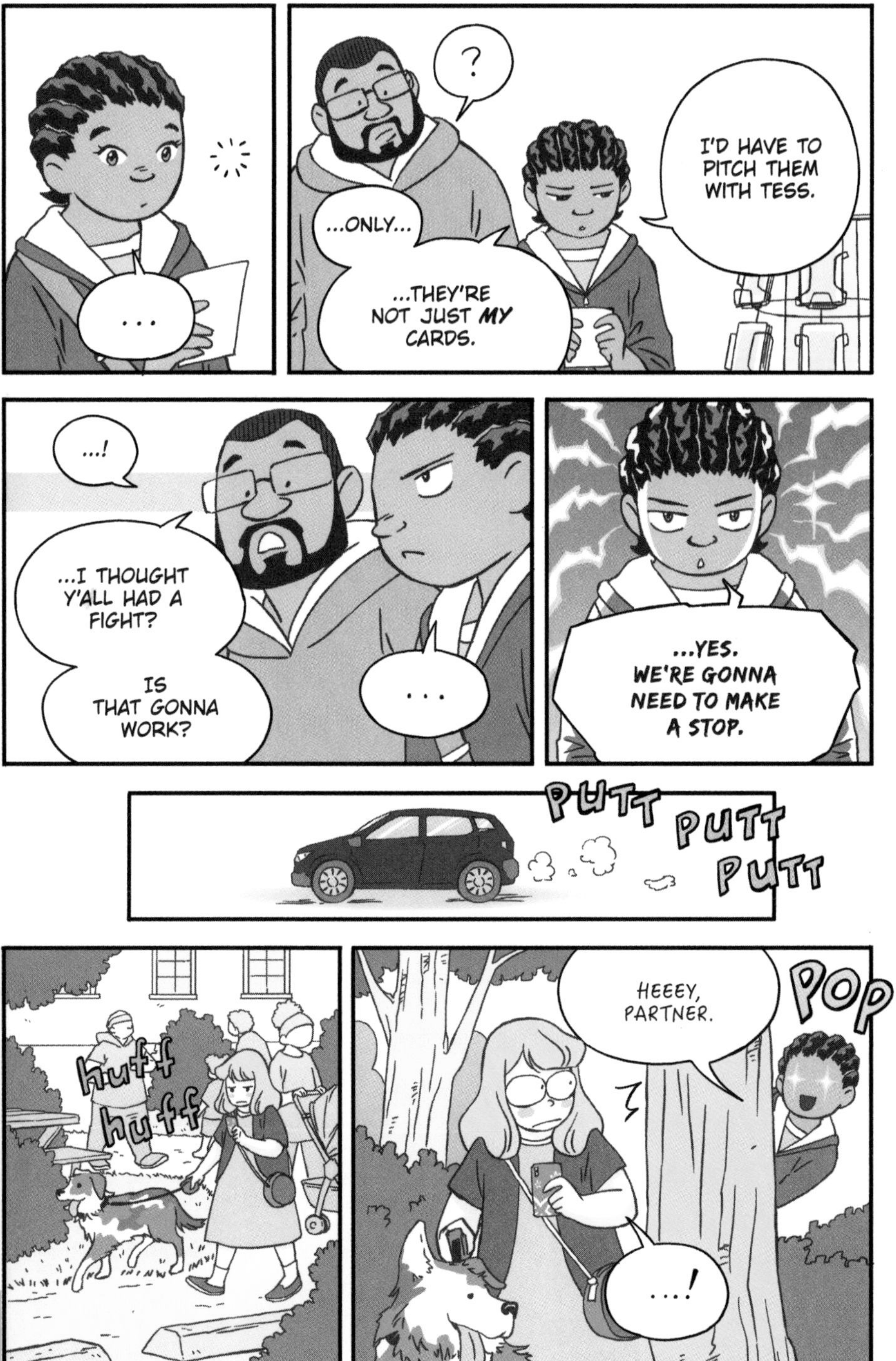
. . .
?
...ONLY...
...THEY'RE NOT JUST MY CARDS.
I'D HAVE TO PITCH THEM WITH TESS.
...!
...I THOUGHT Y'ALL HAD A FIGHT?
IS THAT GONNA WORK?
. . .
...YES. WE'RE GONNA NEED TO MAKE A STOP.
PUTT PUTT PUTT
huff huff
HEEEY, PARTNER.
POP
. . . !

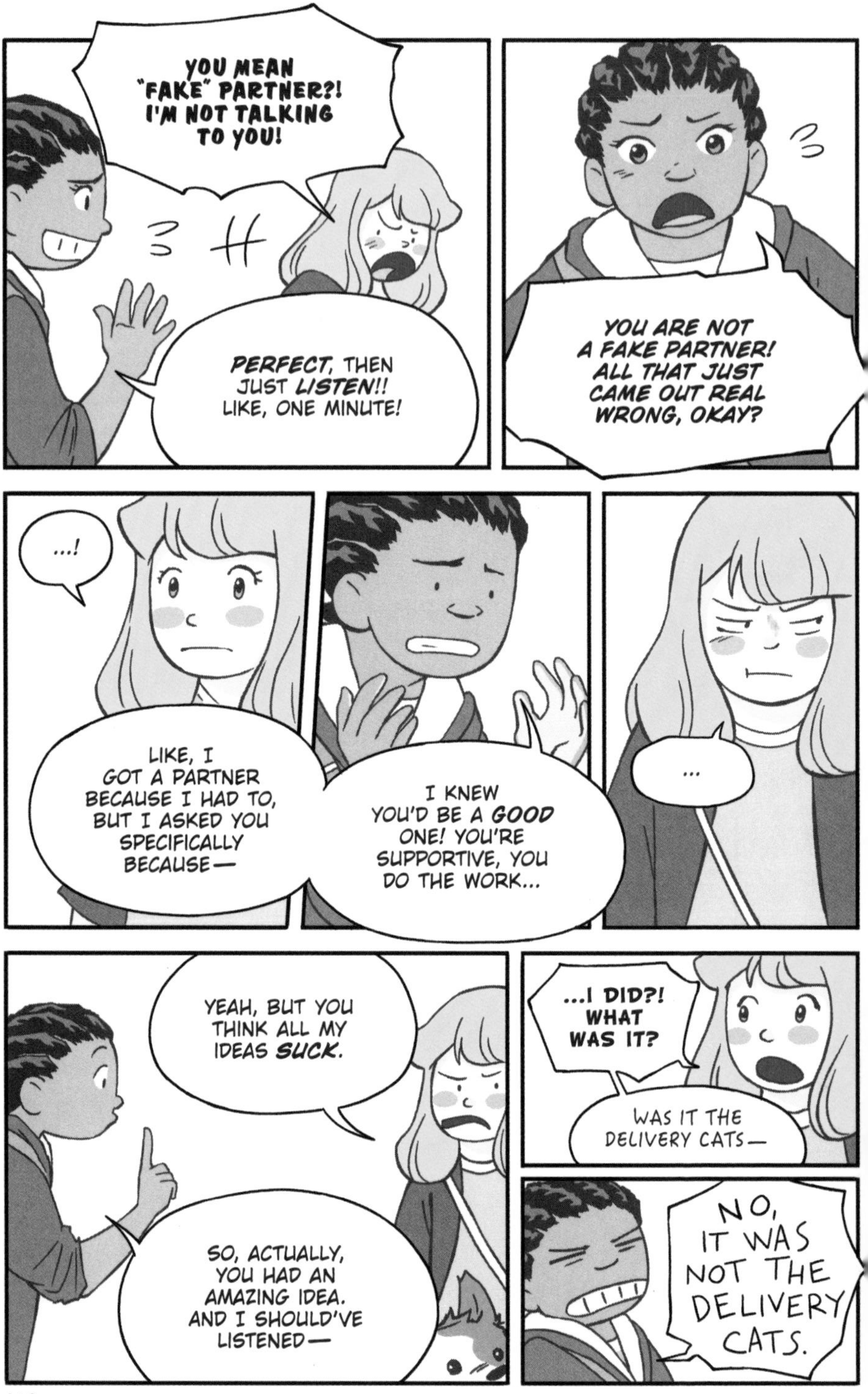
YOU MEAN "FAKE" PARTNER?! I'M NOT TALKING TO YOU!
PERFECT, THEN JUST LISTEN!! LIKE, ONE MINUTE!
YOU ARE NOT A FAKE PARTNER! ALL THAT JUST CAME OUT REAL WRONG, OKAY?
...!
LIKE, I GOT A PARTNER BECAUSE I HAD TO, BUT I ASKED YOU SPECIFICALLY BECAUSE—
I KNEW YOU'D BE A GOOD ONE! YOU'RE SUPPORTIVE, YOU DO THE WORK...
...
YEAH, BUT YOU THINK ALL MY IDEAS SUCK.
SO, ACTUALLY, YOU HAD AN AMAZING IDEA. AND I SHOULD'VE LISTENED—
...I DID?! WHAT WAS IT?
WAS IT THE DELIVERY CATS—
NO, IT WAS NOT THE DELIVERY CATS.

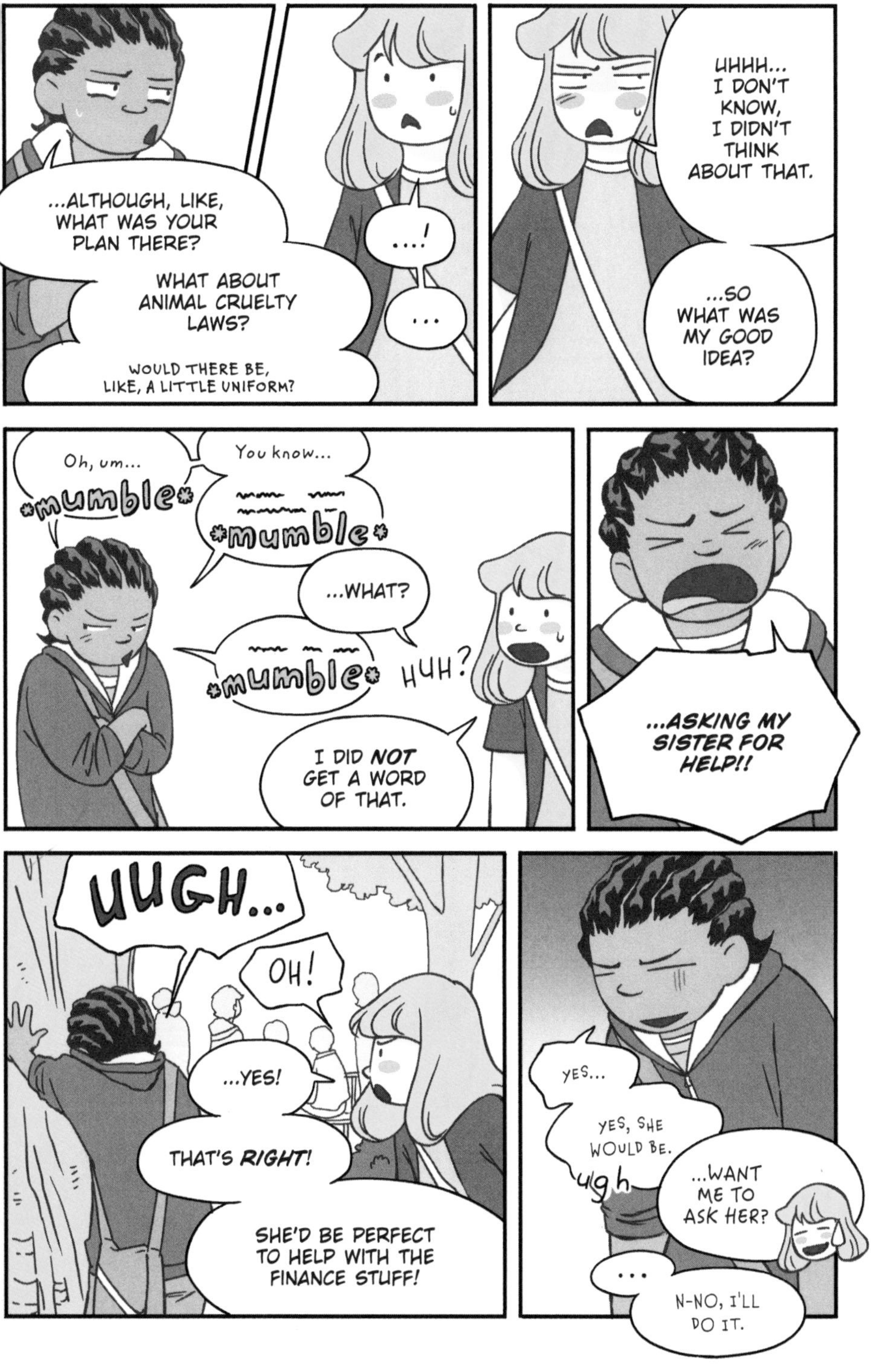
...ALTHOUGH, LIKE, WHAT WAS YOUR PLAN THERE?
WHAT ABOUT ANIMAL CRUELTY LAWS?
WOULD THERE BE, LIKE, A LITTLE UNIFORM?
...!
...
UHHH... I DON'T KNOW, I DIDN'T THINK ABOUT THAT.
...SO WHAT WAS MY GOOD IDEA?
Oh, um... *mumble*
You know... *mumble*
...WHAT?
mumble
HUH?
I DID NOT GET A WORD OF THAT.
...ASKING MY SISTER FOR HELP!!
UUGH...
OH!
...YES!
THAT'S RIGHT!
SHE'D BE PERFECT TO HELP WITH THE FINANCE STUFF!
YES...
YES, SHE WOULD BE.
ugh
...WANT ME TO ASK HER?
...
N-NO, I'LL DO IT.

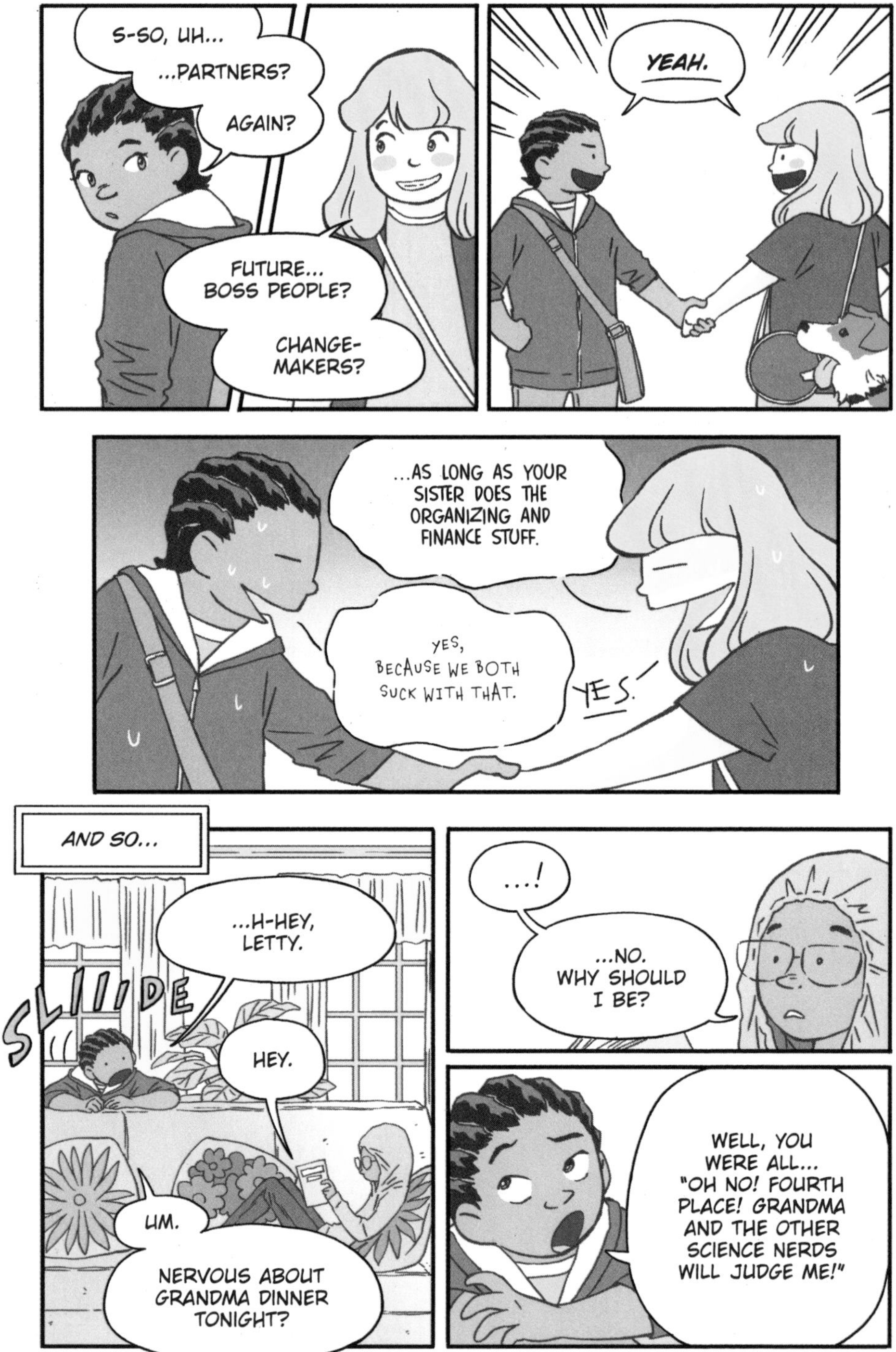
S-SO, UH...
...PARTNERS?
AGAIN?
FUTURE... BOSS PEOPLE?
CHANGE-MAKERS?
YEAH.
...AS LONG AS YOUR SISTER DOES THE ORGANIZING AND FINANCE STUFF.
YES, BECAUSE WE BOTH SUCK WITH THAT.
YES.
AND SO...
SLIIIDE
...H-HEY, LETTY.
HEY.
UM.
NERVOUS ABOUT GRANDMA DINNER TONIGHT?
...!
...NO. WHY SHOULD I BE?
WELL, YOU WERE ALL... "OH NO! FOURTH PLACE! GRANDMA AND THE OTHER SCIENCE NERDS WILL JUDGE ME!"

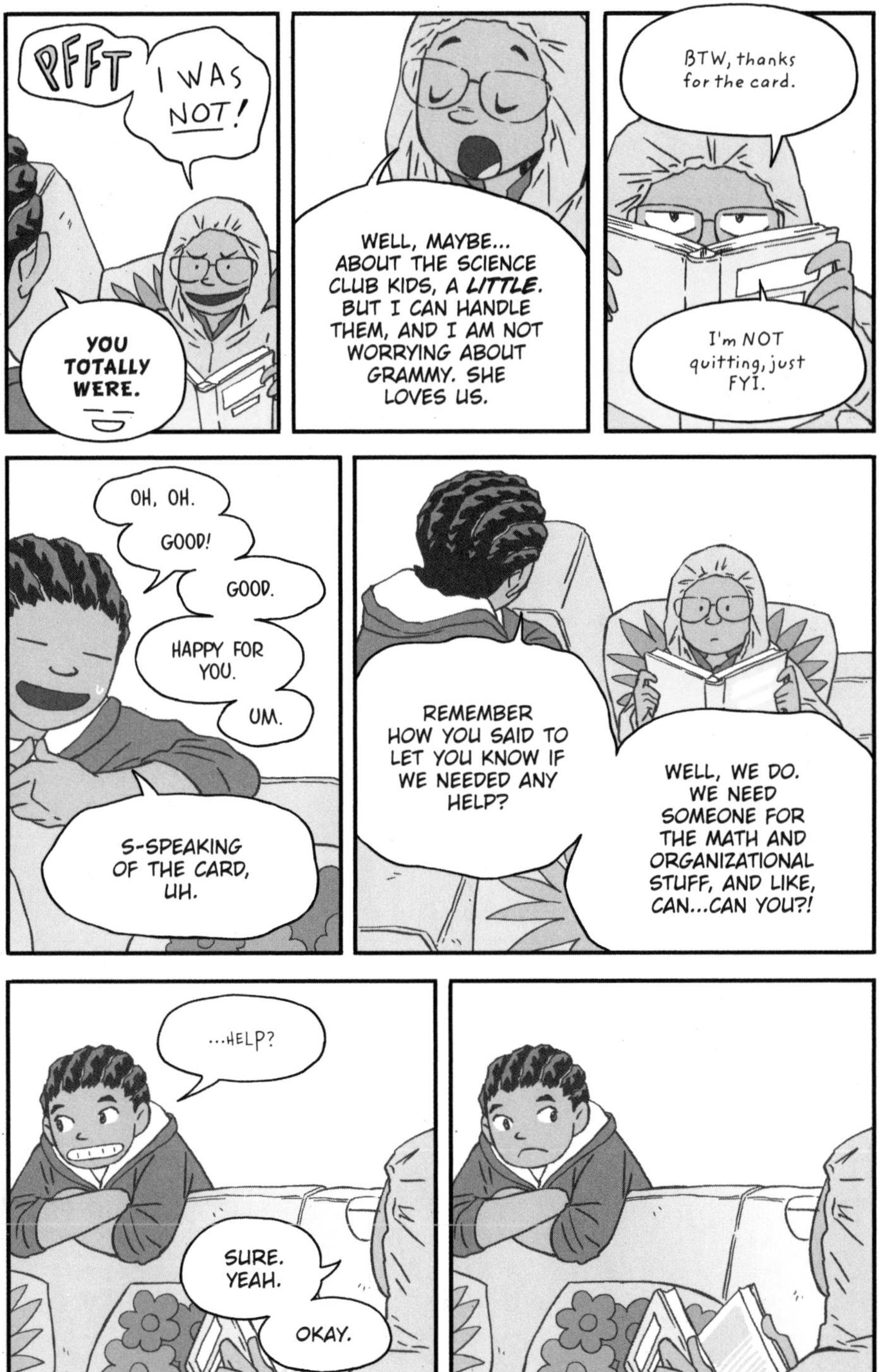
PFFT
I WAS NOT!
YOU TOTALLY WERE.
WELL, MAYBE... ABOUT THE SCIENCE CLUB KIDS, A LITTLE. BUT I CAN HANDLE THEM, AND I AM NOT WORRYING ABOUT GRAMMY. SHE LOVES US.
BTW, thanks for the card.
I'm NOT quitting, just FYI.
OH, OH.
GOOD!
GOOD.
HAPPY FOR YOU.
UM.
S-SPEAKING OF THE CARD, UH.
REMEMBER HOW YOU SAID TO LET YOU KNOW IF WE NEEDED ANY HELP?
WELL, WE DO. WE NEED SOMEONE FOR THE MATH AND ORGANIZATIONAL STUFF, AND LIKE, CAN...CAN YOU?!
...HELP?
SURE. YEAH.
OKAY.

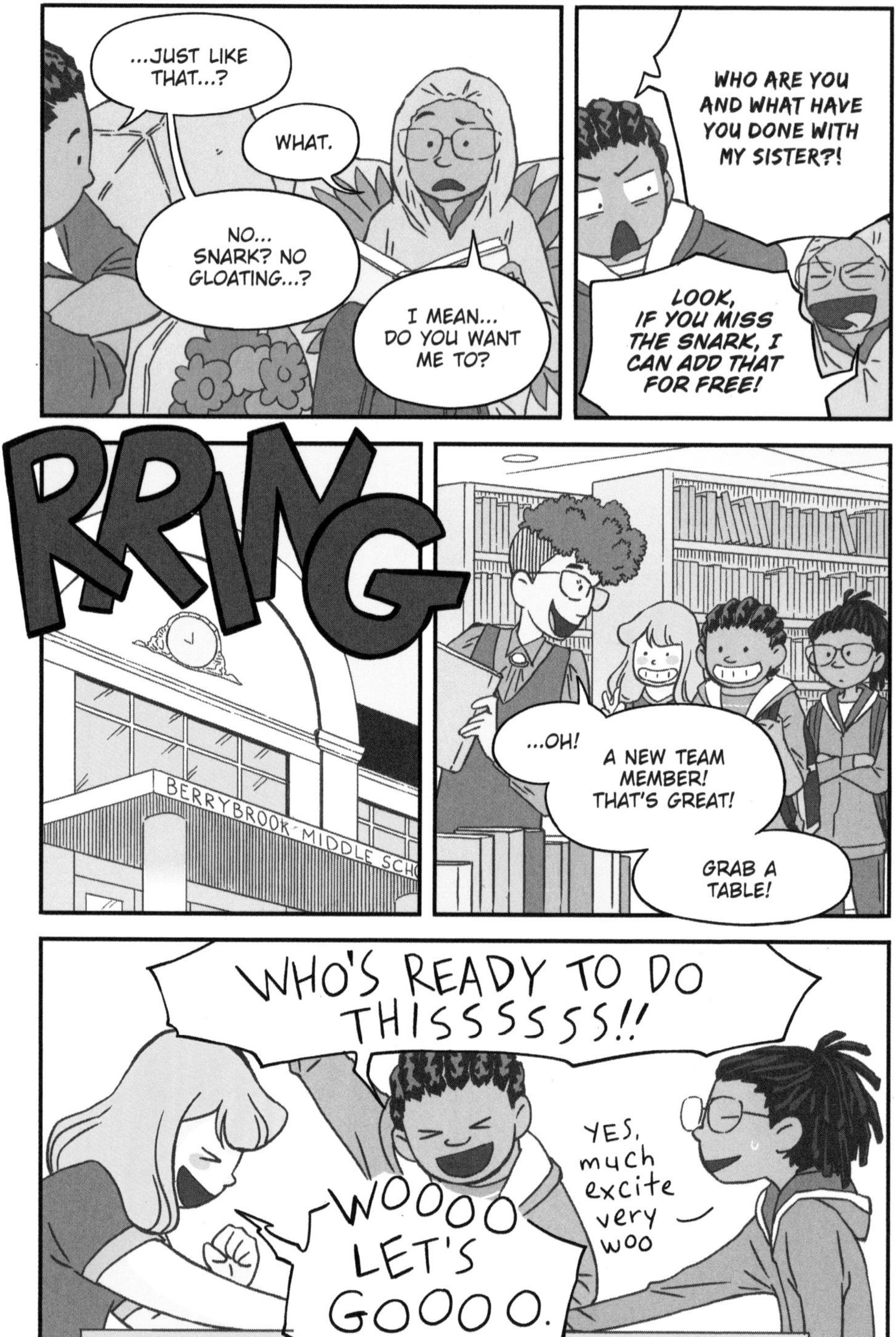
...JUST LIKE THAT...?
WHAT.
NO... SNARK? NO GLOATING...?
I MEAN... DO YOU WANT ME TO?
WHO ARE YOU AND WHAT HAVE YOU DONE WITH MY SISTER?!
LOOK, IF YOU MISS THE SNARK, I CAN ADD THAT FOR FREE!
RRING
BERRYBROOK MIDDLE SCHO
...OH!
A NEW TEAM MEMBER! THAT'S GREAT!
GRAB A TABLE!
WHO'S READY TO DO THISSSSSS!!
WOOOO LET'S GOOOO.
YES, much excite very woo

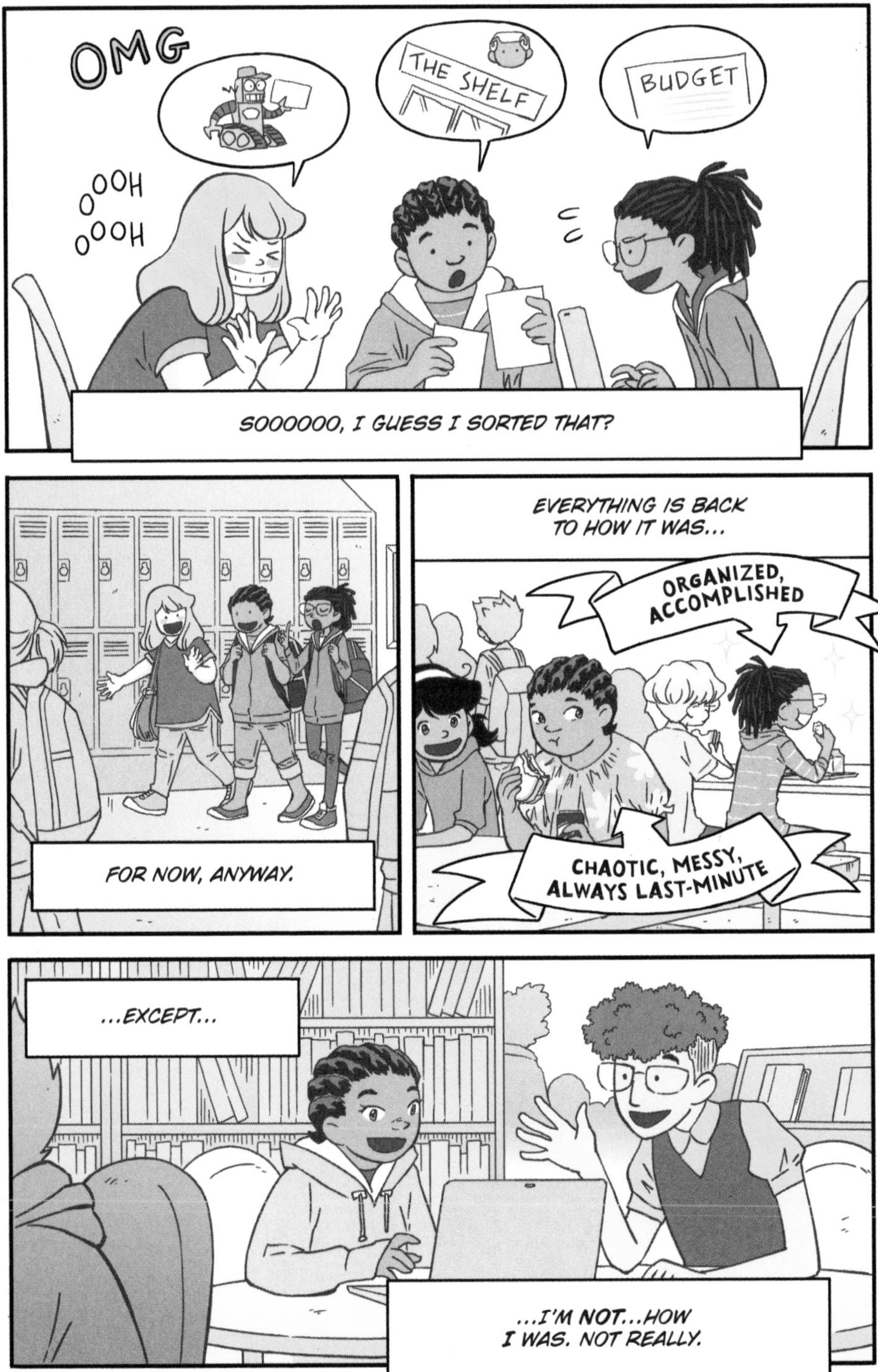
OMG
OOOH
OOOH
THE SHELF
BUDGET
SOOOOOO, I GUESS I SORTED THAT?
FOR NOW, ANYWAY.
EVERYTHING IS BACK TO HOW IT WAS...
ORGANIZED, ACCOMPLISHED
CHAOTIC, MESSY, ALWAYS LAST-MINUTE
...EXCEPT...
...I'M **NOT**...HOW I WAS. NOT REALLY.

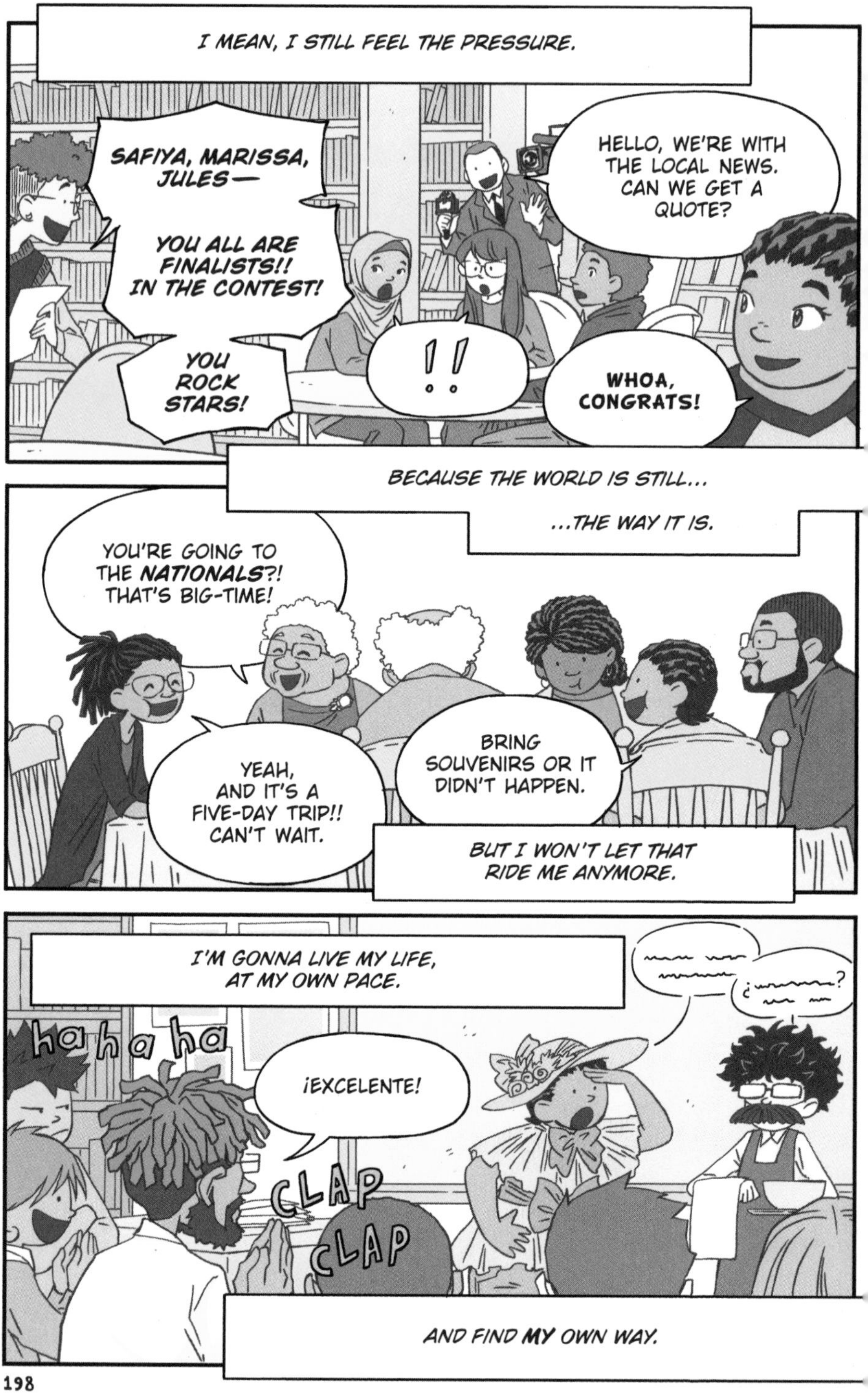

I MEAN, I STILL FEEL THE PRESSURE.
SAFIYA, MARISSA, JULES—
YOU ALL ARE FINALISTS!! IN THE CONTEST!
YOU ROCK STARS!
HELLO, WE'RE WITH THE LOCAL NEWS. CAN WE GET A QUOTE?
!!
WHOA, CONGRATS!
BECAUSE THE WORLD IS STILL...
...THE WAY IT IS.
YOU'RE GOING TO THE NATIONALS?! THAT'S BIG-TIME!
YEAH, AND IT'S A FIVE-DAY TRIP!! CAN'T WAIT.
BRING SOUVENIRS OR IT DIDN'T HAPPEN.
BUT I WON'T LET THAT RIDE ME ANYMORE.
I'M GONNA LIVE MY LIFE, AT MY OWN PACE.
ha ha ha
¡EXCELENTE!
CLAP
CLAP
AND FIND MY OWN WAY.

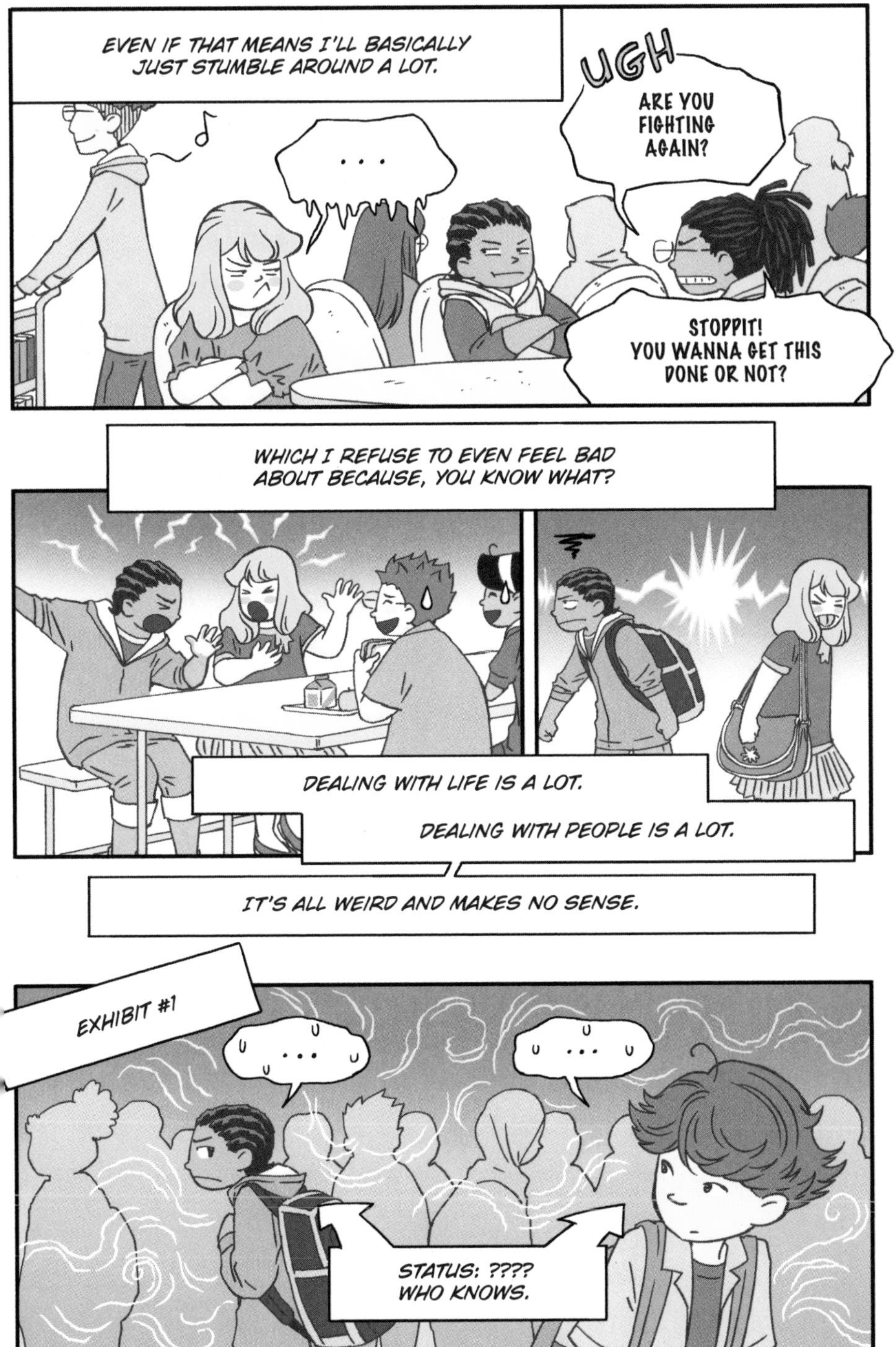
EVEN IF THAT MEANS I'LL BASICALLY JUST STUMBLE AROUND A LOT.
. . .
UGH
ARE YOU FIGHTING AGAIN?
STOPPIT! YOU WANNA GET THIS DONE OR NOT?
WHICH I REFUSE TO EVEN FEEL BAD ABOUT BECAUSE, YOU KNOW WHAT?
DEALING WITH LIFE IS A LOT.
DEALING WITH PEOPLE IS A LOT.
IT'S ALL WEIRD AND MAKES NO SENSE.
EXHIBIT #1
. . .
. . .
STATUS: ???? WHO KNOWS.

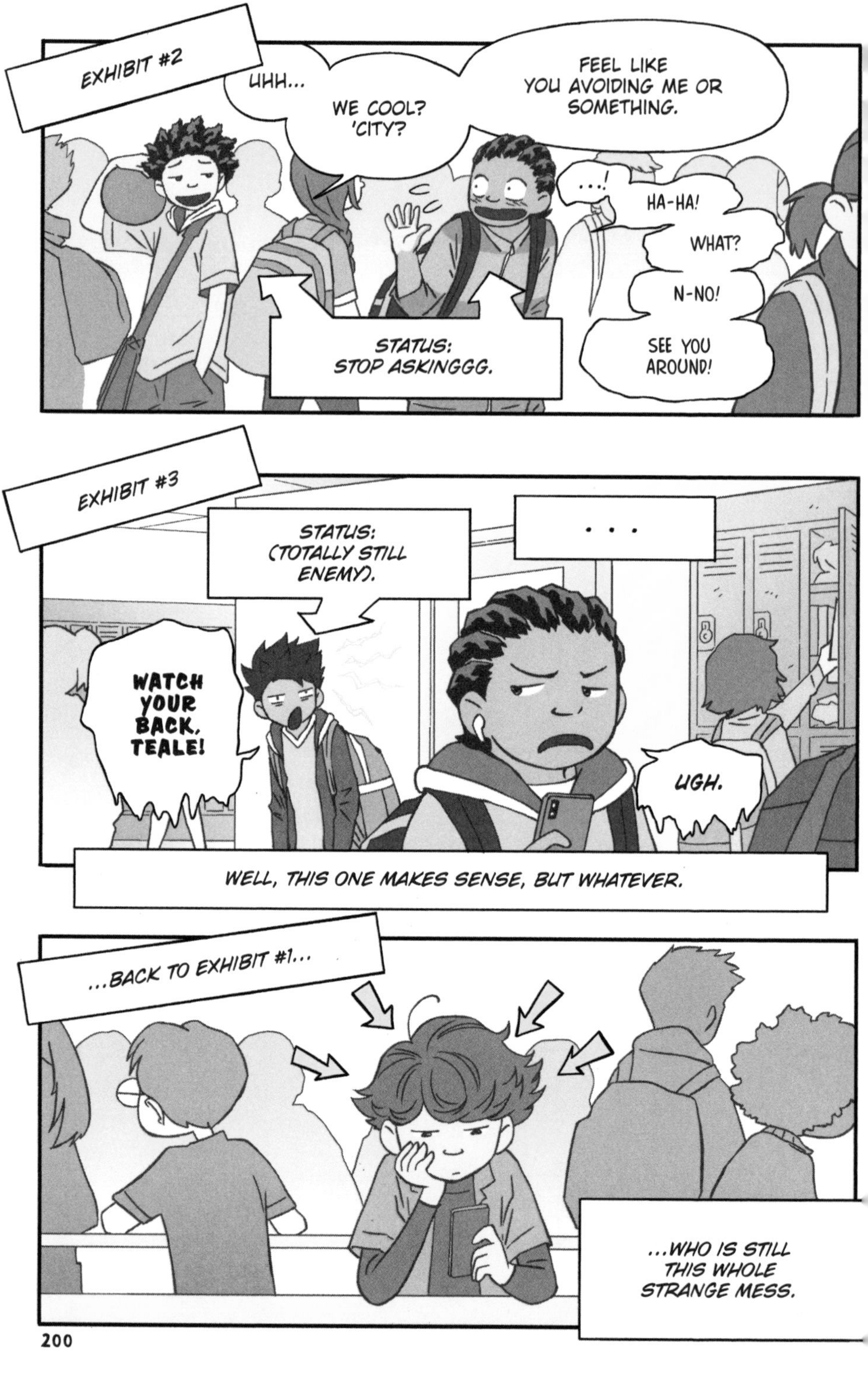
EXHIBIT #2
UHH...
WE COOL? 'CITY?
FEEL LIKE YOU AVOIDING ME OR SOMETHING.
...!
HA-HA!
WHAT?
N-NO!
SEE YOU AROUND!
STATUS: STOP ASKINGGG.
EXHIBIT #3
STATUS: (TOTALLY STILL ENEMY).
. . .
WATCH YOUR BACK, TEALE!
UGH.
WELL, THIS ONE MAKES SENSE, BUT WHATEVER.
...BACK TO EXHIBIT #1...
...WHO IS STILL THIS WHOLE STRANGE MESS.

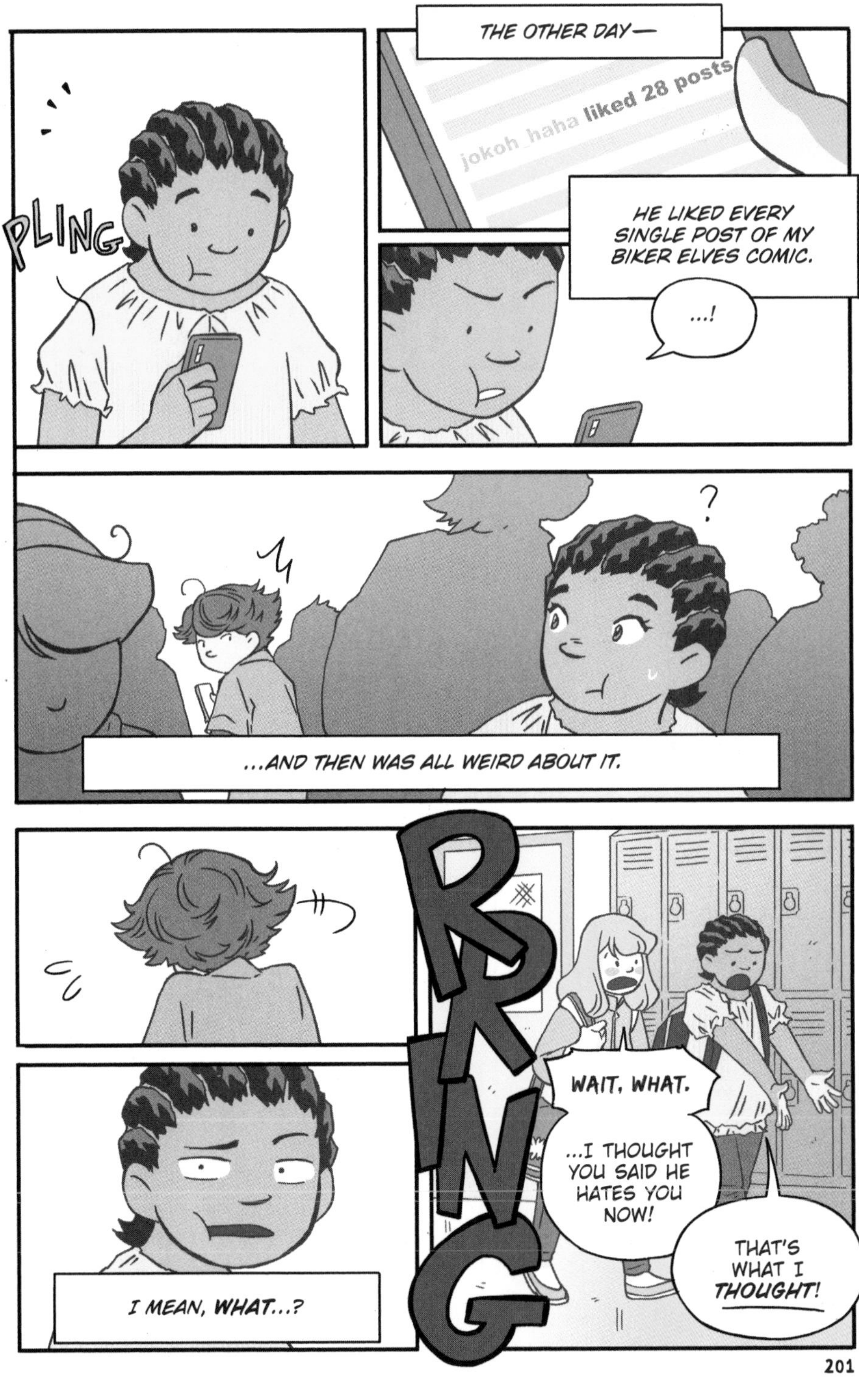

PLING
THE OTHER DAY—
jokoh_haha liked 28 posts
HE LIKED EVERY SINGLE POST OF MY BIKER ELVES COMIC.
...!
?
...AND THEN WAS ALL WEIRD ABOUT IT.
I MEAN, WHAT...?
RRRING
WAIT, WHAT.
...I THOUGHT YOU SAID HE HATES YOU NOW!
THAT'S WHAT I THOUGHT!

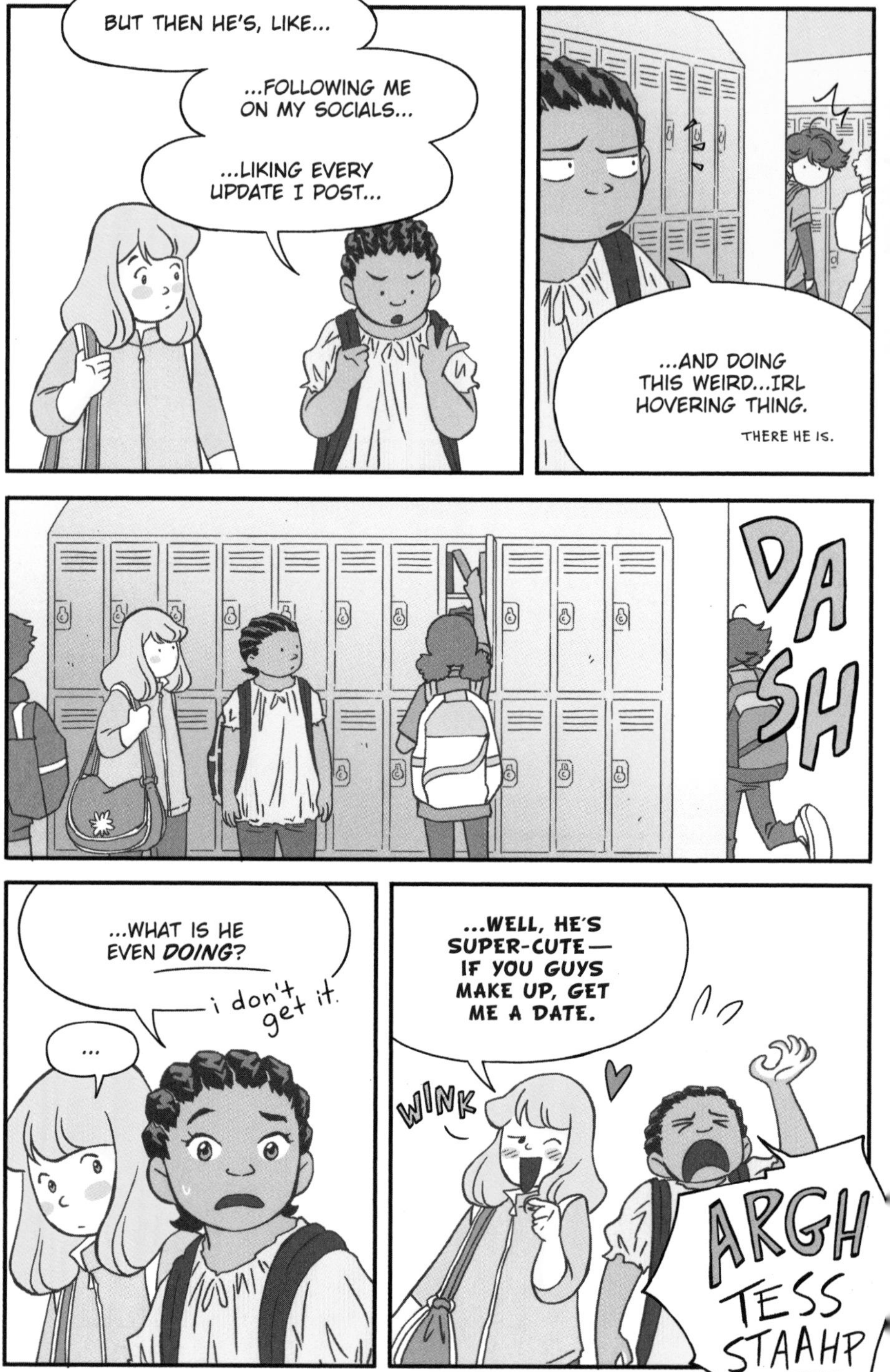
BUT THEN HE'S, LIKE...
...FOLLOWING ME ON MY SOCIALS...
...LIKING EVERY UPDATE I POST...
...AND DOING THIS WEIRD...IRL HOVERING THING.
THERE HE IS.
DASH
...WHAT IS HE EVEN DOING?
i don't get it.
...
...WELL, HE'S SUPER-CUTE— IF YOU GUYS MAKE UP, GET ME A DATE.
WINK
ARGH TESS STAAHP

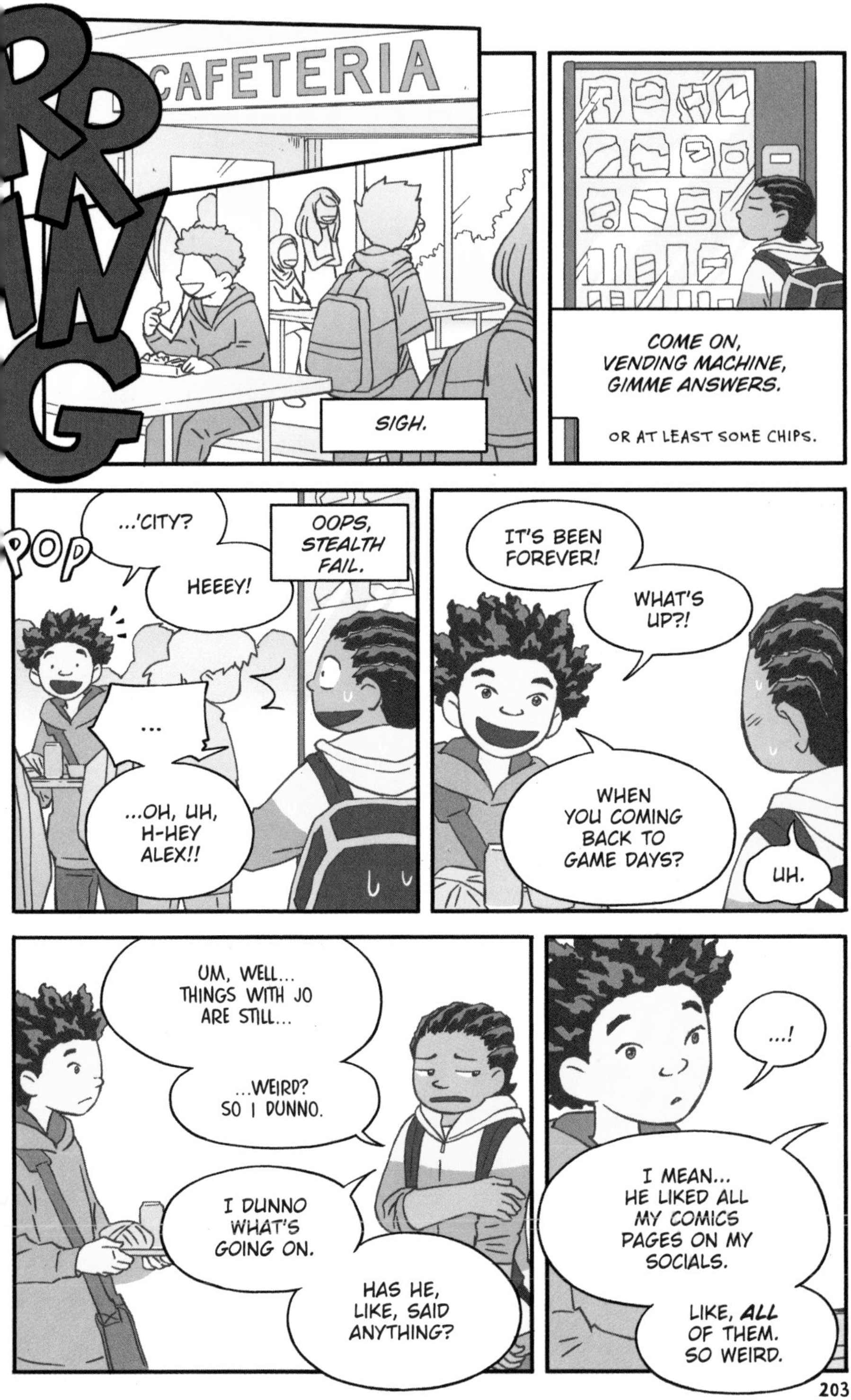

RRRING
CAFETERIA
SIGH.
COME ON, VENDING MACHINE, GIMME ANSWERS.
OR AT LEAST SOME CHIPS.
POP
...'CITY?
HEEEY!
OOPS, STEALTH FAIL.
...
...OH, UH, H-HEY ALEX!!
IT'S BEEN FOREVER!
WHAT'S UP?!
WHEN YOU COMING BACK TO GAME DAYS?
UH.
UM, WELL... THINGS WITH JO ARE STILL...
...WEIRD? SO I DUNNO.
I DUNNO WHAT'S GOING ON.
HAS HE, LIKE, SAID ANYTHING?
...!
I MEAN... HE LIKED ALL MY COMICS PAGES ON MY SOCIALS.
LIKE, ALL OF THEM. SO WEIRD.

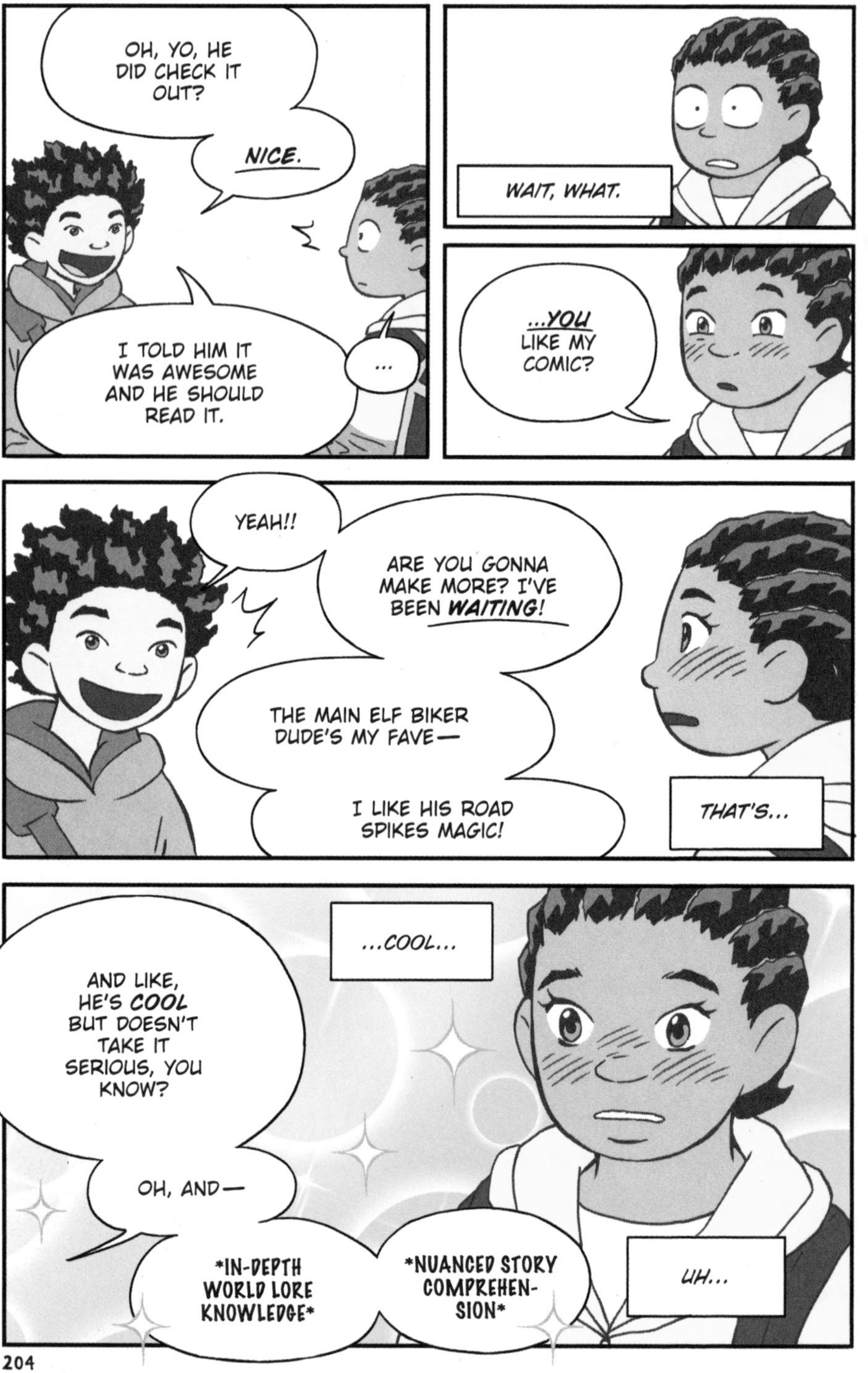

OH, YO, HE DID CHECK IT OUT?
NICE.
I TOLD HIM IT WAS AWESOME AND HE SHOULD READ IT.
...
WAIT, WHAT.
...YOU LIKE MY COMIC?
YEAH!!
ARE YOU GONNA MAKE MORE? I'VE BEEN WAITING!
THE MAIN ELF BIKER DUDE'S MY FAVE—
I LIKE HIS ROAD SPIKES MAGIC!
THAT'S...
...COOL...
AND LIKE, HE'S COOL BUT DOESN'T TAKE IT SERIOUS, YOU KNOW?
OH, AND—
IN-DEPTH WORLD LORE KNOWLEDGE
NUANCED STORY COMPREHEN-SION
UH...

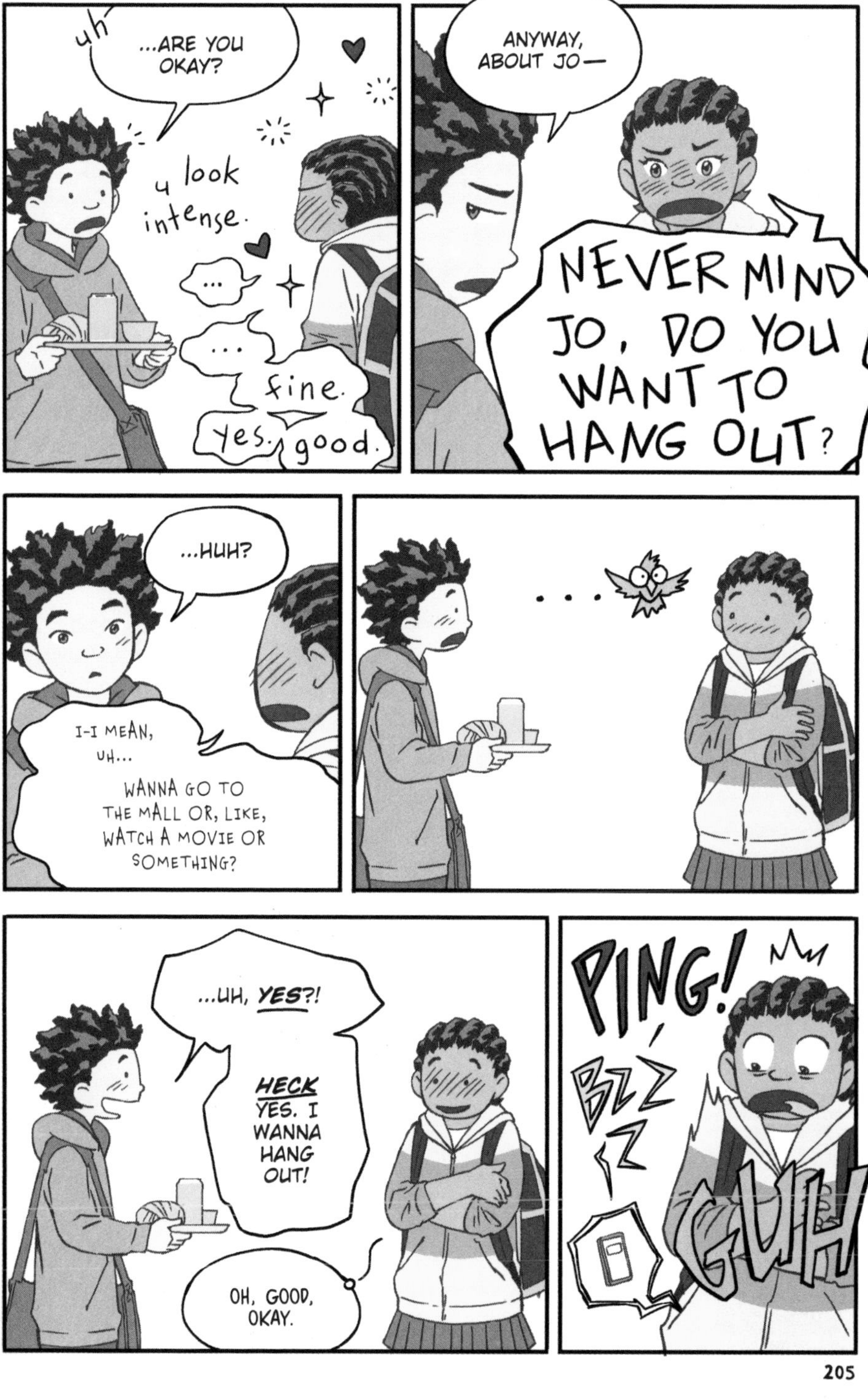
uh
...ARE YOU OKAY?
u look intense.
...
...
fine.
yes.
good.
ANYWAY, ABOUT JO—
NEVER MIND JO, DO YOU WANT TO HANG OUT?
...HUH?
I-I MEAN, UH...
WANNA GO TO THE MALL OR, LIKE, WATCH A MOVIE OR SOMETHING?
...
...UH, YES?!
HECK YES. I WANNA HANG OUT!
OH, GOOD, OKAY.
PING!
BZZZ
GUH

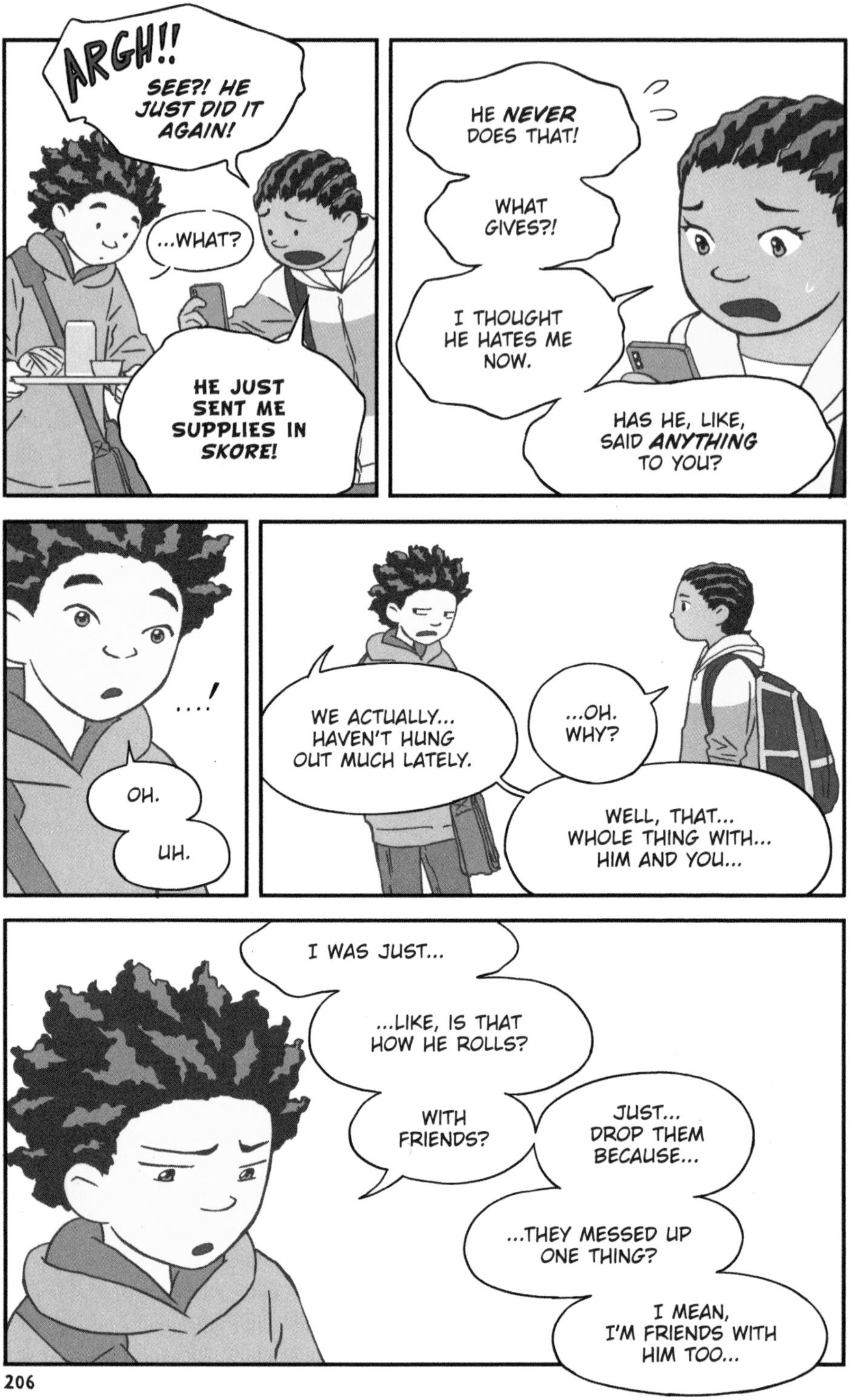
ARGH!!
SEE?! HE JUST DID IT AGAIN!
...WHAT?
HE JUST SENT ME SUPPLIES IN SKORE!
HE NEVER DOES THAT!
WHAT GIVES?!
I THOUGHT HE HATES ME NOW.
HAS HE, LIKE, SAID ANYTHING TO YOU?
...!
OH.
UH.
WE ACTUALLY... HAVEN'T HUNG OUT MUCH LATELY.
...OH. WHY?
WELL, THAT... WHOLE THING WITH... HIM AND YOU...
I WAS JUST...
...LIKE, IS THAT HOW HE ROLLS?
WITH FRIENDS?
JUST... DROP THEM BECAUSE...
...THEY MESSED UP ONE THING?
I MEAN, I'M FRIENDS WITH HIM TOO...

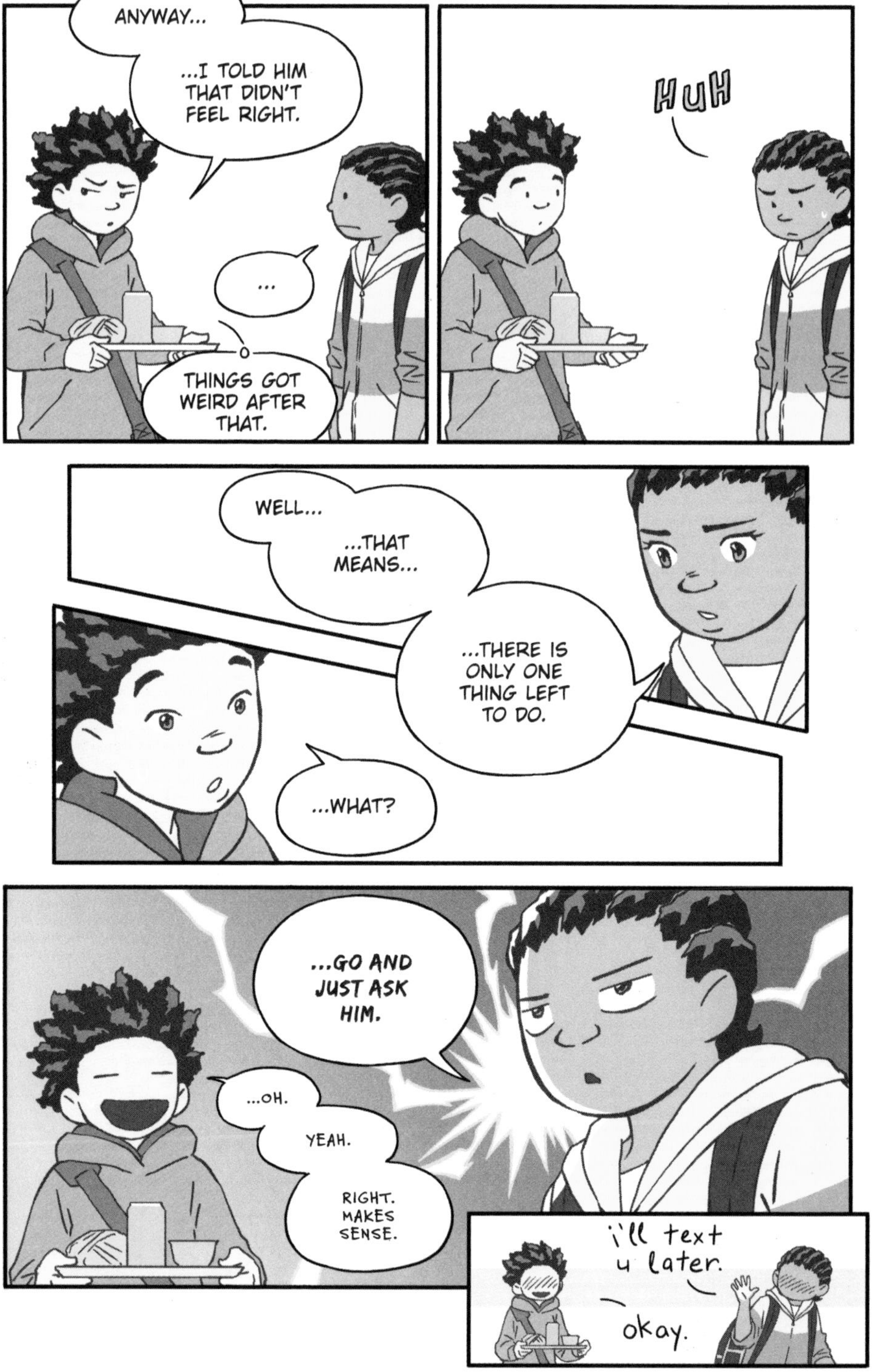
ANYWAY...
...I TOLD HIM THAT DIDN'T FEEL RIGHT.
...
THINGS GOT WEIRD AFTER THAT.
HUH
WELL...
...THAT MEANS...
...THERE IS ONLY ONE THING LEFT TO DO.
...WHAT?
...GO AND JUST ASK HIM.
...OH.
YEAH.
RIGHT. MAKES SENSE.
i'll text u later.
okay.

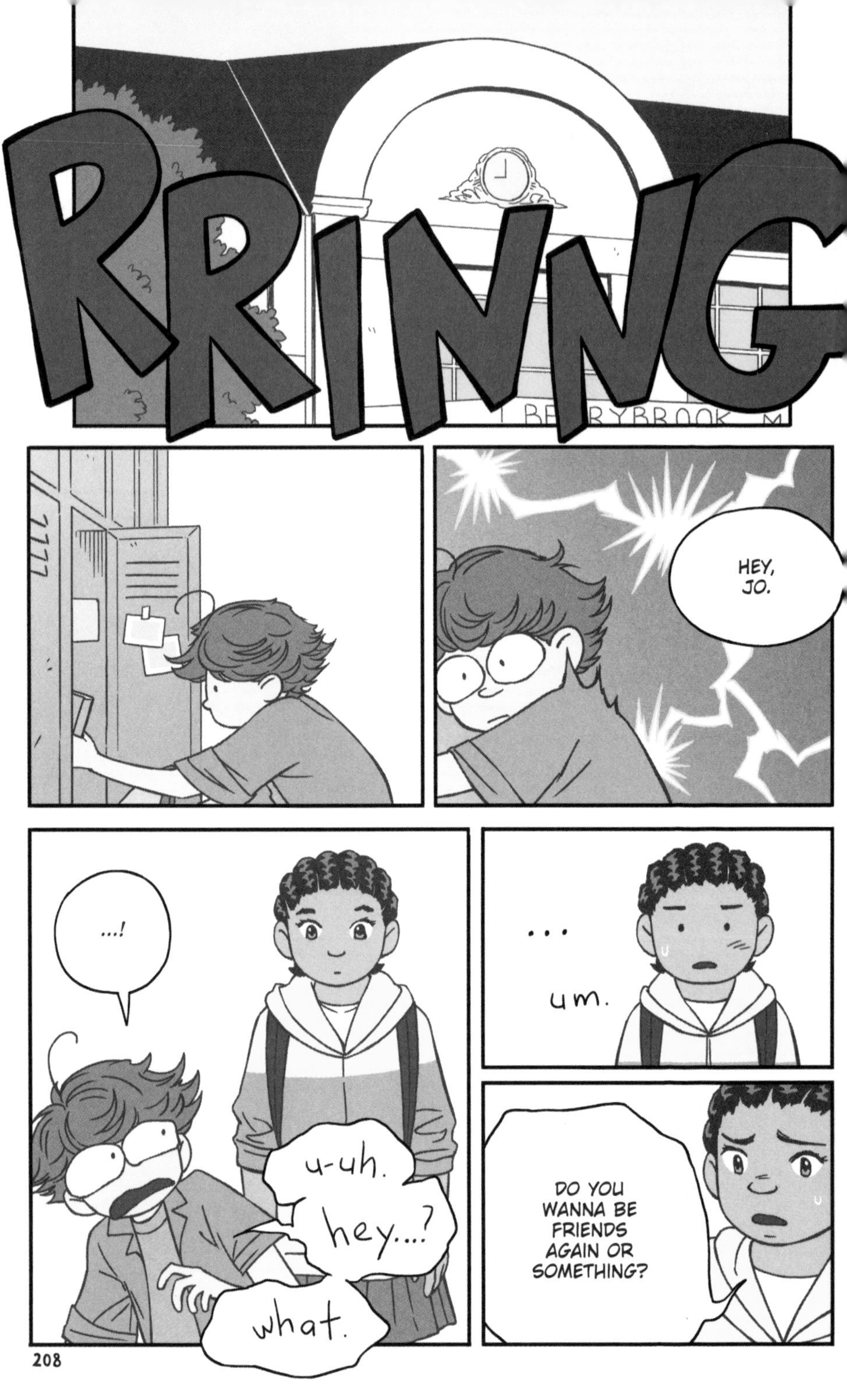
RRINNG
BERRYBROOK M
HEY, JO.
...!
...
um.
u-uh.
hey...?
what.
DO YOU WANNA BE FRIENDS AGAIN OR SOMETHING?

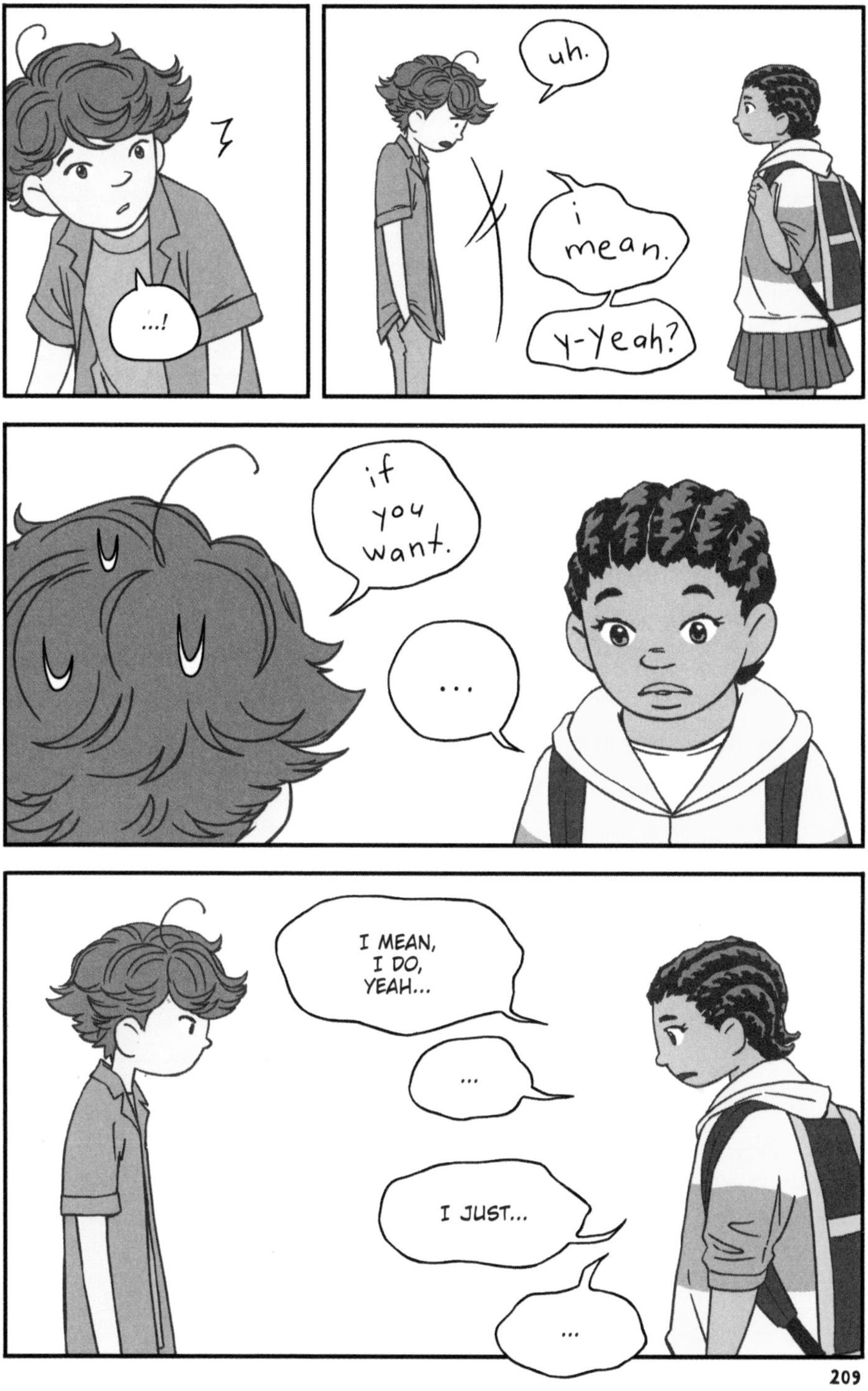
...!
uh.
i mean.
y-yeah?
if you want.
...
I MEAN, I DO, YEAH...
...
I JUST...
...

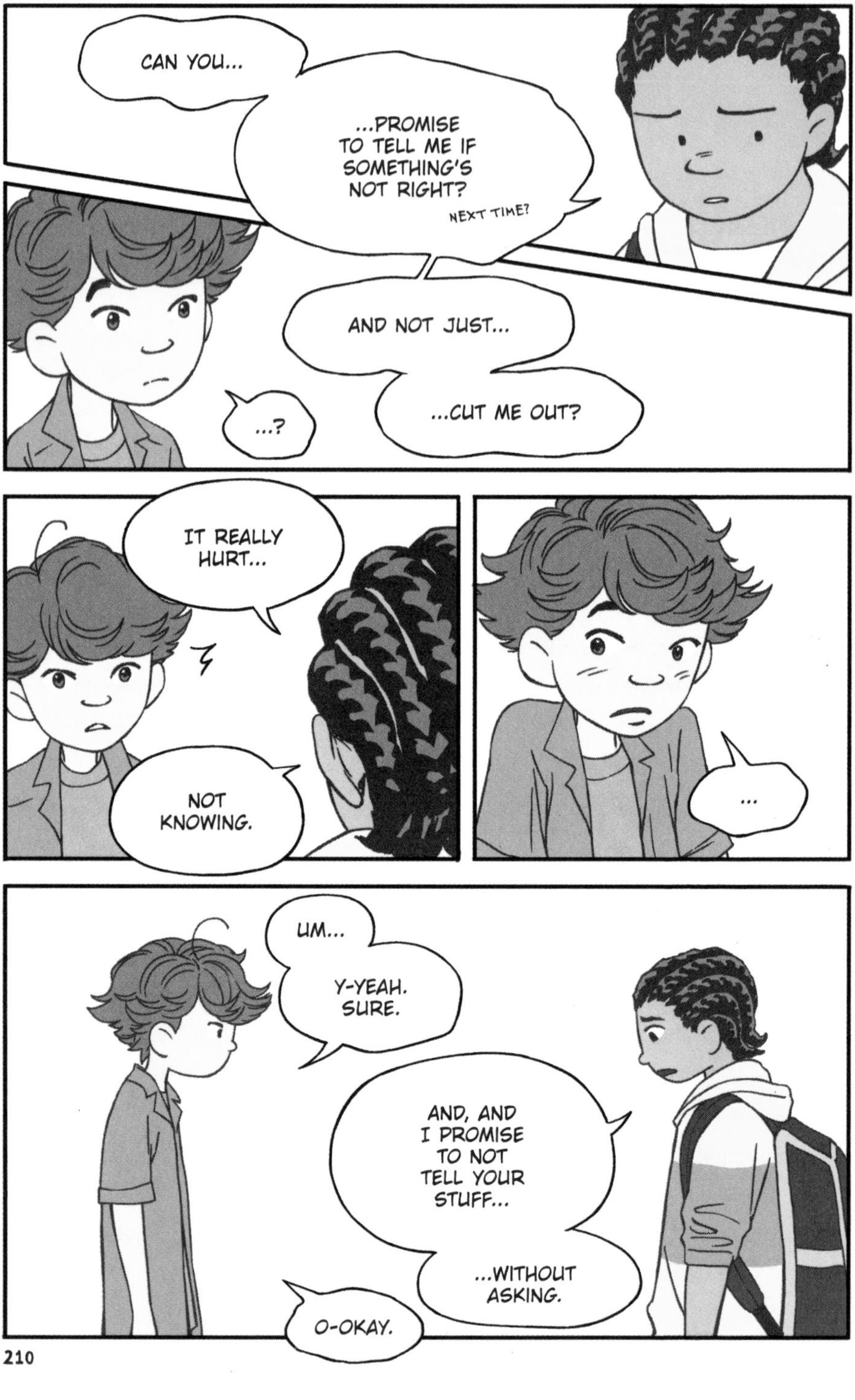
CAN YOU...
...PROMISE TO TELL ME IF SOMETHING'S NOT RIGHT?
NEXT TIME?
AND NOT JUST...
...CUT ME OUT?
...?
IT REALLY HURT...
NOT KNOWING.
...
UM...
Y-YEAH. SURE.
AND, AND I PROMISE TO NOT TELL YOUR STUFF...
...WITHOUT ASKING.
O-OKAY.

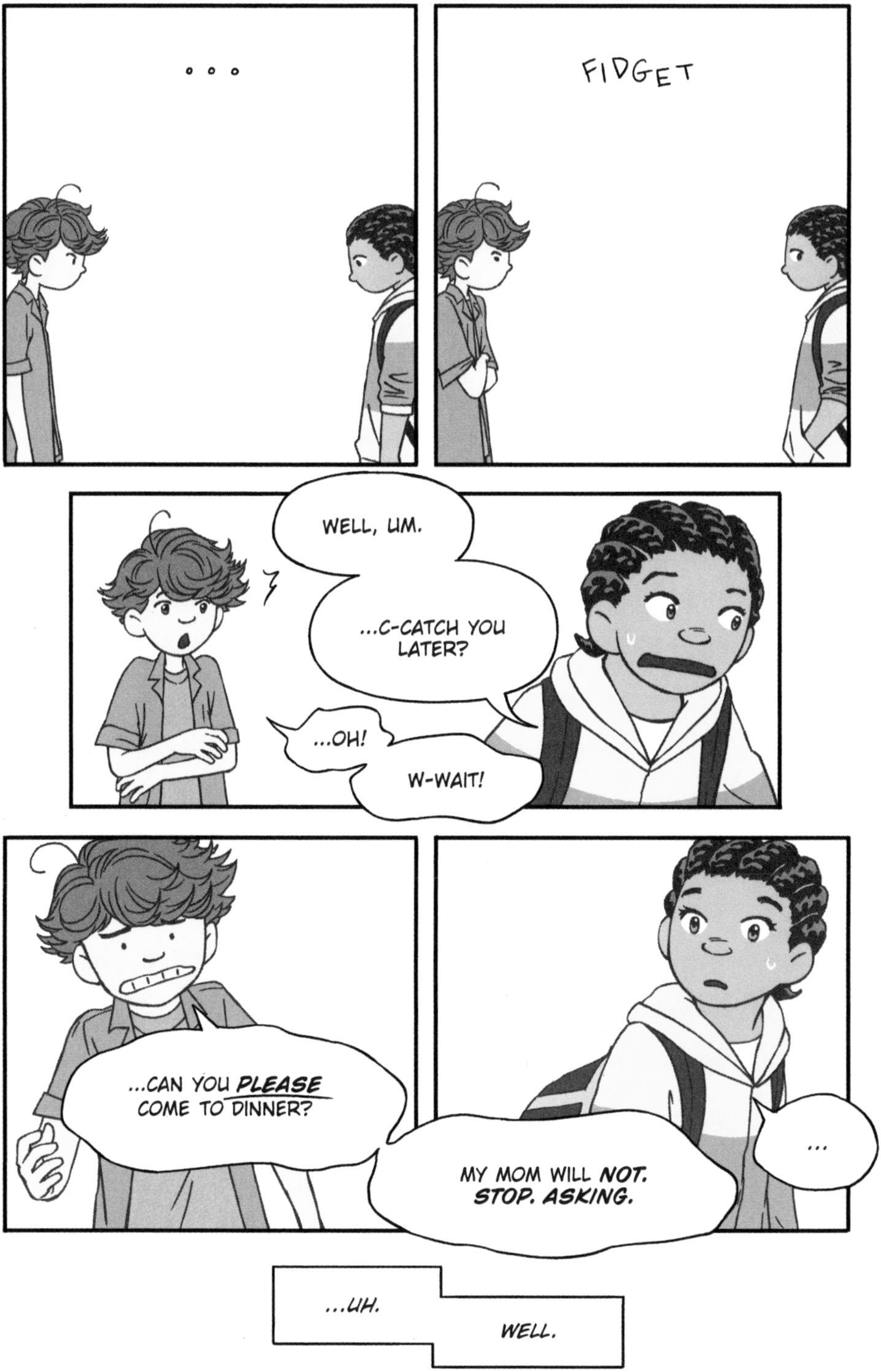
. . .
FIDGET
WELL, UM.
...C-CATCH YOU LATER?
...OH!
W-WAIT!
...CAN YOU PLEASE COME TO DINNER?
MY MOM WILL NOT. STOP. ASKING.
...
...UH.
WELL.

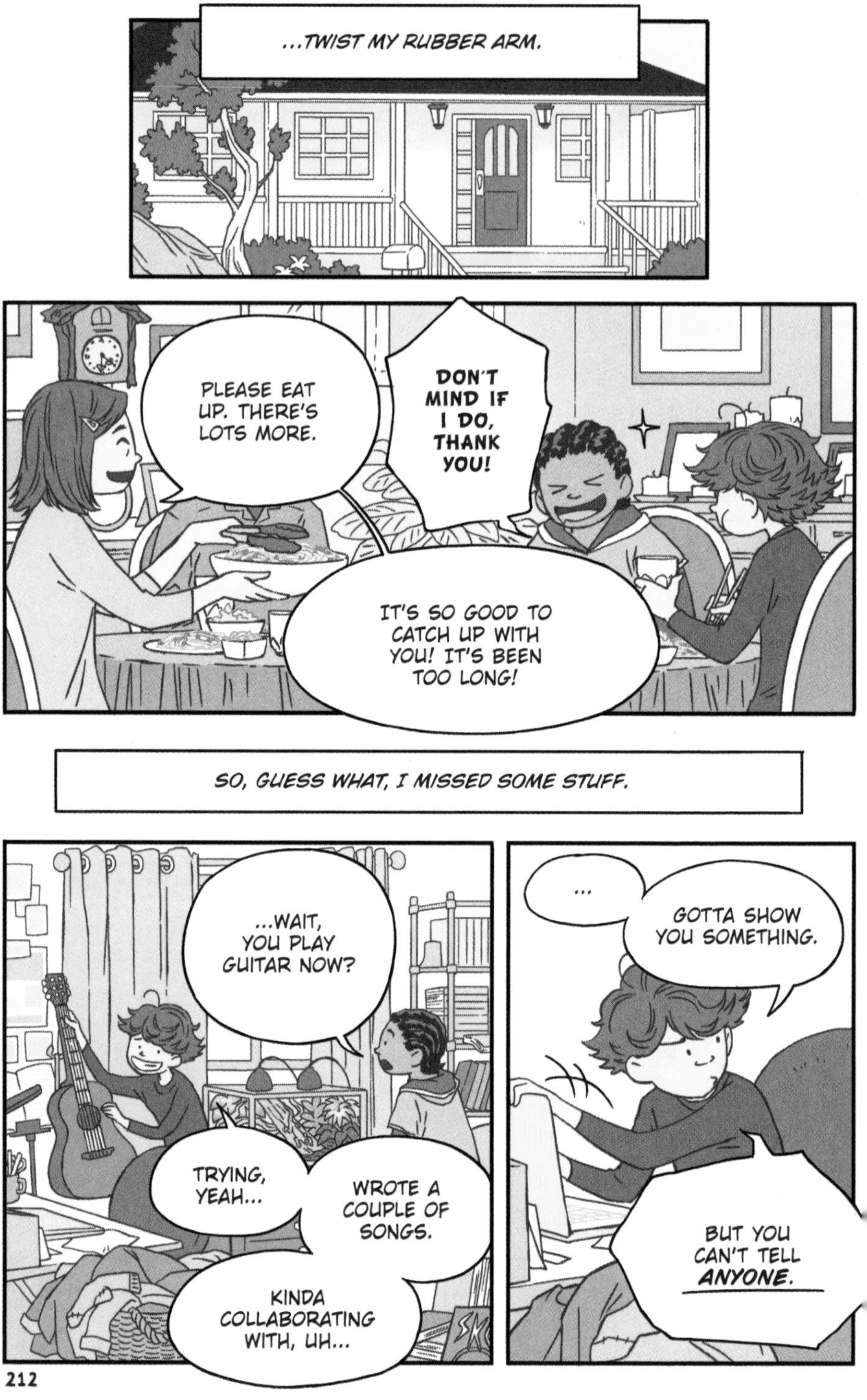
...TWIST MY RUBBER ARM.
PLEASE EAT UP. THERE'S LOTS MORE.
DON'T MIND IF I DO, THANK YOU!
IT'S SO GOOD TO CATCH UP WITH YOU! IT'S BEEN TOO LONG!
SO, GUESS WHAT, I MISSED SOME STUFF.
...WAIT, YOU PLAY GUITAR NOW?
TRYING, YEAH...
WROTE A COUPLE OF SONGS.
KINDA COLLABORATING WITH, UH...
...
GOTTA SHOW YOU SOMETHING.
BUT YOU CAN'T TELL ANYONE.

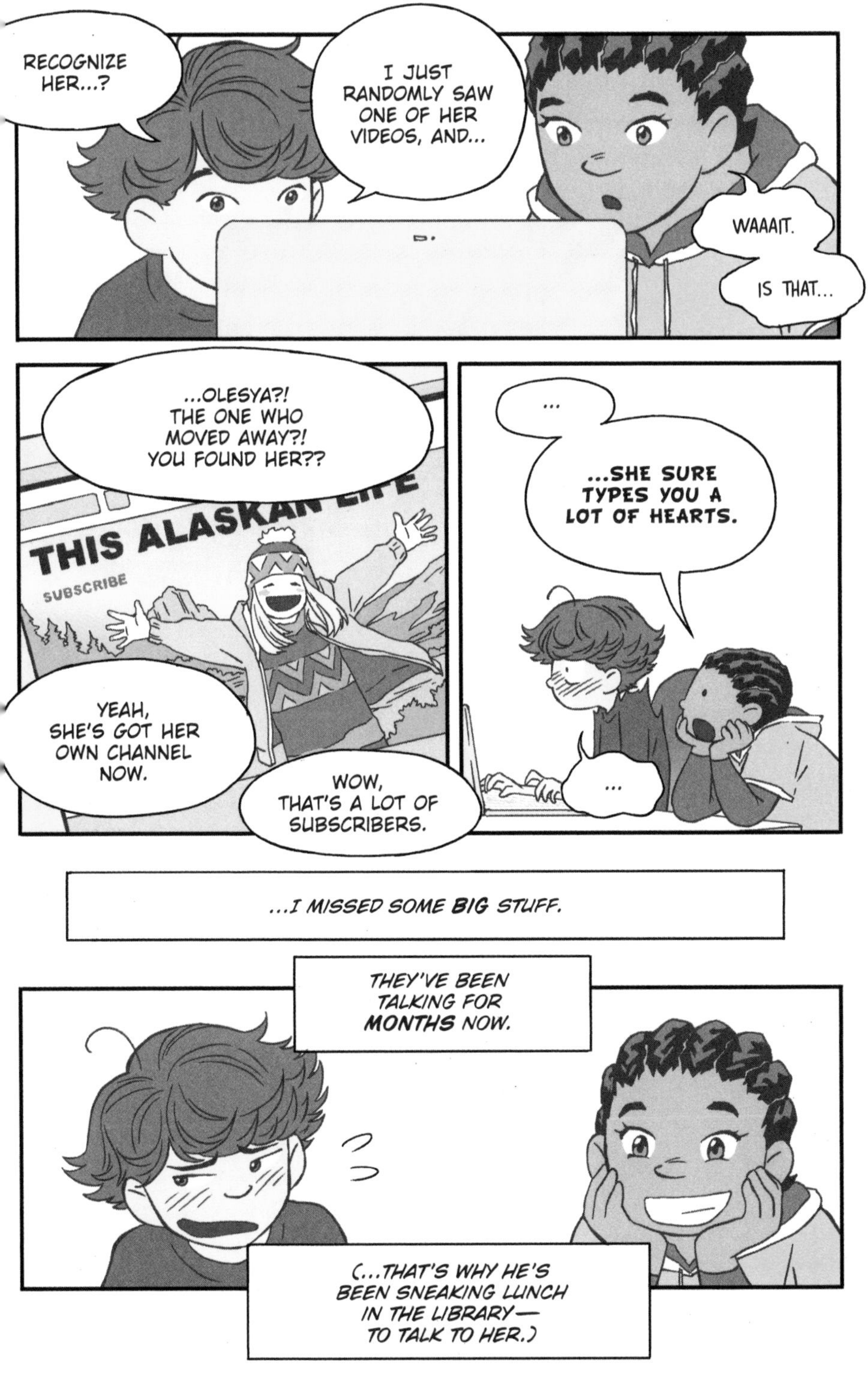
RECOGNIZE HER...?
I JUST RANDOMLY SAW ONE OF HER VIDEOS, AND...
WAAAIT.
IS THAT...
...OLESYA?! THE ONE WHO MOVED AWAY?! YOU FOUND HER??
THIS ALASKAN LIFE
SUBSCRIBE
YEAH, SHE'S GOT HER OWN CHANNEL NOW.
WOW, THAT'S A LOT OF SUBSCRIBERS.
...
...SHE SURE TYPES YOU A LOT OF HEARTS.
...
...I MISSED SOME BIG STUFF.
THEY'VE BEEN TALKING FOR MONTHS NOW.
(...THAT'S WHY HE'S BEEN SNEAKING LUNCH IN THE LIBRARY— TO TALK TO HER.)

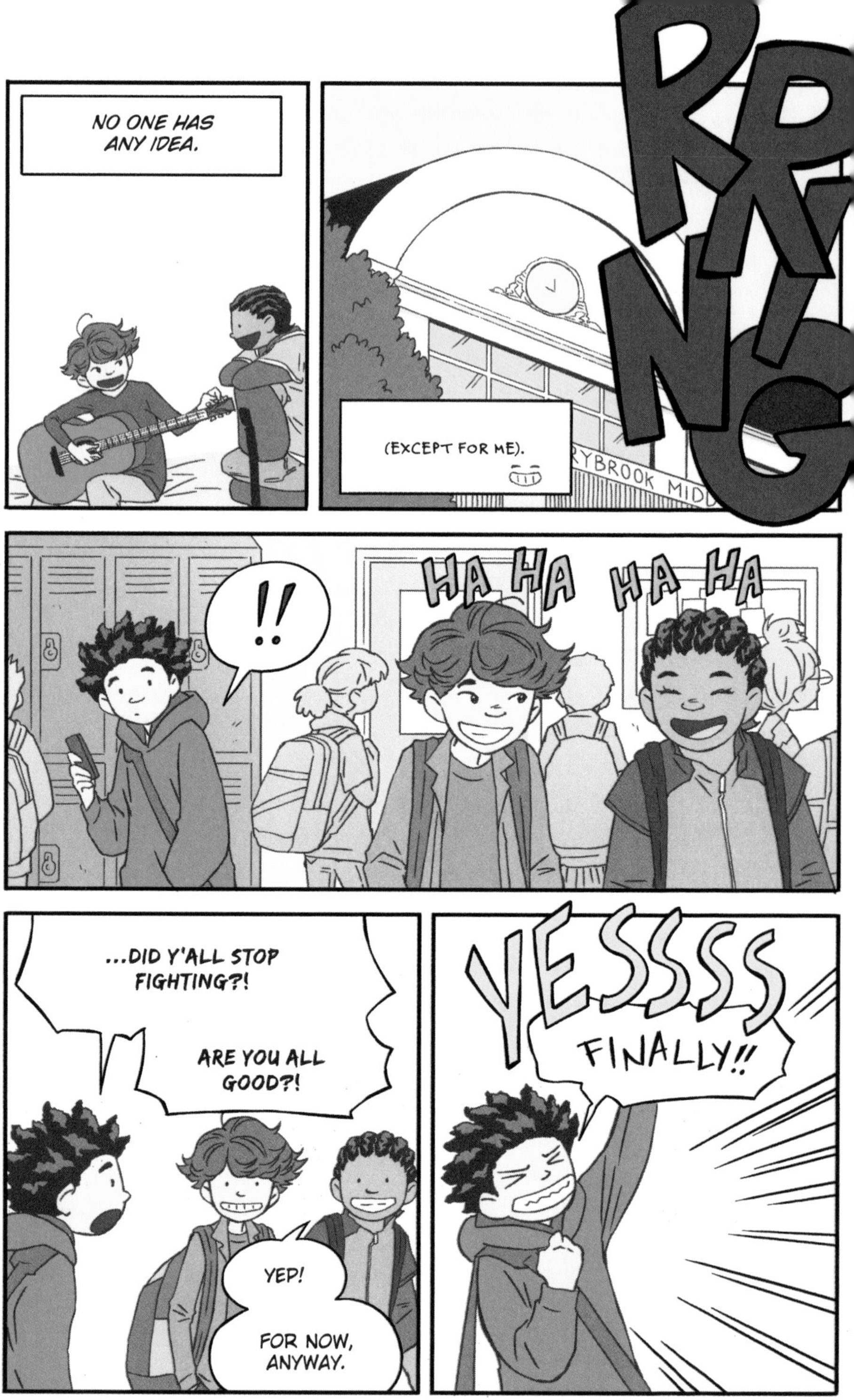
NO ONE HAS ANY IDEA.
(EXCEPT FOR ME).
RYBROOK MIDD
RRING
!!
HA HA HA HA
...DID Y'ALL STOP FIGHTING?!
ARE YOU ALL GOOD?!
YEP!
FOR NOW, ANYWAY.
YESSSS
FINALLY!!

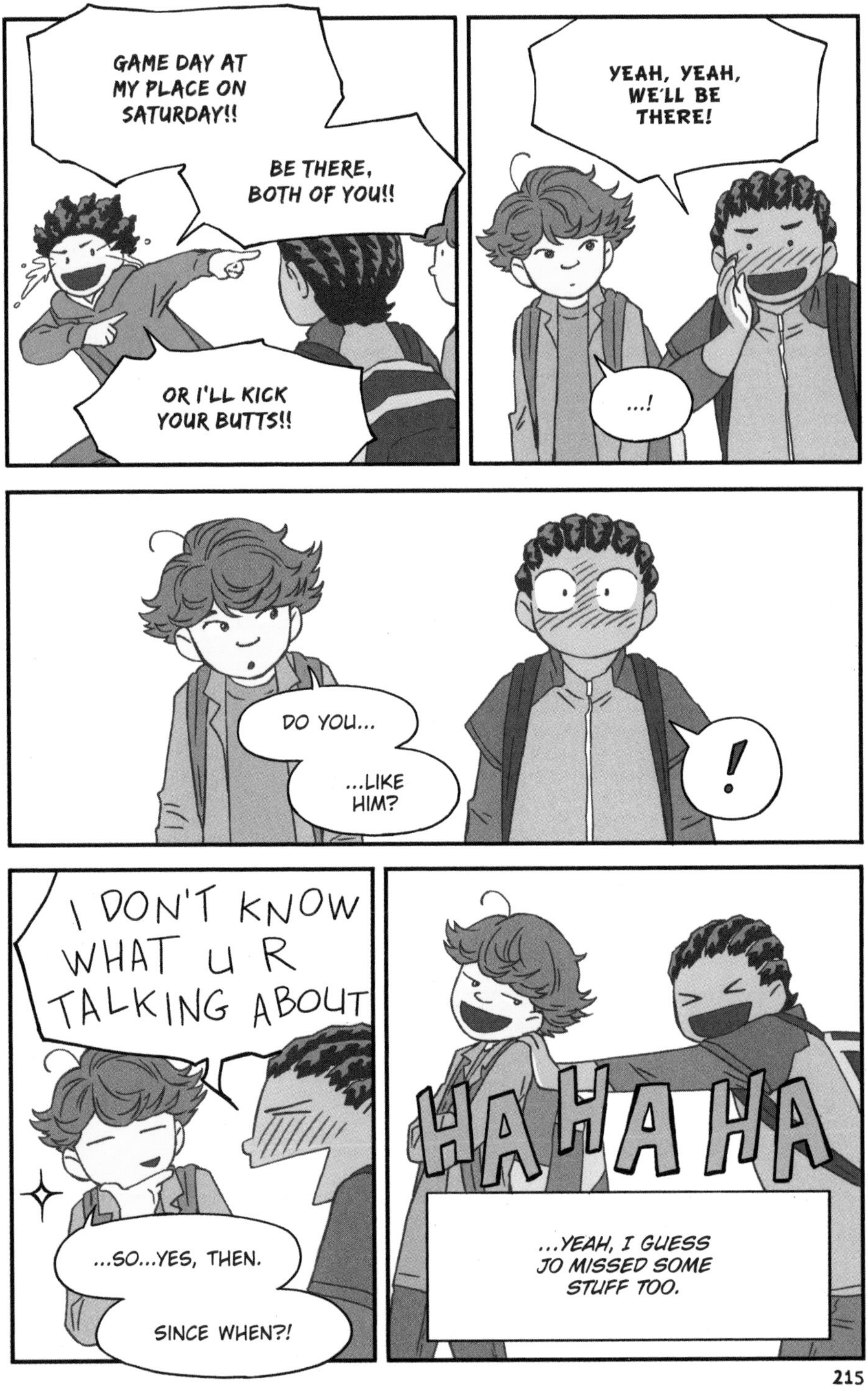
GAME DAY AT MY PLACE ON SATURDAY!!
BE THERE, BOTH OF YOU!!
OR I'LL KICK YOUR BUTTS!!
YEAH, YEAH, WE'LL BE THERE!
...!
DO YOU...
...LIKE HIM?
!
I DON'T KNOW WHAT U R TALKING ABOUT
...SO...YES, THEN.
SINCE WHEN?!
HA HA HA HA
...YEAH, I GUESS JO MISSED SOME STUFF TOO.

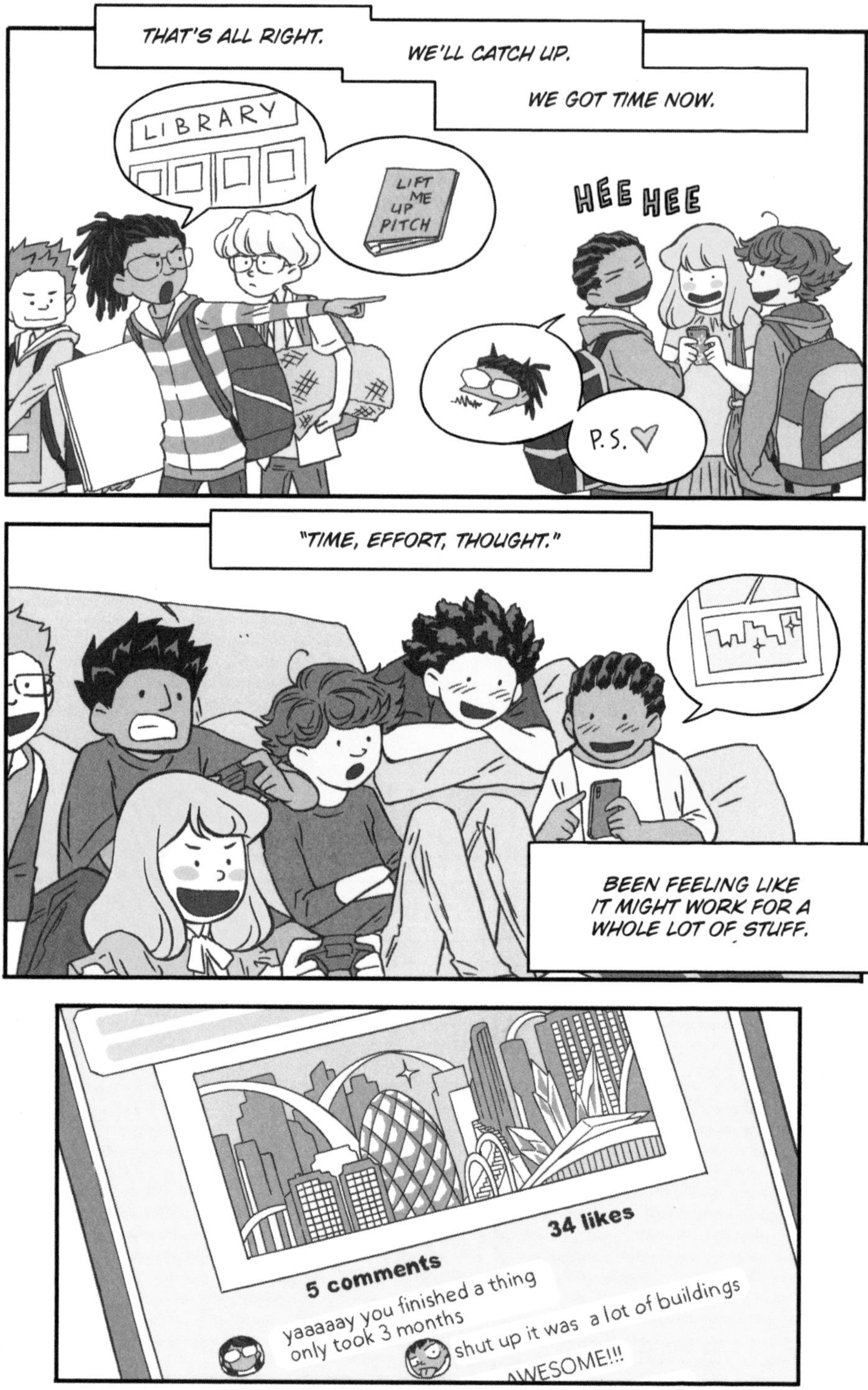
THAT'S ALL RIGHT.
WE'LL CATCH UP.
WE GOT TIME NOW.
LIBRARY
LIFT ME UP PITCH
HEE HEE
P.S. ♡
"TIME, EFFORT, THOUGHT."
BEEN FEELING LIKE IT MIGHT WORK FOR A WHOLE LOT OF STUFF.
34 likes
5 comments
yaaaaay you finished a thing only took 3 months
shut up it was a lot of buildings
AWESOME!!!

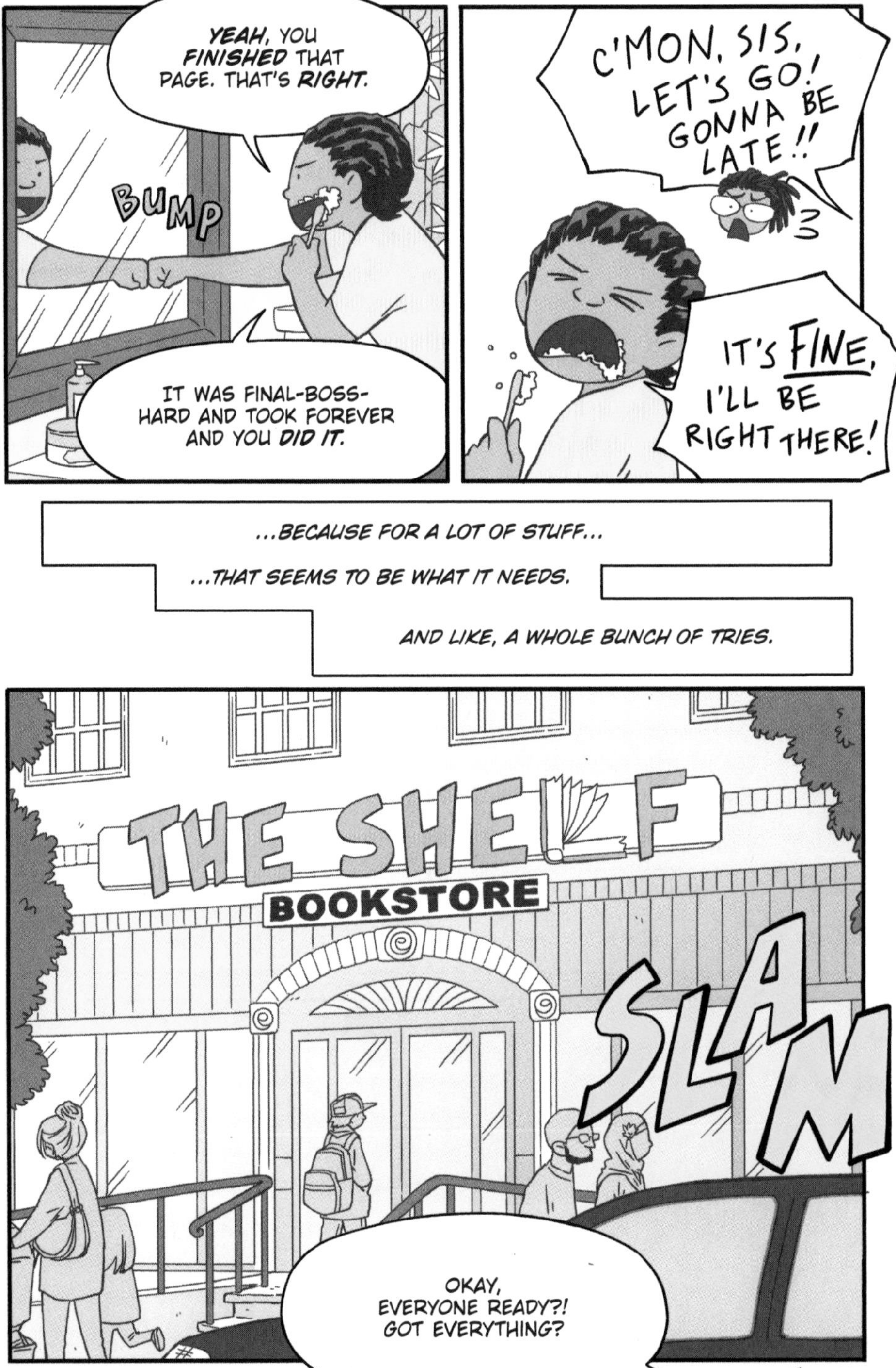
YEAH, YOU FINISHED THAT PAGE. THAT'S RIGHT.
BUMP
IT WAS FINAL-BOSS-HARD AND TOOK FOREVER AND YOU DID IT.
C'MON, SIS, LET'S GO! GONNA BE LATE!!
IT'S FINE, I'LL BE RIGHT THERE!
...BECAUSE FOR A LOT OF STUFF...
...THAT SEEMS TO BE WHAT IT NEEDS.
AND LIKE, A WHOLE BUNCH OF TRIES.
THE SHELF
BOOKSTORE
SLAM
OKAY, EVERYONE READY?! GOT EVERYTHING?

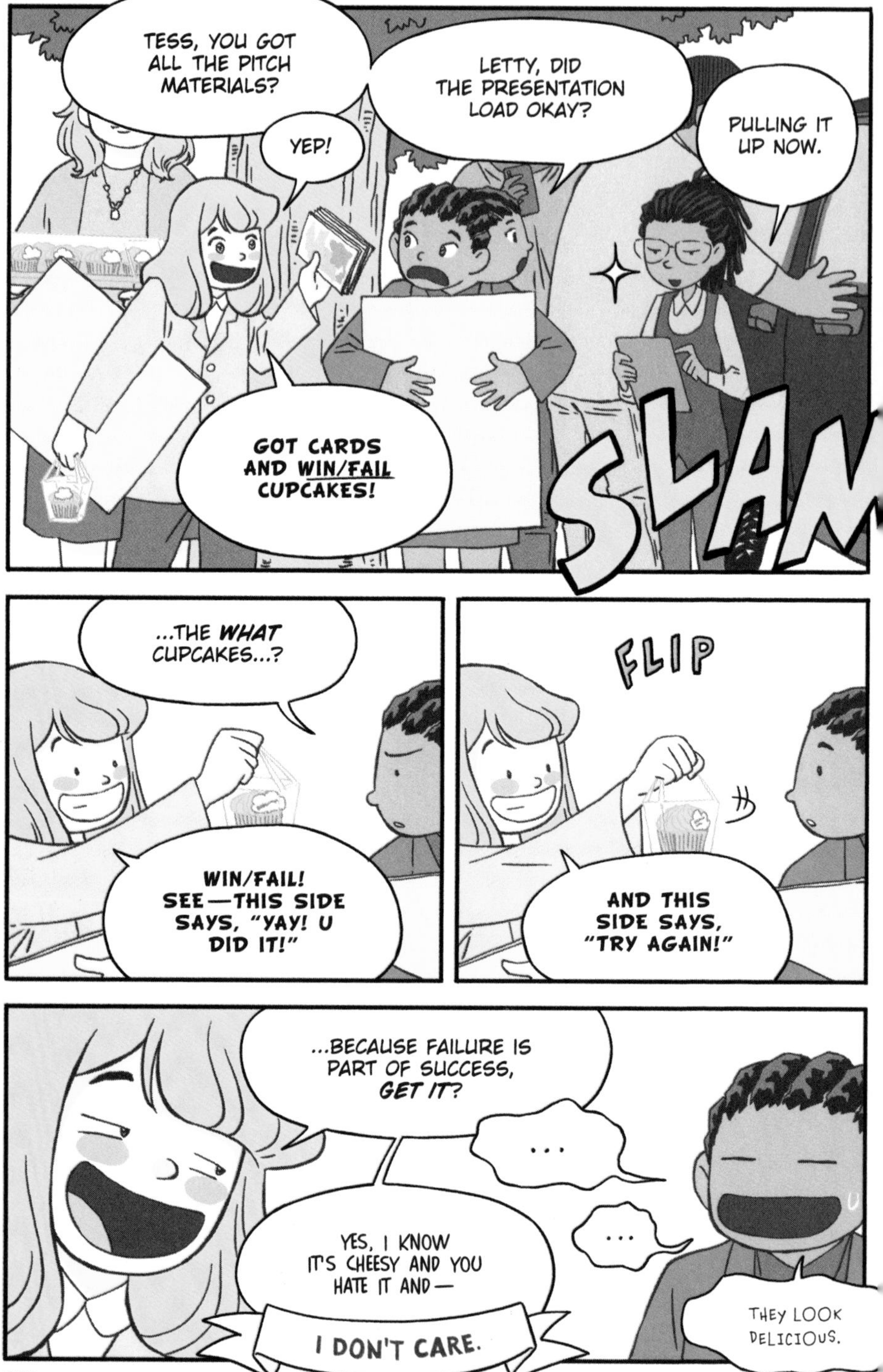
TESS, YOU GOT ALL THE PITCH MATERIALS?
YEP!
LETTY, DID THE PRESENTATION LOAD OKAY?
PULLING IT UP NOW.
GOT CARDS AND WIN/FAIL CUPCAKES!
SLAM
...THE *WHAT* CUPCAKES...?
WIN/FAIL! SEE—THIS SIDE SAYS, "YAY! U DID IT!"
FLIP
AND THIS SIDE SAYS, "TRY AGAIN!"
...BECAUSE FAILURE IS PART OF SUCCESS, *GET IT?*
...
YES, I KNOW IT'S CHEESY AND YOU HATE IT AND—
...
I DON'T CARE.
THEY LOOK DELICIOUS.

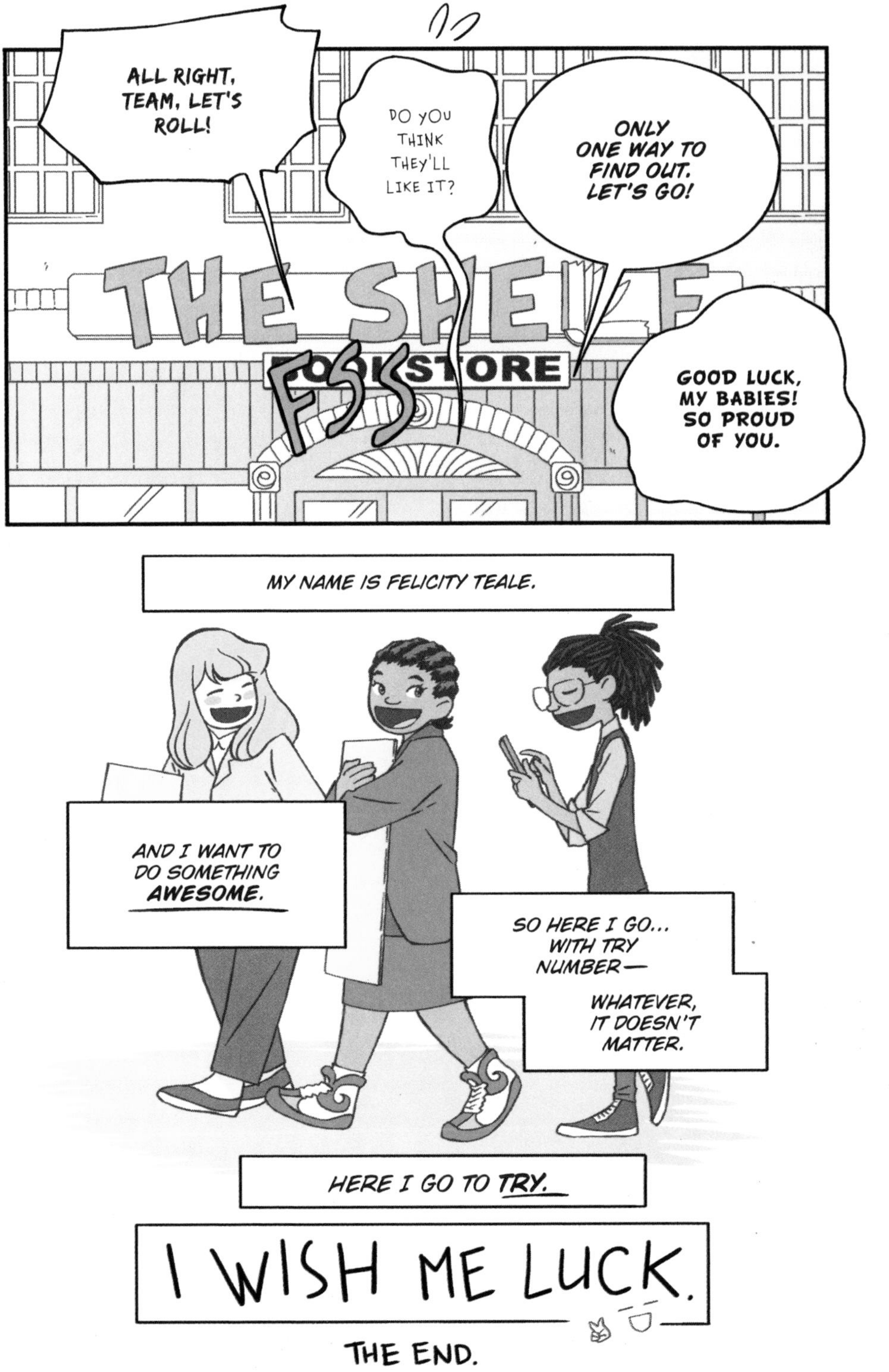
ALL RIGHT, TEAM, LET'S ROLL!
DO YOU THINK THEY'LL LIKE IT?
ONLY ONE WAY TO FIND OUT. LET'S GO!
GOOD LUCK, MY BABIES! SO PROUD OF YOU.
FSS
MY NAME IS FELICITY TEALE.
AND I WANT TO DO SOMETHING AWESOME.
SO HERE I GO... WITH TRY NUMBER—
WHATEVER, IT DOESN'T MATTER.
HERE I GO TO TRY.
I WISH ME LUCK.
THE END.

Svetlana Chmakova was born and raised in Russia until the age of sixteen, when her family immigrated to Canada. After receiving a Classical Animation diploma from Sheridan College, she quickly made a name for herself with graphic novels such as the award-winning urban fantasy *Nightschool: The Weirn Books* and the manga adaptation of *Witch & Wizard* by James Patterson. Her acclaimed Berrybrook Middle School series, which has been nominated for multiple Eisner Awards, has captivated readers of all ages since the publication of its first volume, *Awkward*, in 2015 and has made her one of the most renown creators in the world of middle grade graphic novels. In 2020, she revisited her beloved world of *Nightschool*, populating it with a whole new cast of characters for younger audiences with the first installment of her new series, *The Weirn Books: Be Wary of the Silent Woods.*

☆ THANK YOU! ☆

to my mom, for always carrying pencils and paper for tiny-tot me in your purse, wherever we went. You kindled an artist and I hope your soul sees me putting that to good use. I miss you so much.

to my dad, for always letting me be what I needed to be and for giving me the space to try things and make mistakes. Thank you for giving me All The Books, art supplies, and for taking me to my first ever comics convention.

to my husband, Patrick, for stoically enduring the chaos of my book production schedules, for holding things together when I couldn't, and for all the hugs when I really needed them.

to JuYoun, for the endless rereads of my messy scripts and for always gently nudging me toward my better work. Thank you thank you thank you, for everything you do.

And a HUGE special thank you to:

Melissa

Effie

Young

Judy

Mya, of Salt and Sage Books

Yen Press Production Team

~Svet!
June 5, 2022

GALLERY

PRACTICING TIK-TOK DANCES
...?
MOM

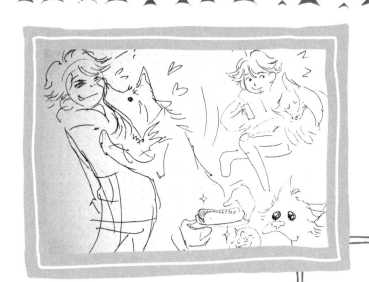

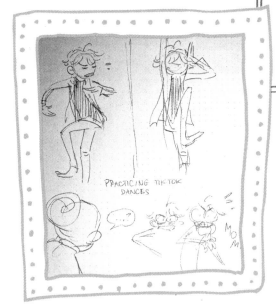

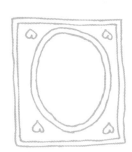

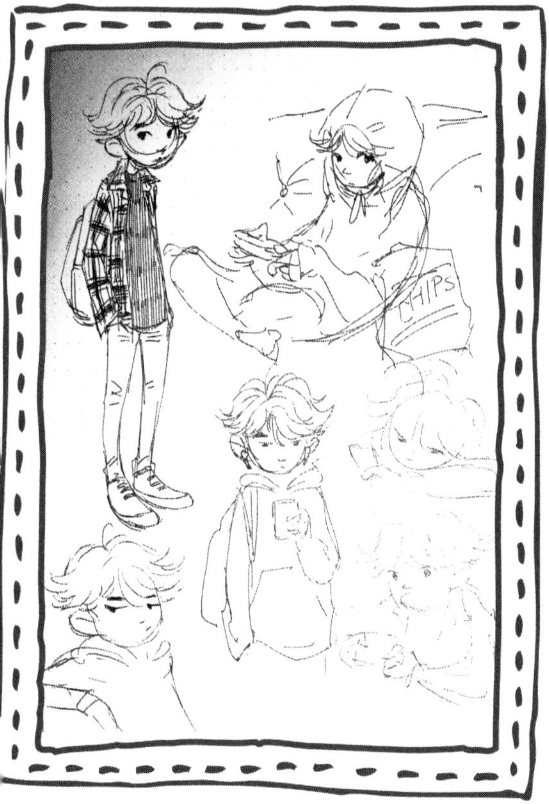

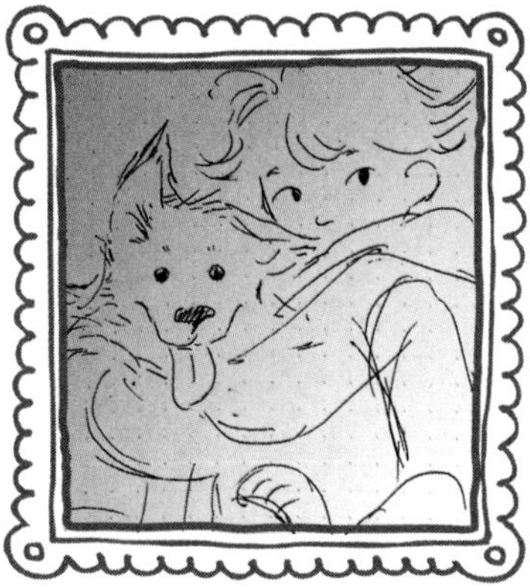

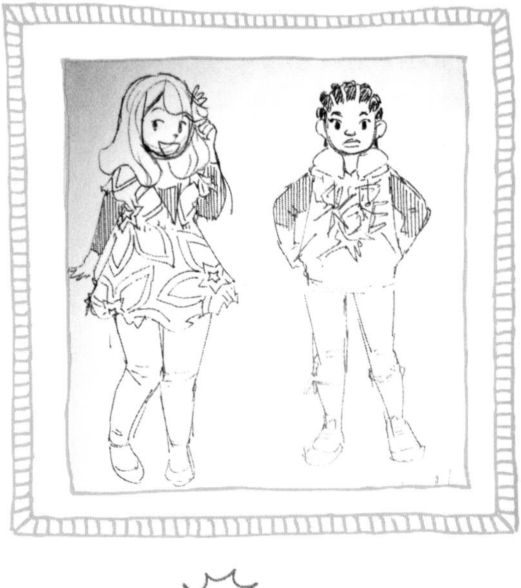

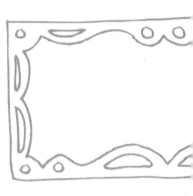

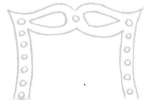

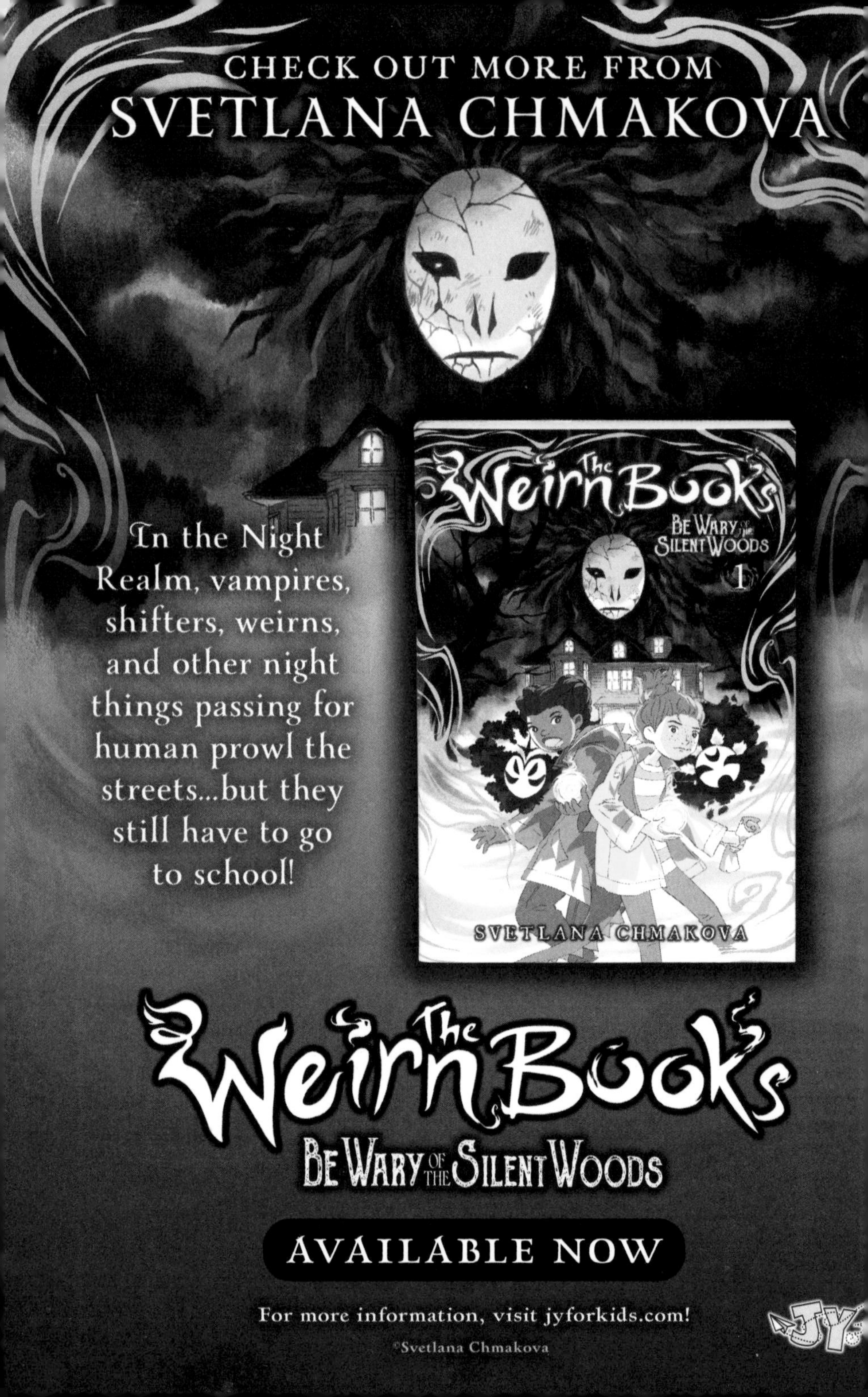
CHECK OUT MORE FROM
SVETLANA CHMAKOVA
In the Night Realm, vampires, shifters, weirns, and other night things passing for human prowl the streets...but they still have to go to school!
The Weirn Books
Be Wary of the Silent Woods
1
SVETLANA CHMAKOVA
The Weirn Books
Be Wary of the Silent Woods
AVAILABLE NOW
For more information, visit jyforkids.com!
©Svetlana Chmakova
JY